Demons of Fame

THE COMPLETE SERIES

EVA CHASE

Demons of Fame: The Complete Series

First Digital Edition, 2022

Cover design: The Write Wrapping

Ebook ISBN: 978-1-990338-60-1

Paperback ISBN: 978-1-990338-61-8

Caught in the Glow

DEMONS OF FAME #1

One

I saw my first Glower when I was seven years old.

I should have been in school, but late that morning Mom picked me up in the silver Mustang after a quick word with the attendance secretary. "We're going to give your dad a little surprise, Avery," she told me with a swish of her chestnut hair. "Bring him lunch and our love."

Even if I didn't have the life experience to put the pieces completely together, I knew she was hoping for more than that. I knew Dad had been home less and less the last few months, and that when he was around, he moved through the house as if underwater, weighed down by an ocean of gloom. No hugs, no low rumble of a laugh, no stealthy tickle attacks. I knew Mom was worried about him and that she looked more tense than playful as her slender hand gripped the gearshift. I think I knew, without being able to put words to it, that this wasn't so much about giving as asking. Asking Dad to remember us. To remember that we loved him. To remember that he loved us back.

I sat next to Mom in the front seat—where I was only allowed to sit under special circumstances, which I guessed this qualified as—as we cruised past palm trees and white stucco walls toward the building that held Dad's current studio space. It was summer, and as hot as L.A. gets, but she left the top down. Scorching wind charged with the smell of baked asphalt and mesquite smoke whipped through our hair and licked away my sweat. I felt relieved when Mom turned the wheel to take us into the little parking lot around back of the reclaimed warehouse. Dad and air conditioning waited on the other side of the dun brick walls.

I think for a moment I believed Mom might have found some magic trick to turn what was happening to our family around. Stepping out onto the concrete in that teal sheath dress with her chin held high, she looked as if she could conquer kings.

The warehouse building had great acoustics and crappy security. Someone had propped open the back door with a cinder block. Mom clutched the bag of take-out Vietnamese subs with one hand and my fingers with the other, and we strode down the long gray hall, cool air washing over us with a distant hum and a whiff of mildew. The heels of Mom's pumps tapped out a determined beat.

Grigory, the guy Dad called his "personal bouncer," was stationed at the far end, outside the biggest studio room. He looked characteristically grim. The left corner of his mouth twitched slightly upward when he saw us. That was the closest I ever saw to a smile when he was on duty. Off... He could throw back a six-pack and whoop so loud it shook the next-door neighbor's windows.

"So he's here," Mom said, sounding reassured, as if she'd been afraid he might not be.

"Just him, Mrs. Harmen," Grigory said, giving her a respectful dip of his head. Mom had told him to call her Cath about a hundred times, but he never did when he was on the job. "He told the guys not to come in today, said he wanted to work through some riffs on his own."

"Well, let's see if he's ready for a break and a bit of company," Mom said with a strained grin.

Grigory stepped aside so we could go in. The entry way led through the control room with its consoles and monitors—dark, empty, with such a feeling of abandonment it sent a prickle down my spine—and into the big live room that had several isolation booths sectioned off along the side walls. I spotted the band's drum kit past the open door of the closest booth and couldn't resist stepping inside to run my fingers over the acrylic glass shells. I liked the feel of the lacquered mahogany kit Dad kept at home better, but my hands still itched to grasp the sticks and rap out a quick beat.

"Avery," Mom said, drawing my attention back. She was craning her neck. The same question crossed my mind that must have been running through hers: where was Dad?

I rejoined her, and we walked a circuit of the room, Mom peering through the little windows above my head on the doors. I counted them, as if the number of the booth would tell me something.

It was at the fourth, near the back of the room, when a strangled, alien noise wrenched from Mom's throat. The bag of subs fell from her hand as she jerked at the door handle.

The door swung open. When I remember that moment now, it glides in slow motion, gradually revealing a pair of booted feet, sprawled legs in rumpled jeans, untucked tee, jawline grizzly with a three-day-old shadow. But probably it happened much faster than that.

My dad was slumped in the corner. Rubber band around his bicep. Syringe on the floor an inch from his limp fingers. My voice caught in my throat, squeezed into a ball, and burst out in a shriek.

"Daddy!"

Then I saw, as if I'd need to blink to clear my vision before the figure would come into focus, that Grigory had been wrong. Dad wasn't alone. A woman was crouched beside him. Long pale hair, slim pale limbs, all shimmering as if lit from within. Her mouth was pressed to Dad's chest, lips parted, with a rasp like the drawing in of a deep breath. That spot on his chest was shimmering too, and as it flared brighter, the woman flared with it. The angles of her face, of her body, flickered and blurred. For an instant she looked like a he. Then her features seemed to smooth until she had no sex at all. Until she was nothing more than a skeleton of light.

My legs had frozen with panic, but Mom moved. She threw herself at the glowing woman-man-thing with a howl and swinging fists. The thing looked up at her, searing irises in a glowing oval of a face. I don't remember it having a mouth, but I swear I could tell it was smiling. That smile haunted me in my nightmares for years afterward.

The glowing thing disappeared a second before Mom fell on it, crackling away into the air like an electric shock. Mom threw herself down beside Dad. "Roy," she said, over and over. "Roy." Gripping the sides of his face, sobbing between each repetition of his name.

His head lolled in her grasp. His eyes didn't gleam. There was no light in them at all, only filmy blue irises and vacant pupils that burned into my memory as my own eyes spilled over with tears.

That was the day I learned that artistic passion could consume a person, literally.

Two

"ARE YOU SURE THIS IS A GOOD IDEA?" I SAID.

My Tether Society supervisor glanced over at me as we waited for the elevator he'd just summoned. He was probably thinking it was a little late to be bringing up doubts. He couldn't have known this one had been circling through my head ever since he'd handed me my new client file: Colin Ryder, singer-songwriter-rocker, on the verge of international stardom at the tender age of 19.

It *was* a little late to suggest turning back. We were already standing in the lobby of one of L.A.'s most exclusive condo buildings, cool air with a hint of jasmine wafting around us. Two security guys were eyeing us from across the marble floor even though we'd shown our IDs and confirmed we were on the approved visitor list. But Sterling obviously knew this was an especially dicey situation, or he wouldn't have been here. Normally I'd have come to meet a new client on my own.

"Why are you concerned?" he asked, tilting his head to the left the way he always did when contemplating a problem. His dark brown eyes, nearly the same shade as his acne-scarred skin, considered me calmly. Thoughtfully. "Because you knew each other?"

I shook my bangs from my eyes, wishing I'd kept the doubt inside me the way I'd managed to up until now. I didn't want to be a problem. The fact was, though, that Ryder was only my second official client since completing training, and all evidence suggested he was going to be a tough one.

"No," I said. "There's no way he'll even remember me. But if he wouldn't play nice with the last two people you assigned to him, why would he listen to me?"

The door slid open and we stepped into the elevator. Sterling hit the button for the upper penthouse. I wriggled my toes in my ballet flats, looking at the little indents the wheels of my suitcase had made in the pile. Real velvet, if I wasn't mistaken. Very posh indeed.

"It took those two trial runs to narrow down Mr. Ryder's particular... issue," Sterling said, with one of the famous meaningful pauses my best friend and fellow Society member Fee had been known to imitate behind his back. "He seems to have a particular allergy to authority figures. Placing him with someone his own age, someone he can see more as a... supporter, rather than a superior, we think will allow us to maintain the necessary presence in his life. At least until you can arrange a more permanent solution."

Herbal "supplements"? An earring or watch embedded with malachite? A tattoo that included just the right construction of lines and shapes? The end goal of every Tether Society assignment was to introduce a personalized method of warding off Glowers that would allow the client more independence, which benefited both them and us since it freed us to help more of those who needed it. There were a variety of ways to accomplish that independent warding. But given Ryder's resistance to the idea that he might need any sort of help at all, I had trouble believing I was going to talk him into a permanent lifestyle change or regular fashion statement any time soon. Especially when one of the Society's other most unshakeable guidelines was that we didn't try to explain to the client *why* that change was necessary. Which, fair enough—I wouldn't have believed in demons slipping into our plane of existence to suck the life energy out of creative talents if I hadn't been able to see it happening with my own eyes. A client who thought you were crazy *definitely* wasn't going to listen to you.

Sterling was studying me again. I dragged in a breath and realized I'd balled my hands in the skirt of my purple-and-green striped sundress. I let go, smoothing it down.

"You've done well with your past placements," Sterling added. "I'm sure you can handle Mr. Ryder."

He didn't sound sure. He sounded resigned. My stomach twisted with the sinking feeling I'd had since I read about the two Tethers who had already failed with Ryder in the last six months.

I wasn't a shiny new strategy. I was a last ditch effort.

Well, I was here now. I had to see this through. Fee and Mateo were the only other Tethers under twenty-five, and they were enmeshed with other clients. The Society needed me to make this work.

The elevator bumped to a halt. When we stepped out, there was only one door in front of us: a thick cherry wood slab at the other end of an entry hall. Sterling rapped his knuckles against it. A slim, forty-ish woman jerked it open before his hand had dropped back to his side.

Ryder's manager, Marissa Fitch. Her photo had been in the file.

"Good," she said by way of greeting, the faint crows feet at the corners of her blue eyes—way too vibrant, had to be contacts—crinkling when her gaze fell on me. I'd spent enough time in Tinseltown to read the signs of cosmetic work left on her skin: Botox stiffness in the cheeks, red tint of dermabrasion around her mouth, not quite hidden under the foundation powdered all over her face. I wouldn't be surprised to find those crows feet gone if I saw her again a month from now. In an industry that sold image as its bread and butter, even the people behind the scenes competed to set a certain standard.

"So this is the replacement?" Fitch said as she motioned us in. Her skeptical tone and her wording directed the comment solely at Sterling, as if I were nothing more than a new fridge or faucet. I decided not to be offended. Checking out the sights held more appeal anyway.

Beyond the stainless steel and ebony shine of the kitchen and the semi-circle of white leather sofas beside it, floor to ceiling windows offered a view of the city toward the glittering water of the ocean. The sliding doors past the eight-seater dining table stood open, letting in a tickle of the warm autumn breeze laced with a tang of salt. The doors led out onto a terrace where padded loungers circled a small private pool.

Nice. Extravagant, but extravagances I could appreciate. My previous two live-in assignments—one in training, and my first official one—hadn't been with clients this flamboyant.

My gaze drifted from the windows to the electric guitar leaning against one of the sofas. A Fender Stratocaster, also *nice*. An acoustic I couldn't determine the make of sat half-hidden on one of the dining room chairs. A couple amps were stacked near one of the inner doors. I wondered if Ryder had a studio set up right here.

A shiver of excitement raced through me at the thought, and

then my stomach clenched all over again. There was another reason I'd been hesitant to take this job. Ryder would be the first musician I'd worked with. And not only that, he was a rocker like Dad. Like I'd once imagined for myself. I was going to be surrounded by reminders of that every day for who knew how long, living here.

"...just didn't realize quite how *young*," Fitch was saying to Sterling when I tuned back in to their conversation.

I caught her eyes before her gaze could dart away from me. "I'm nineteen," I said. "Old enough to do everything but drink, which I wouldn't be doing on the job anyway. The last guy in here was thirty-five. How well did that work out?"

Fitch's lips pursed. We both knew it had "worked out" with Ryder upping his antics until he'd ended up in the hospital getting his scalp stitched up after a drunken brawl in a prime Hollywood nightclub two weeks ago. I'd bet she'd rather not have to go through the song and dance of trying to downplay another incident like that to the tabloids.

"Miss Harmen is fully trained and very capable, I assure you," Sterling said. "I think you'll find she provides more of a... moderating influence, rather than aggravating."

"I should hope so," Fitch said. "That's what you were hired for. If Colin doesn't get his act together soon and get on with recording that album, the label's going to cancel his contract and none of us will get paid."

As if the biggest thing at stake here was a paycheck. Fitch had no idea the Tether Society offered any service beyond keeping troublesome or sensitive clients on track and steering them away from non-demonic dangers, but she still could have placed a few items ahead of her commission on her list of priorities. Ryder's future career? His health? His life?

A giggle carried out of the hallway that branched off from

the living room. Fitch stiffened, her head jerking around. A young woman with sun-bleached hair and nothing but a short silk robe covering her hourglass figure ambled into view. She was grinning at someone behind her, so she didn't see us until that someone caught up, catching her by the waist. Then she glanced up and yelped in surprise.

"Colin," Fitch said dryly. "I did mention we had a meeting at noon."

Colin Ryder eyed her over the blonde's shoulder, and then shifted his heavy-lidded gaze to Sterling and me. He had been smiling before, but now his full lips tensed into a flat line. The shaggy black hair that had fallen into his amber eyes did nothing to hide the resentment in that stare, like a knife on my skin.

He straightened up, the lean muscles in his bare shoulders and chest flexing as he let go of his companion. *He* was wearing nothing but bright red boxers. And oh, the body he had on display was even more fine than his publicity shots had suggested. My skin warmed, and I yanked my attention up from the band of fabric just below his taut stomach to his face. Which was pretty fine too, I had to admit, even looking as pissed off as he did right now.

"Wait for me back there," Ryder said to the blonde, swatting her rear, and she darted out of view the way she'd come. He glanced around, picked a pair of rumpled jeans off the floor near the wall, and stepped into them, not seeming to mind that he had an audience. He stalked the rest of the way to the kitchen island on bare feet. He was looking only at me now. A puzzled line had formed on his brow.

The warmth tingling over my skin prickled up my neck. Maybe he did recognize me. I'd assumed he wouldn't, given that I'd only spent one semester at the Rushfield Academy for the Performing Arts and that had been more than five years ago. I'd hardly been a focus of attention while I *was* there. Mom had enrolled me under her maiden name to try to avoid any talk about Dad—mainly from the teachers, since no one in my generation thought much about Roy Harmen, twice platinum blues rocker, dead before they'd graduated from kiddie pop. The only thing remotely striking about my looks was my honey-brown hair, which I'd kept short and blunt cut back then, a style that made me wince when I looked at old photos.

Colin Ryder, on the other hand, had made a splash from the start. He'd smuggled a guitar into the cafeteria in the first week of classes to serenade some girl who'd caught his eye, and after that display of his wicked fingerpicking and his low rich voice with just the right hint of a rasp, everyone had wanted to team up with him for group work. His smooth tan skin and bright eyes hadn't hurt his popularity either. He hadn't been this muscular at fourteen, though, I found myself noting. He must be working out a lot.

Crap. I was checking him out again. Thankfully he wasn't eyeing me anymore.

"*This* is my new babysitter?" he said, leaning an arm on the polished granite countertop of the island and raising his eyebrows at his manager. "She looks like she'd do better sticking with elementary school kids."

This time it was annoyance that prickled up my neck, but Sterling chose to ignore the comment. "Mr. Ryder, this is Avery Harmen. Avery, Colin Ryder. She'll be the Tether Society advisor assigned to you for the remaining duration of our agreement."

I squared my shoulders and offered my hand across the countertop. Ryder refused to return the gesture, his gaze still fixed on Fitch. I drew my arm back. Well, if that was how he wanted to play this...

"I heard you found advisors older than you to be too… intimidating," I said, making use of a Sterling-esque pause with a smile and an eyebrow arch of my own. "I trust you won't have the same issue with me."

Provoking him was a gamble, but it seemed to work. At least I got a blink in my direction, as if he'd suddenly remembered I was an actual person and not a piece of gear he was discussing with the others.

"*I* didn't hire you," he said, and turned back to Fitch. "Why can't we just—"

"You signed the agreement too," Fitch said, cutting him off. "It's in your contract with Spright Records. You renege on that and all this"—she waved her hand to the expanse of the penthouse—"goes away in a flash. We've been over this, Colin."

"I don't need someone watching over my shoulder," Ryder said with a scowl. "I take care of myself. They knew what they were getting when they signed me."

"Well, I think they did expect they'd be getting an actual album out of you," Fitch remarked.

They stared each other down for a moment. Ryder sighed and looked away, his jaw tightening.

"Don't think of Avery as a chaperone," Sterling said in the quiet tone that was his most persuasive. "She's here to assist you —to make sure you're in the best possible position to make the best possible music."

"Fine. She stays in the same room as the others? The cleaner changed the sheets." Ryder snapped his fingers at me. "Assistant Avery. There's beer in the fridge. Grab two bottles and bring them to me and my friend, last door down the hall. Pronto."

He sauntered off, passing the fridge as he went.

Fitch rolled her eyes heavenward. "Your room is the first down the hall," she said. "It's very nice. Is that all you brought?"

I prodded my single carry-on sized suitcase with my toe. "I've found it's easiest to start light and then grab anything else I need once I have the lay of the land," I said. "Why don't I get Mr. Ryder and his 'friend' their beverages first? Got to keep the client happy."

As I moved, Sterling touched my arm, leaning close. "You can do this," he murmured. "Tether him."

Three

I held the two beer bottles by their necks in one hand, sweating glass slick against my fingers, and knocked on the door at the end of the hall. A giggle carried through it, followed by Ryder's low laugh. He opened the door with a defiant expression. His face softened fractionally when he saw the beers, as if he hadn't expected I'd actually bring them.

"Thank you, Miss Harmen," he said in a dismissive tone, relieving me of the bottles.

Dismissive was fine. Dismissive I could work with. For now, I didn't need him to like me, just to tolerate my presence. The rest could come later.

I checked out the room Fitch had said was mine, the door closest in the hall to the living room. She hadn't been lying—it *was* nice. The same pale polished hardwood as the rest of the penthouse, the same spectacular view, though I was glad for the filmy curtain that would give me a little sense of privacy when I wanted it. I sat on the bed and bounced. Good mattress, firm but not hard. Mom liked to burrow into pillow tops, but those always made me feel as if I were drowning.

The room's location was good too. Voices filtered through the wall as Ryder and his companion wandered past. I'd be able to hear his comings and goings pretty well from here—and therefore ensure the goings included me.

I peeked into the hall in time to see the two of them wandering out onto the terrace, hand in hand. Ryder was still in only his jeans, the woman in that tiny robe. At least he wasn't already testing the boundaries of this new arrangement. As long as he stayed in the penthouse, I didn't care what he did here.

I fished my phone out of my pocket as I unzipped my suitcase. Fee answered on the second ring.

"Avery!" she squealed in an over-bright voice that told me in just three syllables that she was already two sheets to the wind and reaching for a third. Bass thumped in the background amid a warble of voices.

"Are you hitting the clubs early, or did you just never leave last night?" I asked. "It's not even one in the afternoon yet, you know."

Fee laughed. "Gotta keep up with the shiny Starlet. She doesn't care much about clocks. Hey! You had your appointment with rocker boy today, didn't you? Is he as fine as his photos?"

That sounded more like my usual Fiona. True, she'd always been the adventurous type, but since she'd started tethering her current teen wild child client last winter, a little extra wildness had seemed to rub off on her. But Sterling wouldn't have left her on the job if her extracurricular activities were a real problem. And hey, at least at twenty-one she was drinking legally, which was more than I could say for the guy outside my bedroom door.

"He's even fine-er," I said, tugging open one of the drawers on the pine dresser to shove in my socks and panties. "And also asshole-er. He's only agreeing to having me here because the label's threatening to cancel his album." An album I was somehow going to have to convince him to hurry up with recording, along with protecting his soul. "I have a feeling this is going to be a long one."

"The best ones are," Fee said. "The more juice they've got in them, the more the Glowers want them. I'll probably be with Kady until I'm thirty. Or she is."

If she makes it that far, I thought but didn't say. Fee had guarded the kid well so far—put off three Glowers trying to mark her already. We could never be sure a Glower wouldn't come back, but Fee was good at convincing them it wasn't worth the energy they'd have to expend.

"When you find out where he likes to hang, give me the deets and maybe there'll be some overlap. We could do a double client-date!" Fee laughed.

The comment reminded me of our last one-on-one get-together, one that we'd had to cut short because of a last-minute visit Fee had agreed to with her mother for reasons she hadn't gone into.

"Hey," I said, "did you sort that thing out with your mom?"

"What? Oh, yeah, no big deal."

Her voice, suddenly terse, told a different story. Fee had kind of a weird relationship with her parents, at least from what I'd gathered mostly reading between the lines. A few years after they'd gone the Chinese adoption route with her, they'd unexpectedly found themselves pregnant with a kid of their own, and I got the sense Fee wasn't quite convinced they saw her as a full part of the family. It didn't help that her mom was always on her case about one thing or another.

"Well, I'm glad it's okay," I said tentatively.

"Me too!" The background voices warbled louder. "Ack, sorry, got to go, Ave. Keep me in the loop!"

"Of course."

I finished unpacking, hanging the few dresses, shirts, and skirts I'd packed in the ample closet and plunking my heels and sandals on the built-in shoe rack, setting my laptop on the table in the corner, fluffing my duck down pillow on the bed. In this line of work, I didn't find myself at the house I technically still shared with Mom very often. The pillow was the one piece of home that came with me everywhere.

My stomach muttered, reminding me that I'd been too tense to force down an early lunch. Fitch had assured Sterling and me that "the people" kept Ryder's fridge fully stocked and that I could take whatever I wanted from it. I slipped out and padded into the living room, glancing toward the terrace to confirm that my client was still on the premises. My gaze snagged on that smoothly muscled back, and my feet halted of their own accord. Heat crept through my cheeks.

Ryder and his companion were braced against the terrace wall, him facing her as she perched on the concrete edge. Her legs were wrapped around his waist, her spine arching against the metal railing as he pressed his mouth to her collarbone. The shoulder of her robe had slipped down to her elbow, and one of Ryder's agile guitarist hands was teasing her breast. From the expression on her face, eyelids low and lips parted, his mouth and fingers were playing one very enjoyable melody on her body. I couldn't see his face at all, only that bare back and his shadow-dark hair in its jagged line across his neck.

It was hard not to stare. I'd seen people making out in public before, sure, but not... not like that. Not so nakedly, so fervently. Just as I was about to drag my eyes away, Ryder's hips shifted, the low-slung jeans edging lower. The woman let out a breathy gasp loud enough to penetrate the windows, and I realized they weren't just making out.

Ryder rolled his hips with another thrust, and the woman moaned. My cheeks outright flared at the same time as a warm little ache formed between my legs.

I spun on my feet and marched back to my bedroom. He'd probably meant for me to see. To let me know he wasn't changing his behavior one bit in consideration of my being here. Message received. He could sex up his lady friends all over the penthouse if he wanted, it wasn't going to scare me off.

Though I was going to have to wait until the exhibition was over before I'd have the stomach for lunch.

It was midnight when I heard the whisper of socked feet passing my bedroom door. I'd left it a smidge ajar in anticipation. I'd turned out my light an hour ago, but I was sitting on my bed reading the assigned chapters for one of my distance courses on my phone. The bitter taste of the unsweetened coffee I'd gulped down after dinner lingered in my mouth.

I'd been ready to stay up all night. It was almost a relief not to have to wait that long.

Of course, a *real* relief would have been if Ryder had knocked on my door and let me know he planned to go out.

I got up and headed for the living room. Ryder startled as I flicked on the main lights. They flooded the room, catching his figure in the foyer, one sneaker on, the other still in his hand. Alone. He'd sent his blonde companion off a few hours ago.

Crossing my arms over my chest, I gave him a onceover as he glanced back at me. Tight dark jeans, tighter royal blue tee.

"Good," I said. "Looks like I'm already dressed appropriately enough for wherever *we're* going."

As I ambled over, Ryder muttered something under his breath that was probably obscene. He really did have an awful mouth on him, fine as those full lips were.

"I could try telling you to go back to bed," he said, "but that'd be a waste of air, right?"

"I see you're familiar with the protocol," I said. "FYI, next time a little advance heads up would be appreciated. But you'll just try to sneak quieter, right?"

He grimaced and pulled on his other sneaker. "Well, let's go," he said. "I hope you can keep up."

Beyond the twinkling lights of the lobby, a car was already waiting for us: a classic Mercedes with a maroon paint job. Ryder slid into the back without a word, so I guessed he'd given his driver directions ahead of time. The tinted divider window was shut. I sank into the leather seat beside Ryder, and the engine revved.

My hands moved automatically to buckle my seatbelt. When I looked over at Ryder, expecting a sarcastic comment about playing it safe, he was doing up his own. He noticed me staring and smiled at me for the first time since yesterday's meeting, flashing even white teeth.

"I take my risks on a case by case basis."

"Good to know," I said.

Wherever we were going, it wasn't far from the condo building. I figured about fifteen minutes had passed before the car stopped. Ryder leapt out onto the sidewalk, and I scrambled after him. The squat brick building before us was pulsing with red-and-violet lights and a frenetic electronic beat. Its name was etched in shadows on the pitch-black sign: The Catacomber.

Ryder strode straight in without a backward glance. Steeling myself, I followed suit.

This club wasn't in the same category as the polished, upper echelon place where he'd gotten into the fight last month. I wondered if he'd picked that place specifically because of the extra publicity that would come with his stunt, or if he'd picked this one because he thought it would unnerve me.

Beyond the Catacomber's dim entryway, a short flight of steel stairs led into a dance pit. And pit was the word for it. A crush of bodies jostled and collided beneath the stuttering colored lights. To my surprise, an actual band was playing on the battered stage at the far end, an East Asian guy with a bleached fauxhawk crooning into the microphone as a green-haired girl beside him produced an eerie digitized melody from her keyboard. A drum machine thumped behind them.

A metallic tang mingled with the smell of perspiration in the air, prickling my nose as I trailed after Ryder down into the fray. He went straight through the crowd toward the stage. I took an elbow to the ribs and a smack of sweat-damp hair to the face as I pushed after him. I must have drunk too much coffee, because my head was starting to throb in time with the beat, the precursor to a caffeine headache. I closed my eyes for a second, and winced as a heel stomped down on my foot.

Give me another ballerina next time? I thought in silent supplication to the Society administration. *A middle-aged character actor? A classical violinist?*

I'd expected Ryder to stop at the stage. Instead he hopped right up with a heft of his muscular arms. Fauxhawk looked startled but not upset to see him. They knocked fists and slapped each other's backs like friends, and the green-haired girl pointed to the scruffy canvas curtain at the side of the stage.

Ryder ducked behind it and came back out fiddling with the knobs on an electric guitar.

"Hey music addicts!" Fauxhawk shouted to the crowd as his partner adjusted the winding electronic melody. "We've got a surprise special guest joining us for a song or two."

Damn it. If I'd known he was going to perform in a place as uncontrolled as this, I might have called for backup. At least I'd have tried to lay down a few ground rules beforehand. As it was, all I could do was drift to the edge of the crowd and watch.

An orange spotlight beamed down on Ryder as he stepped to the front of the stage, his lips already curled into that same slanted but sure smile I'd first seen nearly six years ago, that first week at Rushfield. "Oh my God," said a young woman swaying with her friends near me. "That's Colin Ryder, isn't it?" She raised her arm and shrieked, and her friends did too.

The hum of voices in the crowd around us had gotten louder. Ryder wasn't a household name yet, but that last single off his indie debut—and the swaggering, smoldering video that had accompanied it—had put him in the sights of anyone with more than a passing interest in the rock scene.

He wasn't looking at the crowd now, his head thrown back as his fingers danced over the strings as if he were channeling inspiration from on high. Fauxhawk had started singing again. The notes that ripped from Ryder's guitar entwined with the ragged vocals, the keyboard melody, and the artificial drums into something dense and complex and, if I was going to be completely honest, beautiful. I found myself swallowing thickly.

The guy could play. Say anything else you wanted about him, he could *play*.

And that was exactly why the Glowers would want him.

I'd barely had time to be swept up in the song when my gaze caught on a figure in the crowd who stood out from the rest. A petite woman with light red hair and creamy skin, whirling in a shimmery black dress that was more gaps than fabric. To my eyes, it wasn't only her dress that shimmered. So did the whites of her eyes, the breath that escaped her lips as she peered up at Ryder, and the pale flame of her hair when she shook it around her face. No one around her could see it, but they'd had enough instinct to leave a careful space around her.

My stomach twisted. The Glower couldn't have been here waiting for Ryder, I didn't think, given that his appearance seemed to be a surprise to everyone but himself. Either she'd been considering marking one of the band members, or she'd been drifting, absorbing the shreds of energy any crowd like this gave off. But she'd noticed him now. Whenever she raised her glittering eyes, she was looking at him.

Double damn it.

There was no immediate emergency. Before a Glower could affect any permanent damage, it had to open a connection. Offer some common point of interest or temperament to make the target enjoy its presence. Insinuate itself into the target's inner circle by offering little glimpses of the highs of creative exhilaration it could provide, holding off on siphoning that energy back for the time being. Only then could it suggest a marking, in whatever misleading language it thought it best to couch the deal in, and expect the target to accept.

Once it got to that point, once the target was marked, there was no going back. No one at the Society had found a means to break that connection once a Glower had created it. And the Glower would use that bond to suck away all the spark and joy from its target's life, feeding them just enough inspiration at intervals to keep the spiral going, until the target crashed at the bottom. Like Dad had.

A Tether could moderate the effect of a mark, but it was still a terminal condition, our presence no more than a palliative treatment. A client who'd have held on for two or three years before the Glower sucked them dry might survive as many as ten with our involvement. But that was the best outcome we could hope for. Eventually the Glower always claimed its final price.

The safest approach was to interrupt the marking process before it could even begin.

A Tether had a choice to make when they spotted a Glower who hadn't yet made a move on their client. I could wait, hope she'd find some reason to decide against pursuing Ryder, and only intervene when there was something concrete to intervene against. Or I could try to nip this in the bud, which would either save me some hassle down the road or ensure a lot more hassle. Some Glowers got excited by the idea of a challenge—at least at first, before they'd sunk much energy into the pursuit. They knew someone like me wouldn't be here unless there was real treasure to protect.

I considered for only a moment, and then started toward the shimmering woman. In a place like this, crowded and completely unfamiliar to me, I couldn't be sure of seeing if she did make a move. Even if she came back stronger next time, if I could get rid of her just for tonight, next time we might be on more favorable ground.

I squeezed past a couple who seemed more interested in groping each other than dancing and a bunch of teens in retro goth gear and parked myself in front of the Glower. The little pocket of space she'd carved out for herself suited me just fine. Thanks to Dad's genetics I was a big-boned five foot eight, which gave me at least half a foot on her. But it wasn't as if the physical realm was her primary arena.

Her eyes flicked over me and away, disinterested. I leaned close enough to be sure she'd hear me.

"Time to leave, demon."

Her gaze darted back to me, a gratifying amount of shock coloring her expression. Then she grinned, sharp and quick.

"He is as precious as he looks, then, is he?" she said, with a husky voice that sounded too big for her delicate frame.

"You weren't here for him."

"I think I am now." She licked her thin lips with another glimmer of breath.

My hand had slipped into my purse. I tugged the knotted string out of one of the pockets and curled its end around my forefinger.

"This one's off limits," I said, at the same time as I whipped out my hand in a gesture so practiced it came automatically, flinging the string around her. I caught the end with my other hand and completed the ring before she'd had time to do more than widen her eyes. Then she was gone, with a faint crackle and a sputter of sparks only I could see.

Anyone around us who'd noticed her would find themselves imagining she'd vanished by normal means into the crowd. I collected the string into its usual loose loop as I turned toward the stage, feeling the gritty texture where the strands had been rubbed with oregano and rosemary. My heart was thumping, the adrenalin rush carrying away my impending headache, but I didn't feel triumphant.

Banishings were temporary. The ring cut the Glower off from all the energies of this plane, destroying its ability to hold human form. It'd need at least a few hours, maybe as long as a day, to recover. Then it would be back, on the hunt again. But this was the strongest attack I had.

Every Tether wished we had a way of obliterating the

demons permanently, but in however many centuries the Society had been aware of the Glowers, no one had found an effective method. It seemed they left the most vital part of their essence on whatever plane of existence they came from, which meant we couldn't touch it. To my ongoing frustration, I could only affect the forms they created here.

At least we should be long gone from here by the time this Glower recovered. If I was lucky, it hadn't caught Ryder's name. It hadn't seemed experienced with Tethers, so the banishing might have intimidated her—and even if it was familiar with the Society, there was a good chance the knowledge that he was protected would put it off.

I couldn't count on that, though. And there would always be others.

While I'd been distracted, the band had finished their song. Fauxhawk laughed as Ryder bounded across the stage, wringing the most intricate solo that guitar had probably ever produced from his instrument. His cocky smile was gone, replaced by a smaller one, as if just for himself. For an instant, he looked like a little boy enamored with his favorite toy. A hint of pride and maybe a bit of affection flowed through me.

I'd protected that boy from the worst fate I knew of.

Ryder ended with a flourish and raised the guitar over his head, all pomp and posturing again. The crowd cheered. He stared out over the pit, his gaze searching—for me? To avoid me, not to find me, I'd bet. With my next blink, he was jogging off-stage.

Oh no, he wasn't getting away that easily. I pushed my way through the crowd, ignoring the glares and muttered complaints. I'd almost reached the far end of the pit when Ryder reappeared at a side door. He glanced over his shoulder, and his eyes found mine. He smirked with a clear declaration of challenge. Then he was off, skirting the dented Formica bar.

The crowd was thinner along the fringes. I didn't have to push so much as weave to stay on his trail now. Ryder ducked through another doorway to the left of the bar, this one hung with a sheet of thready gauze.

When I slipped after him some fifteen seconds behind, I found a smaller, darker room on the other side. A few candles in wall-mounted brass sconces provided the only illumination. The club patrons here were sprawled or hunched on overlapping rugs layered across the concrete floor. I scanned them as I walked, my toes curling as the soles of my flats caught on damp and then crunchy patches in the fabric. None of the figures was Ryder, but there were two more doors at the other end of the room, both of them with *Private* scrawled on them in yellow paint. The one on the right had just been clicking shut when I'd come in.

When kind of goose chase was he leading me on?

I raised my chin and shoved open the door as if I belonged there. The hall beyond was lit by a single bulb. The air was dank and still. No sign of Ryder, but I could see a few rooms branching off farther down.

I strode forward. I'd almost made it to the first doorway when a stocky guy with a buzz cut and a 'roid rage stare stepped from it into my way. His jaw jutted.

"What are you doing back here?" he snarled.

I held up my hands, taking a step back. "I'm just looking for a friend. He came through this way."

The guy loomed, taking in my sundress and the short-sleeved jacket I'd thrown over it, the rise of my chest with my nervous breath, his gaze lingering on my hips. I tensed.

"You know, I bet Mal would like to decide what to do with a

piece like you," he said with a smile that was more a baring of teeth. Then he lunged at me.

"Hey!" a voice rang out from behind him. I was already in motion. As the guy came at me, I shifted sideways, planting my feet. Heel of the hand to the solar plexus. Other hand grasping the shoulder. I let out a huff of breath as my muscles heaved, but it wasn't even that difficult. The guy's lunge had given me all the momentum I needed, and he was top heavy. He toppled feet over head, landing on his back on the hard floor with a smack of flesh and a pained grunt.

He snatched at my ankle, but I was already dancing past him, out of range. Right into the figure who'd just emerged from the second room.

Ryder caught my arm, his grip tightening as he stared at the guy on the floor. He let out a hoarse chuckle.

"I think we'd better get going," he said.

Four

"I still think that me rescuing you from an untimely end makes a much better story," Ryder said ten minutes later, stretching out his legs in the back of his Mercedes. The faint shadow of stubble on his jaw added to the roguish look he was obviously going for.

"That was the plan, right?" I said. "Get me to follow you in there, make me look like a fool in front of their security guy, put on a show of saving the day to prove you're not the one who needs protecting?"

He tipped his head, somehow managing to look disarmingly sheepish and completely unrepentant at the same time. "They know me in there—Ed would have backed down if I told him to. I wouldn't have let you actually get hurt." He lifted his gaze to mine with a quirk of his eyebrow. "Though apparently you've got the kung fu skills to take care of yourself no problem."

"Basic self defense," I said. "It's part of the standard Society training."

"You just toppled a guy twice your weight without losing your cool," Ryder said. "I think that's a little more than basic."

The admiration in his gaze sent a tickle of warmth through me. I clamped down on the sensation, on all thought of how attractive the guy sitting across the car from me was. Inside me, I built a little wall with the word *client* emblazoned on it, and shoved every emotion not strictly professional behind it. Maybe I couldn't help noticing my client was hot, especially when he decided to turn on the charm, but I could keep that from interfering with the job. This wasn't the time or the place for it.

"He underestimated me," I said. "He was careless, the way he came at me. That always helps. Anyway, now you know I wouldn't stand around and let *you* get hurt—as long as you let me keep up with you."

I readied myself for a snarky remark about being defended by a girl, but instead Ryder smiled, with a hum in his throat that did something funny to my gut before I heaved that feeling behind the *client* wall too. "A female bodyguard," he said. "I could get into that."

I flicked out my foot to give him a light kick to the calf. And then winced. The shock of pain distracted me from pulling my leg back in time. Ryder caught my ankle and lifted my foot onto his knee.

"Are you okay?" he asked. "Someone did a number on your shoe."

A dark smudge of a heel print marred the ivory fabric. I made a mental note to wear thicker footgear for our next late night lark.

"I got stomped on pretty good in the crowd," I said. I tried to yank my foot away, but Ryder kept a firm but careful grip on my heel. He slid off the ballet flat and sucked in a breath. Even in the hazy streetlight filtering in from outside, I could see the splotch of a bruise forming across the flesh from the base of my toes to my anklebone.

"Let me make it up to you," Ryder said. "I've been told I give excellent foot massages, Miss Harmen."

Told by his blonde babes? I hesitated, and he ran his thumb along the arch of my foot with just enough pressure to send a pleasant burn through the muscles. Well, he did owe me. I might as well take advantage of this momentary generosity. I wasn't going to lose my cool over this, if that's what he was hoping.

I shifted in the seat, twisting as far as my seatbelt allowed and relaxing against the door. "All right. But call me 'Avery.' 'Miss Harmen' makes me feel like I'm either six or sixty."

"Noted. Same goes for you. I mean, if you're going to call me by name, go with Colin. I'll also accept 'genius,' 'rock god,' etc."

He flashed that grin at me, and I rolled my eyes. It was easier to keep the distance I needed if I thought of him as Ryder. Then he went to work on my foot. His thumbs glided over my skin, steady and sure, gentling around the bruise. The stretch of the muscles sent a fresh warmth tingling up my leg. I reached for a topic to take my mind elsewhere.

"So you know the people in the band that was playing?"

"Yeah. Raging Minister. Shirou and I have been friends for ages. He introduced me to the woman who ended up making that snazzy video for 'Burning Starlight.' I'm doing my best to pay him back for the favor. I contributed a little guitar work for the demo they've got making the rounds too."

For some reason I wouldn't have expected that sort of reciprocity from him, not when he was busy being the hot new rock god, and the realization gave me a jab of guilt. We hadn't gotten off to a good start, but I couldn't blame him for resenting being assigned a "babysitter," as he'd put it. Apparently he treated his friends well, famous or not. It was sad how many celebrities I'd met who didn't give anyone "below" them so much as the time of day.

"They had a nice sound," I said as a peace offering, and Ryder nodded. He dug his thumbs deeper into the muscles of my foot, and for a moment I gave myself over to the massage. The rumble of the car filled the space around us. My eyes drifted shut.

Then Ryder pounced.

"So why did you leave Rushfield Academy, Avery?"

He rolled out the question in a languid voice, as if it were just an offhand curiosity, but when my eyes popped open, he was studying me.

So he did know me. For the first time since yesterday's meeting, I felt truly off balance. It took me a moment to gather myself.

"I didn't think you remembered," I said, affecting the same nonchalance. "I wasn't there that long. Or maybe you made a point of keeping tabs on all the girls?"

Ryder shrugged, not rising to the bait. "I made a point of noticing all the fantastic drum solos. There weren't so many of those."

He meant the winter showcase. We freshmen had all performed for everyone in our year, mostly in groups. I'd formed a temporary girl band with a throaty singer and a slick-fingered bassist. We'd decided we'd each freestyle a solo during the song.

The memory of that evening flooded me, unbidden: the exhilaration that had rushed through me as I'd hit my cue, my arms flying out with the sticks like extensions of my body, the beat building around me and echoing through me...

I swallowed, willing the memory away. Ryder's fingers had crept up from my foot to my calf, running over the tense muscle there. It felt good, but in a way that made me abruptly uncomfortable. He was too close.

"I think that's enough of a massage," I said. He didn't resist when I tugged my leg back.

"So?" he said. "Why'd you leave? It couldn't have been that they decided you didn't have the talent."

"I decided it wasn't where I wanted to go with my life," I said. Vague but true.

"You decided you'd rather be doing *this*?" he said, gesturing around the car. "Chasing after jerks like me?"

The fact was I'd have been a Tether either way. There weren't enough of us who'd happened to witness a Glower in the midst of a killing—the only method by which a human being gained the ability to see them for what they were—for the Society to be picky about who they recruited. I'd already been in training when I started at Rushfield. But I couldn't explain that to a client.

"Most of the people I've worked with aren't jerks," I said. "*You're* not really a jerk. And this is important too." Then, before he could press further, I decided to turn the interrogation back on him. "So why are you avoiding recording your album, Colin?"

He narrowed his eyes at me. "Who says I'm 'avoiding' it?"

"Your manager. Your record label. As I understand it, the deal was signed six months ago, and you've only laid down three tracks."

"I wasn't finish touring," he said. "I've had events."

I'd tossed the question out without much thought, but suddenly, hearing the edge in his voice, I was hit with the certainty that getting a real answer was the key to understanding Ryder's problem. The key to getting through to him. "And?" I prompted.

He paused. "And I'm not ready yet."

"What does that mean?" Mom said to me two days later, across the patio table where we were winding up a quick cafe lunch. I'd just finished relating a truncated version of my backseat conversation with Ryder. "How is he not 'ready'?"

"Beats me," I said. "I asked him that, and he clammed up, and by then we'd gotten back to his building. But maybe just getting him thinking about it was enough of a push. He's in the studio now, after all."

I'd escorted him to the concrete cube of a building a couple blocks down the street from this cafe late this morning, after which I'd been freed from my duties long enough for this lunch with Mom, who was briefly between clients. Ryder was supposed to call me if I hadn't dropped in before he was done. But I'd chosen an eating spot from which I could see the studio doors, just in case.

Mom shook her head, her graying chestnut curls bouncing. "This generation of musicians, I don't know..."

I gave her a skeptical glance as I popped the remainder of my raspberry tart into my mouth. The buttery pastry dissolved on my tongue. "You expect me to believe that Dad never got all 'artistic temperament' or 'procrastinating in search of perfection' when he was working on an album?"

"Well, maybe he did. Those aren't the parts you tend to

think about, looking back." She rubbed her lips, the creases at the corners of her mouth deepening. It wasn't a good day to talk about Dad, then—not that many days were.

"You're not finding Ryder too much of a challenge?" she said before I could come up with my own change of subject. "I know it must be a lot of pressure, with his resistance to help and knowing you're the third one in there."

"I think Sterling was right," I said. "It helps that we're the same age. He's been a lot more easygoing since the stunt at the nightclub." I wasn't sure I could hope for that armistice to last, but I was going to enjoy the relative peace for as long as I could, starting with a very enjoyable bake on the penthouse terrace yesterday afternoon.

Ryder wasn't the type of client who responded well to pushing, that much was clear. Right now, the best strategy looked to be getting in my barbs when his banter called for it while waiting for him to warm up to me more. I'd know he was open to a little more influence when he started seeking me out instead of the other way around.

"I've just seen how Sterling gets when he hits a tough case," Mom said. "I don't want him laying more expectations on you than you can handle. It's only your second official assignment. And none of us can work miracles."

"I'm *fine,* Mom," I said, and reached across the table to squeeze her hand in emphasis. She squeezed back firmly enough, but the thin bones felt fragile in my gasp. "You don't have to worry about me."

She would anyway. That's what happened when you blamed yourself for losing one person you loved by not watching them closely enough. But at least she respected me enough to ease off when I called her on it.

Her smile turned mischievous as the waitress delivered the

bill—which Mom promptly snatched up, ignoring my protest. "I'm not the only one thinking about you," she said, pulling a few bills from her embroidered wallet. "I was at the Society offices this morning. Mateo asked about you."

"Mom," I said with a groan. "You know that's not going anywhere. We *broke up*, months ago."

"You two seemed happy together."

"We were," I said. "For a while. But, you know, you spend more time with a person and sometimes you realize they're not what you really want."

She opened her mouth, and I held up my hand. "I'm not getting into any more detail than that."

She made a disgruntled sound. "Well, you're young, you have plenty of time. It's not as if I'd want you settling down at this age. I still think you should ask for some leave after you're done with Ryder. Following clients around day and night, doing your college courses over the internet, you're never going to meet anyone. Not just boys. Friends. Or you could have experiences outside the city—that you picked, not tagging along with some celebrity's idea of a good time."

"Maybe I will," I said. "Let's see how long it takes me to set up Ryder with more permanent protection first."

I gave her a hug before she flagged down a taxi, and then headed to the studio. At the thought of seeing Ryder, guitar slung across his chest, lips tipped close to the microphone, a little spark of anticipation tickled through me.

I definitely wasn't thinking about Mateo anymore. But I was going to have to keep a close eye on that spark. I tossed it back behind the wall before it could flare any brighter.

I was half a block away when my phone rang. Sterling. I paused outside a designer clothing boutique and raised it to my ear.

"Hey," I said. "What's up?"

"What is going on with your client?" Sterling said, his voice clipped and practically vibrating with urgency. "I just received a call from one of the producers. Getting him into the studio only to have a meltdown won't earn us any good will with the label."

A meltdown? I started walking again, the soles of my shoes smacking the pavement. "I don't know anything about that," I said. "I was having lunch with my mom—I didn't think he'd need me right *there* while he was recording." Glowers couldn't enter private buildings without an invitation unless they'd already marked someone inside. But I hadn't been thinking about the trouble Ryder could cause all on his own.

"Apparently he did," Sterling snapped. "You know how much difficulty we've been through with Ryder already, Avery. You've got to stay on top of him. You know that erratic and aggressive behavior—"

"—is a warning sign," I finished for him, my chest clenching. "I know. He's not marked. I promise."

"Make sure he stays that way," Sterling said. "It's bad enough when we lose a client—worse when it's someone that young. And from the way the staff at the label are talking... we could lose their faith entirely."

He hung up. My fingers clenched around the phone for a second before I lowered it. If the record label decided the Society wasn't serving its theoretical purpose, then they wouldn't hire us for any of their musicians, and we couldn't shadow people without some sort of official permission. All those potential Glower targets would be left with no one to watch out for them.

I was coming up on the front doors of the studio when Ryder burst past them, his eyes wild and his mouth twisted tight. In the first instant when his gaze snagged on me, it was as if he had no idea who I was. My stomach flipped.

"Hey," I said. At the sound of my voice, the clouds in his expression parted just slightly. He turned on his heel, toward the parking lot and the blue Audi he'd driven us here in.

"Don't ask," he said. "I don't want to talk about it."

Five

I KEPT MY MOUTH SHUT UNTIL WE'D LEFT THE AUDI IN THE condo building's underground parking garage, but as we boarded the elevator, I couldn't resist making an attempt.

"Is there anything—"

"No," Ryder said, cutting me off. "Just leave it alone."

He stood the way he'd driven, his hands clenched, his shoulders braced defensively as if preparing for an attack. I let the issue go. I could try again after he'd had time to wind down.

It was a pleasant October temperature outside, but the penthouse was sweltering when we walked in, the afternoon sun blazing through the windows at full force. "The maid should have switched on the air conditioning," Ryder muttered, fiddling with the control. He grabbed a bottle of beer out of the fridge and stalked to his bedroom.

I stood for a moment by the kitchen island, sweat beading on my skin. *I* felt wound up, as much as I had when the security guy had confronted me in the club the other night. Something was going on with Ryder—I could see that. Something more than fickle artistic temperament. Something I had to tackle before a Glower latched onto it as an opening. With any negative emotion—pain, anger, fear—they were eager to offer their services as a cure-all. And it'd seem like one up until they dug their claws right in.

But I couldn't tackle Ryder's problem until I understood what it was.

I paced the length of the living room a few times as the air conditioning edged back the heat. Through the sliding doors, the sparkling water in the pool caught my eye. I glanced at the hall, but it didn't look as though Ryder planned to go anywhere any time soon.

In my bedroom, I quickly changed into the bathing suit I'd brought and swept my thick hair back into an elastic. Then I strode onto the terrace. The pool wasn't deep enough to dive, so I settled for a loose cannonball. The whip of the air and the cool smack of the water brought a smile to my face. I broke to the surface and crossed the pool with a brisk front crawl.

After thirty laps, the tension in my muscles had dissolved into a satisfying ache. I lay back and floated for a while, watching spots of white cloud drift across the stark blue expanse of the sky as I drifted in the pool. The faint prickle of ocean salt in the breeze mingled with the chlorine tang.

When I finally got out, my fingers had pruned, and probably my toes too. I was walking across the rippled limestone tiles to the towel I'd draped on one of the lounge chairs when Ryder pushed aside the sliding door and stepped onto the threshold. He leaned against the steel frame of the doorway with an ease that suggested his mood had improved and gave me an obvious onceover. The path of his gaze traced a warm line down my body, dispelling the remaining chill of the water. The corner of his mouth curled up.

"That's a suit for soccer moms," he said. "Scared of showing some skin?"

The warmth turned into a flash of annoyance—and maybe a bit of embarrassment. I grabbed my towel, resisting the urge to wrap it around me to hide my body from his scrutiny. I thought the violet two-piece was about as flattering as any swimwear was going to get on my figure. The long lace-up top gave a little more substance to my chest and the boy shorts bottoms slimmed my hips, while leaving my better assets—legs, waist— bare. By any reckoning, I was more pear than hourglass... unless you counted my shoulders, which were the sort of broad that made strapless outfits completely inadvisable.

Just because I was aware of my limitations didn't mean I was ashamed of them, though. Maybe my figure wasn't ideal, but it wasn't a *bad* one either. I pressed the towel to my face and then draped it over my shoulders. "It's comfortable," I said, setting my hands on my hips. "I'm not here to show off."

"That's a shame." Ryder tapped his lips with his thumb and then ambled up to me. He stopped just a foot away, close enough that my skin tingled with the awareness of his body. "It wouldn't take much," he said. "A couple of inches off here." His thumbs skimmed in a semi-circle near the lower hem of the top, almost but not quite touching the fabric. If I'd exhaled deeply, he'd have grazed the underside of my breasts, but I'd started holding my breath the moment he'd reached for me. An image flickered through my mind: seeing him out here with the blonde that first day, his hand caressing *her* breast, his lips on her neck. More warmth flooded me.

Ryder's hands dipped down to draw lines in the air beside my hips. "Another inch or two off here. You could turn some heads."

Maybe, but that wasn't the basis on which I bought my

swimwear. And it occurred to me, as I fought to steady my suddenly racing heartbeat, that he didn't really care about that either. He knew how easily *he* turned heads. He was counting on having an effect on me. This was nothing but another little power play.

I gathered up the warmth and the tingle and stuffed them behind the wall inside me. Normally I'd have shot off a snappy retort and walked away. But that satisfied smile and the playful quirk of Ryder's eyebrows sent a different sort of impulse through me.

"You know," I said, letting the impulse carry me, "I think you should be more concerned about what *you're* wearing."

He glanced down at his fitted T-shirt and jeans. "What's wrong with them?"

I tugged my towel forward around my neck to make sure it wouldn't fall when I moved. "Well," I said, "they're about to get soaked."

As I said the last word, I set my hands against his chest—possibly enjoying the feel of the firm muscles beneath my fingers for just a second—and shoved.

Ryder had been standing right by the edge of the pool. He toppled into the water with a splash even more magnificent than I'd imagined. In its wake, he came up sputtering and swiping wet hair from his eyes. Then he started laughing, his amber eyes even brighter than usual as they caught mine. I found myself grinning back.

He launched himself at the side of the pool, sweeping his hand toward my ankle. I dodged him easily. Even as I laughed, my breath evened out and my heart quit its giddy beat. He was still a head-turner—even more than usual now, with that wet shirt clinging to those powerful arms as he pulled himself out of the water—but that didn't concern me.

I patted the rest of myself down with my towel and then offered it to Ryder. He accepted it with a crooked smile. "That's the least you owe me," he said, but his eyes were still amused. As he ran the towel over his dripping hair, the twanging I recognized as his ringtone carried from inside the penthouse.

"It's a good thing I didn't have that in my pocket," he said to me with a waggle of his finger and headed in. I lingered on the terrace a few minutes longer, leaning against the wall's railing and staring toward the sea, until I was certain that every not entirely professional feeling in me had subsided.

When I stepped into the living room, Ryder was just hanging up. My heart sank. If after the recording session his expression had been stormy, now it held a full-out tsunami. He wiped his hand across his mouth with a jerky motion as if he'd eaten something bitter, not looking at me.

"Bad news?" I said cautiously.

"You could say that," Ryder said. "My parents are going to be in town tomorrow. We're having dinner."

"How'd you end up at Rushfield when you didn't live in L.A.?" I asked Ryder as we waited for the elevator the next evening. He'd told me yesterday, before holing up in his bedroom with door firmly closed, that his parents were coming from Sacramento, where he'd grown up.

He shrugged, the collar of his shirt bobbing beneath his freshly shaved jaw. A hint of his aftershave lingered in the air: piney with a touch of mint. He'd dressed up a little, a button-up shirt with thin silvery lines through its forest green fabric over his usual dark wash jeans, black monk straps instead of sneakers, shaggy hair slicked back from his eyes. He looked as fine as always—not that I had checked him out or anything—but I was pretty sure I liked the rumpled, casual Colin Ryder look better. Given the stiffness in Ryder's posture, I suspected he did too.

"Everyone knows that Rushfield is one of the best schools for the arts," he said. "And everyone knows L.A. is the best place to be if you want to get into show business. So I saved my pennies for a trip down here to audition and managed to get a scholarship ride."

"And your parents didn't mind you moving all the way across the state at fourteen?"

"Nah," he said with a nonchalance that sounded forced. "I was driving them crazy in the house with all the guitar practice anyway. They're happy as long as I make an appearance when they summon me."

The elevator dinged, and the door opened. As we stepped in, Ryder peered at his reflection on the mirrored wall and frowned.

"So I guess they're not much into the music scene themselves?" I ventured.

"Top 40 radio as background noise, that's about the limit of their interest." He gave a rough chuckle, and then slid a curious glance toward me. "I guess it's... different, growing up right in the middle of the industry."

The thought of Dad made my breath catch for a second before I could answer. "Well, there are different problems too. Expectations. Comparisons. Pressure. And parents are still parents. It's not as if seeing a musician's career from the inside made my mom less nervous about me maybe taking that route."

Ryder paused, scuffing his shoe against the velvet carpet. "Sorry," he said. "I shouldn't have just tossed that out there. I know about your dad— I didn't mean to bring up bad memories."

I guessed he'd done a little research after I'd turned up at his door. "It's okay," I said, and found, because he sounded sincerely concerned, that I meant it. "It was a long time ago."

Silence hung between us as the elevator dropped the last several floors. As it eased to a halt, Ryder exhaled and said, "Well, here we go. They'll probably keep the visit short. I was planning to meet some friends at a club when we're done."

"Whatever you want," I said, "as long as I come with. I'm not trying to cramp your style, you know. I'll be around if you need me, but I can fade into the background when you don't. I won't get in your way."

He nodded and surprised me by saying, "Thank you."

So I was feeling pretty good about my progress as we crossed the lobby to the wide glass wall that stretched across its front in a mimicry of the penthouse's windows. Ryder was accepting my presence without protest, offering actual consideration to my feelings. Trust and respect—that was the foundation I needed.

We were almost at the doors when my gaze caught on a petite form on the sidewalk outside. My arm automatically whipped out in front of Ryder as I halted in my tracks.

"What's wrong?" he asked, giving me a puzzled look and then peering outside. I motioned him back a few steps, and he followed, but his forehead had furrowed.

Standing beyond the tall windows, some ten feet down from the lobby doors, was the Glower I'd seen at the club my first night with Ryder. She'd pulled her sleek, light red hair into a high ponytail, rimmed her eyes with thick liner and painted her lips crimson. Beneath her cropped leather jacket, a bustier that looked more like lingerie than a proper shirt clung to her ample chest. The pale skin above it glittered, and so did her pale blue eyes as she peered through the lobby windows. The angle of the sunlight would be reflecting her surroundings back at her, or she'd have spotted us already.

She was confident. Glowers didn't have to keep the same appearance each time they traveled to this plane, though they often had a template they preferred. This one wasn't worried about my recognizing her if I was with Ryder, which she should have realized I was likely to be.

Ryder let out a low whistle. "Hot chick at two o'clock."

"Hot chick you're steering clear of," I said firmly. "I know her. She's trouble, and not the kind you'd like. The last couple guys she went after ended up in the hospital missing a few appendages."

It was probably metaphorically true, and it was from the Society's set of standard lines for warning off a client. Frame the Glower as a criminal of some sort, unstable and ill-meaning. It was the explanation closest to the truth that an ordinary person would believe when they couldn't see what we could.

"I don't know," Ryder said, sidling past my still-extended arm. "A little time with a girl like that might be worth a bit of a trade."

Was he kidding me? "I'm not joking," I said. "Can you keep it in your pants for one minute? I'll get Security to escort her away from the—"

"Oh, come on, Ave," he said, his gaze still fixed on the Glower. "I promise I won't talk to her, all right? But the car's right there. I think I can manage to walk past a woman half my size without sustaining any bodily injuries."

He strode forward. "Ry— *Colin*," I snapped, grabbing at his arm, but he'd already barreled past me. *It isn't your body I'm worried about getting injured,* I thought as I dashed after him.

He was already pushing past the lobby doors when I caught up, too late to drag him back without a commotion. So I hurried out with him, clinging to the fragile hope that we might make it to the waiting car without the Glower noticing us.

"Hey!" Ryder said, turning toward her as he grasped the door handle. He raised his other hand and saluted her. "Looking good."

My teeth gritted. The Glower looked over and grinned wide. Ryder kept moving, at least, ducking into the car before she'd taken more than a step toward us. My stomach was churning, but I followed him in, I threw her a glare meant to remind her of how easily I'd kicked her out of this plane of existence the other night before. She halted, watching the car pull away. Still smiling. My fingers curled into my palms.

If she hadn't been sure he lived here before, she knew it without a doubt now.

"Don't give me that look," Fee said as I let her into the penthouse a couple days later. She held up her arms, bangles the same bright magenta as her structured skater dress clacking around her skinny wrists. "You can't invite me to his *building* without letting me see his place. That would be a total violation of the friend code."

"I think the Tether Society code might have something to say about client privacy," I retorted, but I was mostly teasing. Hell, if I screwed up this assignment, Fee might *be* Ryder's Tether before much longer.

I'd invited her to brunch at the bistro downstairs not because it had particularly good food but because despite Ryder's promise to hang out up here all morning, I didn't feel comfortable so much as crossing the street from where he was. Not after seeing the Glower staking out the place the other day. Not after he'd already ignored my warning about her once. We obviously still had some work to do in the trust and respect department.

Fee shook back her fine black hair as she circled the kitchen island. She poked at the pots dangling from the rack fixed high on the wall. "These look like they've actually been used."

"They're not just for decoration," I said, but I couldn't blame her for being surprised. Most celebs in a position to have their fridges stocked by outside help didn't deign to touch the kitchen appliances. Ryder usually ate out for dinner, but I'd seen him make a few breakfast omelets and lunchtime pastas since I'd arrived. He washed the pans and pots afterward too, which was even more impressive. I guessed six months after the big deal, he wasn't that removed from regular life yet.

"A rock star who cooks," Fee said, raising her delicate eyebrows. She peered across the length of the living room. "Pretty sweet. So you didn't get *any* dish on his parents?"

"*Fee*," I protested, dropping my voice. I was mostly sure Ryder was still sleeping off last night's partying, but only mostly. If he was awake... Fee's voice was known to travel.

She grimaced at me and gestured for me to go on.

"It's not as if I was part of the conversation," I said, keeping my tone low. "I was sitting at the other end of the restaurant. Do you hang around for the Starlet's family dinners?"

"The Starlet doesn't have family dinners," Fee declared. "She has family shouting matches and family bodily target practice sessions. I swear, they make my family look almost functional. I nearly got clocked in the head by her mom's purse the other day." She touched her temple gingerly. "So where *is* the rock god? Don't I get to meet him?"

"Definitely not if you're going to talk about him like that," I muttered. "Come on, Fee, let's—"

The intercom buzzed. I paused, glancing toward the hall that led to Ryder's bedroom. No sound of stirring reached me. At the next buzz, I hit the answer button.

"Yes?" I said.

"There's a package here for Avery Harmen."

I blinked. I hadn't been expecting anything—and I'd have remembered giving someone this address as mine. I shot Fee a look, and her eyes widened.

"Oh, no," she said. "I know nothing about this."

Maybe it was from Mom, or someone at the Society? Or maybe my Glower 'friend'—could she have found out my name?

My gut clenched. I guessed I'd have to see.

"Okay," I said into the intercom. "Bring it up."

Fee poked around in the cupboards while we waited. The courier employee who came to the door handed me a cardboard box with my name and Ryder's address on it. I signed for it and watched him leave, checking for stray glimmers. Nothing. I frowned. The box itself was non-descript, not even a company logo printed on it.

"That's the kind of box they ship adult toys in," Fee said with a nudge. "Avery, darling, is there something you're not telling me?"

"Shut up," I said, but I was kind of glad she was here in case the box's contents were meant as a threat, not a gift. She trailed after me as I went to my bedroom, where I could minimize how much Ryder might be exposed.

I set the box on my bed. The tape ripped off the flaps easily enough. I jerked them open... and lowered my head with a groan.

"Bathing suits?" Fee said, lifting out a bikini top that was little more than two triangles of fabric, and then another. The first was leopard print, the second a dark pewter with a metallic shine. She cocked her head. "These aren't exactly your usual style. Maybe you *do* need to tell me something, Ave."

"I need to tell you that Colin Ryder is infuriating," I said with a wince. "He decided my current suit isn't risqué enough. I guess he figured just telling me that wasn't sending a clear enough message."

Fee gave me a measured glance. "*Is* something going on with him? I mean, it'd be totally understandable if you were into him. There can be fun in infuriating."

"Nothing's happening," I said, but a blush had crept across my face. Fee jabbed my shoulder.

"But you like him," she said. "Don't deny it."

"Maybe he grows on a person a little," I said, waving her off. "I'm pretty sure acting on that would be against the Society rules. Not that *he'd* be interested in acting."

"Ah, the only rule anyone there really cares about is whether you keep the client safe," Fee said. "Sometimes you can do that better if you bend the smaller rules. No one's complained about my approach yet."

She flipped over the tag on the top she was holding, and then flopped onto the bed with a cackle, twirling it around her finger by the strap.

"It's the right size!" she said. "Go, Avery! Colin Ryder bought you skimpy bikinis and he was ogling you enough to figure out exactly how big your boobs are."

"Or how big they're not," I grumbled, checking the other top. She was right. He'd guessed my size correctly.

Fee kept laughing, covering her eyes as she gasped for air. As I stared at her, a chill prickled over me. It was kind of funny, sure, but not *that* hilarious.

"Fee, are you on something?" I said carefully.

She managed to stop laughing after a few sputters and peeked at me through her fingers. "What?"

"Did you take anything? Before you got here?"

"I might have popped a pill in the cab. Mmmm, yes, I think it's starting to kick in." She sighed at my expression and stretched her arms against the bedspread. "What does it matter, Ave? It's nothing hardcore. They just add a little... sparkle to the day."

"And having brunch with me is such a chore that you needed to add sparkle to it?" I said. The question came out more bitterly than I intended.

"Don't take it as an insult," Fee said. "It's not about you. I'm just having fun."

"Fee..."

She pushed herself upright, looking suddenly serious, but in a slightly spacey way that only chilled me more. Her gaze didn't quite focus on me.

"I should be allowed to do that, right?" she said. "Have fun? We've got the most depressing job on the planet and we have to constantly be making sure no one stops the clients from having *their* fun, so, why not?"

"How can you have seen everything we did in training and think like that?" I said.

"Because I'm not getting *really* messed up." She frowned. "This is about your dad, isn't it?" she said with a matter-of-factness that felt like sucker punch. "Nothing's going to happen to me, Avery. No Glower is going to come along and suck me down into the spiral of darkness. It's completely clear I don't have a creatively talented bone in my body. I'm one hundred percent safe. So don't be a spoilsport about it. Please?"

It wasn't about Dad. It was about my best friend of seven years, the person I'd shared joys and worries with since we started training a few months apart—the girl who'd told me jokes after a session had me on the verge of tears until I was crying with laughter instead of pain, the girl whose jitters I'd hugged away the day before her first official Tether assignment started, the girl who'd never once treated me as if our two year age difference and the vaster gap in various life experiences made me any lesser—acting like someone I didn't know. Acting like hanging out with me wasn't a sparkly enough activity to be worth her time while sober.

"I'd just rather you weren't high when we're hanging out," I said. "That's all."

"Well, I'm here like this now," she said. "Are we brunching or what?"

"We're brunching," I said, kicking the box of bikinis under the bed with the resolve to pretend it had never arrived. But as I walked Fee to the door, my stomach was tying itself into a string of knots.

It was hard enough trying to tether Ryder. I didn't know how to tether my best friend too.

I woke up the next night to a pair of stiletto heels clattering down the length of the penthouse's hall. A woman's voice was shouting something—muffled by the walls, but I made out a few choice words: "prick," "loser," and "waste of my time." I sat up, wondering if I needed to intervene.

Ryder had seemed cozy enough with the thankfully not at all shimmery young woman he'd picked up after another impromptu performance at another grimy nightclub. I'd ridden in the front of the Mercedes with the driver so I didn't have to watch them making out on the other side of the privacy screen. She'd been hanging off him, cooing over his biceps while he mixed drinks, when I'd retired for the night. Obviously something had gone wrong. And abruptly. A glance at the clock showed me I'd been asleep less than an hour.

The shouting got more muffled as the stilettos reached the living room. I pushed aside my sheet and tiptoed to the door. I couldn't see Ryder or his lady friend when I peeked out, but I could hear them just fine now.

"I think you'd better go," Ryder was saying, in a tired voice that suggested he'd said the same thing several times already.

"You think I'm not good enough for you, Mr. Hotshot Rock Star," the woman hollered back. "Well the real fact is you're not good enough for *me*. There are all sorts of guys in this city who'll give a girl what she asks for."

"And I'm sure you know that from experience," Ryder said mildly.

"Oh, screw you."

There was a clang, as if she'd thrown something that'd hit one of the steel window frames. Then Ryder's voice, as cool as before: "I guess I will, because I'm definitely not screwing *you*."

The woman made an inarticulate sound of rage, and then the door slammed. After a moment of silence, Ryder spoke again, calling down to the front desk as far as I could tell. "Sam, there's a girl coming down who's not in the, ah, best of spirits, and has a few drinks in her. Can you make sure she gets safely into a cab? …Thanks."

The phone clicked as he set it down on the counter. If he'd gone back to bed then, I would have gone back to mine.

But he didn't. He sighed, and his bare feet padded across the floor, farther away from me. I stepped into the hall in time to see him slump onto the sofa. He tipped his head back against the cushions, pressing the heel of his hand to his temple. I hesitated, and in that moment he turned and saw me.

There was no point in pretending I hadn't heard the

argument. I walked over to the sofa. "What was that about?" I asked.

"She—" he started, and laughed hoarsely, as if he couldn't believe what he was going to say. "She wanted to do it without a condom. Said it was more 'personal' that way or some crap. And then she pitched a fit when I said I wasn't interested in getting that kind of personal with someone I'd known less than three hours."

"Oh," I said, glancing at the door as if it'd reveal anything about the woman who'd stomped out past it. "Does that... happen a lot?"

"No," Ryder said. "Not really. Not in my experience so far, anyway." He paused. "Because it's the guy who's supposed to want that, right? And now I'm thinking it must be ten times more miserable trying to get laid without complications if you're famous and a woman."

"Well, thankfully neither of us will have to find that out firsthand," I said, and he cracked a sliver of a smile.

"By choice, in your case," he said.

"Yeah, because there are *so* many celebrity drummers."

"Is that why you gave it up? Too little promise of stardom?"

I rolled my eyes, but the offhand comment gave me a twinge. It'd been the exact opposite reason. The thrill of performing for an audience, of being welcomed into the spotlight, had felt too close, too much. Too dangerous.

Everyone always said I had a lot of Dad in me. I didn't want to find out just how much I took after him.

"Sorry we woke you up," Ryder added. He paused, his eyes narrowing at my outfit: loose T-shirt dress over nylon leggings. "Is that what you normally wear to bed?"

My turn to offer a flicker of a smile. "I've got to be ready in case I need to chase you on another sudden excursion out of the building." Whip a belt or a sash around my waist and the outfit would be outright presentable.

"Well, you don't have to worry about that tonight," he said. "I'm done." He turned back toward the windows, edging further down on the sofa as he stretched out his legs beside the ottoman.

I could have left him then, returned to my bed. But there was something almost mournful in his gaze as he contemplated the dim glow of the city lights catching in the haze of smog beyond the windows. If he needed to talk, if he was willing to talk, I wanted to let him. Maybe he'd give me a better clue of what else he needed.

That was what I was here for, after all. To tether him, to give him something solid to hold on to, to ward off the temptations the Glowers could offer of heights that came with too far a fall.

I sat at the other end of the sofa, leaning against the arm and crossing my legs, leaving a careful space between us. I didn't speak, just contemplated the view with him. He rubbed his forehead.

"I don't even like them," he said after a minute, so quietly I wasn't sure I'd heard him right.

"What?" I said. "Who?"

"Those girls. The ones at the clubs. The ones I bring back here. I don't even really like them."

That sounded like an awfully simple problem to solve. "Then why do you hook up with them? Why not, you know, hook up with girls you *do* like?"

He seemed to consider the question, sucking his lower lip under his teeth with a suppleness that sent the wrong sort of shiver though me. I fixed my gaze on his eyes.

"It's easy," he said. "They're easy. They're right there. They come to me. I know exactly what they want. I don't even have to think about it. I mean, it's fair. They don't really like *me* either, just the idea of hooking up with a 'hotshot rock star.'"

Somehow that answer surprised me. Because, I realized as I said it, "I didn't take you for the type to prefer easy."

He rolled his head over against the back of the sofa so he could look at me. Those amber eyes were far more penetrating than I liked. "No?" he said. "What type do you take me for?"

I thought of the guy I'd seen fingerstyling an improvised solo on a cafeteria table five years ago. "The type who figures out what he wants and then goes for it, no matter how far away it seems."

He made a faint sound that might have been a laugh. "And you figure you know me pretty well after hanging around here for all of a week?"

"I knew you from a distance for four months, at Rushfield," I pointed out. "I know you're the only person from our year there who's pulled together an indie album that got radio play, and not only that, was good enough that the record labels came knocking with big checks. You're not going to tell me *that* was easy, are you?"

"No," he said, still holding my gaze. He sounded almost puzzled, as if he'd forgotten how he'd ended up here. "I guess it wasn't."

Something had shifted in the way he was looking at me. It wasn't the suggestive eyeballing he'd given me the other day in my bathing suit, but the intensity of it sent a pleasant prickle over my skin all the same. He eased himself more upright on the sofa, sliding half a foot closer to me with the same movement, and my breath stuck in my throat. I scrambled to my feet.

Ryder raised his eyebrows at me. Maybe I'd misinterpreted the gesture. But one thing I knew for sure was I had no intention of acting as a stand-in for the woman whose attentions he'd just dismissed. That wasn't going to help either of us.

"I'm beat," I said. "I'd better crash."

His look followed me as I sidled around the sofa. Guilt gnawed at me. I wasn't sure if he'd recognized my rejection for what it was. I wasn't even sure what exactly I'd rejected.

It didn't matter. He was still my client. I was still his Tether. And even if I hadn't been, I didn't want to see him hurting.

Fee was right. I liked him.

So I offered him as much as I felt I safely could. I reached over the back of the sofa and gave his shoulder a light squeeze. "If you miss easy, there'll be plenty more of that tomorrow, right?"

His lips quirked up. "I guess so."

I didn't look back, but I felt his eyes on me the entire time it took me to walk to my room.

Seven

"You really don't have to stick around if you've got other things to do," Ryder said as he parked his Audi beside the studio building the next day. If last night's odd conversation had affected his opinion of me at all, he hadn't shown it so far. "You shouldn't have to put your whole life on hold to follow me 24-7."

"That's sort of what the job is," I said. "Anyway, after last time..." I shot him a pointed look.

He set a hand on his chest over his heart and raised the other palm forward. "I solemnly swear I'll behave myself for at least the next three hours. I'm in a much better mood today. See?" He dropped his hands with a grin that was broad and authentic enough to set off a fluttering in my chest.

I clamped down on the feeling, but I couldn't help smiling back. "Maybe I want to see the brilliant Colin Ryder at work," I said as I got out of the car. The truth was, I wouldn't have left regardless of whether I believed him. Even though I hadn't seen his Glower groupie since the day his parents had visited, I couldn't believe she'd given up. I wasn't leaving him unguarded until I was sure she was no longer a problem.

"It's really not all that exciting," he said as we strolled up to the building's entrance. "A lot of recording the same bits over and over with just a little tweak each—"

"Colin," I interrupted gently, "I was hanging out in recording studios practically from birth. I know how it goes."

"Oh. Right." His eyes made a little twitch toward me, and I knew he was remembering my dad—and the official story of how he'd died. Of Mom and I finding him ODed in *his* studio.

After a moment's hesitation, Colin recovered his grin. "Well, you can't say you didn't ask for it then."

Two members of his backing band were waiting in the primary live room. "Marcy," Ryder said, prompting me to offer my hand to the chubby brunette in a faded Nine Inch Nails tee. "Our excellent bassist. And Joel, drummer extraordinaire." A guy who looked to be in his early twenties tipped his newsboy cap to me. The angular face behind his pale scruffy beard struck a chord of recognition in me.

"Kevin's on his way," Joel said, and added for my benefit, "He's our keyboardist and second guitar."

"Joel," I said. "You look familiar. Have we met?"

Ryder knuckled the other guy's shoulder. "Rushfield grad, couple of years ahead of us. He helped with some of the orientation our year."

Joel's eyebrows leapt up. "You're a Rushfieldian?"

"Well, I— sort of. I wasn't there very long."

"You didn't tell me that," Joel said to Ryder, and then to me, "Don't ask me how I got roped into backing this young upstart."

"He broke my favorite guitar ten minutes before I went on during the sophomore showcase," Ryder said, *sotto voce*, leaning toward me. "He's felt so guilty about it ever since, it seemed only fair to let him make it up."

Joel guffawed. "I broke a *string*," he retorted, elbowing Ryder with the ease of a long established friendship. Then he turned back to me. "What Colin did tell me is you're ace with a kit."

I glanced at Ryder, who gave me an innocent shrug. "I only spoke the truth."

"I haven't actually played in a while," I admitted.

"Hey, you know, Joel's got a nice set-up," Ryder said. "I bet he'd let you kick around with it while we're waiting for Kev. Just for old time's sake."

My gaze slid to one of the isolation rooms. I knew instinctively which one would house the drum kit. The door was half open; from what I could see, and there was no reason for him to lie, Ryder was right. It was a nice kit. But he was eyeing me so eagerly it made my skin go tight.

"Sure," Joel said. "It'd be cool. We don't see a lot of girl drummers." At Marcy's snort, he reddened. "Not meaning I'd be surprised if you *are* good. Just sometimes there's a different approach—it's interesting to hear."

He took a few steps toward the room as if he expected me to follow, and my heart did with a flying leap. I swallowed thickly, curling my fingers into my palms.

"That's okay, really," I said. "I'll only embarrass myself."

Joel stopped. "Well, if you're sure. The kit'll still be here later if you change your mind."

I was spared further debate by a stocky Indian guy bursting past the door. "I am here! Kevin has arrived!" he announced, and a portly man whose dome of a shaved head shone white in the overhead lights stepped out of the control room—the producer, I guessed.

"All right, let's get 'Far Out' down so we can finally move on to the next track, people," the bald guy said, his focus mostly pointed at Ryder. I took that as my cue to fade out of the room.

I lingered in the back of the control room for the first hour, watching the band through the window as the producer called out instructions and suggestions to them and to the sound engineer at the mixing console. He mostly ignored me. Ryder hadn't lied—it wasn't the most exciting process to watch. Even with the best music, hearing a riff or a strip of melody adjusted and re-adjusted became less than thrilling after the first dozen times.

Ryder, at least, seemed into it, closing his eyes as he crooned into the mic, dancing his fingers over the fret board of his guitar with the same boyish smile I'd seen that first night when he'd crashed the performance in the Catacomber. Seeing that enthusiasm again sent the same tickle of affection through me. And then a flash of heat, when he stepped closer to the window, his eyes seeking out mine.

I gave him a little wave, and the producer looked at me for the first time since I'd come in. Frowning.

I didn't want to be responsible for distracting the star performer. And apparently I could use a little cool down. I slipped out to stretch my legs and wandered down the narrow hall that led to the two smaller studio areas. One of the studios was in use, the other vacant. I peeked inside the latter and was about to turn back when a glimmer of movement drew my gaze.

A thirty-something man dressed in janitor khakis emerged from one of the iso rooms, pushing a wide broom. But he wasn't any janitor. His white-blond hair and pinkish skin exuded the same shimmer as the redhead who'd been staking out Ryder.

Glower.

It could have *been* the redhead in a different guise, but something about him—the frequency of the light that emanated from him, the tone of his movements—told me it wasn't. So he might not be here with any particular target in mind, yet. I guessed this place made a good front for scoping out potential marks. In that uniform, it wouldn't have been too hard to convince someone to give him access to the building.

I stepped into the live room, closing the door behind me. The Glower looked up at the click. "Just finishing up," he said, but his voice cut off on the last syllable as he registered my expression. "Ah. Hello."

"Do you want to just leave or are we going to have to make it a production?" I asked, folding my arms over my chest.

He gave his broom another push. "If you're here playing guardian angel, you don't have to worry. I'm not interested in whomever your charge is."

"I don't want you being 'interested' in anyone," I said.

"Well, I'm afraid that's a condition I can't agree to." He reached the corner and turned to look at me again. "Your kind really are unfair to mine, you should realize. Though I suppose I can understand it, circumstances being what they are. Who was it for you, who died while you watched and left you *seeing*?"

My back stiffened. Of course the Glowers knew how it worked: that their final act of feeding changed something in the minds and eyes of anyone who witnessed it. It hadn't occurred to me they gave the process much thought beyond trying to ensure there were no witnesses, though.

When I didn't answer, he went on. "That doesn't make the best first impression. But there's so much more to it than that. A symbiotic relationship. An exchange of energies. We give them what they want most."

"Obsession?" I said. "Addiction? Depression? Sorry, I'm not buying."

He shook his head. "Inspiration. Genius. Joy. The best work of their careers."

I'd heard that line before. It always made me think of those last few months I'd had with my dad. Of the absences and the unexpected rages and the pained distance even when he was in the same room. My throat closed up.

"You give a few hours of inspiration and then drain away all the joy it brings them for yourselves," I said. "You leave them with *nothing*. A few hours for weeks of misery—you call *that* fair? Spare me."

"And yet so many are glad to accept our price." He peered at me, gray eyes shining like coins under water. "Are you simply afraid that your loved one would have made the same choice even knowing the outcome?"

My hand dropped to my purse, my fingers clenching. I took a step toward him. "*You* don't get to talk about my 'loved ones.' I doubt you know anything about love other than what it tastes like when you steal it away." My voice was shaking. I took a breath, steadying myself. "Now are you going to leave easily or not?"

"Are you going to try to banish me?" he asked. "That would be interesting."

He was holding the broom handle casually, but close enough to his body that he could use it to obstruct any move I made. This wasn't like with the Glower in the club, who hadn't anticipated my attack. I slid my hand into my purse to run my thumb over the string with its knots and treatment of herbs, but I left it there. He'd just as likely snap it in half before I completed the circle.

"No," I said. "But I'll stand in this doorway as long as I need to, to make sure you don't go where you're not wanted."

The Glower let out a low chuckle. "I'm done here as it is," he said. "So I'll take my leave, because I choose to. I told you already, I'm not after your charge. Though if you really care about protecting the people you shadow, perhaps you shouldn't stand in the way of those who can deliver them all the glory they're dreaming of."

His form wavered, and then vanished. The broom handle tipped over against the wall. And I stood there for several minutes more, breathing around the ache in my chest, until the burn of tears behind my eyes retreated.

That night's club was as bright as Ryder's previous haunts had been dark: stark white walls and ceiling, blurred mirror of a floor, yellow and orange lights radiating and reflecting at me from every direction, making the dance hall look like an inferno. Even the DJ in his little booth in the corner was dressed in white. The air conditioning blasted over the dancers, thick with ozone.

Ryder had thrown himself into the throng the moment we'd walked through the doors. I could barely keep track of his lean form amid the figures undulating around him, but I wasn't sure it'd be wise to try to rein him in. He'd been in a strange mood since we'd left the studio. Since before that, actually—I wasn't sure when it had shifted. After my confrontation with the Glower, I'd spent a couple hours working through online course material on my laptop in the hall outside the control room, and when I'd returned Ryder had been off in an iso room perfecting a guitar solo. I'd thought he looked all right when he'd come out... But at some point in that last stretch of recording, we'd exchanged a look, and I'd seen the clouds creeping in. On the drive home and in the penthouse afterward, he'd been quiet. Pensive, as if he were stewing over something.

Now it seemed he was throwing that something off into the universe. I bobbed on my feet along with the rattle of the bass, edging around the wilder dancers as I followed Ryder's circuit of the room. I caught up with him near the far corner in time to see another guy drop a couple pills into his open hand.

I halted, my stomach twisting. We weren't supposed to forcibly interrupt clients' recreational activities as long as they weren't excessively dangerous and no Glower influence was involved, but that didn't mean I enjoyed watching Ryder tip back his head with his hand to his mouth. A reddish light slid down his throat with the bob of his Adam's apple. He brushed his hand over his hip and then raised his arms in the air.

"The rock star is in the house, and it's time to *party!*" he hollered, springing back into the crush of bodies. His whoop carried over the thrum of the music. I sighed and took up the chase again.

"Colin Ryder, coming through!" he was shouting a minute later, still waving his arms. Whatever he'd taken, it'd hit him fast. I followed him back and forth through the crowd as he made several more announcements of his presence. Then he paused where a small circle had cleared in the middle of the dance floor. I squeezed through the throng to his side.

A break-dancer was going at it in the middle of the ring, spinning and flipping with a speed that left me breathless just watching. Every tiny gesture echoed the frenetic pulse of the music with painstaking accuracy. The guy should have been on a stage, not performing for a tiny audience of random club-goers.

As the dancer whirled onto his feet, I caught the manic brilliance in his eyes—the artificial energy of a high, maybe from the same stuff Ryder had taken—and a different sort of spark. A glimmering spot in the middle of his chest, flickering with beat of his heart. My own chest clenched up.

The dancer was marked. My gaze darted around and settled on the spiky shimmering hair of a young man at the other side of the ring. A young man whose eyes glinted like glass as he watched his meal.

I didn't know either of them. Probably a guy like this, a street dancer who hadn't grabbed enough attention to catapult into the wider public eye, would never have had a company or a manager with enough stake in his future to seek out the Society's services. And there simply weren't enough Tethers for us to seek out and protect every artistic flame burning in so many souls across the world. The smaller stars made for smaller feedings, but they were easier prey too, and there were plenty of Glowers happy to settle for that.

But I was here now. Maybe I couldn't do much, but every bone in my body balked at the thought of turning a blind eye.

I'd just started moving toward the Glower when the dancer pulled off one last tumble and posed on his head for his applause. The crowd hollered and clapped, but the ring was already contracting around him. The dancer leapt upright, sweaty and grinning. The Glower came up behind him and rested a hand on his mark's shoulder.

Before I could even let out a shout, the Glower had taken it. All the joyous energy of the moment, of a performance well-received, coursed in a quivering stream from that flicker in the dancer's chest to the Glower's hand. The Glower smiled even as his mark deflated, the exuberance I'd seen an instant before draining away, the triumphant grin sagging.

Bile collected in the back of my throat. I took another step toward them as the crowd shifted around us, thinking I could at least offer the dancer some reassurance or encouragement that might give him the strength to resist a little longer. Then I heard a familiar whoop, far enough away that I tensed.

Ryder had charged off again. I hesitated, my teeth gritting, and turned my back on the dancer to go find my client.

There, near the wall now, the lights painting bright streaks in his dark hair. I couldn't deny the flash of relief that passed through me seeing him. And not seeing any other Glowers nearby. Pain in the ass though he was being, the thought of watching *his* delight sucked away made my stomach turn.

A few minutes later, a hint of smoke prickled my nose. I assumed it was some creative cologne until the flavor of it crept over my tongue as I dragged in a breath, and the shriek of a fire alarm cut through the throbbing beat.

The crowd shifted with a sudden surge, tossing me in the opposite direction. Real smoke was gushing up from somewhere to the left of the DJ's booth. Real smoke and real flames, dancing with sharper edges amid the still blinking club lights. Holy hell.

Someone screamed. The crowd surged again with the strength of a tidal wave. I stumbled backward, only managing to keep my balance by grabbing the arm of a woman who immediately jerked away. My head whipped around. Where was Ryder? He'd been right beside me a minute ago.

I tried to turn toward the place I'd last seen him and stumbled again, caught in the rush toward the doors. My heart thudded. If I wasn't careful, I was going to end up so much ground meat under all those feet. I craned my neck as the current carried me onward.

The guy next to me flinched with a bark of protest, and then Ryder shoved past him. He grasped my elbow. "You okay?" he said by my ear. His expression had sobered, his amber eyes alert as he scanned the figures around us.

"Yeah," I said. "As long as they keep those doors open."

The crush forced us closer together. Ryder slid his arm around my back protectively. Even as the contact sent a tingle through my body, it occurred to me how odd it was for him to be suddenly so cool and collected, considering the high he'd been coasting on for the last half hour.

The smoke wafted over us, following the air and the bodies streaming toward the entrance. A club employee had propped the doors open and was motioning everyone out with waves of a couple glow sticks. "We'll all be fine. Easy does it!"

A siren was pealing through the night air when Ryder and I finally lurched onto the street. He steadied me as a few of the other club-goers hurtled past. I spotted the Mercedes down the street. Ryder dropped his arm, but I felt his hand hovering near my waist as we headed over. His strides were solid, even.

Something was *definitely* odd.

I turned to him as we reached the car. "That wasn't much of a night out. Were you thinking we'd drop in someplace else?"

He was looking past me to the club. The fire truck had just pulled up, the last few patrons spilling out toward it. I couldn't tell if the smoke I still smelled was in the breeze or on his shirt.

"No," he said. "I think that was enough excitement for one night."

I studied him as his driver headed back to the condo building. Ryder rubbed his eyes once, but that looked more like fatigue than anything else. Otherwise he sat still, his hands folded, his gaze following the lights of restaurants and bars on the streets we cruised down as I became more and more certain.

I held my tongue as we crossed the lobby and rode the elevator to the top. An image swam up—that swipe of his hand by his hip after he'd downed the pills.

When we got into the penthouse, Ryder ambled across the room toward the terrace. I caught him by the dining room table.

"Hey," I said, touching his side. "Tell me something?"

His abdominal muscles tensed under my fingers as he swiveled toward me, the heat of his body seeping through his shirt, but I had other things on my mind. I was just hoping the contact had distracted him a little from my real intentions. Because the next thing I did was dip my hand into his front pocket.

"Avery?" he said with a husky note I'd never heard in his voice before. *That* got to me, a little tremor through my nerves, but I'd already found what I was looking for. I tugged my hand out, two white-and-blue capsules pinched between my fingers.

"Why did you buy these just to put them in your pocket?" I said, holding them up. We were close enough that his startled exhale grazed my wrist. "Why did you *pretend* to take them? To be tripping?"

He snatched at the pills and I skipped backward. Then, letting impulse take over, I marched to the kitchen sink and dropped them down the drain, hitting the button for the food disposal. I stalked back to where Ryder was still standing by the table, his face frozen in a mask of indifference.

"Are you going to answer the question?" I said.

He let out another breath. "It's too hard to explain," he said. "You wouldn't understand. What does it matter to you anyway? Shouldn't you be glad I wasn't really high?"

"I'm definitely not going to understand if you don't even try to tell me," I said. "And of course it matters. I'm supposed to be... to be looking out for you. How can I do that properly if I don't know what's real and what's you pulling slight of hand tricks?"

He dropped his gaze, swiped his fingers through his shaggy

hair, and then looked at me again. "It's just the job," he said. "That's why you care."

There was something needy in his eyes, a plea I didn't totally understand. But it pulled a little ache into my gut. I opened my mouth and hesitated, and Ryder shrugged.

"Of course," he said flatly. "Well, don't worry. I can 'look after' this just fine on my own."

The words slammed down, cutting me off, crushing any progress I'd made with him in the last ten days. They knocked the breath out of me. So it wasn't that hard to honestly say, "No. Colin, I'd care—even if they took me off duty right now, I'd want to know you were okay. Just because it's a job doesn't mean you're not a person to me too."

He took a step toward me, closing that distance again, and this time there was no ignoring the solid presence of him, that piney aftershave mingling with the smoke still clinging to his clothes.

"Yeah?" he said softly.

"Yeah," I said. "I mean, at times a highly irritating person, but frequently one I actually enjoy being around."

A sliver of a smile touched his lips. "You're never going to cut me a break, are you?"

"Do you want me to?"

He paused. "No. I want..." The sentence hung unfinished in the air between us. Then, without warning, he caught me by the waist, spun me to the side, and sat me on the edge of the table. I barely had time to let out a stutter of a laugh and a "What—" before his lips captured mine.

In the first few seconds of the kiss, my thoughts fragmented. The wall I'd built so carefully inside me crumbled to dust. There was nothing in the world but Ryder, and he was everywhere, and that was all I wanted. His mouth, hot and demanding against mine. His fingers tangling in my hair. The length of his torso flush against me. His hips between my knees, the seam of his jeans rough against my skin where my dress was riding up. One of his hands traveled from my hair over the back of my neck and down my spine, pulling me even closer. As I gripped his shoulders, my lips parted, welcoming. His tongue glided past, teasing out mine. My fingers twined around the soft curls at the base of his neck and tugged accidentally. The pleased sound he made in his throat sent a jolt right through the core of me.

It was that little jolt that woke me up. A shock of panic raced through me.

It didn't matter how good this felt. He was my client. I had to keep a clear head around him. I had to be on my game.

He was Colin Ryder, who went through lovers like lattes, and my heart was already panging at the thought of letting him go.

This was dangerous.

I pushed back with a gasp, the loss of contact radiating through me. Ryder—oh, who was I kidding, I couldn't think of him as anything but *Colin* after we'd been entwined like that—stared at me, his chest heaving. His hands slipped to my waist as if to tug me back toward him, and I caught them, shifting so I could hop off the table beside him. My legs wobbled under me. My pulse was skipping wildly. I had to tear my eyes away from his, so bright and wanting.

"I can't do this," I said. "I *can't*."

Then I fled to my room.

Eight

I'D NEVER FLOWN ON A PRIVATE JET BEFORE. THE ONE THE record label had sent for Colin and his crew, to deliver us to Austin where he was scheduled to play at a fundraiser music festival they thought would give him good "exposure," was all soft silver-gray carpet and creamy leather seats: a sofa that could have seated eight stretched alongside sets of more traditional, if larger, airline chairs with mahogany tables perched between them.

I was sitting in one of the latter, theoretically working on an essay for my sociology course, though I'd been rewriting the same paragraph for about forty minutes. Colin was lounging on the sofa just beyond the edge of my laptop's screen, tweaking the tuning on an acoustic guitar and chatting with Joel, who was tossing one of his drumsticks between his hands. Marcy and Kevin had retired to the smaller seating area beyond the washrooms. From the eyes they'd been making at each other since we took off, I figured it was better I didn't interrupt whatever they'd gotten up to over there.

So I stared at the screen and tried not to let my gaze wander past it to Colin's striking profile. It'd been five days. I'd rebuild my wall of professionalism brick by brick. But I still couldn't brush my hand over my mouth without that kiss flashing back to me at full force.

It was my fault. I'd played along with his flirting. I'd let the flames of attraction burn too long before dousing them. I should have held that wall steady, patching up every crack the second a wisp of unwelcome emotion started to trickle past it. Now... Now no matter what I did, that moment would always remain between us.

My phone buzzed in my pocket, jerking me from my regrets, and I startled. I'd forgotten it was even on—private jets didn't come with the standard, and apparently unnecessary, warning to turn off all cellular devices. I pulled it out and hesitated at the name on the display.

Why was Mateo calling me?

Well, only one way to find out.

"Hey," I said, and noticed Colin glance over. I shifted in my seat, wishing there was a room where I could take the call in private. "You have the honor of being the first person to ever speak to me on the phone on a plane in flight."

Mateo chuckled. "A historic moment," he said, his hint of a Colombian accent almost lost in the background static. "So you can talk?"

"Yeah," I said. "What's going on?"

"I... It's been a while since we caught up. I'm on a bit of a break between clients—Sterling has me helping digitize all the old records. As exciting as that is, I thought I'd check in and see how the new job is going. If you *want* to talk. I know Sterling's been on a tear about this Ryder guy."

So Sterling had been venting about Colin around the office

too. My fingers tightened around the phone. "I'm fine," I said. "It's going fine." *I have no idea what the hell is going on in my client's head ninety percent of the time, and it's requiring a major ongoing effort to keep my hands off him, but otherwise...*

I certainly couldn't have said that last bit to Mateo, even if I'd been alone. He and I had broken up because he hadn't been comfortable opening up more with me, but technically I was the one who'd called it quits. He'd acted disappointed but not especially broken-hearted, and after a couple months of distance we'd fallen back into the friendly work dynamic we'd had before we started dating, but I had no idea what was going on beneath that. That'd been the whole problem when we were together: Mateo had stoicism down to an art form, and it'd been hard to feel at ease with someone who wasn't willing to start sharing his deeper thoughts and feelings with me even after a year of dating.

I hoped this call really had been motivated by Sterling's blustering and not by the thought of exactly who my new client was.

"So you're hanging in all right?" Mateo said.

"Yeah. It's, you know, the job. Sterling's given me more to stress about than the client has. Hey, have you talked to Fiona lately?" I'd texted Fee a few times since our awkward brunch and left her a voice mail two days ago, but I still hadn't heard back. Which was really not like her.

"She came by the office for a moment yesterday," Mateo said. "She's— Well, she's Fiona."

From the reluctance in his voice, I suspected he meant the new Fiona, not the Fee I'd trained in with. If Mateo could tell how much she'd changed after just a few minutes around her...

Fee had asked me to leave it alone. Sterling was keeping an eye on her too—and if he decided there was a real problem with her behavior, she *had* to listen to him.

I bit my tongue to keep from asking if Fee had said anything about me. "Okay."

"Well, I'd better get back to the paperwork. You call me, okay, if you ever need to talk anything out?"

"Of course," I said. A lump rose in my throat. I wouldn't, but I was touched that he'd offered.

After I put away my phone, I turned back to the laptop, but sociological theory seemed even more irrelevant than before. I dropped my head into my hands, replaying my last conversation with Fee in my head. Random chatter about the presentation of the bistro's food, about some new fashion designer who'd opened a shop near the Society's office, about the Starlet's hot new bodyguard. All skimming around the surface of the issue we'd been avoiding coming back to.

She must have been able to tell I hadn't really let it go. Why else would she be avoiding me?

Damn it, Fee.

I looked up at the sound of a body dropping into the seat across from me. A body I was now more familiar with than I really should have been. Colin raised his eyebrows at me and motioned to his ear as if holding a phone. "Everything all right?"

I was surprised he'd come over to ask. We'd been doing a bang up job of pretending nothing had happened the other night on his dining table, mostly by speaking to each other as little as possible. He must have wondered if the conversation had been to do with him or with the upcoming gig.

"As far as I know," I said, forcing myself to meet his eyes with a smile. Pushing away all thought of how the lips that had formed the question had felt against mine. "And I'd like to point out that I'd prefer it stayed that way. No stunts today, right?"

"Now, why would you think you have to say that?" Colin

said with a grin I didn't entirely like. Then he got up and went back to the sofa—without actually answering the question.

I had a feeling this was going to be a longer day than most.

"What do you think, Austin? Are you rocking with me?" Colin hollered, strutting across the outdoor stage. I braced myself against the scaffolding, but at the roar of the crowd on the lawn, he just brandished his guitar and launched into another song.

I let out the breath I'd been holding. So far, so good. Colin's half hour set was drawing to a close, and he'd done nothing Sterling or the record label could complain about. My gaze wandered over the stage to Marcy wailing on her bass, Kevin pounding chords on his keyboard, Joel's sticks flying over the drum kit with a precise power I couldn't help admiring. A twitch ran up my arms. It had been so easy to release any tension that was gripping me back when I still played regularly. I'd just sit down at Dad's old home kit and give myself over to the rhythm and the flow.

Yeah, I missed it. That didn't mean going back to it was a good idea.

I pulled my attention back to the crowd. We had two Glowers in attendance—which was to be expected given the number of bands involved in the festival, but I'd still have preferred to see none. A black guy with neat cornrows and a wide-collared suit had been hanging out near the fringes of the crowd since the set before Colin's, his eyes sparking every time he blinked. And a strawberry blonde girl—if she'd had a human age, it couldn't have been more than eighteen—had been moshing by the front of the stage for the last fifteen minutes, hair flashing and face tilted back. She looked taller and curvier than the redhead who'd been chasing Colin before, but that didn't mean it wasn't her. I didn't know yet just how dedicated that Glower was, and I wouldn't be able to get a sense without a close encounter. I hoped it wouldn't come to that.

An odd twang split the air. My gaze jerked back to the band. Colin was still singing, but he was staring down at his guitar—at one of the strings, snapped. A tight little smile curled his lips as he drew in a breath. The crew probably had spares somewhere, that was standard, but with just a couple minutes left in the set, there wasn't much point in stopping to search for one now.

"Well, look at that," he said instead of continuing the song, and his tone made my back go rigid even before he brought down his hand, wrenching across the remaining strings. Another snapped. Colin laughed, but it was a rough humorless sound. The rest of the band kept playing, their eyes on him, Joel paling, Marcy biting her lip. *They* clearly knew this wasn't leading anywhere good.

Before I could even consider stepping onto the stage after him, Colin yanked the guitar strap over his head. With a swing of his corded arms, he slammed the instrument into the stage. Then he stomped his heel down on body—I winced at the crunch of splitting wood—and jogged backward a few paces to take a running kick at it. His foot sent the crumpled guitar spinning toward the far speakers.

"That's all I've got for you tonight, Austin," Colin shouted into his mic, and hurled that away too. The other instruments petered out as he stalked off stage without so much as a glance at his bandmates. Or at me.

I hurried around the scaffolding as Kevin retrieved the mic. "I guess that's a wrap, folks," he said. "Thanks for listening to the great Colin Ryder!" An edge of sarcasm colored his voice.

It'd be just great if Colin alienated the rest of the people he needed to make his album along with his producers and the label.

Some of the crowd had spilled around the sides of the stage. I wove through the clustered figures, silently cursing every person who just stood there in my way, oblivious until I said, "Excuse me?" Finally I reached the back, where a set of stairs allowed access on and off stage.

Colin was already gone. Of course he wouldn't have waited for me. I turned on my feet, and it occurred to me that I hadn't spot-checked the Glowers before I'd taken off after him. I wasn't sure they'd stuck around for that last minute while he was throwing his tantrum. One of them could have come around back here to intercept him...

No. If someone had confronted him, he'd still be here. He'd probably headed to the trailer he'd been given as a dressing room, one of the many in their rows beyond the chain link fence.

I loped over to the gate, flashed my ID to the security guards, and counted rows as I hustled past trailer after trailer. Colin's had been near the back. Seven rows down, two over. Right—

My legs stalled as I came up on the seventh row.

Colin was there, standing outside the trailer door. And with him was the Glower girl from the crowd. She was leaning into him, peering at him coyly through her lashes as she walked her fingers up his arm. Her lips were moving too, with words too soft for me to make them out. They glittered in the air like shards of glass caught in the sunlight. Colin's head tipped closer to hers, and I knew.

She was asking the question to mark him—in the Glowers' twisted way, obscuring exactly what sort of deal she was proposing. And by every appearance, Colin was about to accept.

Nine

I WASN'T PREPARED FOR THE RUSH OF EMOTION THAT HIT me, seeing the Glower so close to Colin—both his body and his soul. The usual surge of protective instinct, the fear even as I bolted toward them that I wouldn't move fast enough to save him, that was familiar. But something stronger, deeper, wrenched through me alongside them.

He hadn't even flirted with another girl in front of me since that night we'd kissed. I couldn't have known how much it would ache to watch his hand drift toward her waist, the distance close between their mouths. As if she'd ripped him away from me and stolen my place.

So I might have used a little more force than I'd have otherwise brought to bear when I grabbed the Glower by the shoulders and yanked her away from Colin. She stumbled into the side of the trailer opposite. Sparks flickered in the air at the impact. I stepped in front of Colin, my lungs heaving to catch my breath after my mad dash. She straightened up and faced me with a gleam dancing like fire within her glare.

"Avery," Colin said, so low and pained I couldn't help jerking my gaze away from the Glower. Had she marked him after all? No glimmer of a mark shone in his chest, or his face as I searched that too, but the tension in his jaw and the raw wildness in his eyes made my chest clench up. What had she said to him? What had she promised?

I could find that out later. I turned back to the Glower, shifting into a defensive stance when she eased a step closer. "It's time for you to leave," I said. "You're not welcome here."

"Don't you want me to stay, Colin?" she purred, looking past me to him, his name silvery sweet from her lips. In that moment I was sure she was the same Glower who'd been watching him before. I swallowed hard.

Colin drew in a breath, and hesitated. Worse than a no, but better than a yes.

"Colin needs to get ready for the gala dinner," I said. "He doesn't have time to entertain visitors right now."

She kept her gaze on him. "You should go," he said quietly, and my muscles sagged in relief.

The Glower's lips pursed. For a second I thought she was going to fight. Then she shrugged and flipped back her shimmering hair.

"Some other time then," she said with an edge of challenge meant just for me, and sauntered off.

Colin pushed open the trailer door. As I followed him in, nerves still jangling, he spun on me. The apparent anguish I'd seen in him before had vanished. His eyes were hard in the dim light.

"What the hell was that?" he demanded as the door thumped shut behind us. "I'm not allowed to have any fun now? She was just offering a good time."

"Believe me, it would have been anything but good if I

hadn't gotten here when I did," I said. "You have no idea who she is. That's why you're *supposed* to wait for me to check things out before you start making new 'friends.' And while we're asking questions, maybe you can tell me what the hell you were doing on stage just now? It didn't look like bold macho bravado, if that's what you were going for. It looked like you were having a psychotic episode."

Colin's mouth flattened. "So?" he said. "It'll get people talking. If the label complains about it, they're idiots. All publicity is good publicity, isn't that what they say?"

The defiance in those words would have fed my anger if I hadn't caught a hint of that earlier rawness in his voice. I paused, taking in the set of his shoulders, his hands balled into fists at his sides. The erratic rise and fall of his chest, as if he'd been the one racing over here. Under my scrutiny, his mask wavered, something like panic flashing through his expression.

"What's going on, Colin?" I asked, my own voice softening. "Please. I want to help, but I can't when you're stonewalling me like this." Like every time I thought we'd come to a basic understanding and then he did a U-turn on me.

"It's nothing," he said. "Stressful day. Blowing off some steam."

"It looked like more than that."

"Well, I can't help that," he said. "There's nothing else to tell."

I didn't believe him, but by now I knew if I pushed harder he'd just double down on his denial. "Okay," I said. "It's probably not that big a deal." As long as it didn't keep happening. "Can you at least promise you won't take off on me like that anymore? If you decide you don't want to talk to me, or even look at me, whatever, that's up to you, but you've got to let me keep up."

"So you can protect me from the groupies?" he said with a crooked smile.

"You know I haven't stopped you from hooking up with other people," I said. "You have to trust me that I know which ones to avoid."

"She didn't look all that dangerous to me."

"Because she wouldn't want you to see that. That's how predators work—by convincing everyone else they're part of the herd."

I expected Colin to ask what sort of predator this one was, readying myself with one of the pre-approved stories I had memorized, but he just sighed. The dejection in his posture sent a pang through me. Was he really *that* disappointed to have lost out on what he'd thought was a quick roll in the hay?

"Anyway," I added before I could think better of it, "I thought you didn't really like those girls."

He gave me a look then, so serious and intent that you'd have thought my response could determine the fate of nations. It took me back to our conversation in the penthouse right before he'd kissed me. When he'd seemed so concerned about whether I cared and why.

"I'm not getting offers from anyone else," he said. "If those are the only girls who want me, then those are the girls I have."

In that moment, with his gaze fixed on me, every inch of my skin tingled with my awareness of him, even though he was standing five feet away. My lungs contracted.

It wasn't true. He had to know that wasn't true.

Or maybe he didn't. All he knew was that I'd broken off our kiss and barely exchanged more than small talk with him since. He didn't know how often the memory of the kiss had played through my head. How my heart had flipped at the sight of him with the Glower girl.

Which was exactly why I shouldn't even be thinking about this. Falling for him wasn't going to do either of us any good. And just the thought of those lips on mine again was enough to make the wall inside me tremble.

So I was going to tell him that? That I wanted him too much to give in to it? *The job,* I thought, but that excuse no longer felt the slightest bit solid. *The only rule anyone really cares about is whether you keep the client safe,* Fee had said, and I knew she was right. She spent hours with her client drunk or high and no one at the Society had complained. All I wanted to do was make out with mine, and that wasn't going to prevent me from being able to protect him.

In fact, it might *help* me protect him. Glowers had a knack for picking up on their target's emotions, sensing their weaknesses. This Glower had clearly decided the best way to get to him was not through drugs or insecurity or pride, but desire. If he focused that desire on me, even for a little while, maybe she'd find him not so easy a catch after all. Maybe she'd give up. Maybe it'd give me the time I needed to find a more permanent solution he'd agree to.

Wasn't a little heartbreak worth it if I saved his soul along the way?

I sucked in a breath, abruptly lightheaded. Then I reached inside me and kicked over that wall. "They're not," I said, holding Colin's gaze as the truth of my words coursed through me. "They're not the only girls who want you."

He stepped toward me, still studying my face. I had to raise my chin to keep my eyes on his. My heart was thudding so hard I could feel it right through to my fingertips.

"No?" he said.

"No."

His voice dropped. "You said, before— "

"I thought I couldn't let myself. I changed my mind."

"Really." Colin smiled again, with an echo of both that cocky grin of challenge and the boyish enthusiasm that came over him while performing. It was an intoxicating combination. His head dipped and his breath tickled over my cheek. His hand rose to the collar of my shirt, his thumb brushing my collarbone as he fingered the button there. The contact sent a tremor of anticipation through me. "I'm just that irresistible?" he said.

My laugh came out breathless. "If that's how you want to see it."

"Hmmm." He slid the button from its hole and traced his fingers down to the next, just above the center of my bra. His body was so close to mine that the scent of him filled my nose with each breath, the faded pine and mint of his aftershave under the musky sweetness of the sweat he'd worked up on stage, and yet that was the only point where we were touching. "I don't know how much I really care, as long as I can keep doing this."

Second button undone. Down to the third. I exhaled shakily, but somehow managed to keep my voice even. "You want *me* that much?"

Colin chuckled low in his throat. "Avery, I've wanted you since I watched you toss that jackass on his back in the Catacomber." Then, as the third button came loose in his grasp, he ducked his head and pressed his mouth to the crook of my neck.

Heat swelled in my chest and below as he kissed his way across my left shoulder and then down over the modest swell of my breasts toward the right, tugging my shirt further open to clear the path. A sound like a whimper crept from my throat, more needy than I'd ever heard myself. Had I really considered denying myself this?

My fingers curled into his shirt, my breath stuttering as he grazed my skin with a hint of teeth, a flick of tongue. My lips had parted, neglected in the still air.

"Colin," I whispered, pleading. He nipped the corner of my jaw. Then my hands were clutching the sides of his head, drawing his mouth to mine.

We kissed slow, deep, lingering, not the headlong rush of the other night. His arm tucked around me, pulling my body against his until I was drowning in him. I still wanted more. My hand trailed down his side and slipped under his shirt. I reveled in his pleased hum as I traced the taut muscles along his torso, the fine curls of hair down the middle of his chest, faintly damp from his recent performance.

Colin reached for my shoulder without breaking the kiss, coaxing my bra strap to the side until it trailed down my arm. Then his hand slid under the loosened cup to cradle my breast. His tongue glided out to caress mine as his thumb teased around my nipple. I moaned, my hips flexing against his of their own accord, the deepest hottest ache gathering between them.

I'd never slept with a guy on a first date—and I hadn't been on *anything* you could exactly call a date with Colin. But I'd never been with a guy whose touch lit me up like his did. We'd been circling around each other for weeks. Maybe this wasn't moving fast but the urgency of having waited so long.

His mouth left mine, trailing a slow hot line down my throat as he pushed aside the other bra strap. His fingers stroked the side of my breast as his thumb had its way with the nipple, edging back and forth around the hardened nub, each movement sending an electric pulse of pleasure through me. A cry lodged in my throat as his lips caught its partner. His tongue mimicked the rhythm of his thumb, slick and fleeting, and all I could do was hold on to him, my legs starting to tremor.

"Good?" he murmured against my sensitized skin, and I let out a giggle that hardly sounded like me at all.

"I think," I started, my hands closing around the hem of his shirt with every intention of yanking it off and pulling his bare chest against mine through another kiss, and someone knocked on the trailer door. Barely two steps away.

I flinched, my body going rigid. Colin raised his head without moving away from me and glanced toward the door. I registered the closed shutters on the windows with relief. I'd been so caught up in him I hadn't thought of privacy.

The knock came again. "Col," Joel said, "we're due in fifteen minutes. You coming?"

The dinner. I'd forgotten that too. I pulled back, shooting Colin a pointed look. He grimaced.

"Yeah," he called to Joel. "I'll meet you there."

We stood there for a few moments, the air filled with the rasp of our settling breaths, until I was sure Joel had left. Colin turned back to me.

"Avery."

"You should get cleaned up and go," I said, even though every cell in my body was urging me to leap right back into our interrupted embrace. "Not because I actually want to stop what we were just doing. But... It'll look *really* bad if you throw a fit at the end of your set and then don't even turn up for the second half of the event."

"Who says I care how it looks?" he grumbled, bending to nuzzle the shell of my ear. I braced my hands against his shoulders, easing him back so I could look him in the eyes.

"Maybe you don't care," I said, "but you should. And *I* care. If you pull a no-show, I'm going to be in more trouble than you are."

That last comment hit home. Colin made a face, but he

trailed his hands around to the front of my shirt and started doing the buttons back up. I tugged my bra straps up, swallowing a sigh as the cups pressed over my still-tender nipples.

"But we're not done," Colin said, and waited until I met his eyes. "Us. This. You're not taking off on *me?*"

"No," I said with a twinge in my heart and more honesty than he knew. "You've got me."

For now he was looking at me, not thinking of the women out there, especially the ones with glimmers in their eyes and on their breath. That was what mattered most.

Sterling was waiting for me when the plane landed in L.A., standing just inside the sliding doors beyond the tarmac, his face nearly as dark as the night amid the glow of the interior lights. I let the band and the scattering of security and airport personnel who'd come out to meet them pass me by. Colin shot me a curious glance, but he was deep in hushed conversation with Joel, who'd gone tight-lipped and edgy after a phone call a few minutes before landing.

Sterling fell into step with me behind the others. "Is everything okay?" I asked, bracing myself. It was past midnight. I was tipsy from the gala dinner's wine and the other sorts of glances Colin had directed my way throughout the flight. The last thing I wanted to do right now was talk with my boss. Especially when seeing Sterling reminded me that regardless of my intentions, I doubted *he'd* explicitly approve of my new arrangement with my client.

"That's what I'd like to hear from you," he said. "I was

informed that Ryder had some sort of... fit during his performance this afternoon."

I found myself rising to defend the exact behavior I'd chastised Colin for six hours ago. "He's doing the rocker thing. Smash the guitar. Play the prima donna. It wasn't anything extreme."

"Has he drawn attention?" Sterling said tightly.

I didn't need to ask what sort of attention he meant. "There's been one Glower hanging around," I admitted, my stomach knotting as the image of her fingers trailing up Colin's arm flashed back to me. "But I haven't let her—it—get close to him." *Much*. "I have the situation under control." *Not really at all. But hopefully more so now.*

"Avery," Sterling said, stopping, so I was forced to stop too. He peered at me with a frown. "You know how tenuous this situation is."

Which was exactly why I couldn't tell him how uncertain I was. What was he going to do to fix this—send in another mentor figure who'd raise Colin's hackles all over again? I'd made more progress than the last two Tethers had in a fraction of the same time. I *would* get the situation under control.

"I do," I said. "He has some personal issues to work through before I think we'll be able to pitch anything that'll protect him long term. But he's opening up."

"All right," Sterling said. "Record anything you notice, then. If we lose him, I want Spright Records to understand it was due to circumstances beyond our purview."

"Do you really think they'd give up on the Society's services across the board?" I asked, a chill trickling through me as I remembered his comments the week before.

Sterling's jaw tensed. "The representative I've been speaking with said as much during our last conversation."

My stomach clenched further as we started walking again. Too much depended on this, on me and Colin.

"I don't want you letting Ryder out of your sight from here on," Sterling went on. "Unless he's asleep or in the bathroom, you should have a direct view."

I nodded. Easier said than done, but I didn't want to admit that either. I'd just have to up my game. For Colin, and for all the other musicians who needed the label to keep their faith in us. "I can do that."

"Good."

The band had reached the doors that led out to the drive where our cars would be waiting. As they spilled onto the front walk, Colin halted to let me catch up, still with Joel, who was gesturing urgently with his hands as he talked. Sterling motioned me off to the side where we could see them through the window. He touched my arm, his grip terse.

"Don't let him end up like your dad, Avery," he said. "They've taken too many good ones so young already."

A lump rose in my throat. "I know," I said.

He tipped his head in dismissal. My heart was heavy as I pushed past the doors. It lightened slightly at the almost shy smile that crossed Colin's face as I joined him and Joel by the Mercedes.

"Joel's crashing at my place," he said with a hint of apology in his tone. "He and his boyfriend had a big argument, and since we both need to be at the studio tomorrow morning anyway..."

"It's fine," I said, giving his arm a little nudge. Putting a temporary pause on what we'd started in his trailer might not be a bad thing. The longer it dragged out, the longer it'd be me he was focused on, not that Glower in her various personas. "Are you all right?" I asked Joel as we squeezed into the car.

The drummer shrugged. His pale face was still taut. "I'll survive."

"He'll come around, right?" Colin said, his tone breezy but his gaze concerned as he studied his friend's expression.

"He always does," Joel agreed. "I just hope at some point we can start skipping the blow up phase." He glanced at me. "Philippe doesn't like how unpredictable my schedule's gotten. He doesn't get that you have to give what the industry demands or you're out."

Colin grimaced. "And I haven't exactly helped. I'll try to keep the recording sessions on track."

"Don't worry about it," Joel said. "We were playing together before I even met him—he needs to be more flexible." But there was a jerkiness to the wave of his hand that showed how much uneasiness he was holding in.

"Then I promise you this," Colin said. "When we get back to my place, I am going to kick your ass in Halo so hard you won't be thinking about anything else."

Joel laughed and Colin grinned, and for the rest of the drive I could almost believe everything *was* fine. Then we pulled up outside the condo building, and an odd glint caught my eye beyond the corner of the lobby.

I hung back as Colin and Joel headed for the elevator, peering through the scattered lamplight. My gaze came to rest on a slight figure in front of the low rise next door.

The Glower. Back in her L.A. form, pale redhead. She caught me looking and fluttered her fingers at me with a thin smile. The knots in my stomach retied themselves. Couldn't she give Colin a break for just one night?

At least she hadn't tried to approach us. She was smart enough to realize that would be overkill, I guessed. Even without Glower sight, a person could sense something was off with enough exposure. She wouldn't want to risk irritating Colin when she'd been so close to marking him.

Maybe because of Sterling's last remark, a memory swam up in my mind: Dad slumped on the studio floor, the glowing figure leaning over him, draining the last spark of his life. I spun on my heel and strode across the lobby.

"Mr. Ryder's having an issue with a stalker," I said to the security officers by the front doors. "Young woman, short, slim, light red hair—maybe you've noticed her hanging around before? She's got the place staked out from down the street. Can you get her to move off?"

I doubted it was their jurisdiction when she wasn't right outside, but you didn't pay the prices to live in a building like this and get staff who questioned many requests. One of the guys marched out. He returned a minute later, brow furrowed.

"She must have left," he said politely, but I could hear a note of doubt in his voice. "There's no one out there, Miss."

Oh. My face warmed as I understood. She hadn't been here for Colin after all. This had been about taunting—and, if possible, embarrassing—me. And I'd walked right into her snare.

Ten

Just as we reached the studio the next morning, Colin's phone rang. I knew the instant he said, "Hello," with that dry edge to his tone that it was one of his parents. His voice dropped as he spoke, though he wasn't saying much more than, "Yes. I know. I know. Of course." He motioned for Joel and I to go on ahead of him.

We lingered outside the studio doors as Colin's expression became progressively more clouded through the Audi's windshield. My spirits sank. I'd thought this was going to be a good session up until now.

"Do you know the whole story with his parents?" I asked Joel tentatively. Maybe Colin had shared more with him than he'd been willing to with me.

Joel scuffed his sneaker against the pavement, his hands in his pockets. "I've just gathered that they're jerks. He's always in a crap mood after he talks to them—or worse, sees them." He made a face. "I think it's a money thing. They don't care what he's doing as long as he shares the wealth. And they seem to want a lot of it. 'Least that's the impression I've gotten. Don't tell him I told you that."

Colin got out of the car, shoving the phone into his pocket. "All right, let's get this over with," he said as he strode over.

That stormy attitude smoldered on through several awkward false starts of a new song, three conferences with the producer during which Colin did most of the speaking, his voice constantly rising, and finally an argument that started with Kevin mixing up the harmonics and ended up with all four of the bandmates snapping at each other and waving their hands as they gave evidence on who exactly was screwing the entire album up the most. I cringed as I watched through the control room's window. The producer sighed and rubbed his forehead.

"Hey," he called into his mic. "Let's call a half hour break. Take a walk, have a breather, simmer down, and then we'll start again."

Joel immediately stalked out of the building. Marcy and Kevin wandered down the hall, still muttering to each other. Colin threw up his arms, and then hauled his preferred electric guitar into one of the iso rooms.

I slipped out, thinking I'd try talking to him—as much good as that usually did—but the iso room's door slammed shut just as I stepped into the live room. I stood there for a moment, inhaled, exhaled, and decided I was better off letting him be, at least for the first half of this break. Maybe I couldn't see him, but there was no way into that room except through this one as long as he was unmarked. He was safe enough. And there was no way I was getting through to him until he'd cooled off a little.

I leaned against the wall, running through possible openers in my head and rejecting them in turn. After a bit, my gaze crept to the drum kit beyond one of the other iso room doorways. My fingers itched. A little musical therapy was exactly what *I* needed to get my thoughts sorted out.

Well, why not? I'd made out with my client and the world hadn't ended. Joel had offered to let me play the other day—I didn't think he'd be offended if I took him up on the offer now. I'd just tap away a little, no big deal, and maybe the perfect solution to this mess would come to me.

I ambled over, leaving the door open so that if Colin came out I'd see him. The sticks felt good in my hands, light but substantial. I perched on the seat, spinning one stick and then the other, taking in the weight and length of them. Then I rested my foot on the pedal and launched into a basic warm-up exercise.

My fingers started to ache after just a couple minutes—I loosened my grip, reminding myself not to clutch—and I wasn't as fast as I'd once been, but the lack of practice hadn't erased the muscle memory. My rusty arms flowed through the motions as if they'd been waiting for a kit to appear before them. I let them leap from the practice rhythm into the drum section from one of Dad's songs, a more complex beat that made me stumble a couple times before I got the hang of it again. The stretch and burn of muscles I hadn't used much in the last few years felt even better than I'd remembered. My mind drifted with it for just a moment, and when I jerked my attention back to the world around me, Colin was leaning against the doorway, watching me with a triumphant smile.

I dropped my hands to my lap, and he straightened up. "Still good," he said. "I figured you would be. You don't just lose skills like that."

"I guess not," I said. It'd been other things I'd been afraid I'd lose if I kept going. I stood up. "Is everyone back already?" It'd only been ten minutes.

Colin shook his head, his smile fading. "I just wanted to tell you I'm leaving."

"Well, if you're taking a walk, I'll walk with you."

"No," he said. "I mean really leaving. We're not getting anything decent done today."

My gut twisted. "You've hardly been here an hour," I said. "If you take off on people again and again, then—"

I hesitated, and he folded his arms over his chest. "Then?"

"Then maybe they stop showing up at all," I said quietly.

His mouth flattened. He glanced behind him, checked that the sound out of the room was switched off, and then jerked the door shut with a click of the lock.

"Maybe I don't want them showing up," he said. "Maybe what I need is a better band."

I didn't think he'd have cared whether they heard him say that if he'd really meant it, but it seemed unwise to point that out. "This isn't really about them, though, is it?" I said. "You're pissed off because of that conversation with your parents."

"It's the band too," Colin said with a twitch of his hand toward the live room. "The song isn't *right* yet. I can hear it. It's not *there*. But they all want to just lay it down with what we have and move on."

"It's not as if you're carving it into stone," I said. "You can always leave it as a rough cut and go back to it later when you've got a better idea of the shape of the album. People do that all the time. My dad sometimes re-recorded songs from scratch at the end of a session. It's no big deal."

Colin paused. "I guess," he said. "I've never... The first album, we basically produced it ourselves. I didn't have a label breathing down my neck."

"Well, it's still your music," I said. "You still get a say. I don't know exactly what's in your contract, but unless your manager is a total incompetent, the label can't just release whatever they want. And they'll *want* you to be happy, because happy musicians give better PR. Do you really think they'd be putting up with the crap you've been pulling otherwise?"

He rubbed the back of his neck, looking suddenly sheepish. It was kind of an adorable look on him. My pulse fluttered.

"Probably not," he admitted. He drew in a breath and released it slowly. I could see the tension easing out of his muscles beneath the thin fabric of his T-shirt. But he lingered, as if he were dreading going back out. His gaze wandered around the room and back to me.

"Is that why you do this job?" he asked. "Because of your dad? Trying to save us unstable creative types from our self-destructive impulses?"

My smile tasted bittersweet. "That's part of it." You could claim that technically Dad's death was all of it. The only reason I could fill this job was because of him, because I'd been there as the Glower stole the last of his soul. I didn't know how any person could see something like that and not want to do everything in their power to stop it from happening to anyone ever again.

"I'm sorry," Colin said. "I know I've been making the job more difficult for you."

I smiled more easily at that. "It's always difficult," I said. "And this one *has* come with occasional perks..."

I couldn't suppress the giddy feeling that tickled through me seeing the way his amber eyes brightened as I walked up to him, the way his lips quirked up. I didn't *want* to suppress it. It was better to think about this, about the living boy in front of me, than about those long dead and gone. I set my hands carefully on Colin's chest, just above his stomach, and tipped my head to catch his gaze again.

"You know," I said, "that half hour break isn't up yet, and you've spent most of it stressing out. I think you need to clear your head."

His grin curved higher. "I don't suppose you have some suggestions for how I could manage that?"

"Maybe one or two." Being this close to him only made me more dizzy, but in a good way. And there were things I hadn't gotten to do yesterday before we'd been interrupted.

I slid my hands to the bottom of his shirt and tugged it up. Colin helped me peel it off, watching me with hungry curiosity. Waiting to see what I would do next. I splayed my fingers against his bare skin, feeling the muscles tremor beneath my touch, breathing in piney aftershave and a salty-sweet smell that might have been soap or shampoo or just him. I thought about yesterday afternoon in the trailer.

Turnabout was fair play. I was at the perfect height to kiss his collarbone. I trailed my lips along it across the center of his chest, tasting the soft skin over hard bone, while I traced the silky firm planes of his abdomen with my hands. Colin made a rough noise in his throat. He brought his hands to my head, twining his fingers in my hair. Not directing, just following. His fingertips sent pleasant shivers through my scalp with each caress.

I bent my head to one of his small nipples, grazed it with my lips, and was rewarded with a ragged inhale. With a smile I suspected looked rather wicked, I closed my mouth around it, testing the pattern of his breath with the delicate scrap of my teeth, a slide of my tongue. Then I traveled across the wispy hairs of his sternum to repeat my experiment on the opposite side.

"Avery," Colin muttered, his grip on my hair tightening, and offered an inarticulate sound when I pursed my mouth around the other nipple. I savored the feel of the nub against my tongue, the taste of his skin, that same salty-sweetness.

"Good?" I murmured, echoing his question from yesterday, and he groaned.

"You know what would be even better?" he said, and let go of my hair to catch my waist. As I raised my head, he spun us around, lifting me at the same time to brace my back against the wall. Our bodies conformed together, his hips holding mine in place. Then his mouth was crushing mine.

I kissed him back just as hard, my fingers intertwining behind his neck. His tongue licked into my mouth and out again, and mine chased after, mingling with his. His hands ran over my sides and under my shirt. He broke the connection of our lips just long enough to yank the shirt up and off. Then he was kissing me again, deep and needy. Every nerve in my body was singing. I didn't know which I liked better, this fierceness or yesterday's tenderness. I just knew I didn't want it to stop.

My thighs tightened around his as he eased me off the wall, steadying me with a hand on my hip as the other found the clasp of my bra. With a practiced ease I didn't let myself dwell on, he unhooked it and tugged it off too. We pressed against the wall again, bare against each other from head to waist. He shifted his weight, and the feel of his skin grazing my breasts made me whimper.

He kept his right hand on my thigh, thumb massaging in a loose semicircle, as the left slipped between us. His fingers traced around my breast teasingly, closer and closer to the point that was begging for contact. Then he snagged the nipple between his fingers, rolling it gently. I arched against him, moaning, and he clutched me tighter to him. To the hard length I could feel through his jeans and my leggings, flush against the core of me.

Colin released my lips to nibble down the side of my throat, trading hands to fondle my other breast. I grasped the hair at the top of his neck and tugged the way I had accidentally the first time we'd kissed. His hips jerked against mine with an electrifying pressure.

"Avery," he said against my shoulder. "Avery." As if he'd lost all capacity for speech except my name. A laugh escaped me, transforming into a gasp as he rolled his hips against me again. The room spun around us. His thumb ran along the waist of my leggings, hooking inside it by the small of my back.

"Can I...? Can we...?" he rasped, so desperate and wanting it stole my breath. I nodded, my head bowed to his, and he leaned in to capture my mouth with another kiss as he eased the clinging fabric down over my panties.

That was when the speaker near the ceiling crackled on.

"We're reconvening in the live room to discuss a plan for the rest of the morning," the producer's voice hummed out. "Ready to join us, Colin?"

Colin's hand stilled on my rear, and I tipped my head against the wall with a cringe. Thank God for soundproofed walls. Colin nuzzled his face against the side of my neck with a hoarse breath.

"We really need to pick our locations better," he said, and the laugh that comment provoked softened my disappointment. I dropped my feet to the floor as he tugged my leggings back up.

"Or our timing," I pointed out, letting my fingers trail down his chest one last time before I bent to pick up our discarded clothes. "Is your head clear?"

He chuckled as he walked to the intercom. "Of band drama, yeah. Now it's full of you."

"Well, go put that energy into your performance," I said. "I'm not going anywhere."

He shot me a look that seemed oddly startled before he

pressed the talk button. "I'll be out in a jiff," he said. I wondered what the rest of the band had made of our disappearance, and then decided it didn't matter. Because Colin was ambling back toward me, taking his tee from me and balling it in his hand as he leaned close for one more kiss.

"You'll be watching?" he said.

"The whole time." As Sterling had ordered. I watched Colin even now, as I reassembled my own outfit. Taking in the hesitation in his glance toward the door after he'd pulled on his shirt. The hint of tension creeping back into the set of his jaw. We'd been so close just a minute ago, and already I was losing him.

I stepped toward him, touching his arm. "Colin," I said, and he looked at me. "You're amazing. So this album is going to be amazing. Remember that, all right?"

Eleven

"So what's good here?" Mom said, and I tried not to stare as emergent rock star Colin Ryder gave my mother ordering tips across the ivory restaurant tablecloth. I was still somewhat bewildered by this turn of events. Mom had called me while we were driving home, and as I'd been telling her I wasn't sure when we could get together next, Colin had pointed out that he and I did need to eat dinner, and somehow that had ended with us arriving at a posh downtown establishment that had required Colin pull a blazer out of the car trunk to be allowed in—though I suspected he'd had to slip the maître de a sizeable tip to overlook the jeans.

I wouldn't have pictured him hanging out in a place with polished silverware and vested wait staff, but he'd said this was one of his favorite restaurants. I wasn't sure if he was trying to impress me or Mom, or maybe both of us.

Apparently Mom was already impressed. "Are you going for a similar sound with the new album?" she asked Colin after the waiter had taken our orders and glided off. "I thought your first was wonderful—there was an energy in it that too few new acts manage to capture these days."

Colin grinned. "I'm honored to hear that. I know anyone who took the name Harmen has got to have good taste."

"Oh." Mom flushed a little, fidgeting with her fork. But before I could get out the words to change the subject, she brushed aside her feathered bangs and glanced up at him again. "You're familiar with Roy's work?"

"Sure," Colin said. "My uncle was a big fan—he's the one who gave me my first guitar and started teaching me to play. And I try to listen to anyone whose music was respected, regardless of the decade. If you don't know your history, you end up writing the same stuff everyone's already heard."

A small smile crept across Mom's face. "Roy used to say something a lot like that."

"Hey," Colin said, "he toured with the Stones once or twice, didn't he?"

"He did," Mom said, her smile brightening. "That was before we were even married—I was so worried they'd think I wasn't 'cool' enough, the girlfriend tagging along and cramping his style—I wasn't used to the life yet. If that kind of tour doesn't prepare you for it, nothing will."

Within a few minutes, he had her laughing as she told tales of Mick Jagger and Keith Richards' backstage exploits, some of which Dad had gotten himself wrapped up in too. Some of which *I'd* never heard about. By the time we'd finished our appetizers, Colin had gotten it out of Mom that Dad had been close buddies with Eddie Vedder until an argument over pizza toppings, that she'd once helped Dad flee a hotel where his band had trashed the room, and that I'd conducted my first drum performance on his lap at age three as he guided my hands through the motions. Mom paused there, dapping a shrimp in the last bit of cocktail sauce, still smiling even though her eyes had gone misty.

"There were a lot of good times," she said. "Can you excuse me for a minute? I think I'll use the facilities before the main course comes out."

Colin leaned back in his chair as he watched her go, and then glanced at me with a grin. "Your mom's awesome," he said.

I laughed. "I'm almost as surprised as you are." Which wasn't entirely true—I had always thought she was pretty awesome—but this was a side I hadn't seen before. Maybe I shouldn't have always been so careful about bringing up Dad. Maybe it was good for her to remember the times before everything had gone wrong. I hesitated, studying Colin before venturing, "Unlike your parents?"

"Ah, yeah. Like I told you before, they just don't get music." His tone was casual, but he shifted straighter, a stiffness creeping into his posture. "If it hadn't been for my uncle... They thought all the lessons and practice were a waste of time. If I'd listened to them, I never would have tried to get into Rushfield."

"That must be hard," I said. Even though I didn't play anymore, I couldn't imagine loving music as much as I did and not being able to talk about it with Mom. "But now that you've proven it's not a waste...?"

"They figure I got lucky. All they really look at is the cash that came with the deal."

Like Joel had said. I must have grimaced, because Colin made a dismissive gesture with his hand. "It's fine. When you've always been struggling to make ends meet, it's hard not to focus on the money. I get it. Hell, for the first few months after "Burning Starlight" took off, I had panic attacks about spending the earnings on anything that didn't seem 'necessary.' I don't mind sending some back home. The house needed work. They needed a break from stressing. I *want* them to be comfortable. I just..." He stopped, and for a moment I thought he was going to leave it there. He rubbed his mouth, contemplating the tabletop. Then he looked at me again. "It's like somehow I stopped being their son. Or even a person. As far as they're concerned, I'm an ATM."

He didn't have to tell me how much that hurt him. I could hear it in the roughness in his voice, see it in the twisting of his napkin between his fingers. My heart squeezed. I lay my hand over his.

"You know one of the best things about the music industry?" I said. "There's a ton of crap that goes on and a lot of competition, sure, but there's also a community. You connect with people, you find a different kind of family. After my dad... passed, there were always colleagues, people who'd respected him, who came by and helped out. We always had people to turn to. There'll be people like that for you too."

"I know," Colin said. "I had a bit of that... There was this one guy, a British rocker, who visited Rushfield—after you'd left. He liked what I was doing, introduced me to some people in town, just hung out and let me ask all kinds of dumb fifteen-year-old's questions. It was nice."

Something in his voice made me pause. "'Was'?" I said.

"We were supposed to hang out when he was back in town one time," Colin said. "But he— I found out— He'd hung himself."

My grip on his hand tightened. "I'm sorry," I said.

Colin exhaled and shrugged. "Lots of messed up people in this business, right? I guess that's why we all get along so well."

The self-deprecating smile he gave me looked genuine if pained. I didn't know what else to say. Then I caught sight of Mom emerging from the restroom nook at the back of the restaurant and eased back my hand. Colin looked up. When he saw her approaching, his expression settled back into its previous relaxed contentment.

None of what he'd just told me had been in the Society's file on him. I guessed the mentorship hadn't been especially public, and he hadn't warmed up to his past Tethers enough to start dishing about his family situation. Suddenly a large portion of what we'd been through, the things he'd done and said over the past few weeks, didn't seem quite so strange.

In some ways, he really was adrift. He *needed* a Tether, even if he'd thought it was the last thing he wanted. He needed someone to bring him back to earth when he started spiraling off in frustration, someone to remind him he wasn't alone.

When Mom sat down, we fell into the same light chatter, Colin drawing out a few more tour stories and then answering some of Mom's questions about pulling together his indie debut, me mostly listening. As the waiter cleared our plates, Colin got up, saying he needed to make a trip to the little boys' room. As soon as he'd walked away, Mom turned to me. The look on her face made my stomach flip. I braced myself for bad news.

"What?" I said.

"It's nothing yet," she said. "And I hope it stays nothing. I'm glad I got to meet him. He seems like a young man who should be going places."

That preamble only made me more nervous. "*What?*" I repeated.

"Sterling got a call from the record label a couple of hours ago," she said. "It seems one of Ryder's bandmates has been complaining about his behavior, wanting out. On top of everything else... They told Sterling that if they haven't seen improvement within the week, they're cancelling his and all their other contracts with the Society."

My skin went cold. Cancelling the contracts meant pulling me. Leaving Colin for the Glower who'd already almost marked him.

"They can't," I protested. "He's in danger. I'm getting somewhere with him, Mom, but there's no way I can make sure he's protected if I only have another week and then I'm gone."

"Well, hopefully it won't come to that," she said, her eyes downcast. "I just wanted you to hear, because I know Sterling is too caught up in the big picture to think to say it, that no matter what *does* happen, this isn't your fault. You have to remember that. Ryder's just been a difficult case, and the label's been unreasonable. You've done the best anyone could have expected. I can see you've gotten through to him so much more than the last two must have."

But it might not be enough. I sank down in my chair, my gut churning.

I'd never let myself imagine I was going to be with Colin forever. It seemed inevitable that his interest in me would be fleeting. What I hadn't considered was that I might be the one leaving *him*.

Two hours later, I was sitting at my desk in Colin's penthouse, debating whether to answer Fee's last text. It was the first conversation we'd had since that brunch, but I could tell from tonight's particularly creative grammar and spelling that she wasn't all there. Apparently she and the Starlet were out at some party for planning the after-party to that party? She wasn't making a whole lot of sense. *Wish u cud b here*, she'd sent a few minutes ago. *100xx grate times. Freekin awe mazing peeps.*

I wished she were anywhere but there. I wished I knew what

to say to her that wasn't a total lie and wouldn't sound like I was judging her. I didn't want her to end up shutting me out all over again... So it seemed safest not to say anything. To pretend I'd gotten busy and hadn't been able to respond. Maybe we'd find a chance to get together sometime soon and we could have a real talk.

I couldn't stand sitting there with the phone staring at me, though. I glanced out into the hall, but Colin was still holed up in *his* bedroom, which he'd wandered into after his manager had called as we'd come in from dinner. The length of that conversation made it feel ominous too, especially in light of what Mom had told me. I couldn't believe Joel would have turned on Colin while still acting so friendly to his face. Was it Marcy who'd been complaining about him, or Kevin?

An itch crept through my muscles. What I really wanted was a good run on Dad's drum kit, but I had other ways to burn through unwanted energy here.

I changed into my bathing suit and ambled out onto the terrace. After a couple laps in the pool, the burn I'd needed start to tickle through my body. I swam on, back and forth across the short distance between the walls, focusing all my attention on the sweep of my arms, the rhythm of my breath, and the tang of chlorine.

When the burn shifted from pleasant to painful, I rolled onto my back. Floating on the cool water, the hazy night sky spread above me, I felt far away from everything else in the world. From everything that might weigh me down.

At a faint splash, I lifted my head, letting my feet drop to the slippery tiles of the pool bottom. Even at the deeper end I could keep my chin above water if I stood on my tiptoes.

Colin had just sat down at the edge of the pool, setting his legs in the water. He must have noticed me out here a little while ago—he'd had time to change into his swim trunks. He smiled at me and I smiled back, somehow feeling less vulnerable cloaked in the ripples of the water, even though he had the higher ground.

"What did Fitch have to say?" I asked, trying to keep my worries out of my voice.

"She's arranged a last minute gig," he said. "Opening act at a concert this weekend. Some issue with the original band, they had to pull out. We're supposed to try out some of the new material on the crowd. It'll be good to see the response, I guess."

Not bad news, then. I smiled more freely. "I'm looking forward to it. I always prefer hearing songs live."

He squinted at me and raised an eyebrow. "You're still wearing that old suit. What happened to the new ones I got you?"

"I don't know what you're talking about," I deadpanned, and he flicked water at me with his foot. I grinned, gliding a little closer. "I'm not exactly in the habit of taking your orders, in case you hadn't noticed."

"You know, I actually had noticed that."

I caught his ankle before he could splash me again and nudged it back toward the wall. "It was a nice thought," I allowed. "But those bikinis are for girls who aren't me. I am the shape I am, and I'm fine with it, but I'm not going to dress like I'm someone else."

His expression turned serious as he looked down at me. "Have you really never had a guy make you feel you had a body worth showing off? That's just not right."

"It's not like that," I said. "I've had boyfriends; they made me feel... appreciated. There are just different kinds of showing off."

He made a dismissive noise. "Not appreciated enough, then. That's obviously why those boyfriends aren't still around."

"Nah," I said. "They just weren't right."

"You never got serious?"

"Well, the last one..." Mateo. My chest tightened, but only briefly. I kicked away, making a leisurely circuit of the pool. "We were together for almost a year. I would have gotten more serious, if things had been working out. But he just... He was very reserved, I guess. And even when we'd known each other a long time, whenever I'd bring up any more personal subjects, he never felt comfortable enough with me to share on the same level. I figured if he still didn't feel that deep a connection after a whole year, it probably wasn't ever going to happen."

I felt Colin's gaze following me across the water, though he was silhouetted in the dusk by the penthouse lights slanting through the window behind him. "Anyway," I added, "I don't think there's something wrong with the way I look. I just know there's a difference between me and someone with the sort of looks that get people throwing themselves at them every hour of the day. Like someone else around here, not to name any names."

Colin snorted. "Well, in my opinion anyone who overlooks you is the one missing out."

"Oh yeah?"

"Yeah." He slid into the water, landing with a slight bounce of his feet, and meandered toward me where I'd paused in the shallower water. "You're got that Joanna Newsom vibe going on, quirky-pretty, *real*, not trying to force yourself into some box someone else designed."

"Or some bathing suit someone else thinks I should wear?" I suggested, and he sprang at me through the water, catching my wrist.

"Touché," he said, tugging me toward him. "And you know what? Come to think of it, I'm okay with other people missing out. Less competition for me."

I laughed, with a little hitch of breath as his arms came around me, his skin slick but warm in the cool water. He sank onto one of the steps leading out of the pool, pulling me over to perch on his lap.

"I was thinking," he murmured, his lips grazing my cheek, "that there is no one but you and me on this entire floor of the building, and the door is locked, and my phone is turned off, which means I'm pretty sure there is no chance whatsoever of another unfortunate interruption."

A tingle ran through me as much at the words as the feel of his lips. "Interesting," I said. "I take it you have thoughts on how we should use this golden opportunity."

He didn't bother to answer, just tilted my mouth toward his.

There was something electric about kissing in the water, the faint chill on our lips playing against the warmth of our mingling breaths and the heat of our tongues. The way his fingers glided over my skin. The smooth ripple of the muscles in his shoulders, across his back, over his chest as my hands charted a path of their own. I pulled him closer, losing myself in the next kiss and the next. An ache of longing was already spreading through my body, but I wasn't going to hurry this. If this was it, if we went all the way and it turned out the once was enough to satisfy him, I'd never have another moment like this. So I was going to savor it for as long as I could.

He shifted me on him so I was straddling him before trailing his hands over my wet hair and down my back, and then cradling my face again to angle the next kiss into something even deeper. His fingers traveled down to the neckline of my top, finding the bow that tied the lacing there. With a tug, he'd loosened the knot.

"I have to admit, I do like this particular feature," he said against my jaw before kissing the crook of my neck. A breathless giggle escaped me. My head tipped back, the water buoying it, as his lips followed the curve of my throat and his fingers coaxed the lacing from each set of eyelets, one by careful one. The top hovered looser around my chest with each release.

He was good like this, I thought. He was good with me. Happy. Relaxed. Maybe, if what we had didn't end here—if I could hold his interest at least a little longer—maybe I could save him from more than just the literal demons out there. Maybe I could help him hold it together through the next week, make peace with his band, turn over a new leaf for the record label. Just... settle down a bit. And then, even if he broke my heart, even if he went back to chasing the "easy" girls at the concerts and in the clubs, at least I'd have guarded that happiness for whomever he decided to share it with next.

The idea came with a pang, but then Colin cast the last piece of lacing away and the sides of the top floated free. The caress of the water over my bare breasts stole every other thought from my mind. Colin slid his hands under them, smoothing his thumbs back and forth across the curve of my flesh, letting the tickle of the current tease my nipples hard until I could barely stand it.

I yanked his mouth back to mine, my fingers twisting his hair as we kissed and then gripping his shoulders. As he eased his hands up, the textured pads of his thumbs, creased and calloused by guitar strings, replaced the cool sweep of the water. I moaned into his mouth, and he drank the sound away.

My legs flexed against his as I sank deeper into his lap, where the hardness that pressed against me told me just how much he wanted this too. He brought one hand behind me, holding me even more firmly against him while his other hand continued to flick and fondle in its delicate torture. I arched into him and we both gasped.

"I love the sounds you make," he whispered, his fingers tracing down my thigh and back up again, and without intending to I cast my gaze toward the terrace wall. Toward the spot where I'd seen him in an embrace not unlike this with the blonde who'd been here my first day.

"Avery?" Colin said, and I realized I'd tensed against him. I let out a breath and jerked my gaze away, back to the desire in his bright eyes. When I leaned in to kiss him, he caught my cheek, holding me a few inches distant.

"What is it?" he said.

"Nothing," I said. "Nothing that matters."

"It matters," he said firmly. "I don't want— If we're moving too fast, if you're not sure—"

"No," I said, with a rasp of a laugh that must have convinced him, because his grip loosened enough that I could lean my head against his, forehead to temple. "It's not that. It's nothing like that." *I'm more sure I want you than I've been of anything else my entire life.* If I said the thought that had actually crossed my mind, would that kill *his* wanting? Transform me into the sort of uptight, jealous girl he'd want to run from, not to?

I couldn't screw this up. He needed *me*, at least for now.

"Avery," he said again. I could feel his heart thumping against my hands where they'd fallen to his chest. "Please. You can tell me."

I swallowed. "I just... I know it's not a fair thing to think, okay? And it's not as if I'm totally inexperienced. But I—I've never almost had sex in a recording studio, or had sex in a pool, or— It's new, and I *like* it, but you, and however many other girls there've been… It seems like this must be the same old thing for you."

Colin's hand stilled where he'd been stroking my hair. I closed my eyes, abruptly afraid that he was going to push me off him.

Instead he pulled me to him, wrapping his arms around me and conforming my body to his in an embrace that felt oddly chaste given what we'd just been doing—and yet at the same time more intimate than any we'd shared before.

"It's different," he said quietly by my ear. "It's new for me because I've never been with you."

Those words weren't enough to erase my unease completely. But they were something, and it wasn't as if I actually wanted to stop. I shifted back to find his lips with mine, but he cupped my face first, kissing my forehead, the tip of my nose, one cheek and then the other, before he finally met my mouth with his. I kissed him hard, my arms tight around him, but nothing I did could hold back the sensation of falling.

Just let this not be the last time, I thought. *Let it not end here. That's all I ask.*

For several minutes, we just kissed—harder, softer, tongues teasing in and out as the heat built back up between us—until I was pressing into him again, those two layers of fabric the worst impediment I could imagine. Colin's hand edged along my bathing suit bottom between us, his thumb dipping lower and lower until it pressed against the most sensitive point of my core. I cried out, my hips canting against his, and he groaned. He circled that point with steady strokes, radiating pleasure through me until I was throbbing with it. My head spun.

"Please," I whimpered, not caring how I sounded.

Colin groaned again and kissed me as he slid the bottoms

down, over the curve of my thighs. The water tickling between my legs sent a fresh pulse of pleasure through me. He set his hand there, the heel of his hand taking up that gentle circling, his fingers stroking lower.

"We're not actually going to have sex in the pool," he murmured. "Chlorine and condoms—bad mix. But I'll be damned if I'm stopping now. I'm going to make you feel better than any guy has in your life."

He already had, but I wasn't going to say that. I was hardly capable of speech. I moaned and swayed against him as he glided his fingers across my opening.

"Do you want to feel me inside you?" Colin said, and a laugh broke from my throat so tight it was almost a sob.

"Yes," I said. "God, yes."

He penetrated me as I gasped out the second assent, one of those skilled fingers sliding in and up until it found a tender spot inside that brought a fresh moan to my lips. I rocked against his hand, any shred of self-control I'd possessed disintegrating. He ran his fingertip over that spot again and again, the heel of his hand never ceasing its work without. I clutched his shoulders, his back, unable to do more than whimper a plea for release as tremors rippled from my core.

"Come for me, Avery," Colin said, low and ragged. He eased a second finger in to join the first. "Let me see you let go. Please."

The hunger in his voice tipped me over the edge. I cried out, my hips clenching as a final wave of bliss surged through me, trembling from my core down to my toes and up through my chest to tingle across my scalp. Stars danced behind my eyes.

As the ripples carried through me with the final thrusts of Colin's fingers, I melted against him, boneless in his embrace. The water lapped at my shoulders. He kissed me roughly as he withdrew his hand, gathering me against him. I leaned into him, my breaths shuddering through me, as those same fingers traced spirals over my spine.

"Good?" he said, and I found I had regained myself enough to chuckle.

"The best," I said, and his arms tightened around me. As I came back to myself, it occurred to me that he couldn't say the same.

I wasn't accepting that.

I tugged my bathing suit bottom back up, mostly because that was easier than squirming the rest of the way out of it, and settled over Colin again. Holding his gaze, I lay my fingers against his breastbone and trailed them down over the dark curls on his chest and stomach to the hard length of him still encased in his swim trunks.

"Your turn," I murmured.

As I closed my hand around him, his head tilted back with a choked sound, his eyelids fluttering to half-mast. I kissed his throat as I stroked him through the fabric of his trunks. Then, impatient with the obstruction, I yanked them down his hips to free him. His breaths turned shallow as I explored the silky hardness in my grasp, my thumb flicking over the tip and back again. He twitched beneath me at the gesture and arched his hips into my touch. Then he pulled my head back to his, kissing me with an edge of teeth against my lips, devouring my mouth.

I wrapped my fingers around him, finding a rhythm, shivering as I imagined that hardness inside me. "Tell me what you need," I said, grazing my lips along his jaw.

"Just like that," Colin muttered. "So good, Avery. God."

At another twitch, I firmed my grip, and the guttural sound that escaped him told me I'd taken the right tack. "Don't stop," he said in a strangled voice. "Almost. Ah. Faster. Yes."

As I sped up my rhythm, a moan broke from his lips and his hips spasmed beneath me. The flesh in my grasp quivered and pulsed. I kept going, slowing, gentling, but not letting him go, as the haze of his release dissipated into the water.

Colin closed his hand over mine, drawing it back to his face. He kissed my palm and adjusted me against him so our bodies connected perfectly. As if we'd never been meant to fit anywhere else. It was dizzying and lovely, and I never wanted to let him go.

I closed my eyes with my head bent next to his and squeezed away my tears.

Twelve

I'D DONE A DECENT JOB OF KEEPING MY WORRIES AT BAY the next morning, coasting on the good vibes from yesterday's encounter and the knowledge that Colin was heading back to the studio without a fuss. But I couldn't help noticing the way his gaze skimmed the sidewalk outside the condo building as he pulled the Audi out of the parking garage onto the road. The way his brow knit as if he were puzzled to find it bare.

My gut twisted. I could only think of one person he might have been expecting to see there: our red-headed friend. He'd seemed warm enough with me this morning, smiling so wide it sent a flutter through my chest when we'd met in the kitchen, stealing a couple kisses as we both ran around getting ready to leave, resting his hand on my back as the elevator had carried us down. Was he already thinking ahead to his next fling?

"Looking for someone?" I made myself ask, keeping my tone casual.

"Traffic seems lighter than usual," he said, which wasn't

really an answer. Then he drove around the corner and left the building and the Glower's recent haunt behind.

When we pulled into the studio parking lot, Colin glanced up at the building with a clenching of his jaw. We had more immediate problems.

I took his hand as he raised it from the gearshift. "Take it easy, all right?" I said. "Whatever you record today is going to be great, because you're great at what you do, and if it isn't quite great enough, you can fiddle with it later all you want."

His lips curled up, and he lifted his other hand to brush his thumb over my cheek. "Orders received, boss," he said teasingly.

As he leaned in to kiss me, the producer stepped past the main doors and turned our way. I stiffened, instinctively pulling back. My heart was suddenly racing. If people found out just how close Colin and I had gotten, if news traveled back to the wrong person at the label or at the Society, it was possible that alone would get me pulled off this job.

Colin frowned. He followed my gaze and dropped his hand from my face. "Right. Time to get to work!" he said with a cheer that sounded forced.

"Colin," I said, and didn't know how to continue.

"I get it," he said. "Professional appearances and all that." He shoved open the car door and stood up with a jerk.

Despite that, the day seemed to go well enough. Colin put his smile back on as he greeted the producer. In the live room, he bantered with the rest of the band and the sound engineer, gamely moved from one verse to the next even though I could tell he wasn't totally pleased with the vocals, and even diffused a fight that started brewing between Marcy and Joel. Still, the whole time I never quite relaxed. Maybe because I wasn't convinced *he'd* actually relaxed. He was putting on a good front, sure, there was something just a touch off in his behavior—a distant flavor to his calm that felt somehow false, as if he were maintaining it only by keeping part of his mind distracted. Distracted with what, I had no clue.

That uncertainty sat heavy inside me, distracting *me* enough that I momentarily forgot the one rule Sterling had drilled into me the other day. *Don't let him out of your sight.* When we were heading out in the late afternoon, Colin paused with his hand on the outer door and asked if I could grab the bag of picks he thought he'd left behind, and I went automatically. It was a little favor, one small thing I could offer him unreservedly.

I'd spent a couple minutes poking around the iso rooms when Joel asked me what I was looking for and then commented, "I don't think he brought his own today. He borrowed one of Kevin's picks."

My stomach plummeted. With a hasty, "Thanks!" I bolted for the door.

I should have realized. I should have known Colin wouldn't have asked me to leave him on his own, even for a minute, over something that small. Not unless he had an ulterior motive.

I burst past the outer door and halted as my breath caught up with me. The stutter of my pulse settled, leaving only a dull hum of unease. Colin was still in sight, standing a few paces from the door and talking with a woman who was definitely not a groupie, at least not one like any I'd seen before. She looked to be in her mid-thirties, with chocolate-brown hair in a blunt bob that cut across her cheeks and a loose plaid shirt tucked into skinny jeans that ended in a pair of worn work boots.

And her tan skin sparkled in the sunlight with an effervescence no cosmetics could have produced.

"It's been a while since I saw an up-and-comer who impressed me," she was saying, her thumbs hooked casually in her belt loops. "We like to add a little fresh blood to the mix when we can. We jam together once or twice a week, usually."

"What's going on?" I asked, ambling over to rejoin Colin. I wanted to grasp his hand, to tug his attention to me, but he had both slung in his pockets out of reach. His eyes stayed on the Glower.

"Natalie saw me play at the Catacomber a few weeks back," he said. "She wanted to invite me to come play with her and a few indie folks she knows."

"Nothing official," "Natalie" put in. "Just a little friendly sharing of ideas and inspiration. We all vibe off each other and come away with something better."

She smiled then, thin and bright, and my gut pinched. It was the same one—the same Glower as before, the redhead, the strawberry blonde—just another new look. I couldn't have proven it, but I felt it right through to my bones.

Had she been able to sense she needed to change her strategy from a distance? Or had she gotten close enough to him to use her Glower sensitivity sometime before today without me noticing? She'd obviously known to take a different approach before she'd arrived here this afternoon.

If she'd shown up ready to fawn over him with sexual overtures, I could have hoped simply walking over would have blocked her gambit. But I'd been encouraging Colin to find a new family for himself in the community just last night. How could I shut her overture down in a way he'd accept? How could I *keep* it shut down? I could offer him my body, my heart, everything I had in me, but I couldn't be more than one person —a person who wasn't even part of the music scene anymore.

Joel and Kevin wandered out, glancing at us curiously as they headed to the parking lot. "In fact," the Glower went on, tapping her hip, "we're getting together tonight, if you want to stop by and test the waters." She tugged out a business card and handed it to Colin. "That's the space we use. Just buzz up."

"That'd be—" Colin started, and a burst of panic jolted through me. I might be just one person, but I had to at least try every tactic I could, other consequences be damned. His soul was on the line right now.

I curled my fingers around Colin's elbow. "We have that thing tonight," I interrupted, soft and even, and he turned to me for the first time since I'd come out.

"Thing?" he said with obvious confusion.

I squeezed his arm and bobbed up on my toes to press my lips to his.

I didn't want to overdo it, but I did need him to feel the promise I was making. To remember the desires between us still unfulfilled. I leaned close enough that my breast grazed his chest, tangling my fingers in his hair to give him that tug I knew he loved as I parted my lips, and then I eased back. Joel or Kevin let out a catcall behind us, and they both laughed, but I didn't care. Colin was staring at me and only me, hunger lit in his amber eyes. He seemed to study me for one long, heart wrenching moment. I looked back at him as openly as I could, hoping he could see the affection and longing that brief touch had sent rushing through me. This wasn't just a tactic. I was every bit as hungry as he was.

His Adam's apple bobbed. "Right," he said with a rasp. "The thing." His gaze darted to the Glower. "It sounds like a great opportunity. I'll get in touch to find out another good time to drop in."

"My number is on the back of the card," she said. He gave her a curt nod and a wave, already swiveling toward the car, his hand closing around mine. His thumb traced back and forth across my knuckles as we walked, a promise of his own, and a slow flush crept over my body.

We barely spoke on the drive back. Every time I thought of opening my mouth, all I wanted to be doing was kissing Colin again. When we stopped at a red light, he reached over to touch my knee, his fingers drifting over my inner thigh. The second time, he edged my skirt a little higher, and the third time even higher, until I thought I would melt into the seat.

Outside the condo building, he tossed the keys to the valet and practically dragged me to the elevator, not that I had any intention of dawdling. Just as he'd stepped closer to me, a white-haired resident in a jogging suit loped on, pressing the button for the fifth floor.

Colin and I stood there silently, our arms brushing, my heart thumping, as the numbers lit up one by one. The jogger got off. The door closed. Colin let out a rough sigh of relief and caught me in his arms. He kissed me against the elevator wall, one hand pressing me to him, the other sliding over my hip and along my thigh, raising my leg against his. I could feel him against me through his jeans, already hard. The sensation sent a thrill through me. I teased my fingers down his chest, kissing him back just as eagerly.

Whatever this meant, wherever it ended, I needed it. This. Him.

We dashed for the penthouse door, and Colin kicked it shut behind us. Before the lock had even clicked into place, he'd tugged my face to his to continue those desperate kisses. I broke from him with a ragged breath to yank his shirt over his head; another kiss and he'd discarded mine. He walked me backwards to the hall as he disengaged my bra, the muscles of his shoulders quivering with anticipation beneath my fingers, his tongue demanding as it swept around mine.

Before I'd had more than a glimmer of doubt at the thought of taking this encounter into the bedroom I'd seen at least two other women sharing with him, he nudged open the door to my room.

"Is this okay?" he said hoarsely, his hands running up over my stomach to the base of my breasts, and there wasn't much I wouldn't have agreed to in that moment.

"Just don't stop," I said, with a catch in my throat as he rolled one nipple beneath his thumb.

We sank onto the bed, shoving aside the tangle of sheets I hadn't bothered to smooth this morning, still kissing. Colin straddled me, tearing his lips from mine to lick and nibble a searing path down my neck and over my collarbone, capturing the other nipple in his mouth. As he laved it with his tongue, I arched my neck back with a gasp. For a hazy minute I surrendered to his attentions completely. Then my fingers slipped down over the tight muscles of his abdomen to the top of his jeans. I gripped the buckle of his belt determinedly.

"Not yet," Colin murmured. He trailed his mouth to my other breast, and then down, over my stomach where it dipped to my belly button, his hands traveling up my thighs under my skirt. His thumbs hooked around my panties and edged them down, inch by torturous inch, as each press of his lips eased closer to the core of me. I whimpered, bowing up to meet him. He pushed my skirt up to my waist and then his mouth was there, devouring the hottest, hungriest part of me.

I cried out as his tongue flicked over the sensitive nub there, a jolt of pleasure radiating through me. He dipped lower to lap my opening, and my hips bucked. Much more and I'd have come apart right then, but that wasn't what I wanted. We'd waited long enough.

"Come here," I said with a tug of his hair. Colin swept his

tongue over me again, forcing a moan from my lungs. Then he surged up over me, our bodies flush, my taste musky on his lips as we kissed. I reached for his belt again, and this time he didn't stop me. I felt the hitch of breath from his chest to mine as I released the buckle and popped the snap beneath. His length pressed against the zipper as I slid it down. I trailed my thumb over the thin fabric of his boxers and he groaned.

"I want you," I heard myself saying. "Please."

Colin let out a shuddering laugh as he kicked off his jeans. "You don't have to ask twice."

He straightened up, kneeling over me as he retrieved a packet from his wallet. I took the opportunity to ease down those boxers and coax out his erection. I hadn't really seen him in the pool last night, through the water and its reflections. I traced the veins corded through the silky skin that seemed at odds with the hardness of him, loving the hum my touch drew from his throat. He ripped the packet open and paused, gazing down at me.

I rested my hand over his, and we slicked the condom over him together. He conformed his body to mine again, kissing my jaw, fondling my breasts, as the solid length of him rubbed between my legs, provoking a hum of my own. I raised my knees to his waist.

"Please," I whispered, and he guided himself in.

My eyes drifted shut and a sigh slipped from my mouth as he filled me, hard and hot in all the best ways, sliding easily against the abundant wetness inside. He moved slowly, teasingly, until all I felt was him, above me, within me. I opened my eyes and found him watching my face with an expression so tender it called butterflies into my chest.

"Colin," I said before I'd realized I was going to speak.

"Yeah?" he murmured.

I couldn't say the words that had been on the tip of my tongue, that ached in my throat. He'd think I was ridiculous. It'd only been a few weeks. Maybe those words weren't even true. But I wanted to give him something to answer the affection in his eyes.

"I'm happy," I said.

His smile sent warmth through parts of me I hadn't thought could get any hotter. "Me too."

He pulled back and pushed into me again, a little faster, and a little faster. My legs squeezed around him. I rocked with him, urging him on, and he groaned. He gripped the curve of my hips and tilted them up so he could angle even deeper. His length pressed against the sensitive spot inside, building and building to that magical peak.

"You feel so good, Avery," he muttered against my cheek. "So damn good."

I ran my fingernails down his back and his muscles trembled in response. I had no capacity for words left at all. I arched higher, embracing him with everything in me. He nipped the corner of my jaw, thrusting harder, and I hit my release. Pleasure rolled through me, making my legs shake and my breath quaver. Colin moaned, his hips jerking.

I coasted on the pulsing tingles of the aftermath for a few dreamy moments as he slowed inside me. Then he withdrew, but only for a second. He lay back and carefully gathered me against him, his chest still heaving and his breath rasping as he kissed the top of my head.

I wasn't sure how long we lay there like that, sprawled together, naked except for the skirt bunched around my waist. I nestled my head against his shoulder, gliding my fingers up and down his sternum, lost in the warmth of him and the feel of skin against skin, the salty-sweet smell of him mixed with the lingering hint of pine. For that short stretch of time, I almost believed it could be this simple: him and me and no one else. No Glowers, no demanding record label execs or Society supervisors, no restless bandmates. I almost believed that nothing else could touch us, let alone harm us, as long as we could breathe in the same rhythm.

Then Colin cupped my face to brush a strand of hair back behind my ear, and I felt his body tense against mine as if he were readying himself.

"Avery," he said, "I need to tell you something."

"What?" I said. It was a struggle keeping my voice from breaking over that one word, but I managed it. The possibilities flitted through my head as my hand stilled on his chest. He wanted to be sure I understood this didn't mean anything beyond the act itself. He needed me to know it couldn't happen again. He was going to ask for me to be reassigned. I wanted to be prepared for the worst.

"I know what you're doing for me," he said. "I know what you're trying to protect me from."

That statement was so distant from anything I'd been expecting that I couldn't help laughing. "From your particularly reckless impulses?" I suggested. "From ill-advised decisions? I'm pretty sure we covered that in the introductions."

"No," Colin said. "I mean I know about the ones that glow."

Thirteen

"WHAT?" I SAID, SITTING UP BESIDE COLIN IN THE BED. My heart thudded against my ribs, a hollow echo of the thrum that had filled my body not so long ago.

Colin gazed up at me, his head propped on one arm, those amber eyes as captivating as ever beneath his thick lashes. His muscled chest rose and fell where my fingers were still resting on it. He lay his hand over mine, grasping it and holding it there.

"I thought you should know," he said. "I've felt like an ass, pretending not to have a clue. And you shouldn't feel like you have to keep trying to protect me. I know what they are. I know what I'm doing."

My mind was still reeling. The warmth of his skin against mine provided none of its earlier comfort. "I think I need you to back up a little," I said. "You know this how?"

"Well, I— I'm sure you have a better understanding of how the whole thing works," Colin said. "But as far as I've figured out... The British rocker I told you about, the one who mentored me a bit? I adjusted that story."

My memory tripped back to that conversation over the restaurant table. Oh. *Oh.* "You said you found *out* that he'd hung himself..."

"I found him," Colin said, his voice going rough. "Right after. He'd given me the key to his house in the city before he left, in case I needed a break from the dorms sometimes, and I went over as soon as I heard he was back in town, didn't even wait for him to get in touch. And—" He stopped, his gaze sliding away as his expression clouded in remembrance.

Oh, Colin. I could picture him—the lankier, ganglier, though no less charming younger version of himself—bounding up the front steps to the door, rushing inside eager to reestablish that connection with the makeshift musical family he'd started to construct, and then...

Despite my shock at his revelation, my fingers tightened around his in sympathy.

"I guess that's how it happens?" he said. "Being able to notice them? You were there, when your dad..."

I nodded. "No one knew?" I said quietly. "That you'd found him?" If his discovery of the death had been reported anywhere, the Society would have reached out to him the way it had to Mom and me, to find out if a Glower had been involved and if he'd gained the sight.

"I was freaked out," Colin said. "I could tell he was gone. I didn't know what the thing I'd seen was or what it might do to me. So I took off. I called 9-1-1 from a payphone and hiked back to the dorms. Never told anyone I'd been there."

He drew in a breath and looked at me again. "I figured it out. There are so many of them in this city, when you're in certain crowds—I saw how they acted, what they said to people, what sort of people they went after, and what came out of that...

I might not know as much as your Society does, but it's not that hard to pick up the basics."

"Then why the hell have you been acting like such an idiot?" I burst out, unable to contain myself. My hand slipped from his as I threw both of mine in the air. "Talking to them, letting them get close to you—that one in Austin would have marked you if I'd gotten there any later!"

"Marked?" Colin said, frowning.

"That's what we call it," I said. "When they... latch onto one person, so they can feed off their energy more quickly. When you see someone with them, who has a little glowing spot, right here." I touched my chest over my heart, the place where the break-dancer's body had glimmered the other night in the club. "It's not something you can play around with, you know. Once they've got a line in you, there's no way to break it. None that we've found, anyway."

He rubbed his eyes with a broken laugh. "I didn't know it was that easy."

"That's why I'm *here*," I said, "and the people the Society sent before me. Why didn't you say something to begin with? We could have explained the stuff you don't know, what to watch out for, how to ward them off, where to—"

"Avery," Colin said, cutting me off. He caught my hand again, rubbing his thumb over my palm. His eyes had gone so serious my voice died in my throat. "That's what I'm trying to tell you now," he said softly. "I don't want to watch out. I've been trying to get their attention, to look like an appealing target, so one of them will *want* to mark me."

The words knocked the air from my lungs. Because I knew the instant he said them how true they were. Like a shift in the light that turns what appeared to be a mishmash of shapes into a coherent picture, all the crazy inexplicable things he'd done since

I'd started this assignment—the grandstanding in the clubs, the faked highs, the shout to the Glower outside the condo building —no longer looked so inexplicable. In fact, they made a horrifying sort of sense. Even today, he must have seen the Glower outside and sent me off on the wild goose chase for the imaginary picks because of that, knowing I wouldn't give her a chance to talk if we went out together.

The only part of the picture I still didn't understand was...

"Why?" I said, staring at him. "Why would you want—" The thought of seeing that glint in his chest, watching the life drain from him through it, hit me with a wave of nausea so overwhelming I lost the thread of my words. I swallowed thickly.

"Why not?" Colin said. "They give something back. They give people the jolt they need to take their career to the next level, or to get it back when they've mostly lost it. Brian—he was almost a has-been when I met him, and then suddenly he was writing songs like a maniac. He turned out a new album in no time, and everyone loved it. He was getting new fans, he was touring again—"

"And then the Glower took all that away," I said, my stomach still churning. I couldn't believe he was saying this. "You know that, right? He didn't kill himself, not really. They only give their marks a boost so they can feed on the excitement, the high of creative success and the attention that comes with it, and they're so hungry they don't care if they leave the mark feeling empty afterward. Feeling like he's got to try harder, reach farther, push himself to the fraying point to get back that high... And then as soon as he does, the Glower sucks it all away again. It's like the worst possible addiction, where the rush only lasts long enough for people to know how much they want it, and all the rest is the pain of withdrawal. It wrecks people. It gets harder and harder for them to pull themselves together, and then before long the Glower pushes a little too hard, and they drown in drugs, or throw themselves into stunts too wild to recover from, or simply decide they can't take it anymore..."

"Because they don't know," Colin said. He sat up, the sheet pooling in his lap. "*You* don't tell them. They don't understand what's happening. But I could negotiate. I'd go in with my eyes open."

"That wouldn't help you once you're marked," I said. "As soon a Glower gets a mark on you— You wouldn't have any control at all, Colin. They take whatever they want and there's nothing you could do to stop them."

His mouth flattened. "Well, maybe I'm okay with that too, if it means that for at least a little while I'm making songs worth listening to, music that'll last. Can't I decide for myself if that's worth the trade-off?"

He was sitting just a few inches from me, the musky-sweet smell of the sweat we'd worked up tickling off his bare skin, the eyes that for a second had seemed to look right inside my soul fixed on me, and abruptly I wanted to squirm away. My heart felt as if it were about to wrench in two. Who *was* this guy? I didn't know him at all.

"I can't believe you," I said. "You knew, the whole time, and you let me—"

I couldn't bring myself to finish the sentence, but the wave of my hand—to the bed, to the two of us—must have said enough. Colin's expression shuttered.

"I let you *what?*" he said, and there was a darkness in his voice I'd never heard before.

I hesitated. "I..."

He got up, snatching up his boxers from where they'd fallen on the floor. "So that's all this was? Seduce the client to get between him and the Glowers? Whatever it takes to get the job done? Sorry I inconvenienced you."

"No!" I said. "No, Colin, I— That's not—"

"I don't want to hear it," he said as he yanked on his boxers and grabbed his jeans. "I've had enough of this already. Don't you see, that's why— This is the world. People want you there so they can take whatever it is they need for themselves—their reputation, their *job*— No one really gives a crap, and I'm supposed to think that's worth sticking around for? I'd rather go out in a quick blaze of glory that *I* chose, thanks."

I scrambled off the bed as he headed for the hall. "Colin!" I said, and he yanked the door shut between us with a bang.

I stood there for a moment, gripping the handle, my skirt drifting down over my naked legs. Colin's footsteps thumped down the hall toward his bedroom. That door slammed. I cringed and let go of the handle. Then I tilted my head against the door, squeezing my eyes shut against the mess of pain and horror inside.

When Colin still hadn't emerged from his bedroom a few hours later, the knots in my stomach had shifted enough to make room for a gnawing of hunger. I crept out and grabbed a carton of leftover chow mein from the fridge. I ate it cold, perched on one of the stools by the island at the edge of the haze cast by the fixture over the front door. That light had already been on, and turning on any of the others felt like too immense a task. Besides, the chilled noodles sliding down my throat and the gloom of the deepening evening around me fit to my mood.

It was going to be okay, I told myself. Colin would cool down eventually, and when he did I'd explain to him what I'd really meant and erase the hurt I'd seen in his eyes before he stormed out.

Some part of me didn't really believe that, though. Or it didn't believe that explaining myself would be enough to fix everything our last conversation had broken.

Even if he understood that I cared about him, that he'd meant far more to me than any job, I'd heard the determination in his voice when he talked about getting marked. If he wanted it that badly, if he was that convinced it was the only way, if nothing I'd said already had made a difference, I wasn't sure *anything* I said or did could change his mind.

I'd only choked down a few bites of the chow mein when my phone rang. The sound emanated from my purse on the floor just inside the doorway, where I'd dropped it in our headlong rush as we'd come in. The mouthful I swallowed stuck in my throat before going down. I got up and retrieved the phone.

The call display showed it was Fee calling. My thumb hovered over the answer button. A few months ago I'd have been overjoyed to see her name on the display, to know I could talk through this catastrophe with her. Now, my gut clenched at the thought of hearing a waver or a slur in her voice that'd tell me she wasn't really with me at all. But I brought the phone to my ear anyway.

"Hey," I said.

"Is this Avery?" said a girlish voice I didn't recognize.

I frowned. "It is. Who's this? Why are you on Fiona's phone?"

"This is, um, Kady Forrest? Fiona was working with me?" The voice trembled. "I just— I didn't know what to do, and you're the first person in her favorite contacts, I've heard her talk about you before, so I thought if I was going to call anyone—"

Kady Forrest. The Starlet, Fiona's client. "What's going on, Kady?" I interrupted, keeping my voice as calm and level as I could even as I clutched the phone. For her to be calling me, for her to sound that way—it terrified me to imagine what could have pushed her to it. "Just tell me what happened, from the beginning."

She dragged in a breath. "My parents and my sister had to go out of town for a couple days, so Fiona was staying with me. We've just been hanging out, watching movies, nothing crazy, I swear—but I think she must have taken something. I don't know what. She started getting all loopy after she came back from the bathroom, and then all of a sudden she, like, fainted, and now I can't get her to wake up. I mean, she's still breathing and everything, but she doesn't seem *okay*, you know. But I wasn't sure, if I called an ambulance or something, maybe I'd get her in trouble. Maybe she'll just wake up on her own..." She trailed off uncertainly.

My mouth had gone dry, but I had years of Society training to kick in and carry me through. In this line of work, drug overdoses were a potential hazard even with unmarked clients. I'd just never expected to have to apply that training to a fellow Tether. To my best friend.

"Okay, Kady," I said. "You say she's breathing—like normal, or slow? Is she making any strange sounds?"

"No, nothing weird," Kady said. "And I think it's normal breathing."

"Do you know how to take a pulse? Can you tell me how hers feels?"

There was a muffled rustling as she must have knelt down. "I think so. I... Okay. Um. I don't know. Maybe it's a little slow?"

"How does her skin feel?" I asked. "Cool or warm?"

"Warm. But she was sweating. Her hair's damp."

"Did she throw up or anything like that?"

"No. No, if she'd seemed really bad I'd have called an ambulance." Her breath hitched with a suppressed sob. "I just want her to be okay."

I walked across the living room and back, debating with myself. Kady was right: Fee probably would get in trouble with the Society, with Sterling, if he found out she'd passed out like this while supervising her client. I didn't know if she'd ever forgive me if I made the decision to call this in. And it didn't sound as if she were in critical condition. Maybe she'd just nodded out. Maybe she *would* wake up perfectly fine on her own.

If only I could see her for myself, to be sure...

"Kady, where are you?" I said.

She gave me an address in Brentwood. Not that far from here. In a cab, I could probably make the trip in under fifteen minutes.

"Listen," I said, "just keep an eye on her, and I'll come and see how she's doing, and then we can decide—"

I halted, the awareness of the closed door at the end of the hall prickling over me. Colin might have turned in for the night, but I didn't know that. I couldn't leave him alone right now, not after the fight we'd just had. He might walk right out of here and into the Glower's waiting arms.

Damn it.

"No," I said. "Wait. I..." I paced to the dining table and back, trying to formulate a plan that would protect everyone I cared about. Maybe Kady could bring Fee here? Hauling her unconscious body across town—no. "I can't," I said. "I—I can probably call someone else who'll come help." Mateo might be free. I thought he'd understand. He and Fee were friends too. "Can you just—"

Footsteps sounded behind me. I turned to find Colin standing at the edge of the living room, fully dressed, his face weary. My heart stuttered.

"What's wrong?" he said.

I didn't want to lay this on him on top of everything else. "I can handle—" I started, and he cut me off with a jerk of his hand.

"What's wrong, Avery?" he said firmly.

"My friend Fiona, she's at a client's house, she took something and passed out," I said.

His expression didn't shift. "And you want to check on her."

"It doesn't have to be—"

"I'll take you," he said before I could protest more. "Let's go."

Fourteen

THE STARLET'S HOUSE WAS A BIG COLONIAL NUMBER NEAR the park, with an intercom at the gate I had to buzz her from before Colin could steer the Audi the rest of the way up to the house. I leapt out the second he hit the brakes at the top of the drive. Kady opened the door as I was pounding up the front steps.

"I think she's getting worse," she said, her mouth twisted and her pale face ruddy with tear tracks. Despite her fashionably mature shag haircut, she looked so very young. Fourteen? Fifteen? But already on TV screens across the world.

And this was the life that came with that sort of fame.

"It's just been the last couple minutes," Kady said as she tugged me into a huge entertainment room. A semi-circle of suede sofas faced a flat screen TV in a built-in oak shelving unit that filled the entire opposite wall. Fee was sprawled next to one of the sofas. My chest contracted. Fee was so full of life most of the time it was easy to forget how small her actual body was.

Lying there now, eyes shut, jaw slack, and limbs akimbo, she looked like a child's doll tossed carelessly aside.

"She made this sound, like coughing," Kady said, jittering from foot to foot. "I rolled her onto her side. That's what they always say—to make sure the person doesn't choke—"

"That was good thinking," I told her. I crouched next to Fee and touched her forehead. She felt clammy, her skin damp and faintly cool. The fringe of her fine black hair was plastered to her temples.

"Fee?" I said, shaking her shoulder. "Fee!"

Her eyelids didn't even flutter. Her chest was still rising and falling, but erratically—one breath, then a pause, then two right after each other, then another longer pause. I slid my fingers down her neck to the pulse point. Her heartbeat was steady but sluggish. Not good.

I sat back on my heels, a chill washing over me. She needed medical care. I couldn't say for sure she'd die without it—but I couldn't say for sure she wouldn't, either. And I'd rather have Fee alive and never speaking to me again than gone forever.

"We should get her to emerg," I said.

"The UCLA hospital is ten minutes from here," Colin said by the doorway, and I startled. I'd been so focused on Fee I hadn't noticed him following Kady and me in. "We can drive her there faster than waiting for an ambulance."

And bring the Starlet? That would be a mess. I glanced at Kady, my gaze catching on the green stones in the studs in her ears. "Fiona gave you those earrings?" I said.

She touched them, looking puzzled. "Yeah."

Malachite. That was something. "Keep them on," I said. "For... for luck, for her. And don't leave the house. Can you promise that? I'll call the Society; they'll send someone over as soon as they can."

"Okay," Kady said. "I don't *want* to go anywhere. Is she going to be okay?"

"I don't know yet," I said. "I think if we get her to the hospital soon, she should be."

"Then go," she said. "Just, when you know how she's doing..."

"Someone will call you," I said. "I promise. We're going to get her taken care of, Kady. Don't worry. The doctors will know what to do. It was really good that you called me."

She nodded, hugging herself, her face still drawn. Colin was already lifting Fee, cradling her head against his shoulder. Slim as she'd always been, as I saw how easily he picked her up I realized she must have gotten even thinner with all the partying. Those bold structured dresses she favored would have helped hide the change.

I steeled myself and pulled out my phone as we hurried to Colin's car. Sterling responded to my emergency code text twenty seconds later.

"Avery?" he said, sounding as if I'd woken him up.

"I'm with Fiona," I said. "She's... We're taking her to the emerg at UCLA."

I could almost feel him snapping alert. "What?" he said. "Tell me everything."

My last glimpse of Fee that night was the soles of her bare feet gliding away as the emergency room nurse wheeled off her prone body on a gurney. Sterling had just arrived. He stopped next to me, looking after Fee and then glancing over at me— and at Colin beside me. His brow burrowed. When he spoke, his voice had the low flat inflection that told me he was deeply displeased.

"You'd better get your client home," was all he said.

I wasn't sure how much he was upset at me, or Fee, or the situation in general. It didn't seem wise to ask. He'd have taken care of everything else that needed doing, and I guessed the real reckoning would come later. I bobbed my head.

"Let me know as soon as they're sure she's all right," I said.

"Of course." He turned away.

I trailed after Colin down the echoing hall and across the parking lot. Neither of us spoke as we got into the car. I slumped in the passenger seat. Colin started the engine and turned us back toward his condo building. As the streetlamps flashed by overhead, my mind drifted back to a similar drive some five hours ago. One just as quiet, just as tense, but in a totally different way. A lump rose in my throat.

It had been a beautiful day, and now it was a wretched one. How had it all fallen apart so quickly?

We stood at opposite ends of the elevator, a distance that felt yawning. I kept a couple paces behind him as we stepped into the penthouse. Colin turned over the deadbolt, and my gaze fell on the shirt crumpled on the floor near the kitchen counter— the shirt he'd pulled off me between kisses earlier than evening —and somehow that was the thing that broke me.

I took a gulp of air that turned into a sob and dropped my face into my hands as if I could catch the tears and push them back in. They just kept coming, streaming between my fingers and down my cheeks with each hitch of my breath. My legs wobbled. The space around me felt so empty I was sure Colin had walked off and left me to my pain until a hand tentatively touched my back. I turned toward him instinctively, and he drew me closer, his arms loose but fully around me, his thumb stroking over my hair against the nape of my neck. I gripped his shirt, unable to stop myself from sobbing harder.

"It'll be okay," he said. "She'll be okay. I've seen people survive after being way more gone than that."

That didn't mean they always did. But the words sank in, gradually, giving me at least enough of a defense to barricade myself against that fear. My tears started to slow. I wiped at my eyes and my nose, conscious of the wet streaks I'd left on Colin's shirt. When I'd gathered myself enough that I trusted myself to look at him, I eased back.

"Sorry," I said.

"You don't have to apologize," he said, but he didn't meet my eyes, and his voice was stiff. "She's you're friend. Of course you care about her."

I heard the echo of a past conversation that had happened here in this room, when he'd challenged me about how I cared about *him*. Did he really think Fee was the only person I was frightened for?

Colin stepped away, heading for his bedroom. He'd made it halfway there before I managed to force out another sound.

"Can we talk?" I said.

He stopped, but he didn't turn back. The set of his shoulders looked like a wall. "I think I said everything I needed to," he said.

"Well, then maybe you need to listen," I said. "Because there are things I still need to say."

He sighed, but he faced me then, braced as if he expected me to hit him, his expression wary. I'd hurt him that much, with just a few thoughtless words.

He'd cared that much, that my words could hurt him.

I swallowed hard. "I think you got the wrong idea about what I started to say, before. There are two things I want you to be absolutely clear on." I paused, grappling with the words. "I was attracted to you from the first time I saw you at Rushfield," I went on. "Even more, the first time I saw you here. I didn't fake how much I wanted everything we'd done together. And it isn't just the physical stuff—I've been around you, I've seen you—not always in the best situations, but enough to know you're funny, and kind, and passionate about the actual music, not just getting famous, and all sorts of other things that make me *like* you. You made me remember that I can't just bury myself in work and school all the time, that I should be enjoying my life too."

"But?" Colin prompted.

I risked stepping a little closer. He didn't move to meet me, but he didn't draw back either. "I wanted to be with you," I said. "I did. But I'm not the sort of person who can get into some casual fling and then just walk away. I knew the more involved we got, the harder it was going to be when it was over."

"What made you so sure all *I'd* want was a fling?" he asked.

I gave him a look. "Oh, I don't know. Maybe the fact that the first day I was here, you made sure I'd see you having fun with your friend on the terrace. Or the fact that you had a different girl here less than a week later. Or that less than a week after that, you were practically drooling over that woman I didn't know you knew was a Glower. And it wasn't as if you were talking long term plans or grand romance with me. How do you *think* I got the impression you weren't looking to settle down?"

Colin opened his mouth, and closed it again. "All right," he said after a moment. "I guess that's fair. I never really... It was to try to get their attention. The Glowers. They seemed to like the stars who ran a little wild." I raised an eyebrow, and to my surprise he blushed. "And, okay, I did get some enjoyment out of it."

"Then there's the other thing you have to know," I said. "Yes, maybe if I weren't doing this job, if we'd met under normal circumstances and you didn't have Glowers hovering around you, I wouldn't have wanted things to move so fast. Maybe I'd have wanted to take a little time to be sure I wasn't getting in over my head. But I didn't hook up with you *because* of the job. It wasn't to get some glowing performance report or a quarterly bonus. I was worried about you, for *you*—I hated thinking that what happened to my dad could happen to you—I *cared*. I cared so much I couldn't help thinking that protecting you and your happiness any way I could was worth getting my heart broken."

I stepped forward again, right up to him, my eyes locked with his. I still couldn't read any acceptance in his face, but he stayed there.

"So I'm sorry," I finished, my voice shaking, "if I got a little angry at the thought that you didn't care about yourself the same way. But you can't say I was using you to get something for myself. I gave you *everything*."

I pressed my hand to his chest in a little shove for emphasis, and he caught my fist. "Avery," he said, his voice strained. I found myself blinking away fresh tears. He traced his thumb over my cheek, brushing aside one that had slipped out. His jaw flexed. Then all at once he was cupping my face, pulling my mouth to his.

The kiss was rough and needy, but that was fine. I hadn't thought Colin Ryder would ever be kissing me again. I kissed him back with the same fervor, my arms looping behind his neck.

He lifted me, groaning as our bodies pressed together, and carried me the few steps to the sofa. As he lay me down on the buttery leather without breaking the next kiss, his hands were already sliding up under my shirt. I hadn't bothered with a bra when I'd pulled it on, hadn't thought I'd be leaving the penthouse tonight and had been too panicked over Fee to think of it before. He found my bare breasts with a hum of pleasure that rippled from him into me, and pinched the nipples between his thumb and forefinger with a pressure that made me gasp. My hips canted against his, provoking another groan.

There was no gentle teasing this time, no slow burn. Colin dropped his hand to venture beneath my skirt, exploring the dampness already spreading on my panties. I whimpered a plea against his mouth. His lips crushed against mine as he yanked the panties past my knees, fumbling with his jeans a second later. I didn't care. I was ready. He paused just long enough to retrieve a condom, and then it seemed before I'd even had time to gather my breath he was pushing inside me, all the way to the hilt.

He thrust hard and desperate as his kisses, but even so his hand stayed between us, massaging the nub above my core. I moaned, lost between those sparks of pleasure and the electric fission within. The room spun around us. As I bowed up, the hard length of him found that sensitive spot within. Just that one touch sent a pulsing, shuddering wave of release through my body. Colin arched over me, thrusting a few more times before his breath stuttered with his own release.

I looked up at him braced above me, the muscles standing out in his corded arms, as the stars faded from my vision and the heat of the moment faded away. He met my gaze. Still inside me, softening but no less filling me, and yet I could see in the distance in his eyes that I hadn't reached him. Not really, not in the ways that mattered. And with that every other part of me felt empty.

He withdrew with a gentleness completely at odds with the way we'd come together and eased back on the sofa, tugging his clothes back into order. I guessed I might as well do the same. I found my panties dangling from one ankle and slid them up under my skirt, trying not to think of him, of the act that should have been intimate and now somehow felt the opposite, as the fabric settled between my legs.

"That's the last time we should do that," Colin said, staring straight ahead. "However I feel about you or you feel about me, I'm not changing my mind about getting marked. And you obviously can't accept that decision. So there we are."

The pang of loss I felt was nothing compared to the tension I could see in his face, coiled through his shoulders. I found the ache in my chest was for him as well as for me.

"Then there's one more thing you have to know," I said. "You don't need any Glower's help to make music people are going to love, that's going to last. You've got a gorgeous voice, you play like you were born with a guitar in your hands. You don't need them for anything."

Colin's brow knit as he glanced at me, and I realized with a shock that he honestly didn't believe it.

"You can say that," he said, "but I know how I got here. It's the same way I got that Glower interested in me. I put on a good show, I act a little crazy, and people take notice. It's got nothing to do with the music I'm making. That's what people liked about me at Rushfield, that's what got Brian's attention, that's why the record label thinks they can make money off me. If I'd just been sitting with a guitar on a stool in some coffeehouse, no one would have given me the time of day."

I doubted that. "You don't think it's possible it could be both?" I said quietly. "That you could be good at getting people's attention with the way you act, *and* good at making music?"

He lowered his head. "I'm not saying I'm crap. I'm just saying... This is my big break. This could be the one time I get this much money and press thrown at me. And when I'm in the studio, playing, singing, nothing sounds *right*, nothing sounds like a song that'll be more than a brainworm in someone's ear for a few weeks until the next thing comes along. I want to be more than that, while I have the chance. While it *matters*."

I reached for his hand, and he let me take it. I clasped it between both of mine, resting it on my knee.

"You know," I said, "I don't think—most people at the Society don't think—that the Glowers actually make anyone more talented. They'll puff you up with extra confidence, push you past the fear that you won't be good enough, that you'll screw up, anything that holds you back from the best you could do. But that talent is in there either way. There are ways you can reach that best without them."

"You think," Colin said. "You don't know."

"No," I acknowledged. "There aren't any Glower manuals lying around, and they'd obviously *like* people to think they're offering something sparkly and magical. But I can tell you I've never seen anyone produce something after they were marked that's *so* far beyond what they were creating before that I can't imagine they could have come up with it otherwise."

"The thing is," he started, and hesitated. "Why did you stop drumming, Avery? Really?"

Somehow I hadn't expected that question. It hit me like a jab in the gut. But he needed honesty.

"I was scared," I admitted. "I... Dad played a lot of different instruments, let me try out all of them. I could have taken up anything I wanted. But I picked the drums, after the Glower took him, because that seemed safe. He always used to joke with the guys in the band about how no one ever looks way back on the stage to the drummer's little fortress. I thought I could just play and enjoy doing that, and the rest of that stuff, the stuff that broke him down, it wouldn't get to me."

"But it did," Colin said.

"Yeah. That winter showcase performance at Rushfield—it was the first time I ever played in front of more than a handful of people. I *knew* I was playing well. And it felt... It felt incredible. Not just the playing, but knowing how many people were watching, knowing they were into it... I finished and all I wanted was to do it all over again."

"Yeah," Colin said with a hint of a smile. His hand turned in mine, squeezing my fingers. "I know that feeling."

"It scared me," I said. "Because I wasn't sure, even knowing about the Glowers and what they did, that I wouldn't be tempted. If I liked the feeling that much, wanted to keep feeling it that much, I didn't know if I'd be strong enough to deal with the times when people weren't interested in listening. When I was struggling to play anything they'd be interested in. Because everyone has those low points. So I stopped."

"You see," Colin said, "I can't do that. I can't be scared like that. The music... It's the only thing I have. If I don't give it everything I can, there's no point. So I want to go all in, whatever it takes, whatever I have to use or give up. You made your choice. I'm making mine. Can't you understand that?"

My throat closed up. I didn't know what to say. I could feel, in that moment, that nothing I did say would make him see things any differently. At least not right now.

"I can understand that's how you feel, even if I don't agree with what you want to happen," I said after a moment. "But can you just— Whatever you feel you need do, can you hold off for just this week? Show up at the studio, keep laying down tracks, do that opening act gig as if everything's good? Because if you start acting out again, before that... I don't know if you're still going to have a record to be putting out there."

"They're that close to canceling the deal?" he said, and I lowered my head. He sucked air through his teeth.

"All right," he said. "Until after the concert. It can wait that long, now that I know how close I am anyway." He let go of my hand and stood up. "I guess you should get your things. There's not much point in you staying here when I don't need the protection."

I watched him walk away knowing this could be the last time we were in the same room together, and every step was like a needle to my heart.

Fifteen

As I walked to the cafe where I was supposed to meet Fee, the mid-day chatter on the sidewalk around me felt jarringly bright in contrast with the coil of dread in my gut. Early that morning while I was settling back into my room at home, Sterling had called me to let me know Fee had been discharged from the hospital, and Fee had texted me an hour ago asking to me have lunch with her. The request had been so brief I hadn't been able to read her mood. I hesitated as I came up on the place, clutching the purple teddy bear with Get Well T-shirt I'd grabbed at a gift shop. Then I dragged in a breath and pushed inside.

Fee was perched on a stool at a table near the front of the cafe, her elbows braced on the tabletop. She glanced over as soon as I came in and hopped to her feet with an energy and a smile that reassured me. The flush was back in her smooth cheeks and her dark eyes were clearer than I'd seen in months, but she still felt too thin when I hugged her. I guessed that part of recovery would take time.

"I got this for you," I said as we sat down, handing her the teddy bear. Fee took it, studied it, and raised her eyebrows at me.

"I'm not an invalid, you know," she said.

"I know," I said, blushing. "I just thought you'd like it."

"Good," she said. "Because I do, and there is no way you're taking it back." She squeezed one arm around it as she flagged down the waitress, and some of my dread dissipated.

I considered the menu and asked for just the soup of the day. After this lunch, I was due to meet with Sterling for the first time since Colin had "fired" me, and my dread about *that* had stolen most of my appetite. Fee mustn't have been feeling one hundred percent yet either, because she only ordered a coffee and a salad instead of one of her usual platters.

"So... how are you doing?" I said after the waitress had left.

Fee shrugged, fingering one of the sugar packets. "It wasn't exactly the greatest experience of my life, but I think I'll be back to normal pretty fast."

"Are you going back with the Starlet?"

She nodded. "Yvonne's there now, but Sterling okayed me to pick things up again next week. I pointed out how much progress I've made and the great 'rapport' we have. He wants me to stop by the office for regular drug tests until further notice, though."

I hid my flicker of relief. "That sucks."

"You don't really think that," she said, eyeing me. "You're probably dying to say you told me so."

The dread swelled up like a punch in the gut. "No, Fee," I said. "Not at all."

"Then why are you acting so weird?" she demanded. "You've hardly looked me in the eye since you came in."

I opened my mouth, paused, and forced myself to say, "I

just wasn't sure— I was scared you'd be angry with me. Because I got the Society involved. I didn't want to, Fee, I swear, but I didn't know what else to do."

"Oh." Fee blinked at me. I made myself hold her gaze, and realized there was nothing accusing in it. She reached across the table and grasped my wrist. "Of course I'm not mad at you, Ave. I'm *glad* that I could count on you. You have no idea how good it is to know that I've got at least one friend who cares about me enough to do whatever it takes to make sure I'm all right, even when I've been kind of a jerk to her and she's not sure I'll even appreciate it. You did the right thing. I'm the one who was acting stupid. I didn't want to worry about anything, so I wasn't paying enough attention to what I took or how much or where it came from."

"Okay," I said with an exhale of relief. I set my hand over hers. "I just didn't want to lose you. And... don't beat yourself up too much, okay? I'm certainly not in a position to criticize anyone for getting carried away in the middle of a job."

Fee's eyebrows leapt up again. "Oh, really? Apparently I've been *way* too distracted. What happened? Spill!"

My throat closed up at the memory of Colin's face as he told me to go. "I don't think I'm ready to talk about it yet," I said. Other than the awful talk I was going to have to have with Sterling in less than an hour. The thought of it rubbed against all the painful spots still raw inside me. "I'll give you all the details when I've got my head sorted out."

"Promise, bestie?" Fee said with a playful gleam in her eyes.

"Promise," I said, smiling back at her as the flicker of relief became a flood.

"So you've returned home," Sterling said the second my butt hit the chair opposite his desk. He stayed standing, pacing slowly between the bookcases on either side of the narrow office, past the photos that hung on the back wall of him with clients famous enough that I could recognize them on sight.

"It seemed like the only reasonable option," I said.

"It's never *reasonable* to abandon a client without even checking in with us," Sterling said, halting to lean over his desk. His hands fisted on the glass surface. "What were you thinking, Avery? You know how hard we've been working on Ryder's case. First you drag him off to Fiona's... misadventure, and then you up and leave?"

My spine stiffened. "I was thinking," I said carefully, "that if the client told me directly to leave his home, I ought to listen to him. Especially when he already knows exactly what we're trying to protect him from, and he's stated that he doesn't want or need our assistance."

Sterling hesitated. "He knows...?"

"He *knows*," I said. "He knows everything—about the Glowers, what they do, why they do it—almost as well as we do. There was some British musician, a rocker named Brian someone, who was marked and hung himself in his house here in L.A. about four years ago? He was mentoring Ryder. Ryder found him, saw the Glower with him. This whole time, he's known exactly what we were trying to do. What we were trying to protect him from. He's been making things hard on purpose."

Sterling's expression had frozen. He shook his head, as if he could erase the facts I'd laid out by denying them.

"He *wants* to be marked," I told him. "I can't stop him if he's making a conscious choice."

That remark broke Sterling's daze. "Of course you can," he

said, rapping his hands against the desk. "That's your job. You find a way to change his mind. I don't care how. We lose him, and we lose all of Spright Records' business."

My job. Even as guilt prickled through my stomach, another question pushed in front of it. "Is that really what's most important? Their *business*?"

"You know what I meant," Sterling said. "The well-being of every artist they work with, from now until as long as they keep producing records. Think of all the lives that are riding on this, and then return to your post and make something work."

I stared at him. His eyelid twitched, his dark skin slightly grayed beneath the mottling of acne scars, and suddenly he didn't seem intimidating so much as desperate. Almost... pathetic. Before I'd made any conscious decision to react, I was springing to my feet.

"This isn't on me," I said. "I did my best."

Sterling's face hardened. "That is not how a good Tether thinks. If you give up—"

"*I did my best*," I snapped. "I got him to open up to me. I found out what's going on. That's way more than the two guys before me managed to accomplish. Why aren't you bitching them out?"

Now Sterling was staring at me. "Avery," he said, but I wasn't in the mood to listen. My talk with Fee was still whirling in my head. I'd been a real friend to her, I'd looked out for her, by doing what I knew I had to in order to get her out of that mess, even though I'd been terrified of how she'd think of me afterward. Why had I been so hesitant to be a real friend to myself all this time? It didn't matter how scared I was of what Sterling would think if I stood up to him—I wasn't going to be able to keep being any sort of Tether if we went on like this. It was time for *him* to listen.

"You've been acting ridiculous since you first put me with Ryder," I said with a slash of my arm through the air. "Putting all the responsibility on me, making me feel like the world depends on my pulling this together, reining him in, protecting him from *everything*, not just the Glowers. The way you've been treating me, *you* might as well be a Glower, pushing and pushing to get what you want no matter how it affects anyone else. Well, maybe if you'd eased up I wouldn't have felt I had to push things with him so far, so fast—maybe we'd have found some kind of balance without everything blowing up in my face. But that's what happened. That's the mess we have now. And I've done everything I can to fix it, so if you've got some great solution in mind, why don't you get on with it?"

I headed for the office door, my heart thudding, not quite sure what line I was drawing. Would I be able to come back to the Society if I left this conversation here?

Would I *want* to, if I couldn't?

My fingers had just closed around the knob when Sterling cleared his throat. "I apologize," he said in a low voice. "I didn't realize... There's been so much pressure... Of course it wasn't fair of me to displace so much of that pressure onto you."

I turned to face him. "Okay," I said.

The silence stretched for a moment. "With Ryder," he started, "you could— "

I held up my hand to stop him.

"I don't want anything to happen to him, Sterling," I said. "I really don't. But I think I've played every card I can with him. I gave it everything I had, and I couldn't change his mind. If someone's going to, I don't think it can be me. I'm not going back."

Sterling paused, and then nodded. "I'll see what I can work out. And... why don't you take the rest of the week off? I think you need that, and you've certainly earned a break. We'll start talking about possible new placements on Monday."

I was pulling into our driveway when the enormity of what I'd just done fully hit me. I'd chewed out my direct supervisor. I'd compared him to the demons we were dedicated to fighting. I'd refused the job he'd wanted me to do.

And he'd backed down.

A startled laugh burst out of me. I tipped my head forward almost to the steering wheel and squeezed back the tears that tried to follow. After several shaky breaths, I felt more like myself again. But also, as I stepped out onto the pavement, so much lighter.

Mom wasn't home. She'd started with a new client a few days ago, one who required overnights at least to begin with, so I might not see her for a while. I ambled through the house we'd moved into a couple years after Dad's death. Though he'd never inhabited it himself, his presence lingered in the framed photos on the mantle, the platinum records hanging in their place of honor over the stairs, the worn armchair I could still remember curling up on his lap in, snuggling against his broad chest. And then, of course, there was the drum kit in the spare bedroom, which Mom had never gotten around to moving into storage even though I hadn't played on it more than a few times a year since I'd left Rushfield.

I stopped in the doorway, looking at it. That familiar itch crept through my fingers as I remembered playing on Joel's kit at Colin's studio. The memory brought back Colin's smile when he'd caught me, the way *his* fears had seemed to ebb as I talked about later chances to rework songs, the heat of the connection between of our bodies when we'd been pressed together against the wall. A tingle raced over my skin, followed by a wave of grief.

I hadn't been lying when I'd told Sterling I wasn't going back to work with Colin, but I hadn't been lying when I'd said I didn't want anything happening to him either. I'd said everything to him I could think of. If only there were a way to make him *see* what he'd be sacrificing, that he didn't need to...

Instead of resisting my earlier impulse, I let my feet take me into the room. I sat down on the stool, picked up the drumsticks, and spun them in my hands. That old fear shivered through me again. What would I end up willing to sacrifice, if I let myself be drawn in to the passion for music the way Dad had?

Then I thought of standing in Sterling's office, telling him where I drew the line. I thought of kneeling over Fee's prone body and making the call to get her to the hospital. A resolve hardened inside me.

I didn't need to be scared. I was strong enough to stand up for myself, for what I knew was right. I'd proven that.

Maybe the question I should be asking was, how much was I sacrificing if I let fear stop me from following my passion?

My mind tripped back to my last conversation with Colin. *I can't be scared like that*, he'd said. But he *was* scared. He was terrified—that he didn't have the talent, that he couldn't deliver the album he desperately wanted to. It was fear that had driven him to this point, not ambition or greed or ego.

And why would he listen to me telling him to be brave, to face those fears, when I was still cowering myself?

An idea blossomed inside me. As I brought the sticks down

on the drums, it spread through my body with the gentle but eager warmth of hope. At first I struck the drums' taut surfaces tentatively, but I gathered energy as I settled into the rhythm I knew by heart.

I didn't have time for caution. I had five years of practice to catch up on and only three days to do it in.

<h1 style="text-align:center">Sixteen</h1>

EVEN DURING THE OPENING ACT, THE CONCERT HALL WAS packed. I was pretty sure my ribs were bruised where some guy near the bar had elbowed me, and I'd narrowly escaped a stiletto to the toes, which had prompted the memory of that first night in the club when I'd gotten my foot bashed up and Colin had tended to it.

It was hard to stop my thoughts from cycling back to him, over and over. After weeks together, I hadn't seen him in nearly four days. I hadn't really been prepared for the way my heart would leap when he walked onto the stage with that usual cocky cool, the overhead lights turning his amber eyes to gold. As his fingers danced over the guitar strings, I remembered them running over my skin. When he closed his eyes as he launched into the first chorus, losing himself in the song, I saw the generous, yearning boy I'd gotten to know outside the spotlight, and my heart outright ached.

The band was onto the fifth song now, Colin pouring his enthusiasm into the microphone as he pelted out the second verse, bleeding his joy into his guitar. I didn't know why he couldn't hear what he did, unaided by any supernatural power, for everyone listening. All I could hope was that he'd start to believe after tonight.

I'd hung back from the stage during the first few songs, not wanting him to see me—and not wanting someone else to see me either. The Glower was here, back in her redheaded form and corset top, gleaming and swaying right by Colin's feet. He bent down to clasp hands with the fans he could reach as Kevin charged into a solo on the keyboards. When Colin's fingers touched the Glower's, even from across the room I saw how their eyes locked. My breath caught in my throat.

Colin nodded, but when he straightened back up, her spark didn't travel with him. She hadn't marked him yet. But I didn't think I'd imagined the agreement he'd offered her either. He was going to give himself over soon. Maybe even tonight.

Unless I could change his mind.

I glanced down at the grimy piece of paper I'd begged off one of the roadies: the set list for Colin Ryder's opening act. Six songs and then, as I'd hoped, one encore. He'd been mixing his established material with some of the new songs, and the encore was one of the tracks I'd heard them recording. But there were still at least a couple obstacles up ahead.

As the band launched into their sixth song, I headed backstage, flashing my Society ID at the security guy guarding the door. I found a spot in the wings on the side of the stage near Joel's post. Music always sounded different backstage, when you were standing in the eye of the storm rather than being washed over by the forward surge of it. It felt more real, hearing the parts weave together around me.

I pulled my hair into a ponytail as I waited in the shadows. The song ended with a final chord and a crash of the cymbals.

Colin waved to the audience and made a show of walking off stage—in the opposite direction from me, to my relief. Joel ambled toward me, gulping from a bottle of water. He stopped just beyond the curtain, his forehead furrowing when he saw me.

I didn't have much time to make my pitch. The crowd was already hollering for Colin's return. "He's going back on, right?" I said. "To do 'Far Out'?"

Joel nodded. "Where've you been the last few days, Avery?"

"That's— It's complicated. This is going to sound sort of weird, but will you let me take over the drums for the encore?"

He blinked and glanced at his kit. "That's kind of out of the blue. No offense, Avery, but, I mean, it's my job."

"I know," I said. "And I'm not trying to take it. It's just this once." The shouts outside were getting louder. Colin walked back onto the stage, and the crowd cheered. "Please," I added. "It's for Colin. He's... been working through some things. You know how he's been acting since he got the deal. I think seeing me out there with him will help get him back to where he needs to be."

Joel paused, visibly torn. Marcy and Kevin had already rejoined Colin on stage. Kevin was peering toward Joel.

"Please," I said again.

Joel rubbed his face. "You're right about him being off. And he was better when you were around. You know the song?"

"Well enough, I think. If I ruin it, you can blame it on me. Say I forced you at gunpoint."

"Let's hope it doesn't come to that," he said with a laugh. "All right. Go at it."

I delayed for a second to grab him in a quick hug that left him chuckling and dashed to the kit. Colin turned just as I was picking up the sticks. He stiffened and then stalked over.

"What are you doing?" he demanded in a low voice.

I looked right back at him and raised the drumsticks to indicate I was ready. "I'm going all in," I said.

He stared at me. I didn't break my gaze from his. "Colin!" Marcy hissed, and he snapped out of his shock. He swiveled and strode back to the front of the stage, holding the microphone aloft in a salute before hooking it into the stand.

"Let's end this party right!" he called out, and dropped his hands to his guitar.

With Colin's back to me, my awareness of the massive crowd beyond him expanded, rolling over me. In that first instant, it was suffocating. All those shifting bodies in the hazy light past the reach of the spotlights. I sucked in my breath, my palms abruptly clammy. It was me they were watching now, even back here in my fortress of drums. I was part of the storm.

I almost missed my cue. The guitar's chords penetrated my daze, and even as my pulse stuttered, my arms moved automatically. I'd practiced every song of Colin's I could—the ones on his debut, the ones I'd heard in the studio to the best of my memory—for hours over the last few days. I knew this beat.

My hands stumbled once, and a cold sweat broke over me. But as the guitar and bass and keyboards swelled in their melody, as Colin's voice carried through the hall, the storm rushed up around me, and I didn't mind. I was here. I was adding my noise to the song, for all those hundreds of figures cheering us on. My throat choked up, but the rest of me was floating.

I hadn't realized it at the time, but I'd lied when I'd told Sterling I'd done the best I could. *This* was the best I could give: the music that had hummed through my veins since before I was born. And as I threw myself into the seven stroke roll of the chorus, I knew that I was never going to give it up again. Not for fear, not for a Glower's temporary promise. I wasn't scared anymore.

At least not for myself.

Colin turned from the microphone, his eyes half shut, bending over his guitar as his fingers swept into the bridge. Then he shot a flash of a grin back at me. And if I'd been floating before, right then I started soaring.

———

"Good night, L.A.!" Colin shouted to the crowd as we waved our goodbyes. My arm wobbled, my body as shaky as if I'd played through a full set, not just one song. Giddy and nervous. Unsure of what would come next.

We headed off stage as the roadies hurried out to prepare for the main act. Joel clapped me on the back as soon as I reached the sidelines.

"I don't think any tall tales are going to be necessary," he said.

"There you are," Colin remarked mildly. "Decided to take a little break?"

Joel shrugged, smiling. "Avery made a case I couldn't dispute. You *were* always saying we should hear her play."

"Yeah," Colin said, and laughed. He took my hand, his fingers twining with mine, and gave me a tug that asked me to follow.

He didn't speak to me as we ducked down the stairs and hurried along a narrow hall that smelled like Doritos and floor polish to the dressing rooms. There was just the rasp of his breath as he wound down from the show and a faint tremble in his muscles when his arm brushed mine. I wanted to hope, wanted to so badly it seared through my chest, but nothing was settled between us, not yet.

The Glower girl was standing beside one of the dressing room doors. Colin's, I guessed. She smiled when she saw him, but her eyes glittered fiercely. My hand tightened around his.

Colin brushed right by her. "You should leave," he said with dip of his head toward her as he opened the door. "I've got plans for tonight that don't include you."

"Do you think—" she started to purr, and reached as if to caress his arm. She halted when he raised his eyes. Something in them must have shut her down cold. She smiled again, sharply, her breath shimmering past her bright teeth, and spun on her heel. For a few seconds she was ambling away from us, and then she seemed to meld into the darkness beyond the stairs.

Plans for tonight. The words echoed in my head as Colin ushered me into the dressing room. Just *tonight.* Was that an invitation for her to come back tomorrow?

He closed the door and locked it. My gaze traveled through the concrete-walled room, which was just big enough for a table beneath a well-let mirror, a furry rug, a rolling wardrobe, and a pair of metal chairs. Then Colin was standing in front of me, his eyes shadowed and familiar musky-sweet scent tickling off his skin with its sheen of stage sweat, and I couldn't look anywhere else.

"Avery," he said, and swallowed audibly. He didn't move, as if he wasn't sure what to do, what I'd accept. Where we were going. It made me think of the first night we'd kissed, his uncertainty that I'd want him. I set my hands on the table and hopped up, letting my legs dangle, knees splayed. Then I held out one hand to him.

Colin stepped closer, stopping at my knees. His fingers

settled on my waist, and his head bowed, not quite low enough to reach mine. My pulse thumped.

"Missed me, did you?" he said softly.

"You could say that," I said.

"Good. I missed you too. I..." He hesitated. "You played, Avery. In front of an entire packed hall."

"I did," I agreed.

"I thought you were scared."

"I was. But I had other feelings that mattered more."

He brought his hands to my face, trailing the backs of his fingers over my cheek, down my neck, across the strap of my dress and the peak of my shoulder, along my bare arm. The contact sent a warm shiver though me, but I resisted the urge to pull him closer.

"It felt different, playing with you," he said. "I could hear... The song's still not quite right, but I could hear how it could be."

"You probably always knew how to make it right, somewhere in there," I said. "You just hadn't found the way to it yet."

"You don't want any credit for helping me get there?"

"A thank you in the credits? A cameo in a music video?"

The corner of his mouth quirked up. He loosened the elastic holding my ponytail and slid it off so my hair drifted over my back. "That wasn't exactly what I had in mind."

"No? Maybe you could show me then."

He threaded his fingers into my hair and tipped my head, his lips finally finding mine. He kissed me slowly, tenderly, not at all like the night I'd been remembering. But better, because I didn't have to stop him. I didn't have to be scared of him. It was me he still wanted. Just me.

I kissed him back, running my thumb over the damp curls

at the back of his neck. He shifted closer, and the skirt of my dress edged up my thighs with a tantalizing tickle of fabric. A whiff of his piney aftershave made my head spin. *Yes, yes, yes,* every inch of my body was wailing, but I realized I had one more thing I needed to tell him before we went any further. One more thing I needed to know.

I eased back, my hands at either side of his jaw.

"I'm falling in love with you," I said.

Colin drew in a startled breath. Before he had to answer, I hurtled onward.

"Maybe I haven't known you very long, but I think I know you well enough to say I want to be with you. Not just now. Through the recording sessions and the contract negotiations and all the ups and downs that come with this business. For all the celebrations and all the disappointments. I can handle that. I just can't... I can't watch some Glower siphon away the things I love about you bit by bit. I've already had to watch that once, and it's the worst thing I've ever been through. I don't know if I could survive it a second time. You have to understand that doesn't mean I don't care about you. But that's my limit."

He was silent for a long moment. "I've been thinking a lot, since the last time we talked," he said. "About... whether I really need to go that far. Whether I could go all in on my own. I didn't really think so until—the way I felt tonight— Will you play with me again? I want you *there*, being part of my music, not just watching."

I hadn't known until he said it how much I'd wanted him to ask. How much I wanted to say yes. "I think you'd have to talk to Joel about that," I said. "It's his gig. He might not be pleased about me stealing it." I paused. "I do want to keep playing, though, one way or another. I think I'm supposed to."

Colin nuzzled my cheek. "So if I, let's say, found Joel an

even better gig, and there happened to be an opening in my band...?"

I laughed. "I'd still have to sort some things out with the Society. But it would be my honor."

"Okay," he said. "I want to try. To see what I can really do, myself. If... If I end up deciding I can't make it to where I want to be that way, that I need to make some kind of deal, I'll tell you first. I'll understand if that means you have to leave. The last thing I want to do is hurt you, Avery."

"I'm not afraid of that anymore either," I said.

He smiled. "Good," he murmured. "Because I've already fallen for you."

His words tingled through me, and then he was kissing me again, more insistently than before. As I tugged him to me, welcoming his tongue with mine, his fingers caught the zipper at my back. They drew it down over my spine with an excruciating slowness, the dress parting against my skin. He left it at the hollow of my back, pressed his palm there to conform our bodies even more closely together, and then reached for the straps. As soon as they were sliding down my arms, he ran his thumbs over the cups of my bra, seeking out my nipples. Even through the thick cloth, his touch sparked against them. I hummed in encouragement as they hardened.

My own hands slipped down Colin's back, following the lines of muscle until I reached the hem of his shirt. I leaned back to help him pull it off. He took advantage of our momentary separation to dip his head and gently nip my throat. I sighed. The sound turned into a moan as his fingers dipped inside the bra, nudging it down so he could fondle my breasts unimpeded. My head and shoulders drifted back against the mirror, the glass cool against my flushed skin.

Colin unclasped the bra and tossed it aside. He licked one

nipple and sucked it into his mouth, his hands sliding up under my dress at the same time. They glided over my outer thighs before slipping between my legs. I arched into his touch. He stroked the needy nub there before brushing down over my opening, stroking the dampening fabric as I clutched his bare shoulders.

When he tugged my panties down, his mouth followed in a scorching trail of kisses to my stomach. He paused just long enough to hitch the skirt of my dress a little higher. Then he was kneeling before me, his mouth on me, laving that sensitive nub and drawing a gasp from my lungs. I arched again, braced against the mirror, as he slicked his tongue over my opening. He sucked and nibbled, savoring me gently but purposefully. Pleasure swelled in my core. His fingers caressed the sides of my thighs as he dove deeper, flicking his tongue right inside me. A jolt of pure bliss shot through me.

"Colin," I said, my voice quaking. "I'm going to—"

"Please," he whispered against me. He teased his tongue over my nub and down again, and my pleasure peaked. My fingers tangled in his hair as I bucked to meet him. He kissed me while the waves rocked through me, over and over until they finally ebbed. I sagged against the mirror.

"We're not done," Colin informed me, setting off on a path of kisses up my torso. "*You're* not done."

I wasn't going to argue with that. I dragged his face to mine, kissing him hard, wanting him to feel every shudder of the bliss he'd given me. He lifted me off the table onto my feet.

"I realized I've never seen you completely naked," he said, already guiding my dress down my legs. "I think it's time we fixed that oversight."

I grinned. "As long as you join me."

He offered a happy murmur as I yanked off his belt and

unzipped his jeans. As he stepped out of them, he swept me up and laid us down on the thick rug. It was softer than I'd expected against my back.

"Okay?" he asked.

"Not quite," I said, and shoved him over as I rolled onto my knees. Leaning over him, I kissed him on the mouth before charting my own path down his throat, across his chest, delaying to run my tongue across each nipple, smiling at the hitch of his breath.

"Avery," he mumbled as I reached the dip of his taut stomach, followed by an inarticulate sound as I jerked down his boxers and took the length of him in my hand. I stroked up and down that silky hard flesh, circling my thumb over the glistening tip and sliding the wetness there back over the shaft. His hips quaked and his erection twitched as I lowered my mouth over it.

I didn't have much practice at this particular act—Mateo had always gotten awkward when I'd suggested it—but I was happy to experiment. I eased my lips down Colin's length, and the groan he made reverberated into me. As I raised my head, I teased the soft skin with the edges of my teeth before rolling my tongue around him.

"Oh, God," Colin said, sounding choked. He gripped my hair with a tug that made me look at him. The blatant desire in his eyes sent a bolt of electricity through me.

"If you keep doing that, I'm not going to make it," he said roughly.

"Make it to what?" I teased, even though the core of me was aching all over again. I slicked a finger up and down his length. He drew me up beside him as he kicked off his boxers. We kissed fast and desperate, wetness seeping between my legs at the feel of him pressed against me. His hand traced the curve of my waist to my hip.

"I want inside you," he said.

"Who's stopping you?" I muttered, and Colin laughed. He kissed me again, more deeply this time, drawing it out until I was quivering against him. Then he fumbled in his discarded jeans for his wallet.

I raised my hips as he penetrated me, hooking my ankles behind him. That first thrust came so hard and eager I moaned. He thrust again, gliding deeper and deeper with each cant of his hips, until mine were arching to meet his every stroke. He kissed my cheek and my neck. His teeth grazed my shoulder, and I dug my fingers into his back.

His hand slid beneath me to lift me so we connected even more tightly, and he hit that wanting place inside me even more firmly. I cried out as my pleasure surged, and surged higher, until it seemed I'd never find the end of it. Then with one final plunge it crashed over me, and I came apart, pulsing and gasping against him. Colin sped up, his swift strokes carrying me through the aftermath, his sides tensing and trembling beneath my hands. With a cry of his own, he followed me into release. His thrusts slowed until he settled onto me, his head tucked against my shoulder.

After a moment, he rolled onto his side, pulling me with him. We cuddled on the rug as our breaths slowed together. I was walking my fingers along his bicep, taking an obscure enjoyment from feeling the firm surface of the muscles beneath his smooth skin, when a knock rattled the door.

"Mr. Ryder?" an unfamiliar voice said. "Someone sent down a bottle of wine."

Colin pressed his face to my chest, shaking with silent laughter. "That's a new one," he whispered to me. "Thank you," he called out toward the door. "Can you leave it outside? I'll grab it in a bit."

"Um, yeah. Sure."

As the footsteps shuffled away outside, I tipped my head to look into Colin's eyes, brushing back the dark hair that had fallen across his forehead.

"I have the feeling that's going to happen to us a lot," I said.

He studied me with a smile spreading across his face. "That's a price I'm willing to pay if it means we're *doing* this a lot. I guess we'll just have to get used to it."

Then he drew me in for one more kiss—one I knew for sure was far from the last.

The Morning After

A COLIN RYDER POV BONUS SCENE

Colin

Normally on days that didn't require an alarm I woke up gradually, easing into consciousness bit by bit. But that morning, the first morning I had Avery in my bed, I came out of a vague shape of a dream in a snap. My eyes popped open, and my body tensed. My heart thudded for the few seconds it took for me to roll toward her.

She was still there. Relaxing against the mattress with a smile I couldn't restrain, I took her in. Her bright brown hair was spilling over the pillow, her lean arms curled up as if to shield her face, her angular chin pointed toward them. Disappointingly, I couldn't see much below that, because the sheet was pulled up to her shoulders.

Her rosy lips were slightly parted. Another time, I might have leaned in and kissed them. The urge rose up to refresh my memory of her softness, her taste. The problem was, she looked so serene it provoked a competing urge: to shelter and protect. I was going to feel guilty if I woke her up. And I was pretty sure there wasn't any type of kissing I knew that wouldn't lead to that.

I debated with myself for a minute. Through the gauzy curtain beyond Avery's form, the sky was still dark—as dark as it ever got over L.A.'s lights. What with yesterday's performance and the activities we'd occupied ourselves with afterward, last night had been a long one. She needed the rest.

And the last thing I wanted was to give her any reason to think sleeping over was a bad idea.

Even though it was early, *I* felt wide awake. I groped on the end table for my phone. Five o'clock. *What the hell, brain?* I set my head on my pillow and shut my eyes, but my pulse still hadn't settled. It thumped away at an erratic tempo as a restless feeling crept through me. I'd left something important undone, it insisted without bothering to mention what. I frowned and squeezed my eyelids tighter.

After a few minutes I was no closer to sleep. With a grimace, I slid out of the bed and grabbed a pair of jeans and a T-shirt I'd left draped over the bedroom's chair. The *what* I needed to do had started to solidify in my head. I snuck out and dressed in the living room while contemplating the fridge. Fortification for the feat I was about to attempt sounded like a good idea, but I wasn't hungry. I wasn't sure I was actually about to do anything. I might end up standing around like an idiot and coming back here no different than I'd started.

But maybe not. They seemed to know when they were wanted. And I knew this one wanted me. I'd thought back to the craving in those pale blue eyes more than once in the last few weeks. Before, I'd found it reassuring. Now it sent a queasiness curling through my stomach.

All right, I *definitely* wasn't hungry.

I eased the door shut behind me and played punchy guitar riffs in my head as the elevator descended. Sam nodded to me from behind the security desk in the lobby. I walked past the two security guys near the entrance and ambled out onto the sidewalk as if it were a perfectly normal time for a stroll. Those guys had seen pretty much everything anyway—quite a bit of it from me.

The pre-dawn air was comfortably cool. Just a hint of a breeze tickled over my bare arms. I glanced around and decided I'd take my stroll around the block. If that didn't conjure her, well, I'd decide on a new plan of action then.

I set off with my hands in my pockets, trying not to feel like an idiot already. I'd just made it to the corner when a curvy figure with shimmering red hair stepped out of the shadows into my path.

"Looking for someone?" the Glower said, peering at me through long eyelashes that shimmered too.

She was wearing the same outfit she'd had on at the venue last night: a low-cut corset top under a leather jacket, skinny jeans. A look I might have appreciated at other times. On other girls. The sheen that seeped from within her ivory skin was chillingly inhuman.

It always had been disturbing, I thought with another twinge of nausea. I should have taken it as a warning. I'd just let myself get so caught up in the thought of what the Glower could give, I hadn't let myself imagine what she'd take.

"Yes and no," I said. I held my ground as she sidled closer. There wasn't anything she could do to me if I didn't agree.

"What does that mean?" she asked, cocking her head.

"I was looking for you," I said, "to tell you I don't want to see you around here again. I want you to back off, find some other sap to chase after. I'm not interested in what you're peddling."

"Oh," the Glower purred, "but you have no idea how much I could do for you, Colin. If you'd only give me the chance to—"

"I do know," I interrupted. "I've always known what you're really offering. I'm not as naive as most of the marks you go after. I *see* you. Just like I saw the thing like you that killed my mentor."

She stilled, her flirtatious air fading as she studied me. "Oh," she said again, in a completely different tone. "Well, I suppose that does alter the situation."

"Exactly," I said. "So enough of this—enough of the stalking, the come ons. I thought I wanted it, but I've changed my mind. There's no point in you hanging around."

"That depends." She stole even closer, raising her hand to trail her fingers across my arm. The hairs on the back of my neck rose, but I suppressed a flinch. Show no weakness.

"If you changed your mind once," she went on, "you could change it again, don't you think? That girl, what will she matter in the long run? It's your music you love the most, and I can help you take it everywhere you've dreamed."

I'd braced myself for this, dreaded the moment when I'd find out how I reacted when she dangled that carrot. The words hit me—

And I felt nothing. Not even the slightest tickle of temptation. A laugh tumbled out of me with the relief of it. How easy it was to turn her down.

For so long I'd thought she was right. I'd thought the music was all I had, and that the only way I could hold on to it, shape it the way I wanted, was with the boost someone like her could offer me. But I didn't believe that anymore. This conversation would give me far more control over my career than she would ever have given me if I'd given in.

From here on, the music I made was going to be totally mine. No label, no cranky bandmate, no family pressure, and definitely no Glower was going to take that away from me.

"You have no idea what you're talking about," I said. "Avery already means more for my music than you ever could."

"For now," the Glower said.

I caught her hand as she reached for me again and pushed it toward her. "For the foreseeable future," I said firmly. "I don't want you bothering us. I don't want you bothering her. Do you really think pissing me off is going to convince me of anything? If I *do* change my mind again, if I'm in a buying mood, you'll know. So go find something more productive to do with your time."

She pursed her lips, but she kept back. "You make a reasonable argument," she said after a moment. "*When* you change your mind, when you realize you can't ascend to the heights you wish for without me, I'll be here."

With that, she turned and sauntered off. Her hips swayed as she turned the corner. Then she'd disappeared, swallowed up by the shadows between the streetlamps.

I felt lighter all over as I walked back to the condo building. Maybe she was right—maybe I couldn't get as far as I wanted without her help. But I'd be damned if I wasn't going to figure that out for myself. By myself.

Well, not completely by myself.

When I came back into the bedroom, Avery had turned onto her other side, facing the window. I stripped to my boxers and sat down at the other end of the bed to slide my legs under the sheet behind her. With the movement, the sheet slipped below the scooped neckline of her chemise to reveal the shadow of her cleavage. And suddenly a different part of me was on high alert.

No, I chided myself. *No waking her up, not even for that.* But as I lay down, she shifted, pushing closer to me. Her bum brushed my rising hard-on, and my skin went hot. I looped my arm around her waist and breathed in the faint lilac smell of her hair. If she was *already* awake…

"Morning," she said drowsily.

"Morning," I replied. And then—there might have been some guy alive who could have resisted at that point, but I was not him—I nuzzled her hair to the side so I could kiss her neck. "What do you say we make it a good one?"

Avery hummed happily and squirmed even closer to me, making me even harder down below. "I assume you've got a suggestion for how to accomplish that?"

"I might have a few ideas." I nipped the crook of her neck before nibbling my way up to the tempting spot just behind her ear. She hummed again as I teased it with my tongue. I grazed my hands up from her waist to her breasts, rubbing my palm over one of her pert nipples through the soft fabric. Her hum turned into a sigh.

"Colin," she murmured in that pleading, wanting voice that shot straight to my heart—not to mention my dick. I stroked all around the delicious curve of her breast and back over the nipple. Then I extended my arm farther, pulling her tighter against my body. Her breaths shortened as I brought the other nipple to its peak. She moaned, reaching back to clasp my thigh.

With a growl against her neck I couldn't suppress, I tugged the chemise down and cupped her bare flesh. She pressed against me as I continued to kiss and caress, until I couldn't stand the friction any longer. I let go of her breast to explore beneath the hem of her chemise.

She wasn't wearing panties. That discovery alone made me twice as hard. I dipped my hand between her legs. My fingertips circled the sensitive point there until she was whimpering and arching against me, and then I cast them lower. She was slick and ready. I eased a finger inside her and had to swallow a groan.

Avery was apparently more ready than I'd realized. With a shaky exhalation, she rolled over and pushed me onto my back. Then she was straddling me, hands on my shoulders. That teasing wetness slid against me.

As I grabbed a condom from the end table, she leaned down to trail her lips across my chest. I touched her cheek to bring her mouth to mine, kissing her long and deep as I prepared myself with my other hand. Then she was sinking down onto me, and I could barely think at all.

It had never felt like this with anyone before. So close, so in sync, as if the heat between us had melded us together into two halves of the same being.

I thrust up to meet her as she rocked against me. Pleasure surged through me. I gripped her hips, easing her forward as I urged her onward, watching her until I saw her eyelids flutter, her skin flush along her neck, and knew I'd found the perfect angle to send her soaring.

Both our breaths were ragged now. I flicked my thumb between her legs, just above the place we were joined. It only took a few more caresses before I felt her clench around me. As she cried out, the sound sent me tipping over the edge at the same time. I came with her, pumping up into her until I was sure I'd carried her through.

Avery sighed and bowed down to lie on me. I collected her against my body, fitting her to me until she was a part of me again. Then I tilted her face toward mine so I could kiss her forehead, her cheeks, her nose. She gazed at me, satisfied desire making her hazel eyes languid.

"Where did you go?" she said.

I was so caught up in her that at first I didn't follow the question. "What?" I said.

"You got up and went out a little while ago. With your clothes, so I'm guessing it wasn't just for a glass of water."

"No. I—" I hesitated, and the instinct to lie rose up. It was what I'd been doing any time I was asked about the Glowers for years. It was what I'd done with Avery for most of the time I'd known her.

Thinking that with the warmth of her body so entwined with mine, my gut twisted with guilt. I'd sworn to myself I was done lying to this one person.

"I went out to talk to my Glower 'fan,'" I said.

Avery's expression didn't change, but I felt the faint tightening of her muscles where they rested against mine. I barreled on before she could imagine anything worse. "I wanted to tell her to stay away from us. I made it clear that I know what she is and that I'm not interested anymore. It seemed to work."

"You know, they can take any sort of interaction as encouragement," Avery said. "And that one has been particularly stubborn."

"Well, if it turns out talking to her didn't work, I'll just ignore her from now on. Is that what you'd officially recommend?"

I raised an eyebrow at her and was relieved to see her lips twitch upward. Her body had started to loosen against me. She laid her head on my shoulder, her breath tickling over my throat.

"From now on, yeah," she said.

"It was just getting to me, thinking about her lurking out

there. Not knowing when she was going to make another move. I wanted to get it over with."

Avery nodded, hugging me tighter. "I understand."

With those words, my heart quivered. Because I believed her. I'd been alone in this for so damn long, but now I had her. She'd seen all the things I'd seen. I could tell her anything without her thinking I was insane.

She understood.

All that crap the Glower had said about Avery not mattering, not being able to offer me enough—it couldn't have been more wrong. I had seen the Glower, but Avery had seen *me*. Even when I was acting like an ass, even when I'd told her to give up on saving me, she hadn't written me off. She'd stood by me.

I doubted many people got to find someone that amazing in their entire life, and I'd found her at nineteen. How the hell had I gotten so lucky?

I tangled my fingers in her hair and drew her up so I could kiss her on the lips. Our mouths melded and parted, our noses still touching. There was one more thing I wanted her to understand.

"I love you," I said.

A smile spread across Avery's face that was brighter than any supernatural glow. She nestled closer to me and whispered by my ear, "I love you too."

Caught in the Rush

DEMONS OF FAME #2

One

For a fifteen-year-old, the Starlet had excellent taste in parties. When the car reached her family's gated mansion on the way back from the after-after do at some blockbuster TV producer's house, I was giddy from the lights and the music and a particularly close dance with a swoon-worthy A-lister. No booze or drugs necessary for that kind of high.

Miss Charity Reece was a little tipsy in the more standard formulation: one more glass of champagne than was completely wise. But that was why she had me—so she could have the not-completely-wise times any fifteen-year-old was entitled to and still survive stardom with her soul intact.

"They think I'm a baby," she muttered, fidgeting with the tastefully knee-length hem of her dress.

"Who?" I said. There were a lot of people she could mean. Maybe even me. Charity hadn't exactly been thrilled two months ago when she'd found out the execs behind her hit tween sitcom had hired her a shadow to tag along every time she left the house, though I thought she'd warmed up pretty quickly in the time since then. The Tether Society kept assigning me to the "wild child" divas because I always managed to work it out. I might be somewhat reformed in my slightly older age, but it didn't take long for the girls to recognize me as a kindred spirit.

"Everyone!" Charity said with an expansive if unsteady wave of her arm, and then clarified, "All the people at that party. All they saw was some stupid teeny-bopper who needs a laugh track so people will watch. They're never going to consider me for anything *real*."

I studied her. With those expertly highlighted blonde waves, pert ski jump nose, cupid's bow lips tinted glossy pink, and youthful body in sequined skater dress... she *was* a teeny-bopper. But her frown was serious. The hint of jasmine and amber floating in the air reminded me of the quick wrist-scrubbing I'd advised her on before we'd left, because she'd slathered on her new perfume on a bit too thick. Her new perfume that was much more mature than the breezy sweet florals she used to like. Something was going on with her.

"Getting tired of the sitcom scene?" I asked as the car pulled to a stop outside the garage.

"Ex*haus*ted," she said, rolling her eyes. "When do I get to take on a role that's about more than giggling over boys and freaking out about pop quizzes? No one thinks I could pull it off."

"So what?" I said. "If there's something you want, you just go for it. *Show* them what you're capable of. No one can hold you back from doing that except yourself."

"You really think so? What if I screw it up?"

"I think so," I said. "And anything worth doing means taking a little risk. That's the fun part."

I shot her a grin as we climbed out. Then my gaze stopped

on the compact silver Mazda parked on the other side of the drive. I'd never seen it here before.

"Oh!" Charity said, spotting it at the same time. "Will must have come right after class. I didn't think he'd get here until tomorrow."

A baritone voice carried from the direction of the house. "I thought I was going to get to hang with my little sister tonight. I guess you've gotten too famous for me, huh?"

Charity dashed toward the guy who'd just stood up from the bench by the door. He strode forward to meet her, picking her up and spinning her in a circle as she wrapped her arms around his broad chest. I stayed back by the car, watching, but I had to smile at the obvious familial affection. It wasn't a sensation I had much experience with.

I hadn't met the Starlet's brother before—the last time he'd been home was winter break—but I'd picked up the basic info from conversations around the house. William Reece was twenty-two and in his last year of the engineering undergrad program at Stanford, about to graduate *summa cum laude*. I was familiar with his looks from the photos around the house, but it was different seeing him in the flesh—rather appealing flesh, I had to say. The sandy-haired guy now ruffling Charity's blonde waves was built like a quarterback: tall and muscular, but not *too* bulky. Just the way I liked 'em. The sibling resemblance was plain in the delicacy of his nose and mouth, which contrasted with the rest of his square-jawed face to make him look equal parts strong and sensitive. Be still my heart.

Then Will raised his head, and his pale green eyes swept up and down my body before locking with mine. A warm shiver tickled over my skin. There was definitely nothing delicate about that gaze.

When he spoke again, a thread of tension resonated through

his words. "Is this the time you're usually getting home on a Thursday these days, Char?"

He was still looking at me. Lacking a little in the friendliness department, apparently. I stared right back at him as Charity shook her head.

"Nah," she said. "I got a special invitation, thanks to one of the guys on the show—not a regular deal. Mom and Dad don't mind. And Fee keeps an eye on me."

Then she was looking at me too, with a mischievous grin. Her brother raised an eyebrow.

"I'm glad to hear that," he said with an edge of skepticism.

I wasn't sure how exactly I'd gotten off on the wrong foot before I'd even opened my mouth, but if he expected me to cower, he had the wrong girl. I gave him an even smile.

Charity clapped her hand over her mouth to cover a yawn and then giggled. "I've gotta crash, Will," she said. "We'll hang tomorrow, 'kay?"

"I'm holding you to that, sprout," he said, finally bringing his attention back to her. He gave her hair one last ruffle and watched as she swayed up the steps. When she'd disappeared into the house, he turned back to me.

"She was drinking?"

I shrugged. "It was a party. I made sure she didn't go overboard."

"She's *fifteen*."

"Exactly. Let her live a little." I cocked my head at him. "Are you going to try to con me into believing you never touched a drop of alcohol at that age?"

He grimaced, which meant I'd got him. And that he wasn't so impervious. Hmmm. He was here for a week—it was awfully tempting to test whether he had a wild side lurking under that stern exterior.

I shifted my weight from one hip to the other, and his gaze darted over my body again, less deliberately this time. He jerked his eyes back to my face as he caught himself. Ah ha. My smile widened. That seemed like a good place to leave him for now.

I reached for the car door. "I'd better let Paul take me home."

"No," Will said. "I'll drive you. There are a few more things I'd like to talk about."

He gestured to the chauffer. The engine rumbled, and the sedan whipped down the drive. Paul had a home to get back to too.

Will motioned me ahead of him to the silver Mazda. Well, if he wanted to check out my ass, he could go right ahead. I sauntered over to the passenger side.

I had to give the guy a little credit for the car. It was nothing flashy, which meant he hadn't taken advantage of his sister's recent sizeable contributions to the family fortune.

Will stalked to the driver's side, unlocking the doors with a press of a button. I dropped into the seat carelessly enough that my dress rode up my left leg to mid-thigh. Nothing truly immodest, but it earned me another glance as he got in beside me. He might not be keen on making friends, but I was pretty sure he liked what he saw.

He set his hand on the steering wheel. "Where am I taking you?"

When I gave him my address, he started the car and pulled it smoothly past the gate and onto the road. Steady, deliberate, precise. I couldn't help seeing the potential there.

"How old are *you* even... Fee?" Will said.

"Fiona," I said. "And twenty-one. Perfectly legal, not that I was doing any drinking myself." Not of the alcoholic sort, at least. The bitter taste of the last shot of coffee I'd thrown back still lingered in my mouth.

"No?" he said, with a return of the skeptical tone and a different sort of glance.

"Not a drop," I said. "Never do on the job." Not there or anywhere else, nor powder nor pills, not since waking up in a hospital five months ago with a tube down my throat after chasing a high a little too avidly. That was not an experience I planned to repeat. "Do you need me to get out and walk along the white line?"

"I think we can skip that," Will muttered. Then he added, "I should be concerned, shouldn't I? One moment Charity's lucky to book a commercial, and the next she's on magazine covers and getting mobbed by fans. With all those stories about child stars going off the rails... She's my little sister. There are some lessons I don't want her to have to learn through experience. Okay?"

I wondered what he'd say if I told him the main experience I was in the business of protecting kids like his sister from was having their creative spark and all the enthusiasm and *life* that came with it drained away by demons. That I was here to make sure she stayed out of an early grave. That just tonight I'd steered her away from the Glower who'd talked his way into the first after party.

Probably accuse me of being drug-addled after all and demand I never set foot near Charity again. The one problem with the job—well, there were plenty of problems, but if we were talking top five or so—was that telling anyone outside the Society, even your own clients, what you actually did would make you sound insane.

"I get it," I said instead. "And I promise she won't go off the rails on my watch. I know what it's like being that age and stir-crazy. I got up to all sorts of stunts when I was her age, as terrifying as you obviously find that idea. I survived, and I'll make sure she does too."

"Well, *that's* reassuring," he said, sounding as if he meant the exact opposite.

"What can I say that would be?" I asked. "This is my job. It's what I'm paid for. And I care about doing it right. I care about Charity. I'd throw myself in front of a bus to protect her if I had to. All right?"

I hadn't meant to get quite so impassioned about it. I bit my tongue. Next thing you knew I'd be blurting out the whole truth that hospital wake-up call had driven home with a lovely shot of terror: I didn't know who I'd be without this job, without knowing there was one thing I could do that contributed something to the world. If I screwed up again and lost it, I'd be losing myself too.

Will was silent for a long moment, so I knew he'd heard the emotion I hadn't meant to bring into the conversation. I kept my mouth shut, watching the view beyond the window as if nothing out of the ordinary had occurred. We stopped at a red light, and he shifted in his seat.

"So I assume you get some kind of training for a job like this?" he said, but his tone was apologetic enough that I forgave the suspicious phrasing.

"More than you might think," I said. "Self defense, first aid, conflict resolution. The Society prepares us well."

"And how does a person get into this field in the first place, Fiona?"

Catch a Glower in the act of sucking someone's life away, end up able to spot them for the rest of your life. With so many Glowers, so many stars for them to target, and so few of us Tethers to get in the way, it wasn't as if the Society could afford to be much pickier than that. I wasn't sure they *would* have kept me on after the hospital incident otherwise.

So I was just going to keep proving they'd made the right decision.

"I've heard the horror stories too," I said, somewhat honestly. "I grew up in the city, knew people who went into the biz. I figured if I didn't have the talent to be a star myself, I might as well look out for the people who do."

"So you're a woman of no talents?" Will said lightly.

"I didn't say *that*." I discarded several too-suggestive remarks before settling on, "The ones I have just aren't the sort they put you on magazine covers for."

"Ah," Will said, with a pause that suggested he might have considered the possibilities. He eased the car onto the curving driveway outside my building and stopped across from the door.

I turned in my seat, resting my hand on my bare knee. "So do I still have a job, Will?"

He flushed an endearing light pink. Just when I thought I couldn't find him any more enticing.

"I wouldn't have—" he started, and then amended, "It wouldn't be my decision anyway."

"That's not really an answer."

He met my eyes. "As long as you seem to really be looking out for Charity, I'm not going to complain."

That wasn't quite an answer either, but I'd take it. I was pretty sure it was progress, at least. Enough that I felt comfortable saying, "Well, I'm off duty now. If you feel you need to get to know me better, you're welcome to come up for a nightcap."

The *complete* whole truth was, I still craved the rush that the powders and pills had used to give me. I'd just found other ways of getting at it. It'd be a welcome change, scratching that itch some way other than my usual making-eyes-over-a-tonic-water as I scoped out possible one night stands at the nearby bars.

I'd looked back at Will steadily as I said the words, calm and casual, letting him decide how much to read into the invitation. So I had a clear view of the darting of his gaze down my body and the bob of his throat as he swallowed. If I were the betting type, I'd wager it'd been a good long time since Mr. William Reece had gotten himself laid.

"I don't think so," he said, with a roughness in his voice that hadn't been there before.

I smiled at him mildly and got out, smoothing my dress back down over my legs. "Maybe another time then. Thanks for the drive!"

I ambled to the door with the slightest roll of my hips. The sound of the engine revving didn't reach me until I'd crossed the lobby. I let my smile widen then.

Maybe Will and I weren't going to be friends, but I was looking forward to my next visit to the Reeces' a little more than before.

Two

THE SHRILL RINGTONE I'D ASSIGNED TO STERLING RIPPED apart my dreams at five-thirty the next morning. I groaned into my pillow and stretched my arm to the bedside table to find out what had possessed my Tether Society supervisor to try to reach me at this ungodly hour.

"Yes?" I said, making no effort to disguise the grogginess in my voice. Normally I wouldn't have been *that* far off from waking up on my own, but after last night's late partying, I'd been counting on getting every shred of sleep I could squeeze in.

"Please tell me you didn't know about this," Sterling said. His normally measured voice quivered with urgency. "This is the last sort of publicity any client needs... but especially yours, at her age..."

A spike of adrenaline propelled me upright. "What?" I said. "What's happened to Charity? Sterling, I have no idea what you're talking about."

His sigh managed to convey relief and exasperation at the same time. "Check the Cinema Wonder website. You'll see."

Well, given that instruction, it didn't sound as if she'd come to any physical harm. I grabbed my laptop off the floor. After a quick fumble with the keyboard, I'd brought up the site. My stomach dropped.

"Oh crap," I said when I was capable of speech, followed by several mental curses I preferred not to express aloud to my supervisor.

Charity was staring out at me from the main page of Cinema Wonder, a major industry blog. Staring from where she lounged on a scruffy armchair in a shredded dress that played peekaboo with the indigo bra and panties she was wearing underneath, raccoon-eyed and violet-lipped, her sleek blond waves rumpled and streaked with cocoa-brown.

No, not just staring. She *glared* at the camera as if daring the viewer to complain. Aggressive, not seductive. At least no one could call that porn.

When I clicked through to the full posting, I found five more poses in the same outfit, a couple equally aggressive, a couple more sullen, and one in which the awkward angles of her slender arms and the slant of her mouth suggested such fragility and sadness it wrenched at my heart even though I knew—I did know, right?—that she was only acting.

That's when understanding dawned.

"What could she possibly have been thinking?" Sterling was saying. "Those photos... Who took them? When did this happen?"

"I don't know," I said. "Not while I was around. But I think I know why she did it. She's been talking about wanting people to take her more seriously—to treat her like a real actress and not just a child star. I guess she figured this would do the trick."

I had to give the Starlet props. Pulling this stunt off had taken balls. But at the same time, my stomach kept on sinking.

She might as well have sent up a signal flare for any Glower trolling for a new target. Here was a girl who wanted more than she had, those photos said. A girl who was hungry in a way the demons could use to sate their own hunger.

I dragged in a breath. Well, it'd really only be one at a time I had to deal with. Glowers never shared a mark. Any that turned up would scuffle amongst themselves until only one was left to start the pursuit in earnest. I had plenty of experience handling that. Charity would come out of this fine.

"These kids and the internet," Sterling muttered. "Adults and the internet! We may as well be offering the Glowers online shopping for ideal marks. You do have her... social media locked down, don't you?"

It seemed to me the Society might have found some ways to spin the internet revolution in our favor, but it'd only been recently we'd even switched to sending in digital assignment notes instead of hard copies. I guessed that backwardness wasn't a total surprise when the standards had been set long before computers existed.

"Of course," I said. "Charity doesn't even know the passwords to her 'official' accounts—her publicity team is handling those—and her private accounts are restricted to friends we vetted. No Glower is getting to her that way."

"One crisis averted, then," Sterling said. "Her agent has been yelling my ear off. Sort this out, please? You need to keep control of your client while she's this vulnerable."

"I *know*," I said, more sharply than I meant to. Sterling probably had plenty of opinions about me and control—or lack thereof—even beyond what he'd expressed to me at length after my accidental overdose. But I'd still done right by my last starlet client, gotten her consistently dedicated to the herbal "supplements" of oregano and rosemary that would block any mark a Glower tried to place on her, and the Society had declared her safe to go unmonitored other than monthly check-ins. I'd get Charity there eventually. You couldn't hurry things with a hotheaded teenager. I should know.

After I hung up, I contemplated my pillow for a few seconds before hauling my ass out of bed. I wasn't due at the mansion for another couple hours, when the Starlet would be leaving for the day's rehearsals, but I showered and dressed, shoveled down some breakfast and chugged a large mug of coffee, and then summoned a cab on the Society's bill. I'd almost forgotten about Delectable Older Brother until I rang the doorbell and Will answered.

"So this is your idea of keeping her on the rails?" he said without preamble, his glare echoing his sister's in those photos.

I nudged him aside with a hand to his chest—as deliciously solid as it looked beneath his crisp collared shirt, I couldn't help noting—and marched in. "It has nothing to do with me," I said. "I'm not the one who's supposed to be keeping an eye on her when I'm off duty for the night."

He frowned. "Our parents wouldn't have—"

"They obviously missed something," I said. "I know *I've* never let her out of my sight anywhere near long enough for her to conduct a photo shoot. Where is she? I should talk to her."

"In her room," Will said. "I'm not sure—"

I didn't wait to find out what he wasn't sure about. As I headed past the kitchen to the basement stairs, I heard the Starlet's father on the phone, his voice rising. "What do you mean, there's nothing you can do? She's a minor, and we never gave our permission..." Talking to someone at Cinema Wonder, I assumed.

It wasn't as if having the photos taken down there would do much good now. No doubt a thousand plus fanboys had already saved them for sharing, and they'd be reposted all over cyberspace by noon.

The back half of the mansion's basement was the Starlet's private domain: a bedroom nearly as big as my entire apartment, an equally spacious lounge and entertainment room that served as a guest room when I needed to spend the night, a washroom for her dedicated use, and a little patio area outside with steps leading up to the main level backyard. I found Charity sitting at her vanity just beyond her open bedroom door, lipstick tube in hand, contemplating her reflection in the mirror with an expression that suggested she'd been so occupied for a while already.

She was usually still buried under her duvet when I showed up at the regular time, and it had been a later than usual night for her too. Maybe she wasn't quite awake yet.

She startled when I came in. A guilty flush washed over her cheeks. "Fee," she said. "You're early."

"Considering you just blew up the internet, I thought we needed a little time to talk before we headed to the studio."

Her blush darkened. "Is it *that* bad?"

I crossed my arms and leaned against the doorframe. The Starlet looked so nervous I couldn't help giving her a crooked smile.

"No," I said. "The world isn't going to end because you took a few edgy photos. When the hell did you arrange that? Who took them?"

She tugged a lock of hair over her shoulder. "I have a friend who's really into photography. We did the shoot back in November when I was hanging out at his place. I just got nervous about letting him send the photos out."

"*Him?*" I repeated, thinking of the revealing dress.

Charity rolled her eyes. "Don't be like that, Fee. Anyway, he likes *boys*."

"Hey," I said, holding up my hands, "I'm just looking out for you, doing my job." November. Before I'd even been on the job. At least I knew for sure none of this was my screw-up. "So why'd you give him the go-ahead now?"

She looked at the mirror again. "When we did the photos, I thought I was just goofing off. But... I really like them. It's been bugging me more and more, the stuff I said to you last night. How everyone wants me to keep being that sweet ditzy Miracle Mina character all the time. The scripts my agent sends me, they're all aimed at, like, ten year olds, you know? And you said that thing about just going for it, showing people what I can do —and I knew you were right. So I told him to send them out, whichever place he thought would get them up the fastest." She laughed. "I didn't know it'd be *that* fast."

I winced inwardly. Okay, maybe it was kind of my screw-up.

"You know, when I said that, this wasn't exactly what I had in mind," I said.

She paused, biting her lip. "You think it was too much?"

"I don't know," I said. Seeing her uncertain because of my uncertainty, when mine wasn't because she'd done anything wrong but because of the god-awful Glowers she shouldn't have had to plan her life around, something clenched up inside me. "No. You know what? Taking some photos like that isn't so crazy. You *should* be able to change how people see you, let them know there's more to you. It's your career. It's just, when you change things up out of the blue like that... there are people who are going to use it as an excuse to be jerks. But that's not your fault, okay? It'll just mean I'm a little extra busy."

"Okay," Charity said quietly. "I'm sorry I didn't tell you first."

I wasn't. If she had, I would have been duty-bound to change her mind. I waved her apology off. "Just be extra careful about who you talk to the next little while. Stay close to me when we're out. All the usual precautions, even more than usual. Then we won't have any problems."

I hope.

When I stepped back into the hall to let her finish getting ready for the day, Will was standing near the lounge room. I closed the bedroom door behind me. He ambled to join me as I headed for the stairs.

"Nothing to do with you?" he said.

"Was I supposed to psychically realize she'd done a secret photo shoot before I even started working with her so I could make sure none of my comments ever inspired her to pull the trigger?"

I stopped at the foot of the stairs and rubbed my temple. The adrenaline had carried me along pretty well so far, but that buzz was starting to fade.

Will's forehead furrowed as he scrutinized me. "You look a little out of it," he said.

"I'm running on about three hours sleep," I replied. "Sorry I'm not perfectly perky. Another coffee will do the trick."

I must have let more of my irritation show than I'd have preferred, because Will blinked, and then grimaced the way he had when I'd called him on his teenage drinking habits. "Right," he said. He glanced toward his sister's bedroom, and his expression softened. "Do you really think she could break out from kiddy shows?"

I raised an eyebrow at him. "Why not? If that's what she wants, and she's willing to put in the work..."

"Yeah," he said, looking a bit abashed. "Of course she can.

Just, maybe be a *little* more careful in how you phrase the inspirational speeches in future?"

"No kidding," I said. "I'm the one whose job just got harder, remember?"

I discovered just how *much* harder several hours later as I stood near the base of the stage where the Starlet was giving an interview for an entertainment news show.

The good news was, the invite proved her photos had already started to get her the attention she was longing for. This wasn't the type of show that usually brought on teeny-boppers. Charity's agent had called right after we'd arrived at her studio to let her know this show had wanted her to step in after a last minute guest cancellation, no doubt hoping to cash in on the sudden wave of publicity around her. So far Charity had handled herself exceptionally well. She'd fielded the unavoidable questions about the photo shoot with an explanation she'd honed in conversation with her agent—a little teenage rebelliousness mixed with a desire to expand her career horizons. Even Will, who'd shown up to watch his little sister in action, looked relatively relaxed where he was sitting amid the audience.

So everyone seemed to be having a good time except me, and that was thanks to the seven Glowers I'd already spotted in that audience. Sprinkled here and there amid the three hundred or so seats was a glinting face, sparkling hair, a laugh at a joke that sent a glittering breath into the air. Normally if more than one demon came to a place interested in the same target, they'd have been eyeballing each other as much as the star, trying to suss out their rivals for an advantage. This bunch didn't seem at all concerned by the competition. Two of them were even sitting next to each other, in the forms of a preteen girl and her apparent father.

I'd never seen Glowers behave like this before. Which meant I didn't know what to expect from them next. I didn't like that fact one bit.

I had the itch to pull out my phone and call someone. Not Sterling—he was already freaked out after the photo thing, and I'd given him enough grief in the last five months besides. Avery? I'd just talked to my best friend a couple days ago, and while she was a Tether too, she hadn't mentioned any weird Glower encounters. Of course, she might have been a little distracted by Lover Boy, a.k.a., former client/current rock star Colin Ryder, who'd just gotten back to the city after a month-long tour. Maybe Mateo? As the other member of our trio of young Society colleagues, he was the only other Tether I'd trust not to tattle to Sterling about my uncertainty, and he *did* have a year more experience in the field than me...

As I toyed with the idea, the interviewer stood up to shake hands with Charity, their talk concluded. I left my phone alone, figuring it wasn't likely anyone I could call would tell me anything useful anyway. Thinking on my feet was part of the job. Whatever the Glowers threw at me, I'd deal.

I joined the Starlet and a couple of the show's security people in front of the stage for the brief meet and greet the Miracle Mina producers had insisted on in exchange for Charity's time. As she flourished a Sharpie, a large portion of the audience got up from their seats and swarmed toward us, waving photos they wanted her to sign or calling out endearments. I'd have found it more warming to see how quickly her fans had responded to the news of her appearance if that swift spread of information hadn't brought the Glowers out too. It wasn't easy tracking seven different glimmering faces in the crowd.

As I hovered behind her, Charity leaned in for cellphone selfies, scrawled her signature over the photos, and answered breathless questions with her usual grin. At least she seemed to have regained her confidence after all the fuss this morning.

When the first of the Glowers, the girl-shaped one with fake dad in tow, approached, I tensed. But all the "girl" did was gush out a few compliments and briefly squeeze Charity's hand. The dad-Glower leaned over to say something about arranging an appearance at the girl's supposed school, and I cleared my throat.

"Bookings go through Charity's agent," I said.

They backed off without my even having to reveal that I knew what they were. Okay, maybe this wasn't an emergency situation after all.

I shifted on my feet as another demon worked its way to the front, this one wearing the appearance of a thirty-something Indian guy in a sharp suit. "I'm producing a film I think you'd be perfect for, Miss Reece," he said the second he reached Charity. "It would give you a real chance to show your range."

Charity beamed, turning toward him, and my heart skipped a beat. "Scammer," I murmured in her ear. Then, to him, "Talk to her agent."

"I think Miss Reece has shown she can handle career decisions on her own," the Glower said, looking down his nose at me.

Yeah, *that* didn't sound shady at all. I grasped his wrist, making sure the ring around my middle finger touched his bare skin. The ring with a speck of malachite embedded in the silver on the underside, too small to affect the Glowers except that close, but enough to shake his connection to this plane when I forced the issue. He stiffened, his gaze jerking from Charity to me.

"Or maybe you could just leave," I suggested, giving him my fiercest smile. The Society hadn't found any way of completely destroying Glowers—because they weren't even from this world, and so couldn't be *that* deeply affected by it, the reasoning went —but we could make sticking around very unpleasant.

The Glower stepped to the side, toward me. "I don't mean any harm," he said.

I laughed. "Right. Charity's got better things to do than listen to you. Take off."

"You misunderstand," he said, and sidestepped again. He was trying to draw my attention away from the Starlet, I realized abruptly. I pulled away from him in time to see another Glower with the guise of a young woman draping her arm over Charity's shoulder as she spoke into her ear. Shit.

Even in that first second, a glint traveled from the woman's hand into Charity. A spark of inspiration the demon was hoping would light up Charity's enthusiasm for whatever opportunity she was pitching. That was how they always worked. Excite the target's creativity until they were hooked on the Glower's company, propose the marking in the wrapping of some minor bargaining, and then leech them dry for however long the mark lived thereafter. Oh, sure, from time to time they topped up the mark's drive with hits of supernatural inspiration, which seemed to make the Glowers think they'd created a totally fair arrangement, even though the mark barely had time to enjoy the creative highs before the demons drained every positive emotion out of them again. Even though after a few years of that, every mark found a way, accidentally or deliberately, of permanently ending the torture—by ending their life.

I couldn't let this one getting her hooks one smidgeon farther into Charity.

"Hey!" I snapped, squeezing past one of the security guys,

my pulse skittering wildly. There wasn't time to think, so I followed my first instinct. I smacked my hand with the ring against the most sensitive point on the Glower's false body: the crook where the neck met the head.

The woman flinched as if I'd sent an electric shock through her. "Fee," Charity said, staring at me, but I was busy glaring at the Glower.

"Enough chatting," I said. "Let's give the other fans a turn, all right?"

"Is there a problem with this one?" the security guy asked.

"I haven't done anything!" the Glower protested.

I stepped right into her face. "And you won't get a chance to," I said in a low voice. Amid the figures still gathering around us, another silvery sheen caught in the corner of my eye, and another. My heart thumped harder. What if the next one got even pushier? No one was going to believe me calling all of them criminals to keep them away.

The only answer was to get the Starlet away from them.

Sucking in my breath, I spun around. "Everyone!" I said, clapping my hands together. "We're going to have to cut this short. Charity has an important engagement to get to. We're so sorry."

"I don't—" Charity said, and I shot her a look that made her clamp her mouth shut. She raised her hand to wave to the people who hadn't reached her yet. "Thank you so much for coming to see me!" she said. "I hope I'll get to talk to you another time." Then the security people were ushering us away.

Three

"What was that about, Fee?" the Starlet asked as Will drove us back to the mansion. She turned in the front passenger seat to peer back at me. "Why'd we have to leave like that?"

"People were getting too pushy," I said. "When you've been doing this a while, you start to see the signs that the situation isn't going to stay secure for much longer. It's better to be on the safe side with some things, you know."

"I guess," she said. "I just feel bad for the people I didn't get a chance to see."

"You'll have lots more appearances," I pointed out. "Your fans know you're busy—anyone who blames you, they're the jerk."

The corner of her mouth slanted up at that. She swiveled forward in her seat and spent most of the rest of the ride chattering to Will about the day's rehearsals and costuming, occasionally calling on me to back up an observation, and asking him about a report he'd been working on for school that apparently had something to do with robotics. I mostly gazed out the window at the cityscape we were cruising through. My pulse had steadied, but I still felt uneasy.

When we got to the house, Charity gave me a quick hug and hurried inside. Will hadn't gotten out of the car. After a moment, I realized he was waiting for me.

"I can just call a cab," I said to him through the open window.

He shook his head. "It's not that far. I don't mind."

So I took the seat Charity had just vacated, stretching my legs out under the glove compartment. I watched the muscles in Will's arms and shoulders shift as he pushed the lever into drive and turned the wheel. The itch from yesterday came back. Man, it would be nice to have a little distraction from unsettling Glower antics.

"Do you lift or something?" I said, tipping my head toward those impressive biceps. "Or is engineering work a lot more physically intensive than is generally publicized?"

I thought I saw a hint of that endearing blush touch Will's face. "You could say that," he said. "I find an hour in the gym clears my head and helps me focus for the rest of the day."

"And the more superficial effects mean nothing to you, of course," I said. When he glanced at me, I raised my eyebrow and grinned so he knew I was giving him a hard time only in jest.

"I'll concede that there are other benefits unrelated to my studies," he said, and grinned back. My heart fluttered. Hell, he was gorgeous when he smiled. I had to figure out how to get him in a good mood more often.

"Do you have to do that very often?" he asked a moment later, his gaze back on the road. "Make up an excuse to get Charity out of someplace?"

"No," I said truthfully. "But it was a different sort of crowd than we see at her usual events. And after a big development like those photos going out, with people's opinions of her maybe shifting... I didn't want to take the chance of the situation going wrong."

He nodded. "It's really important to you," he said. "Protecting her. I could tell, when you were moving people off—you weren't messing around."

"Of course I wasn't," I said with a prick of annoyance. Had we still not gotten past that point of doubt?

The self-deprecating smile Will shot me a second later melted my irritation away.

"I'm apologizing," he said. "Apparently badly. I haven't been giving you much of a chance. I should have seen that you wouldn't be doing a job like this if you didn't think it mattered."

I decided I could accept that. "She's a good kid," I said. "She shouldn't have to deal with the assholes out there." Or the demons.

"You know you have my full agreement there."

"You could have kept an eye on her a lot more easily from UCLA, you know. Although I guess it's pretty hard to turn down an offer from Stanford?"

He gave a short laugh. "Yeah. It was the dream. And I didn't know her career was going to take off like that. She was only eleven when I got in."

I'd seen one of Charity's commercials from around that age. It was hard to believe that sweet, gawky preteen was now raking in a couple million dollars a year. "Well, she's got your parents here," I said.

Will made a noncommittal sound that I took to mean he'd observed the same thing I had—the elder Reeces were a little too awed by Hollywood to be completely impartial guardians. But then, that was why Charity had *me*.

"I think you've still got her ear if you need it," I said, remembering the way Charity had lit up seeing him yesterday night. "She obviously adores you. I wouldn't fire you as a big brother just yet."

His gaze twitched toward me, and for a second I wondered if I'd misjudged my play on yesterday's conversation about job security. Then the corner of his mouth curved up, the same way Charity's did when I nudged her from just the right angle.

"Well, thanks," he said dryly. "I appreciate the vote of confidence."

We reached my building a few minutes later. Will eased the car to a stop and paused in a way that glued me to my seat. He looked at the steering wheel and then at me, with an intentness that shoved all my worries about the Glowers and the Starlet to the back of my mind. A tingle raced over my skin.

"Last night's invitation still stands," I said.

That comment earned me a more definite blush. Will opened his mouth and closed it with an audible swallow. I could have sworn he was going to say yes when he opened it again, but instead what came out was, "They'll be expecting me back at the house."

I had nothing against quickies, but I didn't think we were quite at the point where I could mention that outright. "Well, good night then," I said, and patted his knee with just enough of a linger that I felt the warmth of his leg through his khakis. "Thank you for the drive."

The heat I'd seen in his eyes followed me all the way up to my apartment.

"*Seven* of them," Avery repeated. "All after her in the same place?"

I nodded as I sipped my iced tea. "Maybe more. I got her out of there before they all had a chance to make a direct approach."

Avery frowned, her brow knitting with those two cute little worry lines she got way too often. Less often since Colin Ryder had entered the picture, though. He'd even inspired her usually-over-dedicated self to ask for a week off from Tethering so she could join him on a leg of his winter European tour and celebrate her twentieth birthday with a whirlwind tour of Paris instead of the movie-and-a-bite-out with me that had been the most she'd generally let herself indulge in. I guessed I could give him credit for that.

She swept her long, gold-brown hair back over her shoulders, another nervous habit. "I've never seen that before," she said. "But, I mean, I'm only on my third real client. And none of those clients made some move while I was working with them that caused a big, sudden change in how people would be thinking about them. Maybe it's normal in a case like this. Did you tell Sterling?"

I made a face. "I put the facts in my daily report, but I didn't talk to him directly. You know how he is when he thinks something's going wrong. I might get Mateo to ask around. He knows the older Society peeps better than I do."

"Maybe they were all just scoping her out, not planning on making any claims until they got a sense of how vulnerable she is," Avery suggested, poking her straw at me. "Now they know she's got protection. They should back off."

"That would definitely make my life easier." I wasn't going to count on it, though.

"Have you been talking to Mateo much lately?" she said after a pause.

"We chat by text maybe once or twice a month," I said. "Just to catch up. I haven't seen him since he started with the rapper client. Why?"

Avery shrugged and rubbed the side of her mouth. "I don't know. The last few times I saw him, something felt a little off. As if he was upset. But he didn't say anything."

Of course he hadn't. When it came to Avery, the guy was obviously hopeless. "Maybe he's jealous," I said.

"Of Colin? I started dating him *months* after Mateo and I broke up—and we broke up by mutual agreement! I don't know if I've even mentioned Colin to him. You don't really think..."

"You're too much of a peacemaker, Ave," I said. "If he's stressing about that or anything else, he's sorting through it on his own, because that's what he's decided to do. If he wants something from you, well, it's on him to speak up for once, right?"

"I just don't know if he knows how to," she muttered, but then she let out her breath as if dismissing the subject. Her phone, which she'd left face up on the cafe table, beeped. She glanced at it, typed out a quick message, and looked back at me as she set it down. "*You're* not stressing out about the Glower thing, are you? If you are, you really should touch base with Sterling."

The worry lines had deepened. Between that and the cautious note that had crept into her voice, I suspected she was thinking about my little derailing in the fall. Wondering if a problem like this could push me back over the edge into drinking and drugs, but not wanting to say that outright in case she offended me.

Avery and I had known each other for years, started training at the Society around the same time, talked with each other about everything... but since the night she'd had to haul me to the hospital, it'd been like a sheet of glass had formed between us. We saw each other, talked to each other, but we didn't quite connect.

I liked to think snarky things about Colin, but the truth was any distance between us was my fault. I knew that. I just hadn't quite figured out how to say that to her. I wasn't even sure saying it would make anything better. Maybe that was why I hadn't tried.

"I will," I said with a smile that felt a little stiff, and her phone beeped again. Avery ignored it. I kicked her leg under the table.

"Lover Boy?" I said.

"His jam session ended early," she said. "I already told him I'm hanging out with you. I'm supposed to meet him at the Society later anyway—Sterling's still working on converting him into a part time Tether."

"Any progress there?"

She smiled in the dreamy way that told me she was fondly remembering some moment with Colin. "He has committed to keeping an eye out for Glowers and providing guidance on the fly to any other musicians he runs into, and to reporting back anything that seems concerning. He doesn't *want* to see anyone getting marked."

"That sounds fair to me." If I had rock star talents, I doubted I'd want to be Tethering full time. I considered my mostly finished iced tea, which was getting gross now that the actual ice in it was melting. We hadn't decided yet whether to order more than the cheese plate we'd shared. I didn't feel hungry.

"You know, we've had a good chat already," I said. "He's only in town for, what, another couple weeks? Go see him, make the most of it."

Avery cocked her head. "Are you sure, Fee? I've got another hour. We could window shop or take a walk through the park if you just want to get out of here."

So she could watch for signs to reassure herself I wasn't relapsing? No, thank you. "I've got stuff to catch up on at home," I said with a flick of my hand. "And I'll see you again soon."

I tried not to think about the way she hugged me, the hesitation in her sturdily athletic body, as if mine had become more fragile than she'd used to believe.

"That was so *good!*" the Starlet exclaimed, flopping back on the couch as the credits for *Juno* rolled on her lounge room TV. After most of Saturday off, I'd been with her for an evening event and now overnight, because the rest of the family was out of town for some second cousin's wedding the work event had excused Charity from. Technically, I'd have trusted her to stay home on her own, but the contract said I wasn't supposed to leave her except under the supervision of her parents—and given the swarm of Glowers we'd encountered the other day, I'd found I didn't mind.

We'd just spent the last couple hours vegging out with microwave popcorn and the movie, which by some horrible oversight no one else had shown her yet. Charity was the perfect eager movie viewer: cringing dramatically at the awkward moments, covering her eyes and peeking through her fingers when things got tense, squealing with glee when the characters found a little happiness. I felt fully validated in my choice.

"That's what I want to be doing," she said now, pointing at the TV. "Movies like *that*. I could have been Juno, right?"

"Sure," I said automatically. Then I paused, and made myself really picture it. "Yeah. I can definitely see that. You'll get there, Char."

"I want to be there *now*," she said with a sigh.

"Your mom said your agent had a long talk with you this morning. Was it not as good as she seemed to think?"

Charity brightened a bit. "It might be. He said he's gotten a bunch of calls since the photos went up, possible auditions for some movie roles, that sort of thing. But nothing I can try for right away. He's off in France for most of the next week—he said he'd start making definite arrangements after that."

"A whole week?" I said teasingly. "I think you'll survive that long. It'll still be *work*, you know. And it's better not to want things too much. That's how you get taken advantage of."

"Yeah, yeah," she muttered. "When did you get to be such a downer? What about taking risks?"

"It's a balance," I said, the back of my neck prickling. There was an edge of real annoyance in her voice. I needed to make sure *I* kept her ear. "You take risks, and then you're careful in considering the outcome. I'm sure there are some good opportunities in there, or your agent wouldn't have mentioned them."

Charity was still frowning, but she rested her feet against my thigh, tapping me with one and then the other. "Do you even get it, Fee?" she said. "What do *you* really want to do, other than this? Acting? Directing? Screenwriting? Isn't there anything you'd take any risk for if it meant getting closer to that goal?"

"I don't think I'm the Hollywood type," I said. "Not that way."

"Well, you should have something. You could learn how to

build crazy machines like Will. Or be a lawyer and argue with people all the time like my dad. Or plan weddings like my mom. Or anything. You've got to want to do more than follow people like me around all the time."

"Says who?"

"Says, I don't know, the deity of not being bored out of your mind your whole life?"

I poked the sole of her foot. "Keeping up with you isn't exactly boring."

"You know what I *mean*," Charity said.

I did. I just didn't want to answer the question. What did I really want? To keep doing this job, knowing I was helping the few people I could. To have fun, get in some thrills and be swept up into that shiny happy version of myself who didn't care that underneath I was just a scrappy Chinese adoptee who'd gotten mediocre grades and eschewed official extracurriculars for activities that verged on criminal. To accomplish the latter without compromising the former.

I was staying pretty busy just with that. And I didn't have the spark people like Charity, or Colin Ryder, or Avery had, that drew people in when they performed on the screen or a stage. Lots of people didn't, after all. We got by the best we could and took our enjoyment from baser pleasures. There was nothing wrong with that.

The thought of such pleasures brought my mind back to Will. "So your brother is building 'crazy machines'?" I said, figuring a change in subject was in order anyway. "It sounded like you two were talking about robots the other day."

"Something like that," Charity said. "From the way he talks, I guess real life robots aren't half as interesting as movie robots. But he's into that stuff. And some company in San Francisco has already said they want to hire him as soon as he's graduated.

They're working on pretty cool projects—like, floating cars or something science fiction-y like that. It was all Mom and Dad talked about for pretty much a whole month after he got the offer." She paused and peeked at me through her lashes. "Why? Are you interested in him, Fee?"

I gave her feet a shove. "Don't be like that," I said with a grin. Even though in the back of my mind I was wondering if he'd give me a drive home tomorrow. If the third time might be the charm to get him up to my apartment.

"It'd be okay if you were," Charity said slyly. "His last girlfriend was *so* annoying."

"I'm definitely not looking to be anyone's girlfriend," I said. That much I could say completely honestly.

Four

When my restless thoughts woke me up on the lounge room futon at seven the next morning, not the slightest sound was coming from the Starlet's bedroom. I knew from past experience that she made the most of her Sundays off. I'd be lucky to see her emerge before ten.

I didn't mind. That meant I got most of the mansion to myself for a few hours. The rest of the family wasn't due back until mid-afternoon.

I padded up to the kitchen in my sleep tank, combing my hair with my fingers. The stainless steel fridge there was always well stocked, even though I never saw the Reeces cooking. Opening the door and leaning into the cool air, I weighed the possibilities. Real maple syrup? Yes, please! French toast, here I came.

A downside of being short: I had to push the stepstool over to the counter to reach the upper shelf that held the mixing bowls. A downside of new construction homes: the goddamned floors don't creak. I didn't realize I had company until I'd stepped down from the stool and turned to place the ceramic bowl on the kitchen island, and my gaze hit the tall, rumpled-haired figure in the doorway. I almost dropped the bowl.

"Hey!" Will said, seeing me fumble, and leapt forward to steady it. His fingers brushed mine for a second before I got my grip on the bowl and set it down where I'd meant to. I got a faint whiff of citrusy cologne, faded since yesterday's application under an earthy, musky smell that was just the man.

Will took a step back, taking his warmth with him. "I didn't mean to startle you," he said. "I didn't expect anyone to be up this early."

His gaze traveled down my body and jerked back to my face, leaving a different sort of warmth in its wake. It must have been obvious I hadn't expected to run into anyone either. The tank only barely hit my thighs. If he'd come in while I was grabbing the bowl, he'd have been treated to a great view of my hot pink panties.

He was only wearing an undershirt and boxer briefs. The instant my brain registered that, I had to squash the urge to check out his package. He definitely filled out that thin white tee well.

"I thought you were staying overnight after the wedding," I said. Oh, crap, were the 'rents home too?

"I don't sleep well in hotels," Will said. "I decided to drive back last night. Got in a little after one—it sounded like you two were already out, or I'd have come down to say hi."

Okay. It was just him then. My heart was still knocking in my chest, but there was nothing anxious about that rhythm now. I'd waited three days to get this guy stripped down, and I wasn't known for my patience. Charity would be sleeping for ages yet. Who needed my apartment? We had a whole house to play in.

"I can go," he said.

I grabbed his hand as he turned to leave. He stopped the second our skin collided. A tingle ran over mine.

"Why?" I said. "It's your house. I don't mind."

He looked at me with that intentness I'd seen in his green eyes Friday night in the car, when I'd thought he might agree to come up. "You need help making breakfast?" he asked. The teasing note in his baritone voice sent another tingle through me.

I traced my thumb over the lines of his palm to his wrist, feeling his pulse jump, and smiled. "You know, suddenly I'm feeling a different sort of hungry. If you're up for helping with that."

"Fiona," he said, and didn't seem to know how to continue. His gaze tripped down my body again.

"Will." I stepped closer to him, close enough that I could smell that mix of citrus and earthy musk again, feel the anticipation humming through his body. He didn't move away. I let go of his hand and placed mine on his waist. The muscles there tensed at my touch.

"When was the last time you did something without planning it to pieces beforehand?" I said.

"A while," he admitted, his voice rougher now.

I tipped my head back so I could look him right in the eyes. "Well, this is where I'm at," I said. "If you're not interested, that's fine, I'll stop right here, no hurt feelings. But what I'd really like? Is for you to bend me over that counter and take me so hard I'll forget I've ever been with anyone else. It's up to you."

I dropped my hand and turned back to the island. Listened to the rasp of his breath as I untied the bag of bread. The moment stretched, and I started to think he really was going to walk away.

I was just glancing over when he moved, a blur of motion, his hands grasping my waist. He whirled me to face the opposite counter, setting my feet on the stool I'd left there with a carefulness at odds with the heat of the body now flush against me from shoulders to ankles.

"Like this?" Will said, his breath on my cheek, and deep down I began to ache. Yes, yes, yes.

"It's a good start," I said. I inhaled sharply as he pressed his mouth to the side of my neck. Leaning back into him, I griped the edge of the counter as he kissed his way from the corner of my jaw to the crook of my shoulder. His hands slid up from my waist, the hem of my tank teasing my hips as it rose with them, his fingers slipping around to cup my breasts. He massaged them through the thin cotton. His forefingers hooked across my already taut nipples, flicking up over them and down again. He pinched them, and then teased his teeth along my shoulder. I moaned as I arched against him. Here was the wildness I'd hoped I'd find in Mr. William Reece.

Will released my breasts for just long enough to tug the straps of my tank down my arms. The neckline jumped over my nipples, and then his hands were there again, skin to skin, his thumbs circling the peaks until another moan rippled out of me. I inched my feet apart on the stool as I reached back to grab his boxers. More. Faster. I wanted to be carried away from the kitchen, the house, away from every part of me except the heady rush building inside me.

He was hard, a solid length that twitched by my inner thigh as I ground against him. With a choked sound, he brushed his fingers down my stomach to curl around the mound between my legs. I gasped, pressing into him again, and he groaned against my neck. His hand dipped inside my panties, all the way between my legs to where I was hot and wet for him. The heel of his hand kneaded my clit as he fingered my opening.

"Don't stop," I said, panting. I wanted all of him, filling me, now. I swayed against the counter as I yanked my panties down and bit back a cry of frustration when I felt him hesitate.

"I don't have—" he said, sounding dizzy. "We can't just— I have to get—"

Oh. Relief flooded me—and validation for the sort-of snooping I'd done a few sleepovers ago.

"Don't go anywhere," I said, and pointed. "Silverware drawer, under the tray, at the back."

Will hesitated, and then reached. The drawer was close enough that he could keep his fingers on me, his arm around me, as he yanked it open. He nudged up the tray and pulled out a condom packet, staring at it and then at me.

"*I* didn't put them there," I said. "I was looking for the peeler, and…"

He let out a strangled laugh. For a second, from the look on his face, I was afraid the thought of what his parents might be getting up to in this same kitchen would kill the mood for him.

I trailed my hand down the front of him to the hard-on straining against his boxers, and everything fled his face except the hunger. He tugged me to him, planting a kiss on the other side of my neck as his fingers slid inside me. It wasn't enough. I leaned forward, bare nipples grazing the cool granite of the countertop, and heard the tear of the foil.

His hand caressed my thighs, sliding the tank up to my waist. Then his length was pushing against me from behind, teasingly, just the tip easing in. I arched toward him and he sucked in a breath.

"God," he said. Then he was thrusting into me, hard and hot and stretching me in just the right way. He gripped my hip with one hand as the other glided up to fondle my breasts again. I leaned my arm against the counter for balance, a whimper escaping my throat as he withdrew and surged into me, faster. Just what I needed. The ache inside swelled up to my chest and down to my knees with a buzz of pleasure.

More. I lowered my hand to the curls I kept carefully trimmed and rubbed my clit to send a fresh shower of sparks through my nerves, imagining it was his hand. He was all over me, brawny chest against my back, fingers circling my nipple, breath on my neck, and inside me, deeper and deeper.

I cried out, louder than I meant to. And then suddenly it *was* his hand between my legs, working that sweet spot as he held me to him, his hips pumping even faster. I sagged against the counter as a final wave of ecstasy crashed over me, washing through me—washing everything else away.

Will clutched me, the hardness inside me seeming to expand as he came in turn. He leaned over me with a ragged exhale.

The part after the best part was sometimes the worst. The high of the orgasm ebbed, leaving me aware of the edge of the counter digging into my stomach, the length on him inside me softening, the dribble of my wetness that had seeped down my inner thigh. But what really mattered was what he did next. I braced myself for embarrassment, excuses, disdain—any of the many defensive reactions that could rear their heads after things had, well, come to a head this quickly.

If he shut down on me, it wasn't my fault, I reminded myself. It was only about him.

That wouldn't stop it from hurting a little.

Will withdrew, his hands coming back to my waist. As I straightened up, he slipped them around my body and turned me to face him. Before I could check his expression, he'd cupped my face and brought my lips to his.

His kiss was gentle but assured, deepening as I tilted my head to return it. A flutter ran through my chest. It seemed weird that a kiss could affect me when we'd already been about as intimate as any two people could get, but then, it was also kind of weird that we'd only kissed properly now, after getting that intimate. I stopped bracing and gave myself over to the sensation, winding my arms around his neck.

When he broke the kiss, he barely moved, his head tipped close to mine. Our noses touched.

"I've never done anything like that," he said quietly.

I grinned. "Is that my cue to tell you that you performed more than adequately? Because that was exactly what I needed."

I felt more than saw his grin in return. "I wonder how long *I've* needed that."

"Well, it doesn't have to be the last time. You're around for the rest of the week, right? Maybe we'll... run into each other again."

He chuckled, a low sound that provoked the same flutter his kiss had. "I think I'd like that," he said, and kissed me once more, firmly enough that heat flooded my body and I started to wonder if maybe he'd be ready for another go right now.

Then, through the buzz in my head, I heard the thud of a door through the floor beneath us.

I recoiled. "Charity," I said, and Will stiffened too. I jerked my tank's straps up over my shoulders and snatched up my panties as he shoved himself back into his boxer briefs. He grabbed my hand just long enough to give it a quick squeeze before he loped off toward his room, presumably to get dressed. I spotted the empty condom packet just as the Starlet reached the top of the basement stairs—caught it, shoved it into the trash can, and swiveled to give her an innocent smile as she reached the kitchen doorway. She stretched her arms and yawned.

"What are you making?" she asked, giving me a vaguely suspicious look as she took in the open but abandoned bag of bread.

I motioned her over, holding on to the high of the rush still singing through my veins. "French toast. You want some?"

Five

I called home every Sunday. Not because I really enjoyed talking to my parents, not because there was much about my life I felt comfortable sharing with them. It was mainly to prove I could meet at least one criterion on the "good daughter" expectations list. I wasn't going to let them complain that I never called them, not when Mom already had such an extensive stockpile of other grievances.

"You're still doing that new TV assistant position?" she said this time, as if I were likely to have switched careers in the last week.

"Yeah," I said. "It's going well."

Her silence was heavy with disapproval. She'd wanted me to be the sort of person who *had* assistants. But I couldn't exactly tell her what I really did.

"I hope you're keeping an eye out for other opportunities," she said.

Time to change the subject. "How's Daniel?" I asked. The kid brother and I weren't close, but that wasn't his fault. Mom and Dad had stopped encouraging me to include him in my activities once they'd realized how few of those activities they wanted even *me* to be getting up to, and for the last four years, high school and various clubs and teams had kept him pretty busy anyway. We'd had a couple of good chats about dating and girls before I'd moved out, but otherwise, I didn't have much to offer. He was already golden.

Even more so now, it turned out. "Oh, he's just gotten his acceptance to Princeton!" Mom said. "So exciting. He hasn't decided whether he's going there or one of the others yet, but we're so glad he has the option."

"Definitely," said the daughter who hadn't even applied to colleges.

"You know," Mom said, "he's going to be performing at the music academy's spring recital—that Chopin piece he's been working on. You should come. We don't see you enough. He'd be so pleased."

Daniel had taken to the piano about as well as I *hadn't* taken to the cello. I doubted he cared that much whether I came to watch him—I doubted Mom really cared other than that my showing up would be a sign that she'd raised her daughter right in at least a few ways. But he had talent. I'd liked hearing him practice when I still lived at home. You could hear how he got caught up in the music, in a way that swept up anyone listening properly too. And as much as our parents' company could grate on me, I didn't want to drop out of his life completely.

"Text me the date and time," I said. "I'll see."

"The hours you work," she said, and I knew she was shaking her head.

"It's the nature of the job."

"You need to have a life for yourself too," she said. "How will you fit anyone else into it?"

"I'm not looking to right now," I said.

She paused. "Fiona, you would tell us, wouldn't you, if it's something like... If you have more 'alternative' interests..."

I rolled my eyes at the wall. "Mom, I'm not gay. I like guys plenty. I'm just not planning on settling down any time soon. I'm only twenty-one!"

"Oh, well. You know your father and I were married when I was twenty-three. Maybe that isn't in vogue these days, but you don't want to miss the good ones."

"I'm sure there'll be a few left when I'm ready," I said.

"As long as you're careful," she said.

But careful wasn't any fun, I thought when I hung up a minute later. I took my precautions against pregnancy and STDs, of course, but beyond that...

My mind tripped back to that morning. To Will behind me in the kitchen. Inside me. To the kiss afterward, his hands gentle against my face. A sudden warmth flooded me.

I shouldn't be thinking about the *kiss*. I dragged my mind back to the moments before, and a different sort of warmth sparked between my legs. The phone conversation had left me edgy, but there were plenty of ways to release tension solo. I flopped down on the bed with a grin already curling my lips.

"I can't believe David Garrand actually wanted *me* to come," the Starlet said, squirming in her seat. I glanced across the car at her and smiled. She was all lit up beneath the carefully applied make-up and meticulously styled hair. Her agent had called this morning right before he'd taken off on his French adventure to say Garrand, who'd won an Oscar last year for the most recent film he'd directed, had specifically asked if Charity Reece could attend a soirée at his Beverly Park home. Apparently he'd seen the photos and her recent interview, and was intrigued by her decision to transform herself.

"There'll be other directors there too, and producers, and actors—people who work on *real* films..." Charity jittered as Paul pulled the car up to the estate's gate. "What if I say something stupid, Fee?"

"You won't," I said. "And if you do, everyone will forget because of all the smart things you say before and after. You've got this."

"You really think so?"

"I know so. Just try to play it a little cool. Someone talks about a possible role, no definite answers, you'll discuss it with your agent." It seemed unlikely that a Glower could have snuck into a private gathering of industry bigwigs, but you never knew. And the industry bigwigs could be predators of a different sort.

"Right," Charity said with a sharp nod, and proceeded to do herself proud from the second she stepped out of the car. She drew her spine up straight in her tasteful but still youthful silk dress and strode toward the open door from which music and light were already streaming. I hustled after her, taking in the sculpted lions near front steps, the marble tile in the entry hall, and the crystal chandeliers. Garrand had only risen to the top ranks of Hollywood in the last few years, but he'd obviously been making the most of his box office earnings.

A couple dozen people were clustered in the room just off the hall, where ebony side tables were laid with platters of hors d'oeuvres, a pot of fragrant orchids perfumed the air, and a man in a white dress shirt was pouring wine liberally. I gave the place a quick scan as Charity accepted a glass with a giggle and a wink from the waiter. I knew that actor over there, and that producer had been at the same do as Charity the other night, and there, looking much like he had on my TV when he'd climbed the stage to accept his Oscar, was Garrand himself...

My back stiffened and my heart skipped a beat. Yes, there was David Garrand, director of the hour. And beside him stood a slim young man whose black hair was slicked away from his pale face—a pale face that shone more than could be attributed to the chandeliers. His eyes glittered when they caught my stare.

I jerked my gaze away. My throat had gone dry. A longing rose up in me to grab one of those wine glasses and down the contents in one gulp, but I clenched my hands instead.

Garrand was marked—the glowing spot just above his heart told me as much. Marked by the Glower lingering at his side, no doubt. The director looked happy, smiling and joking with his guests, but that demonic sickness was in him, latched too deep for any Tether to dig it out. As they always did, the Glower would be puffing him up now and then—giving him those extra bursts of inspiration to drive his passion. And as always, any intense positive emotion the man felt in the aftermath, exhilaration or pride or joy, the Glower would be sucking out of him. It had to be early days, or someone in the Society would have noticed and put out a warning. Soon there'd be nothing left inside him but gloom and pain.

That was the fate Charity would face if I didn't keep her safe.

As far as I'd learned, though, a Glower never marked more than one person at the same time. Maybe they couldn't. So that guy should be no threat to her.

Even as I tried to reassure myself, my gaze hit another shimmering form gliding in from the patio. This Glower was wearing the guise of a middle-aged woman with an arched Roman nose and an elegantly coiffed bob. She glanced around the room, considering the Starlet for longer than I liked.

A young actress, around my age I estimated, sidled up to

Charity and said something that provoked a grin. My heart sank. The actress had the same glowing mark on her chest as Garrand. A Latino-looking guy with a Glower sheen to his brown skin came up behind her a moment later, trailing his fingers over her shoulders. I shivered as if he'd touched me. Then *another* Glower ambled into the room from down the hall, this one with the appearance of a teenage girl.

My stomach started to churn. I eased my way over to Charity's side, trying to keep track of both the woman Glower and the girl in my peripheral vision. They didn't seem to be attached to anyone here.

What the hell was going on? Several independent Glowers showing up at Friday's interview was one thing. But this—this looked like collusion. Had this all been Garrand's Glower's idea? To invite Charity and put her in a setting where she'd be more open to flattery and eager for approval, and then let a few Glower associates at her? Did Glowers even *have* associates? I'd never heard of that either.

Well, I could puzzle over that later. Right now I needed to protect my client. I supposed I should just be glad the Glowers hadn't taken on the appearances of real people Charity would recognize and have a particular stake in talking to—they were capable of it, though pretending to be a real person created too many complications to be practical in the long term of hooking and feeding on a mark, which was presumably why they didn't try more often.

The actor and producer I knew both seemed like safe, maybe even helpful, conversational companions. I'd just extricate Charity from this conversation and make some introductions.

"Oh my god! You're Charity Reece, right?" the girl Glower said, springing to the Starlet's side as I reached for her elbow.

The Latino-looking Glower sidestepped, bumping into me as if by accident and knocking my arm away.

"Hey," he said with that unnatural glint in his eyes. "I haven't seen you at David's parties before."

"I'm here with Charity," I said, my heart thudding. "Chaperone. And there's someone she needs to—"

"Well, that's no fun," the Glower's actress mark said, interrupting me as she joined him. "Have you seen the rest of the house? It's *amazing*. Here, I'll give you a little tour."

"No, really, that's okay," I said, taking a step back. The girl Glower had pulled Charity over to the side tables. I turned toward her, and the actress grasped my forearm.

"I'm serious," she said. "The greenhouse is just fabulous, and there's a whole room full of sculptures. David loves to show it off."

She was obviously in on the scheme too—and my tricks, my ring and the knotted string in my purse, wouldn't work on her, even if I thought I could get away with using either of them without this turning into a scene Garrand could use to eject me right out of the house. I gritted my teeth.

"Let me just get Charity, and we'll all look together, then," I said. The actress didn't release her grip even when I gave my arm a tug.

"It looks like she's busy right now," the actress's Glower said, nudging me in the opposite direction. "Let's not interrupt her if she's making friends. Everyone here will look out for her. She can see the rest of the house another time."

I twisted my wrist and managed to extricate myself from the actress. "Thank you," I said to her. Marked or not, complicit or not, she was still part of Charity's industry, still someone who could affect her career. "I'm sure the house is great. But I've really got to stick close to Charity for now—contractual obligations and all."

Before she could argue more, I hustled over to the side tables. Charity was just plucking up a shrimp, nodding as the girl Glower gabbed on.

"Char," I said, tapping her shoulder. "I think it'd be good for you to talk to—"

A sudden thump of bass filled the room. Garrand's Glower raised his hands by the stereo system and hollered over the music, "Let's make this a real party!"

A few of the younger guests whooped in approval and started bobbing to the beat. The girl Glower squealed and grabbed Charity's hand. "Come on, we've got to dance!" She yanked her into the middle of the room. I hurried after, tracking the woman Glower who was strolling to meet them. Charity glanced back at me, but at the same second the girl Glower whispered something in her ear, and she threw her head back with a laugh.

"Charity!" I said, and Garrand's Glower stepped into my way. He caught my arm as I tried to dodge him.

"I hope there isn't any problem," he said, peering down at me from his substantial height.

My skin went cold. All the Glowers here had to know what my real job was. They also had to know that at a private event like this, where the danger lurked amid Charity's colleagues rather than a bunch of unruly fans, I couldn't raise a real fuss, declare them too dangerous and haul her off. Not when so far all they'd done was talk to her and get her dancing. Not without ruining the trust I'd only just built with her—and maybe making her look bad in front of all the people here who *didn't* have ill intentions.

Which was exactly why they must have arranged it this way.

In that moment, I wished with every bone in my body that the Society had some sort of emergency phone service set up, like those bad date apps. Text a quick code and have someone call up Charity with urgent business she needed to take care of elsewhere. Get us both out of this mess with our reputations intact.

But there wasn't. There was only me. So I'd have to do whatever I could.

"I need to talk to Charity for a minute," I said, trying to push past the Glower. He shifted his arm so my malachite ring only brushed his sleeve. The Latino-looking demon shifted to flank him.

"Aw, she's fine," he said. "You know what? You need to relax. Let's get you a drink."

"No, thank you," I said, but they were already ushering me to the wine table, one on either side of me. I jerked my arm away from Garrand's Glower and saw the producer I knew watching me with a puzzled expression. I dragged in a breath, struggling to keep my cool.

"Excuse me," I said firmly, and managed to slip around the Glower this time. The girl and the woman were both hanging close to Charity now, all of them swaying with the music, her head turning one way and the other as she followed their joint conversation.

"Hey," I said, coming up behind her. The woman Glower shot me a look that could have frozen magma.

"Fee!" Charity cried, with a loopy smile that told me she'd downed at least one more glass of wine since we'd come in. "Diana's been telling me about a new cable TV series she's developing. It sounds really cool. You should tell her," she added to the woman.

"Actually, Miss Reece, we're just going to borrow your friend for a minute," the Latino-looking Glower said, resting his hand on my back.

I recoiled. "Leave me *alone*," I snapped. Unfortunately, the music had dipped to a lull just then. My voice carried through the room. Conversations muted as several pairs of eyes turned our way. Charity flushed red.

Shit.

My pulse was outright racing now. I couldn't let them take me away from her, but I didn't know how much longer I could argue without making things even worse.

A memory wavered up. My heartbeat rattling the way it was now, my skin burning with a fever, and Mom's arms around me, rocking me as she murmured soft words by my ear. Those only times I'd ever felt I really mattered to her, regardless of whatever else I'd done wrong—when I was sick.

People forgave a lot if they thought you were suffering.

I grasped at the idea desperately, letting my legs wobble and pressing my hand to my gut. "I'm really sorry, Charity," I said. "I don't know if it's something I had at lunch, or a stomach bug, but—I don't think I can stay."

Guilt pinched at me as the shock on her face softened into concern.

"Let's sit you down," Garrand's Glower said, because of course he was hovering around us too. "Maybe you'll feel better with some rest. You could even lie down in one of the spare rooms."

Oh, they'd like *that*, wouldn't they? I shook my head, keeping my eyes fixed on the Starlet. "I really think I should go. I think I might—" I clamped my lips shut with a wave of nausea I wasn't entirely faking. Charity tensed. She wouldn't want her chaperone puking all over David Garrand's floor, or bed, or anything. That was *not* how she'd prefer her visit be remembered.

"No," she said, to my relief. "I should make sure Fiona gets home and comfortable. I'm sorry we're leaving so early... You have a business card?"

The woman Glower smiled thinly as she handed one over. "Be in touch soon," she said.

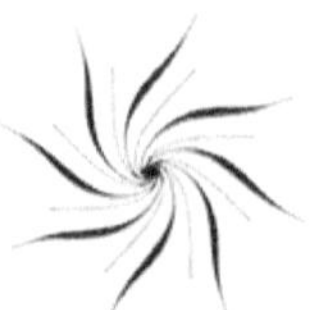

It was eleven at night when I got home. I called Sterling and, unsurprisingly, his voicemail answered. "It's Fiona," I said. "Call me when you get this. I need to talk to you about my client."

I kept pacing after I hung up, though I'd already crossed my living room at least twenty times as I'd debated whether to call at all and it hadn't made me feel any better so far.

On the drive back from Garrand's place, I'd managed to convince the Starlet that while I wasn't well enough to socialize, I didn't need any special medical help either, just to get home. I'd also made her promise not to call the supposed TV producer but to pass her info on to Charity's agent—"I've heard things about that one," I'd told her. "She talks big, but she doesn't have anywhere as much clout as she pretends to. He'll know how to get the right details from her." I thought Charity had believed me and would stick to her agreement, but then, she'd already proven how easily she could take me by surprise.

Just like the Glowers had.

I couldn't keep doing this. I couldn't keep Charity safe when they tag-teamed me like this. I'd used up my best excuses and gotten us away by the skin of my teeth, but I couldn't keep pulling out the same stories every time we left her house. She was already disappointed at how much I'd made her miss out on this week. And who knew what the demons had in store for us next?

Sterling and the other senior Tethers would figure it out. They would have a strategy. Probably it would include removing me and sticking someone more experienced with the Starlet, but that was what she deserved. Someone who knew how to actually protect her.

Telling myself that didn't loosen the knots in my stomach.

The intercom for the lobby door buzzed. I paused in my pacing, staring at it. Had Sterling been in the neighborhood and decided to drop by instead of calling?

I pressed the answer button. "Hello?"

"Fiona?" a familiar low voice said through the hum of static. "It's Will. I, ah— Can I come up?"

This was unexpected. On edge as I was, the nervous pause in his words sent an eager little jolt through me. I buzzed him in.

A minute later, he was knocking on my apartment door. When I opened it, he peered at me, seeming to study my face for several seconds before I raised an eyebrow at him and he ducked his head, looking abashed. And good. He always looked good.

"I don't want to bother you," he said. "But Charity said you weren't feeling well, and that you seemed upset at the party—she was worried—so I thought I'd check on you. Make sure everything's all right?"

"I do have a phone," I said, with a smile to show it wasn't a criticism.

"Yeah, I know." He scratched the back of his neck. "When I'm concerned about something, I like to be able to see the person I'm talking to."

I couldn't really complain about that. I'd barely seen him since two days ago, that morning in the kitchen. I had the urge to reach out and run my hand down that plane of a chest, to remind myself how it felt against me.

But he was here because he was *concerned*. About Charity. About me?

Suddenly I couldn't stand the thought of lying to yet another person. At least not as thoroughly as I had with Charity. He cared about his sister. He'd understand. Maybe he could even help.

"Do you want to come in?" I said.

He looked at me and I looked at him. My skin tingled at the sight of the heat behind the concern in his lovely green eyes. I'd bet good money he was remembering the other morning too. I moved to the side, and he stepped in so I could shut the door.

His gaze followed me as I ambled into the living room. Intent, as if the way I moved would answer his questions all on its own. I drew in a breath and found it easiest to jump in without a bunch of lead up.

"I wasn't really sick," I said. "I'm *not* really sick. I just had to get Charity out of there. It seemed like the way that would embarrass her the least."

Will frowned. "What happened?" he said, a dark note creeping into his voice.

"Nothing concrete. There were just people there who... didn't mean her well. I thought that director was trustworthy, but it seems he's fallen in with some of the predatory types. Those tales of Hollywood exploitation do have some truth to them."

"Do we need to step in?" he asked. It took me a moment to register that "we" was him and his parents, not him and me.

"No," I said. "I've handled it." *For now.* "And I've contacted my supervisor to consult on any further precautions we might need to take." I paused. "Actually, if you could just keep an eye on her at home... Make sure she doesn't make any calls that sound like business, set up any meetings, without talking to me or her agent first?"

"Of course," he said. His broad chest rose and fell with a long exhale, and the urge to touch him rose up inside me again.

"I guess this hasn't been quite the relaxing break you were hoping for," I said.

"Well, I wasn't expecting it to be *that* relaxing, given the amount of work the profs laid on us ahead of time. And it's not your fault." He met my eyes again with that same intentness. "Thanks. For looking out for Charity. You're obviously doing a good job of it."

Those last words prickled at me. My smile twisted. He had no idea how lost I'd felt in the midst of that party.

But I *had* gotten her out. I was going to make this situation right. Maybe I deserved those words.

I deserved a distraction, one final bit of fun, didn't I? This might be the last time I ever saw him.

"So now that you've checked on me, do you have to go running back to all that schoolwork?" I said.

The corner of his mouth curved up. "Why, did you have something else in mind?"

That teasing half grin gave me all the encouragement I needed. I set my hand lightly on his sternum and glided it down over the brawn I could feel through his T-shirt. "It did occur to me that maybe you could stick around a while. Now that you're here and all."

"You make a good point," he said with a new roughness in his voice, but then he seemed to hesitate. I held his gaze, letting my hand linger on his waist. He shouldn't have any doubt where I wanted this to go.

He swallowed audibly. Then he brushed his fingers over my hair and pulled me into a kiss.

I pushed up on my toes so he didn't have to bend far, throwing myself into the warmth of him. His kiss was as good as I remembered, forceful but somehow considerate at the same time. He coaxed my mouth open so the hot shock of his tongue could flirt with mine, and a pleased shiver ran through me. But I hadn't started this just to kiss.

I walked backward, tugging him with me into the bedroom. On the threshold I stopped long enough to peel that T-shirt off him. I ran my hands over his bare chest as I kissed him again, exploring his muscular shoulders, the hard little nipples I tweaked to provoke a pleased noise in his throat. The trail of hair that disappeared into his jeans was a few shades harder than the blond on his head and enjoyably coarse against his smooth skin. I let my hand follow it down, all the way to the corded length of him hardening behind the fly of his jeans. He groaned as my fingers cupped him.

We kept kissing, kept edging toward the bed, while I released that belt, slid it from his pants and tossed it aside. He found the zipper at the back of my dress and pulled it down. The cool air tickled over my bared skin. The backs of my legs hit the foot of the bed as his hand reached my ass.

I shrugged out of the dress and kicked it aside before hopping onto the bed. All I had on now was a lacy black bra and lacy black panties, cut to emphasize my curves. My shoulders and knees might be a bit knobby, my elbows pointy, but he wasn't looking at those, oh no.

I held out my hand, and Will climbed onto the bed after me. He kneeled over me for another kiss. The jeans had to go, I decided. I pushed him onto his back, unbuttoned them, and jerked them down his hips. He sat up to help me tug them the rest of the way off. Then I looped my arm around his neck and sank onto his lap so his hardness pressed between my legs, only two thin layers of fabric between us.

God, I needed this.

Will kissed my throat, making me hum, while he reached behind me to unclasp my bra. The moment he'd tossed it aside, he flipped us over again. As he laid me against the mattress, he bent to pepper kisses across my collarbone. I curved my hips up, missing the contact, and he gripped my waist.

"Not yet," he said, ragged but firm. "We do this my way this time."

I made a sound of protest. "And what's your way?"

He kissed the very top of one of my breasts. "Slow." The other. "Savoring. What's the rush?"

The rush is everything, I thought. The rush was what carried me away. But as he slipped his thumb over the base of my breasts, teasingly close to but not quite touching the peaks, a different sort of rush started to build inside me. Like an undertow gathering power as it massed into the biggest possible wave. I decided I could give slow and savoring a try.

I grazed my fingernails over his scalp and across his shoulders as he kissed his way down my sternum. His thumbs circled closer and closer to my nipples. Then they glided over them with a whisper of a touch. I moaned, arching toward him, and he finally gave me what I wanted. His lips closed around one nipple, his tongue lapping over it as he rolled the other under his thumb. Letting go, he sucked the other into his mouth and squeezed the first between his fingers at an angle that sent a bolt of pleasure through me, so intense I gasped. He licked and laved and teased with his teeth until I was whimpering for release. I grasped his head and yanked his mouth back up to mine.

His lovely torment didn't stop there. As his tongue tangled with mine, his hands kept up their caresses until they'd found every sensitive spot on my chest. I raised my legs to hook them behind him, and he leaned into me, his length so hard against my panties. I arched up to increase the pressure, sliding my hand down to trace the top of his boxer briefs, trying to pay him back with a little torment of my own. Will eased himself up and down against me, the fabric creating a delicious friction.

I didn't want friction, though. I wanted him inside me. I growled low in my throat, and Will chuckled, breathless. Then his hand dipped down between us to my clit. He circled that sweet spot through my panties and drew a choked moan from me. Down his fingers crept over the dampness spreading from my opening. Up again, snaking under the fabric to explore me skin to skin. He kissed me deeply as one finger slipped right inside me, and I almost bit his lip. He stroked that finger up and down, his thumb grazing my clit above, until I was trembling and aching. I pulled my mouth from his.

"I want you," I said. "*Now.*"

Evidently his patience only went so far too. He pulled my panties off, and I scooted up the bed to grab a condom from the bedside table. I tugged down his boxers, unable to hold back my grin as his hard-on sprang free. I brushed my fingers up and down the soft, veined flesh, grinning wider when he twitched. Will let out a moan of his own as I flicked my thumb over the moisture beading at its tip.

"What happened to now?" he said.

"Slow," I said. "Savoring."

I ripped the packet and eased its contents over him. Then I raised my legs again. He guided himself in.

I was so wet, but he was big. The stretching feeling came with a different sort of friction, even more delicious than the other. I moved with him, urging him onward, deeper. He slid all the way in with a rumble from his chest and then slowly withdrew. In and out, stroking me from the inside with that solid length of him until I was whimpering again. His own breaths came harsh and shaky now, sweat beading on his skin where my hands roamed over his shoulders, his back, those teasing hips. Every time the pleasure within me seemed about to crest, he slowed again just slightly, and the wave built higher, and higher, until it was everything. Just him and me and the hot heady sensation swelling through me.

"You feel amazing," he murmured. "God. I've got to—"

He sped up, thrusting harder, deeper, and I careened over the edge at last. The orgasm washed over me like a shower of sparks, my toes curling, every nerve singing. I shuddered with it, my hands tight on his shoulders. Will surged against me, lifting my hips to adjust his angle. The wonderful fullness of our joining provoked one more jolt of pleasure before he came with an inarticulate sound of bliss.

He stayed inside me, slowing but still pumping into me. Our bodies seemed to melt together. Every muscle in mine had gone slack.

Will rolled us onto our sides and cupped my face for another kiss. All I wanted to do in that moment was nestle into the bed with his warm citrusy-earthy smell around me and let myself drift away.

A nervous tremor tickled through me at the thought. I never asked the guys I picked up to stay. It gave them the wrong idea. It had the potential to give *me* the wrong idea.

But Will wasn't some stranger. And we both knew any arrangement we made wouldn't outlast the week. It might not even last past tomorrow, depending on what Sterling said. Why not let myself indulge just this once?

When our lips parted, I traced my fingers up his side. Something clenched in my chest. I found I couldn't meet his eyes, could only look at his mouth as I said, "Stay?"

Will shifted. For one heart-wrenching second I thought he was pulling himself out of the bed. Then his hand caught the corner of my blanket and tugged it up over us, and he settled back beside me.

"Happy to," he said quietly, hooking his arm around my waist.

I woke up early, like usual. Will had rolled over sometime during the night, but his back was still a warm presence just inches from my body. I followed the line of it from his neck to his tailbone, my hand hovering in the air without touching him. His sandy hair was rumpled, his face soft with sleep. I didn't want to break that peacefulness.

My bladder insisted that *I* needed to get out of bed, though. I slipped off the other side and padded to the bathroom.

When I'd been apartment hunting at eighteen, flush with money saved from my first few Tether Society paychecks, I hadn't been extremely picky. I'd been looking for a place with big windows for lots of sunlight, in a neighborhood close to the rich 'hoods, but not in them, so I could count on getting to work relatively quickly without paying celebrity prices. Other than that, the only feature I'd cared about was the bathroom. Maybe it shouldn't have mattered anymore, but back at my parents' house, with a bedroom door that didn't lock, the cramped upstairs bathroom had been my only real refuge when I needed a half hour's peace without having to worry about my parents barging in.

When I'd seen what this apartment offered, I'd put down my deposit on the spot. Who could argue with a counter wide enough for various assorted toiletries, a claw foot bathtub, *and* a shower stall so big that I could stretch my arms straight out before I touched the walls on either side, with a rainfall showerhead that had quickly convinced me I was never going to settle for anything else?

I turned on the shower, adjusted the temperature until it was nice and steamy, and stepped into the stall. The trails of water trickling over my skin stirred echoes of Will's touch last night. I smiled, soaking up the sensation for a minute before I reached for my shampoo.

I'd just rinsed the conditioner out when the bathroom door clicked open. Will's figure showed as a beige blur on the other side of the frosted glass.

"Nice set-up," he said, evidently taking in the space, and then paused. "Can I join you?"

That hesitation I'd noticed last night was back in his voice. As if he were worried he was making some sort of imposition I'd take offense to. It was sweet, but I'd have to disabuse him of that idea.

"What are you waiting for?" I said. "Do you need an engraved invitation?"

He chuckled as he ambled over. I backed up to make room as he slid the stall door to the side. He hadn't dressed when he'd gotten up. I let myself ogle him freely while he ducked into the spray. The water pattered over him, darkening his eyelashes, streaking down his brawny chest. He shook back his wet hair with a swipe of his hand and grinned at me. Then he bent to press his slick lips to mine.

As we kissed, I ran my hands over the trails the water had already charted, enjoying the glide of the moisture on his solid flesh. My fingers teased down until I could graze my knuckles along his length, smiling against his mouth as he rose to half mast at that one touch. He nudged me against the wall, pressing closer, skin to damp skin. His lips nibbled along by jaw.

"You make me want to do things I'd never have considered before," he said by my ear, so low it was almost a growl.

"I did tell you I had some talents," I said, and felt his laugh in the hum of his chest against mine. His hand traveled down my ass, smoothing over the curve of it.

"You know, I didn't come here expecting this to happen."

My turn to laugh. "Wasn't I clear enough about what I was offering Sunday morning?"

He nipped my neck as his fingers eased between my legs. "I thought you were sick," he muttered. "And... this isn't *exactly* how I've hooked up with girls in the past. You called me out on planning things ahead of time. I'm not known for my impulsivity, let's just say."

"But impulses are so much fun." I followed one of mine, to brush my hand under his hard-on to stroke his balls, and he really did growl.

"Not going to argue that," he said. "I think I've needed a little more thrill in my life."

"You want thrills?" I said, sliding my hand back up the corded length of him. "We can do better than this. Or are you really telling me you've never made out in a shower before?"

He made a disgruntled sound before admitting, "Not without discussing it beforehand. Not with someone I've known less than a week. I suppose this is all business as usual to you?"

He said it lightly, no judgment in his tone, but the question made my throat tighten all the same. Because I didn't like the idea he might think I was completely reckless?

"More than for you, maybe," I said, and offered an admission of my own. "There's not usually anyone here the morning after the shower with. The thing about impulses is, you have to know where to draw the line. Most people I've known less than a week, I wouldn't trust enough to let them sleep over." If they even wanted to, which was hardly a given.

Will's fingers paused where they'd been caressing me between my legs from behind. For an instant I thought I'd said too much, implied more than I'd meant. Then he kissed me again, tipping my head back against the tiles as his fingers slid around my thigh to cup me completely. I moaned, shifting to meet him as he swiveled the heel of his hand against my clit. His tongue twined with mine as his forefinger swept inside me.

"Stay there," he said before kissing his way down my neck. I exhaled shakily, leaning back against the wall with no desire whatsoever to be anywhere but here.

Will licked the droplets from my skin down to my sternum before detouring across my breasts. As he sucked one nipple into his mouth, so forcefully it shocked a gasp from my throat, his finger hooked up to find the most sensitive spot inside me. Pleasure spiked through my body. I gripped his shoulders, my hips driving into his hand. In just a moment I was lost in his caress, the edge of his teeth testing the skin around my nipple and tickling across to the other, the heat of his breath mingling with the shower's steam.

He didn't linger on my chest long. After another nip and a lap of his tongue to bring the other nipple to its peak, he sank lower, kissing the flat plane of my stomach, the dip of my belly button. Then he crouched on the floor and pressed his mouth to the spot where his hand had been rubbing a second before. I cried out as his tongue licked over me there. My fingers tangled in his hair. *His* finger kept up its slow, savoring pace up and down inside me.

He kissed me hungrily, lips and tongue and breath, leaving me whimpering. My hips shuddered of their own accord. He steadied me with his other hand as he leaned even closer. His tongue darted over my opening, and my legs started to wobble. I could do nothing but cling to his head as his mouth had its way with me, steam misting the rest of my skin, pleasure radiating through me.

"Don't stop," I heard myself saying—panting, really. "Don't stop." His tongue flicked right inside me, and the wave of ecstasy broke, crashing through me so hard my knees gave out. I would have fallen if he hadn't been holding me.

Will kept his mouth on me until my shaking subsided. As he straightened up, I shoved myself off the wall and pushed him against the one kitty-corner. I pressed my lips to his chest, his nipples, the strip of hair down the middle that widened as it hit his abdomen. The spray pattered against my back.

"Fiona," Will said. I tapped his waist to hush him.

"Stay there," I said, repeating his earlier instruction, and licked the tip of his hard-on into my mouth. He sagged against the wall with a groan.

This was one act where I'd always believed in slow and savoring. I swirled my tongue carefully around that tip as I raised my hand to graze the underside of his length. So soft and yet so hard. Hardening even more, with a twitch that made me smile, as I edged my lips a little farther down. Will's breath stuttered. Yes, I had talents.

As I took him into my mouth, I gripped the base of his hard-on more firmly. He was too big for me to suck him all the way down. From the moan that escaped him as I swirled my tongue again, he didn't mind. I began a steady stroke of the base as my lips began to echo it, back and forth, in and out, my tongue caressing that tender spot below the head and then all around him once more. His hips began a pumping motion in time with my strokes. I sped up by increments, a little faster, a little more pressure, until he was trembling. His hands dropped to my head, his fingers sending tingles through my scalp as they twined in my wet hair.

"Yes," he murmured. "Hell. Fiona, I... I'm going to..."

So considerate even when I had him writhing against my shower wall. I didn't need the warning. I sucked him into my mouth so deep he hit the back of my throat, and his hips jerked. With a gasp, he came. I swallowed until his movements stilled. Then, with a quick swipe of my lips, I started to stand up. He caught me partway and lifted me to meet my mouth with a kiss.

"What do you think?" I said when we broke apart, blinking away the spray. "A worthwhile impulse?"

Will laughed, his face still close to mine. "The best I've ever had."

"I'll see if I can't think up a few more for you to follow before this week is over." My imagination had already conjured up a couple possibilities.

I left him in the shower to do his own washing. After toweling myself off, I wandered into the living room in my satin bathrobe. I'd just started coffee brewing in the kitchen when my phone rang. I'd left it on the table.

It was Sterling's ringtone. My pulse jumped. I'd managed to forget leaving him that urgent message last night. And the events beforehand that had led to me leaving the message.

In the warm morning light, with the pleasure of Will's attentions still lingering, those doubts seemed miles away. Had I really been on the verge of calling it quits? I drew in a breath and brought the phone to my ear.

"Hey, Sterling."

"Is everything all right, Fiona?" he said without preamble, that slightly panicked quaver already threaded through his voice. My back went rigid.

It was true that I'd gotten overwhelmed last night, because I hadn't been prepared. That didn't mean I was the screw-up he obviously still expected me to turn into. I could handle the situation with the Starlet now that I had a better idea what I was dealing with. Sending someone else in to deal with Charity now that she was comfortable with me might screw everything up more. And I suddenly had no doubt that was the first step Sterling would take if I suggested I was in over my head.

"Yeah," I said. "I... I just thought you'd want to know. I saw a couple celebs who are marked but not recorded, at a do with Charity yesterday. David Garrand and—I don't remember her name, that actress who played Mary Jane in the last Spider-man movie?"

"Oh," Sterling said, with a pause that told me he was noting it down. "And they were definitely marked, not just... in the company of..."

"Yeah," I said, a chill running through me at the memory of that fatal glow around their hearts. Telling us we were too late to save them.

"We'll keep a close eye on those... situations, then," he said. "Is that all? You sounded upset in your message."

"Never pleasant seeing people like that, you know," I said, trying to sound perky and confident now. "Otherwise it's just the same as I've mentioned in my reports." I glanced toward the bathroom. The shower was still running, but I didn't want to take any chance of Will overhearing. I dropped my voice. "The

Glowers, working together. At the party, Garrand's had brought a couple others, unattached, to scope out the people there."

"I did see your mention of the interview audience, but I didn't realize their actions were that coordinated. You think they're purposefully colluding?"

He hadn't challenged my explanation for my message. That gave me the confidence to say, "Yes. Definitely. I went into more detail in my report from last night. It's something for the other Tethers to keep an eye on."

"Certainly," Sterling said. "That is very odd. I don't believe we've ever seen truly... cooperative behavior from them in the past."

"That's why I thought you should hear about it right away," I said.

"Yes. Of course. I'll let you know if I learn anything from elsewhere that you might find helpful in such a case. You still feel your current assignment is... viable?"

I hated that uncertain pause. "Definitely," I said again, with all the certainty *I* could muster. "We're getting along great, and everything's under control."

May Heaven smile on me and help me keep it that way.

Seven

I was watching the Starlet's dress rehearsal from the sidelines just before lunch break the next day when someone tapped on my shoulder. I startled and turned to find Mateo smiling sheepishly at me.

"Sorry," he said with his light Colombian accent. "I wasn't trying to scare you."

"No worries," I said, relaxing. It was good to see my fellow Tethers once in a while. When you spent too long only in the company of people who had no idea Glowers existed, it was easy to start feeling a little insane. And while Mateo wasn't the most expressive guy around, he always had a steady, reliable air that I found reassuring.

Then my mind leapt to the possible reasons he might be visiting. *Avery*. I tensed again. "What's up?" I said. "Is something wrong?"

"No, no," he said, holding up his narrow hands. "My client is doing a stint in rehab, so I've been on office duty—Sterling wanted me to check in. He said you've seen some odd behavior from the Glowers?"

I hadn't gotten around to mentioning that to Mateo directly yet. "Yeah," I said. "I mean, nothing's been off here so far." I motioned around the sound stage. The episode's director was talking to Charity and the actors playing her brother and her crush in the living room set-up, getting ready for another run-through of their lines and positioning. The rest of the staff were scattered around the room, a few in quiet conversation, others using the break to grab a fresh coffee or bottle of water from the table near the back.

"But a couple times now, there've been a few of them working together," I went on. "One trying to distract me while another gets the Starlet's ear. Or a bunch of them coming at her with different angles. It makes it harder to call them out, you know? I can say *one* person at a party or wherever can't be trusted, to get her away from them, but if I have to start acting like every second person she meets is a problem, she's going to think I'm just paranoid and stop listening. Have you seen anything like that with the rapper?"

Mateo started to shake his head, and then paused, rubbing the short black curls at his temple. He frowned. "Actually, there was... A couple of days before he decided he needed to check into rehab, he was doing a concert with several other up-and-comers, and I counted nearly a dozen Glowers in the audience. I assumed that was because there were multiple targets, but I remember thinking it was strange that at least a few of them seemed to be talking to each other."

My throat tightened. I'd thought I'd be relieved to hear I wasn't the only one noticing strange behavior, but apparently some part of me had been hoping mine was just an isolated case, something specific to Charity. If *all* the Glowers were picking up this new strategy, our jobs were going to be a lot harder from here on out.

"Sterling has been talking with the rest of the Tethers," Mateo continued. "He and the other supervisors should be able to figure out pretty quickly whether this is a fluke or a new pattern. And if it's the latter, we'll find ways to address it. They can change—so can we."

"We're just stretched so thin already," I said. There were so many budding creatives we *didn't* get to in time as it was. Like Garrand and the actress at that party.

"I know," Mateo said. "It's a shame we can't recruit Tethers through a normal process."

Relying on identifying people who'd witnessed a Glower kill *was* a rather morbid necessity.

The actors launched into another run-through of the scene, and the bracelet I'd given Charity this morning caught the overhead lights as she tossed up her hand in affected frustration. The chunks of malachite embedded in the silver gleamed. Mateo nodded approvingly. "You've got her taking protective measures."

"For now," I said. "I'm not at a point where I'll be able to convince her it's a good idea to try to wear the same accessory everywhere." For stars who were in the public view a lot and had to be extra fashion conscious, the herbs or something that could be placed more privately, like a tattoo, was usually a better permanent solution anyway.

"We do the best we can," he said, and hesitated. "Have you mentioned the new issues with the Glowers to Avery?"

The flick of his eyes away from me when I glanced at him said more than a thousand words could have. Oh, Mateo. I didn't know why he hadn't fought harder to make their relationship work. She'd called it quits because he didn't seem invested enough, but he was obviously still hung up on her.

"I did after the first time," I said. "We haven't talked since the second. She didn't remember seeing anything similar."

"Okay, well, I'm glad to hear things seem to have settled for now. Call in if anything else comes up. I should be around the office most days in the next week or two if you'd rather avoid dealing directly with Sterling."

He said the last bit with a wry smile, and I knuckled his shoulder. "You know me too well, Jimenez. I'll keep that in mind. Don't work too hard now that you've got the time off, all right?"

"Who, me?" he said, lifting his thin eyebrows, as if we didn't both know he'd done pretty much nothing other than work since the break-up with Avery. Was that really almost a year ago now?

Mateo ambled off, and I watched Charity and her colleagues run through another take. Then the director called lunchtime. Charity bounded off the set to the sandwich trays a couple interns had just carried in. I followed her with my gaze, and my pulse stuttered.

Both of the interns, bringing in a fruit tray and a platter of cookies now, had an unearthly shimmer to their skin. Glowers. The one with the fruit set down her tray and then had to disguise her recoil as Charity brushed past her. She hurried over to join the first near the doors, and a third caught up with them, leaning in to murmur something. It was two girls, one guy, all of them looking twenty-ish. All of them looking mostly at Charity, though they gave a couple of the other actors a onceover. At least the bracelet was keeping them from going right at her. With that much malachite in it, I doubted they'd be able to handle standing closer than five feet from her.

But the bracelet was only a temporary solution.

One of the show's producers had just wandered onto the sound stage. I hurried over to him, trying to ignore the knots in my stomach.

"Who are the newbies, Hank?" I asked as breezily as I could manage as I jabbed my thumb their way. They couldn't have just wandered in—Glowers needed an official invitation to enter private property, which usually gave us some protection against situations like this. But this bunch must have gotten staff approval.

He glanced up from the papers he'd been looking over and smiled. "Oh, excellent, they made it. The old batch of interns just finished up their contracts. It's good to have fresh blood around, I say."

"They all checked out all right, I guess?" I said. He wasn't going to react well to me outright accusing him of not having vetted people thoroughly enough... but someone had clearly screwed up somewhere.

"They're from that performing arts school... Whatchamacallit. Glowing recommendations from a professor there, Wendy said. They're big fans of the show, too."

He nodded to them. The trio had started chatting up one of Charity's co-stars, bright sparkling smiles all around. Just making friends with the cast, it'd look like to anyone other than me. But I saw the careful berth they were giving the Starlet, and the many pointed looks they shot her way.

'Glowing recommendations' my ass. From what I'd seen of their new tactics, I'd bet one of them had played the professor over the phone for all three of them. That was another first. Mateo should have stuck around a little longer.

I dragged in a breath. Hank had already gone back to reading his papers. "What was the professor's name?" I asked.

He shrugged. "I can't recall off the top of my head. Does it matter?"

"They just..." How to say it? "Something feels a little off about them to me."

He looked at me then, with a frown and a stare that reminded me exactly who I was. And who I was, to him, was an inconvenience he'd been saddled with against his objections thanks to some other staff member's concerns for Charity. For all his "just call me Hank" style attempts to put on a chummy persona, he was really a bit of a control freak.

If he could make a case that I was causing unnecessary trouble, he might be able to get those objections heard this time around.

"They just got here," he said. "What's the problem?"

"Just a feeling," I said carefully. "Maybe it's nothing."

"I'm sure it is," he said, and moved on.

Maybe I could track down this Wendy and see if she'd be more open to double-checking the new interns' credentials.

The three of them were still steering clear of the Starlet, but one of the girls had approached Fran, the costume supervisor. They had just a brief conversation, and then the Glower girl went to refill the coffee machine, but a moment later, Fran called over to Charity.

"That bracelet you have on doesn't really fit with the sweater we've got you in for this episode, Charity. We'll need to find you something else."

A prickle ran up my spine. Just a few minutes on set, and they were already scheming to make her more vulnerable.

There wasn't time to go looking for staff members I didn't know. I was going to have to deal with this fast, my way.

"I saw a bracelet that would look perfect with that outfit in the prop room," the other girl Glower said with a brilliant smile.

She probably thought she was being clever, moving things along, but I smiled too, despite the dull ache of nervous anticipation expanding in my chest. The prop room. That would work perfectly for my purposes.

"Yeah," I said, walking over. "Actually, all three of you should be helping with the props for the next scene. I'll make sure you get everything covered."

Charity gave me a curious look—I wouldn't normally have volunteered to go off without her—and the three Glowers narrowed their eyes at me in almost comically identical expressions of distrust. The girl who'd talked to Fran had a vibe to her that felt familiar. I hadn't spent enough time around them to be sure, but I suspected this guise was a replacement for one of the Glowers who'd approached Charity at Garrand's party. She'd know what I was here for, which meant the others would too.

But this was where I could use their status as interns against them. Just as I had to maintain a certain front for everyone around us, so did they. If they mouthed off at me, Charity wasn't likely to feel too friendly toward them. It might even get them fired.

"Are you sure?" the guy Glower said.

"Yeah, Hank just said." I motioned to the producer's retreating back. "Come on."

The Glowers shuffled their feet, but before they could come up with an appropriate protest, Fran said, "Well, what are you waiting for? The break's not that long." And after that there wasn't much they could do but head over to the prop room with me.

As we strode down the hall, I let the Glowers take the lead so I could keep an eye on them. Study their movements and reaction times. I slid my hand into my purse at the same time and wound the knotted string there around my fingers. With three, I was going to have to be *really* fast to banish them all, but I'd be happy even to cull one or two.

Even though people were in and out of the prop room every day, the air that seeped from its doorway had a stale bread smell that made me wrinkle my nose. The trio of Glowers hesitated there until I waved my arm to usher them in. "It's a school scene next. Grab some notebooks, pens, textbooks, that kind of thing. And that bracelet you saw."

One of the girls grimaced, but they marched in as if they were just hoping to get this over with as quickly as possible. Maybe they thought it was the bracelet I planned to mess with. Maybe they didn't think I'd be bold enough to banish people supposedly here on official work.

Either way, they were wrong.

As soon as the last of them stepped over the threshold, I stepped behind her, tossing out the knotted string. She'd barely let out a startled squeak before I snapped it into a complete circle around her. With a crackle, she blinked out of this plane of existence. Heart thumping, I barreled on.

The other two Glowers had spun around, but they hadn't had a chance to react otherwise. I caught the guy just as he started to strike out and thanked my past self for choosing a longer string than Sterling typically recommended. Even though the Glower managed to brush it partly aside, I could still reach the opposite end as it swung around him. I clapped the ends together in front of him, and he vanished too.

When I turned to the third Glower, she was standing with her back to one of the shelving units where a teddy bear peered over her shoulder with glossy plastic eyes. The girl raised her arms, her chin jutting defiantly.

"We'll just come back," she said. The vibration that carried from her voice over my skin made me even more sure I'd encountered her before.

She was right. This was only a temporary solution. They'd gather the energy to reappear on this plane in a day or so, and then they'd be back. But I was showing them they couldn't just waltz into the Starlet's life and get away with whatever they wanted, when they wanted, and damn did that feel good. I eased closer to her, and she braced herself for a fight.

She wasn't prepared for the other trick I had up my sleeve. I'd tipped some of the contents of the little pouch I kept tied to the base of the string into my palm. Now I flicked that handful of dried oregano and rosemary into her face. The Glower cringed with a gasp of pain, her hands flying to her eyes, and I got my opening. I jerked the string around her waist.

And then I was alone in the gross stale air of the prop room.

I brushed my hands together, shedding the last flakes of the herbs, and tucked the string back into my purse. Then, to garner good will, I grabbed a stack of things I figured the set people would want to have on hand for the afternoon. A grin tickled across my face as I headed back to the sound stage.

Whoever asked, I'd say the new interns had taken off, complaining that the work was boring, insulting the actors and the other staff. They weren't here to defend themselves, and their absence would be plenty of proof. By the time they made it back here, they might find the door slammed right in their faces.

Eight

"Are you sure about this?" Will said as we stood on the platform waiting for our train to arrive. "Can't people get arrested for this sort of thing?"

"Well, I haven't been, so far," I said.

He raised his eyebrows. "And how many times have you done this, exactly?"

"It's been a couple years. But let's just say I got in plenty of practice before then. Take comfort in knowing I've got all the tricks down."

When he didn't immediately reply, I took his hand and gave it a teasing squeeze. "I thought you wanted more thrills? If this is too intimidating for you, we can go back to the kiddy rides."

I smiled up at him, but we both knew it was a challenge. His green eyes glinted, and his fingers tightened around mine. "No," he said. "Let's do it."

I'd grabbed him as soon as the Starlet and I had gotten back to her house, with my triumph over the Glowers still humming through me. Making me want even more of a buzz. "Wanna have some fun?" I'd whispered in his ear, and now here we were.

The feeling of his skin against mine, even just palm to palm, made my mind leap ahead with a tickle of excitement to what we'd be doing in a matter of minutes. His uncertainty just made me more eager. I was going to *corrupt* this responsible straitlaced boy, oh yes, I was. Not that he was half as innocent as he was acting right now. I might have led the way, but he'd matched me step for step so far.

The train rumbled into the station. We were the only two getting on at our door. I checked the car and confirmed that, as I'd expected given the time, there were only a few other passengers on board. I picked a row of seats that gave us some distance from the others without taking us too far from the bathrooms and dragged Will down beside me. He leaned close, his bare arm firm against mine. That familiar itch ran through me.

"Relax," I murmured to him. "We don't do much yet. Someone will come by to check our tickets, and then it's only ten minutes before the next stop—not enough time. After that..."

He sucked in a breath nervously, but then he shot me a conspiratorial grin. Wicked enough to send a shock of heat through me. No, not so innocent at all.

The train started to move, a steady vibration seeping through the car. I gazed out the window, keeping Will's hand in mine. In a few minutes, the attendant I'd anticipated wandered in. We showed her our tickets, and she made a notation that meant she wouldn't bother with us again.

As she headed off, I uncurled my fingers from Will's. I'd said we wouldn't really get started until after the next stop, but there was nothing wrong with stoking the flames a little early.

I slid my hand over his lower thigh, grazing the pliant fabric of his chinos just above his knee. Then I started to trace little circles on the inside of his leg with my fingers. Will swallowed. I tipped my head against his shoulder to give me an excuse to scoot closer, keeping my ears perked for movement behind us.

After a minute, I edged my hand a little higher. Will opened his mouth as if to speak and closed it again. Then he reached over and set his own hand on my leg, where the hem of my A-line skirt rested. His fingers dipped under, sending a spark through my skin all the way up to the place between my legs.

Good boy.

The train stopped. I tucked my hand between his leg and mine, and Will did the same. A couple women got on at the other end of the car and stayed there. The train started to rumble forward again. I brought my lips to Will's ear.

"Forty-five minutes to the next stop. Attendant should be by in five. Then it's game time."

He shifted in his seat as we waited. The attendant brushed by us without so much as a glance. I waited until she'd left the car completely before I reached for Will's thigh again, further up this time. He followed suit, easing my skirt up a few inches. Stroking the sensitive skin there. I bit my lip.

"We don't— Right here in the open—" Will said quietly.

I shook my head. "Bathroom," I said under my breath. "But if you don't want to get caught, that part has to be fast. So we get good and ready ahead of time."

He chuckled again, a little raggedly now. "Would you believe I'm not sure I can get any readier?"

"Oh, *I'm* sure you can." I lifted my hand to brush the bulge at the crotch of his pants, and he sucked in a breath.

"Okay," he said. "You're right."

I lay my hand back on his thigh, halfway to that bulge now,

and resumed my gentle circling. He drew his hand further up my leg. The same pressure he obviously felt was building in me as well. I had to fight the urge to sink down into his touch, to speed up the process. The teasing progression while knowing we had to keep quiet amid our fellow passengers was all part of the rush.

I inched my way up, my pulse thrumming faster as I listened to the rasp of Will's breath, and his fingers continued their careful journey along my own thigh. When I reached his hard-on again, I grazed my thumb along it, smiling as it twitched. Will made a muffled sound in his throat. I pressed a bit harder, and then hooked my fingers around it as well as I could manage through his pants, stroking his length from base to head.

Will tilted his head toward me, his breath hot on my forehead as he kissed my temple. Then his hand smoothed under my raised skirt to close the last short distance to my sweet spot. Both of breaths caught as he touched the bare curls there.

My panties were in my purse. Underwear plus train sex just made for complications.

Will trailed his fingers up and down between my legs, and I swallowed a moan. The train rattled on the tracks, making his hand vibrate against me in a way that only heightened the pleasure of his touch. Heat had flooded me from head to toe. I gave his hard-on another stroke, and then tested the waist of his chinos. No belt today—that helped. My fingers crept below the waistband to graze him through the thinner fabric of his boxers.

He covered a groan by clearing his throat. His fingers increased their pressure, sliding over my already wet opening and darting inside. My hips flexed to meet him. His head sank lower.

"I want you," he whispered. "So badly, Fiona."

I was about ready to leap onto his lap myself, spectators be damned. I gave his length one last caress, and then reached for his hand, drawing it from between my legs. My wetness traveled from his fingers to mine as they intertwined.

Will got up the second I moved to stand. I managed to walk leisurely if not completely steadily to the doors at the end of the car. I took one moment to confirm the space beyond them was empty, and then I shoved past them, opened the bathroom door, and yanked Will in with me.

He fumbled the lock shut and grabbed me, tossing me onto the little sink counter as if I weighed nothing at all. I'd barely managed to inhale the warm citrusy scent of him before he was kissing me, fierce and hot. His hands roamed down my front to fondle my breasts through my clothes. I arched against him and slid my own hands up under his shirt. But there wasn't much time for foreplay now. I didn't *want* much foreplay. I wanted him inside me, now.

I gripped the front of his pants and popped the snap. Yanked the zipper down and pulled that hard length of him through the opening in his boxers. The floor jostled beneath us. Will gasped as my fingers tightened around him. He pushed up my skirt and slicked the condom he'd been carrying in his pocket over himself faster than I would have thought humanly possible. Then, as I tugged him to me by the waist, he drove inside me.

I couldn't hold back a whimper of pleasure as he filled me. His lips crushed against mine. The counter shuddered with the movement of the train as he thrust with hard, desperate strokes, as if he'd lose his mind if he couldn't push even deeper inside me. I urged him on with the roll of my hips, the grasp of my hands. My legs wrapped around him, my knees trembling. He caressed my breasts again, and then, as his breath grew even more ragged and his thrusts more frantic, he tucked his hand between my legs to rub his thumb against my clit. A burst of ecstasy rushed through me, and then another, and another, hitting me harder and harder until it blared in my ears. I clung to him, wanting and wanting and aware of nothing else, and the final wave crashed over me, racing through my body like a train itself, leaving me shaking.

Will moaned softly into my ear as he let himself follow me over the edge. He held me to him, pumping a few more times as his rhythm slowed. His lips dipped down to kiss my neck.

"Oh my God," he muttered, the movement of his mouth sending a fresh tingle over my skin. "I will never doubt you again."

I laughed, my head still spinning from the orgasm. "We'd better get back to our seats before someone notices and complains," I said.

He made a sound of frustration, but he eased back. I straightened my clothes as he tossed the condom in the trash and zipped up his pants. The only signs of our mischief as we ambled back into the car to take our seats were the grins stretched across both our faces.

The rest of the way to the next stop, we just sat there leaning against each other, basking in the afterglow. At the station, we got out, checked the times, and spent fifteen minutes drinking bad coffee out of cardboard cups while waiting for our transport home to arrive.

"So you did this a lot?" Will said after we'd settled in on the second train. It was a little busier than the first, but we still had a buffer of a few rows between us and the nearest other passengers.

My stomach clenched. I checked his expression, but he looked only curious.

"There was no way I was going to get away with hooking up with guys at my parents' house," I said, relaxing against the cushioned seat. "It was a bit of an adventure, finding alternate locations, you know? And a risk factor makes everything more fun. Usually with the train I'd be fare dodging too." I raised an eyebrow at him. "Are you shocked by my criminal tendencies?"

He laughed. "I'd be a hypocrite if I was, considering what we just got up to. And I fare dodged once, to get to a concert with some friends."

"Oooh," I teased, walking my fingers up his brawny chest. "*Once*. What a wild child you were."

He shifted closer to me, tucking his hand around my bare knee. It was almost unfair the way my body responded to that simple touch, less than an hour after I'd had him completely. A tingle traveled up my thigh to the sweet spot between my legs.

"Fiona," he said, his voice suddenly serious, "there's something I've been feeling I should tell you."

I tensed all over again at his tone. "What?" I said, keeping my own voice light.

"I... When my parents told me the studio had hired someone to keep an eye on Charity, I wasn't sure what to think —about any of it, I mean. The Tether Society, their whole set-up. So I asked around, checked with my friends who still live in L.A. to see if anyone had any experience with the organization or knew people who did, and usually people would ask if I had the name of the person working with Charity in case they'd heard of you specifically... One of the guys I went to high school with, he's doing a medical residency at UCLA. He was working emerg when you were brought in last year."

My skin chilled. For a second I couldn't speak. "What?" I choked out.

Will hung his head. "He shouldn't have told me. Patient confidentiality. I shouldn't have *let* him tell me. But... friends... and I was just thinking about Charity... So, one of the main reasons I came home for the break was to check you out. To make sure you weren't actually leading Char down the wrong path. That you were stable enough that you could keep her safe if you needed to."

My throat was still tight, my mouth dry. He knew. He knew that five months ago I'd been carried into the emergency room in the throes of an accidental drug overdose. Maybe he'd even guessed I'd been on the job when it happened.

The way he'd looked at me, *scrutinized* me, the first few times we'd talked. His insistence on coming over to see me face to face when Charity had told him I'd been "sick." Now I knew what he'd been looking for. I covered my face with my hands.

"Your parents?" I said as a fresh jolt of panic hit me, trying to remember if they'd treated me any differently since he'd come home. "Did you tell them?"

"No," he said quickly. "I haven't said anything to anyone. I should have told *you* sooner. It wasn't fair, knowing that about you and you not knowing that I did... I'm sorry." His thumb, still on my knee, stroked my skin gently. "It didn't take me long to see that I had nothing to worry about. I don't know what was going on with you then, but I don't need to. It's obvious you care about Charity, and that you take the work you do with her seriously. I know you'd never purposefully put her in a situation where she could get hurt. She told me she's never even seen you drink wine."

"It seemed safest to go cold turkey," I said, my voice muffled by my hands. "I didn't want what happened that night to ever happen again."

"Exactly," Will said. "Because that's not you. Maybe you were a 'wild child,' maybe you like your thrills—I'm not going to criticize you for that. You know where to draw the line. That's what matters."

"A lot of people wouldn't see it that way." I wasn't sure even my supervisor or my best friend saw it that way.

"Well, I'm not 'a lot of people.' I'm just me." He squeezed my knee. "You know, in just the last few days you've made me feel more... *present*, and alive, than I have in ages. I've seen the way Charity is with you—I think you've opened her eyes up too. You help her feel her own power. You make her realize how much she can reach for. You want to talk about talents, I'd say that's a pretty huge one."

I lowered my hands cautiously. Will glanced over at me, his mouth twisted, his eyes worried, as if he were afraid I was going to judge *him* for his admission. Some of my anxiety drained away. I reached up and brushed a few stray strands of sandy hair away from his forehead.

"You think so?" I said.

"Sure," he said, a tentative smile creeping across his face now. "You connect with people. You make them feel they can do more, be more. That's something really special."

No one had ever suggested I was really special before. I couldn't help suspecting his assessment might be slightly clouded by the mutual enjoyment we'd indulged in. But I didn't see any need to argue with him. Not when he was looking at me like that, so warmly intent I felt his gaze from head to toe. The rest of the tension inside me melted. I let my hand slide down the front of his shirt, watching his eyelids dip at the contact.

"If you're just angling to get another 'date' out of me, this much flattery is really not necessary," I said.

He chuckled. "Not flattery. Just honesty." He bent his head toward me, kissed my cheek and then the corner of my jaw. "I do want something, though," he added.

My pulse was already fluttering. "And what's that?"

"I think we can get one more thrill out of this ride," he murmured by my ear. "We've got, what, half an hour before there's a stop?" His fingers teased down the side of my knee and back up again. "I want to make you come right here in your seat. Without anyone around us having any idea what I'm doing to you."

I exhaled shakily. Just hearing him talk about it was making my nerves shiver with anticipation. "Yes, please," I said, and he smiled.

"Relax," he said. "I'll take care of everything."

I sank lower in my seat as he turned sideways in his. He raised his head to glance down the car even as he eased his hand up under my shirt. He traced the outline of my bra and then brushed his knuckles across the cups. My nipples hardened at the muted contact, aching after their previous neglect. I arched into his touch as far as I dared. He gave my ear a gentle nibble as he dipped his fingers inside the left cup. They glided over my skin to circle the peak. His thumb flicked back and forth over the nipple, and I stifled a gasp.

Abruptly, he withdrew his hand. A few seconds later, one of the other passengers strolled by to the bathroom. Will set his other hand back on my knee, running his thumb over it the way he had my breast as we waited.

As soon as the man passed by us again, Will resumed his attentions beneath my shirt, on the other side now. I fought the urge to squirm in my seat as the pressure of his fingers sent sparks racing over my skin. The train jerked on the tracks, and my heartbeat thumped.

Will's hand trailed downward. He stroked my belly all the way to my public bone. Then he pressed against me through my skirt. I swallowed a whimper, lifting my hips toward him.

He smoothed his fingers over my clit and the opening below again and again, the shocks of pleasure amplifying until I thought I would scream. His hand left me, but only for the moment it took him to slip it under my skirt. He hiked the fabric most of the way up my thighs, so it only hid the most private part of me.

He drew in his breath as he slid his thumb over the wetness between my legs. He had to know how much I enjoyed this too—how much I'd enjoyed all of our time together. Had to know I was doing this as much for my desire as his.

Will eased his forefinger inside me. Deeper and deeper, until he hit the spot that sent a pulse of heightened bliss rippling through me. I bit my lip with a sound I only partly managed to muffle. Will stroked that spot while his thumb caressed my clit, and I couldn't stop my hips from arching again. It took all the effort I had in me not to moan. A trickle of sweat ran down my neck.

A second finger joined the first, and then a third, filling me the way I loved. Will's breath became shallow as he picked up his pace, in and out, as deeply as he could reach, always hitting that pulsing spot within. I turned my head and pressed my mouth against his shoulder to hold in a cry of pleasure. *Don't stop. Don't you dare stop.* I couldn't think anything else.

As he pumped his hand faster, he raised his thumb once more and grazed the edge of his fingernail over my clit. Up and down, gentle but sharp. Ecstasy crashed over me, sweeping me up and casting me far away. I bit his shoulder as the orgasm rocked me, throbbing around his fingers.

Will kept his hand on me, in me, as we rode out the aftershock. When I sagged in the seat, he slowed, and slid his fingers down my leg, drawing my skirt down with them. Then he leaned over to kiss my lips, carefully but thoroughly. I drew his tongue into my mouth, not caring about the bitter coffee flavor that matched what he must be tasting on mine.

After the kiss, he pulled back just far enough to speak.

"Watching you respond to me, give yourself over like that..." he said. "It's the sexiest thing I've ever seen."

"It feels pretty damn good too," I said, and he laughed.

I looked up at him as he grinned down at me, and a different sort of feeling crept through my chest. Something as soft and delicate as hope.

I didn't want him to go. He had to head back to Stanford in just a few days, he had a job lined up there as soon as he graduated, but I wanted him here, beside me, *mine*. The thought of letting go of him, of this, sent a wave of sadness through me.

With a flash of panic, I clamped down on that sadness. Shoved it way deep down until it barely touched me.

He *was* leaving. I *was* letting go. And whatever I might want in this moment, I knew that was for the best. Better to leave him remembering all the good he saw in me, with no time for disappointment. That was the way I'd always done this. That was the way it worked.

Nine

"Oh, good, Fiona," Sterling said when I knocked on the half-open door of his office. "Right on time."

The top of his desk was impeccably neat as always, the dress shirt and slacks he was wearing pressed smooth. I'd thought I'd done a reasonable job of dressing professionally when I'd picked out the simple gray sheath dress I was wearing, but standing in front of Sterling I always felt I'd missed something. There was a wrinkle in the fabric by my waistline, or a little thread dangling from the edge of one cap sleeve. My heels were a smidge too high.

Sterling never said anything about my appearance. As I sat down across from him, he just looked me over and rubbed the short wiry hair covering his dark scalp. Also as always, his expression was solemn.

"What's up?" I asked. He hadn't given me any details in the voicemail he'd left me, only asked that I come in after today's shift with the Starlet.

"I read your report on the situation with the interns at your client's production's sound stage," Sterling said, motioning to the laptop open on the desk by his right hand. "This is clearly above and beyond any behavior we've seen from the Glowers in the past."

"I know," I said. "Does anyone have any idea why the sudden change?"

"We've been coming up with theories," he said. "But they're only guesses at this point. A few other Tethers have reported witnessing similar tactics, but the Glowers don't appear to have adopted it widely—yet. It does seem those that have picked up the new strategy are trying it out primarily on the... less mature targets."

A chill washed over me. "Kady's still all right, isn't she?" I said, thinking of my former starlet client.

"We haven't seen any Glower activity around her," Sterling said, with a thin smile I guessed was supposed to convey reassurance. "She's been keeping up with her supplements. I'd imagine they're focusing on those not already fully protected."

That would make sense. I wished they'd leave the partially protected alone too. I guessed that photo shoot had made Charity look like far too tempting a target. "So why did you want me to come in?" I asked. "Is there a new strategy you want me to try in response?"

Sterling steepled his hands on the desk. "I've been giving this a lot of thought," he said. "It seems to me that... considering the precariousness of the current situation... it would be best to let one of your more experienced colleagues take over with Charity Reece."

Take over—take my place with her. My fingers tightened around the arms of the chair. *No.*

A few days ago I'd intended to ask him for this. But now I had the situation under control. I had to show him I could keep it under control. Because I couldn't believe that in making this call he was only thinking about my few years as an official Tether. He was thinking about my hospital trip too.

Charity knew me. She trusted me. Even Will had said I was good for her.

"In a precarious situation, don't you think it's better for her to stay with someone she's used to, someone she'll definitely listen to?" I said. "Couldn't one of the other Tethers just back me up, and I stay?"

"You know how short-staffed we are," Sterling said. "If I pull another Tether off a current client, I'll need you to take over there, or we'll be leaving that client vulnerable."

"I get what you're saying," I said. "But I can tell you that Charity isn't going to like it. When I first started— You know how teenagers are. They test you. And someone older than me, who feels even more like an authority figure than a friend, she's going to resist more."

Sterling nodded. "I recognize that's a risk, but I think the benefit of experience will offset it. And we have to think about *your* wellbeing also. I can only imagine how stressful dealing with this... unexpected Glower behavior has been."

There it was. We wouldn't want Fiona to get stressed out— who knew what she might do!

He didn't want me working at all, I thought, suddenly sure of it. If there'd been enough Tethers in L.A. that he could have fired me and not felt guilty about it on the client pool's behalf, he would have already.

I summoned my steadiest voice, pushing it from a throat gone tight. "I've been managing fine. I dealt with the interns no problem. They didn't even try to show up today. I doubt they'll be let back on set at this point, and the producers will be more cautious about the next bunch they approve."

"It *was* smart thinking, the way you dispatched them," Sterling acknowledged.

"I'm the one who's seen how the Glowers are approaching Charity," I went on, gathering steam. "I'll recognize any problems coming up faster than someone who hasn't. I'm the Tether experienced in working with *her*. I want to do what's best for her, Sterling, and I really think it's a bad idea to swap me out for someone who's a stranger to her while we're in the middle of dealing with this problem. Especially when she's been going through a lot personally, trying to branch out with her image and her career, on top of the Glower issues."

Sterling gave me a measured look. "And if the situation gets worse?"

I swallowed hard, sending up a silent prayer to gods I didn't actually believe in. "Then I'll let you know. I'll swap out if it looks like that's what she needs. But I don't think it'll come to that."

I hoped it wouldn't, so freaking much.

"All right," Sterling said. "You've made reasonable points. But please do inform me of any new... developments. And if you run into a scenario where you need additional help in the moment and bringing another Tether in appears to be a viable solution, don't hesitate to contact the office. We'll do our best to send temporary assistance. Remember, the client's needs come first."

"Of course," I said, my face heating. He had no idea how much I'd already beaten myself up on that score, for what I'd put Kady through.

I stood up when Sterling did, accepted his offered hand for a shake, and hurried out of the office. My stomach gurgled as I pushed past the Society's front doors and headed down the stairs to the street. It was getting late, and I hadn't eaten since a few bites on set several hours ago. As I flagged down a cab, I attempted a long-distance inventory of the contents of my freezer. Did I need to grab something from the grocer down the street from my apartment? I was pretty sure I had at least one frozen pizza left.

I was just sliding into the back seat of the cab when my phone's text alert jangled from my hip pocket. I dug out the phone. Avery had sent me a message.

Hey Fee! Just got off duty. Have the night free. You wanna hang?

My thumbs hesitated over the touchscreen. My body was still jittery from that tense conversation with Sterling. Mostly I wanted to go home and bury my head in my pillow.

Did Avery really just want to "hang," or was she checking up on me? Sterling or Mateo had probably mentioned the new Glower incidents to her by now. Maybe she even knew about Sterling's plan to try to replace me. I could imagine, suddenly, the three of them discussing me behind my back: how stable I was or wasn't, whether I seemed likely to go off the rails again. A sour flavor filled my mouth.

Can't, I texted back. *Crazy week. Will let you know when I can.*

She texted back a sad emoticon that gave me a jab of guilt. Even if she had planned to check up on me, even if she'd discussed me with Sterling or Mateo, it would have been only because she wanted me to be okay. I might not have even been alive if it hadn't been for Avery and her quick thinking the night I'd accidentally ODed.

Well, I couldn't take back the lie now. I slumped against the seat and stared out the window without really processing what I was seeing. The cab wound through the streets to my building with an occasional honk.

I was in enough of a daze when we pulled up to the sidewalk that I didn't recognize the statuesque woman in the carefully tailored pantsuit standing outside the lobby door until the cab jerked to a complete stop and she turned to face it.

Mom. My pulse jumped. It took me a second to gather myself enough to hand over the fare and collect my receipt.

"There you are," Mom said with forced cheer as I climbed out. She patted her pale sculpted curls and adjusted the angle of her sunhat. "I didn't realize you'd be coming home so late."

"What are you doing here?" I said. "Is everything okay? Is Daniel okay?"

My heartbeat only slowed when she pursed her lips as if my concern were absurd. "You're always so distant on the phone," she said. "I wanted to *see* you for once. It has been a long time, you know. And I realized I've never seen the inside of your apartment. It'd be nice to have an idea of where my daughter is living." She smiled, but the gesture was too stiff to lighten her comment.

She was checking up on me. A flicker of anger passed through me, but I quashed it. I'd learned ages ago that there was no more point in getting offended by Mom's behavior than there was in getting upset that a wasp had stung you. It was just who she was. The easiest way to survive was to bite my tongue and move on.

"So I guess I should invite you up, then?" I said with a faint smile of my own.

"That would be lovely," she said, as if I just had.

I suppressed a sigh and led her into the lobby. Now I was doing a different sort of mental inventory—I hadn't left anything shocking lying around, had I? Mom did have some limits to her prying, thankfully. I didn't think she'd go poking around in my bedroom closet where I stashed my vibrator and a few other toys, or in the bedside table that held my supply of condoms and birth control pills. If any male guests had left an incriminating item behind, I would have noticed it by now. It was a few days since Will had stayed over. And of course I hadn't had any illicit substances on the premises in months.

The other consideration was my work. I never kept any records that even hinted at the secret aspects of the Society lying around at home. My reports were on my computer, which was password protected. I should be clear there too.

Still, I braced myself as I unlocked the apartment door, half expecting to find some horrific display of reckless incompetence strewn across the hall floor. A flick of the light switch revealed only the coat rack and a few dust bunnies along the baseboards. Mom raised her eyebrows at those, but she'd lived with my mess in her house for seventeen years. It wasn't as if a bit of dust would surprise her.

"It's a little stuffy," she said as she meandered into the living room. Her shrewd gaze took in the secondhand couch, the small but new TV on its oak stand, the framed cult classic movie posters hanging on the walls. "You should open the windows more often. There's no need to rely on air conditioning when it's mild out."

Even as she spoke, she was moving to a window to open it herself. "Mom," I said, "I'd rather leave them closed, especially at night. The street noise comes in. I'll air out the place some other time. It'll be easier if you give me some advance notice that you're showing up."

"Would *you* show up then?" she said, in a tone that was trying to be teasing but fell flat. We both knew the words held too much truth.

"So how *is* Daniel?" I asked as a change in subject. "Ready for his big performance?"

"He'll keep practicing until the day before," Mom said as she continued her explorations. She peeked into the bedroom—I could picture without looking over her shoulder the tangled sheets, the clothes draped over the closet doorknob, the dresser, and the chair in the corner—and moved on with a wrinkle of her nose. "You know how conscientious he is. Are you coming to the recital, then?"

"I don't know my exact schedule yet," I hedged.

"Well, we bought you a ticket. You'll need to let us know to wait for you outside the concert hall if you decide to come."

She peered into the bathroom next, and that, at least, earned me a slightly awed widening of her eyes and a nod of approval. Mom might not have needed hers as a refuge, but she could appreciate luxury when she saw it. Then she ambled into the eat-in kitchen.

"Do you want anything to drink?" I said. If I'd still had alcohol around, I'd have offered to make her a Caesar, but I guessed I was doomed to be a disappointing hostess in that department now too. "There's water, of course, and I have OJ and Sprite and..." I opened the fridge to jog my memory. "Iced tea."

"Water is fine," Mom said. When I looked up, she was idly sifting through the stack of opened mail and other collected papers I'd left on the formica table. I didn't register the impending disaster until her hands stilled over one unfolded print-out.

"Fiona," she said in her voice of offended sensibilities. "What is this about?"

She held up a medical report: my test results from the neighborhood clinic. My stomach dropped.

I got myself screened for STDs every couple months, just in case—for my own peace of mind and out of consideration of my various partners—and kept the printout on hand in case anyone asked. Mom wouldn't see that as a responsible gesture, of course.

"It was just a precaution," I said, clinging to my bite-your-tongue-and-move-on resolve. "Nothing to worry about, you can see. Everything came back negative."

"Chlamydia," she read off. "Gonorrhea? *AIDS*?"

"Negative," I said again. My jaw was starting to clench. "That's the standard screen, Mom."

She waved the report at me. "And why would you think you need to take this kind of precaution? I thought you weren't even dating!"

"Not that it's any of your business," I said, "but you don't have to *date* someone to hook up with them."

"Any of my business?" she repeated, her voice rising. "Any of my *business*? You're still my daughter, Fiona, and I have a right to be concerned if you're taking part in this sort of... of—"

My control fraying, I cut her off before I had to find out exactly how she'd describe my sex life. The last thing I needed was a lecture from her on top of everything I was already dealing with this week.

"There's nothing to be concerned about," I said. "I'm fine. That paper you're holding proves it."

"This time you're fine. What about the next time? I knew we were letting you move out too early. You just don't think these things—"

"That's enough," I snapped. I pointed toward the door, my arm trembling, before I'd realized what I was going to do. "You should leave now."

Mom stared at me. Her face paled. "Fiona."

"Get out," I said. My voice was trembling now too. Sterling and Avery and her, all in a row—it was too much. Maybe I was a screw-up, maybe I didn't think enough, but it was my life, and

I was living it the best way I knew how, for *me.* "You didn't *let* me move out. I was eighteen. You couldn't stop me. And this apartment is my property, and I'm telling you to get out before I have to call the building security guy to escort you."

Mom's lips flattened. For a second I thought she was going to plant her feet and refuse to budge, to call me on my threat. I wasn't completely sure whether I'd follow through.

Then she dropped the paper as if it were hazardous waste, scooped up her purse, and strode to the apartment door. I trailed behind her, but she didn't wait for me. She stalked out and yanked the door shut behind her without a backward glance. It thudded into the frame.

I hesitated just a second before stepping forward to turn the deadbolt. My heart thudded in my chest, dull and heavy.

She'd left. I hadn't wanted her in here in the first place. She'd been awful. But somehow in the space of her journey to the door she'd left me feeling as if this whole mess was no one's fault but my own.

Ten

"IT'S FRIDAY NIGHT! IT'S PARTY TIME!" THE STARLET hollered as she bounded down the basement hall. I exchanged an amused glanced with Will in her lounge room, where we'd been helping her set up a spread of snack bowls and cans of pop on a folding table. She was expecting a few of her colleagues from the show plus some friends from her pre-fame school days, and she'd been chattering since we got home at a speed that made it obvious she was nervous about this going well.

"This is the first time since she started the show that our parents have green lighted her having more than a few people over at once," Will had murmured to me earlier. I guessed that meant her colleagues and the other friends had never met.

Technically I was off-duty now, and I could have asked Paul to drop me off at home right after he'd driven here. But Charity's frantic energy had wriggled under my skin. I didn't think I was going to be able to relax until I had visual confirmation that her party had gotten off on the right foot. So I'd been conscripted for the refreshment and decoration detail.

"You've met all the school friends before, right?" I asked Will as I unwrapped a stack of paper cups. I'd looked into the names on the list Charity had given me and found nothing worthy of concern, but I figured it couldn't hurt getting a second opinion.

He nodded. "They were all by the old house a bunch of times. They were good kids—I mean, teenagers, but there were never any real problems."

None of them could be Glowers, then. Even if a Glower had wanted to try a con that long, there'd have been no reason for one to be interested in Charity back then. And I'd met Petra, Juliet, and Allison, the girls who played Charity's cousin, best friend, and arch nemesis on the show, personally. I had no reason to worry.

Charity hustled back into the room. "Do you think we need more pillows?" she said, her forehead furrowing. She'd already tossed some on the floor for anyone who wouldn't fit on the futon or chairs.

"It looks good to me," I told her, and she darted out again.

"I think we're done here," Will said, contemplating the table. He stepped past me, trailing his fingers over my lower back, and bent close to murmur, "If you get bored, come find me."

There was a wickedness to the curve of his lips. I would have grabbed him right then if Charity hadn't dashed over with her iPod in hand.

"Can you look at the playlist and tell me if it's too... too much of anything?" she said.

"I'm not exactly a music expert," I said as Will headed upstairs. Maybe I'd end up staying past visual confirmation of party success.

"I just haven't had time to listen to the new bands in a while," Charity said. "I don't want them thinking I'm a dork."

I skimmed through the list and handed the iPod back to her. "Nothing in there screams 'dork' to me," I said. "Chill out a little, Char. These are your friends. They're just going to be happy hanging out with you."

"I haven't had much chance to talk to them in a while either," she said. "I haven't gotten to see them at school since I had to start doing classes with the tutor to get around my filming schedule. I don't even know what most of them think about the photos, or what I've been doing on the show..." She let out a breath. "But it'll be good."

She sounded as if she were trying to convince herself. But then, I wasn't in much of a position to give advice on trusting your friends to think well of you.

"It will be," I said.

"Oh! I wanted to get the ice bucket." Out she ran again.

I gave the room a onceover and decided it was as ready as I was going to get it. As I stepped into the hall, I heard the melody of the Starlet's ringtone carry down the stairs. When I got to the kitchen, she was just hanging up.

"Who was that?" I asked.

She grabbed the ice bucket out of the cupboard. "Oh, just Petra. She and Juliet and Allison bumped into a couple people they knew, wanted to find out if they could bring them along. I figured the more the merrier, right?"

The back of my neck prickled. "Do *you* know these other people?"

"Not well, but Petra said we've all met. They wouldn't be inviting people if who seemed like weirdoes or something. And it's not like they're going to try to scam me—they're just coming to hang out." She paused when she saw my expression. "What, Fiona? You really think it'll be a problem?"

"I was supposed to have final say on everyone who'll be here, that's all," I pointed out.

She made a face. "Oh, come on. I'm not *five*. My parents are going to be here the whole time. No one's going to hurt me."

She was probably right. I hoped she was right. She just wasn't aware of all the ways she could be hurt.

"I guess you've already told them okay, so it's done," I said tentatively. At least I'd have a chance to check out the newcomers before I left. "Next time it'd be good if you asked me first, though, okay?"

Charity rolled her eyes. "You are getting to be *such* a drag, Fee," she said.

My spine stiffened as she hurried off with the ice. I needed her seeing me as a trusted ally right now, not an antagonist. Maybe I'd have to make more time for us to hang out, just the two of us, soon, somewhere Glowers couldn't reach us. Build back the rapport between us that'd been coming along so well.

She might have been a little bit right about my level of caution. What were the chances a Glower had figured out this party was even happening? Charity's social media people would have known better than to mention a private do like this. Although... her colleagues weren't so tightly under wraps.

I pulled out my phone and searched for the girls' public accounts. Petra and Juliet hadn't posted anything in the last couple of days, but my thumb stilled over Allison's feed. *Can't wait to party at my bud CR's place tonight!* she'd written this morning.

Anyone could have seen that and known there was something going down at Charity's house. A chill prickled over me.

Charity had just come up from her final preparations. Before

I could say anything, the gate buzzer sounded. She raced to the intercom. "Hey!" she said breathlessly.

"It's Petra," said the voice on the other end.

Charity stepped out onto the front patio as soon as the gate opened. I followed, tensed but holding on to a shred of hope.

A compact Honda pulled up to the house. It was nothing fancy, and not brand new, but her colleagues were only secondary characters at the moment. They weren't pulling in the same big bucks as Charity. That might have been part of why she was so nervous about having them see her home.

"Char!" one of the girls called with a squeal. She hopped out and ran over to give Charity a hug. Then the Honda's back doors opened, and my whole body went rigid.

Two of the girls who stepped out next shone in the dimming sunlight. It took a moment for me to get past the initial shock of *Glowers* and on to recognition. Both of their guises were familiar: one of the female interns I'd temporarily banished, and the girl who'd chatted up Charity at David Garrand's soirée. They hadn't lied, exactly—Charity *had* met them.

These were our extra guests. And the Starlet had already extended her invitation to include them. It wasn't my property —I couldn't revoke it.

"I ran into Jessica outside the studio," Petra was saying to Charity as she motioned to the Glower-intern. "She's such a huge fan of the show, it's ridiculous they kicked her out just 'cause her mom got sick and she had to leave early the one time."

So that was the sob story that "Jessica" had spun. I frowned, and she smiled coyly at me. Glowers had a supernatural knack for determining what people would want to hear, what would grab their attention or tug at their heartstrings, so they could make their targets feel compelled to go along with their suggestions. Parental misfortune must be a weak spot for Petra.

"And I just met Devine a few days ago, but she's with the same acting coach I had—got into a couple movies that way—and she's really cool," Allison said. "We were texting today and she wanted to hang out, and I thought, why not see if she could come along? She said she met you at some director's house?"

As the girl-Glower from Garrand's party approached, Charity's initially hesitant smile grew. "Right! I remember. Great coincidence. Well, come in. You're the first ones here."

Coincidence my ass.

I lingered in the living room doorway as the six of them clustered there to wait for Charity's other guests to arrive. My hands had clenched by my sides. This was *not* good. I couldn't leave her like this. Her parents were here, sure, but they weren't going to see any reason to hover over every interaction. If I started claiming that both of these girls had wormed their way into Charity's colleagues' lives just to get to her, I was going to sound crazy even without getting into the demon part. But I didn't dare let them out of my sight. It could take as little as a minute apart from the others for one to mark her. They were already focusing most of their attention on her, complimenting the show, her performance, her clothes—and she was eating it up.

"How long have you lived here?" one asked. "It's a gorgeous house."

"Almost eight months," the Starlet said, beaming as she sat down on the arm of the couch. "I helped my parents pick the place." Because it'd been bought mostly with her money, she didn't say.

"Hey," the other Glower said with a snap of her fingers.

"Have you talked to Diana about that role in her project? You were *so* perfect for it."

"No," Charity said. Her gaze shot to me. My veto held less water in the face of friendly approval from elsewhere. "You're working on it, right?"

The Glower nodded. "My biggest role yet. I'm going to be in, like, five scenes. Not a huge part, but I'm getting there. She's still trying to cast the lead, though. I bet you could get it. You need to give me some pointers sometime!"

Charity blushed. "Well, I mean, any time you want to come by—"

Oh hell, no, I was not letting her offer a blanket invitation. I leapt forward to grab Charity's shoulder, cutting her off. "I think I heard the buzzer."

She frowned, glancing toward the door. And then one thing went right for me, finally—the buzzer actually sounded. "Oh!" Charity said. She hurried over to welcome the next bunch of friends.

As she introduced the guy who'd just shown up—her photographer friend, I gathered—and his boyfriend, one of the Glowers started eyeing me. Sensing I was their biggest obstacle, I guessed.

"Hey," she said, giving Charity a nudge and pitching her voice as if she were trying to be discrete, though she obviously intended for me to hear. "Why is she following you around even in your own *house*? Don't you ever get to hang out without a babysitter around?"

She let disdain color her tone. A supernatural spark leap from her lips to Charity's ear. My gut twisted. She was using her demonic power of inspiration—inspiring Charity to believe hostile things about me, no doubt.

Charity bit her lip. "No, of course not. Fee was just helping me set things up. She doesn't usually stay too long after work."

She aimed a pointed look at me, clearly intended to cue me to take my leave. I forced a smile. "I just want the chance to meet all your friends," I said, grasping at the first excuse that occurred to me. "You're still expecting some more people, right?"

"Yeah," Charity said. Her gaze lingered on me a little longer, her expression puzzled, before she turned back to the others. Shit.

Well, I'd bought myself a little time. I still had no idea how to make the Glowers take off. If I could find an excuse to drag them away from the others so I could banish them without being seen... but I was in no position to order them around here. If I intruded on the party too much, Charity might lose her patience and order *me* to leave.

I shifted my weight, my nerves jangling, as the Glowers leaned closer to her on either side again. One tapped her necklace, just a few inches from where the spark would shimmer if she were marked, and the knots in my gut tightened.

Sterling, I thought, crossing my arms over my chest. I could call him. Tell him I needed that emergency backup he'd offered. But how could I justify random other Society employees showing up here when I could barely explain why *I* was staying?

I could at least ask him for advice on handling this, as much as I hated the thought when just yesterday I'd been telling him I could handle this alone. Charity's safety mattered more than my pride.

I was about to pull out my phone when someone touched my back. I flinched.

"Sorry!" Will said quietly. He peered past me to his sister

and her friends. "Everything okay? You look... I don't know. Worried."

I inhaled, readying myself to lie and say it was nothing, and my eyes met his. His warm green eyes, bright with concern, waiting for my answer. Trusting that it would be a good one.

I couldn't tell him everything, but I could use his help. *He* could be my backup. And then maybe I wouldn't need to call on Sterling after all.

I tugged Will a short distance from the doorway so I could talk without the teens overhearing. "You remember I told you we ran into some people I thought might try to hurt Charity," I said. He nodded. "Well, two of them conned their way in with her friends from the show. They're... They're scam artists. The girls think they're just fellow industry people who want to make friends, no ulterior motives. Charity's already getting frustrated with how much I'm monitoring her. I'm not sure she'll believe me if I tell her they need to leave, and I don't really have the authority here."

Will's face had darkened. "I can get them out," he said, and my panic eased just slightly.

"I don't think that's necessary yet," I said. "It'll look really strange if you suddenly decide some of her friends aren't allowed to stay, and I don't want Charity getting upset with you either." Maybe if the other tricks I had up my sleeve didn't work... but I'd save that for a last ditch effort. "If you could just distract them for me for a bit—get Charity talking about something with you so she's not listening to them and whatever stories they're feeding her? There are a couple of things I can try so they'll take off of their own accord, but I don't want to leave her with them unsupervised."

"Of course," he said without hesitation. Even though the whole story must have sounded absurd. Even though I'd given him no proof of any danger. I swallowed thickly, a sudden emotion swelling in my chest. I didn't have time to think about that.

"Thanks," I managed.

As he stepped into the living room, drawing the eyes of all the girls—and the two guys too—I rushed down the hall to the kitchen. I had to open three cabinets before I located the spice racks I'd noticed in passing before. Oregano. Rosemary. There wasn't enough in the stainless steel shakers for me to make a solid loop around the Glowers, even combined with the contents of the pouch in my purse, but that would have been hard to accomplish without the rest of the group noticing anyway. I could still make them uncomfortable.

I glanced toward the basement stairs, thinking of the malachite bracelet I hadn't expected Charity would need today, but I wasn't sure where she'd put it, and I didn't have much time. When the rest of the party arrived, she'd lead everyone down to her domain. I could work with that.

Heart thumping, I started at the top of the stairs and sprinkled a line of herbs from one end to the other. To my relief, the tiny leaves blended into the dappled gray-and-blue tiles enough that I doubted anyone would notice them. Laughter carried from the living room, followed by Will's low voice. He had their attention. Good.

I tossed a few pinches over the stairs for good measure, and then hurried down the hall. Halfway, I laid down another barrier of herbs from one wall to the other. And then another blocking off the hall just outside the living room doorway. The rest of the flakes, I poured into my hand so I could scatter them past the other entrance to the living room without it being obvious what I was doing. Now the only direction they could go without crossing one of those barriers was out the front door.

Just as I was jogging back to the kitchen, brushing the last flakes from my palm, the buzzer sounded a third time. I shoved the containers back into the rack and reached the hall in time to see Charity opening the door to the last two groups of friends she'd been expecting. Thankfully, none of these seven girls and guys was glowing.

"Okay, let me show you my part of the house now!" she said, as I'd anticipated. "There are tons of snacks, and a bunch of movies if you want to put something on, and I've got that karaoke game..."

She ambled down the hall as she talked, and the others trailed after her. As she passed the living room and that first line of herbs, the Glowers halted on their way to joining her. The rest of the group pulled away from them as they edged forward. Their faces paled.

Just one barrier probably wouldn't have stopped them. They'd have cringed walking over it and then moved on. But they must have sensed there was more up ahead. I had no idea how the herbs made them feel, other than it wasn't good. Those plants disrupted the Glowers' connection to this plane of existence the same way malachite and certain symbols did.

Charity noticed that the Glower-girls were hanging back just before she reached the top of the basement stairs. "Hey, Jessica, Devine," she said. "Come on!" The others were gathered around her already.

One of the Glowers glanced toward me, her gaze accusing. I offered an easy grin. Her eyes narrowed. But she didn't move forward.

"I really like hanging out up here," the other said. "Why can't we bring the snacks up to the living room?"

Charity backtracked partway down the hall so she could talk

to them without yelling. "*Everything's* downstairs," she said. "My TV, my music equipment, the game system…"

"Well, we don't need all that, right?" the first Glower said. She scratched one arm and then the other as if an itch had come over her, and then stepped back a pace.

"And my parents will be around up here," Charity went on. "We'll be able to relax a lot more downstairs."

"Yeah," said photographer boy, who I guessed had come visiting before. "It's an awesome set-up. Let's go already!"

Everyone was staring at the Glowers now. They looked at each other, and I could almost read their internal debate. The more they protested, the crazier *they* would look. And if they couldn't convince the others to go along with their request, which was looking increasingly unlikely, they were going to need to keep these people on their good side if they wanted to come at the Starlet in a similar fashion in future. They were as stuck as I'd thought I was a few minutes ago.

The first one turned and outright glared at me. Then she called back, "You know, I just remembered I have something I promised my mom I'd get done tonight. Sorry I could only hang out for a little while."

"I've got to bow out too," the other said quickly. "I just got a text. My boyfriend's freaking out about something. You know, boys…" She offered a weak smile.

Charity blinked at them, momentarily speechless. "Well… okay," she said. "Sorry you've got to go."

She moved forward, but I got there first, hoping to cut off any last minute conversation that might result in a return invitation.

"I'll see them out, call them a cab," I told Charity as I waved her off. "You should get on with your party. I've got to head out anyway. Have fun!"

Charity's stare fixed on me, puzzled again. "Fee," she said, and stopped.

"Yeah?"

She shook her head. "Nothing," she said. "Thanks."

Something in her tone pricked at me. She suspected I'd had a hand in these sudden departures, I was pretty sure, even if she couldn't have guessed how. But there wasn't time to talk things out with her. She headed to her other guests, and the bunch of them disappeared down the stairs. My back started to relax.

"Shall I show you out?" I said to the Glowers.

The one who'd glared at me grimaced. "I think we can manage on our own," she said tartly. They pushed open the door and stalked out. I had no doubt they'd wisp away from this plane of existence the moment they felt sure no one would observe them.

The Glowers' need for an invitation and our vetting of guests had been enough to protect my previous clients in their own homes. It looked like I couldn't rely on that anymore. I *was* going to have to talk to Sterling again. Maybe we could work out a proposal that the Starlet's parents would go for to add a more permanent sort of protection to the property—sigils marked on the drive or the gate, malachite embedded in the ground. The sorts of things it was so hard to explain to anyone unfamiliar with demons that we didn't usually bother asking, considering this kind of incursion was so rare.

Had been so rare. Sterling was not going to be pleased that I'd let those Glowers get even a one-time invitation. No doubt that would be the last bit of evidence he needed to swap me off.

Will came up behind me, slowly enough that I didn't startle this time. He set his hands on my shoulders to run his thumbs over the muscles still tensed there. Another person whose questions I'd have to answer. I let out my breath and braced myself for an awkward conversation about how I'd orchestrated this and who those girls were.

"You want a drive home?" was all he said.

In my surprise, I let myself lean back against him. The warmth of his body tingled over me. But what tingled deeper was the unexpected realization that he might be the only person in my life right now who was willing to take me as I was, no criticisms, no doubts. Just believing in me.

"Please," I said.

Eleven

When we got to my building, I used my key card to wave open the entrance to the parking garage. Will didn't blink. Neither of us needed to say out loud that this was going to be more than just a quick drop off at the door.

He parked in the spot that belonged to me, though in my car-less state no one but guests ever used it. We sat there in the gloom of the garage for a moment, silent. My relief at having dispatched the Glowers had faded on the drive over, leaving only that gnawing uncertainty. They kept getting closer and closer. If I hadn't decided to stick around to help Charity set up...

At least Will had had my back. "Thanks," I said, meaning that, the drive, everything.

He swiveled toward me in the driver's seat. "Those photographs Charity took—is that what's made her more of a target?"

"Probably," I said. "They put more of a spotlight on her. Made people realize she had ambitions beyond what she's already doing. A person who wants something badly is easy to manipulate."

He frowned. "So what do we do now?"

How I wished I knew. "The same thing I've been doing all along," I said. "Keep an eye on anyone who shows an interest in her, keep them away from her if you don't trust their intentions. We need to be especially careful of anyone who claims to be part of the industry. And... after today, I don't think she should have anyone over to the house who you don't know from before, unless I'm there too."

"Do you think the interest will die down after a while?"

"It should," I said. The Glower sort, anyway. "But, you know, the negative attention goes hand in hand with fame. If she wants to pursue a real career beyond the kiddie shows, she'll need to keep putting herself out there. At least she'll get more practice at knowing who to trust herself as she goes."

"Yeah." He sighed and rubbed his face. "I suppose if she gets in a little over her head, it'll be a learning experience if nothing else. I'd just like to think we could step in before she's really hurt."

"Yeah," I said quietly.

"It's weird," he went on. "The way— With her career taking off, all the money she's bringing in— My little sister *paid* for that house. She's fifteen and she's already making more a year than my parents probably have in the last decade."

"I seem to remember hearing that you have some high class job lined up yourself," I said with a nudge of my elbow.

"How...? Charity told you." He shook his head. "That's not exactly the same. There are tens of thousands of engineers in the world. How many movie stars are there?"

"Are you jealous?" I said. "You don't come off as the fame-seeking type."

He chuckled. "No, I wouldn't want to be doing what she is. I'm a lot happier with calculations and circuitry. Straightforward, cause and effect, no worries about popularity or cultivating the right image... But I'll admit it can be hard not to feel everything I *have* accomplished has been overshadowed by her success. Our parents spend more time telling me the latest news with her than asking what I've been up to. I'm proud of her—I'm incredibly proud—but I worked my ass off to get into the program I'm in, to get the sort of job offers I've been able to field... Sometimes it'd be nice to feel they were a little more proud of *me*. Does that sound pitiful?"

A lump had risen in my throat. "No," I said. "That totally makes sense. Does it help if I tell you that when you're *not* around and she is, they talk about you all the time? How wonderful your grades are, this and that award you got, 'work ethic,' 'dedication'... I think sometimes Charity feels the same way you do, just the other way around. Like they think what you're doing matters more than being on some TV show, no matter how much money she's making."

"Really? Actually, that does make me feel better. Not the part about Charity worrying about how they see her, but the rest." He gave me a rueful smile. "What about you? You get along with her so well, you've got to have siblings, am I right?"

My own smile felt like a grimace. "Yeah. Younger brother. The less said about my family the better."

He studied my face. "That bad?"

"Well, I mean, not like they're *abusive* or something." I hesitated. I never talked about my parents with my hook-ups. But Will was a little more than just a hook-up, wasn't he? With his own admission of insecurity still hanging in the air, letting my mouth open and the words spill out felt like simply resetting the balance of disclosure between us. "I was adopted. My parents tried for ages to have kids and thought they'd never be able to. So they went that route. But they had this idea of the stereotypical Chinese girl, polite and obedient and conscientious—that's what they wanted. And they got me. I don't think I need to tell you I was not that at all, from the start. And then when I was four, my mom got pregnant after all, with my brother... and *he* was everything they wanted. Excellent student, never in any trouble, hardly ever argued with them." I stopped there. The lump in my throat had become an ache.

"That must have been tough to watch," Will said softly.

"Well, it was definitely hard not to see they thought I was a mistake." My voice had gone rough. I rubbed my mouth, blinking a couple times at the heat building behind my eyes. I was *not* going to cry. "But whatever. I moved out as soon as I could, and I interact with them as little as possible, so I'm not their problem anymore."

"Fiona," Will said, and I could hear the concern in his voice. Knew how he was looking at me without raising my head. My chest tightened. I didn't want him thinking of *me* as some pitiful thing. I wasn't pitiful. Maybe I wasn't anything all that special, but I had a good enough life.

Too much talking—that was the problem. We weren't supposed to be here for that.

I glanced out the Mazda's back window. The underground lot was maybe half full, a car on either side of us. In this corner, the only way anyone would see us was if they walked all the way to the back of the lot.

An idea formed in my head with a tingle of anticipation that washed the worst of my discomfort away. I let a real smile creep across my face.

"Push your seat back."

"What?" Will said.

"Conversation time is over," I said, peeking at him through my eyelashes. "Push your seat back as far as it will go."

For a stomach-knotting second I thought he might protest the abrupt change in subject. Then that passion I loved seeing lit in his eyes, and his own lips curled upward. He reached for the lever and slid the driver's seat so it almost touched the back seats.

I climbed onto his lap and sat on his knees, facing him. As I raised myself to loop my arms around his neck, he met me for a kiss. Deep and heady, sending a shiver straight through me. Yes, this was the right direction.

Not quite the right position, though. I shifted back to feel for the controls and tipped the seat so it was almost horizontal. Will gazed up at me, eager, curious. I scooted forward, my skirt riding up as my thighs hugged his, and leaned over him for another kiss.

He brushed my hair back from my face and tangled his fingers in it, pulling me even closer. His tongue teased past my lips. As it twined with mine, his hands slipped down to find the hem of my blouse. They smoothed up over the bare skin of my back to the clasp of my bra. After a couple of fumbles, he undid the hooks. The cups dropped forward, and I made a pleased sound into his mouth.

I reached for his shirt as we continued kissing. Just in case, it seemed wisest to leave it on him, but I edged it up until his nipples were bare. I traced the compact muscles over his broad ribcage, his tight abs, those hardening little nubs. He inhaled sharply when I pinched them, and I grinned. Then the heels of his hands found *my* nipples beneath my shirt, creased skin circling over those sensitive points, and all I could do was moan.

He teased with slow, steady strokes until I leaned into him, begging for more. His teeth ran over my lower lip as his thumbs rolled my nipples against his fingers, and I gasped. I settled lower on his lap, letting the hard-on I could feel through his khakis rub between my legs with a wonderful unbearable pressure. Will groaned. One of his hands dropped to my thigh as he arched to meet me.

Our kisses grew sloppier, our breaths more ragged, as we ground against each other. Will yanked my skirt up to remove one layer of fabric between us, and I reached for his fly. He took advantage of the momentary parting of our lips to sit up and tug my breast into his mouth. My hands forgot what they were doing as his tongue licked over my nipple. I clung to his head instead, running my fingers over the soft waves of his hair as he sucked and nibbled one side and then the other, until the heat between my legs felt ready to explode.

I shoved him back against the seat and bent down for another breathless kiss. Then I grasped the button of his pants more firmly. He sighed as I eased the zipper down. In its wake, I trailed my thumb over his hard-on. At my tug, he lifted his hips so I could drag his pants down his legs, far enough that I could sink onto him, panties to boxer briefs, without the waistline chaffing my thighs. I ran my fingers over his chest, kissing his throat, his jaw, as I pressed against him.

"Fiona," he murmured, not pitying or concerned or anything but wanting now. He hooked his hands around my waist, thumbs dipping to skim just beneath the top of my panties. I rocked against him with a whimper. Then I eased my fingers between us to free him from his boxers with a stroke of that silky smooth hardness. He groaned again, nipping my shoulder. But as I flicked my thumb over the liquid beaded at the tip, I felt him hesitate.

"I don't have condoms in the car," he said in a voice strained with disappointment. "We could take this up to your apartment?"

I bowed my head, still gripping him. Feeling him twitch against my palm as I swiveled my thumb over him again. No, I needed him in me, here, now, while my blood was still pulsing past my ears and that high welling up inside me.

I had rules I didn't break. But as I'd already admitted to myself, Will wasn't my usual sort of lay. I ran my fingers up and down his corded length, leaning so close my lips brushed his cheek.

"We don't have to," I whispered. "I get tested regularly, I'm clean, I'm on the pill. If there's no reason for you to think you're not safe..."

He exhaled shakily as I stroked him again. I forced my hand to go still. Hungry as I was for him, I didn't want him making this decision out of blind desperation. I wanted him to be able to think about it, to make a real choice.

After all, I had a lot more reason to trust his evaluation of risk than he did mine.

Will stared up at me with the same hunger that was coursing through me—and a shadow of doubt. His thighs had tensed against mine. My chest clenched. Maybe I'd gone too far, suggested too much.

"I've never done it bare before," he said.

"It's all right," I said quickly. "We can—" Inspiration hit me, and I could have kicked myself for not remembering earlier. "I've got a couple in my purse."

I started to twist to reach for the bag on the floor on the passenger side, but Will caught me, his hands firm against my waist. He lifted one to touch my cheek. "No," he murmured. "I'd like to know what it feels like. I can't think of anyone better to find out with. As long as *you're* sure?"

His words squeezed my heart. It took me a moment to find my voice. "Yes. Yes."

I'd barely finished speaking when he dragged my mouth to his. We kissed hard and hot, his hard-on just as hot against the fabric of my panties. I resumed my caresses, fingers around him. He clutched my hip, arching into me. The contact made my eyes roll back. Then he gripped the edge of my panties again.

"Off," he said, panting.

My head was spinning. The thought of moving one inch away from him felt suddenly impossible. It wasn't as if they were anything special.

"Rip them off," I said. "Tear them right off me."

He gave a breathless laugh and curled his fingers around the fabric. With a jerk, it snapped. I pushed the rest aside, positioned him beneath me, and eased down onto him in the space of a heartbeat.

Will tipped back his head with a rough sound in his throat as he filled me, my wetness coating him, no barrier between us. I sank down and down until he was completely inside. Bracing my hands against his chest, I lifted myself halfway and sank down again, and again, and again, shifting forward just slightly so he glided in even more smoothly. The tight friction from his size radiated through me, drawing a moan from my lugs. Sweat dampened his skin beneath my fingers.

As I picked up the pace, Will reached for my breasts again. He slid his palms up and down over them in time with my rhythm, his thumbs flicking back and forth and then holding over my nipples with tight circles. His hips pumped against mine. The pleasure hummed through my nerves, my veins, until my whole body was trembling with it. I moved faster, letting him thrust into me so hard it shook the breath from me.

"God," Will choked out, pinching my nipples. He surged up

as I pressed down, hitting me even deeper than before, and ecstasy crashed over me. Will gasped at the same time. As I swayed up and down over him a few more times, my arms wobbling, a wetness that wasn't just mine slicked down the inside of my thigh.

I leaned against his chest, and he tucked his head down to kiss me. We stayed like that, intertwined as closely as two bodies could be, while I slowly came back to myself.

"That was amazing," Will said, caressing my hair.

The impulse rose up inside me to snuggle into him and invite him upstairs to spend another night. To fall asleep with those brawny arms around me, that broad chest against my back. A second later, panic shot through me.

Oh, no. I couldn't let myself get that mushy. The guy beneath me was heading back to a school five hours away in a day and a half. And that was good. No time for him to see anything of me but what I wanted him to see. No time for disappointment. I'd leave him with a lovely memory of the thrills and the rush.

I eased myself off him and pulled the hem of my skirt back down to my knees. "It's late," I said. "I should go."

He nodded. "I don't leave town until Sunday afternoon," he said. "I've got a project I really should finish tomorrow, but... I could stop by on my way out of the city, if you're free?"

I had to grin. "Call me."

I'd just stepped out of the shower Sunday morning when my phone rang. Considering how early it was, I was surprised to see Will's name pop up on the screen.

"Hey," I said with a smile when I answered. "Making plans already?"

His tone was so serious it banished any impression I'd had that this was a booty call. "Did you know about this casting director coming by to talk to Charity?"

Casting director? "What?" I said. "No. When?"

"*Now*," he said. "She and her assistant just turned up. Apparently she arranged the meeting with my parents yesterday. One of my dad's friends, a guy who works in entertainment law, he got talking with her and ended up putting her in touch with them. They must have figured because of that connection and since they're here to supervise, they didn't need your approval. But after what you said the other day... And it seemed strange to me that she'd be having the meeting here at the house."

"It is," I said, my skin chilling. Unless this "casting director" had a reason to angle for a long term invitation. "Thank you for letting me know. I'll be right over. Can you take one of your parents aside, tell them I want to meet this woman before they agree to anything?"

"I think I can manage that."

I threw on my clothes in record time and arrived at the mansion with my hair still damp and my stomach empty other than a sensation of dread. I hadn't called Sterling yet, hoping some brilliant solution might come to me over the weekend, and he hadn't responded to my official report. So it was still just me.

Will answered the door, his mouth tight. "They're in the dining room," he said in a low voice. "I told my dad you were coming. Do you need anything from me?"

"No, I don't think so," I said. He rubbed my elbow, and I reached up to squeeze his hand, as if I could take some of his strength with me. "I guess just stick around, just in case."

Voices carried from the dining room. I walked over, briskly but with what I hoped looked like confidence. Before I'd even reached the doorway, I saw the supernatural glow seeping across the floor. My heart sank all the way to my gut.

Well, at least an official industry figure I could put off more easily than a Glower approaching with a more personal connection. I inhaled deeply and stepped into the room.

The five of them—Mr. and Mrs. Reece, the Starlet, the casting director, and her assistant—were sitting around one end of the expansive dining room table. Mr. Reece glanced up when I came in and gave me a short nod. The "casting director," a plump woman with curly black hair, was in the middle of a sentence, gesturing enthusiastically as she spoke, her hands glinting in the morning sunlight that drifted in from the window beside her. She didn't bother to acknowledge me. Her equally shiny assistant raised her eyes and narrowed them.

But it was Charity I couldn't help looking at first. Charity with her make-up and hair done up all tasteful and mature, but not enough to hide the eager flush in her cheeks. She was gazing at the casting director-Glower avidly. My stomach constricted.

I was going to have to kill that hope, yet again.

"I was impressed," the Glower was saying. "It takes a lot of courage and, hmmm, spirit to put yourself out there like that." The photos, I guessed she was talking about. "The producer for this project is very picky, so I just wanted to be sure of your in-person presence before we extended an official invitation to audition."

I closed my eyes for a moment as her voice washed over me. The tenor of it wriggled through my bones. She'd been here before, I was pretty sure. The same Glower who'd been playing intern, if I was going to guess specifics.

"I'd love to give it a shot," Charity said, her eagerness resonating through the words. Her gaze darted up to me. "It sounds like a really cool project, Fee. A web series, but Paramount is funding it, so it'll be a major production."

"And we have a team well-versed in making content go viral," the Glower said to the Reeces, still ignoring me. "A lot of important people in the industry will be watching to see how we do. I think it would be a great stepping stone in Charity's career."

"When would the filming start?" Mr. Reece asked. "Charity has a pretty full schedule at the moment."

"If she gets the part, not for several weeks." The Glower turned back to Charity. "I'd imagine you'll be on hiatus then?"

She nodded. "That would work perfectly."

"Then the next step would be that full audition. We've had several other girls come in, and none have been quite right, so filling that part has become something of an urgent matter. If I give you pages now, could you come in tomorrow morning? We could make it early to fit around your rehearsal schedule."

Her parents glanced at each other. "I have an early meeting I can't get out of," Mr. Reece said.

Mrs. Reece bit her lip. All month she'd been talking about the big out-of-town client she was driving up to consult with for a few days this afternoon. "Well, Fiona will go, of course," she said, brightening as she motioned to me.

Of course. That was my job, after all. I smiled tightly, and the casting director finally glanced at me with a far-too-brilliant smile of her own. Imagining all the obstacles she could throw in my way if it were just the Starlet and me in a building where she controlled everything else. How many other Glowers could she summon to help her land this "deal"?

"Sure," I said, playing along for now.

Mr. Reece jotted down the location and time, and they all stood up, with handshakes all around. I hung back as Charity and her parents walked the Glowers to the door. Charity managed to hold in her excitement until they'd stepped outside. Then she bounced on her feet with a little squeal.

"You should have heard the whole pitch, Fee! I love it. And she really seemed to think I'd be right for the part."

"Charity," I said slowly.

She really looked at me then, and her joy went out like a light. It killed *me*, seeing that.

"Was there a problem with Ms. Colton?" Mr. Reece asked, frowning.

I'd conjured up the story I'd use on the cab ride over. It didn't take much tailoring. "I've seen her before, using a different name," I said. "She doesn't really have any connections with Paramount—probably not with anyone else she said is involved with the project either. She has a lot of different scams she uses… I don't know what she's got going this time, but there's no way this audition is legit. I'm really sorry, Charity."

The Starlet's jaw clenched. For a second she just stared at me. Then she snapped, "You didn't really want it to work out!"

I stared back at her. "What?"

She jabbed her hand toward me. "This whole week you've been acting weird. Getting upset about *anyone* new who wants to talk to me. Freaking out for no reason. I thought you *wanted* me to go after better roles."

"I do," I said, abruptly queasy. "I'm not trying to get in your way, Char, I promise. I'm just protecting you. You're getting a lot of attention now, and a lot of those people are predators. That's how this business goes."

"So nothing that's happened has been for real? Honestly?"

"That interview you scored was real," I said. "And the parts your agent was talking about, that he's going to go over with you when he's back this week—"

"Parts I might not even *get* to audition for. Maybe you'll decide all of those are wrong for me too!"

"Honey," Mrs. Reece said, "I'm sure Fiona is only doing her job—"

"Well, maybe her job is bad for my career," Charity interrupted. She raised her chin, her hands fisted at her sides. "No one's perfect. If I'm going to have to wait until I can work with people who've never done anything sketchy in their entire lives before I get to try out for a part, then I guess I might as well give up now. Is that what you really think makes sense?"

Her father reached for her, but she waved him away. Spinning on her heel, she stalked off to the basement stairs. I watched her golden head disappear into her lair. My gut felt like one massive knot.

"She'll come around," Mrs. Reece said quietly. "It is a disappointment, after everything..."

"I know," I said. "I wouldn't have said anything if I wasn't sure she could get into real trouble with that woman."

Mr. Reece nodded, but I thought I caught some skepticism in the slant of his mouth. It'd be bad enough if Charity stopped listening to me. If her *parents* started believing I was overly cautious, I was completely screwed—and so was anyone who tried to replace me, too. It'd be open season for the Glowers.

How the hell was I going to fix this? I dragged in a breath.

"I think you'd better give her time to cool off," Mr. Reece said before I could speak. "We'll call you if she wants to talk before your usual shift tomorrow."

He moved as if to see me out, and Will materialized into the hallway from the living room. I'd forgotten I'd asked him to stay nearby. His bright green gaze found mine, nothing but solidarity there, and the turmoil inside me settled a bit.

"I wanted to talk something over with Fiona before she goes," he said, and then, to me, "Can we take a walk?"

"Sure," I said.

Mrs. Reece looked curious, but she and her husband just said their good-byes, and I headed out at Will's side. We strolled together with a couple feet between us, past the pool and through the sprawl of the backyard. When a scattering of saplings put us out of view of the house, he took my hand, interlacing our fingers.

"She won't stay upset," he said. "She's been more pissed off than that at me plenty of times, and she always gets over it."

"I don't know," I said. "You're her brother. I'm just the 'babysitter' who showed up a couple months ago."

"Believe me, I can tell that's now how she really sees you.

She's just disappointed. As soon as she gets a chance at a real role, it'll be like this never happened."

I wanted to believe him. He should know, right? He'd been around for Charity's entire life. I exhaled, focusing on his presence beside me, the graze of his thumb over the back of my hand, instead of the gnawing worries inside me.

"I hate having to be the bad guy," I said. "Even temporarily."

"You're not, though. It's the people who'd use her who are the real bad guys. You're the hero." He squeezed my hand with a flash of a smile.

I managed to laugh. "I hope she does see it that way eventually," I said. "I hope she can find some meaty roles to dig her teeth into the way she wants. She's good enough to break out." If the Glowers would get out of her way, she'd have a real shot at making it big. But that was exactly why they wanted her so badly. Talent and passion and youthful exuberance—an immensely satisfying meal to whichever made their mark first.

"From what I heard, her agent is back tomorrow, right?" Will said. "She could be on her way by the end of the week."

That was a nice thought. And I didn't want to worry about the Glowers anymore, not right now, not when these were the last moments I was going to spend with Will before he left. I didn't want to be thinking at all, only feeling. As we approached the stucco wall that surrounded the property, I sidled closer to him.

"So, was this walk just to talk about your sister, or did you have something else in mind too?"

His smile grew with that wickedness that made my heart skip a beat. "I may have had an ulterior motive," he allowed. He stopped by the wall and glanced up at the fronds of the palm tree that cast its branches over from the other side. "I thought... since you're here anyway... One more thrill to end the week?

There's something I've been thinking of ever since we moved into this house, wasn't sure I'd work up the nerve. But I've been inspired."

I grinned back at him. "I'm intrigued. Do tell."

He jabbed his thumb toward the wall. "I can see from my bedroom window—the neighbors have a little oasis set up. Circle of palm trees, fountain, grass all around it. Lots of shady parts where no one would be able to see what's happening there at all."

My pulse quickened. "On the other side of the wall."

"They're gone for the weekend," Will said. "I watched the whole family take off Saturday morning. No one's gone in since." He stepped closer to me, close enough that the earthy-citrusy smell of him surrounded me, even though we weren't quite touching. "Unless a little innocent trespassing is too much for the thrill-seeker?"

"Oh, please," I said. "Trespassing was my favorite game when I was growing up." I hadn't done it in a while, though. Witnessing the Glower drowning Ginny Sinclair had kind of soured the enjoyment I'd gotten out of it. I pushed that memory aside. "Okay, smart guy. How are we getting in, then?"

"I can handle the wall," he said. "I'll help you over?"

He held out his hands to offer me a boost. I didn't let myself hesitate, just stepped onto his palms and let him heft me upward. The wall was only five feet tall, nothing huge. I scrambled over and dropped down on the spongy soil between the palm trees on the other side. Will took a brief running start and heaved himself up and over, his muscles flexing beneath the short sleeves of his button-down shirt.

He grabbed my hand again, tugging me through the trees. "Just over here..."

We emerged into a clearing. The wall sheltered us on one

side, palms on all others, with a thick carpet of grass covering the ground between them. Off to the side in a pool of sunlight, a carved stone fountain burbled. A row of bright red and purple lilies swayed behind it.

Will peered back toward his house. "Here's the spot I can see from my window," he said, standing in the sunlight. "So over here..." He ambled a few paces to the left, where the light fragmented into speckles through the fronds. "Totally hidden."

I followed him. "It seems you've gotten awfully good at breaking the rules all of a sudden. Why's it taken you so long to start seeking thrills, Mr. William Reece?"

He ducked his head, looking suddenly, delightfully shy. "I'm not sure," he said. "I think... I've been focused on certain goals for a really long time. When I was ten, I saw this presentation from some guys at Stanford—these new developments in robotics they were working on—and I basically thought that was the most incredible thing in existence. That must make me sound like a total dork."

I gave his arm a little shove. "Yes. But I'm okay with that."

"So I decided I wanted into that program, no matter what. And my parents, and my teachers when I told them, all they'd say was how hard it was to get in, how careful I'd have to be to keep my grades up, make sure I had the right range of extracurriculars, and this and that... Obviously I goofed off a little here and there. But I was always worried about screwing up that dream."

"But you got in," I pointed out. "You've *been* in, for four years. You're almost done."

"Exactly!" he said with a laugh. "I was so in the habit of sticking to those routines... But I don't have to. If there's any time I can loosen up, it's now. I got what I wanted. And now I want to enjoy where I am."

His voice dropped a little with that last sentence. He dipped his head to capture my mouth with his. I kissed him back whole-heartedly. If this was the last memory he'd have of me, I wanted him enjoying every second of it. I certainly intended to.

He pushed me against the wall, leaning into me until I couldn't feel anything but the heat of his kiss, the solid weight of his body, and the dimpled texture of the stucco behind me. His hands smoothed over my ass and then roamed up my sides, across my shoulders, finding the zipper at the back of the dress. I shifted forward as he yanked it down. The fabric fell to my feet in a mass of fabric. Will lowered his head next to mine, gazing down at my body. He kissed my cheek and then down my neck. I wrapped my arms around him, soaking up his warmth. The teasing of his lips sent shivers through me.

I shouldn't be the only one here getting undressed. I tugged at his shirt and he let me peel it off. Then he eased us down on the grass, the silky blades tickling my bare skin. He kissed my mouth again as he traced his fingers along the top of my bra. I ran my hands up and down his chest and then, still feeling overly naked in comparison, undid his slacks. He made a throaty sound as I touched the already hardening length of him.

"I'd say thrills definitely agree with you," I murmured.

He chuckled. "You're only coming to that conclusion now?"

"Just collecting further evidence."

His breath hitched as I stroked him again. He pulled me closer, and we kissed until I barely remembered where we were. Somewhere in the midst of that, he disposed of my bra. His hands worked over the swell of my breasts and their sensitive points, and I let out a cry into his mouth. I ran my fingers into his soft hair as he trailed his kisses down to my collarbone.

An odd tickling sensation whispered over my ribs to my belly. Will had plucked up a leaf and was tracing shapes on my skin with it. As I watched, he slid it up to spiral it around my breast. I bit my lip as he grazed it over my nipple, drawing it to an even tighter peak.

He kissed me again while he teased the leaf up my neck, along my jaw, over my cheek. Then it fluttered back down to flirt with my other breast. The warm breeze wafted over us, so thick with the scent of lilies it dizzied me. I arched against Will, hooking my leg over his to press myself to his hard-on, and he groaned.

Sitting up, he reached for my panties. He slipped them over my legs as tenderly as his dispatch of them last time had been rough, and kissed the top of each of my feet as he tossed the panties aside. The leaf he trailed up my left leg from ankle to knee, and then the right. Then back to the left, from the knee to the top of my thigh. He pressed a kiss to my belly button before darting the leaf right between my legs. I whimpered, curving my hips toward him, and he flicked it over my clit. After several teasing passes, he replaced it with a careful hand, fingering me as he shifted to meet me for another kiss.

I wrapped my own hand around his length, giving him a gentle pump that made him growl. He kissed me fiercely. I lifted my legs as he rolled onto me and grasped for his boxers. He wrenched them off.

I let my head fall back into the bed of grass as he bent over me. The tip of his hard-on twitched against my opening.

"It's still okay?" he rasped. "Without—"

I nodded before he had to go on, raising my hips in a plea. Without another word, he surged into me.

I cried out as the delicious burn thrummed through me. He slid back and thrust again, gripping my hips and lifting them off the grass so I could meet him at an even deeper angle. A shudder ran through me. I might have been embarrassed by the noises coming out of my mouth if I hadn't been so lost in the haze of pleasure. I tightened my legs around him, pressing into every thrust. My arms quivered where I clutched his shoulders.

"You're perfect," Will muttered, his breath hot on my cheek. "So perfect."

I started to laugh, and an even deeper thrust turned the sound into a moan. "Please," I said. "Please... oh..."

I lost my voice as the orgasm rippled through me, building and building until it echoed from my scalp to my curling toes. Will gave a cry of his own. He buried his face in my shoulder, teeth tapping the bone, as his hips jerked a few more times and he poured himself into me.

We clung there together, skin to sweat-damp skin, as the afterglow washed over me. Will leaned onto his side and tugged me with him. As his heartbeat slowed against the palm I'd rested on his chest, his hand swept across my waist and up to my breasts. I made a noise of protest.

"I don't think I can feel any more after that."

"I think you can," he said. He flicked one nipple between his fingers and swiveled his thumb over its tip. A spark of pleasure raced through me. "You drive me crazy, Fiona. I want to do the same to you." As his hand kept up its teasing torment, he kissed the side of my neck, the corner of my jaw just below my ear. "I want to see how many times I can make you come in the time we have left." His fingers slid lower, and even though the aftershock of the orgasm was still trembling through me, my hips canted toward him in encouragement. A sigh slipped from my lips.

He was going to kill me, but it would be a sweet, sweet death.

"I don't know how I'm going to make it through the next two weeks," he murmured into my hair.

Despite his skillful touch and the fresh jolts of bliss it brought, my mind snagged on those last words. "Two weeks?" I said, and whimpered as his forefinger dipped between my legs. Between the way he turned me on and his come inside me, I didn't think I'd ever been this wet.

"I got you a flight into San Francisco," he said. "I can pick you up there—it's just a half hour from my apartment near campus."

The comment hit me like a splash of cold water. My hand shot down to grasp his wrist and halt his explorations. I pulled back to look at his face. "What?"

Will's cheeks flushed. That would have been endearing if I hadn't been too frozen in shock for any other emotion to penetrate my heart. "It wasn't that expensive," he said. "I wanted to make it clear right off the bat that I'm not some selfish jerk of a boyfriend who'd expect you to spent half the day on the road just to see me."

Thirteen

I SAT STRAIGHT UP, STARING AT WILL. THE BREEZE DRIFTED over me again, and this time it only made me feel more naked. I crossed my arms over my chest.

"Boyfriend," I repeated.

Will pushed himself upright too, more slowly. His expression was so fond it only made the pain in my chest clench tighter. "Did you really think I was going to shrug this off as just a fling? That it didn't mean anything to me? Fiona, I think you're amazing. I want this—I want *us*—to work."

A laugh caught in my throat. "I thought this *was* just a fling," I said. "I don't remember you asking if I wanted to be your girlfriend."

He was looking puzzled now. The way Charity had looked at me after I'd gotten rid of her new "friends": with a trace of betrayal. "Well, I mean, I assumed— After everything we've been doing, the time we've spent together— I didn't realize you needed to be asked."

It was absurd. For so long I'd tried to guard my heart by

never letting myself get attached, never letting any guy trample it, and now it felt as if it were breaking because this guy cared too much.

At least, he thought he did. I could imagine how things would go if I played along. If I took his plane ticket, went up to Stanford to visit him, hung out with all those college whiz kids. Talked for longer than ten minutes at a time. I was amazing at making him feel good, sure. I wouldn't look so amazing at anything else when he saw me side by side with his classmates. I wasn't especially smart or insightful or witty. As soon as he got a few more thrills out of his system, I'd be boring him to tears. Or freaking him out by refusing to play the girlfriend role he was used to. The girl who'd have squealed and thrown herself at him at the thought that he'd paid her way for a visit without a second thought.

Whatever idealized vision he had of me, whatever expectations he might not even realize he'd formed, it wouldn't take long for the relationship he was imagining to come crashing down. I knew how these things worked. We might as well get the crash over with now.

"We were having fun," I said. "For a week. And out of the blue you decide you can make plans for me without asking what else I might have going on—you want me to rearrange my life around you?"

His jaw stiffened. "We *have* had fun," he said. "And we've talked, we've gotten to know each other. Most girls would want that to keep going."

There it was. That hadn't taken long at all. "Well, I don't go by what 'most girls' want." I grabbed my bra and hooked its clasps behind me. "I have a job, I have friends, I have a family, even if I don't get along with them that well. I don't like people assuming I can clear an entire weekend for them on demand.

And I *really* don't like being told who I'm supposed to be and what I'm supposed to want."

I didn't look at him as I yanked on my panties and then my dress. Will was still just sitting there, as if he were stunned. My heart thudded hard. The pain inside me prickled deeper, but it wasn't enough to overcome the edge of panic urging me to get out of here.

"So it didn't mean anything to you?" he said quietly. "Nothing between us mattered to you? *I* don't matter to you at all? Are you really going to tell me that?"

I made myself look at him then, as I clutched the back of the dress he'd stripped off me so passionately just minutes ago and zipped it up myself. I meet those bright green eyes that had made me swoon so often in the last ten days. My throat closed up.

It wasn't true. But at the same time, my pulse was scrabbling in my veins like a rabbit caught in a snare. If I gave him an inch, he might never let me go. And it was going to hurt so much more than this, for both of us, if I didn't end it now.

"Yes," I said, my voice harsh to my own ears. At least that might stop him from noticing the quaver underneath. "We both got off. Good times. I've gotten off with dozens of guys before you. I'll get off with dozens after. You clearly think very highly of yourself, but believe me, you're not that special."

Anger burned every other emotion off Will's face. He pushed himself to his feet, snatching up his clothes and jerking them on. "Obviously I was wrong about you. The last person I want to be with is someone who messes with guys' heads as if seducing them is some kind of game."

I gritted my teeth against the ache that jabbed into my gut. "Good," I said. "Now help me over this wall, and we'll get out of each other's lives, and you can find the sort of girl who's waiting for your grand romantic gestures."

After Will helped me back onto the Reeces' property, he strode on ahead of me. I let him increase the distance between us. My stomach was churning, my skin uncomfortably hot. I was afraid if he pushed me again, the pressure building behind my eyes would burst in a gush of tears.

He'd already headed inside when I reached the house. Paul was waiting in his car on the front drive to take me home. I glanced at the house, wondering about Charity, but my phone had been silent. It seemed I'd pissed off both siblings quite thoroughly.

What I needed, I decided as the car pulled past the gates, was to wipe Will out of my system. Get started on the next in that line of future hook-ups right now. It had always been easy for me to move on before. I just had to remind myself how.

The morning was barely over. I had time. At my apartment, I forced down a quick meal of toast and cheese. Then I showered with care, washing every hint of the oasis encounter from my body. I pulled on one of my favorite pick-up dresses, a deep red number that set off my dark eyes and hair and showed just a peek of cleavage and a hint of thigh—flirty but not too forward. I applied the fresh-faced makeup guys always seemed to respond best to, adding a slight dramatic flair with the length of my eyelashes.

The bar down the street felt too familiar. And it was still earlier than was ideal. I strolled through the neighborhood, checking out the places that were open, taking my time. My queasiness had settled into a dull nausea that only prickled into my awareness if I paused. So I kept walking.

After a long while, I came across a dive bar that was just opening. Alternative folk on the sound system, a soccer game on the TV, a sheen of grease on the wooden table tops. Suddenly I didn't feel up to walking any farther. I plopped onto one of the creased leather-top stools at the bar and asked for a soda water with lime.

As I sipped it, I glanced around. A couple of older guys—older than appealed to me—were watching the game over their beers at the other end of the bar. A young couple was grabbing lunch at a table in the corner. Three thirty-something women ambled in.

No prospects yet. But there was plenty of time.

My heart was still beating too fast. I had to restrain my feet from kicking against the legs of the stool. I reached the bottom of my glass, and the bartender came over to take it.

"Are you sure you don't want something with a little more bite?" he asked.

My body stilled. I stared up at the rows of bottles on the shelves behind him.

I'd gone months without a shot or a glass of wine or even a taste of beer. What for? I was what I was. This morning I'd proven that beyond a shadow of a doubt. So why should I pretend to be anything else?

"Make the next one a vodka tonic," I said.

I couldn't help watching as he mixed the drink. The ice cubes clinked against the sides of the glass. The vodka warbled flowing over them. The soda gun hissed. My fingers curled against my palms where my hands rested on the counter.

The bartender slid the glass over to me. Condensation left a streak of moisture in its wake. The tang of the alcohol rose from within, tickling up my nose.

I slid my fingers around the glass. Peered down into it. My mouth felt suddenly dry. I wanted, so badly, to toss every drop of the liquid between my hands down my throat. But a memory swam up as I swallowed against that dryness: that first moment when I'd woken up in the hospital, my stomach burning, my skin chilled, and my mouth like ash. As if I'd died and been resurrected.

I closed my eyes. Then I wrenched one hand from the glass and grabbed my phone from my purse. I held my breath through each ring, until the click of the connection sounded on the other end.

"Avery," I said, "I need you."

I was still clutching my vodka tonic when Avery arrived a half hour later. The bartender had been side-eyeing me for most of that time and the backs of my legs were sweating against the stool, but I hadn't lifted the glass off the counter. Small victories.

"Let's go," Avery said gently, touching my shoulder. I managed to release the drink. I set a ten on the counter to cover that and the bartender's trouble and followed my best friend out to the cab that had dropped her off.

As soon as we were inside my apartment, I sank onto the couch. Avery sat down beside me, close enough that I could have leaned against her for support, but I felt too tangled up inside to appreciate the physical comfort. I tipped my head into my hands.

"What happened?" Avery said.

I might as well get straight to the heart of it. "I started sleeping with the Starlet's brother."

"Mmhm?" She didn't sound especially surprised. Well, Avery knew me.

"He was hot. And up for having some fun. That was all it was supposed to be."

"And then?"

I sighed, blinking at the tears that were threatening to burst out again. "I liked him. He was sweet, and he seemed like he... like he *respected* me. But then he got it into his head that we were going to have a real relationship and I was going to fly out to Stanford to visit him and all this stuff, without even *talking* to me about it, and I just— I couldn't do it. I can't do it, Ave. I'm not the girlfriend type."

"It sounds like he thought you were the type of girlfriend *he* wanted," Avery said.

"He *thought*. He's barely known me for a week. He didn't have time to see my crappy side."

Avery nudged me lightly with her shoulder. "I happen to believe you don't have a crappy side. No one's perfect, Fee."

"Some are closer than others," I muttered, and glanced up at her. "Haven't you spent the last five months waiting for me to crash again? What happened, my OD, it hasn't gone away. I know you're still thinking about it. Sometimes..." I paused, a lump filling my throat. I might as well say it. "Sometimes I'm not sure if you even want to be friends anymore or you just feel that you have to, to make sure I don't go off the deep end."

Avery's eyes widened. "Fee," she said. "Of course I— You're my *best* friend. Yeah, things have been a little weird lately, but we're still— I haven't tried to push for us to talk and hang out too much because it seemed like *you* wanted some distance. You made a mistake. It happens. It's not as if I haven't made plenty. It doesn't change our friendship."

"Why would you want to be friends with me?" I asked with a sweep of my hands. "I'm a total screw-up, that much is obvious. I have a job I only got by default, the client I'm trying to help thinks I'm messing up her life, I hurt the one guy who actually cared about me, and the second things get tough, I'm off to self medicate myself again. Who the hell wants to hang around that?"

"Okay," Avery said in the no-nonsense tone I loved her for. She ticked off each item on her fingers. "You wouldn't still be working for the Society if you weren't doing at least a decent job. There'd be no point in having you in the field unless you were actually helping people. Clients *always* get annoyed that we're interfering with their lives in ways they don't understand. Yours *love* you most of the time—I could never handle the starlets, and make them feel supported instead of controlled, half as well as you do. It sounds as if this guy hurt you by making decisions for you before you did anything wrong to him. And you stopped yourself from drinking, and everything else. As soon as you saw your using was out of control, you stopped completely, and you've stuck to that for five months. Just by your own will power. Not a lot of people could manage that."

"Lots of people wouldn't need to in the first place," I said, but her words had started to stitch together the parts of me that had felt so broken. I rubbed my face. "And what have I ever done for you?"

Avery snorted, sounding so dismissive the rest of my doubts eased back. "Oh, I don't know. You were the first person to make me feel that I was really a part of the Society, that I belonged there, even though I'd started training before you. You come up with the best adventures I've ever been on. You make me laugh. You've listened every time I've been in a rut and never judged me." She paused. "You should try that with yourself. If it were me, if I'd gotten caught up in drugs or something else that hurt me, you wouldn't decide I didn't deserve friends. You accept everyone except yourself, Fee, and that's not right."

Those last words resonated through me. I dragged in a breath and wiped at my eyes, thinking of what Will had said to me before. *You connect with people. You make them feel they can do more, be more.* If he saw that in me, and Avery did too... maybe there was something to it. I hadn't lived up to a lot of people's ideals, but that wasn't a crime. I'd told Mom to let me live my life the way I wanted... Why couldn't *I* let me do that without beating myself up for it?

Of course, even if I was being a friend to myself, I had to admit I had some problems I needed help with. And losing myself in a drink or a handful of pills or some guy's embrace might let me escape them for a little while, but it wasn't going to fix them.

"I'm sorry for freaking out at you," I said. I leaned toward Avery, and she grabbed me in a hug. I squeezed her hard, taking reassurance from her steadiness. Then I pulled back. "This whole thing with the Glowers, the different strategies they're trying... I feel like I can hardly keep up," I said. "Every time I think I'm on top of it, they pull something new. I don't know if I can keep Charity really safe like this."

"You've talked to Sterling?" Avery said.

I nodded. "Sort of. He wanted to pull me off her case and put someone else on, and I convinced him to let me stay. I have to talk to him again. I just... I *get* her. If he puts some middle-aged Tether in there, she's just going to chaff even more. That's not going to help anyone."

"You get her," Avery repeated. "Then, what do you think she

needs? If you were in her position... what would get through to you?"

Somehow I'd never looked at the situation from quite that angle until now. If it'd been fifteen-year-old me instead of Charity facing what she was, what would I be thinking?

The moment I turned it around, I saw how the next twenty-four hours would play out as clearly as if I'd scripted it. My heartbeat stuttered.

"I'm not calling Sterling yet," I said, the certainty that was rising up inside me carrying me past the lingering pain. "Charity's going to need *me* tomorrow."

Fourteen

DAWN LIGHT WAS JUST STARTING TO TINT THE SKY WHEN the gate outside the Starlet's house eased open. I straightened up in the driver's seat of the rental car I'd gotten as a base for this morning's stakeout.

A slim figure slipped through the opening and closed the gate behind her. The faint light caught in her pale hair. Conveniently, she turned toward me. I'd figured she'd leave early, before there was any chance of her parents being up, and that she'd head this way, since it was the fastest route to the main road. I waited until she got close enough that we could have a conversation, and then I stepped out of the car to meet her.

Charity froze the second I appeared behind the open door. She took a step back, as if considering running for it, but she must have realized there wasn't any point now that I'd caught her in the act. Her chin rose defiantly as I crossed the street to join her.

"What are you doing here, Fee?" she said tightly.

"Making sure you get that career you want so much," I said. "You're sneaking out so you can go to that 'audition,' right?"

Her silence was answer enough. She glared at me.

I sighed. "Look," I said. "You were right. I shouldn't be making all your decisions for you. So I'm not here to stop you from going."

Her eyebrows leapt up. "You're not?"

"Nope," I said, and motioned to the car. "I'll even drive you to the place. I just want you to do one thing for me that will help *you* make the best decision for yourself."

"What's that?"

"Come on, let's get some breakfast and I'll tell you. You're not due there for another hour and a half anyway."

She followed me to the car, and I drove us to a cafe closer to my neighborhood than hers, where the prices wouldn't make me swallow my tongue. After we'd placed our orders—scrambled egg and bacon sandwich for me, yogurt and fruit salad for the Starlet—she tapped the tabletop.

"So what's it you want me to do, Fee?"

I pulled a bracelet out of my purse: a simple silver band with three smooth rectangles of malachite embedded in the curved surface, a match for the one I'd given her last week. I handed it to her.

"How did you—" she started, staring at it.

"It's not the same one," I said quickly. "There's a store the Tether Society works with, they keep certain designs in stock for us—I picked this up yesterday because I figured you wouldn't have yours with you. All I'm asking is that you wear it. Keep it on the whole time you're in the audition. That's it."

Charity's brow knit as she picked up the bracelet. "I don't get it. How does that help anything?"

I'd come up with a story that was true enough to answer

that. "It's a symbol," I said. "The sort of people we need to be wary of, who are looking to use you not work with you, they know the Society will come down hard on them if they hurt one of our clients. That bracelet will tell them you're under our protection. If the audition is legit, it won't matter. But if it's not... They'll see that, and it'll scare them. I'd bet good money the casting director won't shake your hand—I'd bet she won't even come within five feet of you while you have it on. Her assistant either. They might try to convince you to take it off too, to show you're willing to throw that protection away."

"Really? All because of a bracelet?"

"I know it sounds weird," I said. "But just watch how they react. And if I'm right, I hope you'll believe me that they're not people you want to be doing business with."

Charity ran her fingers over the silver surface, and then slipped the bracelet on. It gleamed against her tanned wrist. "And you're going to take me there, so I can see?"

"Yeah. You're calling the shots here. I just want you to have all the info before you decide what you're going to do."

"Okay," she said with a sharp exhale. "I won't take it off. If they act strange about it, I'll leave. But if they don't, I'm doing that audition, and I'll take the part if they offer it to me."

"That's totally fair," I said. "I promise, if that's the way it goes, I won't say another word against them."

We didn't talk much through the rest of the meal. Charity pulled out the audition pages the Glower had given her and read over her lines, mouthing the words to herself between spoonfuls of yogurt. It pinched my heart, seeing her so intent, knowing that hope would soon be shattered. Or, if my gambit failed, her soul might be.

When we headed out, I tried to focus on the road, but I

couldn't help glancing at her from the corner of my eye. Her expression had gone thoughtful.

She had a good head on her shoulders. I knew that, just like I knew *I* had one too. I needed to trust her, to trust that she could draw the line before she fell too far. If she never had to chance to toe that line and pull back from it... She'd never totally trust herself. And she'd hate me for standing in her way. I knew what that felt like too.

I pulled into the small parking lot behind the squat brick building where the Glowers must have arranged a room for this and possibly other operations. Charity hesitated with her hand on the car door.

"Thanks," she said to me. "You'll wait for me here?"

"I'll be right here if you need me," I said.

She aimed a flicker of her usual smile at me and hurried to the building. A wisp of relief washed over me. I hadn't lost her. Not yet.

I waited with my foot tapping the floor of the car until I forced it stop. My gut was tying itself into knots. I could hear Sterling's voice in the back of my head, chewing me out for letting my client wander unsupervised into a place I knew held at least two Glowers. If I'd misjudged the situation, misjudged the Starlet...

I hadn't, I told myself. I knew Charity; Sterling didn't. And if this demonstration worked, we'd be so much closer to making her safe from the Glowers for good.

By the dashboard clock, fourteen minutes passed before Charity hustled back out of the building. Her face was tight, her hands clenched. She jerked open the car door and dropped into the passenger seat. For a second, I was afraid her frustration was meant for me. Then she spoke.

"You were right. They— It was the casting director and her

assistant and this guy who was supposed to read for the other part, and none of them would come anywhere near me. It was like I had some contagious deadly illness! And the casting director tried to talk me into taking the bracelet off, just like you said. Some stupid excuse about how it wasn't right for the character, as if wearing one little thing would make it impossible for her to tell if I could play the part..." She pressed her hand to her forehead. "But it was so weird. They really were scared of it."

"I'm sorry," I said. "I wish it had been legit. I really do."

She peered at me with a keenness that didn't sit well with me. "Is there something else going on, with the bracelet and these people, that you're not telling me, Fee?"

I hated lying to her. But if I tried to tell her the full story, about demons who sucked the life out of creative stars, she'd laugh me out of the car. This was as close to the truth as I could give her.

For now. Maybe someday I could explain more. Maybe we *should* be telling the clients more, trusting the evidence to speak for itself, letting them make more of these decisions.

"I don't think so," I said. "Look, we'll find some real roles for you to audition for. If your agent hasn't gotten any good ones after all, we'll just have to find you a new agent who can, right?"

Charity guffawed. Then her face fell. "Do you really think there are legit people who'll *want* me to work for them?"

"I do," I said honestly. "I'm sure of it. You can't let this get you down, Char. You ended up in the spotlight all of a sudden because of those photos, and that brought a lot of creepy people out of the woodwork. Once they start backing off, it'll be easier to see the real opportunities."

She fidgeted with the bracelet. "I guess I should keep wearing this. Except I'm going to have to take it off for filming. And it's not like it goes with all my outfits." She let out a chuckle that sounded too much like Will's. "Why don't we get my social media people post a picture of me wearing it online? Let all those creeps know you've got my back so they should leave me alone? We could act like it's just to show off some fashion for my fans—they're always asking for more of that stuff."

I opened my mouth to veto that idea—broadcasting information to the Glowers at large would only let them know they had to prepare for that obstacle before they approached her —and paused as her last sentence sunk in. I'd seen some of those fashion posts. *How to dress like your TV faves!* The Starlet's fans didn't want to just see what she wore. They wanted to wear the same things, to be a small part of her world.

And they could be, in more ways than they knew.

Charity was never going to be safe as long as the Glowers were using the people around her to insinuate themselves into her life. Somewhere, some day, I was going to slip. It wasn't insecurity to admit that. It was just a fact.

I'd been thinking my problem was figuring out how to close her off from strangers. But Will had said, and then Avery, that my talent was knowing how to reach people. How to make them feel connected. If the Glowers could use all those connections to Charity to get at her... why couldn't I use those same connections as a shield? I could reach out to the people who cared about her using the exact same technology that had allowed the Glowers to stalk her.

"You know," I said, "I think that's a brilliant idea. Let me make a couple calls first, and then we'll show off your new style all over the internet."

I added a couple of reminders on my phone before starting the engine and turning us toward the studio. I'd need to check with the store to make sure they could arrange a large order of the malachite bracelets from their supplier, and find out when they'd expect to have them in stock. Then we could schedule some posts with Charity's social media rep. *Show your support for Charity and Miracle Mina by getting your own lucky bracelet here!* Picture, link, and Charity's endorsement.

A grin slid across my face. The Glowers had no idea what they were in for.

Fifteen

Two days later, I sat on my couch with my laptop, watching the shares of Charity's photo showing off her "lucky bracelet" multiply by the second. The practicalities had come together faster than I'd dared to hope, and we'd launched the image and its accompanying info just a couple hours ago.

It appeared to be working the way I'd hoped, though I wouldn't know for sure until we had time to see whether people acted on this enthusiasm offline as well as on. But the burst of triumph I'd felt when her fans had first jumped on the post had dampened under the weight of another task I had yet to complete.

There was a more private message I needed to send. I'd had the email window open for nearly half an hour, and I hadn't gotten past the name at the top. I set my teeth and forced my fingers to move over the keys.

Will,

. . .

Charity gave me your email address. She doesn't know we argued. So if you don't want to hear from me, please don't be angry with her.

I hope you'll at least read this, because I think you should know the truth.

I stopped, inhaled, exhaled, and ignored the twinge of longing that shot through me—for a shot of vodka, a powdered artificial high, anything to take me away from the pain I'd caused. I couldn't fix this if I let myself run away from it. Maybe I couldn't fix it anyway, maybe he wouldn't care, maybe I'd hurt him too much, but he deserved the chance to hear it.

The truth is that I was lying when I said you didn't matter to me, that you were just another guy. It seemed like you were expecting so much from me all at once, so much that I hadn't expected, and all I can tell you is that I freaked out. I didn't know what to do except find a way out of the conversation, and the way I found was unkind. I wish I'd reacted better.

I still think you should have talked to me before going around buying plane tickets or whatever, okay? But mostly I freaked out because of things that had nothing to do with you, and that wasn't fair. You remember what I told you about my parents? I guess I'm always a little afraid of disappointing people, even if I try to convince myself not to care what anyone thinks. It's been easier to always be moving on, to never stick with anyone too long, so no one gets a chance to be disappointed. That's the best explanation I can give you. I'm sorry.

Maybe you're disappointed already, or will be. But you know what? That's okay. I am who I am. Part of who I am is someone who really enjoyed spending so much time with you last week, who'd really like to see you again. There were things you said to me that made me realize I should at least not be disappointed in myself. Things that helped me figure out how I could help Charity more than I already was. So even if I don't see you again, or I do but you don't want to talk, I wanted to thank you for that.

That's all I wanted to say. Whatever happens, I wish you well. And I think last week is always going to mean more to me than just about any other time in my life.

Fiona

My hands hovered over the keyboard for several seconds before I found the courage to hit send. The instant I did, panic washed over me. I curled my fingers into my palms and closed my eyes.

I couldn't take it back. My real feelings were flying through cyberspace to Will's inbox right now. And that was exactly where they needed to be.

I hadn't realized how fancy Daniel's recital venue was going to be. His music academy had rented a historic theater not far from downtown for the event. It had a beautiful stone face, fluted columns on either side of the doors, and velvet curtains hanging inside the windows. Thankfully I was never one to dress down. My mauve dress was a little bright amid the bustle of arriving family and friends who seemed to favor grays and dark blues, but I didn't see why anyone should care about that.

I'd texted Mom to let her know I'd be coming, so she and Dad were waiting out front with the tickets. I forced my mouth to smile when she caught sight of me. We hadn't spoken directly since I'd kicked her out of my apartment a week and a half ago. But Mom was good at faking that everything was fine. As I wove through the crush toward them, she gave me a little wave and nudged Dad. He offered a hesitant smile of his own.

When I was growing up, the nervous look I saw on his face would have made me retreat inside myself—to protect myself from the displeasure he never showed as blatantly as Mom, but clearly felt all the same, and to protect *him* from having to confront whatever it was in me that scared him. The thought of what I might do next, I guessed. Of how far I might cross the line.

Seeing his expression now, I held my head higher against the discomfort that prickled over me. He had nothing to be scared of. I'd never actually done anything all that scary. And I was a lot tamer now than I'd been in my teens.

"You didn't call last Sunday," Mom said the second I reached them. No hello or how are you, just straight into her complaints.

"I'm sorry," I said. "It was a crazy day. I figured we'd have lots of time to talk here."

"Well," Mom said with a twitch of her shoulders, "I'd have appreciated a quick message letting me know that."

"You were really that eager to hear about my week?" I said. "You'd just seen me a few days before." And *that* conversation hadn't exactly gone well.

Mom's lips pursed in a way that told me she was

remembering that visit and purposefully not mentioning it. "It's just... I appreciate knowing you're thinking of us."

I paused, studying her. I'd always assumed she'd "appreciated" me staying in touch because it gave her some parental validation. Something in her tone now made me wonder if I'd underestimated her. Would she actually be hurt, not just embarrassed, if I cut her out of my life completely?

Just as a flutter of concern passed through me, she had to ruin the moment. "I suppose, with this very 'active' lifestyle you're leading, it's difficult to keep track of things like days of the week," she added with a jerk of her gaze away.

My jaw clenched, my skin going tight. What I'd actively been doing for most of last Sunday, after getting myself out of that bar, was watching movies and eating takeout with Avery. By the end of the day, it'd seemed inconceivable that I'd ever questioned the strength of our friendship. And it'd been an excellent reminder of why I didn't need to put up with people who saw me as any less worthy.

I readied myself, breathing slow and steady. I'd known this meeting would probably end like this.

"Can I have my ticket please?" I said, and held out my hand.

Mom glanced at Dad, who drew some folded papers from his jacket pocket. He handed one to me. "We are glad you could make it out," he said stiffly. "And Daniel was pleased to hear you were coming too."

"I suppose we should go in," Mom said.

"Before we do," I said. Slow. Steady. Firm. "I think we need a new ground rule. I'm happy to sit with you, *if* you can manage to keep your judgments about how I'm living my life to yourself."

"Fiona," Mom said, her eyes widening, "I never—"

"Don't, Mom," I interrupted. "You've already taken at least

two digs at me, and I haven't been here five minutes. I'm sick of it. So I'm not exactly the daughter you'd prefer. You've had more than twenty years to get over that fact—don't you think it's time you did? I have a job I like that pays well enough that I can take care of all my needs, I never come begging for loans or favors, I've never been arrested or put you in any danger, I've called you every Sunday since I moved out except this one time. If that's not good enough for you, fine. I don't want to hear about it anymore. So you can tell me now whether you can at least pretend to be okay with *me* or whether you're going to keep whining about who you wanted me to be. Because if it's the latter, I hope you'll understand if I pick a different seat."

Mom's mouth opened and closed a few times like a fish struggling for oxygen. "Fiona," Dad said, his thin face grayed, but she held up her hand.

"No," she finally managed in a pained voice. "Fiona's right. Maybe I've been too... pushy." She hesitated. "I think this is going to require a longer conversation than we have time for right now, before the concert. But I can promise not to make any more negative comments tonight. I would like us to be together for this, as a family."

It was the first time I'd heard her refer to me as part of the family in years. I hadn't known how much I'd been missing that. A little light of hope flickered on amid the tension inside me, bringing a real smile to my face.

"Good," I said. "We can talk more later."

We ambled in, past the wood-beamed lobby and into the auditorium with its rows of plush seats. A thick brocade curtain hid the stage. Dad spotted three free seats in a row near the front. As we hurried down the aisle toward them, Daniel appeared at a door beside the stage. He waved to us and hustled over, his thin pale face, like a younger version of Dad's, split with a grin I couldn't help returning.

"You made it," he said, and grabbed me in a hug. "It feels like ages since I've seen you, Fee."

It was, I realized. "Good to see you too," I said with a pang, squeezing him back and resisting the urge to muss his gelled hair as if he were still the little kid I'd grown up with. I'd have to reach way up to do it now. Had he grown another five inches in the last year?

"I hear there are congrats in order, as far as college applications go," I added as he let go.

His cheeks pinked. "Ah, thanks. I'm still not sure where I'm going to go. Anyway, I can't hang around right now, I just wanted to say hi. And I hope you like the piece I'm playing tonight... It kind of reminds me of you."

"That's a little frightening," I said teasingly, and his grin came back.

"Reminds me in a good way," he said. "You're sticking around afterward?"

I could tell, suddenly, how much it meant to him that I did. That whatever my parents said and felt about me, it hadn't rubbed off on Daniel the way I'd let myself fear it had. He'd never stopped seeing me as part of the family.

He was a good kid. I shouldn't let myself forget that.

"Yeah," I said. "I'll be here."

He raised his hand in farewell and darted back past the stage door. I sat down beside Mom with an unanticipated warmth easing through me.

The violinist and the saxophonist who played first and second had skills, but nothing I'd be thinking back to tomorrow. Daniel stepped out next, the lights bright on his white collared shirt and gelled-back hair. My kid brother perched on the piano stool and let his hands rest on the keys with the confidence I'd always envied in him, even though I knew it was part of the performance. He was probably sweating through that collar right now.

Then he started to play. And within a minute I was smiling again, even though my eyes had gone watery.

The piece was playful and erratic, a tinkling of notes here, a long lingering melody there. Keeping you on your toes while it made you ache to find out what would come next.

It reminded him of me, he'd said. Maybe I could believe that. That my ups and downs and irregularities could be that beautiful when the right person was looking at them.

Sixteen

"That is a *lot* of people," the Starlet murmured to me, rubbing her arms anxiously. We were peeking out at the massive line of fans waiting outside the temporary booth the mall had set up for this Saturday afternoon's meet and greet.

"You're a popular girl," I said, but my nerves were jumping too, if for completely different reasons. An event this public would be the perfect opportunity for Glowers to mingle with the crowd and look for opportunities to grab Charity's ear. I hadn't spotted any yet, but given how closely they'd dogged her recently, there had to be at least a few.

She was wearing her malachite bracelet, which would force them to keep their distance from her, at least. It wouldn't help us if they tried to cozy up to the staff or the other fans, as a stepping stone.

"We start in five," one of the event assistants told Charity. The Starlet nodded, tugging shut the door. She dragged in a breath and rolled her shoulders before shooting me a quick smile.

"Tell me again how I did with the reading this morning?"

I had to smile back. Her agent had come through with one of the parts he'd heard about—one that thankfully included no Glower involvement whatsoever, as far as I'd seen. "You were perfect. You hit all the right notes, lots of emotion but with a restraint that fit the character—if you don't get a callback I'll eat my hat."

"I've never seen you wear a hat," Charity said, but she was fully grinning now.

"It's a good thing I won't have to eat one then," I said, giving her a nudge. "But hey, even if that opportunity doesn't work out, it sounded like there are a couple more coming down the pipeline. I did tell you there were legit roles on the way, didn't I? And they're not going to stop."

"Miss Reece?" the assistant said. Charity followed her out to the greeting table while I hung back inside the booth. My smile held as I watched Charity wave to the crowd and heard the hail of squeals and excited shrieks thrown back at her.

The fans were ushered up group by group. They jittered as they beamed for selfies with Charity and made breathless comments as she scrawled her signature on the photos, magazines, and other paraphernalia they'd brought. In the second group, a flash of silver around one girl's wrist caught my eye. She was wearing one of the malachite bracelets too.

Someone had been keen enough to go for it, then.

I continued to scan the line for demons as it surged on toward the table. No unnatural glimmers or sparks gleamed amid the regular mortals. I couldn't believe the Glowers had ignored this event completely—what were they up to?

"Your lucky bracelet is so pretty!" another fan said as the Starlet signed the bottom of her shirt. She waved her own matching band on her wrist, and Charity raised her arm to clink them together.

"I know, right?" said the girl behind her, who was also wearing one. My pulse kicked up as I peered through the crowd with a different focus. Three already—had my idea really worked *that* well?

Now that I was looking for it, I saw the green and silver bracelets around wrists all down the line. I spotted even more as new groups of fans reached the table. In just a few minutes I counted a couple dozen. A sense of triumph tingled over me.

That was why the Glowers were staying away. They couldn't have come within ten feet of the entire event area without all the malachite in this place repelling them right back to wherever they'd come from. I'd built Charity a shield, all right—one they couldn't break through any more easily than they could have walked through steel.

"She looks like she's having fun," a different assistant said, coming up beside me.

"She always likes meeting fans," I said. When I glanced at the young woman, my gaze caught on another glint of silver and green. "You got the bracelet."

She blushed as she twisted it around her arm. "Yeah... Maybe the show is a little young for me, but I love it. And Charity is great in it. It seemed like a fun way to, I don't know, show some solidarity."

"Yeah," I said. This was more than I'd let myself hope for.

People wouldn't wear the bracelets forever, of course. But by the time they stopped, there was a good chance the Glowers would have given up this hunt and moved on.

The event gradually wound down, the end of the line finally coming into sight. I was looking around, making sure Charity hadn't left anything in the booth that she'd need to remember to bring home, when a familiar figure loomed at the edge of my vision. My heart leapt to my throat as I turned.

Will halted a couple paces away, his hands slung in the pockets of his slacks. "Fiona," he said. "Hey." The smile he offered was uncertain, but that green-eyed gaze pierced right through me.

"Hey," I said, my pulse still stuttering. "I didn't know you were coming." I hadn't heard from him at all since I'd sent the email a week and a half ago. I'd assumed that meant I'd burned that bridge too thoroughly to rebuild it.

Maybe I'd been wrong.

"Well, I had these plane tickets I needed to change to something I could actually use... Completely my fault, of course." The corner of his mouth slanted a bit higher, turning his smile wry. "I figured I can never have too much time with the family. And that if you and I were going to talk, it'd be better to do that in person."

"Okay," I said. What sort of talk were we going to have, exactly? I guessed this wasn't the best place for it.

"Charity's been all right?" Will said, nodding to his sister, who was hugging one last fan for a photo. "She got over being mad at you?"

I'd almost forgotten she ever was. "Yeah," I said. "We're back to being best buds."

He laughed, and Charity turned at the sound. "Will!" she cried, and darted over to throw her arms around him.

I ended up in the front beside Paul as he drove us back to the house, since Will had left his car back at Stanford. Charity chattered to her brother about the morning's audition and the other projects her agent was looking into, beaming at his remarks of approval. But when we reached the house, she gave me a pointed look as we stepped out of the car.

"I guess I'll go hang out in my room," she said, her gaze shifting from me to Will. "Let me know if you need me."

Heat pricked at my cheeks as she headed into the house. Her tone had made it clear that she didn't expect us to "need" her any time soon. Will raised his eyebrows at me, and I spread my hands.

"I didn't say anything," I murmured. "She's a perceptive girl."

"Well, because she's a curious girl too, why don't we take this conversation up to my room?"

I followed him up the stairs to the second floor. From what he'd said the last time I'd seen him, I knew his bedroom was at the back of the house, with that view of the neighbor's yard. I turned my back on the window after I'd stepped inside, not wanting to be reminded of the last place we'd been together—the place where we'd broken apart. Will closed the door to give us more privacy.

The room was plain: a double bed with a neatly tucked navy duvet, a couple bookshelves that mainly held storage boxes, a desk that was bare except for a pencil holder. "I wasn't home for the move," Will said as I took it in. "It doesn't quite feel like home yet."

"With that job in Stanford, I guess you'll end up moving out permanently, right?" I said.

"Probably." He paused. "I'm sorry I didn't reply to your email. I thought about calling, but..."

"You like to be able to see the person you're talking to," I said, remembering the comment he'd made the first time he'd come up to my apartment.

His lips twitched. "That, and I wanted you to be able to see me," he said, "while I attempt to properly say what I should have said before. But I should start with—I'm sorry for making those plans without talking to you and for getting upset when you didn't respond the way I was hoping."

The apology was so earnest, his eyes so intent on mine, that any worries I'd still had about where this conversation might go started to fade. "I could have handled it better too," I said.

He waved that admission off. "It made sense that you reacted that way. I should have known making those kind of assumptions was the wrong thing to do in any case, but especially after what you'd told me about your family. I just... To be completely honest, I think I was afraid that if I talked to you, told you how I felt, you'd say you weren't interested in pursuing anything with me beyond that week. And by buying the ticket and acting as if it were a done deal, I'd... make it harder for you to say no. Which is really awful. All I can say in my defense is I wasn't *consciously* thinking about it that way when I did it. I suppose I wasn't really 'talking' to myself either."

He lowered his head, studying the floor. The gesture, so small in comparison with a bulk of his body, sent sympathy shivering through me. Given all the mistakes I'd made out of fear, how could I hold this one against him?

"So I can assume it won't happen again, then?" I said lightly.

He peeked at me sideways. "It definitely won't. Does that mean... you are interested? In more?"

I stepped close enough to touch his arm. His body opened immediately, his other hand rising to stroke my hair as I gazed up at him. "I like you a lot," I said. "Yeah, I want to keep seeing you. I can't say where it's going to go, and I can't promise it'll be all fun and games like most of that week was... Are you sure that's what *you* want?"

Aren't there hundreds of Stanford girls who'd belong at your side more than I do?

I squashed that doubt before it could dig in too deeply. That was Will's call to make, not mine.

"Fiona..." He caressed my hair from my temple past my ear, the contact setting off sparks through my skin. "I meant what I said before. You make me feel more. More myself, more alive, more here. And it's not just that. I love seeing how much you care about people—about Charity, about your family, even if maybe you shouldn't so much with them. I love how hard you fight when you feel you need to. Maybe that seems normal to you, but from what I've seen, there aren't very many people like you out there. I want that. I want you. Even if it's hard sometimes."

"Okay," I said softly. Suddenly all I wanted was to feel him against me, skin to skin, as close as we could get. I eased closer so I could twine my fingers behind his neck. "Should we start now?"

"Start what?" he said with that wicked smile *I* loved.

I cocked my head. I wasn't looking to chase a rush right now. I didn't want to be swept away. I wanted to stay here with him, knowing exactly who and where I was.

"So I'm your girlfriend now," I said. "Where would you normally hook up with a new girlfriend?"

He lowered his head to mine until our foreheads touched. "That's what you want: what I'd normally do? I don't think the thrills should have to stop just because we're putting an official title on the relationship."

"I don't think so either," I said with a smile. "But we've done thrills already. We haven't done the official side. I... I haven't been anyone's girlfriend in years. I'd kind of like to see what that feels like."

He leaned in to kiss me then, gently at first, his lips coaxing mine apart. Then his tongue swept in demandingly to flirt with mine. I gripped the back of his neck, pulling him closer. His hands traced down the sides of my body and around to the small of my back.

"I think we'd stay right here," he said a little breathlessly when our mouths parted. "My room. My bed. Not too loud in case my parents are around. Take our time and explore each other."

"Sounds good to me," I said, and he tugged me into another kiss.

We kept kissing as he walked me to the bed. He stopped to yank down the blind on the window. Then he looked at me in the dim sunlight that seeped around its edges. My skin flushed as his gaze traveled over me with nothing but frank appreciation in his eyes.

He touched the hem of my shirt, and I raised my arms so he could pull it off. Underneath I was wearing the lacy black bra I'd had on the first night he'd come to my apartment. He grazed his knuckles over the thick fabric. Just a whisper of pressure reached through to my skin, but it was enough that my nipples hardened and my heart skipped a beat. Then he cupped my face and kissed me again.

I gave myself over to the kiss—not chasing the high of the pleasure, but taking note of everything that grounded me here: the faint taste of salt in Will's mouth, the hint of roughness on his lower lip, the way his head tilted a little more when I grazed that lip with my teeth. The solidness of his hands on my cheek and my shoulder, of his chest beneath my own hands. The thump of his heart within that chest. My own pulse echoing it.

The textured fabric of his shirt felt like an obstacle. I reached for the buttons, smiling into the next kiss at his hum of approval. One after the other, I cleared a path down his chest until the shirt parted completely. I splayed my fingers against his bare skin, my thumbs noting every ripple of the coarse hair that ran down the middle of it. Then I pushed the fabric over his shoulders so the shirt dropped to the floor.

Will wrapped his arms around me, enveloping me in warmth and a wisp of his citrusy cologne. I teased my fingers up his neck into his hair, and his hum became a rumble. He turned us toward the bed. As he set me down onto the edge of the mattress next to him, he lifted my legs over his so we could stay pressed together. His hand lingered on my thigh, tracing circles through my skirt.

His mouth left mine to travel down my neck and across my shoulder, then dipped down to my collarbone. His hand slid up my back, unclasping my bra. My fingers curled into his hair as he freed my breasts.

"Tell me what feels the best," he murmured against my skin. He ran his thumbs along the undersides of my breasts and stroked his fingers over the tops. Orbited the peaks without quite touching them. I nibbled his earlobe.

"That all feels good," I said. He grazed my nipples, and they strained toward him. "Mmmm, especially that." He brushed them more firmly, and I swallowed a gasp.

I pulled him back on the bed, lying down as he bent over me. He pinched my nipple, and I couldn't catch my gasp at that.

"Too much?" he said, and I shook my head.

"Good," I said. "Keep doing that."

He fondled one side and then the other, flicking and rubbing and pinching again as I arched into his hands. Then he dipped his head. "Yes," I whispered as he sucked one nipple into his mouth. "So good." I gripped his shoulders as an ache of pleasure spread through my chest, searing all the way down to the sweet spot between my legs. He swirled his tongue around the other nipple, and I barely strangled my cry.

He hadn't been kidding about the need to be quiet. His parents *might* be in hearing distance. Somehow that thought made what we were doing feel even hotter.

When he raised his head to kiss me on the lips again, I shifted onto my elbows and nudged him over. He gazed up at me with an eager grin as I considered my next move.

"What do *you* like best?" I asked, sliding my fingers over his chest. I leaned down to kiss the corner of his jaw, the underside of his chin, and nipped my way down his throat until he groaned.

"That," he said. "That's a very good start."

He gave another moan as I slicked my tongue up the same path. "Shhh," I reminded him, and he chuckled.

I kissed every inch of his chest, lingering over his nipples, over the curve at the bottom of his rib cage where the gentle contact made him suck in a breath. When I reached for his slacks, he caught my hand.

"My turn," he said, and flipped us over so he was on top again.

He licked a careful ring around my belly button as his thumbs glided back and forth just above the waist of my skirt. Then he found the side zipper and pulled it down before tugging the skirt off and tossing it onto the floor. His mouth followed the same line his thumbs had, above my panties now. He stroked my outer thighs and then worked his hands inward. Higher and higher, not quite touching the spot right between. I made a noise of protest.

"What do you want?" he said teasingly.

"Touch me. Kiss me. Everything."

He trailed a finger down my panties, and I quivered in anticipation. My hips curved up to meet him as he reached my opening. He increased the pressure, drawing my growing wetness through the fabric. Then he jerked the panties down and set his mouth over my clit.

I swallowed a whimper as he laved me there and then down to the opening below. His tongue darted into me, and I had to bite my lip to keep quiet. "Just like that," I managed to say, and sighed as he dipped his tongue deeper. I tangled my hands in his hair.

He came up for air, replacing his tongue with a slick finger. My hips canted as he found the most sensitive point inside me. He pressed against it with each thrust.

"I want to do what I didn't get to do last time," he said under his breath. "I'm going to make you come, and come again, and again if I can. Unless you have some objection?"

I shook my head, my breath hitching. Then he placed his mouth back over me, suckling my clit as a second finger joined the first inside me. My body was already trembling. Sweat beaded on my forehead as the pleasure built with each surge of his hand, until I was outright shaking with it. The orgasm broke over me with a gasp I couldn't contain and a tremor that rolled from my head to my curling toes.

As the wave subsided, I dragged Will up to kiss me on the mouth. I grasped the waist of his slacks as soon as it was within reach. This time he didn't protest as I undid them and shoved them downward. I grasped his hard-on through his boxer briefs, and he moaned against me.

"You always touch me just the right way," he said.

I stroked his length several times, until the liquid from the tip seeped through his boxers. Then I sat up, wrenching those down too. I took him into my mouth, all the way down, as far as I could. His breath stuttered as I ran my tongue over the underside, sliding my lips up and down him at the same time. I held the base of his hard-on firmly. Each twitch and stiffening made me smile as I used them to direct my attentions.

"Fiona," he rasped, and I could hear the warning in his voice. I didn't want us to end this here either. I caressed his length with my mouth one last time, and then I straightened up. Straddling him, I rubbed myself against the head of his hard-on. He gripped my thighs, urging me onward.

With a ragged exhale, I sank onto him. He filled me, inch by inch, until it felt as if there were no place inside of me he didn't touch.

Will ran his fingers up over my body to cup my breasts as I rocked over him, slowly at first and then gathering momentum. His hips pumped to match my pace. I found the angle that pressed against that sensitive point inside me and let him hit it again and again. My eyes started to roll back. He tweaked my nipples, and a growl broke from my throat. Then his hand slipped down to rub against my clit.

The sudden contact sent me over the edge. As he fingered me there, his length swelling inside me, another orgasm shuddered through my body. A tiny cry escaped me. I braced my hands against his chest, wanting to keep going for him, too shaken by the torrent of pleasure to completely control my movements.

Before the tremors had ended, Will looped his arm around me and turned us. In an instant, he was poised above me, his hardness still inside me. At first he kept his hips still even as I pressed up against him. He kissed me on the mouth and trailed his lips along my jaw and down my neck to nip the crook of my shoulder. His chest lowered until it brushed mine. Then he slid himself out and in, his sweat-slick skin caressing my nipples, his length filling me with that delicious friction. Harder, faster, until I was whimpering with the pleasure building all over again.

"Yes," he murmured, surging deeper. His breath was erratic now. I arched up to meet him, and he slipped a hand under my ass to hold me there. He thrust into me even harder, the way I liked it best.

I made a sound like a squeak, and that was it. The wave of pleasure washed over me once more, melting my bones and turning my muscles to jelly. The sensation kept coursing through me as Will's hips pounded against mine. With a choked sound of his own, he spilled himself into me.

He stroked in and out a few more times as his breath evened out. I touched his cheek, and he lowered his head to kiss me deeply. Then he sank onto the bed beside me, pulling me to him.

I squirmed even closer and ducked my head under his chin. In that moment, I couldn't imagine anywhere I'd rather be than cuddled against his solid body, more sated than I'd ever been in my life.

"I think I could get used to this girlfriend thing," I said, and he laughed.

"Good." He kissed my cheek. Then his voice became more serious. "It is going to be difficult, with you working here and me in Stanford. But... I don't mind driving down every weekend that I can, especially when it means I see the family too."

"Sometimes I could go up there," I said. "When I have a whole weekend free. Or we could meet halfway. You shouldn't have to do all the traveling."

"Of course," he said. "I just... I know you had your doubts about the whole relationship thing. I don't want you to feel that you have to make a bunch of sacrifices for it to work. The company that wants to hire me, they have a few different branches. I might be a lot closer in a couple month's time anyway."

Hearing that made my heart leap in a way I never would have expected a few weeks ago. I set my hand against his chest, feeling the thump of his pulse beneath my palm.

"I've never had any doubts about how much I like being with you," I said.

He tugged me up for another kiss, long and lingering. I settled back into his embrace, letting my eyes drift closed. A quiver of excitement tingled through me.

Maybe this *could* work. Maybe I could be a girlfriend type of girl to the right guy... and maybe Will was that guy.

I was looking forward to finding out.

Caught in the Dream

DEMONS OF FAME #3

One

THE ONE THING I CAN'T FORGET IS THAT I WOULD NEVER have seen my first Glower if I hadn't started that last fight with Rosa. That last, *stupid* fight.

I should have held my tongue. I should have appreciated what I had. It was our first good conversation in weeks. I'd texted her some images from the portfolio of a local artist I'd come across online, thinking they fit the look her dance studio was considering for their upcoming recital. She'd called me to tell me she loved them and that she'd just gotten a callback for an audition. In her excitement, the haze of stress and doubt that had surrounded her for most of the last few months fell away. It was a moment meant to be cherished.

But then she mentioned Isaac in that bright sparkling voice that used to be her normal tone, and all *my* doubts came rushing in. I'd managed to bury them for weeks. It had been easier when I could see how much my girlfriend needed me to be steady for her through her own struggle. Easier to believe I was the one she wanted. That one moment when she tossed out his name so casually was all it took to yank my jealousy back to the front of my mind and into my mouth. And back then I didn't have the self-control to catch it.

"Isaac was there when you got the call?" I said. I think I even interrupted her.

Rosa paused. In the gap when nothing but the fizz of static carried through the speaker of my hand-me-down phone, I felt her sparkle dying.

"Teo, don't start that again," she said. She sounded suddenly weary. I should have stopped and salvaged the conversation. I could have. But my mouth was already moving.

"It just seems weird that he gets to hear your good news before I do," I said.

"It's not like I planned it that way," Rosa said. "You know he has his contemporary classes down the street. We ran into each other after, we grabbed a snack, and that was when they called."

"How many times have you seen him this week?"

"We're just *friends*, Mateo. Jeez. I've told you that a million times. What, do you want me to just never talk to him again?"

Even then, I knew better than to answer honestly. I'm not sure what set me off. Maybe it was the fact that she'd avoided answering the actual question, which made me suspect she'd seen Isaac more than even she thought was normal. Maybe it was the pressure of having held in my concerns for so long. Because I knew the right answer, and yet there I was saying, "Yes. That's what I want. He's after you, Rose—it's not right."

I still remember the sound she made, as if she'd tried to laugh but was too choked up to manage more than a strangled cough. It made my gut bunch into a ball that only got tighter when she started talking.

"Of course," she said. "Because he couldn't actually like me as a person, right? Why would anyone just like *me*? Why should

I get to have a friend who actually understands what I'm going through—the classes, the auditions, everything with the dancing that you don't have a clue about? You know what's not right? It's you turning my good news into a thing to complain about. You can't be the only person I ever talk to, Teo."

My skin went cold all over. She'd gotten pissed off at me before, but she'd never sounded so serious. Finally, my better sense caught up with me. All I wanted to do was take it back. Restart from the beginning.

It's too bad it was too late.

"I didn't mean it like that," I protested, and Rosa cut me off before I could continue.

"Are you sure? Because that's what I heard."

"I'm sorry. I love you, Rosa, that's all. I don't want to lose you. I'm sorry."

"I don't want to talk to you any more today," she said. "There are some things you just shouldn't say. You should keep them to yourself."

And then she hung up on me, an ice-sharp click on the line.

I was left sitting in my bedroom with a silent phone at my ear. Rosa had never hung up on me before either. I lowered the phone, but only to my lap, and sat there waiting for her to call back, to apologize and finish talking things out.

The phone's screen went dark and stayed that way. The chill on my skin slowly sank into my stomach.

She'd been so on edge lately. She'd needed this happy moment, and I'd ruined it. I had to make it up to her.

I called her number, but it went straight to voice mail. She'd turned off her phone—or blocked me? That only made me more worried.

If she wouldn't speak to me on the phone, I'd just have to go to her.

It seemed like a simple enough answer when I decided it. I swung by her house in the suburb next to ours on my longer weekend runs all the time. Biking would get me there faster, though. I grabbed the ten-speed from the porch and took off.

I hadn't paid attention to how hot it was, even with the sun just dipping below the horizon. A humid breeze wafted around me, still carrying the burnt wood smell of the forest fire that had finally died out this morning. Within a couple of minutes, I couldn't think about anything except the ache in my chest and the sweat trickling down my back. I was going to be a mess by the time I got to Rosa, but I couldn't let myself stop. I had a sense, like a stopwatch ticking down in the back of my head, that every second counted.

I still wasn't fast enough. When I finally made it to Rosa's house, panting and drenched, I knew right away she was gone. The old Hyundai she'd scraped together enough money to buy after her sixteenth birthday that spring wasn't in its usual spot by the curb. The streetlamp gleamed yellow off the blob of oil where it had leaked.

There were plenty of places Rosa could have gone, but I didn't have time to check them all. I could make a reasonable guess. When she started feeling the pressure too much, when she got that frantic glint in her eyes like a mouse pinned by a cat's paws, she didn't want to be around people. She liked to drive out into the canyons, onto the loneliest roads she could find. A couple of times this month, I'd sat beside her as the tires bumped and the engine sputtered with each dip of the potholes she didn't slow down for, watching silently until the tension around her mouth relaxed and the color came back into her knuckles where she gripped the steering wheel. I knew her favorite route, even if *I* wasn't old enough yet to get my license and drive it myself.

I didn't really believe I had a hope in hell of catching up with her. I just needed to be moving. Every moment I delayed, fear burrowed deeper into me.

I pushed on past the houses and the streetlamps. By the time I left them behind for dry earth and stumpy trees, the smoky smell had thickened, rubbing my throat raw with every breath. The muscles in my runner's legs were throbbing. I stared down the road through the dimming daylight, willing a pair of headlights to blink into view in the distance.

I was just rounding the first curve into the canyon proper when I saw a different sort of smoke. A plume of it streaked up from the slope beside the road.

Somehow I found a fresh burst strength to apply to the pedals. The road slanted down, and I careened with it, my heartbeat pounding. The wind brought a scorched chemical smell to my nose.

Rosa's red Hyundai lay on its side in the midst of the brush, some twenty feet down the slope from the road. She'd kept going straight where the road turned, smashed through the guardrail, and tumbled on down. From the skid marks, she'd realized at the last second and tried to correct her course. Too late.

The instant I recognized her car, my mind detached from my body. My legs kept moving automatically. I dropped my bike and scrambled down the slope. My hand whipped out my phone, my thumb tapping in the emergency number. I think I shouted her name. It was only when my feet jerked to a halt a few feet shy of the car that my consciousness slammed back into my head with a heave of my breath, as I gaped at the glowing figure slumped in the passenger seat.

The shimmer radiating off the figure's skin blurred his features—and highlighted Rosa's where she lay crumpled against the shattered window on the driver's side. My gaze jerked from the glowing thing to her. Her face had turned sallow around the blood that streaked across it from forehead to jaw. Her eyes were dull beneath her half-lowered eyelids. The soft lips that had spoken my name little more than an hour ago parted to emit a scarlet dribble.

A yell ricocheted up my throat, rough-edged as the rocks that littered the ground around the crash site. Then I recognized the shining head now bending to Rosa's shoulder.

It was Isaac. The boy who'd tangled me up in jealousy nearly every day since Rosa had first mentioned him—a fellow dancer, a guy two years older than me, with that confident smile and that perfectly tousled flaxen hair. But I'd never seen him *glow*. The light seemed to sear from the whites of his eyes and the tips of his fingers as he pressed his hand to Rosa's chest.

My first thought was that he meant to help her. Then I saw that the light in him was searing brighter as another light lit in her—and flowed out of her body into his.

"No!" I shouted as I hurtled the last few steps to the car. My foot caught on one of those scattered rocks. I tripped, catching myself on my elbows as I sprawled. A flash of pain shot up my arms. Ignoring it, I scrambled onto my hands and knees.

Isaac was gone. There was no one on the slope except me, no one in the wrecked car except Rosa's still, bloody body.

I crawled to her side. Her arm was bent at an impossible angle, her pale palm tipped toward the sky. I curled my fingers around her limp ones.

"I'm sorry," I said, as if my apology could turn back time. "I'm so sorry, Rose. I'm sorry."

I must have apologized to her a hundred times as the sirens pealed toward us. I never let go of her hand.

Two

For his first show after his latest stint in rehab, Malignant J was in top form. He swaggered across the stage, spinning out the lyrics of his final encore with a speed I'd always found incredible, pumping up the crowd to a roar with a sweep of his arm. The thick, square-topped silver ring we'd made a point of letting the paparazzi capture since his re-emergence glinted under the spotlights. I'd seen a matching glint on the fingers or dangling from chains around the necks of dozens of fans when I'd surveyed the line outside the venue before the concert. From back stage, watching the audience as they raised their hands in applause, I caught several more.

I doubted anyone in the crowd had a clue that the sigil imprinted on that piece of bling could shake up a Glower's ability to move through this world. They didn't have a clue that demons like the Glowers even existed. Not even Malignant J knew that. But none of them needed to know for the sigil to do its work.

My client was one of the top rap artists of the year, with a reputation for instability and misbehavior—exactly the sort of target the Glowers preferred. They weaseled their way into the lives of creative artists by exploiting every weakness they could, offering glimpses of the supernatural inspiration they could provide to increase the artist's eagerness for their company. Then, when the target was hooked, they presented a deal shrouded in misleading language that amounted to selling one's soul. When the artist accepted, the demons placed a mark that allowed them to more easily inspire the creative highs the artist longed for—and to more easily feed off the energy generated during those highs, until the person was little more than a shell of their former self. In the end, whether through an accident caused by an addled mind or a desperate act to end the downward spiral, anyone marked would die.

When I'd first taken this assignment, a Glower had already been circling Malignant J in the guise of a drug-enabling associate. It had started to earn the rapper's trust by boosting his confidence in moments of doubt with his music. I'd managed to discourage that demon within a week, but there had always been more on the fringes. Yet tonight, with all those rings and their sigils shining in the crowd, not a single glowing figure had come stalking after my client's soul.

Fiona would be happy to hear my report, I thought as I scanned the audience again. This new strategy of using our clients' fan bases to help deter Glowers had been her brainstorm. The best part of it was, if we reached enough people, we'd be protecting at least some of the many artists who hadn't risen to enough prominence to become clients of the Tether Society yet —people like Rosa. With every new campaign, with every new group of people carrying sigils or malachite or the other materials that disrupted the demons' energies, we made the whole world less welcoming to Glowers on the hunt.

Malignant J—or Jayden, as those of us who worked with him closely usually called him to his face—looked pleased with the night's outcome too. He grinned as he raised his mic and gave one last shout-out to the crowd. A wave of cheers and excited screams swelled up in response. Jayden saluted his fans before sauntering off stage into the wings, where I was waiting.

"Great performance," I said, falling into step beside him as he headed to his dressing room. "I think the audience would have stayed with you all night if you'd kept going, they were so into it."

"It felt pretty great, Matty," Jayden said in his low voice that was rhythmic even when he wasn't turning a rhyme. After five months, I no longer had to suppress a wince at the nickname he'd given me, which sounded like it should belong to a child under ten, not a man of twenty-two. "I'm glad to be back."

"You're starting off with a bang," I said. "The two appearances tomorrow, and shows all through the week—it'll be nice seeing Miami again. Your fans there, nothing beats their enthusiasm."

Jayden came to a halt outside his dressing room door. His backup musicians and dancers hadn't made their way into the bowels of the venue yet, so we were alone in the narrow air-conditioned hall. He turned to look me in the eye. It wasn't that hard—though he had at least fifty pounds on me, his broad frame draped in the bulky bomber jacket he favored for performances, we were the same height—but meeting my gaze so directly seemed to embarrass him. He rubbed the back of his neck.

"Matty, look, you're not coming to Miami."

I blinked. "What do you mean? We're scheduled there on Monday."

"*I'm* scheduled there." Jayden paused and sighed. "I figured I should let you know ahead of time. It seems dishonest not to. I talked to my manager, and we're requesting a replacement advisor from your 'Society.'"

He dropped his gaze. I was staring at him. I reined in my reaction, forcing myself to tilt my head casually.

"A replacement," I repeated. "Why? Is there a problem?" I'd thought everything had been going well in the two weeks since he'd gotten out of rehab. He hadn't mentioned any concerns. We hadn't argued. It didn't make sense. And even though he'd been good about wearing that ring regularly, with his substance abuse issues the Society would definitely insist on continued monitoring for at least the near future.

"Not with your work," Jayden said, holding up his hands. "Don't get me wrong, brother. I've said nothing but good things about that. It's just a personal differences kind of thing. We've never really gelled. You've got to know that. We've had some good times, but there's something about you, the way you keep to your own self, it makes me a little tense. I need to be around people I can relax with, you know? Folks with more of a chill vibe. It's not your fault."

"I'm sorry to hear you feel that way," I said. What else was there, really, that I *could* say? My mind tripped back over a long line of memories: hanging with Jayden and the other guys on the road, joining in their banter, always adapting my mood to what he seemed to need. Maybe I'd kept some of my thoughts to myself, but who didn't? I was here to support him, not the other way around.

But I didn't know what a "chill vibe" would be, let alone how to produce one if I hadn't managed to already, so I couldn't promise to start delivering one. Arguing with him certainly wouldn't be very "chill." I swallowed the tightness in my throat and added, "I've really enjoyed working with you. I'll still be listening."

"Thank you, man. I mean it." Jayden clapped me on the shoulder. "I hope they give you some guy a lot less crazy than me to deal with next time. Or maybe one of those hot lady pop stars, hmmm?"

He cracked a grin and tapped his hand against the dressing room door. "Give me ten. The car should be around soon. I expect they'll want you to stay on duty 'til tomorrow anyway."

Normally I wouldn't have let him out of my sight in a venue like this, but with that ring glinting on his finger and its duplicate carried throughout the flood of fans who'd be slowly dispersing around the club, I wasn't worried any Glower would get to him. So I took the dismissal with a nod and left him, climbing the stairs to the private back exit.

I guessed all those times I'd hung back with him before, shot the breeze while he wound down from a show, I'd actually been making him *tense*.

It happened sometimes—a Tether and a client just weren't the right fit. Not that big a deal. But I realized as I reached for the door handle that my jaw had clenched. That I'd gone rigid inside with those words echoing through me.

No, not his words. Avery's, from nearly a year ago.

I feel like you're never really relaxed with me. Comfortable. And if you're not by now, it seems like it's probably never going to happen. Better that we accept that instead of trying to force this to be something it's not, right?

Just not the right fit, me and her, after almost a year together. As she'd seen it, anyway.

But that was long past, and I shouldn't be thinking about it, or her, not any more. I'd be assigned to another client, and life would go on as it always did.

I stepped out into the cool night air of the alley, grimacing at the gasoline smell wafting from the busy road around the corner. The honking of L.A. traffic carried with it, but Jayden's car hadn't turned up yet. A couple of Jayden's bodyguards were standing at the alley's entrance, ensuring that the concert-goers continued on their way rather than sneaking around to gawk. I took in the mural the club owners had hired some street artists to paint on the back of the building. Impressively vibrant, and I liked the use of lines. It was a shame hardly anyone must get to see it.

I turned the other way and realized someone had slipped past the bodyguards. At first glance, I didn't quite mind. The young woman standing in the amber glow of a bulb over the back door of a neighboring building was striking in a very enjoyable way. From her profile, I could see a large dark eye and elegant nose, waves of bronze-brown hair cascading to mid-back, a trim torso and generous hips clothed in a sleek black dress. If I had a type, she hit every criterion on the list. For that instant, seeing her knocked any lingering thoughts of Avery from my head.

Then the woman swiveled toward me, and two things happened simultaneously. I was struck even harder by the beauty of her face and the intensity of our gazes connecting, and I registered what was off about the light falling over her. It wasn't *just* falling over her. The glint in her hair and the shine on her tan skin didn't shift with her movements, but beamed steadily, as if emanating from some source other than the bulb above her.

Because it was. It was emanating from *her*.

The jolt of attraction that had shot through me as our eyes met dissolved into disgust. Not a woman. A Glower, in yet another deceptive disguise.

She smiled welcomingly at me as I strode toward her, as if

we were going to have a friendly conversation. That only made the words to order her gone leap up my throat faster. I was just opening my mouth when she held out her slim hand to me and said, "Mateo. I was hoping I'd find you."

I'd never had a Glower call me by name on first meeting. I paused, sizing her up. I'd definitely have remembered those looks if I'd seen them before, but a Glower could put on any appearance it wanted. More telling was the aura of energy they gave off, a sense impossible to measure but as distinct as a whiff of a scent or a taste tickling over your tongue.

This one didn't feel remotely familiar. Shoulders braced, I accepted her hand for a brief shake to see if the physical contact would tug a memory loose. Her skin was smooth and warm against mine, and indicated nothing else. I let go, brushing my palm against my slacks. She gave no indication that the gesture offended her.

"I have a proposition I'd like to discuss with you," she said with that same slightly wry smile. I'd have found it charming on a real human being.

"I'm not interested in discussing anything with a demon," I said. "It's time for you to leave."

Her voice dropped to a purr. "But how can you know you're not interested when you haven't heard what I'm offering?"

"Sometimes knowing who's doing the offering is enough," I replied and made a shooing motion. "Get out of here. Or are you going to make me call over Security? They're right there."

The Glower sighed. Her breath glittered as it traveled into the air between us. "So closed-minded, all of you Tethers are. I know things about you, Mateo. I could be very useful to you. And to the rest of your Society too."

The fact that she knew my name made it difficult to dismiss that as a total bluff. Why had she come to *me*? But my answer was the same. "Not interested," I repeated firmly, ignoring the flicker of curiosity. It didn't matter why she'd picked me or what she thought she knew. She was trying to manipulate me—that was the only game the Glowers knew.

The club's back door creaked behind me, and Jayden's jovial voice rang out. "Matty, what are you doing? You can pick up the ladies when you're off the clock."

The Glower's gaze darted to my client with more enthusiasm than I liked. My hands fisted. She spoke before I had to.

"I can see this isn't the best time for a full conversation. That's fine. I'll find you again. For now, consider it, Mateo. How often does one of us come to you looking to make a fair deal? Think of all the things I might be able to do for you."

She waggled her fingers at me and ambled away, her hips swaying with her languid stride. I pulled my attention back to my client, who was shaking his head at me. I tried to smile at him, to pretend nothing was wrong, but my mouth was tight.

That last comment, the way she'd said it—it hadn't sounded quite right. Not quite right in a way that gnawed at me.

I turned it over in my head a dozen times while I rejoined Jayden and we climbed into the car that had just pulled into the alley. It was only as I dropped into the seat that recognition hit me.

The strangeness hadn't been in the words she'd uttered or her inflection. It'd been in her voice itself. For that last sentence, she traded the sly sweet murmur she'd been using before for a timbre a little higher, a little rougher, though still sweet enough to my ears for it to twist around my heart.

The Glower had spoken to me in Avery's voice, perfect to a note.

Three

"THERE'S NO ACCOUNTING FOR A CLIENT'S TASTES," Sterling said briskly as he looked up from Jayden's file the next morning. I was sitting on the other side of my Tether Society supervisor's oversized oak desk, my elbows over the arms of the chair, waiting to hear my next assignment. I'd hoped this would be a simple matter of in and out, but despite his comment, Sterling looked less than pleased. His mouth twisted as he turned to slide the file back into the metal cabinet to the left of the desk, and his deep brown skin appeared to have grayed. No, he did not look pleased at all.

I considered pointing out how much I'd managed to accomplish with Jayden, but the thought of speaking made my chest tighten up. If Sterling wanted to know my thoughts on how the assignment had gone, he'd ask. It wouldn't improve his current impression of me if I started blurting out excuses unprompted.

"Well, Mateo." He folded his hands together on the desk. "It seems we need to find a more... appropriate position for you.

I'm not sure placing you with another client is the best course of action."

I'd never imagined I'd hear those words, even in a worst-case scenario. There were too few of us who could see the Glowers and so many clients in need of protection. So many scheming demons trying to turn their heads and steal their souls. What had Jayden said to the Society in confidence that had made Sterling draw that conclusion?

"I'm ready to go back in the field," I said, keeping my voice calm. "I'll even start tonight—I was supposed to work this weekend anyway. There has to be somewhere I could be of use."

"There is," Sterling said. "I'm just thinking it may not be in the field."

"If there's an area of my work in which you think I need further training in first—" I started, and Sterling shook his head.

"This isn't about your ability. I know you're fully capable." The tensing of his lips seemed to turn that statement into a lie. He ran the heel of his hand over his short wiry curls. "I simply feel you could contribute the most at the present moment here in the office. The work you did on the new database was exemplary. Organization is clearly one of your strengths. We should play to that."

"I'd be happy to continue fitting in office hours around my client scheduling the way I did before," I offered. Better that than leave someone unguarded. "With the shortage of Tethers..."

"I think what you'll do here may help with that... situation," Sterling said. "You've been on the job most of the last two weeks —take this weekend for yourself. On Monday morning, I'll have the details of your new assignment ready."

He stood up then, my cue to leave. I got to my feet slowly.

"I hope you know if anything does come up with my performance that concerns you, I'm always open to feedback and improvement," I said, one last try.

"I have no doubt of that, Mateo," Sterling said. "If I were concerned, I would let you know."

There had to be some reason he was demoting me to office duty. Did he really believe I couldn't handle the criticism? I'd never once let my temper or any other emotion get the better of me while I'd been training in, in the two and a half years between Rosa's death and my eighteenth birthday. I'd always kept things professional with my clients, even in the most stressful situations. It didn't make sense.

I found no answer in Sterling's eyes, only resolve. Suppressing a frown, I bobbed my head in acceptance and headed out into the office proper.

It was a small office space, generic in both layout and design, which might have seemed surprising given how unusual our work was, but I'd always thought that was the point. We wanted clients and their representatives, who couldn't have understood what we were really protecting them from, to feel at ease. A row of ten cubicles, five by two, stood beside a small lounge area composed of two armchairs and a couch, all in gray linen. An exposed brick wall next to it offered a tiny bit of character that was offset by the Van Gogh sunflowers print hanging on it, something I suspected the decorator had picked off a top ten list of popular paintings. Beyond the row of supervisory offices I'd just left lay the entrance to the kitchenette and the locked door to the massive records room. I'd spent most of Jayden's rehab time entering the reports from those stainless steel shelves into our new computer database. Occasionally I'd stumbled on an interesting observation, but mostly it had been drudge work.

And that was what Sterling felt I was best suited for.

Other than the cubicle in the far corner that was the permanent station of the Society's receptionist, Yelena, the desks in the main room belonged to whoever happened to need them on any given day. It was late enough this Friday afternoon that the few people who'd been seated at them when I'd come in had left for the weekend—except for Fiona, who was tapping away at a laptop with the frenetic energy she brought to everything she did.

It would have been easier to slip out and avoid questions, but Fiona looked up at the exact moment I glanced at her. She swept her fine black hair away from her face and motioned me over with a grin. At that point, walking away would have raised even more questions.

"What are you working on now?" I asked as I ambled over. Fiona had been spending extra time in the Society office lately, but only because her current client was settling into the protective habits that meant a Tether's presence was only needed for occasional check ins—and because that brainstorm of Fiona's about using the fan bases had taken off so well.

"Look at this," she said, tugging the laptop's screen toward me. I recognized the image on it at once: it was a variation on the repelling sigil etched on Jayden's ring. This was a simpler configuration, drawn with thick black strokes, the ends of the curved lines sharpened to points. Nothing about the website Fiona had brought it up on struck me as familiar, though.

"What are you using it for?"

"Temporary tattoos!" she crowed, and motioned to a description to the right of the image. "They're perfect for the kid and preteen audiences, probably can grab some of the teen demo too. We had a meeting with one of the Disney reps this morning, and I convinced him to introduce the symbol as a wink to 'insiders' in some of their shows and in the general fan club. Then we have them offer swag like this, and we've potentially got hundreds of thousands of Glower repellers all over the country. Those demons won't be able to cross the street in Idaho without feeling the sting!"

"That's impressive," I said, meaning it. "I don't understand why no one thought of trying this sort of strategy before."

"You mean you don't believe I'm just that smart?" Fiona's grin widened to show she was only teasing. "The world is changing. Twenty-five, thirty years ago when people like Sterling were just getting started, there wasn't any way to offer up our own customized merch this easily. The magic of the internet is a wonderful thing."

She'd left her phone sitting face up on the desk. When it chimed with a new text, my gaze darted down. Before I caught myself, I'd already registered the name. Avery Harmen. *Still good for six?*

Fiona grabbed the phone to tap in her reply. I returned to studying the tattoo design, but she'd obviously noticed me noticing, because when she set the phone aside—on the other side of the computer, out of my view—she said, in a slightly apologetic tone that rankled me, "I'll be taking off soon. The boyfriend and I are meeting Avery and Colin for dinner."

"Sure," I said with a shrug. "I've got to get going too."

Avery was by all appearances and reports head over heels for her former client turned occasional bandmate and ongoing boyfriend, Colin Ryder, and I was glad she was happy. I couldn't really be anything else, even if said boyfriend was an increasingly famous rock star. I wasn't competing with him. Avery and I were only friends now.

And if I still got a bit of a twinge looking around the office with her on my mind, when my attention fell on the spot by the couch where I'd first seen her—reassuring a frantic client with that firm but warm manner of hers, flashing a smile at me as they'd left that had made me instantly sure I wanted to get to know her—that was no one's concern but my own.

"Got any exciting plans for the weekend?" Fiona asked with a wiggle of her dainty eyebrows.

I'd expected to still be working, to be honest. "I guess that depends on your definition of exciting," I said. "There's a new exhibition at The Broad I might go to."

"Hmmm," Fiona said. Mischief sparkled in her dark eyes. "Have you met the newbie yet? Sofie?"

"I've heard of her," I said. "She just started training this winter, right? We haven't crossed paths."

"Well, you should try to," Fiona said. "She's cute. Very cute. It'd do you some good to get to know her a little, I think."

One of the few things worse than working with your ex-girlfriend is fellow colleagues who suspect you're still hung up on said ex-girlfriend. I tried to summon a spark of enthusiasm at the thought of very cute newbie Sofie to satisfy Fiona, but it was difficult when I knew essentially nothing about her.

"Sure," I said again. "I'd imagine I'll see her around soon."

Fiona gave me a measured look. I had a feeling I wasn't going to like the next words out of her mouth, but I was saved from having to hear them by the creak of the office's main door. Fiona's head jerked around, and her face lit up so bright I could have mistaken her for a Glower.

"Will!" she said, in that pleased chirpy voice that came out when she was excited. She shut the laptop and darted around the cubicles to clasp hands with the broad-shouldered, blond-haired guy who'd just stepped inside. It was strange seeing the blush that crept into her cheeks as he bent to kiss her. I'd known Fiona since I first started training with the Society, and I'd never noticed her so giddy over a guy. But she'd kept this one around for two months so far.

"Bye, Mateo!" she called with a wave over her shoulder. Will dipped his head to me. We'd never really spoken, but he seemed nice enough. I was glad for Fiona too.

I started after them and hesitated when it occurred to me that Avery and Colin might be swinging by to pick them up.

So what if they did? I pushed myself onward, down the stairs and out onto the street.

Fiona and Will were just getting into a cab by the corner. As I watched it take off, I wondered what I *should* do now that I had my whole weekend free. The art exhibition would only take up one afternoon. I could call up one of the friends I'd had limited contact with since starting Tether work full time and see if I could reestablish that connection, especially if I was going to have more regular work hours for the foreseeable future. My cousin Ricky had been badgering me about hanging out too, but then he'd probably pump me for music industry contacts like he always did.

What I really wanted to do right now, I realized as I headed east, was to take a nice long run. Burn away the knots in my stomach with the pounding of my feet on the pavement and the flow of air through my lungs. I could have jogged to my apartment building from the office, except I'd dressed to look my best for this appointment with Sterling, and these slacks weren't cut for comfortable running.

When I got home, I decided, I'd change and head right back out. The park a few blocks over made for more enjoyable scenery anyway. I could even—

A figure stepped out in front of me from the narrow alley between a pizza place and a vintage clothing shop. I stopped in my tracks, my hands clenching when I saw her face.

The young woman who'd approached me outside the club two nights ago—the *Glower* who'd approached me—gazed at me with a slanted smile.

She drifted forward, the whites of her eyes gleaming.

"No," I said, moving to step around her. "I told you I don't want anything to do with you."

She caught my arm, her grip stronger than I'd have expected. "Mateo," she said, "you don't know what I'm offering yet. I don't want to hurt anyone. I want to help."

I didn't try to restrain my laugh. "Somehow I find that difficult to believe."

I hadn't meant to meet her eyes again, but they drew me back almost hypnotically as her fingers tightened around my wrist. Her irises were a deep shade of brown that was close to burgundy, her pupils dilated.

"You're upset," she said. "Something happened this afternoon. You're afraid someone is unsatisfied with you." Her smile grew. "People are always wanting things from you that you don't know how to give, aren't they? I can teach you it. How to show them what they need. How to set them at ease. Opening people up is our specialty."

I jerked my arm away. "I don't know what you're talking about," I said, as if she wouldn't be able to sense that was a lie. My heart was suddenly thudding. I'd known Glowers could read a person's emotions and sensitivities—I'd seen it happen with clients dozens of times. I'd just never had one direct that ability at me, at least not so baldly.

"I can give you everything you could wish for," the Glower went on, ignoring my protest. Her hand hovered in the air between us. "I'm not asking very much. I only want you to listen. My people are uneasy. We need a change. The current situation between your Society and ours, it is unsustainable."

My people. That gave me pause. "You're speaking on behalf of the others like you?" I said.

"To an extent. There is not much agreement amongst us. But some of us recognize that we can't go on like this. And to make a change, we'll need an ally on your side of the conflict."

"I'm not forming any allegiances with you," I said.

She spread her hands. "Not an ally, then. An open mind? To hear the whole story and decide based on that what you're willing to do after."

I wasn't completely sure what sort of change she was talking about, but one thing was clear: the Glowers were struggling. For one of them to seek out a Tether like me, to reveal even the vague idea of a problem they couldn't handle alone, something had to be *very* wrong.

And I could be the one to find out what, to hear the plans they were contemplating. I could bring that information back to Sterling and the Society's directors. What this "woman" could tell me might be worth ten times more in our battle against the Glowers than even Fiona's massive campaign.

If nothing else did, *that* should settle the question of my strengths in the field.

The moment that hope sparked inside me, I shoved it down under the skepticism I already felt. I couldn't let the Glower seen any enthusiasm, not if I wanted to keep the upper hand. She'd take any chance she could to manipulate me.

"And if I decided that I—we—could do nothing?" I said, keeping my expression terse.

"Then at least I tried," the Glower said. "The deal I'm proposing right now isn't conditional on your response, only that you allow me the time to make my case. Other deals... We could discuss those later, if you chose." She arched her eyebrows suggestively.

"What does 'allowing you the time' mean, exactly?"

"We will work with what time *you* choose to give me. The only restriction is that if you stop listening, I will stop giving."

"Giving what?" I said. She wouldn't still be proposing this if she knew what *I* was hoping to gain from the information she shared.

She turned toward the alley. "Come here," she said. "I'll give you a taste. You don't even have to ask. You just have to let yourself accept. That will be the first lesson."

I entered the alley after her, keeping a careful eye on her movements. She had no reason to try to physically harm me, and there wasn't anything else she could do to me without my permission, but that didn't mean I trusted her an inch. The traffic noise faded along with the daylight between the high walls on either side of us.

"I know just the thing," she murmured, with a roll to her vowels that hadn't been there before. She swiveled toward me again, and her entire body shimmered brighter.

She'd shifted her form. Her hair had darkened to black and shortened to full curls that flirted in layers near her jawline. Her face had lengthened, her skin taken on a deeper tan tone, her lips become more full. The figure below that face was an hourglass now, generous breasts perched above a slim waist, daring the buttons of the green day dress that had replaced her black gown to pop open.

My heart flipped and my legs locked as the unbidden image of those buttons' threads snapping and the dress gaping open to reveal softly curving flesh triggered my memory. It was a familiar form, a familiar face, though one I hadn't seen in several years.

"Miss Bertolini." The name dropped from my mouth before I'd finished thinking it.

The Glower smiled with my seventh grade teacher's coy air. I hadn't *thought* about Miss Bertolini in years, but my body obviously hadn't forgotten her. My first crush. The first object of many nocturnal fantasies as I fumbled through self-explorations beneath my bed sheets.

The Glower had found those memories, just like that.

She reached for me, trailing her fingers down my shirt so lightly the fabric barely grazed my skin, but the contact went straight to my groin. Christ. I was already getting hard.

I stepped back. "No," I said. "I don't think—"

"Then don't think," the Glower interrupted in Miss Bertolini's sultry voice. "Accept. This is a gift. I expect nothing at all in return. All you need to do is stay here and feel."

The worst thing was some part of me wanted to say yes. A part that held my feet in place as she closed the distance between us, as she tipped her head so close to mine that her breath tingled over my jaw and her hand glided down my chest again to caress my waist just above my growing erection. I hadn't been with anyone since Avery, and that fact struck me as suddenly absurd. If this woman could provoke such a strong a reaction in me with a simple touch, what would it feel like to take everything she offered?

"Accept," she whispered, and the dark waves of her hair shimmered with that alien light. Not a woman, I corrected myself, my gut knotting. A Glower. A demon. The same sort of creature that had sapped away Rosa's spirit, pushed her to the edge, and then sucked the last shreds of life from her. And this one was giving me a perfect demonstration of why so many marks we saw ended up not just creatively but sexually involved with those who preyed on them. What could be more addictive than a lover who could sense what you wanted before you even knew yourself and cater their every gesture to your desires?

My thoughts jerked back to the first Glower I'd known. Had

it been like that between Rosa and Isaac? She'd always denied they were anything but friends. But clearly he could have offered her more pleasure than fifteen-year-old me had been capable of in my inexperience. I already knew they'd been closer in at least some ways than she'd ever admitted to me, given the way Glowers always entwined themselves in their marks' lives.

It shouldn't have mattered. Rosa was long dead, and whatever sins she might have committed against me were far more the demon's fault than hers. But the thought that she might not have been faithful to me in any way at all, that even when she was with me in those last few months she might have been longing for his touch just as much as his carefully dispensed artistic encouragement, prickled through me with a sudden chill. I grasped the Glower's hand and pushed it toward her, backing away as I let go.

"No," I said. "If that's how this has to work, then you can forget your deal."

The Glower didn't follow me this time. She frowned, tilting her head as she studied my face. "You are hurting," she said. "I'm sorry. That was not my intention."

The apology startled me in the few seconds it took before the explanation hit me. "You're sorry because you think I'll be less likely to trust you."

She didn't deny it, only blinked at me. "I'm still sorry."

I supposed she was. That was probably the closest a Glower could come to real concern. And to give her credit, she hadn't needed to acknowledge she'd noticed at all.

"There are many ways we can approach my end of the deal," she went on. As she spoke, her glow flared again. When the light cleared from my eyes, Miss Bertolini had faded away, leaving the woman I'd first talked to outside the club two nights ago. "I'm sure we could find one you would be open to. I have no trouble being patient. And I always fulfill my word."

That wouldn't have been enough, if it were her vague promise to help me solve my problems that was tempting me. But I didn't really care about her end of the deal. The Society needed to know exactly what unrest among the Glowers had sent her to me. And I'd just proven which of our wills was stronger. Any doubt I'd still felt fell away beneath a renewed sense of conviction. I nodded sharply.

"All right," I said. "I'll hear you out. Come back to my place, and you can tell me everything there."

Four

I SUSPECTED MY APARTMENT LOOKED LIKE POOR accommodation to a Glower, given that the demons were used to hobnobbing with the rich and famous. My Tether Society salary made possible a certain number of comforts, but I wasn't really the extravagant type. So my savings account was large and my apartment small: an open-concept living area, a tiny kitchen alcove, and a bedroom that fit the queen-sized bed and not much else. There were a few touches of character in the simple, efficient design—the arch of the window frames, the castle-like molding of the baseboards—and I liked the feel of the warm, worn hardwood under my feet. The way the light from the tall windows showcased my growing art collection was a bonus.

If this Glower were unimpressed, she kept her thoughts to herself. She glided through the living room, touching the creased maroon leather of the couch, the matching sateen curtains, the little flat screen TV perched on the glass-topped coffee table next to a mystery novel I'd gotten halfway through and forgotten to bring with me to Jayden's mansion. I couldn't help tensing as her gaze fell on the paintings scattered across the eggshell-white walls.

"Originals?" she said. "I don't know these styles."

"They're newer artists," I said. I made a point of supporting emerging talent with my spending—they needed it the most, and there wasn't anything quite as exciting as finding a piece you could tell showed someone on the verge of mastering their craft, but still with all the headlong enthusiasm of that upward climb. Of course, that made the artists vulnerable in other ways as well. "No one you should bother."

Her gaze flitted away. I shook off the sense that I should be guarding my space from her and ambled over to the kitchen. I wanted some fortification for the conversation ahead of us.

"I'm going to make myself dinner," I said. "Do you want anything?" To the best of the Society's knowledge, Glowers didn't *need* to eat or drink our food to sustain themselves. They fed entirely on the joys and creative energy of their targets—draining those emotions away, leaving their victims as hollowed and depressed as Rosa had become toward the end.

That thought made me want to take my question back, common courtesy be damned.

The Glower shrugged. "I'll try a bit of what you have for yourself, if there's enough."

My fridge's pickings were sparse, cleaned out in preparation for what I'd expected to be even more than a two-week absence. I'd only gotten off duty earlier today and hadn't had time for shopping yet. I gave the counter a quick swipe with a cloth and grabbed one of the bags of frozen vegetables and cans of lentils I kept for days like this. Add enough hot sauce and you almost couldn't tell the difference from a fresh stir-fry. Though I'd never have suggested as much in my mother's hearing.

I had a few beers left in the fridge, but adding alcohol to this mix seemed unwise. I didn't want the slightest chemical interference with my judgment. Instead I poured two glasses of water and carried them to the square birch-wood table in the corner of the living room nearest the kitchen. The Glower stayed standing as I poked at the vegetables in the stovetop pan.

"This will only take me a few minutes," I said. "But you can start talking now. What's happening with your 'people'? Why do you think you need help?"

"We have survived the way we are for thousands of years," she said. "But recently it has become significantly more... difficult. This leads to many more problems even amongst ourselves."

"You're going to have to get more specific than that if you expect me to do anything," I said. "Difficult how? What sort of problems?"

When I glanced over at her, she was grimacing. She had to be aware that the sort of information she was sharing could open the Glowers to attack, even if she hadn't caught on that I was listening for exactly that reason. Well, careful as she tried to be, I'd have to draw their weaknesses out of her.

"Your Society has expanded," she said after a moment, her voice measured. "Fewer of the people we would benefit from associating with are accessible to us. And now you are spreading the materials that are unpleasant to us all through the population."

"Well, I'm not going to apologize for that," I said. "We're trying to stop you from *killing* those people. Is that hard to understand?"

"I think you should let those people make their own decisions about how they direct their lives and whether the heights we can help them reach are worth the resulting fall."

I'd heard that line before. "Let's not pretend you lay out

their options as clearly as that," I said. "You lie and manipulate and use every other trick you can."

She ignored my accusation. "There was a balance before. The changes of modern civilization have increasingly skewed that balance in your favor. We are the ones who are killed."

I couldn't summon any pity when I knew of at least five Glower-caused deaths in L.A. since the start of the year. But the admission grabbed me for a completely different reason. I set down the bottle of pepper sauce I'd been sprinkling over the frying pan and gave her my full attention.

"Glowers can die?"

She grimaced again—whether at our name for them or at the concept of death, I wasn't sure. "All things that live can die," she said. "Without enough sustenance, your people starve. So it is for us as well."

It had never occurred to me that Glowers were mortal, though when she spelled it out that plainly, I supposed it should have. The Society's founders, centuries ago, had recorded various attempts to kill Glowers, all of which had ended in failure, which seemed inevitable when their bodies on this plane were merely temporary constructions. But naturally the demons wouldn't bother with the hunt if consuming that energy didn't sustain them in some essential way. That was a useful fact to have confirmed.

"When the cat is starving because it can't catch enough prey, it seems odd to expect sympathy from the mice," I pointed out. I prodded one of the pieces of carrot with my spatula, decided dinner was cooked enough, and scraped most of it onto the plate I'd set out in preparation. The other small portion I dropped onto a saucer before carrying both to the table. The Glower stepped closer, her mouth twisting.

"We take only what is willingly given."

"As I said before, let's not pretend I don't know better." I motioned to the chair opposite mine. "Sit down. Eat. If you adapted to human food, you'd find it a lot easier to avoid starvation."

The Glower narrowed her eyes at me, but she sat. She poked at the stir-fry with the fork I'd brought for her. "The deal was that you would listen."

"I'm listening," I said. "I didn't promise to *agree*."

"It's simple," she said. "We do not wish to be eradicated. Even if you insist on seeing us as villains, you must be able to understand that. We will do what we must to prevent it. Having even some slight cooperation from your Society would mean we could find methods that might be less harmful to you as well as to us."

So there was a threat imbedded in the plea. I supposed they would have known better than to hope we'd barter unless we stood to lose something otherwise, but if they really did have a "method" that would harm us, I'd imagine they'd have tried it already.

"What are your suggestions?" I asked. "What exactly do you imagine we would do for you?"

Her gaze slipped away from me. Because she didn't have any ideas of her own or because she suspected I wouldn't like them? "You will come to one of our gatherings," she said, and speared a cauliflower floret that was ruddy with pepper sauce. "We have no set agreement on the best course of action, but many have ideas. You can listen there too, and see if there are any avenues you feel it would be reasonable to pursue further."

The thought of walking into a room full of Glowers made my spine stiffen. I chewed my mouthful slowly and swallowed my discomfort with it. I could *learn* even more from a group of

Glowers than from just one. I'd had no idea they conducted any sort of organized gatherings at all.

I doubted I'd learned all I could from *her* just yet, though.

"So the accessories the fans are picking up, the jewelry and all that, you've been finding it difficult to work around?" I asked casually.

The Glower popped the floret into her mouth. Her expression twitched as the hot sauce must have hit her tongue. I had put a lot on. The glow I'd almost stopped noticing on her flickered momentarily brighter before dimming until it was little more than a faint sheen. She gulped.

"Of course it has," she said, jabbing her fork at me, her voice more animated than before. "The last few weeks, I haven't been able to walk down the street without someone passing by carrying some material that tears at me until I want to jump right out of this place. It's... It's..."

"Inhumane?" I suggested dryly.

She rolled her eyes at me, a gesture at odds with her previously cool demeanor, and shoveled down another forkful of the stir-fry. "Cruel," she said. "Sadistic. Is that the sort of human you want to be?"

I hesitated, eyeing her as she set aside the fork by her now-empty plate. *Something* had come over her—an intensity of emotion I hadn't provoked before. Maybe it was only that my question had hit a particular sore spot.

"I'm trying to protect my fellow human beings," I said. "That's all any of us at the Society want to do."

The Glower made a snorting sound. "We'll have to agree to disagree on *that*." She considered me. "You're not like most humans, you know. The ones I've dealt with, at least. That's why I picked you. I hope you'll be able to think differently too."

I wasn't sure if I should take that as a compliment. "You're asking a lot," I said.

"But there's so much I can give as well." She leaned forward, the flick of her tongue over her lips bringing back the memory of her standing so close in the alley less than an hour ago. The corner of her mouth curved up in a teasing smile that felt more like the presence I'd started to get used to, detached and unshakeable. "Tell me, Mateo, how did you become the sort of person who finds it so difficult to accept one of his fondest dreams offered up for free?"

We were thinking of the same moment then. "I don't think *that* was so unusual," I said. "It was an old dream. It was offered in a near public place by a total stranger." A demon, no less.

The Glower waved her hand dismissively. "You would be surprised, then. From what I've observed, most people always want more than they have. You offer them a gift, and they ask what extra comes with it. That's why we get along so well with those clients you're 'protecting.' But you... There is a strange feeling in you about taking what you want. It makes you uncomfortable. You would rather say no, even to yourself. So strange."

If anything was making me uncomfortable, it was this line of conversation. "You did say you'd find another option that I'd say yes to," I said. "Or was that just a con so I'd listen?"

"Oh, that was no con." Her voice dipped to a purr. "I'll meet my end of the deal. I'm going to peel you open and discover what makes you deny yourself, and then I'm going to teach you so many ways of saying yes."

Despite myself, a sudden heat raced over my skin at those words. I didn't want her seeing she'd managed to get a reaction. "I think we've covered enough ground for today," I said, shifting back in my chair.

Before I could finish sending her away, a key clicked in the lock on the apartment door.

Five

I STARED AT THE DOOR AS THE DEADBOLT RASPED OVER. I hadn't seen any notice from the landlord about a visit, and usually he knocked first. What the hell?

I was just getting to my feet, my fork gripped in my hand as a makeshift weapon and my pulse thumping, when the door opened. A familiar hitching laugh carried over the threshold. My apprehension vanished into startled recognition.

An equally familiar stocky figure stepped through the doorway. He was turning toward me as he came in, still holding the doorknob, and he stopped dead at the sight of me. A curse fell from his mouth.

"What's wrong, Enrique?" a female voice said behind him. My eyebrows rose. My eighteen-year-old cousin Ricky glanced from me to the girl and back again, looking panicked as a rabbit in the blaze of a flashlight.

"Something tells me we need to have a talk, Ricky," I said before he could retreat, irritation prickling up from beneath my shock. "Like, right now."

Ricky's face fell. "I was just—" he started, and cut himself off with a strangled noise. He eased back without closing the door. Which was good, because if he'd tried to make a run for it, I'd have come after him, and he wouldn't have made it very far.

"Change in plans," he said to the girl in the cocky voice I'd heard him pull out when telling stories to impress the younger teens at our family get-togethers. "Wait for me in the lobby, okay? I'll be right with you."

The girl murmured what sounded like disagreement, and Ricky made some soothing remarks. A minute later, he came in and shut the door behind him, alone. His shoulders were squared, his full jaw defiantly tight, as if his being here were in any way defensible. Then his gaze fell on the table, and his own eyebrows lifted.

"Got company, cuz?" he said.

The Glower's plate and glass were still sitting there across from mine. I'd almost forgotten her in my confusion. A glance around the room showed me she'd disappeared. Somehow that made me vaguely uneasy, even though I'd been meaning to tell her to leave anyway.

But at the moment I had other fish to fry.

"Not anymore," I said. "I haven't washed up yet. I wasn't expecting company *now*. And from the looks of things, you weren't expecting to see me either. Where'd you get the key, Ricky?"

He shrugged and flipped the key between his fingers. "Your mom has that spare you gave her for emergencies. It's not like she hides it. I borrowed it and made a copy."

So this was more than a one-time transgression? What had been merely annoyance flipped over into anger. "You've been bringing girls here?" I said. "*Here?* For how long? What were you thinking, Ricky? This is my apartment, my *home*, not some hotel room."

"I was thinking it's a helluva lot cheaper than some hotel room," Ricky said, still defiant even as his brown skin went a bit greenish. "Come on, Teo. When I texted you Wednesday afternoon, you said you were going to be away with work until next week. I had no idea you'd be home. You're hardly ever here. *Someone* might as well be using the place. You know what it's like at my house. My mom won't let me even close my bedroom door when I've got a girl over."

And it was pretty obvious what he wanted to do with those girls behind closed doors. On my couch? My bed? I winced. I did not want to picture my cousin in flagrante. "How many times?"

"I dunno. Five or six now? I always cleaned up after, laundry and everything. Your sheets are probably fresher than they ever were when it was just you using them."

"And that's supposed to make me okay with it? Technically this is breaking and entering. You could have *asked*."

Ricky scowled. "I figured you'd say no. I figured you'd act like I was talking about razing the place to the ground, not just having a little fun. Like you're acting right now. You're always such a stick in the mud, Teo."

"I don't think there are many people who'd be cool with their home being secretly used as a love den," I snapped, and held out my hand. "The key. Now."

He hesitated before handing it over. I stuffed the key in my pocket, making a mental note to call my mother tonight and tell her to hide her spare somewhere Ricky couldn't easily lift it again. The gall of the guy.

"I still don't see what the big deal is," he said. "Lending me your apartment when you're gone is the least you could do for family."

"I don't think family generosity is supposed to extend to people you've just caught committing a crime against you."

"Oh, come off it," Ricky said with a swipe of his fist. "It's not like you care about family at all. Everyone talks, you know. You're too busy with your fancy job to come around most of the time. And when have you *ever* been generous with me? You hardly bother to talk to me these days. You know, I don't think you're even that angry I was using your place. You're angry that I have a reason to use it. How long has it been since *you* got any?"

I nearly bit out that I'd been offered an experience probably better than he'd ever had just an hour ago, but I caught my tongue just in time. "It's time for you to go," I said instead, pointing to the door. "I've heard enough. We can talk about this more when you're ready to admit you actually screwed up."

Ricky swiveled and yanked open the door. He barged out without a word or a backward glance, but I could almost see the frustration radiating from his hunched posture. As if *I* were somehow in the wrong for being here and expecting him not to be.

He didn't bother to close the door. I walked over and shut it, a little more forcefully than I intended. I paused for a second with my hand braced against it, and then I turned the deadbolt. As an afterthought, I also fed in the end of the chain lock I rarely used. No one else was coming in here tonight, key or not.

Well, almost no one else. I turned around, and my heart flipped over in the instant before I registered who exactly was standing across the room from me.

The Glower had reappeared by the table, standing there casually as if she'd only just gotten up from her chair. She was frowning at the door. Her dark gaze slid to me.

"Your cousin?" she said. I nodded. "He's a jerk."

In that moment, I was inclined to agree, but hearing the insult drop from her lips, from the lips of a creature who'd done far worse than Ricky would ever have conceived, made me bristle.

"He's being a stupid teenager," I said. "We all go through that stage. He'll grow out of it."

At least, I very much hoped he would.

"You see, that's the sort of normal human behavior I meant before," she said. "He wants your respect, your 'generosity,' your apartment, and he is giving you no respect or generosity in return." She cocked her head, her gaze still fixed on the door as if she were replaying the incident in her mind. "There was something else he wanted that he didn't say. Something he's upset you haven't given him."

She looked at me questioningly. I supposed I should be relieved that there were limits to a Glower's powers of observation. Distance weakened what they could sense—I'd already known that. And physical contact strengthened it. She must have dug Miss Bertolini out of my mind when she'd grasped my arm by the alley.

"It's something I can't give him," I said.

"What?" she asked, curiosity intensifying the unnatural gleam in her eyes. "Why not?"

My gut went cold. I hadn't even thought— Christ, even Ricky could be a target.

"You won't have any dealings with him," I said. "That has to be part of *our* deal. You ask for and take nothing from anyone in my family, ever, and you keep your 'people' away from them to the best of your ability too."

"Done," she said, with a faint crackle in her voice, as if her agreement had been electrically charged. The forcefulness of it left me with no doubt that the promise was binding. "Will you tell me now?"

I hadn't had anyone I could really vent to about Ricky's demands since he'd started coming on strong last fall. My mom got edgy about tension in the family, and my dad's go-to solution was "Just give him what he wants."

Airing familial grievances to people outside the family just wasn't done. But I wasn't talking to a *person* right now. So it felt acceptable, maybe even a relief, to say, "He sings. He wants to be a pop star." The next Romeo Santos, he figured. "He thinks I have connections in the industry, that I could set him up."

"Don't you?"

"Not directly—not the right people for the sort of music he wants to make. And even if I did, I'm not supposed to leverage the Society's work into personal favors."

The Glower stepped closer. I only realized she was reaching for my hand a second too late to jerk back. Her fingers brushed over my knuckles, so gently the shiver that contact provoked was almost pleasant. She peered into my face.

"That's not the only reason. You don't want to help him."

Well, why shouldn't I admit this too? "He'd embarrass himself," I said. "I've heard him... Maybe with vocal training and more practice, he'd be bankable, but right now he wouldn't even make it onto American Idol. And the original songs he's written, the lyrics are awkward, the music itself... I don't know a *lot* about that business, but I've been around people in the industry enough to know what they're not looking for."

"But you haven't told him that," the Glower said. It wasn't a question.

"No," I acknowledged. "Why would I? All it would do is piss him off, and then piss the rest of the family off on his behalf. You saw how upset he got because I criticized him for *breaking into my apartment.* How do you think he'd react to me criticizing his career fantasies?"

"It doesn't seem he reacts well to the other answers you're giving him."

"There's no easy answer. Trust me, if I told him his music sucks, I'd never hear the end of it from everyone in my family."

I was still clutching the copied key. I dropped it onto the table and ran my fingers through my hair as if I could wipe the confrontation with Ricky from my mind. My heart hadn't stopped thudding. Although maybe that was partly the Glower's fault. She was standing only a couple of feet away from me. I didn't trust her. She made me apprehensive. But I'd have been lying if I'd said there wasn't a little attraction mingled in. She'd picked her form too well.

"It still bothers you, what he said," she remarked. "But you *aren't* envious of him. You don't like that he thinks that you are?"

Envious? Oh, of Ricky's regular female companionship. *How long has it been since you got some?*

I smiled tightly. "I don't like being a family pity case. It's complicated."

That wasn't entirely true—it was relatively simple. I'd been with Avery long enough that she'd come to several family get-togethers. Everyone had liked her. My mom had liked her a lot. So when she'd stopped coming, the comments had started. And they'd only gotten more probing and concerned the more time passed without me bringing a new girlfriend around.

I just didn't want to talk about that.

"Ah," the Glower said, and my stomach tightened as I wondered just how much she'd gathered in my silence. She raised her hands as she eased across the last short distance between us and hooked her arms behind my neck. I flinched backward, reaching to push her away.

"Wait," she said softly as my fingers closed around her forearms. "Just listen."

I hesitated. Those burgundy-brown eyes held mine, deep amid the gleam of their whites. The warmth of her body, just inches from mine, tingled over me. Her thumb grazed up and down over the back of my neck, and that touch felt better than I wanted to admit. I closed my eyes to shut out the eerie shine of her. I didn't have to look at her to listen.

"You've done what I asked," she said in the same caress of a tone. "You listened to my concerns. I will need you to listen more, but for now... I think it is long past your turn to receive. I can make it so easy for you. I can give you what you want most."

I felt the shift, like a ripple in the air between us. The faint smoky-sweet smell of the Glower morphed into a far-too-familiar delicate floral tang. Lilac.

I knew before I opened my eyes. Maybe I'd known from the very first moment she'd presented her deal that she would offer me this. My breath jarred against the catch in my throat.

"Mateo," the Glower said, in a voice that was not her own. My heart squeezed. I swallowed thickly, and forced my eyes open.

It was Avery's face tipped toward mine now, from the dark-chocolate eyes to the angular jaw with its point of a chin. Avery's soft arms looping around my neck. Avery's body by mine, strong-shouldered and small-chested, within a sundress that bared her cleavage. Avery's shampoo smell tickling my nose. Avery's voice lingering in my ears.

"Mateo," she said again, letting her body press against mine. "Here I am. What are you going to do with me?"

The guise wasn't quite right. I noticed the slight roughness around the edges as the shock of it wore off. Even when playing seductress, Avery wouldn't have dropped her voice quite that low. Her skin had an end of summer tan instead of June's lighter shade. And of course the shimmer the Glower couldn't quite suppress sparkled through her bright brown hair.

I saw and heard all that, and yet, as she leaned into me, I went hard to fast I lost my breath.

"No," I said. "I don't want this."

The Avery-Glower canted her eyebrows exactly the way Avery would have. "You want nothing more."

She might be right. I couldn't deny, with the gentle firmness of her body embracing me, that what I felt for the girl whose image she'd taken was far more than friendly. This girl, this girl. This girl with her even temper and her unrestrained laugh, this girl whose calm practicality hid a playful streak a mile wide, this girl who'd never made me feel I was anything less than enough, who even in the end had assumed our failure was her fault. God, I'd missed her.

Every nerve in my body was humming with the need to find out just how true to life this vision of her was, in every way.

And yet—

"It isn't right."

"It isn't *real*," the Avery-Glower said. She trailed her hand down my cheek, and my pulse stuttered. "What you do in a dream can't be right or wrong. It just is. You don't have to worry about what she thinks, how she'd feel. Nothing you do will affect her at all. All that matters is what *you* want. The only one you can hurt is yourself, if you pass up this chance."

She dipped her head to press her lips to the bend of my neck. Exactly where Avery had liked to. My skin caught fire. I clenched my jaw.

"This is a dream, and I am all yours," she murmured against my throat. "Anything you do, I'll love it. There is nothing you need to hide or pretend. Give me everything. Please."

That last word in Avery's clear voice broke my control. My hands leapt to cup her face, pulling her mouth to mine. Lord, she even tasted like Avery, the Avery of my memories: hot and peach-sweet. She sank against me as if her body would fuse with mine, and I nearly went mad right there.

I kissed her hard, and she gave back just as good, her tongue darting out to meet mine through a muffled moan of pleasure. My hands dropped to the neck of her sundress and skimmed down over her discrete but incredibly appealing curves. My palms hit her nipples through the thin cotton. She hadn't bothered with a bra, and they were already tight. As I stroked the nubs harder, her hips swayed against mine. My erection throbbed.

It isn't her, a voice in the back of my head insisted, but all that followed the thought was relief. The Glower was right. This was nothing more than a dream. I had spent too long suppressing what I truly wanted to pass up this one indulgence.

"What do you want, Teo?" she whispered as our lips broke apart. "I'll give you anything you want, if you let me. You can tell me."

I exhaled with a shudder. My fingers slid to her waist, the flare of her hips. And I decided. No more thinking. No second-guessing.

"I want you naked," I said. "The dress, whatever you have on underneath, all of it off."

The Glower grinned in a way that was both Avery and not, more like the woman who'd propositioned me in an alley. She slid back half a step so she could reach for the zipper at the side of her dress. She held my gaze as she inched it down, as she slipped the spaghetti straps from her arms and tugged at the bodice, as the fabric leapt over the swell of her breasts, skimmed her hips, and pooled at her feet. Then she grasped the sides of the modest panties she was wearing and pulled them off too.

I couldn't stand to just watch any longer. I pulled her into another kiss, our bodies colliding. My hands traced over her smooth skin down her back and across her hips. I dipped a finger between her legs, and my erection stiffened at the feel of the moisture there. She was already wet for me. She arched into my touch, her head falling back. I kissed her shoulder, her collarbone. Wanting all of her, now.

"Don't stop," she said with a whimper. She lifted one leg beside mine to press even closer against my groin. The movement triggered an impulse I hadn't known was in me. I grabbed her by the waist and boosted her onto the kitchen counter. Her legs splayed around me, at just the right height for the head of my erection to strain against her. Just the right height for me to sweep one of her breasts into my hand and bring the nipple to my mouth.

She cried out, rocking against me. My body ignited. I chaffed my teeth over her nipple and around, and she moaned. Her fingers trailed down my torso, and my muscles tensed momentarily at the thought that she meant to tug aside my shirt. But they just rested there, curling and uncurling against my sides as I had my way with her other breast.

She swayed against me again, and my head whirled. "I want inside you," I said, my voice an unfamiliar growl to my own ears.

"Yes," she said. "Please, yes."

Her hands were already at my fly. They jerked it down, her fingers slipping inside, taking me with Avery's eager but careful grasp.

If it had really been her, if any of this had been real, I would have carried her to the bed, stripped down myself, been with her skin to skin. But my body thrummed with the need to be in her now, like this, her nakedness against me clothed.

I surged forward as she guided me out, and somehow she was right there to meet me. I plunged inside the tight wet bliss of her with a groan. She pushed to the edge of the counter to meet me, to let me sink into her as deeply as I could. Her fingers tangled in my hair as I thrust and thrust again, her hot little breaths panting by my ear between gasps of pleasure. I nipped her shoulder as I delved even deeper, and she squirmed against me as if desperate for release.

"Oh, God, don't stop," she said. I let out a laugh that was more a sigh. At that moment, stopping was not a word in my vocabulary. My own pleasure built as she started to tremble against me. She bucked toward me with every thrust, faster and faster, until I was panting too. Then she clenched around me, her head dropping back as she hit her peak.

The feel of her losing herself around me pushed me over in turn. I choked on a breath as I spent myself inside her. Then I slumped, one hand braced against the counter to keep my balance, the pleasure melting my muscles.

"There," the woman in my arms said in a voice that was half Avery's and half the Glower's. "I knew we could find the right starting point."

When I straightened up, withdrawing from her on wobbly legs, she still wore Avery's form. Avery's gaze met mine as Avery's lips curved into a satisfied smile that was far more sly than anything Avery herself would have worn. The cool air of the apartment drifted over my skin, and I became abruptly aware of the honking of cars on the street four floors below, the daylight dimming to dusk as it streaked past the curtains behind us. All the ways this moment *was* real and not just a dream.

All the heat that had flooded me a minute ago washed away,

leaving me chilled. No warmth remained except a burn behind my eyes.

The false Avery hopped down from the counter, shifting as she did with a momentary flash of brilliance into the Glower's previous form and black dress. She brushed her hands together with an air of efficiency. Because that's what this had been to her—of course that was all this had been to her: a job, one she felt she'd done well. I supposed she had.

"I'd like you to go now," I said.

Her forehead furrowed as she looked at me. "If that's what you want," she said in her own measured voice. "We should discuss, the gathering you need to attend—"

"I'll come to your 'gathering,'" I said. "I'm sure you'll know where to find me when it's time. Please just leave me alone until then."

I kept my gaze low, but I could feel the puzzlement in her stare. Let her be confused. Let her see humans weren't as straightforward as Glowers liked to imagine. Just let her *go*.

"All right," she said after a brief hesitation. "Thank you."

I blinked, and the space before me was empty. I raised my head. My hand was still on the counter, the counter where I'd—

I yanked my palm away. My throat felt thick. My eyes burned hotter.

What had I let myself do? And what unholy bargain had I just entered myself into?

Six

Heading into the Society office Monday morning, I nearly walked right into a curvy young woman who was standing just inside the doorway.

"Oh!" she said, scooting out of the way. "I'm sorry, I zoned out for a second there." She paused, considering me with large blue eyes framed by waves of red-blonde hair. A shy smile crossed her face. "You must be Mateo. I'm Sofie. I started training in a little while back."

"Right," I said, remembering Fiona's nudges the other day. And Fiona had been right—with those eyes, that smile, and the sprinkling of freckles across her peachy-pale skin, Sofie was cute. But the complicated turn my love life had just taken made it difficult to note that fact with any deeper enthusiasm.

I'd come to terms with those complications enough that I could reflect on Friday's encounter with only a flicker of discomfort. What I'd done with the Glower in her guise *hadn't* been real. I had to think it might even be helpful to me, if not exactly in the way the Glower had suggested. I'd gotten that lingering desire for my ex-girlfriend out of my system. A brief liaison with the Glower herself, if that was what she wanted to offer, could kick start the moving-on process I obviously hadn't gotten far enough along with on my own, and there was no reason I shouldn't take that as a side benefit to gathering information for the Society. What better way to rebound than with someone I couldn't possibly hurt? Maybe that was using her, but no more than she was using me. I couldn't let my conscience gnaw at me too much over a creature who had none herself.

And after that was over, maybe I could look the right way at a girl like Sofie.

She held out her hand, and I shook it before glancing around the office. Other than Yelena, who was murmuring into the phone, the office's cubicles were empty. I'd come early hoping to catch Sterling right away, since he was almost always here early too, but I could see his office door was firmly shut.

"Are you meeting someone here?" I asked Sofie.

"Yeah, um, Mrs. Tsung asked me to come in to discuss trial placements." Her brow knit. "Isn't it weird that this place looks so... normal?"

I couldn't help smiling at the way she'd echoed one of my most frequent observations. "We've got to meet clients or their representatives here sometimes," I said. "They'd have some doubts about our professionalism if the office looked like a den of mystics."

"Right," Sofie said, with a crooked grin and a shake of her head. "I'm still getting used to the whole idea. What's *really* weird is being able to see things hardly anyone else can. Demons around us all this time, and until seven months ago I had no idea they were here... or how many people they were hurting."

I heard unspoken pain in the rough edge that had crept into

her voice. A glimpse of what lay behind the cute girl exterior. I wondered what had happened for her to be here now—whose death she'd witnessed, what they'd meant to her—but Society policy was not to ask. It was understood that if a fellow Tether wanted to volunteer their experience, they would. Most didn't. I'd talked about Rosa with a few of the Tethers who'd trained me in only out of necessity and with Avery only briefly. She'd told me about finding her dad with the Glower when she was little. I didn't even know Fiona's story, or Sterling's.

It was better to focus on the people we could still save.

I was about to make some polite enquiry about how Sofie was finding training when the door squeaked behind us. Mrs. Tsung hustled in.

"Sorry to keep you waiting, Sofie," she said. "The traffic was hell this morning."

"It's not problem," Sofie said. "I only got here a few minutes ago." She gave me a quick nod and another flash of a smile. "It was good to meet you, Mateo. Fiona says we of the younger generation need to have each other's backs."

"Yeah," I said, my own smile twitching at the thought of what other suggestions Fiona might be making to her. I gave her a little wave as she followed Mrs. Tsung to one of the supervisor offices. Just as I turned toward the neighboring door, it opened. Sterling's dark head poked out.

So he *was* in. I wasn't used to him keeping his door closed.

"Ah," he said when his gaze landed on me. "You're here. Good. I can get you started."

I headed for his office, but he motioned me to one of the cubicles down the row from Yelena's. As I sat in the chair there, he pulled another over to join me. He tugged the keyboard toward him, woke up the monitor, and opened a new application. The interface that appeared on the screen wasn't one

I recognized. Obviously whoever had designed it had been thinking only of function—it was far from pretty. The flat gray window held two rectangles with multicolored lists of names on one side, and a simple calendar and a vacant box on the other.

"Thanks to the archiving you helped with earlier, we've been able to develop a program that presents that data in a more... organized fashion," Sterling said. "Every client we've worked with as of the Society's current incarnation is listed here, along with the available notes on their progress with their Tethers, permanent solutions found, and current status." He clicked on one of the names in the lower left list, and the vacant box filled with text. Sterling waved the cursor toward the menu bar at the top of the screen. "You can search and sort by all the relevant parameters. And you can also work in the other direction, by consulting the list of Tethers." He clicked on a name in the upper list. Fiona Wilde. Immediately the days in the calendar shifted into an assortment of hues to reflect her schedule times and locations as the text box displayed the details of her current client. I assumed if I scrolled lower it would offer a list of her past clients as well.

Sterling double clicked on the text box and then the calendar, showing me how they expanded for easier viewing. "This is great," I said. "But it's finished. What is it you want *me* to do?"

"It isn't finished," Sterling said as he gazed at the screen with a faint smile. "The programming of the application, yes, but its utility has only begun. Now that we can so easily compare variables, I want you to start working with this data. For the moment, I have three primary goals. One, to go through the lists of existing and past clients and determine which criteria appear to be most important in determining their success or lack thereof with any given Tether. Two, to go through the list of clients awaiting Tethers and use the criteria you've already identified to help prioritize who should be next in line and what qualities they might need in a Tether. Any factors you notice that you believe might be important but aren't currently searchable, make a note of. Ultimately we want to be able to quickly and efficiently arrange assignments so the clients most at risk are set up with the best match of Tether as quickly as possible."

I'd been dreading this job, but hearing the intensity in Sterling's voice, imagining the system he was describing, it was hard not to get caught up in his enthusiasm. The Society had always tried to consider fit of personality and circumstances when assigning Tethers, of course, but that had mostly been guesswork and instinct. I supposed we simply hadn't had many research-minded people in our ranks, and we couldn't exactly recruit someone who didn't understand and give them access to our most private information. But Sterling was striking out on new ground. With this software, we had more than a hundred years of records to quickly scan through. All our successes—and all our failures. We could certainly learn from both.

"You said you have three goals," I said. "What's the last one?"

Sterling hummed. "It's bothered me for a long time that we have to leave so many potential clients unprotected for so long— and that we end up losing so many to the Glowers. I want you to compare the schedules of the Tethers currently assigned to a client with the needs of those on the waiting list, and see if there might be a way that at least some of us could handle two simultaneously. Look at the times when Glower sightings and encounters have been reported, when a Tether actively needed to intervene, that sort of thing. There may be periods when it is more sensible to have someone... unaware of the exact nature of the protection needed keeping a basic watch so that our Tethers can be freed up to tackle the riskiest scenarios across a greater number of clients."

If we could double our reach, guard twice as many people— Well, we couldn't hope for that huge a change, not with the particularly high risk clients needing 'round the clock surveillance, but still, it would be a coup. Between that and Fiona's new strategy, we might come close to shutting out the Glowers completely.

That thought reminded me of one particular Glower who was concerned about that exact "problem." In the back of my mind, I saw her sitting across the table from me. *We do not wish to be eradicated.* I might hate her methods of surviving, but I could understand that feeling. And I'd seen how just about any conscious being reacted when it seemed every option was lost.

The Glowers were getting desperate. If we pushed them even further out, at least some of them would fight back. Right now I had no idea how. We'd nearly lost a few clients, including Fiona's, the last time the demons had adjusted their strategies.

"I'm sure there are even more possibilities with this application," Sterling was saying. "I want you to keep your mind open as you're working through the initial objectives and bring any further ideas to me for consultation."

"Of course," I said. I had a further idea right now—it was why I'd come in early, after all. Sterling slid the mouse to me and shifted his weight as if to stand, and I quickly cleared my throat. "There's something I need to talk to you about already. A Glower approached me."

Sterling went still. Even though I'd shed most of my shame over Friday's encounter, I had to resist the urge to fidget under his keen gaze.

"Approached you with what intent?" he said.

"She's worried about our new strategies for warding them off. Apparently a *lot* of them are worried. We've put them on the defensive. She warned me that if they're left to their own devices, they might launch some sort of counterattack, but they're hoping we'll negotiate a sort of 'compromise' to prevent harm on both sides."

Sterling frowned. "And you agreed to this?"

"All she's asked me to do so far is listen to what she and some of the others have to say," I said, my nerves steadying as saying the words aloud reminded me of how much I'd already accomplished. Sterling didn't need to know about the more intimate side to our arrangement. "I haven't agreed to do anything else for her or them. I don't expect I'll be tempted to. My thought was that I could gain some insight into their plans, what counterattacks they might be planning, and, well, everything about them that we don't already know. Our understanding is pretty limited."

"Because there isn't a single Glower out there who can be trusted," Sterling said. "You've never had their focus directly on you. It seems to me—"

He halted with a sudden intake of breath. His eyes went distant for a moment, and his jaw quivered.

"Sterling?" I said.

He gave his head a little shake and rolled his shoulders. "I apologize," he said. "Something unrelated popped into my mind —a task I need to take care of. We can finish this discussion first."

"I know not to trust her," I said. "I've been careful in my dealings so far. I've been able to defend my clients for years— why shouldn't I be able to defend myself as well? At least I know what the Glowers really are. If we want to protect as many future clients as possible, I don't think we should throw away this opportunity because of a slight risk."

Sterling nodded. His expression had gone thoughtful. He rubbed his jaw. "You really think this Glower will reveal true information to you."

"She already has," I said. "She told me about their worries, after all—and that they're getting together to discuss strategy in a coordinated fashion. She confirmed that they can starve to death if we prevent them from taking marks. She wants me to come to one of those gatherings—imagine how much I could find out there."

He was imagining. I could see it: the same intentness he'd aimed at the computer application now directed at me. "It is quite an opportunity," he said. "You're sure you're comfortable continuing?"

"I'm happy too," I said firmly. "I want to contribute everything I can."

"All right," he said. "I want you to be on your guard at all times. Don't agree to *anything* she asks from you without discussing it with me first for an outside perspective. If anyone should be able to handle this, it's you." He clapped his palm against my shoulder as he stood up. "Good work, Mateo."

The praise washed through me, lightening my spirits more than I'd felt since Jayden's dismissal. I turned back to the computer, back straight, chin up. Now all I had to do was prove I'd been worthy of that confidence.

Seven

I'D JUST REACHED THE FRONT DOOR OF MY APARTMENT
building the next evening when the Glower emerged from the
shadows at my right. She was wearing the same guise I'd seen on
her twice already: tumbling bronze-brown hair, Grecian features,
sleek black dress. As she sauntered over, I let go of the door
handle and stepped back so I wouldn't block any other residents.

"I need you," she said in that silky cool voice. "Our meeting
is about to begin."

My spine had stiffened as she'd drawn closer—closer than a
person would normally stand to anyone they hadn't been
intimate with—even as other parts of my body prickled with a
warmer sort of awareness. I drew in a breath, settling into that
sense of attraction. It was good to be able to feel it for someone
other than Avery. The more I felt it for others, the less my
feelings for her would matter. And it wasn't the *Glower* I was
attracted to, only the beguiling shell she wore. There wasn't
anything strange about that. I wasn't going to forget what lay
beneath it.

"Your meeting?" I said, and then the rest of my brain woke up. The gathering she'd told me about. "Right now? A little more notice might have been nice." I wasn't prepared. But then, how much could I really have prepared to join a gathering of Glowers? I had no idea what to expect.

The Glower cocked her head at me. "You asked me to leave until it was time," she said. "So I did. Does that upset you?"

I hadn't realized she'd take that instruction so literally. Good to know for the future. "No," I said. "It isn't that important. I can go now. How are we getting there?"

If I'd imagined some sort of magical transport might be involved—whisking away on a wind of teleportation, stepping through a doorway drawn in a seemingly solid wall—she disappointed. "I'll give the directions," she said, and flagged down a passing cab. She motioned for me to get in first and leaned over to murmur an address to the driver when she'd climbed in after me.

The cab set off with a stomp on the gas pedal, jolting us back in our seats. The Glower shook herself, chuckling as if the sensation had amused her.

"So what exactly is going to happen at this gathering?" I said. The cabbie took us around the corner onto the freeway a little too tightly, and I gripped the door handle as I swayed. Well, his driving skills made it easier to remember our conversation here wasn't private. "Do the other... Do your 'friends' know I'm coming? Is there anything they'll expect me to do?"

"Just listen," the Glower said. "Those who need to know do, but even they have many doubts about this opportunity. So show them that you're willing to at least consider our perspective. We won't accomplish anything if we don't start from there."

Just listen. I'd been able to manage that before. Still, imagining walking into the midst of a crowd of Glowers made my skin crawl. I'd seen several in the same place before, but never more than seven or eight, and then in the midst of a larger throng of human beings. This would be my first time being in the minority.

"How many will be there?" I said.

"There have been more each time," she replied. "The last time, sixteen of us. Now I hope to see at least twenty. We've been spreading the word—not just in this city, but farther. Our current problem affects all of us."

The Society had never been able to put together a reasonable estimate of how many Glowers were on the prowl locally or around the world. It was impossible to make a count when they could change their appearance so easily. I might be able to recognize when I'd seen one before looking differently, but I couldn't transfer that awareness to anyone else. With more than thirty of us working in L.A. right now, it was impossible to say whether it might be thirty different Glowers who pursued our clients across a week or the same few in a variety of guises. We couldn't even judge accurately by the death toll, given that a Glower-inspired death looked exactly the same as a non-supernatural suicide or overdose or accident unless someone had been around to witness the demonic presence.

I'd have liked to think that a figure of sixteen was reason to take heart. But when we'd rarely seen the Glowers working together even in pairs before a couple of months ago when they'd changed things up, I couldn't assume that was the majority of them and not just the small percentage who could manage to get along in a group of fellow Glowers for more than a few minutes.

I could try to find out, though.

"If we were going to make an arrangement, we'd want to be sure most of you would be following it," I said. "How many would we need to see joining in to have that guarantee?"

"If we make an arrangement, the gatherings won't matter," the Glower said. "As soon as some of us have an easier way, the others will fall in line. I told you—no one wants to starve."

I wasn't sure how to ask the question more directly without tipping her off that I had other motives for digging for information. "How long have you been getting together to discuss this topic?" I ventured instead.

"It started with four of us a few months ago," she said. "So you see, we have already made some progress toward cooperation."

Not the sort the Society appreciated so far. "Was it your idea?" I asked, struck by a sudden curiosity. What made one Glower see the benefits of "cooperation" amid a community of lone predators?

She shrugged, a gesture that looked artless and graceful at the same time. "I contributed," she said, and didn't go on. Was that a sore spot for her?

"And you meet *here*," I said, turning my gaze to the cityscape beyond the window. "Not... where you come from. Or is that just for me this one time?"

"*Here* is more conducive to certain types of activities," the Glower said. "Discussion being one of them."

Before I could ask her why that was, the taxi's wheels screeched. My body jerked forward at the cabbie's slam of the brakes. Thankfully, my seatbelt caught me, snapping tight against my torso with a pinch of pain. My companion hadn't bothered to put hers on. She whipped forward at the sudden stop, throwing out her arms to shield her head. Her elbows jarred against the back of the seat in front of her. Her shoulders shuddered.

"Sorry! Sorry!" the driver said. "This idiot..."

I glanced through the windshield to see a sports car weaving in and out of the lane ahead of us.

The Glower straightened herself up with a giggle. The sound was so unexpected—and so breathlessly human—that my gaze darted to her. She pushed her hands back through her hair, letting them linger over the thick waves, and met my eyes with an oddly playful light dancing in hers.

"Well, I didn't expect the trip to be quite this exciting," she said with ripple of amusement in her normally even tone. For a second I felt as if I were looking at an actual young woman. Despite the glint in her eyes, her unnatural glow had retreated. An exhilarated flush had colored her cheeks. It was disconcerting.

"L.A. drivers," I offered. The Glower leaned forward to peer out the window.

"I don't normally take cars," she said. "Perhaps I should more often."

Of course she didn't normally. She normally flitted through our reality like the supernatural intruder she was.

It appeared that body could feel *something* though. "If you put your seatbelt on, there's a lot less chance of getting battered," I said.

She shook her head, grinning. "And limit the experience? No."

I wasn't sure what to make of that, but her enthusiasm made me feel almost feeble for wanting very much to limit my experience of being thrown about in a cab. "To each their own."

"Yes," she said vehemently. "We all find our own way— there's no need to criticize that."

She seemed to be speaking about concerns beyond this taxi. But the cabbie took an off-ramp then, and a moment later we were pulling to a stop outside a small used bookstore.

The Glower bounded out onto the sidewalk with a smile, her strange new energy still animating her face. She sucked in a breath of cool evening air and strode forward. I followed her through the building's side entrance and up a narrow flight of stairs to an empty second floor studio apartment that looked as if it hadn't been occupied for years. Dust bunnies congregated in the corners, and a moldy patch was spreading across the dingy ceiling over the vacant spot where a fridge should have stood. Given the faintly sour smell that reminded me of wet dog, the last inhabitants hadn't been thorough in their final cleaning. Even the Glower wrinkled her nose.

Before I could ask if this was where they usually met, a faint popping sound vibrated into my ears. Three figures appeared in the middle of the room an instant later.

"Who picked *this* location?" my Glower said, answering my unspoken question. The apartment was obviously new to her too.

One of the arrivals, who'd taken the form of a tall, stiff-postured man with gray sprinkled in his chestnut hair, looked her up and down. He frowned.

"It meets all of our needs," he said in a gravelly voice. "When did you last eat? I think you've been spending too much time on this side."

My Glower waved off his concern. "I'm looking after myself." The last word she said was a blurring of syllables I could barely make out, though the first sounded like *Zut*. His name, I guessed.

Zut turned his penetrating gaze on me. "So this is the Tether you scrounged up."

My hackles rose at the disdain in his tone, but I kept my own voice professionally calm. "From what I've heard, I might be your best chance to solve the problems you've been having. But if I'm not welcome here, I can leave."

"No," my Glower said, grabbing my forearm. "You'll stay." The shimmer on her body flickered brighter.

Zut inclined his head. "I did not mean to cause offense," he said, in a way that left me with no doubt that he absolutely had. But I wasn't here because of him.

And I didn't really want to leave. No Tether before me had gotten a chance like this. My pulse thumped faster as several more shimmering forms emerged from their plane of existence into mine, gradually filling the room with their glowing bodies and their murmurs. My companion had said she'd hoped for twenty, and by the time Zut clapped his hands together in a motion for silence, there had to be at least two dozen demons in the room. The hairs on my arms were standing on end at the feel of their combined presence. I wondered how many of them were local and how many might have come from haunts farther afield —and whether I could find out. The Society saw regular activity and had established branches in other major entertainment centers as well as L.A.: New York, Portland, Vancouver, and overseas cities like London, Tokyo, and Melbourne.

At Zut's gesture, the Glowers began talking one at a time, but in a language that must have been their own. It was flat in inflection and spoken low in the throat, so liquid I couldn't distinguish the syllables any more easily than I had with Zut's full name. From the expressions that accompanied their comments, they were sharing information they found distressing. Most of them were scowling, their movements short and jerky.

My companion didn't seem troubled by my inability to

follow the conversation. She chimed in a few times, her own demeanor returned to her usual subdued state, without a glance at me. After several minutes of that, I tapped her shoulder to catch her attention, and she patted my arm as if to say, "Not yet." My skin was itching with the slithering voices around me when she finally raised her voice louder than before and switched to English.

"We are all seeing difficult times," she said. "That is why I have brought this man here." She pointed to me. "He is part of the 'Tether Society' that causes so many of our difficulties. He has agreed he will listen to our concerns and consider ways we might address them."

One of the Glowers in the crowd muttered something in a dark tone, and my Glower answered him in their own language sharply but firmly.

"Let us discuss what type of arrangement we might reach with the humans," Zut said. "Put forward your ideas."

"What if we agreed to leave the humans guarded by the Society alone?" a Glower in the form of an older woman said. "If they show themselves, we would back off. And in return they would stop the additional 'protections' that reach farther."

"Yes!" another joined in. "Then we could have the lesser ones without interference. There would be plenty."

Plenty to feed on. The itch of my uneasiness niggled deeper. The Society was never going to accept any deal that would leave potential victims in harm's way. *I* would never accept it. But saying so outright might shut down the conversation completely. I was here to learn.

"How do you choose your marks normally?" I asked, as if that would help me decide how I felt about the proposal.

"The best sustenance from the brightest flames," someone near me murmured, and a few others hummed in concurrence.

"That doesn't matter," my Glower said before anyone else could speak. "It is true, there would be enough for all of us if we kept away from you and you from us."

"Or perhaps there could be a limit of time," another Glower suggested. "The Society could protect a person for five years, or ten, to let them see what potential they can achieve on their own, and then we would be allowed to offer our assistance unimpeded. They should *all* be given the free choice."

As if any choice was free when the person being offered it didn't know about the demonic manipulations directing their insecurities and desires.

"We could have one area where the Society doesn't interfere," a third Glower put in. "A large enough metropolis would give us a broad range."

"Or we could agree to spread out our feeds between multiple people, so that they are not drained as quickly."

My hands clenched involuntarily. They were speaking so casually, as if it weren't people's lives they were talking about. No, people's *deaths*. Setting aside an entire city for them to siphon the energy out of as if the creative minds there were cattle herded to a slaughter. Murdering them more slowly rather than all at once.

Maybe I should have taken heart that they were considering adjusting their behavior to our preferences at all. But I heard nothing that told me they cared how we *felt* about their actions or the consequences that followed them. Did they really think we'd happily hand people over for them to kill just to make our jobs a little easier?

My Glower might have picked up on my growing revulsion, or maybe she simply felt it was time for the conversation to take a turn. "What do you feel would be the best proposal, Mateo?" she said to me. "You know the elders in your Society. Do you think they would see possibility in any of these ideas?"

I steeled myself and shoved my horror down. I could have ended this charade of a negotiation now, but hearing all those Glowers speak only made me more determined to find a way to stop them. And my best chance of doing that was finding out more about them. I just needed to string them along until they revealed a greater weakness than we already knew.

"I can mention the ideas to my superiors—carefully, of course—and see what their reactions are," I said. "I'm sure they would, ah, appreciate any scenario that decreases our workload. It might help if I understand better—how often do you *need* to feed? And how many of you are there, that we would need to accommodate for?"

The Glower who'd suggested they get a whole city to themselves opened his mouth, but Zut broke in first. "We can discuss the details once we have narrowed down the strategies. Will you remember all we've said? We should be making a record, I suppose."

"I can take care of that," I said quickly. I pulled out my phone and opened the notes app. The Glowers started talking again, tossing out ideas for how to reorganize their meals as my thumbs darted over the touchscreen. Zut studied me with such obvious suspicion it seemed unwise to ask another blatant question.

I'd get the information I wanted. I just needed a way to talk to the others apart from him.

$$Eight$$

"SO THERE WILL BE MORE GATHERINGS?" I ASKED MY Glower as a different cab carried us back to my apartment building. Zut had continued his careful watch over my movements until she'd declared it was time for us to leave, but I wasn't about to give up.

"We will reconvene in perhaps a week," the Glower said. "You're willing to attend another?"

I nodded. "I was thinking it might be more productive if I could speak to a few of you at a time, in a less formal situation. To get different perspectives without the pressure of a larger audience." Without Zut hanging over us poised to interfere with my questions.

"That might be possible." Her expression went distant. I wondered what sort of logistics went into arranging such a gathering.

"Can you reach out to them?" I asked. "Or... I don't know how you normally communicate."

"I have ways," she said vaguely.

When the cab stopped at my building, the Glower got out too, smoothing the skirt of her dress down over her thighs. I brought my gaze back to her face and found her smiling at me slyly.

"Then I'll see you when you're able to get a group together?" I said.

She leaned close and stroked her fingers down my arm. My pulse jumped. "I haven't forgotten your end of our deal, Mateo. Shall we take this upstairs?"

My reaction to her touch was strong enough that I almost protested. But that was what I wanted, wasn't it? To react to someone else. To rewire those pathways in my brain. With her, it would be simple, harmless, and purely physical. I could handle that.

"All right," I said.

She didn't make another move until we'd stepped into the apartment. She ambled into the middle of the living room as I locked the door. When I joined her, she set one slim hand on my chest, right over my suddenly thudding heart. The shimmer in her hair started to brighten, a lilac scent tickling my nose. I jerked back.

"No," I said. "I don't want that again. Don't make yourself look like anyone I know. Or knew. The way you already are is fine."

The Glower's eyebrows rose slightly, but her hair shifted back and the lilac smell faded away. "If this is what you'd prefer," she said.

I wasn't sure what I'd *prefer*, but I had no doubt that dreaming about Avery wouldn't help my situation. The woman in front of me, the stranger the Glower pretended to be, that was who I needed to focus on.

I touched her face, the soft skin of her cheek, and ran my

fingers into her hair as I tugged her in for a kiss. Her lips parted against mine, welcoming. Her tongue slipped into my mouth, and just like that, I was hard. Hell, this creature had power.

I drew back to catch my breath and found myself remembering the exact wording of our deal. "You said you were going to show me how to set people at ease, give them what they need," I said into the space between us. "Is this supposed to accomplish that somehow?"

She chuckled, low and light, and bent her head toward my neck. "Before you can make others feel they can open up, you need to know how to open up yourself, Mateo," she murmured, brushing her lips against the corner of my jaw. "And you don't know that at all. You are so closed, I wonder if *you* even know what you really want."

That comment echoed my earlier thought so closely that my chest clenched despite the shiver that had passed through me at her kiss. "And this is the best way to find out?"

She trailed her lips carefully down my throat, and I closed my eyes. Maybe I didn't care. I didn't actually expect a Glower to find a solution. Who I was... was just the way I was.

"You and I, we'll open you up physically, and we'll see what else comes out to play," she said. "It's the easier direction to start in. We can be a little more focused this time."

She nudged me toward the bedroom door. I went, taking her hand to pull her with me. On the bed, I reached to kiss her again, but she pushed me back.

"Lie down," she said. Watching her with curiosity and apprehension mixed, I stretched out on my back, my head propped on the duck-down pillow. She climbed over me. Her dress rode up the curves of her thighs as she straddled my waist. "This time, you don't have to do anything. Nothing except tell me what you like. When I should keep going. When

I should switch tacks. Whatever makes you feel best. There's nothing you could ask for that would bother me. If you think it, say it."

That didn't sound hard at all. But when she leaned forward, setting her hands on either side of my head, and said, "Tell me where I should kiss you, Mateo," my pulse stuttered with a familiar jolt of panic. She dipped closer. "There. What is that?"

"Nothing," I said firmly. I set my hands on her hips, sliding down over the taut muscles there to the hem of her dress and up again. This was a dream. This was a figment of a woman. Nothing I said made any difference to her at all. "On my neck," I said, feeling the lingering tingle from before. My heartbeat hiccupped again, but only faintly this time. "Kiss me on my neck."

She pressed her mouth to that point just below my jaw again. Her breasts rested against my chest as she kissed her way slowly along the tender flesh, charting a path from one side of my throat to the other. Then she worked her way down to the hollow at its base. My breaths turned shallow. My hands rose to her waist, pulling her tighter against me. The stroke of her tongue sent sparks through me with each caress. A different want rose up inside me.

"My mouth," I said. Without asking for further clarification, she caught my lips with hers. She reached down my body and eased her hands up under my shirt, pausing as if waiting for a protest, but I felt no need to keep my clothes on this time.

I raised my arms and she broke the kiss to pull my shirt off. I grasped the zipper of her dress.

"I want to feel you against me," I said. "Just skin."

She shrugged the straps over her shoulders as I pulled the zipper down. The dress pooled around her waist to reveal a dark purple strapless bra that barely contained her small, pert breasts.

"What do you want?" she whispered, and I realized another urge had bubbled up inside me.

"I want to touch you," I said.

She lowered herself to me. "Whatever you want," she said. "You can have everything."

I eased my hands into the cups and pushed the bra down. Her nipples turned to pebbles against my palms. I left them for just a second to find the hooks and release the bra completely. Once I'd tossed it away, I returned my attention to her chest. Pushing myself up on an elbow, I took one of those nipples into my mouth as I rolled the other beneath my thumb. She gave a little gasp. She tasted sweet and smoky, as if she'd bathed in sugar and ashes. Was that some fantasy I hadn't known I'd had, that she'd conjured up for me? I didn't want to ask.

She rocked against me, edging further down my body to press herself against my groin. With a groan, I released her breast and yanked her mouth back to mine. My hand on her back, I pulled her flush against me. My erection strained against my slacks between her legs. But when her fingers fluttered down my sides to the hem of my pants, I found I wasn't ready for that release quite yet.

"Touch me again," I muttered against her lips. "The way you just did."

"Like this?" she said, tracing those fingertips back up my torso. Such a small motion, and yet the contact sent tremors of warmth through me from head to toe.

"Yes," I said. With each request I made, the words came easier. "Just like that."

She kissed my neck again as she repeated that gentle caress. My hips jerked up, and she chuckled softly. Then she ground down against me, making my breath catch. A deeper hunger surged up.

"I want to be on top of you," I growled. "I want to be *in* you."

She tipped to the side and I rolled us, coming to rest over her body. I wrenched down her dress. She squirmed the rest of the way out of it as I tugged off her panties in turn. Then she was clutching the top button of my slacks, her eyes rising to mine in question.

"Yes," I said. "Please." I didn't think I could take much more of this without bursting.

I dipped my hand between us as we disengaged the rest of my clothing together. The folds between her legs were wet and ready for me. As I teased a finger inside her, she lifted her hips in an invitation I had to take. With a desperate sound, I guided myself in.

Our mouths crushed together as I pushed into the hot tight center of her. I thrust slowly, building speed, keeping a restraint I hadn't managed before. She felt so good I didn't want this to be over that quickly. I wanted to stay here in the agony on the verge of release long enough to write over the desires of the past, the desires I'd never be able to fulfill in reality again. Long enough to hold off the clearing of my head when I had to think about *who* I had taken this pleasure with.

Somehow she didn't feel close enough. "Hold on to me," I said between pants. She wrapped her arms around me. "Tighter."

She clutched at me, bucking her hips to meet my thrusts. My head started to whirl. I swallowed a moan. One of her arms slipped from my side, and a pang shot through my chest.

"Don't let go," I managed to say.

As she pulled me to her again, I went even harder inside her. I rocked faster, unable to hold myself back any longer.

"Come for me," I murmured.

A sigh escaped her lips. She contracted around me, and I couldn't take any more. I gave over to my own release, coming and coming until I slumped over her with a rasp in my throat.

She looped an arm around my shoulders, running her other hand over my side in that fluttery way I'd asked her to repeat. Igniting me even after I'd just come apart.

"There," she said. "Wasn't that a relief—to say what you want, and receive it?"

"It was," I admitted, but the haze in my head was already retreating. I rolled us onto our sides, caressing the curve of her back down to her hips. *Her* breath was barely disturbed.

I'd asked her to come, and she'd given the impression of it almost immediately. As if on command. A question I hadn't thought to ask before gnawed at me.

"How does it feel for you? I mean, does it—do you enjoy it?"

"It is an act it takes us time to adjust to," she said. "There is nothing quite like this when we are amongst ourselves. But with practice, many of us take some pleasure from it. I do."

Not as much as I did, I thought. I cupped her breast, circling her nipple with my thumb. "So what do *you* like?"

She stilled my hand with hers. "That isn't the point of this exercise."

This exercise. The words stung me in a way I hadn't thought would be possible. Of course I'd known this was all a transaction. But she'd seemed so eager... That had all been part of the fantasy. The dream. I should have remembered that *none* of it was real.

A sense of selfishness prickled over me. I'd always found it hard to get much pleasure from sex unless I knew my partner was equally engaged. Even a partner like this one, apparently.

"What if what I wanted was to make *you* feel good?" I asked. She shook her head as she eased away.

"Then you succeeded," she said. "I did." She sat up, unabashed in her nakedness. "You did well, Mateo. I think you said almost everything."

Almost. What did she think I hadn't? I started to think through every moment since we'd come into the bedroom, but I was distracted by her sliding off the bed. She picked up her dress.

"You're going now?" I said.

She gave me a look that was almost amused. "Do you want me to stay?"

I didn't. I might be able to accept what we were doing as two consenting adults of some form, but that didn't mean I wanted to cuddle with a demon. The selfish shame prickled deeper, even though I doubted she cared one bit.

"I don't even know your name," I said. "You have one, don't you?"

For a second, she looked startled, for the first time since I'd met her. Her lips parted and pressed together again. Then she smiled. "It would be difficult for you to pronounce. The closest and easiest you could say is 'Kess.'"

"Kess," I repeated. "Kess, do you think—"

I glanced up, and she was already gone. All at once I wasn't even sure what I'd meant to ask her.

I had been focusing on successful Tether-client relationships in my survey of the Society's records, but the next morning after I sat in what had become "my" cubicle in the office, I found myself pulling up the failures. The clients we hadn't saved—the ones the Glowers had consumed. Their discussion yesterday of ways to stay "fed" was still ringing in my ears.

I'd developed a few theories about what led to our successes that the data had borne out so far, but I needed to consider the more depressing side of our work to get the full picture. I braced myself as I scrolled through the first profile.

Lord, she'd only been eighteen. A pop singer who'd gotten her start four years earlier when one of her online videos had gone viral. She'd been matched with a Tether at fifteen after she'd gotten a major label deal, but obviously something had gone wrong, because she'd ended up marked by a Glower less than a year later. She'd spiraled downward faster than most who had the benefit of the Society's assistance, bottoming out with one handful of pills too many.

I headed to the bottom of the entry to consult the detailed timeline notes and halted. The entire field for Tether reports was blank. No mention of the client's behavior before the marking, of how it had happened, or of the events afterward. Not even an account of her death.

It'd only been a few years ago. There must have *been* notes. Surely we hadn't lost them? I hadn't entered data on the failures when I'd been helping out, but every record I had entered into the system had come with at least some details.

I brought up another file from the list. Then another, and another. They were all blank except for the base details. What was going on?

Frowning, I got up and went to Sterling's office.

Sterling was bent over his own laptop when I came in, his expression clouded, but when he saw me he smiled. "Ah, Mateo. How's our new endeavor coming along?"

"It's coming," I said, finding myself smiling back. Maybe it wasn't the work I'd imagined myself doing, but at least it was something useful I could contribute until my investigations into the Glowers bore more fruit. "It's taking a while to sift through all the data, but I'm starting to see patterns. About the data, though—we seem to be missing some."

His brow furrowed as I explained. He brought up the program on his own computer and checked the files to confirm. Then he looked at an administrator code I hadn't had access to on my end. "I entered this batch of files," he said. "I'm sure the records were there, or I'd have made a note that they were missing. It was May 15th... Ah."

He sat back in his chair, looking grim. I couldn't think of anything special about May 15th. "Did something happen then?" I asked.

"It was— Well." He seemed to shake himself out of a memory. "I must have been particularly distracted. It's my mistake. I'll dig up the paper copies and get these entered properly."

"I don't mind taking care of it, if you have other work to get to," I said, puzzled. I'd never known Sterling to completely blank on a task. He was usually the one whipping the rest of us into shape. But I guessed everyone had an off day now and then.

"No, it's my responsibility," Sterling said. He stood up and waved me out of the office ahead of him. "I don't think it'll take more than a few days. You have other records to continue to go over in the meantime?"

"Yes, plenty," I assured him.

I hesitated by my chair as he strode to the records room. May 15th. I took out my phone and checked the calendar app. I'd been with Jayden for an appearance in Chicago that day, nowhere near Sterling or the office, so I had no idea what might have gone down.

As I lowered my phone, my gaze caught on a figure stepping past the office's front door. My heart lurched.

"Hey, Mateo!" Avery said with a little wave. Her smile faltered, and I realized I was gripping the top of my chair as if I needed it to keep me steady. Maybe I had needed it. My pulse was still pounding. I let go, willing my body to relax and my mouth to form a friendly grin.

I'd talked with my ex-girlfriend dozens of times since we'd broken up, as was inevitable when we both worked here. It'd never been a problem before. But this time... This was the first time I'd seen her since seeing "her" naked on my kitchen counter last week. I swallowed thickly. I could will away a lot of things, but I couldn't erase those memories completely. Less than seven days ago, I had and I hadn't been kissing those lips, touching the warm skin that right now was hidden beneath a navy shirt dress.

I hadn't thought before, but I did now—how would *Avery* feel if she had any idea what I'd done, how I'd used her likeness?

"Time off from a client?" I said, hoping I didn't sound strange.

"Just a little breather," she said. "I've got to get back in a half an hour. I'm just picking up something Fee said she'd leave for me."

I nodded. "Is the new assignment still going well?"

"About as smoothly as you can ever hope," she said, and her smile brightened. Seeing that made my pulse skip in a way it hadn't in months. "I've already been talking with her about the supplements—she might not need me much longer!"

She started for the row of cubbies at the back of the office where we passed around "mail" that couldn't be digitized, and paused. "Oh, I should check: Are you coming to the summer mixer? I don't think we got an RSVP from you."

Every year at the beginning of the summer, one of the Tethers hosted a get-together intended for us to blow off steam and celebrate our victories since Christmas time. I remembered getting the email about it, remembered seeing that Avery and her mom were hosting this year. I'd been in the middle of an event with Jayden, so it wasn't surprising I might have forgotten to respond.

I hadn't been to her house since we'd broken up. I hadn't been to a mixer since we'd broken up. And she'd probably be there with Colin.

Despite my earlier reaction, the punch of nausea that thought gave me took me by surprise. I gritted my teeth. Whatever buried feelings that ill-advised encounter had stirred up, I had to get rid of them. I'd had my chance with her already. I'd fumbled it. She deserved to be with someone who made her happy. None of that had changed.

"It's the Saturday after next, right?" I said, and Avery nodded. "Yeah, I'm free. Sorry, I wasn't sure when I first got the invite, and then it slipped my mind."

"Great," she said, and walked on. I dragged my eyes away from the soft sway of her hips and stared at my laptop screen.

It was Kess who'd stirred up those feelings. But I was the one who'd stupidly gone along with her role-play. Never again.

And maybe if I continued spending my time with her more wisely, she could burn the same feelings right out of me.

Nine

I LOVED MY FAMILY. I REALLY DID. IT JUST SOMETIMES seemed as if there were far too many people in it. Or maybe the problem was how many of them repeated the same comments whenever they saw me.

"By yourself again, Teo? It's been a while since you brought a girl around."

"Not ready to settle down yet? Don't wait too long, or all the good ones will be snatched up."

"What happened to that lovely young woman you used to always be with?"

"Your *mami* is going to be getting worried she'll never see any grandkids."

And on it went as I worked my way around the big buffet table set up in the park for my Aunt Paola's birthday picnic. We three dozen or so of the Jimenez clan and assorted branches had taken over the BBQ area down the hill from the playground, which was closed off by a yellow plastic fence for repairs. My aunt's grandchildren were racing around the trees here instead. My Uncle Alex was grilling hot dogs alongside fish tamales, filling the air with a mix of smells distinctly American and Colombian. The voices around me spoke in a similar mishmash of English and Spanish, mostly varying by age. My dad had made a big deal about practicing English at home with me and my younger brother and sister after we'd started school, because he'd seen how his accent and grammatical stumbles had hurt him while looking for work. Some of his siblings had taken a similar approach, some had been more relaxed, but everyone here spoke at least a little of both languages.

Ricky hadn't been lying when he'd pointed out that I missed a lot of these get-togethers, but with a family this big, there was some notable event to celebrate practically every week. I tried to make it at least once a month. I might have begged off a bit more often than usual in the last year, though. Even when I'd had my lingering feelings for Avery under control, listening to every second person bring her up either specifically or vaguely could feel like walking down a hazing line of memories.

I'd gone for a long run this morning, and the pleasant burn of that exertion made it easier to smile and nod and change the subject. I asked my cousin Veronica how her mother-in-law had liked the painting I'd helped her pick out as a housewarming gift and exclaimed over the marker drawings my little nephew Sergio had brought along to show me. And when my mom caught wind of my Aunt Lizbeth berating me for my "careless" single lifestyle, she had no problem asserting her actual opinion.

"Mateo will make a good choice, and that takes time," she said. "Besides, please, I'm much too young still to be a grandmother."

So it might have been a *mostly* enjoyable afternoon if Ricky hadn't strutted over to me while I had half a corn cake in my mouth and shoved a CD case into my hand. I gulped down my mouthful.

"What's this?"

"My demo," he said, eyeing me defiantly. "I know what you've said before, but I didn't have anything real then. You've got to know at least one producer you could pass this off to with a good word. A friend of mine knows a guy who has a studio space in his basement, got me a little time as a favor."

When I didn't answer right away, just looked at the CD, he shuffled his feet. "Okay, and I'm sorry about the other day, all right? I was out of line. I just, you know, it threw me off that you were there, so I wasn't thinking straight."

"All right," I said. "I appreciate the apology. But I really don't know anyone I could give this to, Ricky."

I was a little afraid to hear what his recording might sound like too—would a semi-professional set-up have offset some of the eccentricities of his vocals or only amplified them?

"Oh, come on," he said.

"No, really. I'm not even working with a client right now, and the last one in the music scene was a completely different style—*and* I never met his producer in the first place. It's not like I'm hanging out with label execs on the job."

He grimaced. "Well, you should still hold on to it. Maybe one of your coworkers will end up with a good connection. Or maybe you'll run into someone. I don't want to miss any chances."

"Sure," I said. "Just don't count on it." I could at least listen to it. There was a tiny possibility he'd gotten his act together in the... month? since I'd heard his last cringe-inducing performance. "Are you sure this is your best material, what you want to lead with?"

"Of course," Ricky said. "It's great. You've heard me. It's just a matter of getting noticed now."

I was spared any further discussion in that direction by my Great-Uncle Carlos, who came up behind Ricky and tussled his hair as if the guy was still an elementary kid and not a technical adult who'd just graduated high school. "So good to see cousins getting along," he said. "Why don't you bring that nice girl of yours anymore, Mateo? Ava, was that her name?"

"Avery," I said. "We're not together anymore, *Tio Abuelo*."

"She was such a lovely young lady. Whatever you did wrong, you make it up to her."

"It's not like that," I said. "We just weren't the right fit for each other. Hey, what's this I heard about you joining a new bowling league?"

Before he answered, Ricky's eyebrows shot up. He was looking over my shoulder.

"Wow, who brought that babe?" he said.

I turned, and my stomach flipped. My Glower "friend" was sauntering down the hill toward us. The flared spaghetti strap dress Kess was wearing today managed to show off every curve while still maintaining enough modesty not to shock my older relatives—her shoulders were bare but not her cleavage, and the sleek blue fabric only hugged the top of her hips before flowing down to brush her knees. Her lips were curved into her usual smirk.

I might have been gratified by the way Ricky's eyes bugged out when she continued her stroll all the way to my side and reached to take my hand, but I was preoccupied wondering what the hell the Glower was doing in the midst of my family.

"Mateo," she said in a silvery voice, "I'm sorry I'm late."

Ricky cleared his throat, obviously expecting to be introduced. My great-uncle studied me curiously. I ignored both of them. Gripping Kess's hand, I dragged her a few steps away from the rest of the group. Not fast enough. Several heads had already turned toward us.

"What do you think you're doing?" I demanded under my breath.

"I had a feeling you needed to be rescued," she murmured in reply. "Are you so upset to see me?"

I wasn't, I realized, which no doubt she'd already known. I was getting tired—of Ricky's demands, of the rest of the family's well-meaning concern—and her arrival was an excuse to leave. But still...

"I told you to leave my family out of this."

"And I haven't said a word to any of them," she said, peering at me innocently through her lashes.

Technically she hadn't broken our agreement. I still didn't like her being this close to them. "Stay here," I ordered, and moved to head off my father, who was ambling our way.

"Who's this?" he asked with a knowing smile.

"A *friend*," I said. "I've got to head out a bit early. Where's Tia Paola?"

He glanced around. "Oh, she went to take a few of the little ones to the ice cream truck."

I'd already talked with her earlier. I doubted she'd be very offended by my ducking out without a direct farewell— especially if she heard I'd ducked out with an attractive young woman. "Can you give her my apologies and tell her I'll see her at the anniversary party in a few weeks?"

"Of course," Dad said. He clapped me on the shoulder and gave me a wink. "What is it they say? Don't do anything I wouldn't do."

"Ha. Right."

"Are you sure your 'friend' wouldn't like to share our meal, now that she's here?" he added.

I might be hearing about my "lack of manners" from my mom for a month if she didn't. I scooped an empanada onto a paper plate. "Just a little," I said. "I think she already ate."

"Mateo," Ricky said, coming over, and I held up my hand to stop him.

"Sorry, cuz, I've got to run," I said. "I'll see what I can do about the demo."

The mention of his music was a cheap ploy, but it satisfied him enough to make him pause while I performed my escape. I rejoined Kess and directed her up the hill.

"For me?" she said, peering at the empanada.

"If you want it," I said. She accepted the plate from me and bit the pastry gingerly. On her second bite, she must have gotten a chunk of pepper, because her eyes widened. She coughed into her hand.

"Sorry," I said. "My mom likes to make them spicy. So what exactly do you mean, you 'had a feeling' I wasn't happy?" I didn't think I'd been *that* uncomfortable—and I hadn't thought Glowers could sense emotions unless they were nearby. "Have you been following me?"

Of course, I didn't know exactly how our planes of existence overlapped. She'd been aware of my entire conversation with Ricky in my apartment the other day. How often did they just *watch* us, present but invisible? Glowers couldn't enter a private space without being invited, but out in public like this, little restricted their movements.

Kess laughed, more freely than her usual dry chuckle. "No, no," she said with an expansive wave of her arm. "When we've spent some time with the same person, we can become more sensitive to their moods. And you, Mateo, are a moody one."

Her mood had changed again—the way it had in the cab when we'd nearly crashed, and before, when she'd eaten the spicy stir-fry. It had changed now right after she'd bitten that chunk of pepper. Was it something about the shock to her physical senses?

She glanced over her shoulder toward the picnic. "So why is it you're so eager to protect people who make you uneasy?"

That question itched at me in a different way. "I don't dislike them," I said. "And I wasn't actually that bothered. Maybe you're being too sensitive."

She took another bite of the empanada and waggled a finger at me. "There's something about them that rubs you the wrong way."

"They have a lot of expectations," I said grudgingly. "It can be a *little* overwhelming when I'm not meeting many of those."

"But my arrival helped somewhat with that?"

It was hard to see the vibrant sparkle in her eyes and deny it. "Maybe," I allowed. She grinned and hooked her arm around mine. The slide of her smooth skin sent a flush of warmth through me, and suddenly my answer was much more than maybe. I needed that heat to burn the thought of Avery right out of me. I couldn't be turning into a quivering mess every time she turned up at the office.

When we reached the top of the hill, I meandered a short distance farther to the short plastic wall around the playground. Then I turned to face Kess. I let myself follow the instincts I would have applied to an actual woman, lifting my hand to tuck an errant lock of her hair behind her ear.

"So are you going to disappear now that you've 'rescued' me or were you thinking of sticking around a while?" I asked.

She ran her fingers lightly up my side, the way I'd asked her to in my bed the other night, and the earlier flush became a flood of heat. She smiled up at me. "You're so *tense*, Mateo. I'm still keeping my end of the deal. I can help you let out what you're holding in."

I wanted her to be the one spilling secrets, not the other way around. But that laughing, animated persona had faded into cool composure again. My gaze drifted over the fence and settled on the little merry-go-round—just a metal disc with handle bars on a spinning base—in the sand on the other side of the wall.

She knew how to affect me so well. What I wanted most was for that to go both ways. To open her up, to learn everything I could about her kind... To know she was giving herself over just as I was when we came together. I'd seen ways of affecting her too. The food, the sense of motion. It had been accidental until now, but maybe I could make it happen.

"Come here," I said, tugging her toward the wall. I vaulted over, and she followed suit before I had the chance to offer her my hand.

"You wanted some play time?" she said as she took in the abandoned playground. The partly disassembled swing set lay on the ground to our left, but the rest of the equipment had already been updated. I guessed the last of it would be finished after the weekend.

"There are different sorts of playing," I said with a smirk to echo her own, and led her to the merry-go-round. "Ever ridden one of these?"

"I can't say I have," she said, raising an eyebrow. She stepped on gamely. "How does it work?"

"It's very simple," I said, and pushed one of the bars. Kess let out a low chuckle as the disc began to rotate, carrying her away from me.

I gave each handlebar that passed me another heave, until the merry-go-round was really flying. Kess clutched the bar in front of her, laughing openly again, the skirt of her dress rippling up around her legs. Even with the sun beaming down over us, the gleam in her skin dimmed.

I'd done it. There had to be something about intense physical sensations—maybe they connected her more fully to the human body she'd created? I'd need to report this to Sterling.

But that was Monday's concern. "Faster!" Kess said, and raised one hand to the wind as I shoved the bars with all my strength. A chuckle tumbled from my lips. My own breath was coming short from the effort, but I couldn't help grinning with her.

After a minute, I stopped and let the merry-go-round spin on its own momentum. Kess let out a little cheer as she whirled away from me, her hair whipping around her face. Then, as the disc swung her toward me, she hopped off, grinning as wide as I was. Her eyes danced with a light that had nothing to do with any supernatural power. I didn't think about it or decide, I just moved, cupping her face to kiss her.

She kissed me back with an eagerness that felt different from the calculated passion she'd given me before. Her tongue darted between my lips to tempt mine, and I deepened the kiss. Her fingers twisted into the fabric of my shirt. With that one gesture, I wanted her more than I ever had before.

I wanted her like *this*, giddy and wild. Who knew how long it would last? I broke the kiss to survey the playground and dragged her into the plastic fort formed between a slide and a set of climbing bars. The roof was just high enough that I could stand inside without hunching. The sunlight reflected off the bright walls and turned Kess's skin a faint purple tone. She hummed as I kissed her again and pressed my body to hers, her back against the wall. Her hand snaked under my shirt.

"No," I said before she could get very far. "This time is about you."

She pouted playfully, that excitement still sparkling in her eyes. "That's not the deal."

"The deal is you're supposed to help me show what I really want," I said. "What I really want right now is to find out what makes *you* moan. You can feel that's true, can't you?"

She nodded, her gaze locked with mine. I eased my hand up her side and rubbed my thumb across her breast. "I want to know the best ways to touch *you*," I said.

I could barely feel her nipple through the layers of fabric. I yanked down the strap of her dress and lowered the neckline until I could displace that strapless bra as well. Her breast leapt into the muted sunlight.

Kess's eyes slid shut as I rolled her nipple beneath my thumb. I pinched it with a forefinger, but her expression barely altered. "That's nice," she said.

I wanted more than *nice*. I softened my touch, stroking that stiffening nub more and more lightly, until I was only grazing the very tip.

A flush had started to creep up Kess's chest. I caressed her over and over with that gentle pressure, and a whimper worked its way up her throat. She swallowed as if she'd tried to contain it. Her eyelids fluttered.

Watching her, seeing her get truly turned on, was turning *me* on too. My erection had risen beneath the fly of my pants, straining against the fabric, but I wanted more from her first. I continued my soft, slow exploration of her breast as I tugged the bodice of her dress down to free the other. Then I was holding both of them, that sweet smoky smell filling my nose as I leaned close to kiss her cheek. Her breath broke into little pants as I teased both nipples into harder peaks.

"Mateo," she murmured, pleading and also somehow startled. I thought of her comments about enjoying sex the last time we'd seen each other. I might be the first person who'd provoked this much of a response in her. Who'd taken the time to figure out how to draw her into her body, and what brought that body the most pleasure.

The thought sent a rush of exhilaration through me. I glided my thumbs around her nipples as I bent to nibble the crook of her neck and was rewarded with my first moan. Her arms looped around my neck, holding me to her.

"What do you want?" I said against her skin.

She arched into my hands. "I don't know. But I want you to find out."

I found her lips again, kissing her hard. Every part of me ached to be inside her, but I wasn't done exploring.

I let go of one breast to slip my hand down and under the skirt of her dress. Kess made an encouraging noise as I slicked my finger over the dampening panties I found beneath. I kept up the same light pressure that had worked so well already, flicking my thumb against her and venturing lower with feathery caresses, until she was pressing into my hand. Her hips brushed my erection, and I had to swallow a groan of my own. I tucked my hand right inside her panties and received another moan from her. Her hands roamed over my back, my sides, clinging to me as her hips swayed.

"Mateo," she said, and there was nothing in her voice but longing now. My body turned to flame. I pulled her panties down and undid my belt. As soon as she heard the click of the buckle, she reached for my fly, still gripping me tightly with her other arm. "Yes," she murmured. "Yes. Oh!"

I'd thought she'd been wet for me before, but as I slid inside her now, the hot slickness of her nearly melted me. I kissed her lips, her jaw, her temple as I eased in and out of her, trying to maintain the same slow and gentle rhythm despite every muscle screaming at me to pound away to my release. It was her arms, clutched around me, that let me hold on. Her leg, hooked around my hip, pulling me even closer. The frantic gasps escaping her lips with increasing frequency. As if she needed me, needed what I could do for her. As if nothing mattered but this.

A tremor traveled through her body against mine. The gasps collided into a cry. I sped up my thrusts, and she clenched around me, her embrace tightening at the same moment. Her arms locked in their embrace as the shivers rippled through her. Then she relaxed against me, her lips brushing my shoulder.

"Now you," she said in a tone that was almost tender. "I want everything."

The last bit of my control snapped. I pushed her hard against the plastic wall and drove faster into the sweet slick friction of her body. She whimpered, her fingers digging into my back. Then she was shuddering around me again as I came inside her, shuddering too.

"Oh," she said. "*Oh*." In that moment she sounded somehow lost.

We came to rest against the wall once more, my sweat-damp forehead against her hair. As my thundering heartbeat slowed, I eased out of her. But I found I didn't want to move any farther away. Her foot dropped to the ground, but her arms stayed wrapped around me. Her breath tickled my cheek. I touched the side of her face, struck by an unanticipated sense of concern.

"Kess?"

She didn't answer with words, only raised her hands to the back of my head to tug my mouth to hers. We kissed slow and deep, tongues and breath mingling, until *I* was lost. I drew back, my thoughts spinning. My gaze dropped to her bare shoulder, struck by a beam of light that fell through a gap in the play fort's ceiling. To the skin there shimmering with a glow that was not of this world. The haze in my head started to clear.

The woman in front of me wasn't my date or my girlfriend

or even my lover. She wasn't even a *woman*. Even if I had provoked some feeling in her that she hadn't experienced before, she'd only gone along with this encounter because of the deal we'd made. Because she wanted help from me in return. None of this meant anything more to her.

I tucked myself back into my pants and pulled up the bodice of her dress without looking Kess in the eyes. As she bent to straighten her skirt, I backed up a step. I'd gotten caught up in the moment. Now I needed to focus.

"Have you been able to set up another get-together, with even a couple of the other Glowers?" I asked.

I tried to keep my tone casual, but Kess's head jerked up as if she'd heard something odd in it. She studied me for a moment. If any sign of the vulnerability I'd thought I'd seen in her expression before had lingered, it vanished completely then. When she replied, her voice was flat.

"Not yet. I'm not in charge of the others, you know. I can only ask and see what they will agree to."

"All right," I said. "I just— It seemed as if you all were in a hurry to get this settled."

She tipped her head, her hair glittering even in the shadows of the fort. "Have you talked to your superiors at the Society about our initial suggestions?"

She had me there. I opened my mouth intending to lie and thought better of it. She'd probably be able to tell.

"I'm waiting for the right moment," I said instead, which was mostly true. "You have to realize they're not going to be the most... enthusiastic about the idea of a compromise. I'm going to have to be careful how I present it."

"What we're asking will make things easier for them too," she said. "If you simply adjust your approach so that you aren't obsessing about protecting *every* person that might interest us, so many of our conflicts will be eliminated immediately."

"It would only be easier if we could turn off our concern for the people we'd theoretically leave for you," I had to retort. Did she really not see how big an ask this was?

"Your over-generous sympathies are not our fault," she said tartly.

"And your inability to 'feed' yourselves in the way you'd prefer isn't ours," I said. "You realize you're asking us to completely change our moral code as well as our approach, so that your kind can continue getting pretty much exactly what you want the way you want it, don't you?"

"This is the way we live," Kess said, staring at me. "It's how we've always lived. You are the ones who've made it harder for us."

Something tightened in my chest. I couldn't stand talking to her about this any longer. If I heard her make one more callously oblivious comment, I was going to end up telling her just how ridiculous the whole idea of a truce between us and her kind was, and then I'd lose any chance of learning more.

"And human beings have always wanted to survive, and you've made that harder for us," I said quietly. "Look, Kess, I don't know what the rest of the Society is going to say about this, but if you actually want to find a way for us to work around each other, it has to be a real compromise. It's ridiculous for you to expect us to bend to accommodate you if the most you're willing to offer is a slight restriction of *who you kill*. Especially when *you're* the ones afraid of starving. That's all I'm saying. You can tell the rest of the Glowers that before I talk to them again."

I ducked out of the fort, away from her inhuman gaze, and stalked away.

Ten

I WAS IN A CAB ON THE WAY TO AVERY'S HOUSE FOR THE summer mixer when my phone rang. Ricky's name appeared on the screen. I braced myself before answering.

"Teo!" Ricky's voice rang out. "Listen, man, forget about the demo for now. I got hooked up with some connections of my own."

A ribbon of dread wound around my gut. "What do you mean, Ricky?"

"One of my friends met this guy, turns out he's some exec producer type dude, he works for this label—anyway, my friend told him about me, and he called me up, and he thinks I've got real prospects. We're going to meet next week to hash out the deets."

"*He* listened to your demo?"

"Yeah, I emailed him the file. And even before that, he said he could tell just from the way I talk that I've got the kind of voice a lot of people in the industry are looking for right now."

That didn't sound remotely legit. I closed my eyes with a wince. I'd listened to Ricky's demo last week, the night after he'd given it to me. Honestly, I didn't think there was anything wrong with his vocals that some training couldn't fix, but right now they veered off key at random intervals, and the backing music he'd pulled together sounded like something out of a porno film. The slight echo created by the basement "studio" he'd recorded it in didn't help.

No doubt this "producer" was a hack who saw my cousin as an easy mark. The Glowers weren't the only predators that used the hopes of the thousands of aspiring performers in this city for their own selfish ends, only the most lethal. I didn't want Ricky losing the contents of his bank account any more than I wanted him losing his soul.

"What's the guy's name?" I said. "You've got to be careful in this business. I can run it past people I know, make sure he's the real deal."

"I think I can tell a scammer when I talk to one," Ricky said. "Why would you assume that? This could be my big break!"

"I know," I said quickly. "It's just that when someone approaches *you*... It's a really common tactic, that's all. Maybe I'm just being paranoid. Will you give me the name? If he's legit, it won't hurt anything for me to confirm that."

Ricky grumbled to himself before saying, "You're always so down on everything. All right. It's Peter Martinez. He's worked with some big names. You'll see."

"I hope you're right," I told him truthfully.

After I hung up, I tipped my head back against the seat. I hadn't heard that name before, in a good context or a bad one. At least Ricky had brought it up with convenient timing. I could ask around at the party. Most of us had worked with a client in the music industry at some point, and a few Tethers specialized in that area. At very least, one of the more senior Society members might be able to point me to someone else I could contact to check the guy's credentials.

The house Avery shared with her mother, Catherine, looked the same as it always had: a modest split-level, beige with mauve trim. An awkward sense of deja vu tickled over me as I walked to the front door—every other time I'd made this approach, it'd been with Avery at my side or knowing she'd soon be there—but thankfully nothing more. I could handle this. No problem.

Music hummed through the door. When I rang the bell, Catherine answered. She greeted me with a smile, accepted the bottle of wine I'd brought, and ushered me into the warm glow of the living room. Nothing in her manner suggested she found the shift from girlfriend's mother to fellow colleague uncomfortable, and I relaxed even more. Their home full of heavy rugs and cozy furniture had always put me at ease.

More than a dozen Society members were already scattered through the room, sipping from wine glasses or beer bottles and chatting in clusters. Sterling was standing near the window with Yelena and another senior staffer. Most of the others I hadn't seen often outside of these biannual events, but that was business as usual. The Tether career could be an isolating one.

One of the women I'd gotten to know during my training raised her hand to me in greeting. I joined her cluster, exchanging small talk for a few minutes, and then mentioned Ricky's producer. The guy beside me frowned.

"That name sounds a little familiar, and not in a way I like," he said. "Listen, I'll give you the number of a former client of mine who knows everyone in the industry—he'll have the details if there are any."

"Thanks," I said, relieved to at least have a starting point, even if it sounded as though this former client was going to confirm my suspicions. Then, as I glanced around, my gaze snagged on Avery's bright hair where she stood in the kitchen doorway, framed by the starker light behind her.

She wasn't alone. Colin Ryder was standing next to her, looking every bit the rebellious rock star with his knowing grin and skintight jeans. He put his hand on the small of her back as her mother came over to say something to them, and even as I clenched up inside to shield myself from the pain... I realized I didn't feel more than a twinge.

Part of me still wanted to hate him, I couldn't deny that. But I could see that the way he touched her was affectionate, not possessive; that his expression when he looked at her showed nothing but total adoration. He even made Catherine outright laugh in the several seconds I was watching, where I'd always found it a feat to get more than a soft chuckle out of her. He fit there in a way I guessed I hadn't.

"Sickening, isn't it?" Fiona said cheerfully as she came up beside me. "Hey, Mateo. Good to see you outside the office for once."

"Same to you," I said, and found it was easy to smile back at her. Whatever anyone might have said about the odd arrangement I'd come to with Kess, clearly it had helped wash any remaining longing for Avery out of my system. Still, I turned my back on the happy couple so I wouldn't be tempted to keep watching. I grabbed a beer off the side table and caught myself just shy of offering Fiona one. She'd gone cold turkey on alcohol along with other recreational chemicals since her hospitalization last year after an accidental overdose.

Fiona plucked up a can of Coke and raised it to me. "Cheers!"

I clinked my bottle against the can. "You're not really one to talk," I said, heading her off before she could get started on *my* love life. "You've had hearts in your eyes for weeks. Where's the boyfriend?"

"Oh, well." She grimaced. "I couldn't bring Will, of course, since he doesn't know about the whole 'exactly what we do.'"

"Right," I said, embarrassed. I hadn't given that problem much thought—Avery was the only girl I'd dated more than briefly since the Society had recruited me. Not giving my family the full details of the job felt par for the course, but to hide that big a secret from someone I was intimate with? That would seem more like lying. "Are you ever allowed to tell him?"

"The Society strongly advises against," she said, in a tone that suggested she was repeating Sterling's words. "Which I guess makes sense, because what are the chances someone who can't *see* the Glowers is going to believe they exist, rather than thinking we must be delusional cultists or something? And that could get the Society into all sorts of trouble. We don't talk about work that much anyway, especially now that I'm on to a new client and his sister's doing well. But... yeah, if we get more serious, I think it's going to be tough."

"Some people manage," I pointed out. Sterling was a bachelor as far as I knew, but Yelena was married, and so were several of the older Tethers—and not all to colleagues.

"We'll see how it goes," Fiona said. "It's only been a few months, after all." She shrugged and grinned, and then her eyebrows leapt up. "Ah, there's Sofie!"

Uh oh. "Fiona," I started, but she'd already rushed over to grasp Sofie's arm and drag her to join us. Seeing that Sofie looked twice as awkward as I felt eased my trepidation.

"Thirsty?" I asked to break the ice. "There's a large selection of beverages."

Sofie gave me the same shy smile as when we'd first met. "I guess I'll have some white wine. Thanks." She peered around the room as I poured her a glass. "I'm glad you two are here. I feel like I hardly know anyone."

"We all feel that way," Fiona assured her. "That's why we have these parties—to remind ourselves there are more than five of us in the whole Society! Oh, I've got to ask Cath something —I'll catch up with you two later."

I restrained myself from giving her the evil eye as she flitted off. I could only hope her matchmaking intent wasn't completely obvious to Sofie.

Sofie took a gulp of her wine and laughed. "Ah, that's better."

"We're all very nice," I said.

"I'm sure," she said, her smile a little freer now. "It's still a lot to take in. I'm *slowly* getting the hang of all this."

"Have you started your trial placements yet?" I said. I'd spent a year in tutoring with a senior Tether and taking classes on everything from self defense to conflict resolution before I'd been allowed to interact with an actual client, but that was because I'd been underage when they'd brought me in. The absolute earliest any Tether went on the job with supervision was sixteen—I'd been nearly seventeen for my first placement— and no one took on a solo assignment until they were eighteen. I'd gathered the training was sped along in tandem with more hands-on learning if you were already of age. The faster we could get more Tethers into the workforce, the more lives we saved.

"My first, just this week," she said with a nod. "It's a pretty low key situation. She's an author—thrillers, but still... But that's definitely the part of the job I've enjoyed the most so far. Seeing how we can actually help people, after what we saw."

That hint of melancholy I'd noticed in the office had crept

into her expression again. "Yeah," I said, my voice going a bit rough as I thought of my own introduction to the world of Glowers. "The rest of it gets easier too. I promise."

She gave me a look as if she were wondering the same thing about me I was about her—how had we gotten here? But she must have gleaned the etiquette around that question, because she just said, "That's good to know. How long have you been doing this?"

"I started training when I was fifteen," I said. "So if you count from then, a little more than seven years now."

"Oh," she said, her eyes widening. "Then, I mean, you were pretty young."

"Fiona and Avery started younger," I said. "I'm glad the Society was there to help me understand what I'd seen. And, like you said, to show me I could make something good come out of it."

"Yeah..." She swirled her wine and seemed to decide it was time for a new topic of conversation. "Is it mostly people in the performing arts we end up working with? I like movies and music and theater and all that, but I'd *really* love to watch a painter or a sculptor at work. I suppose most of them don't become well known enough to be targeted?"

"We do get some clients in those areas," I said. "Different Glowers have different tastes. Are you a visual arts aficionado, then? I'm a bit of a collector myself."

"Are you?" She really brightened then, and I was struck by how not just cute but pretty she was when enthusiasm drew her out of her shell. "To tell you the truth, I wanted to be *in* that field, before... I like to draw, was dabbling with oils and acrylics in high school. I was thinking of trying to get into a fine arts program for college, but, well..." The light dimmed. "Sometimes circumstances get in the way, right? Anyway, it's not as if many people make a living painting pictures these days."

Seeing the Glower-death hadn't been the first life-changing experience she'd gone through, then. I didn't feel any more comfortable prying into that area, but I could honestly say, "Well, if you still draw, I'd love to see your work sometime. I mean, if you don't mind showing it. I have pretty eclectic tastes. Half the stuff in my apartment I got from the UCLA shows."

"Yeah?" She considered me a little more intently than before. "I haven't done anything in a while, but if I start up again, I think I would like to know what you make of it."

A whisper of warmth traveled through me. Before I could decide what it meant or what to do about it, Sterling's brisk voice rang out behind me.

"Mateo!" He tapped my shoulder. "Come here, I'd like you to tell some people about the... project you've been working on."

"We should talk more later," Sofie said to me as I gave her a gesture of apology. Sterling paused to sip from his glass of red wine and motioned for me to follow him across the room.

I didn't see exactly how it happened. The living room had gotten more crowded in the half hour or so since I'd arrived, and we had to dodge a few new arrivals while offering our greetings. But it didn't seem Sterling actually tripped. One moment he was walking steadily along and the next, with a twitch of his hand, his glass was tumbling to the floor.

Voices dropped at the snap of cracking glass. Sterling halted, staring at the ochre and ivory rug and the splatter of wine that had splashed it and his tan trousers. His hand shook. He pressed it to his side and was just kneeling down by the glass when Catherine hurried over.

"I'll take care of that," she told him, brandishing a dustpan and a handheld vacuum. "Why don't you look after your clothes before they stain? I think the bathroom's free."

"Thank you," Sterling said. He still looked a little bewildered, but before I could say anything to him, he'd spun and was striding toward the side hall.

I grabbed a handful of napkins off the refreshment table and dabbed at the puddle as Avery's mother plucked up the larger pieces of glass. Thanks to the rug, the glass hadn't shattered that badly. The woman I'd talked to earlier brought over a can of soda water, which we rubbed into the rug's pile after Catherine had vacuumed up the few smaller shards. Soon little more than a shadow was left.

"There," Catherine said as we straightened up. "I'll give it a more thorough clean tomorrow, but I don't think there's any harm done." Her forehead furrowed as she glanced the way Sterling had gone.

The party chatter rose around us again. Sofie had ambled off somewhere, and I wasn't sure which people Sterling had wanted me to talk to—or even, really, what he'd wanted me to tell them. In the past week I'd come up with some firmer theories for criteria to use when matching Tethers to clients and a couple of proposals for dividing Tether work time, but nothing I'd be confident encouraging anyone to implement yet. With records going back over a hundred years, there was a lot of data to wade through, even with the new interface simplifying matters.

I ate a couple of cocktail shrimp and finished my beer. A niggling of my bladder informed me that I shouldn't have chugged that mug of coffee right before leaving my apartment. I wove through the crowd to the hall and saw the bathroom door was shut, light seeping from the gap beneath it. After waiting a minute, I turned toward the staircase. I knew where the upstairs bathroom was from my previous visits, and I doubted Catherine would be offended by my making use of it now.

I was just passing the second door in the upstairs hall when a wordless exclamation carried through it. My surprise made me stop. So I was standing there and remembering that door led to Avery's bedroom when the exclamation was followed by her low laugh, petering into something like a sigh.

"I'm supposed to be co-hostess of that party downstairs, you know," she said. Her voice was muffled but audible amid the silence in the hall.

"I haven't seen you in ten days," said a husky voice I knew immediately was Colin's. "I missed you."

"And I missed you too," Avery said, sounding amused. "That doesn't change—*oh*."

Whatever she would have said next was lost in a gasp and a faint thud. Suddenly I could picture exactly where they were: the desk at her wall beside the door—leaning against it, or she was sitting up on it while he... did whatever he was doing to draw those sounds out of her.

I should have walked on. But a strange calm had settled over me, and I was too busy marveling at that, at how easily I could accept what I was hearing. I really was over her. I'd been worried, after our tense conversation in the office, that my emotions had been wrenched out of whack all over again, but no, I was fine. This was fine.

Maybe I wasn't completely convinced—maybe I kept standing there to prove to myself how over her I was. What a mistake.

"We *are* going to work out a way for you to tour with me more often," Colin murmured. "You're the most important person in my life, Ave, and I want you around for as much of it as possible. But for now I'll settle for letting the guests entertain themselves while we make up for some of that lost time."

Avery didn't protest again, only hummed a sound of agreement. Then her moan carried through the door. My gut knotted. I propelled myself around and marched back down the stairs, wiping at the sweat that had formed on the back of my neck.

The first floor bathroom door was open now. I hurried over and shut it firmly behind me. In the harsh light of the bulb over the mirror, I splashed cold water on my face. Then I gripped the edge of the sink, staring down at the gleaming porcelain.

It wasn't Avery's sigh or her moan that was replaying in my head. It was Colin's voice. Colin's words. *You're the most important person in my life, and I want you around for as much of it as possible.*

How many times had I wanted to say that to her? How many times had the sentiment been on the tip of my tongue before my pulse had started to clang like an alarm bell warning me it was too much, too soon, too *something*?

She hadn't minded hearing it from him. Why had I been so sure she'd mind it from me? What the hell was *wrong* with me that I'd let her go rather than force out a thought he'd said so easily?

My breath steadied, and as it did the smell of vomit drifted into my nose. I made a face and covered my nose as I finally relieved myself. The toilet looked clean enough, but obviously someone had already downed a little too much alcohol and faced the consequences. My stomach was roiling now as well.

I stepped back into the hall, and the sight of the figures crowded in the living room made everything inside me clench tighter. All those people I was supposed to chat up and make friendly with, without ever saying anything completely real.

Because I never did, did I? Jayden had said it right. When it came down to the things that really mattered, I kept to my own self. I didn't know how to do anything else.

The thought of going back out there, going through the motions with that thought in my head, made me feel like *I* might vomit. I couldn't keep up the act, not any longer tonight.

I slipped down the hall to the back door and made my escape.

Eleven

I'D BEEN LIVING IN THIS APARTMENT BUILDING FOR MORE than two years, coming and going on my own most of the time, but for some reason as I stepped into the lobby that evening in the deepening twilight, I felt so alone it knocked the breath out of me. I stopped by the row of mailboxes to gather myself and then pushed on into the flood of yellow light near the elevator.

As I approached my door at the end of the fourth floor hall, a figure emerged from the shadow in the corner. I found I wasn't at all surprised to see Kess, even though she hadn't come around since our argument in the park. Of course she'd appear when I was feeling like this.

She didn't say anything as I unlocked the door. When we were inside, she took my hand. I followed her to the bedroom and sat down on the edge of the mattress next to her. She raised her fingers to my cheek.

There was something so oddly gentle about that gesture that it made my chest ache. Lord knew what she made of the mess she must see inside me right now. I considered her shoulder, the neckline of her usual black dress bold against her lightly tanned skin. Her collarbone looked more delicate than I remembered.

"Mateo," she said softly, and my gaze flicked up to her eyes. She looked *sad*. Just another mask? But when she stroked my cheek again, all I wanted to do was burrow my head against her neck and hold on to her. She was here, for me. And even though she had ulterior motives, she'd always come to me without any expectations of who I was supposed to be, what I should offer her of myself, other than that it was me.

With a sense of stoicism that seemed mildly ridiculous to me even in the moment, I clamped down on my desire. "I'm fine," I said. "You don't have to be here."

She let out a snort of disbelief. "You're hurting," she said, and her hand stilled. "I know what you need."

Despite her words, she hesitated. Her mouth set in a determined line. Her fingers trailed up into my hair, and I lowered my mouth to hers. The smoky sweet taste of her teased over my lips as I eased us down on the bed. I didn't know if she would ever be able to keep her promise to "open me up," but at least here, when all we spoke of was physical pleasures, I'd learned how to say anything I wanted.

She drew back, dipping her head to kiss her way down my neck. Then the planes of her face, the waves of her hair, shimmered brighter. In the second while my tongue tangled in my mouth, the scent of lilac had already surrounded me.

"Mateo," she murmured in Avery's voice, sliding Avery's hand under my shirt.

"No," I said, and pushed away from her to the edge of the bed. "*No*. I've already spent too much time thinking about her. Please don't."

Kess lay silent beside me. When I thought I could trust that she'd have shifted back, I rolled onto my side to look at her. She was staring up at the ceiling with that same sadness in her face—or maybe it was confusion, or frustration.

"I'm sorry," she said.

It surprised me that she was apologizing rather than trying to cajole me into accepting what she offered. It surprised me more that she sounded truly regretful. Maybe some small part of the brief connection I'd felt with her last week had been real. Had lasted.

"No matter how I'm feeling, no matter what you see in me, I *never* want you to do that again," I said.

She tipped her head in a slight nod. As my gaze traveled over her, it occurred to me that these features, this body, had been chosen to cater to me too. Hadn't I thought when I'd first seen her how well she fit every physical preference I had? I couldn't believe that had been a coincidence. She'd read my desires and turned herself into another sort of dream.

"What do you really look like?" I said, before I quite knew the words were going to come out.

Her eyes darted toward me. Now she definitely looked confused. "You know we don't have any true visible manifestation in your world," she said.

"Of course. But—you have a... a default appearance, don't you? Most of your kind that I've interacted with, they had a particular look they used most of the time, unless they had a reason to change it." I ran my thumb over the curve of her shoulder. "This isn't yours. You made this for me."

She didn't disagree. "I think you'd like my usual 'look' less," she said.

"Maybe," I said. "But I want to see what you made for yourself."

"Why?"

"I... You can see so much of me, inside and out," I said,

realizing the answer as I spoke. "It'd be nice to see *you* properly, at least on the outside."

I thought I might have to invoke our deal again. But then Kess sighed. She turned toward me, letting her hand rest on my waist. Then she shimmered again.

It was different from watching her turn into Avery. That change had been jarring and unnatural. What happened before my eyes now felt somehow private, like a secret shared. As her hair gleamed straighter, shorter, darker, as her cheeks narrowed and her lips thinned, I had the same sensation as if I were watching someone undress for the first time—only the sense of it prickled deeper, maybe because she'd worn that former guise on a deeper level than any clothes she'd put on. It had clothed her down to the bones.

Her body stayed nearly the same height, but its shapes became more boyish, her hips slimming to match her small breasts. Only her eyes remained completely the same, with those dark burgundy-brown irises fixed on mine.

When the shimmer dulled and I knew she was done, I studied the new and yet known woman beside me for a minute without speaking. She was right that between the two forms the other would have been more likely to turn my head. But she already had my attention now, and this one, even if it was a guise of another sort, felt more true. More like a person and less like a fantasy.

"Why this?" I asked, abruptly curious. I couldn't imagine what it would be like, being able to choose every aspect of your appearance. "Why this face, this body?"

Kess shrugged. "There was... When I first wanted to come into this world, I was watching, and I saw a woman on the street. She looked different from most of the others. As if she were sure that whatever she was doing, it would turn out the way she wished. I liked that. So when I was thinking of how I would like to appear— I knew better than to make an exact copy, and I've adjusted here and there since, but I borrowed a lot from her."

"How long ago was that—when you first came?"

Her gaze drifted away from me. "I don't remember," she said, her brow knitting. "It's... Time feels different for us than it seems to for you, as we go back and forth... I'm not sure I was taking enough notice to know."

Something in her voice dredged up the loneliness I'd felt in the lobby. As it echoed through me, I took her hand.

She focused back on me then, her eyes narrowing, but with a small smile to soften her expression. "I'm meant to be helping *you* open up. Enough talk about my history." She drew in a breath, and said, "Tell me about Avery."

My fingers tensed around hers. "What about her?"

"Why aren't you with her, if she matters so much to you? Why do you keep thinking about her, when you aren't with her?"

I wondered if a Glower could possibly understand the full complexities of human relationships. But she'd asked. I'd never told anyone the real reason Avery and I had broken up. What could it hurt, to let it out? It might even help.

"I really liked her," I said, feeling out the words. "No, I loved her. I just... Whenever we started talking about anything serious, about the future, what we wanted out of life... All I could think of was her. The most important thing was that I wanted her there with me. But, I mean, we hadn't even been dating for a whole year yet, and I was worried I'd sound obsessed, or desperate." My throat tightened, remembering how some of those conversations had ended. Avery's puzzled looks when I'd clammed up or changed the subject. Her following my lead all the same. The hurt I'd started to see in her eyes. But even that hadn't been enough to convince me to let her in.

"I thought it would put her off, showing her how invested I was," I went on. "So I kept avoiding the subject. And then that ended up putting her off. She wanted me to be honest with her, and I couldn't, so she decided it wasn't working. I guess it wasn't." But she'd been dating Colin—was it even six months yet? And he'd been able to say those things tonight without the slightest hesitation. "I still feel like an *idiot* for not figuring out how to get what I was feeling into the right words. If I couldn't talk with her like that..."

If I couldn't with her, when part of what I'd loved about her was how unbreakable she'd seemed, how safe that had made me feel around her, then how was I ever going to get there with anyone?

"It sounds as if she wanted to be with you," Kess remarked. "Why did you think she'd be upset that you felt the same way?"

"I don't know," I said, but that wasn't true. No doubt Kess realized that too, because she squeezed my hand encouragingly. "It doesn't make sense. I know it should be easy to just spit things out, but I've tried. It's the worst with girls I've been interested in, but really, with anyone... When the conversation gets too close, too much about feelings, it's as if I have a panic attack. I lose my breath, my pulse goes crazy. I'm surprised I can even tell you this much."

Only I wasn't. Of course if I could talk to anyone, it would be her. What did opening up to a Glower matter when she wasn't a real part of my life, just a figment slipping in and out, just a practical arrangement, just a dream? There was nothing here for me to lose.

"It wasn't always like that," Kess said.

Yes, there was that reason too. I wondered how much of it she had already sensed.

"No," I said. Then I found this part was hard after all. Not because of the girl I had to talk about, but because of what had taken her. My heart started to thud, but I forced myself to speak. "My first real girlfriend. Rosa. I screwed up with her because I didn't hold back enough. I wanted more of her time and attention than she was ready to give. I was insecure because she was almost a year older than me and meeting guys who were older than her, who had more in common with her than I did... And when I got jealous about the other people in her life, when I told her how I felt, she started shutting me out. She started turning to someone else. So I didn't just put her off. I pushed her toward the Glower that killed her."

My voice faded as I forced out the last words. I closed my eyes. I'd never said it that plainly out loud before.

Kess was quiet for a long moment. Then she caressed my jaw, her thumb gliding over my cheek.

"You're afraid of hurting someone else," she said, "so you let yourself be hurt instead."

"I guess that's one way of looking at it," I said with a choked laugh. "At least it's more fair that way."

She eased closer, until her body was pressed against me. "I won't hurt you," she murmured, and touched her mouth to mine.

Because I won't let you, I thought. But I gave myself over to the kiss, to the feel of her skin beneath my fingers and the heady shiver of hers traveling over my back. Just for a little while, there was a relief in pretending to believe.

First thing Monday at the office, I called up the number I'd gotten from my colleague. The man who answered turned jovial when I mentioned who'd referred me, but his voice darkened after I told him the name of Ricky's "producer."

"That asshole," he muttered. "Tell your friend to steer well clear of Martinez. He's got a whole racket going on where he gets hopefuls paying for studio time and equipment rentals and all that at inflated fees, and of course he's getting kickbacks across the board, and after he's milked them for all they're worth, he suddenly decides they're not 'progressing' enough and kicks them to the curb."

My heart sank, more with resignation than anything else. "All right," I said. "I'll tell him. Thank you for passing on the warning."

"Not a problem. I'd be happy if that leech never gets his hooks into another desperate amateur. Listen, if this friend of yours is any good, direct him to me and *I'll* take a listen. I'm mostly on the production side these days, and if it's not my thing I might know someone else who'd jump for it."

"Thank you," I said again, startled now. You never knew how former clients were going to feel about the Society, but some were a generous lot. "I'll see if he wants to take you up on that." After I made sure Ricky had something decent to show.

I was just hanging up when Sterling sank into the chair at the cubicle next to mine, rotating it toward me at the same time. His face looked drawn, or maybe he'd just lost a little weight and I hadn't noticed before. He frowned.

"Where did you disappear to Saturday night?" he said. "You mustn't have stayed more than an hour."

"I wasn't feeling well," I said, which was as much of the truth as I was willing to admit. And then, taking in his expression, "Was there a problem?"

"I wanted you to talk to some of the other senior staff," he said. "It's important that they understand what we've been working on and how involved you've been. It's not often so many of us are... on hand at the same moment."

"Well, it's not as if I have any definite solutions yet," I said, motioning to the computer. "Wouldn't a presentation go over better if I could lay out a real plan of—"

"I think it would be useful for them to see where you're heading," Sterling interrupted, so brusquely I snapped my mouth shut. "They should know how much you've already contributed. Now I'll have to arrange an official meeting..."

"I'm sorry," I ventured when I was sure he was done. "I didn't realize it was that important to you." It would have been nice, if it had been, for him to have let me know before the party so I could have prepared something specific to say, but it didn't seem wise to mention that given his current mood.

"Ah," Sterling said, his face softening slightly as he studied mine, "I suppose it's done now." A glint of curiosity lit in his dark eyes. He leaned forward and lowered his voice. "How has your other project been... progressing? Have you learned anything valuable about the other side?"

The other side—the Glowers. My mind slipped back two nights to Kess arching over me on the bed, her bare skin gleaming where I'd pulled down her dress, the eager gasps slipping from her lips. A flush washed over me. I hoped it didn't show.

"I don't know how valuable the information will be," I said, "but I have learned a few things so far. To begin with, their ideas about reaching some sort of agreement with us all assume we'd just leave some segment of the population for them to hunt freely."

Sterling made a noise of disgust. "It'll be a cold day in hell before that happens."

"I know," I said. "But I haven't told *them* that yet, so they'll keep talking to me. I'm supposed to meet with a bunch of them again later this week." At least that part of my conversation with Kess, in the moments before she'd vanished from my bedroom, I didn't have to be embarrassed about. "I've also noticed—intense bodily sensations seem to bring out more of a... personality, you could say, in them. More emotion."

"Bodily sensations?" Sterling repeated.

"Like eating something very spicy," I said quickly. "Or—one time I was in a cab with the Glower who initiated the deal with me, and the driver had to slam on the brakes, really jolted us. Anyway, I don't know if that's something we could use, but it's been interesting to see."

"Indeed." Sterling rubbed his jaw. "I haven't heard of that effect before, but then, I suppose when our goal is to keep the clients *away* from the Glowers, it's unsurprising we haven't observed a wide range of their non-predatory behaviors. Have you seen this generalized across all of them?"

"Well... No, I think I've only seen it with that one. Because she's the one who's been around me the most."

"You should try to gather some data on the others' reactions, then. It could simply be a ploy of some kind. You've been staying on your guard, I assume?"

"Of course," I said automatically, and guilt followed like a kick in the gut. I didn't think Sterling would see it that way if he'd known what I'd been getting up to with Kess, how much of myself I'd revealed to her.

Could I really say it was only physical, after that night? After I'd confided things to her I'd never told anyone before? A chill trickled through me, carrying away any heat that had lingered from those memories.

I'd thought I needed her to help me get over Avery, but that was already done. I couldn't let myself be stupid enough to think she'd really fix my problems beyond that.

"I'll try, with the others," I went on, a new resolve forming inside me. "And I'll see what else I can find out about their current plans and organization—at the moment they seem to be pretty scattered still. But I'm not sure I should continue the 'deal' much longer."

Sterling's eyebrows rose. "Why not? It sounds as if you're learning much that's useful."

"Well, I—"

My throat choked up. My heartbeat sped to a familiar frantic rhythm.

Familiar because this was how I'd felt every time I'd thought I might tell Avery how much I wanted to be with her. Every time I'd attempted to offer Jayden or my other clients a deeper sort of conversation.

I was going to see the disapproval on his face, hear the disappointment in his voice, know I'd changed his opinion of me and our working relationship irrevocably. And that idea terrified me.

My hands clenched under the desk. Kess had been wrong that night. I didn't clam up to keep the hurt all to myself. I wanted to save other people discomfort, sure, but I was also protecting myself from their ill opinion and whatever other consequences might follow from saying what was truly on my mind.

And maybe in doing that, I was risking setting people up for even more hurt than I was sparing them from.

I reached for the words and pushed them past the tightness

inside me. "You know what they're like," I said. "The way they can read how people are feeling, where they're vulnerable. And they get better at it, the more time they spend around the same person. Sometimes it... gets to me. *She* gets to me. I don't *think* I'd do or say anything that would compromise the Society, but I —I can't promise that when I don't know what she might try next."

Sterling considered me for a long moment. Then he reached over and clapped me on the side of the arm. "I believe in you, Mateo," he said firmly. "You don't give yourself enough credit. And the information you're gathering right now, the... means by which you're gathering it, it's more than anyone else has dared to attempt in decades. We shouldn't let ourselves shy away from breaking new ground. That's the only way we can get the upper hand. Hold steady."

He stood before I'd come up with a response. "I look forward to your next report," he said, and walked to his office without waiting to see if I would reply.

Twelve

"Is something wrong?" I asked Kess five minutes into our cab ride to this evening's Glower gathering spot. It wasn't a question I'd have normally thought to ask a demon, but she was displaying so many signs I'd have taken for agitation in a human being that I couldn't help myself. She'd been more than friendly when she'd greeted me in her "real" guise, with an open smile and a playful squeeze of my hand that had left me wondering if she'd had some kind of intense altercation on the way to meeting me. But after she'd instructed the cabbie on our destination, she'd started staring out the window with a muted frown, her foot tapping the back of the front passenger seat and her hands wandering to tug at her hair and smooth her dress.

It was hard not to contrast that fidgetiness with the cool and controlled air she'd exuded on our way to the first gathering—until the cab's near-accident, at least. Was there something she hadn't told me that made this situation different?

At my comment, her hands and her foot immediately stilled. "No," she said. "Well, I'm not entirely certain what to expect.

Some of the others have been talking amongst themselves. I think we should be united if we are going to have any success, but achieving that cohesion is another matter."

I wasn't sure how this was a change from last time, but now that she'd given me the opening, I didn't want to lose the chance to work in a few other questions. To use our connection the way I'd told Sterling I would.

"Until recently, you did seem to all operate independently. I guess the recent coordinated efforts to get through a target's defenses were part of a new strategy a bunch of you decided to try?"

"Hmmm," she said, and for a few seconds I thought that was all the answer she'd give me. Then she added, "Many didn't like the idea and choose to continue alone. They are the hungrier ones."

I supposed that amounted to a "yes."

"It might have been a poor choice in the long run, however," she said. "We provoked your Society into making changes as well. And now here we are."

"It's possible we'll all come out of this better off," I said.

She gave me an oblique look. "I don't know," she said in an equally colorless tone.

She'd always been the one cheerleading this idea of a "compromise." I'd never heard her sound so hopeless. Despite myself, a twinge of concern that wasn't just for my career ran through me.

"Why the change in heart?" I asked, keeping my tone light but studying her face.

She wavered, her mouth opening and closing. I resisted the urge to reach for her hand. "I shouldn't have said that," she replied finally. "Our position is still the same."

"Kess..."

"What do you want me to say?" she asked, those dark eyes suddenly fathomless.

I wanted her to tell me the truth. I wanted to have a conversation that wasn't part of some deal. But I was never going to get that with her. It was ridiculous to even think it.

"I guess I'll see what happens at the gathering," I said.

With more than a little trepidation, I followed her into the back room of the out-of-business bowling alley where the cab dropped us off. This time several of the other Glowers were already waiting for us—including, to my disappointment, Zut. He looked me over with an expression somewhere between disdain and disinterest and said, to Kess rather than to me, "So, our Society representative is with us again."

"Of course," Kess said. "That was the point of this."

More Glowers emerged from the shadows around us. At a glance I thought there might be as many as thirty in the dim, dusty room already. My nerves started to itch with the instinct to back away from them, but I held my ground beside Kess and Zut.

"I'm not certain about that," Zut said as his gaze fell on me again. "Before we have any further discussion that this *boy* can overhear, I'd be interested to know if he has offered any of our proposals to the rest of his Society."

I looked back at him, managing not to glare. At least I could say, with what was technically honesty if you counted Sterling as standing in for the whole Society, "I have. They didn't feel any of them benefitted us enough to be worth the trade off. If that is the best you can suggest, then we'd prefer to continue as we are."

"Ah, so now you expect us to help you?" he said, pitching his voice to the crowd as if he'd caught me out somehow. His tone irritated me more than anything before, especially when I heard the disgruntled murmurs that passed through the crowd in response.

Kess had averted her gaze, her shoulders tight. She'd known they were getting less welcoming, not more. That was why she'd been so doubtful. If even *she* didn't think this could work...

"I'm sorry," I said, "but did I misunderstand something? Hasn't this all been about you asking *us* to help *you*? How would it make any sense for us to agree if we weren't getting something out of the deal too? You may be able to take everything your marks have in exchange for a brief ego boost, but our expectations are a little more reasonable."

I hadn't thought it would be possible for the Glower to get any more rigid, but his posture stiffened as I watched, his eyes sparking brighter. "And what do you think would be 'reasonable'?" he said icily.

Hell, I might as well say it. "Fewer people *dying* would be a good start."

The murmuring grew louder. Zut waved at the others, but they only lowered their voices rather than going completely silent. He turned back to Kess. "This is the progress you've made?"

"I suppose you think you could have done better," she retorted, her jaw clenching. "Is this your demonstration of how to negotiate: going on the attack when we've only just arrived?"

Zut's face darkened. Then he shook his head. "This was an absurd venture to begin with."

"Hey," I said, holding up my hands. "You were the ones who approached me."

"And that approach was clearly a failure. That is fine. If your Society will not negotiate fairly, you will find out soon enough how much we can hurt you."

I couldn't believe they had some viable offensive that they'd willingly held in reserve. We could take them. We were already beating them. But as he spun as if to stalk away, I remembered negotiation wasn't my only goal here. There was something else Sterling had asked me to investigate, and Zut had set himself up perfectly.

"What do you mean by that?" I said, letting my voice rise as if I were really upset. Zut ignored me. Good. As he started to walk toward a cluster of his companions, I leapt forward and grabbed his elbow. "Answer me!"

I yanked him back far harder than was necessary if I'd only meant to get his attention. But what I'd meant was to send him staggering off-balance. He stumbled and nearly fell as he whirled around. Then he snatched the front of my shirt.

"You are *nothing*," he snarled, his previous cool disdain completely shattered. "We are the ones with the power. I have no use of you at all."

Then he thrust me away, shuddering as if he could cast off that rage like a dog shaking off water. My heart was thudding, but I had to swallow a smile. At least I'd gotten one answer out of him, whether he'd liked it or not. It seemed intense, abrupt physical sensations could affect any of the Glowers, shocking them out of their demonic detachment, loosening their self-control. Maybe that was why they'd always avoided physical confrontations with us.

And Zut wasn't just enraged. He was hiding fear under his anger. I could see that in his blustering, in the haughty way he marched off again. That reassured me too.

I glanced at Kess. She was staring after Zut, her mouth twisted. The voices of the other Glowers rose around us, mostly in the warbling language I didn't understand, but I heard "Tether" and "Society" thrown around with enough revulsion that I doubted much more discussion would be possible.

"I guess that's my cue to leave," I said.

"No. Just wait in the alley," Kess said. "I'll speak to him."

When she emerged several minutes after I'd left the room, I could tell from the slump in her posture that she hadn't succeeded. "You shouldn't have tried to harm him," she said.

"I didn't," I said. "I only wanted him to talk. He was threatening me."

She exhaled slowly and cocked her head at me, and I reminded myself that she could read me too. "He made you angry," she said. "You dislike him."

I dislike all of you, I thought, but with her fathomless gaze fixed on me, I no longer felt entirely sure of that. "So what now?" I said instead.

She looked at the building, her forehead furrowing. She wanted to be inside in the discussion, I could tell. But still she hesitated. Because she didn't like how Zut had treated me?

I might have lost the others, but I still had her, maybe more than ever before.

"I can wait longer," I said. "I'll still listen to *you*. You go in and see what they say, and I can hang out in that coffee shop on the corner. Find me there after, and the two of us can talk about it. All right?"

Even though I meant every part of that honestly, the startled gratitude on her face made me feel a little sick about the motivations I hadn't admitted to. "Thank you," she said. "I don't think it will take very long." And then, in a gesture that from the jerkiness of her movement seemed to surprise her as much as it did me, she bobbed up to brush my lips with hers.

I was so occupied with my phone when Kess came to find me a half hour later that I didn't notice her arrival until she was standing right beside me at the bar-height counter along the coffee shop's side window.

"Hey," she said in the new, softer voice I was only just getting used to, touching my arm.

"Sorry," I said automatically. I set down the phone and rubbed my face. "Just my cousin giving me grief. Did anything useful come out of the rest of the gathering?"

"Not by my definition." She hopped onto the stool next to me. "To be honest, they spent most of the time complaining about the Society and very little talking about how we might work together."

"Well, to be fair, if you got a bunch of Tethers together, we'd probably mostly complain about you," I said, but I could tell even as the words came out that the joke was falling flat. I added quickly, "What came up in the very little bit about working together?"

"Repeats of some of the ideas you heard last time. And one suggested—" She stopped, looking as if she'd tasted something disgusting.

"Suggested..." I prompted.

"It isn't worth repeating," she said. "I certainly wouldn't consider it an acceptable proposal." When I raised my eyebrows at her, she sighed. "One thought perhaps your Society could leave the younger artists alone, on the premise that those who are strong enough to make a name for themselves without assistance from us are the ones most deserving of later protection."

I winced. Sure, let's just ignore the fact that the young artists were also the ones with the least experience to help them make wise decisions. "A survival of the fittest take. Very nice." I couldn't find it in me to be disappointed, though. I'd never really believed anything good would come of these "negotiations." That wasn't why I'd waited here. "And that comment your leader made about hurting us—did he give any details on how he plans to do that?"

"He's *not* our leader," Kess snapped, an angry flush I'd never seen before coloring her cheeks. She seemed to catch herself and turned to gaze out the window into the dusk. "He didn't mention it again. But I think it was only words. He wouldn't be joining these discussions if he already had another feasible strategy. You shouldn't worry."

"Thanks," I said, unexpectedly touched. I'd wanted that information, and yet I couldn't help wondering what Zut would think of her telling me.

"The reason we don't normally work together is that we all have our own thoughts," she went on in a lower voice. "He speaks only for himself."

Not for me, I thought she meant, even if she couldn't bring herself to say it outright. I studied her as she peered at the street outside.

"What would you say?" I asked. "If it were up to you, if you could decide a compromise for all of us... what proposal would you think was acceptable?"

"I don't know," she said. "Maybe there isn't one."

Her tone was so distant it sent a shiver through me. I was abruptly sure she was imagining her own death by starvation. And here I was, trying to use her in essence to plot that death. A lump rose in my throat.

"Kess," I started, and didn't know how to follow it. She'd never done me any harm. I could maybe even say she'd been kind. But then there were all the people she'd known—marked, fed on, destroyed—before me. She was an inhuman creature, a demon. No matter how good a show she put on for me, I couldn't let myself forget that.

She nodded to my phone. "What does your cousin want now?"

I paused, and decided to accept the change of subject. "It's not what he wants," I said. "Oh, maybe it is. He's texting me about this 'producer' he's set a meeting up with tomorrow, and he wants me to be all excited about it, but I've already found out the guy's a scam artist. I just don't think Ricky will listen if I try to tell him that on the phone. I told him we should grab drinks —I'm supposed to let him know when I'm free—I'll find a way to bring it up then."

Kess was silent for a moment. Then she said, "What is it that you'd want for him? What would make you feel you didn't have to worry about him?"

I considered. "I guess I'd like to know that he's realized he has a ways to go before he's professional level, and that he's focusing on developing his skills rather than on getting famous right off the bat. But I can't make him change his attitude just by wanting him to."

"Still, I think you should tell him what you believe: that he isn't ready yet, but there are ways he could become ready."

"It's not that easy."

"I think it is." She slid off the stool. "In fact, I think it's the next step in our deal. You need to open up to him at least enough to be honest about that and find out what results."

I opened my mouth to protest again, but stopped as my thoughts tripped back to my conversation with Sterling two days ago and the realization that had struck me then. Why didn't I want to have this conversation with Ricky, really? Because I thought I'd make things worse for *him*, or just because I was worried it would make him angry with *me*?

"I don't know if he'll listen to the becoming ready part instead of getting caught up in the idea that I don't believe in him," I said. "Then he won't listen to me at all." And he'd go running back to his phony producer.

"I might be able to help with that," Kess said. "If you'd let me."

I looked at her sharply. Nothing in her tone or expression suggested she made the offer with any ill intent. Still, I couldn't keep the terseness from my voice when I asked, "What do you mean, 'help'?"

She raised her chin. "I know how you feel about my... abilities. But I can use them with precision. I won't hurt him. I won't leave him wanting anything he can't achieve on his own. I swear to you I'll only give him a nudge of encouragement, without any harm, physical, mental, or otherwise, now or in future."

The words rang with a conviction I believed. "Why?" I said.

"Because you are still here, trying to help me," she said simply.

The knowledge that I was here to do exactly the opposite curdled in my stomach, but I let it sit there. We went out to hail another cab, and I texted Ricky the address of a west end bar I thought he'd like the atmosphere off, that wasn't too far from his parents' house.

I spotted him as soon as we walked in. He was hanging over the bar counter chatting up a Amazonian bartender who looked both ten years older than him and completely underwhelmed by his flirting. I guessed he'd flashed his fake ID at her, because she set a foaming beer mug on the counter in front of him. I hurried over.

"Hey, Teo!" Ricky said, beaming with a jovial temper it pained me to think I was about to kill. He leaned over to acknowledge Kess. "And it's a real pleasure to meet *you*." He gave me a sly grin, and I remembered that with her appearance changed to her regular guise, he didn't know this "friend" was the same one he'd met a week and a half ago. He must think I'd really upped my game.

Kess's smile was more amused than anything else. "Let's get a table," she suggested. "It's so uncomfortable being crammed against the bar."

I clued into her real motivation when we reached one of the square wooden tables in the middle of the amber-lit room and she immediately took the seat kitty-corner from Ricky. She wanted to be close so she could work that Glower magic on him. The thought made my skin tighten, but I forced myself to continue. It was better to get the bubble bursting over with quickly.

"So I talked with my colleagues, and one of them referred me to a former client who's now working as a producer with Warner," I said. "He knows a lot of people in the industry, and he recognized your guy's name."

I couldn't help pausing there as my pulse kicked up to the base of my throat. I swallowed, gathering myself, and Ricky's smile dimmed. "And?" he said. "What did they say?"

"Anyone this Martinez guy said he's worked with, he was lying," I said. "He's never gotten anyone any deals. He just milks people for money in kickbacks until he figures he's gotten all he can, and then he ditches them. I'm sorry."

Ricky scowled, his fingers clenching around his beer mug. But to my surprise, what he said next was, "Are you sure?"

None of the venting or accusations I'd braced myself for. Maybe I hadn't given him enough credit.

That thought must have been why, when I answered, "Yes, completely," I found myself adding even though I hadn't meant to, "But the guy I talked to, he's the real deal, and he said he'd take a listen when you're ready to try for the big time..."

Ricky's face had already lit up all over again. "Yes!" he said. "I knew you could make something happen if you gave it a shot. That's amazing! You're the best, Teo. I'm sorry I've been hassling you so much about this, it's just, I want it to happen so bad— A producer at Warner! Wow."

"Ricky," I said quickly, holding up my hand. "I—" I felt myself start to stutter, and steadied myself, my back tensing. "I don't think you should go for it yet."

"Why not?" Ricky said. "If I've got this chance now, I've got to jump on it. Isn't that what they say?"

"This guy isn't going anywhere," I said. "And I..." My voice faltered. Under the table, Kess slid her hand over my knee. I glanced at her, and she met my gaze unwaveringly.

She was right. The demon had seen this situation more clearly than I had. I needed to spit it out.

I drew in a breath, ignoring the twisting in my chest. "And I think you need to work on your vocals, and your arrangements, before you go for the chance. Go for it when you can show him the best you can do. I don't think you're there yet."

"What are you saying?" Ricky demanded. "How would you know? It's not like you ever want to see my performances."

"I listened to your demo," I said, as gently as I could. "It's not that I don't think you could get there, Ricky. I promise I'm not saying that. But I think some vocal training, that sort of thing, it could make a big difference in whether a label decides you're worth the investment."

"Why should I have to go for extra help?" Ricky said. "I'm not good enough with what God gave me to work with?"

His face had shuttered the way I'd always been afraid it would. My heart thudded. But Kess reached across the table and grazed her knuckles over Ricky's wrist. In the hazy light, I could make out a tiny flicker of her glow traveling into his skin, where it vanished.

"You can prove to the guy who tried to scam you that you're better than he thought you were," she said. "You can *do* better than he thought you could. Who gets to a professional level at anything without some training?"

"Exactly," I said, jumping on that thread. "There's no shame in it, Ricky. *Most* of the people you hear on the radio had professional help developing their talent. It's a normal part of the process."

Ricky stared at Kess and then me. After a moment, his shoulders eased down. He gave me half a smirk. "Right," he said. "Of course I'll be even better if I put more work in. I'll blow everyone away after I'm through. That's what I want."

Was it really that easy? He didn't need anything more?

I'm not good enough? he'd asked, and maybe that was what his blustering had been about all along. Not pride or defiance but the fear that he couldn't make it, a fear he'd been running away from instead of facing. I couldn't exactly criticize someone else for that.

And all he'd needed was a little supernatural boost of confidence to carry him through it.

"Great," I said, gathering myself. "I actually know a woman —she worked with a singer I had as a client—she's really good, she'd help you figure out the best approach for your voice and make it work for you in not even that much time. It'd at least be a good place to start." I hesitated. "She is pretty pricy—I can help out with that. Early birthday present."

"Really? You'd do that?" Ricky grinned again, and for the first time in years I saw the tag-along kid I remembered growing up with, before he'd taken on the swaggering bravado. "I thought— I don't know, I thought you figured it was a stupid idea, me even trying."

Was that the impression I'd given him? "No," I said, suddenly choked up. "I never thought you shouldn't try. I just thought you were rushing in too fast. That's all. Of course you've got to try for the things that make you really happy."

"You know, I've got to call that idiot and tell him tomorrow's meeting is off. Don't want him hassling me. I'll be right back." Ricky got up and hustled to the door so he could speak away from the music thumping overhead.

Kess's hand brushed my knee again. She smiled at me, and I couldn't help smiling back. Then I thought of the glint traveling from her into Ricky, and my spirits sank.

It was still *him*, wasn't it, if all she'd done was "encourage" him? But how long would that encouragement last? Could I really be sure that was all she'd done? Maybe I shouldn't have let her near him at all. I'd been so touched by her offer and her apparent concern that I hadn't thought it through as carefully as I should have.

"We make a good team," Kess said, but her smile had faded too. She looked down at the martini she'd ordered, her sleek ebony hair drifting over her cheek and obscuring her eyes.

"Yeah," I said. "I guess we do." Just a very temporary one.

Thirteen

"ARE YOU GOING HOME NOW?" KESS ASKED AS WE STOOD on the sidewalk outside the bar. Ricky had just taken off to meet some girl he'd promised he'd see tonight. I had been thinking I was ready to head back to the apartment, but there was a note of regret in the Glower's voice that made me pause.

"Did you have something else in mind?"

She hugged herself, an oddly frail gesture from her. It was full night now, but in the patch of darkness where she'd stopped beyond the reach of the streetlamps, the glow of her body was little more than a glimmering. She hadn't seemed to pass much energy to Ricky, but maybe it had drained her more than I'd thought.

That possibility pinched at my gut with a guilt I couldn't quite define. For using her or for letting her affect him? Maybe a little of both.

"I went to Magic Mountain this morning," she said then, as if that answered my question. "I've gone in the past, to wander and... take in the excitement, but I never bothered with the rides before. It's extraordinary, the feeling when you drop over a cliff or spin upside down, isn't it?"

I'd only been to the Six Flags amusement park a couple of times, as a teen, because I'd never been much of a rollercoaster fan—my stomach didn't agree with them. But I realized she had answered my question in a way. Of her own accord, she'd gone looking for those intense sensations to ground herself in this world. She'd *wanted* to feel more. Was that why she'd been in such an odd mood this evening?

I wished I could have seen her face, heard her laugh, as the rides swept her along. If that was what she was looking for, I could give her something else, now. Take her further away from the creature who traded confidence for souls.

"It is," I said, and raised my hand to a passing cab. "Come on. I've got an idea."

"Where are we going?" she asked as we climbed in.

"You'll see." I leaned forward, my turn to murmur directions to the cabbie.

The traffic was with us, but the drive still took nearly half an hour. Kess gazed out her window at the city lights, but she looked calmer than she had on our way to the meeting. After a while, I reached over to take her slim hand in mine. Just to see how she'd respond. She glanced at me with a blink of surprise, and then smiled, her expression so pleased and open it was hard to remember what she was.

Maybe she wasn't that entirely anymore. Maybe she was changing.

She stroked my palm with her thumb as the cabbie drove on. The gesture could have felt merely affectionate, but from her it sent a shiver of anticipation up my arm and prickling down to my groin.

I'd brought her to this point. I'd woken her up from the cool detachment she'd worn before. I didn't know what that meant for her or me or anything, but I couldn't deny that it thrilled me.

When the cab stopped and we got out, the salty ocean wind whipped over us, gusting through Kess's hair. She beamed and ran straight over the boardwalk to the sand. There, she spun on her feet with an eager gasp as she waited for me to catch up.

"Yes. I should have thought of this place. Thank you."

The moon was a sliver and the stars dulled by smog, but even in the darkness I could make out a few vague figures a little south of us on the beach. I tugged Kess north, toward the spot where the craggy rocks nearly touched the ocean's edge. I'd discovered this place with a girl I'd had a short fling with in senior year—hadn't been back in ages, but it had always been deserted when we'd come.

The spray of the surf tickled my face as we scrambled over the line of rocks. On the other side, I stopped and stripped down to my boxers, grabbing a stone to prevent the wind from snatching my clothes. When I turned to Kess, her dress was shimmering away, leaving only her strapless bra and panties. The purple looked black in the night. She arched an eyebrow at me in challenge and dashed into the waves.

I ran after her. A laugh jolted out of me as one of those cool waves smacked me in the chest. The surf roiled around us, casting us up and back and drawing us deeper again. Kess dunked her head and came up sputtering, flinging back her sleek hair. She bobbed in the water like a pale beacon, the only clear form in the darkness. Glowing paler with each toss of the ocean.

My eyes stung and my mouth was laced with salt, but I was grinning. I managed to plant my feet on the silty ground. Kess grasped my arm. Another wave pushed her into me, and suddenly we were kissing, salt tang on our tongues as they slid hotly together. Her body trembled against mine. I wrapped my arms around her, craving every hitch of her breath, every quiver of a muscle that told me she was an equal partner in this pleasure. In that moment I wanted her more than I'd ever wanted anyone—Miss Bertolini or Rosa or Avery or any of the girls in between.

The surf jostled us apart. Kess clasped her hand around mine and yanked me toward the beach. We stumbled out onto the drier sand, both of us panting with laughter, and then she pulled me to her again. I cupped her face, kissing her hard, letting myself think of nothing but the shudder of her breath against my bare chest, the slick skin of her arms looping around me. She dipped her head to my shoulder, my sternum, with frantic presses of her lips, as if she were starved for me. This couldn't be just part of the deal. The same desire that coursed through me radiated from her every movement.

A seagull cried overhead, and Kess flinched. She glanced upward.

"Just a gull," I said. "Probably hunting for dinner."

Kess's gaze shifted toward the ocean. "Fish," she said. I couldn't make out anything but the roll of the larger waves, but maybe her Glower eyes were sharper than mine. She stared into the darkness for several seconds, her heart thudding in time with mine. The wind chilled the moisture on my skin everywhere except the places we were touching. I traced my thumb down the side of her face.

"Hey," I said softly.

She turned to me again and glided her hands down my chest in a way that brought me to attention down below. But the tremor that ran through her as she tipped back her head to receive another kiss felt different from the quivers before. I eased back, searching her face. Before I'd even opened my mouth, she jerked her head to the side and shoved herself away from me.

"No," she said.

I froze. "Kess?"

She crouched down on the sand, burying her face in her hands. "How can you stand to even look at me?"

The question was so unexpected that a baldly honest answer dropped from my mouth. "You're beautiful."

"No, I'm not." She sucked in a breath with a rasp of a sob. A wail broke from her throat, so pained it wrenched at my heart. I knelt beside her and touched her quaking back, but I was afraid to do more. I didn't know what had upset her. Maybe it had been me.

"What is it?" I said as steadily as I could manage. "What can I do?"

She just shook her head. She was sobbing freely now between gulps of air. The darkness that had felt so intimate a few moments ago now seemed far too vast and uncertain.

"Here," I said, for lack of a better idea. "We'll go." I tugged on my clothes as quickly as I could, not caring that my wet boxers dampened my pants. Kess didn't look up, but she must have registered what I was doing, because when I returned to her she'd recovered her dress.

"Can you walk?" I said. When she didn't answer, I took her gently by the arm. She let me draw her upright. Her sobs quieted, but she kept her hands over her eyes as we staggered back toward the road. Her entire body was shivering.

The cabbie who responded to my hurried call gave us an odd look, but made no comment as I helped Kess in. She huddled beside me, periodically twitching away and then settling against my body again. I stroked her damp hair and gave her space as she seemed to need it. What else could I do?

By the time we reached my apartment building, Kess's shudders had almost completely subsided. She crawled out of the cab and followed me to the elevator, staying close but not touching me. When I flicked on the living room light inside the apartment, she blinked hard. Even with her eyes red-rimmed and her hair plastered to her head, what I'd said before hadn't been a lie. She was beautiful. But that obviously wasn't what she'd meant.

She took a couple of steps away from me, toward the windows. I moved to close the curtains.

"I'm sorry," Kess said in a low voice. "That was... unfortunate. I'm not quite myself. It's been a long time since I— since I fed. I think that's all."

We'd talked about the Glowers' general need to "feed," but the subject of her personal habits in that area hadn't come up. I hadn't wanted to ask. But I had to, now, bracing myself for the answer. "How long has it been?"

"Properly?" she said. "With a real connection? I suppose... close to two months, by your time. I can consume wisps of what I need—at the amusement park, places like that, where there's so much energy in the atmosphere—but it's not quite the same."

So that was the other reason she'd gone to Magic Mountain. Almost two months. She hadn't marked anyone, fed on anyone, since before she'd approached me. A stronger relief that I'd expected washed over me.

"Why haven't you?" I said.

She gave me a baleful look. "It has not been as easy recently, as you know. And after we made our deal, I decided to hold off. I knew how you felt about it, and it seemed uncharitable to go against your most important principle while I was asking for your help. And then…" She sank onto the couch as if all the strength had fled her body. "And then it started to feel wrong, completely. I have hurt so many—I have ended so many lives —" Her voice broke off with a choked sound. "I am a monster. You think so. I disgust you. You can put it out of your mind for a time, when I make myself appealing enough, but it's true. I don't know… How we live, it never seemed to matter before. It was just the way we live. We made our deals and your kind made your choices and that was nothing but fair. Only I'm not sure of that now. But I still hunger. I don't want to feel it, but it doesn't go away."

Her hands clenched on her lap. She hadn't looked at me since she'd started talking. My throat had closed up. What she'd said about me, it *was* true. I hated the thought of what she must have done to survive this long—I'd hated the thought of what she might be doing, what prey she might be stalking, when she hadn't been with me. Even now, despite the anguish in her voice, I was hearing Sterling's caution about ploys in the back of my mind. Did she really feel this guilt or was this an act to earn more good will from me?

But what purpose would that act serve? After this evening's meeting, she hadn't sounded as if she had any hope left of the Society reaching an agreement with the Glowers—because of their behavior, not mine. If she'd been going to break down as some sort of strategy, why not then?

It didn't feel staged. She wore her distress so rawly that even my moment of doubt sent a stab of guilt through my stomach.

I'd done this. I'd woken her up. And apparently along with the excitement and exhilaration there came anguish too.

"What do you need?" I heard myself saying. "To feed, properly? You don't need to kill anyone—you could live off the same person for years. Do you have to mark someone? Or can you take enough to sustain yourself without that?"

She raised her head, her thin eyebrows drawing together. "I don't need—the permanent connection only makes the process easier. I can... take directly from anyone who agrees and gives freely."

"All right," I said without letting myself second-guess. "Then feed from me."

Her eyes widened. "No," she said. "You don't really want—"

"I do," I insisted. I held out my hand to her, though I had no idea if she needed physical contact. "Go ahead."

She looked at my hand and then back at my face. "Why? Why would you do that?"

"Better that it's me than some soul on the street who doesn't know what he's giving, don't you think?" I said. "I'd rather it didn't come to that, if you have a choice." I hesitated. Then I made myself add, "And I don't like to see you suffering."

I wasn't going to enjoy the process—I'd seen enough marks deflate into despondency after a Glower had drained them to know that much. But just this once, I'd be back to my normal mood tomorrow. If that small sacrifice could carry her through another month or more, it was worth it.

For a long moment, she didn't speak, only contemplated me. Her jaw worked. Then she stood up. "It can't be just any sort of energy. To really feed, I'll need to... inspire you."

I hadn't thought about that. There was a reason they hunted creative talents specifically. "I'm not an artist," I said.

"Everyone has at least a little potential," she said with a muted smile. She curled her fingers around my wrist. "I swear I will cause no permanent effects or connection. Are you sure about this?"

I didn't think she'd needed to offer that promise, or that

question, when I'd already made the offer. So when I said, "Yes," it was with no doubts at all.

I'd expected something obvious, dramatic—a tingle of electricity shooting up my arm, a spectacle exploding in my mind. What actually happened was only that her grip tightened slightly around my wrist. As I waited, my gaze roamed the room and settled on the cluster of paintings on the far wall. An itch crept up inside me. I shifted forward, and Kess let go of my arm.

"They're too close together," I said with a sudden certainty, striding over. "If I just—" I whirled, hurried to a drawer in the kitchen, and pulled out my mounting tools. Back in the living room, I removed two of the paintings from the wall, tugged out the nails, and set new ones a small distance to the side. My heart beat faster, excitement buzzing through me, louder with every movement. I hung the paintings and stepped back to take them in. Satisfaction swelled around the excitement. "There. That balances the shapes and lines even more effectively."

My attention veered to the wall beside me. With a fresh burst of insight, I tapped a spot beside the large acrylic landscape I had hanging there. "I need something else here. Nothing too big or bold... A sculpture. If I got a stand—yes." I could picture it perfectly. I glanced at the third wall. "And if I rearranged those, I could fit in a few more pieces. It'd be a real display. I wonder—I could ask if the student artists I admire would want to show a few pieces here—I could start having people up to see them—with those adjustments to the layout, I think I could make an arrangement that would really grab even a casual appreciator, and then I'd be getting word out about the artists too—"

I pictured dozens of art lovers ambling through my apartment, murmuring over my selections, with a rush that made me almost giddy. Then Kess touched my elbow. "Mateo," she said. As I blinked at her, my excitement dimmed. By the time I'd taken another breath, the living room appeared no different than it always had—nice enough, maybe a little pedestrian. Nothing spectacular, that was for sure. And I didn't really *want* people I barely knew tramping through my home, did I? Why had that seemed like a good idea?

Oh.

I stared at Kess. "That was— Christ." It had crept up on me so surreptitiously I hadn't even registered how unusual those feelings were for me, and yet it had build so fast from her one little nudge into a manic vision of grandeur.

No wonder people whose lives revolved around their ability to create would give themselves over to that high, agree to anything the demon offering it asked.

But unlike the marks I'd observed, I hadn't been left diminished by the feeding. I felt pretty much exactly as I had before Kess's nudge.

"Thank you," she said. "I think that will hold me over for some time."

"You didn't take everything you could have," I said. "Usually, with the marks—they're emptied afterward, of everything they felt good about." I could even appreciate that the new arrangement of paintings on the far wall was in fact more pleasing to the eye and take a little pride in that. Kess's "encouragement" had set me off, but my sensibilities had directed me from there. "Why didn't you take more?"

Kess gave a little chuckle, as if she didn't quite believe what she was going to say. When she spoke, it was so softly I barely heard her.

"I don't like to see you suffering."

A new sort of feeling unfurled inside me: an ache of longing I didn't know how to put into words. Kess gazed up at me as I touched her cheek, so still I wasn't sure how she'd respond next, but when I bent my head to hers she rose to meet me, catching my mouth with a passion not quite as urgent as on the beach but just as potent.

Somehow I still needed to hear the words. "Tell me the truth," I said, like a breath between our parted lips. "Do you want this? Do you *want* this?" Not for what you think you'll get later in return. Just for yourself.

My hands trailed down her body, and she pressed against me. "Yes," she whispered. "Please. Everything."

I bowed my head as she peeled off my shirt, and she paused with an odd sort of care to brush my rumpled hair from my forehead, to kiss me on my brow. I eased down her dress and unclasped her bra. Her breath caught with a whimper when I grazed my thumbs over her breasts. There was something experimental about the way she kissed my neck, my chest, testing my skin with the edges of her teeth and the wetness of her tongue. Her gasps inflamed my skin as I teased her nipples until they were as hard as my erection. She dug her fingernails into the muscles of my back, grinding against me, and my moan echoed hers.

I picked her up and braced her against the wall to press us even closer together, but that position felt too temporary, too casual. "Bedroom," I muttered, and she nodded. Her arms tightened around me as I carried her through the doorway.

I set her on the edge of the bed and tugged her dress the rest of the way off. She leaned forward to mouth the planes of my stomach as she undid my belt. The feel of her hands brushing over me to slide down my pants made me even harder. I nipped her shoulder, her sigh rippling through me, and pulled off her panties. As she scooted back on the bed to make room for me to join her, her eyes roamed over my naked body with a hunger I had no problem at all obliging.

When I leaned over her, she slipped her hand down to grasp my erection. I muffled my groan with a kiss. My fingers tangled in her hair as she stroked me. She pulled away from me to sit up, her hand still on me, her smile widening as I twitched in her grip. Then she bent and slicked her tongue up my member from base to head.

I couldn't stop my hips from jerking, even as the rest of me tensed. "Kess..." I'd usually dissuaded my partners from that particular act, because it conjured up the uncomfortable memory of Rosa's revolted grimace after we'd tried it once. That was not a sight I'd ever wanted to provoke again. But Kess sucked me into her hot mouth with a hum so eager it was impossible to question her enjoyment. She worked up and down, taking me deeper and deeper, her tongue tracing tantalizing patterns on my sensitive flesh, until it was a wonder I could think at all. I let my head fall back and my body drift on the sensation.

Kess raised herself slightly, cocking her head as she pumped me with her hand. "I never thought about it before," she said. "How wonderful it is that the simple touch of a mouth can give so much pleasure."

I choked on a sound of that pleasure as she swirled her tongue around me again. "Just as wonderful to receive it as to give," I managed to say. As I could happily demonstrate. I clasped her hip, urging her body toward me. She must have realized my intention, because she stretched out beside me as she continued attending to my erection. I kissed a path up her thigh, dipping my head as I reached the delicate folds between her legs.

She gasped with a flood of heat over my groin as I set my

mouth there. The sound ignited me. I flicked my tongue over the nub above her opening, reveling in the way that gasp broke into shuddered panting. Remembering how she'd responded best to my touch before, I kissed her gently, grazing my lips over her opening and back to that nub again. She tasted there the way she tasted everywhere, only stronger, that sweet smoky smell that in that moment I thought must be the flavor of stardust.

Kess sucked me down again. I felt her pleasure in the tightening of her lips around me, the clutch of her hands on my hips as I brushed her nub with the very tips of my teeth, the muffled noises that trembled from her chest. My head was already whirling. As she pursed her lips around me and squeezed her fingers around the base of my erection, the pleasure inside me swelled to bursting.

"Kess," I said, my voice strangled. She only increased the pressure. My hips arched, and a moan broke from my throat as I came into the welcoming wetness of her mouth. She caressed my side tenderly as she stroked me through my release.

It took me a minute to recover. As my head started to clear, I brought my mouth to her sweetness again. She cried out freely now, squirming against me as if we could fuse together. I laved my tongue over her, licking and suckling until she was clutching me with all her strength. "Oh," she murmured. "Mateo." She trembled against me, and I felt the muscles in her thighs clench. I kissed her more firmly, working over that nub until the last quivers faded away.

Kess turned herself around so she could kiss me on the mouth. The salty taste on her lips reminded me of the ocean. She wrapped her arms around me. When the kiss was over, she tucked her head under my chin. For several minutes we lay there entwined, our heartbeats slowing together. My eyelids drifted down, heavy with sleep. It had been a long day.

Kess's lips brushed my chest as she spoke. "May I stay?"

It hadn't occurred to me until she spoke that she might think she had to ask that question. It hadn't occurred to me how much I wanted her to. I guided her head back just far enough for me to kiss her forehead.

"Please," I said. She settled back against me, holding me to her as if she never intended to let me go.

Fourteen

THE BIRDS BROKE INTO MY AWARENESS FIRST, A COUPLE OF them squawking right outside my bedroom window. Then the thin morning light grazing my eyelids. I blinked, stirring on the bed, and it was only then that I realized I was alone there.

I hesitated, as if, if I lay still enough, Kess might reappear. But she was gone, the space on the mattress beside me empty, lukewarm like the air when I touched it.

Not just gone, but gone for a while.

The realization hit me like a punch in the stomach. I flopped back against my pillow, closing my eyes, as the dull ache spread up through my chest.

Of course she'd left. Why had I let myself believe she'd do anything else? She probably didn't need to sleep, and I doubted demons got much out of cuddling. What had I been offering her, really, that she'd have wanted to stick around for? Chances were she hadn't stayed five minutes after I'd drifted off.

Why had she even bothered asking to stay? To make me think everything we'd shared before that had been real?

My memories of the night were blurry. We'd gone to the Glower meeting, and to meet Ricky, and then down to the beach...

A deeper discomfort washed over me, knotting my gut. I'd let her work on Ricky. I'd let her *feed* from me. What the hell was wrong with me?

I'd wanted to believe she cared—to excuse how much I'd opened up to her, to replace my pain over losing Avery, maybe for reasons I hadn't fathomed yet. The nausea tickled up to my throat. I pushed myself out of the bed.

It wouldn't happen again. I'd learned everything I could from her and the other Glowers anyway. I didn't need to talk to her again. I definitely didn't need to kiss her again.

There was a moment when, despite my conviction, I held my breath as I stepped out of the bedroom, some part of me holding out hope that I'd find Kess emerging from the bathroom or making coffee in the kitchen or the normal sorts of things an actual person might do after spending the night.

She wasn't there. I was alone in the apartment. There was no sign at all she'd ever been here.

Other than the rearranged paintings on the living room wall. I studied them again in the brightening sunlight and had to admit that they did still look better than they had in their previous configuration. I scowled at them.

I gulped down reheated coffee from yesterday with a wince and hustled out of the apartment. I could grab breakfast later. Right now I needed to talk to Sterling. I'd already proven I couldn't trust myself to keep my head around the Glower. He'd know what safety measures I should put in place to prevent me from making another mistake.

Even now, I couldn't stop thinking back to the affection I'd thought I'd seen in her expression last night. The gasps that had sounded so full of desire. What sign had I missed?

The most obvious one. She was a Glower. A monster, as she'd said herself. That should have been all I'd needed to know.

I was walking so fast when I reached the office building that I nearly bumped into Avery coming out onto the sidewalk. I backed up a step to let her by, but she paused. The last thing I wanted right now was those knowing eyes evaluating me.

"Mateo," Avery said with her usual warm smile. "Hi! Sterling's got you coming in early these days, I see."

"I— Yeah, basically," I said, pulling myself together. It wasn't as if I could explain the truth to her. "Why did you come in?"

"Just dropping off a book I told Yelena I'd lend her—got to go catch up with the client now." Her gaze turned searching, and I felt myself tense before she'd even opened her mouth again.

"My mom mentioned she saw you leaving the mixer," she said. "She thought you looked upset. Did something happen, Mateo, or— Is everything okay?"

I must have looked nearly as scattered as I felt—I'd barely wet my hair in the shower, and I'd pulled on the first clothes my hands had found. As much as I tried to control my expression, some of my frustration with myself might have leaked out. But I had to wonder if there was more behind the concern in her voice.

It was possible she'd heard my footsteps in the hall while she and Colin were hooking up. Possible she'd put together the timing of that with my disappearance.

"I wasn't feeling well that night," I said, keeping my voice steady. "That's all."

She bit her lip, a gesture that had used to make me think about kissing her. It didn't anymore, but that was no relief, because all it did was remind me of another set of lips I'd enjoyed kissing far too much.

"Are you sure?" she said. "We're good? Because if something's wrong, then—"

"Avery," I snapped before she could go on, "can you just leave it alone for once?"

She swayed back as if I'd slapped her, and I supposed I might as well have. "Sorry," she said. "I just— I'm sorry."

Before I could say anything else, not that I had any idea what to say, she spun and hurried away. I watched her go, a prickle of shame layering on top of my present wretchedness.

Well, the day couldn't possibly get any worse, could it?

When I got up to the office, Sterling's door was shut. I knocked, praying for a swift answer. Yelena looked up from her cubicle.

"He's not coming in today," she said.

My heart plummeted. "What? Why not?"

"He called in about ten minutes ago," she said, motioning to her headset. "Apparently he has an out-of-town meeting he forgot to add to the master schedule. He didn't know yet if he'll even be back tomorrow."

"Oh." So I might be on my own until Monday. Four days. I could keep my head on straight for that long, couldn't I?

I wasn't really sure.

"Was there something urgent you needed to discuss with him?" Yelena asked, her brow furrowing, and I realized I was still standing there at Sterling's door like a man adrift. "He should have his phone on him if you need to reach him—you can at least leave him a message."

"Nothing that urgent," I said. I *was* sure this problem required in-person assistance.

I glanced down the line of office doors, but I didn't trust any of the other supervisors the same way. Sterling was the one who'd worked the most closely with most of us younger trainees, maybe because he was one of the younger senior staff himself. I'd gathered he'd been brought into the Society when he was a teen, like me. And he was the one I'd already discussed Kess with, who'd approved my deal with her. I didn't want to get him in trouble over this.

Kess hadn't been visiting me every day. I should be able to make it until tomorrow, at least. And if Sterling didn't show up then... I'd come up with a new plan when I had to.

I sat down at my desk. After several minutes of meandering, I managed to lose myself a little in the work, following the threads I'd started to tease out to determine whether one particular quality or another had resulted in successful Tether-client pairings on a broad scale. Checking what other factors might have gotten in the way if one hadn't. The most definite pattern I was seeing was that there was no guarantee of success.

But Sterling hadn't been off base either. A few criteria did appear to make the relationship go *more* smoothly in almost every case I looked at, like a Tether's capacity for patience and a client being adverse to risk-taking, but anyone could have predicted that. More interesting was the interplay I was starting to notice between personalities. The way someone like Fiona, for example, had clashed horribly with her first training client, a middle-aged stage actress, but always seemed to bring out the best in the teen stars she'd started to specialize in. If I could find more patterns like *that*, I could start to label every Tether and client based on their key characteristics and create better matches without having to wait to see how things worked in the first few trial pairings.

I'd distracted myself from the rest of the world enough that I didn't hear any movement toward my desk until the floor creaked right behind me. I startled, and Sofie hopped back, raising her hand in apology.

"Sorry," she said. "I didn't mean to surprise you. Is this the project Sterling was talking about at the party?"

"Yeah," I said, leaning back in my chair. "I mean, sort of. This is the data we're using. We're trying to come up with a system for matching clients with Tethers more effectively."

"Well, that definitely sounds like a good thing," she said.

"Is your thriller author giving you trouble?" I asked.

She laughed and shook her head. "No. I've got the next couple days off, actually. I was just coming by to bring the paperwork Yelena needed to set up my regular payments." Her voice dropped. "It's still weird to me that we actually get paid to do this."

"It's a job," I reminded her, but I found I was able to smile at her conspiratorial tone. "And hey, the clients can afford it."

"I guess so," she said. "I couldn't believe the house this woman lives in."

"You'll get used to it. Just wait until you end up with an A-lister or a Billboard-topper."

"I guess I'll have to work my way up to the big leagues."

"I don't know," I said. "It seems like you're getting along pretty well already."

Her cheeks pinked at that. She looked at her feet, and it occurred to me that she hadn't needed to stop to talk to me at all. Maybe she was just looking to connect with more people in the Society... or maybe she saw something she particularly liked in me.

With that thought, guilt jerked at my gut.

Guilt because of *Kess*? As if I were betraying her somehow by so much as noticing another woman existed?

An actual woman, who if she liked me, liked *me*, not how

she thought she could use me. My jaw set. I was allowed to notice Sofie. Hell, if it hadn't been for the messed up situation I'd gotten myself into, I probably *would* have asked her out.

So what was stopping me?

The question came with a sudden rush of relief. Of course I could. I could ask out a regular human woman on a regular human date and erase Kess from my life as easily as my interlude with her had helped erase my ties to Avery. What better defense could there be than simply moving on?

"Hey," I said, "if you're off, do you want to get together Friday night? We could grab dinner, and I'll see what else is going on. There might be a gallery showing worth seeing."

Sofie's gaze darted up to my face. She tipped her head. "Get together—like a date?"

"It doesn't have to be," I said. "I'm happy hanging out as friends. But, if you're up for that..."

The flush in her cheeks deepened, but her smile turned slightly mischievous in a way that made me even more glad I'd asked her. "Yeah," she said. "I'd like that a lot."

Fifteen

"You know, I wouldn't have thought I'd be into that kind of stark imagery combined with such vibrant colors, but she really made it work," Sofie said as we strolled down the street. We'd just left the independent gallery I'd found out was hosting an opening, after having met at a Korean restaurant Sofie had recommended. She'd seemed reserved at first, but as soon as we'd stepped into the gallery space, something vibrant had started to shine in her too.

"I have a thing for artists who aren't afraid to play with the more saturated hues," I said. "I mean, too much and it can get in the way of all other intent, but sometimes subtle just doesn't cut it."

"I guess I have a soft spot for subtle," Sofie said, bumping me lightly with her elbow. "I would have taken you for the subtle type too, I've got to say. Quiet and thoughtful. Or have I just not seen your saturated side yet?"

"Oh, I have so many sides you've haven't seen," I said with a grin. The ease of flirting with her—so straightforward, so *normal*

—sent a thrill through me for the instant before the remark dragged up a memory of Kess. Of the purr of a voice she'd used in our early meetings. *I'm going to teach you so many ways of saying yes.*

I shoved the echo away. Sterling had been absent again today, but looking forward to tonight's date had kept me focused. This was where I belonged. This was the sort of life I was supposed to be leading.

"So do you go to shows very often?" Sofie asked, tugging me out of my thoughts.

"I made it to more when I first moved out and was building up a collection for my apartment," I said. "It's difficult to find the time around the Society assignments. Although I might have more opportunity now that I'm doing mostly office work. One thing I'll say for that: the schedule's a lot more consistent."

"I can see how that would be a plus. I'm not exactly overjoyed about this extended weekend shift I'm starting tomorrow." She rolled her shoulders as if working out tension.

"Do you need to head home?" I said, as much as I didn't want her to. It was nearly midnight, but the last few hours were the first time I'd felt fully grounded in weeks. Maybe Kess had been a dream and nothing more, and I was just a guy who went on dates with regular women and talked about art and made them smile.

"Not yet," Sofie said, as one of those smiles lit up her face. "I'm going to enjoy my freedom a bit longer, I think. So tell me more about your personal collection. Any artists I'm likely to know?"

"Probably not unless you've been paying close attention to the local scene," I said. "If I've got a theme, it's catching an artist in their first year of professional shows. I like the rawness you see then—you can picture where they're going, and how they're reaching for it... So most of the pieces I've bought, those artists haven't had a chance to have their careers really take off yet."

"I like that theme," Sofie said. "There'd be something exciting about catching the beginning of the journey. So much possibility."

"Exactly."

She paused with an intake of breath. "Well, maybe you can show me your collection sometime. I'd like to see what other sides of Mateo Jimenez it reveals."

It occurred to me, though she couldn't have known it, that with the direction we'd set off in, we'd ended up not far from my building. I could invite her up to my apartment right now. I had the feeling she'd say yes.

I imagined walking her through my living room, telling the story behind the purchase of each of the pieces hanging on the walls... as if it were the private gallery I'd envisioned two nights ago on the wave of Kess's inspiration. My stomach clenched up. It was one thing to amble around the city with another woman, but to bring her right into the space the Glower had inhabited so fully, so recently—it might take more time to detach myself that far.

Still, I let us continue our stroll toward my building. Sofie commented on an exhibition she'd seen a couple of months ago, and I talked about a client I'd worked with in training who'd made found object sculptures, and before I'd made a definite decision, the familiar concrete face of my home loomed before us.

"Well," I said, "this is me."

"Oh!" Sofie turned toward me, a shade of disappointment on her face. I didn't really want this conversation to end either. My gaze dropped to her lips, pert and faintly glossy. I ought to kiss her now. The thought sent a quiver of anticipation through me. Maybe everything would seem more certain if I crossed that line.

I drew her to me, and she leaned into me with a gentle press of her mouth. Her lips parted against mine, a trace of herbal tea from the gallery lingering on her breath, and with a jolt every nerve in my body seemed to fire at once. Fractured impressions flitted over my skin and through my mind—what the curve of Sofie's breast might feel like in my hand, the brush of Kess's nipples against my chest, the stiffening of my groin now and then. Imagined and remembered caresses blurred together. I wanted to coax her open and explore her from head to toe; I wanted gasps and bare flesh; I wanted Kess's gleeful grin as an ocean wave crashed over her naked shoulders.

I pulled back a little more abruptly than I'd meant to. Sofie peered up at me as if waiting to see what I'd do next.

I couldn't do this. I slung my hands in my pockets in the hopes of both obscuring my arousal and hiding the trembling that had spread through my arms, and said in a voice that sounded impressively calm to my ears, "I can call you a cab. They usually get here pretty fast."

"All right," Sofie said. To my relief, she looked only regretful, not offended or concerned. She waited while I pulled out my phone and made the call. Then she said, "It's been a really enjoyable night. I hope we can do this again."

"Me too," I said, and if we left out the least five minutes, I was completely sure I meant that.

I waited with her until the cab showed up. When she looked up at me to say good night, the question in her eyes made me step in to kiss her again. But it was brief, a perfunctory brushing of lips, and then I was waving as the cab carried her away.

My heart beat with a sickly thudding as I headed up to my apartment. My nerves were still jittering, as if someone had rewired my senses so they didn't quite align with the outside world. Which was probably why, at the touch on my back when I slid my key into the lock, I whirled as if braced for an attack.

Kess stared at me, raising her arms in supplication. Looking at her, at the pale pretty face I'd fallen asleep to two nights ago and searched for yesterday morning in vain, the fragments of frustration and uncertainty and shame inside me condensed into a hard knot of anger.

I didn't trust myself to speak in the hall, where the neighbors might hear. I opened the door and stepped into the apartment, and Kess followed me.

"If I'm interrupting something," she started, in that low sweet voice that was just another lie.

"What are you doing here?" I said, cutting her off. "What do you want, Kess?"

"You're upset," she said. I couldn't tell if that were an answer or merely an observation.

"Yes, I am," I said. "But I don't really want to discuss it with you. So can you just go?"

Her brow knit. "You're upset with *me*. I thought..."

"You thought what?" I prompted when she didn't go on.

"The woman you were with. You were happy, and then you were not."

I didn't understand what she was getting at, but it didn't matter. What struck me instead was that she knew. She knew I'd been out with Sofie. She'd been watching us? Or merely gleaning all she needed to reading my emotional responses from afar? I wasn't sure which made me more disturbed.

"Because of you," I said. "I couldn't just be happy with her *because of you*. This... game, whatever it is we've been playing at —you've messed with my head—one kiss and my body goes crazy—that's not me."

"No," Kess agreed, with a gentleness that only made my gut clench tighter, "it's not. But it's not so surprising that your responses have changed, is it? You kept so much inside, tamped down, for so long, and now you've learned how to let those feelings out, but you're not used to managing them. It should only take time, to find a balance. Isn't it better, to be opened up?"

I shook my head. "Not like this. I didn't feel like I could even control myself."

"You'll get used to it," Kess said. "Most people I've encountered manage to live while juggling all their emotions all the time." She paused and tilted her head with a sly smile. "Or you could simply not bother with 'people' anymore. Stay with those who don't mind if you lose control."

"What's that's supposed to mean?" I said. "I should spent all my time with *you*?"

I meant it sarcastically, but Kess stepped toward me. She laid her arms across my shoulders as she gazed into my eyes, and my pulse started up its heady thrum again.

"Would that be so terrible?" she murmured. "I can be anyone you want, without you ever having to be afraid of the consequences. I can be her, and you can take what you wanted to right now."

Before she'd even finished speaking, her shimmer brightened, her hair paling to Sofie's shade, her face rounding, her nose shortening. She rose on her toes at her diminished height to go in for a kiss, and my stomach lurched. I yanked myself away from her.

"No," I said, closing my eyes against the cloned image of my colleague. "Don't do that. I don't want *her*."

That was the problem, wasn't it? Nausea welled up as the truth of it hit me. I'd had a nice time with Sofie. I'd enjoyed talking to her and I found her attractive enough, but when I'd kissed her, it hadn't really been her body I'd wanted against mine. The next words I could have said caught in my throat.

I want you.

I snatched at that feeling and forced it down, far beneath the queasiness and the anger. She would laugh if she saw it, if she knew I'd bought into her ploys that deeply. That one part of me I wasn't letting her have.

"Why don't you just leave?" I said. "There's nothing more you can get from me, is there? *You* don't even believe the rest of your kind will be able to bargain with the Society. I'm done listening. So the deal is finished."

There was silence. Then Kess said, "I'm not here for the deal."

She sounded so desolate I had to look at her. Her form had shifted back into the slim, dark-haired beauty that was her usual guise. She was still watching me, but her lips had pressed tight and her body had tensed.

"So what are you here for?" I said.

She laughed, a raw strangled sound that jerked a flutter of concern into my chest despite my attempts to harden myself. "Has it not been obvious enough?" she said. "I sway to your touch. I can't feed because every human I see has a heart that beats as yours does. When my kind speak of their hunger, all I can think of is the pain their hunting causes you. I linger in your world when it means I can stay beside you. I'm here for *you*, Mateo."

I opened my mouth, but nothing came out. My throat had closed up. I swallowed, and the first words that worked their way up were, "You *left*. The other night—"

"So I didn't have to witness your horror when you remembered that you'd let me stay in your bed," she snapped.

"So I could try to convince myself I'm still completely mine. But I'm not. What do you need me to say? Do you want to complain about who changed who? I have helped you find what was already inside you. *You* have turned altered the fabric of my existence. I don't know what I am, what to do with this... this awareness. This *compassion*." She bit out the word as if it were a curse. "It gnaws at me, and yet I can't help clinging to it, because it's part of me now, it's something I would lose. I could do without before, but now I'd know I was lacking it. You did this. You see this, and you still assume the worst of me. That is what I have to live with. The whole world has rushed inside me, and still all I am to you is a monster."

She was trembling now, the way she had when she'd broken down on the beach. My arms ached to wrap around her. But the rest of my body balked. How could I know whether this was real or another version of an act? Maybe she had seen my wanting, no matter how deep I'd buried it, and this was her way of using it.

"You came to me for your own reasons," I said. "You wanted my help. I've tried to give it."

"You've given me plenty," she agreed. "But never without regret. You are so full of regret when you look at me, it's become hard to bear. I thought, if I could find the right thing to offer, the right way to show you, if I could bring more pleasure than distress... But it will never happen, will it? You will never stop regretting, not as long as I am what I am, and I can't change that."

"What are you even saying?" I said, my head spinning. "You think we should *date*? You want to be my girlfriend? You're not human. You don't live like I do. You don't even... You don't even live on this plane of existence!"

"I do more than I did before," Kess said. "But yes, it is absurd, I agree. So I'll honor your earlier request and leave."

She'd made it halfway to the door before the word broke from my lips.

"Wait."

She stopped and looked back at me. I found I couldn't move. This was what I'd wanted more than anything, wasn't it? Her gone for good, so I could go back to normal life?

So why did my heart feel as if it were wrenching in half?

"I'm sorry," was all I managed to say. I wasn't sure what I was apologizing for. All I knew was I hadn't intended to be the cause of anyone's pain, not even a demon's.

Kess watched me for a moment longer. Then she bowed her head and wisped away into the shadow by the doorframe.

Sixteen

I KNOCKED ON THE FRONT DOOR OF STERLING'S BUNGALOW
and eased back half a step, praying for an answer. I'd noted his
home address in the Tether database when he hadn't come in
yesterday, and after last night's debacle, I didn't trust myself to
wait until Monday. He hadn't responded to my phone call or the
voice mail I'd left a few hours ago. Maybe he wasn't back from
his out-of-town event, but I'd had to try this.

After a minute, my hopes sinking, I let myself knock one
more time. I was about to turn and walk away when the door
eased open.

In that first moment, staring at my supervisor standing
stooped and hollow-cheeked in a shirt and slacks with enough
wrinkles to suggest he'd grabbed them from a heap on his way
out of bed, I couldn't speak. All at once the pieces clicked. I'd
always thought Sterling was in his forties—early fifties at the
most—but he seemed to have aged thirty years since I'd last seen
him. Or not quite that quickly, because I *had* noticed some of
that wearing down over the last few weeks, hadn't I? The

trembling of a hand, the gestures that could have been in response to pain, the dropping of a glass, the smell of vomit in a bathroom. The odd urgency he'd expressed about our new project that went beyond even his usual dedication. I'd just been too wrapped up in my own drama to see each one of those signs was part of the same larger picture.

"You didn't really go out of town this week," I said. "You're sick."

Sterling drew himself up as straight as he seemed able to and opened his mouth as if to deny it, but all that ended up coming out was a sigh. "Come in," he said. "I supposed it's time we discussed the... situation fully."

He made a few shuffling motions as he led me into the living room just off the front hall, gathering stray pieces of mail and an empty mug, but the place was just as tidy as his office, the linen couch's cushions smooth and unmarked, the geometric-patterned rug recently vacuumed, the Picasso print over the mantle perfectly centered. After I'd sat down on the couch, Sterling disappeared and returned with two new mugs, both trailing thick coffee-scented steam. I took the one he offered me and cupped it in my hands. Too many questions had tangled in the back of my throat for me to force anything past them.

"Why have you been hiding it?" was the first to work its way out.

Sterling rubbed the side of his head, and his body stiffened. I realized a second after he must have that a few tufts of his wiry hair had fallen out onto his hand. He brushed them away against his knee, his jaw clenching.

"Because I wanted my colleagues to continue to listen to me and not dismiss any... bolder ideas I might propose as the product of a medication-addled mind," he said. "The fact of the matter will come out soon enough. I've been trying to finish everything I need to first, but we all have our limitations."

The resignation in his tone sent a chill through me. "Isn't it treatable?"

"Stage four liver cancer," he said. "The doctors are treating it, yes—I was in the hospital for their most recent attempt on Thursday—but it's a menace. And it moves quickly. I'll be lucky to have another six months. Three is more likely."

Ever since Rosa's crash, I'd thought about death every day: the long, slow, draining deaths the Glowers wrought. It seemed almost inconceivable that someone I knew could die in any other way, of a completely ordinary disease. My hands tightened around the mug. I made myself take a sip just to have something to do while I gathered my thoughts. The coffee trickled hot and bitter down my throat.

"That's why you've been so concerned about the database project, and about pitching it to the rest of the Society staff," I said. "I'm sorry. If I'd known..."

He waved off my apology. "I didn't want you to know. You've still been doing excellent work with it. I have access to the server from here—I've looked over your notes. It's been a relief to see the enterprise I envisioned coming together."

"Why did you give it to *me*?" I said. "Why not go straight to working with the other senior Tethers on it? With more of us sorting through the data, we could at least have moved faster."

"Perhaps," he said. "Perhaps not. Too many cooks, you know what they say... I've spent far too much of my life in meetings with the senior staff, hashing out every detail of an idea before we proceed even one step toward implementing it. I wanted to bring the directors something they could imagine in action from the work already put in. Something so obviously beneficial they'd have no excuse to delay moving forward with it.

And I wanted them to know you were the one who put in that work." He leaned forward, his gaze intent on me. "There will be an opening among the supervisory staff when I need to bow out, Mateo. I'm hoping you'll be the one to take it."

"Me?" I said, startled. "I've only been taking on clients officially for four and a half years. My last client *fired* me."

"So your field skills could use a little... refining. I think we need fresh blood on the decision-making level, to bring new ideas, to take the necessary risks—the developments we've seen this past year have demonstrated that we *need* to fundamentally alter the way we're approaching our work. Your record has shown you to be nothing but committed and clear-headed in the face of complications. And even more important is your ability to manage your fellow Tethers. Your contributions in bringing Fiona's new endeavor to fruition have been noted. As has the grace with which you handled the... dissolution of an intra-office romance."

His smile turned wry, but I couldn't accept that praise. I couldn't even prevent an ironic bark of a laugh from wrenching out of me. I dropped my gaze to my mug, as if the dark liquid there would tell me the right way to explain how badly I'd gone astray.

"You came here because there was something *you* needed to talk to me about," Sterling said after a moment.

I felt him watching me, but I didn't raise my head. "I've made some bad decisions," I said haltingly. "The Glower who first came to me—there were times, the way certain circumstances affected her, as I told you... She started to seem so human that I let it go too far. I let her affect me, I let myself *care* about her. I don't think anything that's happened between us could hurt the Society, but I don't know, in the future— I don't trust myself anymore."

Sterling set his hand over mine. I glanced up at him then, braced for anger or disdain, but there was nothing in his expression except sympathy.

"I'm the one who encouraged you to pursue that avenue of inquiry," he said. "I'm your supervisor. If anyone's judgment should be questioned, it's mine. But I can see you're not marked, and you say you haven't harmed the Society, as much as I would imagine a Glower might have wanted you to. That indicates strength to me, not weakness. Look at how quickly so many people fall in with them. You recognized the risk and you're asking for help. That's responsibility."

"I shouldn't have gotten so wrapped up in the situation to begin with," I started, and he shook his head.

"If there's anyone in this world without a list of should and shouldn't haves, I'll eat my shirt," he said. "Do you want to tell me exactly what's happened?"

My chest contracted. The thought of laying it all out in so much detail made me feel queasy. But he had to know most of it, at least, so I could be sure I *hadn't* done worse than I'd realized. So I could be sure, if he still wanted to promote me after this, that it was with full knowledge of my mistakes.

"Some of it," I said. "Maybe... Maybe all of it, but maybe not right away. But what's most important, what I wanted to see you about, is I need a way to make sure that I can't be influenced by her again. She said, once she'd spent some time with me, that she could sense my emotions from farther away. I don't want her following me like that. I'm not sure how much I might be giving away without even knowing it."

"Well, there's a simple enough solution to that problem," Sterling said. "You need to think of yourself as a client this once, not as a Tether."

He got up and shuffled out of the room again. When he

returned with a leather string dangling from his hand, a malachite pendant gleaming at its base, I could have smacked myself. Of course. Sterling was right—I just wasn't used to thinking of myself the way I would a client. When I was on the job in the field, I wasn't supposed to use the protections we could offer them, because I needed to be able to engage with the Glowers as the occasion demanded and to observe how well the client's protections were working on their own. But now, working in the office, I didn't have that restriction. And it would never have been disallowed on my own time.

He handed the necklace to me, and my pulse gave a little lurch before I forced my hands to rise and sling it over my head. All right, maybe there was more to it than habit. Maybe I hadn't really wanted to shut Kess out.

Sitting with that uncomfortable idea, I tucked the pendant under the collar of my shirt. It rested, hard and cool, just above my heart. At least I was making the right decision now.

"I have a drawer of those from my days in the field," Sterling said. "Always useful to have them on hand. Does wearing it put your mind more at ease?"

I nodded, and he settled back into his chair. "All right," he said. "Tell me what happened, from the beginning."

I dragged in a breath. "You know I told you she wanted to make a deal with me," I said. "Well, what she offered as her side of the deal was to teach me how to open myself up..."

When I got to the theater where Avery's current client was in the midst of a dress rehearsal the next day, Avery was already waiting on the sidewalk outside. She might have looked calm to the average passerby, but I'd known her long enough to recognize the tension in her grip on her purse strap and the slight pursing of her lips. Given the way I'd talked to her the last time we'd seen each other, I couldn't blame her for being wary. If I'd thought I would have the chance to talk to her away from work any time soon, I wouldn't have texted her asking for this weekend meet-up. But after spilling my soul to Sterling, I'd realized I had other reparations to make.

She looked good, her bright brown hair and creamy skin set off by her green wrap dress. I was pleased to find I could see that without any twinge of longing or loss. Maybe *one* good thing had come from my entanglement with Kess.

"What's going on?" Avery said as I joined her. Her tone was mild but cautious. The jab of guilt in my gut dug a little deeper. She'd never needed to be cautious with me before.

"I didn't mean to make this sound like an emergency," I said. "I just— I didn't want to leave things strained between us. I have to apologize for Wednesday. I've... been in the middle of a pretty thorny situation, and I was stressed out. I shouldn't have taken it out on you."

"Okay," Avery said. Her fingers loosened as they slid down her purse strap. "So *are* you okay? You don't have to talk to me about it if you don't want to, but if there's anything I can do to help, you should know you can ask."

She could have accepted my apology and taken off, or stuck to making pleasantries. She hadn't needed to make that offer. And that was why I'd loved her.

"I do know that," I said. "And it means a lot to me." I glanced away from her for a moment, still feeling out exactly how much I should say. "I realize things have sometimes been a little awkward since we, well—"

"It's been fine," Avery said quickly. "I mean, I think it's

normal for a work break-up to be a little awkward. It hasn't been a problem."

She knew, or at least suspected, that I hadn't totally been over her. I was sure of it then. Maybe I would have seen it earlier if I hadn't been so busy convincing myself of the opposite.

"That's good," I said. "I also thought I should make it clear... It wasn't your fault that I never really let you in, when we were together. It wasn't even that I didn't want to. I had... issues, I guess, to work through, because of things that happened before we ever met. But I think I'm getting through them. And I really am happy for you. To be honest, I thought it was going to be hard, seeing you with Colin, but it wasn't. I could see how good you are together. I'm glad that you're with someone who makes you so happy."

That was probably the most personal thing I'd ever told her. Ironic that I'd only been able to manage it now, when we'd been apart for a year. But better than nothing.

"Thank you," Avery said softly. Then the corner of her mouth turned up. "I heard you took Sofie out."

Lord, word traveled fast. I spread my hands. "I like her," I said. "I don't know if it'll go anywhere, but that's okay too. I've got lots of time, and there's no rush. And some people are meant to just be friends."

"Yeah."

I would have hugged her then, except I suspected it was still too soon for that. Maybe later, someday when I'd be able to say we truly were friends and not just amicable exes.

"Well, I'd better let you get back to it," I said.

Avery bobbed her head with that little smile, her demeanor completely at ease now, and ducked back inside. I lingered there a minute longer, taking relief from the sense that I'd handled at least one thing right.

Even with the protection of the malachite, I stayed on my guard the entire weekend. The stone might prevent Kess from reading my emotions, and from the size of it I suspected she couldn't have come within several feet of me without discomfort, but that didn't mean she wouldn't approach me at all. It was only after I slid into a cab Monday morning to head to work that my apprehension eased. The Society's office had enough protections constructed into it that no Glower could touch the place, let alone enter it.

So when my gaze caught on a sleek head of shimmering black hair across the street from the building, I wasn't prepared. It took me a second to catch my breath amid the stutter of my pulse.

"Keep going, actually," I said to the cabbie before he could step on the brake. "Around the corner to the right, and stop there."

He drove on without comment, pulling up to the curb by the coffee shop on the corner. After I'd paid him, I hurried through the coffee shop's side entrance and stalked to the front window.

It was her. Kess was loitering near the edge of the sidewalk, wearing her "true" form and her favorite black dress. As I watched, hidden behind the morning sunlight's reflections on the glass, she paced from one streetlamp to another. At this distance, the fall of her hair shadowed most of her expression. I touched the pendant through the fabric of my shirt. It had hidden me from her too, and still did.

I left the window just long enough to buy an espresso so the barista wouldn't get edgy about me lingering, and then I resumed my watch. What was Kess doing here? What did she want? It didn't look as if she were capable of coming any closer to the office building, which fit my understanding. Had she hoped that my seeing her when I came to work would provoke some particular reaction? Or maybe she'd made some sort of deal with another Tether already.

She stopped again, flicking her fingers against her thigh, her back to me as she peered in the direction I'd usually have arrived from. No, I was almost sure she was waiting for me. Why?

Her words from Friday night rose up in my head. The echo of the anguish in her voice, her eyes, made my stomach twist.

Lies. All Glowers did was lie, to catch people in their snares. I'd seen it with every client I'd worked with. I'd seen it with Rosa and Isaac. The demons didn't care about any of us, about anything other than satisfying themselves.

No matter how much I might have wanted to believe this one cared about me.

Which was exactly why I stayed where I was, watching and waiting too. If I called the office, Yelena would tell me to go banish her myself. Maybe I could. I had the knotted string we used for that purpose in my back pocket, as always. But I'd have to take off the pendant to get close enough to do it. I sipped my coffee, willing it to fortify me. Kess was here because of me. It was my mistake to fix.

I was about halfway through the cup when a woman pushing a stroller came hurrying down the block. From her professional dress and her brisk stride, I guessed she was dropping the kid off at daycare—and maybe a bit late doing it. The toddler in the stroller was waving a small stuffed stegosaurus at everyone they passed.

He'd just waved it at Kess when his fingers slipped. The toy dinosaur tumbled onto the sidewalk. The boy's mother was too focused on checking her phone to notice. The boy whimpered, loud enough that I heard him through the glass.

"We're almost there," the woman said. "Try to be patient."

I drew back a step as Kess's gaze trailed after them, though it was so bright outside I doubted she could have made me out unless she'd come right up to the window. Her head bowed toward the fallen toy. Her body stiffened. Then she darted forward and snatched up the stuffed dinosaur.

"Excuse me," she said, sprinting a few steps to catch up with the woman. "He dropped this."

The woman swiveled and gasped. She snatched the toy out of Kess's hands. "Oh, thank you! You have no idea how much fussing you've saved me. It's his favorite."

She handed the dinosaur to her son, who squealed and squeezed it into a tight hug. Kess stared down at him. From where I was standing, I had a nearly perfect view of her face in that moment. So I saw the flicker of emotion that crossed it. The hesitant curiosity and then, as the boy beamed up at her, a soft smile that if I hadn't known what she was, I would have called tender.

"I'm glad I could help," she said in her low even voice. Even with her ten feet away and a wall between us, the sound of it made my heart wobble.

The woman with the stroller walked on. Kess turned to gaze across the street at the office building. Her face pinched. She shook her head, her shoulders hunching, and spun to walk closer to the restaurant she'd been staked out in front of. In a second, she'd slipped out of my view.

My fingers had clenched around my cup. She hadn't needed to help. But she'd done it anyway. My mind scrambled to find a reason for it to be an act and came up with nothing. Nothing except the possibility that she'd honestly wanted to.

I swallowed the rest of the coffee and tossed the cup in the trash bin. Enough wavering. It might not be wise to take off the pendant and attempt a banishing, but I had to go out there and at least confront her. Maybe I'd get some answers that way. With the malachite protecting me, she wouldn't be able to know what I was feeling, to play with those emotions. I could have the upper hand for once.

I stepped out the door—and halted.

Kess was gone. No glinting figure stood in the shadow of the restaurant or farther down the street. She'd vanished the way only a Glower could, as if she'd never been there.

Whatever she'd been here for, she must have changed her mind. Or decided to try again another time. I'd have to be careful when I left this afternoon.

After my scan of the street convinced me she was completely gone, I hurried across to the office and headed up the stairs. When I reached the main room, Yelena was standing near the water cooler, talking to Sofie. At the sight of my companion in last week's not-entirely-successful date, I hesitated for the second time that morning. I hadn't figured out what I was going to say to her yet.

Then I registered the topic of their conversation.

"Why would a Glower be hanging around the Society office?" Sofie was saying. "You don't think they'd try to *attack* us here, do you?"

"You saw a Glower?" I said. Had Kess talked to her?

Sofie glanced over and smiled. "Oh, hi, Mateo! I'm not sure. I saw this woman from, like, a block away when I was coming up to the building, and I *thought* she had that glow to her, but it wasn't very obvious. She'd walked away before I got closer. It could have been just a weird effect of the sun. Maybe I'm getting paranoid."

"Or they're getting up to more new tricks," Yelena said. "We're shielded well enough in here, but I'd say keep your eyes open the next few days, just in case. And tell the rest of us if you see another one hanging around."

Sofie nodded. "Have they ever tried to hurt the Tethers directly?"

"Only occasionally, if cornered, in the past," Yelena said. "But these days, who knows! You can't trust those things. I'm sure they'd burn this place down with all of us in it if they could."

The image rose in my mind of Kess waving a flaming Molotov cocktail—and immediately dissolved as the wrongness of it wrenched at me. *No*, I thought. *Not this one. You don't know her.*

I realized I'd opened my mouth as if I were going to speak. Both Yelena and Sofie were looking at me. The words caught in my throat. I couldn't say *that*, that I not only had seen the Glower but *knew* her.

A sudden heat prickled over me.

Yes. I knew her. I knew how she laughed like pure joy with the spin of a merry-go-round and how she ran wild with the wind by the ocean and how she sighed when I eased inside her. I knew she'd released me from my lingering longing for Avery and shown me how to help Ricky. I knew she'd been less and less like a Glower with every way I'd found to ground her in this world—I knew she'd sought out ways to keep grounding herself, because she'd wanted to. *Because it's something I would lose.*

I knew she'd seen a sad human child and cared enough to rescue his toy and return it to him. I knew she'd received something from his grin that had warmed her.

I knew she was a Glower, too. I did. And I'd let that fact

overshadow every other facet of her I'd seen, even though I also knew it wasn't the only thing that mattered. I *knew*.

Accept, she'd told me, when we'd first started our dealings. Apparently I still hadn't really mastered that skill. If I could accept that Avery was happier with Colin than she'd ever have been with me, that Sterling might not live out the next three months, then why couldn't I accept that a demon might have the capacity to change?

Everything Kess had said to me the other night, it was true. She'd shown me over and over what she could be, who she was becoming, and I'd been the one who kept turning her back into a monster.

She'd offered me everything I'd wanted—desire, devotion, compassion—and I'd thrown it away because I still hadn't learned to let people in. I was too damn busy trying to protect myself, as if a broken heart were somehow worse than one that never got used.

"Mateo?" Sofie said. "What's the matter? Did you see something too?"

Too much, but not soon enough.

"No," I said, my voice sounding distant to my ears. "Everything seemed all right when I came in." I walked to the windows that looked over the street. If Kess had come back, I could go down and talk to her properly...

The sidewalk was empty. Sofie sidled closer, eyeing me with obvious concern. I was a knotted tangle of pain inside, my legs itching to run until I found the one being who could help me out of it, but I was still aware enough to note that concern and still my feet.

There was something I needed to fix *here*, to make sure I didn't hurt anyone else more than I already had.

"Can I talk to you for a sec?" I said. The way Sofie smiled as she nodded made me wince inside. Yelena gave us a shrewd look and sauntered back to her desk.

"What's up?" Sofie said.

I pitched my voice low so Yelena couldn't overhear. "I just thought we should touch base before things have a chance to get weird. I had a good time Friday, and it'd be great to check out more shows and that sort of thing with you... but I think it would be just as friends." I rubbed the back of my neck. "And, I mean, obviously we don't have to at all if you've got enough of those."

I caught a twitch of her eyelid as she blinked, and that was the only hint that she might have been disappointed. Her smile turned wry. "I had a feeling," she said. "It's fine. I *could* use some friends here in L.A. Especially friends who know the best galleries to visit."

"Good," I said, my heart lightening by a fraction. "I'll let you know when I see another showing that looks interesting."

My gaze veered back to the window as she left to meet Mrs. Tsung. Still no sign of Kess. That frantic itch was wriggling down into my bones.

My computer was waiting behind me. The thought of the vast list of files I still hadn't worked through overwhelmed me. Sterling had just a few months left, and we were inching so slowly toward the sweeping solution he'd been hoping for that I wasn't sure he'd see even its beginning. If only we *could* have made a reasonable bargain with the Glowers instead of spending all this time strategizing around them. Kess had truly hoped we could, I was sure of that now. But there was no bargaining when any way you cut it, people died.

I paused, my hands hovering over the windowsill. Only they didn't have to die, did they? The ghost of Kess's touch on my arm tingled through me. She'd fed from me without doing me the slightest bit of harm. Without marking. Without taking anything more than her nudge had built up inside me.

So there was one more thing I hadn't seen, although to be fair to myself, I didn't think she'd seen it either: she'd already given me the answer to both our problems.

The office's front door swung open then. My heart leapt even though I knew it couldn't be her. But the dark, lanky figure who ambled inside with much less fragility than he'd moved on Saturday was the next person I most wanted to see.

"Sterling," I said, the energy of possibility propelling me toward my supervisor, "we need to talk."

Seventeen

"Explain to me again how you see both the clients and the Glowers benefitting from this arrangement," Sterling said a half hour and a somewhat jumbled conversation later.

I had make a conscious effort to stop my knee from jittering in my chair where I sat on the other side of his desk, like a warped echo of our meeting a few weeks ago. Then he'd been adjusting my responsibilities; now I was asking him to reconsider his. He *had* to grasp this. If he didn't, no one would.

"It isn't simply a matter of giving creative energy and taking the same amount back," I said. "The Glower gave me a little nudge, and that spark of inspiration expanded into something much bigger. So when she 'fed,' she could take all the extra feeling that hadn't been in me before—and nothing else. She didn't have to leave me drained. And I still had—still have—the product of that inspiration."

"Your home decor," Sterling said, in a tone so mild I couldn't tell if he was poking fun at me. I decided to ignore him if he was.

"Yes. Why shouldn't it work the same way with clients? Take, say, a painter. The Glower gives him a little confidence boost that would help him feel comfortable trying different techniques, experimenting with his style, breaking new ground. He spends hours working from that inspiration, getting more and more enthusiastic as he sees what he's accomplishing. Then the Glower comes back and eases him out of the creative high— not so far that he's depressed, still leaving him his normal pleasure with the work he's gotten done. And the work *is* done. He has the paintings he can show and sell and be proud of, knowing they're from his own mind and talents. The Glower doesn't have to worry about starving, and we don't have to worry about them sucking away anyone's soul."

Sterling nodded slowly. He looked as if he were seriously considering it, at least. "Allowing Glowers... access to our clients would go against all the Society's principles," he pointed out.

"Our primary principle is to protect them from harm," I said. "We'd still be doing that. *More* effectively, because any Glower that agreed to the arrangement would be one less that might try to mark them. Or anyone else for that matter."

"Assuming they held to the agreement."

"We'd have to test it out and start slowly, put safeguards in place," I said. "But everything I've observed indicates that Glowers are bound by the verbal contracts they make. I think if they swore officially not to mark or drain anyone, they'd have to stick to that as long as we continued to keep up our end of the deal."

"And do you think the Glowers *would* swear to that?" Sterling said. "They've seemed to enjoy... overindulging in their targets. If what you're saying is true, there was never any need for them to kill their marks—they could have sustained one of those relationships indefinitely."

"I don't know what they'll think of the proposal," I admitted. "I'm sure the one I was dealing with, she'd see the benefits outweigh the restrictions we'd require. And now that we're making it so hard for all of them to latch onto talented people to mark, if we offered access to the top creative minds, a prime easy 'meal' with so much less effort than if they tried to defy us—that would have to be appealing. As for overindulging..." Maybe Kess would be able to tell me. If I could find her. That anxious itch stirred inside me again. "It's possible they have to, and this couldn't work. But it looks almost like addiction, don't you think? Why take less when they *can* take more, and there are other marks to turn to once this one's drained dry? That doesn't mean they couldn't discover that moderation is more satisfying in the long run."

"And if they couldn't, or if they refuse to deal with us for other reasons, then we can simply continue as we are," Sterling filled in.

"Exactly. So how can it hurt to give it a shot?"

"The rest of the Society will find this idea difficult to swallow," Sterling said, rubbing his jaw. "I'm not sure they'll even believe in the basic premise."

I paused. "We could show them," I said. "If I talk to her again, if she agrees—I'd let her demonstrate with me, while they're watching, so they could see for themselves."

Sterling studied me for a long moment. "Two days ago you were afraid of letting her near you again."

"I know," I said. "I—I realized I've been letting fear get in the way of my instincts. The fact is, she never lied to me. I saw no indication that anything she did or said was an act. If I'm honest with myself, I believe she really was changing. It was like you said, with this..." I fished the pendant out from beneath my shirt. "I've been taking the same approach for so long, gotten so used to seeing things—seeing the Glowers—from a certain perspective, it was hard to step outside that frame of reference to recognize what should have been obvious. They're not mindless. They're capable of kindness. She is, at least. That has to mean something."

"And now the rest of us need to change our perspective too," Sterling said with a crooked smile. "I seem to remember also saying I wanted you to join the upper ranks so you could push us in new directions, Mateo. I suppose it would be hypocritical of me to fault you for trying to do just that. You reach out to your Glower... acquaintance and find out if she will agree to give this demonstration. If she will, I promise I'll do what I can on my end."

So with Sterling's blessing, I ducked out of the office early. Kess hadn't reappeared outside the building. I had an entire sprawling city to search. I suspected even the Society would balk expensing at a day-long taxi ride, especially if they found out what it had been for. Instead, I called up Ricky, who was off school for the summer now, and asked if I could borrow his junker Mustang.

"I can't say I don't owe you," he said as we stood in the driveway after I'd arrived at his family's house. He patted the car's patchy side affectionately and handed me the key. "Thanks again for the referral to that vocal coach," he added. "You must have some connections—she managed to squeeze me in for a quick evaluation this weekend. I can already feel the difference from just the couple exercises she gave me to work on before our first real session. Why didn't you suggest her before?"

My first impulse was to brush off the question, to evade. But that was the old me. "I wasn't sure how you'd react," I said. "I was worried you'd only hear that I was saying you weren't good enough yet, and then you'd get angry at me and not listen to the rest. I know that wasn't fair."

Ricky bowed his head and shrugged. "I don't know. I *might* have gotten pissed off. It was just a good time for me to hear it, I guess."

At least partly because of Kess's encouragement.

"So what's with all the hot chicks you've suddenly got lined up?" he said as if reading my mind, peeking up at me with a leer.

"It's just a good time for me with women, I guess," I said, tossing the key up and catching it. "But there's only one I'm really interested in.

"Well, good luck, man." He saluted me as I climbed into the car.

I'd left the malachite pendant at home, so there was nothing shielding me from Kess's awareness now. I'd hoped that alone might be enough—surely she'd be able to sense me looking for her, wanting her to appear, the way she'd sensed my distress in the past? I cruised through the city, stopping at the places we'd spent time together. The club where she'd first propositioned me. The park with its newly updated playground, where I'd watched her wake up to the possibilities of her body. The bar where I'd trusted her enough, if only temporarily, to let her help Ricky. Back to my apartment, where so many memories lingered.

I hesitated in the hall outside my apartment door, willing her to emerge from the shadows. Nothing stirred. Peering into their empty depths, it occurred to me for the first time that she might not want to be found. She might know I was looking and be avoiding me.

Or she might have put me out of her mind entirely, written

me off as a lost cause. Why else would she have walked away from the office this morning?

I didn't want to think that. So I looped the pendant's leather string around my neck again and set off to tour the same locations. She had memories at each of them too—memories she'd suggested she didn't want to lose. And if she couldn't sense me coming, she couldn't run away.

Evening was starting to descend when I finally turned the car toward the ocean. Whatever our brief interlude there had woken in Kess, it had obviously brought more pain than joy. But I had no ideas left.

I parked in the public lot and set off on the long trek from there to the sheltered bay where we'd swum. In the darkening dusk, the only people still on the beach were a group of teens hollering at each other farther down the shoreline and a jogger following the bike path. As I came up on the ridge of rocks that hid the secluded strip of sand from view, I slowed. If Kess wasn't here, I didn't know what I'd do next.

I forced myself to keep walking. Up to the rocks, and then scrambling over them until I'd reached the top of the ridge. As I straightened up, the breath I'd been holding rushed out of me.

Kess was standing in the water just past the line of rocks. She'd swapped her black dress for the blue spaghetti strap frock she'd worn at the park the other day. The surf lapped at her calves and surged up to her thighs with each wave, tossing the damp fabric around her legs. The wind flung her dark hair around her face. She was gazing out over the ocean, her back to me, her arms extended as if embracing the spray.

Watching her, an ache filled my heart that was fondness and desire and hope all knotted together. This was where she'd most wanted to be: in this world, present, soaking up everything it could offer that I had to assume hers did not.

This was the woman I'd fallen for.

I centered all my attention on that surge of affection as I edged down the rocks. She should feel that from me first, before anything else. Then, when I was almost at the shoreline, I tugged the leather string over my head and hurled it into the surf.

It only took an instant. Her head whipped around, and her arms dropped to her sides. She stared at me with eyes even in the failing light I could tell were mostly uncertain. Christ, how I wanted to take that uncertainty away. How I wished I'd never caused it.

I stepped down from the rocks onto the sand, and Kess waded out of the ocean to meet me. She stopped a few feet away from me, and I made myself stop too, as much as I longed to close that last distance between us.

"I'm sorry," I said. "You were right. I pushed you so much further than you pushed me and then I wasn't even willing to believe in you. But I see that now. I believe you. I—I care about you. I don't want to lose you."

Her expression didn't alter. How could I have looked on that sorrow and ever thought it was anything but real? It rolled off of her, as powerful as the waves beside us.

"You hate me," she said. "The rest of it can't matter when you hate what I am."

I reached for her and she backed up a step, so I let my hand fall. "I don't hate you," I said. "I hate... I hate what you did to people before we met. *You* don't even like that anymore. But that's not all you are. There's so much more to you than that. And that's what matters."

She bit her lip, giving me the urge to run my thumb over the soft swell of it. "I didn't tell you everything," she said. "I was supposed to tangle you up in thoughts of the girl you missed, until you'd do whatever we asked."

I found I wasn't surprised. I might have been surprised if she *hadn't* been aiming for an advantage at the start. Only at the start. "But you didn't," I said. "You stopped when I asked you to." Without complaint or protest, and then never tried again. There were plenty of human beings who'd treated me worse than that.

"It hurt you," she said quietly. "That didn't seem acceptable. And... I started not to like that you might desire her more than me."

"I didn't tell you everything either," I said. "The only reason I agreed to listen to you, to go to your gatherings, was because I was hoping to learn something about your kind that would make it *easier* for the Society to starve you."

"Of course you were," she said. "Anyone in your position would have thought the same way. The other—the one you fought with—he expected nothing else. Did you learn anything?"

"No," I said, "but I think I *have* found a compromise that will help all of us. It only depends on— The way you fed from me the other night, only taking the energy I'd built off your inspiration, is that enough to sustain you indefinitely? Can your people survive without ever draining a person completely?"

Her mouth twisted. "There is... The larger the feed, the more exhilarating. And taking a life's last energy comes with a special pleasure. Neither provides a different sort of sustenance. But most prefer to partake of those pleasures."

"But you have a choice?" I said.

She nodded, her expression softening as that thought seemed to sink in. "Yes," she said. "I can choose not to."

"That's all we need," I said, excitement tingling through my chest, and started to lay out the plan I'd explained to Sterling.

Kess's lips parted as I spoke, as if she could taste the possibility in my words. "If we can put that system into action," I finished, "it could mean a totally different world. Glowers acting as real muses, bolstering the artists you're paired with as you've always claimed you do."

She studied my face. "Your Society would let us do this? Would work *with* us, *allow* us to feed…"

"In that moderation," I said. "Do you think the others would agree to it? They'd have to show a lot more restraint than they're used to."

Her gaze went distant as she considered the problem. "I think at least a few would try," she said. "And then, once the rest see how much simpler this is… I don't know for certain. But I can imagine it." Her eyes darted back to mine. "You thought all this through. Even after the way they talked at the last meeting, the way they treated you…"

"If you could change, then they could to," I said.

She reached for me then, and I grasped her hand, squeezing it with every bit of affection and longing I had in me. Letting her feel it all. Her fingers curled around mine. She eased closer, her smoky-sweet scent mingling with the salty breeze.

"And what of us?" she said.

I brought my other hand to her cheek and slid my fingers into her silky hair to tug her to me. As we kissed, she gripped the front of my shirt. Her heart beat against my palm. I wanted to kiss her again and again, but her question hung in the air around us. I eased back and tipped my forehead against hers.

"I don't know how this is going to work," I said. "I don't know *if* it will. But I want you. I want you in my life. I want you reveling in all the parts of the world you haven't experienced yet; I want you asking me questions I've never thought to ask myself. All of it. Everything. I mean, as long as you still—"

"Yes," she said. "Yes." Then she pulled my lips back to hers.

I ran my hands down her body as she pressed against mine, tracing those slim, tantalizing curves. She opened her mouth to me, and our tongues twined together, hot and sweet. I wanted her, here, now, no long hike across the sand, no drive to my apartment.

Kess nudged me backward, maybe having read my desire. Between kisses, we stumbled farther up the beach to where the ridges of rock converged into sheltered alcoves. In the thickening darkness, they made for privacy enough.

We knelt on the ground, her fingers tight in my hair, mine dipping beneath the bodice of her dress to trace the shape of her breasts. The sand was gritty against my knees through the fabric of my slacks, but I found I didn't mind. This wasn't a dream. It was real, every part of it.

I grazed Kess's nipple and she gasped into my mouth. Her hand dropped to investigate the growing erection pressing against the fly of my pants.

"You want me," she said wonderingly.

"God, yes," I said. "So much. I always did."

She arched back as I wrenched her dress down. I stroked her breasts until her breath came in little pants, and then I lowered my head to them. As I laved her stiffening nipples, her moans turned me hard as stone down below. She shivered beneath me, but she kept up her caresses through my slacks, until I was trembling too.

"I want you," I murmured. "I want you."

I slid my hand up her thigh to grasp her panties, and she made short work of my slacks. I stripped off her dress too so I could stretch it on the ground beneath her. The grit prickled against my bare skin now, here, amid the cool ocean wind and the cries of the gulls and Kess's warm eager body curving to meet me. As she drew me from my boxers, I slicked my forefinger into the wet hot center of her. Her hips canted up at my touch.

"Mateo," she said with a whimper, and I nearly came undone right then.

I surged over her and into her. The feel of her pulled a groan from deep in my lungs. As I thrust into her and she rocked against me, our movements formed ripples in the sand around the edges of the dress. I kissed her jaw, her neck. She nipped my shoulder.

"I want you," I whispered against her skin, as if, if I said it enough times, she'd never be able to doubt it again. "I want *you*."

She clenched around me, a cry breaking from her lips. I sped up as she shuddered beneath me. She sank her fingernails into my backside, and I came with a gasp.

"Oh," she said, with a soft giggle that faded into a sigh. Not lost this time. Right here with me.

As my muscles slackened, I rolled onto my side and hugged her to me. Kess nestled her head against my chest. She trailed her fingers up and down my sternum.

"So what do you think we do now?" I asked after a moment.

"What do you want?" she said in a lightly teasing voice.

"Not that game again," I muttered, and she laughed.

"Really," she said. "If you ask yourself what you'd want the next thing we do together to be, what comes into your mind?"

I opened my mouth and realized it really could be that simple. "I want you to come back to my apartment with me. I want to make love to you again until we're too tired to move. And I want you to stay the entire night and wake up with me in the morning."

Her hand rose to brush over my cheek. "I can do that," she said softly.

"What do *you* want us to do next?"

"Well, I think your plan for the immediate future suits me just fine," she said. "And then... When you have your next day off work, I would like to take you to Magic Mountain. That's a thing a real couple would do, isn't it?"

Now it was my turn to laugh. Then I pulled her even more tightly into my embrace and kissed her.

"Yes," I said. "That sounds perfectly real to me."

First Date

A CAUGHT IN THE DREAM BONUS SCENE

"So, I should probably warn you that I'm not actually much of a roller coaster guy," I said, even though it was far too late to be mentioning that fact. I was already standing with Kess in Magic Mountain's admission line, minutes from walking into an amusement park best known for its killer rides. The second and last time I'd been here, eight years ago for a friend's fourteenth birthday party, I'd lost my lunch as I stumbled off one of the first roller coasters the group had dragged me onto and spent the rest of the day enduring their heckling and breathing the vomit smell I couldn't quite wash out of my shirt. Not a fun memory. The sight of the arched tracks looming as we'd crossed the parking lot had made my stomach drop in a rather concerning way.

Kess curled her slender hand around mine, smiling at me. My apprehension couldn't stop my pulse from skipping at the affection shining in her face, brighter than the supernatural gleam emanating from her tan skin, her sleek black hair, and the sky-blue tank top and denim shorts she was wearing today to fit in with the amusement park crowd. I wasn't making any effort to hide my feelings, so her Glower sensitivity had likely picked up the reasons for my anxiety in vivid detail. Oh well. Just one of the many ways it was weird having a demon for a girlfriend, something I was going to have to get used to.

She squeezed my fingers and her thumb stroked my palm. A tingle of heat shot up my arm. Yes, having a demon for a girlfriend was weird, but with this particular demon, it was also pretty wonderful.

"We can stick to the smaller rides," she said. "I don't mind."

"If you *want* to go on the big ones..." I started, but she shook her head before I could suggest that I watch from the sidelines.

"I want to be here with *you*, Mateo," she said. "I want to see you enjoying yourself too. I can come on my own other times if I feel the need."

The shock of abrupt, intense physical sensations helped ground her in this world—my world—where the body she wore was technically only a temporary creation. But the more she'd sought those sensations out, the longer the effect had lingered, until something had changed inside her permanently. I no longer saw the cool, detached creature who'd spoken of feeding on human souls as if it meant no more than grabbing a slice of pizza did. The emotions and compassion I'd helped wake up in her were here to stay.

As far as we knew. The doubt quivered up, and I immediately shoved it away. My official relationship with Kess was barely a week old. The trust we'd established still felt fragile —to her even more than me, no doubt, given that I'd been the one pushing her away for most of the weeks before. That was why it was important for us to do things like this: normal couple activities. We were on our first real date, you could say. And that was also why, I guessed, it was so important to her that we experienced all of it together.

I ducked my head to murmur by her ear. "I enjoy just watching you enjoy yourself."

Her amused hum in response brought back the image of her enjoyment in my bed last night, her eyelids fluttering and lips parting as she came. My whole body warmed, remembering. I would have leaned in to give her as much of a kiss as I felt I could get away with in public, but just then the line ahead of us cleared. An attendant waved us over to the ticket booth.

Once we were inside the park, Kess peered around us, walking with a new spring in her step. Her hand was still wrapped around mine. "What *do* you like here?" she asked. "You pick first."

"We'll take turns?" I said with a smile of my own. "That sounds fair. Hmmm... I think I could handle that one."

I pointed, and she bounded forward, tugging me along. I couldn't help laughing at her enthusiasm. My earlier comment might have been teasing, but seeing how much she loved being here really was more than enough to make me love the place too.

I felt a little ridiculous getting into lines made up mostly of younger kids and their frazzled parents, but at least the rides at the end of those lines left me exhilarated rather than nauseated. I suspected Kess was reading my emotional responses and making her choices accordingly, because she continued steering clear of the monster coasters that dominated the horizon in every direction. After a couple hours, we recovered from the early summer heat in one of the air-conditioned shops, where I bought Kess a plush leopard toy I caught her eyeing. She chuckled at the purchase, but the animal stayed tucked tightly under her arm as we continued exploring.

We shared an ice cream cone—the sight of her tongue swirling over it making me hot all over again—and tried out a few more of the tamer rides. Then Kess steered me to a line-up by a track that arced over the trees around the entry station. A track at least twice as high as the others we'd been on. My muscles tensed.

"We'll just try it," Kess said, recognizing the protest I was biting back. "It doesn't go upside down or anything like that. Just a little twisting around and a couple of drops. I think you'll be fine."

I *had* been fine so far. And it'd been years since the last time I'd attempted a real roller coaster. Maybe my tolerance had improved.

"Sure," I said, but my gut stayed knotted as we edged closer to the front of the line.

When it was our turn to get on, Kess darted to the front of one of the middle cars. At least we weren't going to be right at the head of the train. I dropped into the seat beside her, noting that this was the first ride we'd been on with a security bar that came over our shoulders instead of just sitting near our waists. My heart thudded a little faster.

Kess reached over to set her hand on my leg just above my knee, a faint pressure through my khakis. She gave me a sly grin. "I'll help you get through it," she said. "It's all about the sensation."

I wasn't sure what she meant, but anticipation tickled over my skin. The ride attendant walked beside the train making sure all the security bars were in place. Then the cars eased forward. I exhaled slowly, willing myself to relax.

We'd just started to pick up speed, bobbing up and down over a series of smaller hills, when Kess's hand slid farther up my thigh. My breath caught. I glanced over at her, but she was gazing straight ahead, her eyes closed, beaming as the wind rushed through her hair.

Christ, she was beautiful.

I shut my eyes too. *It's all about the sensation.* Maybe the coaster's lurches and drops would be more bearable if I focused on what I was feeling right now instead of worrying about what lay ahead.

The train slowed, and our weight shifted back as it carried us up one of the steeper hills. My heart started to hammer again, but I kept my eyes closed. Then Kess trailed her hand up right over my groin.

Her thumb stroked up and down over me, and with that simple motion I was hard. I swallowed a groan as she repeated the caress. My heart was still thumping, but that had little to do with the ride now. I had the urge to sink deeper into the contact, but the seat's restraints held me in place. I could only sit there helplessly as she cupped my growing erection, her touch setting off sparks through every nerve.

And then the train dropped over the crest of the hill.

Shrieks broke from mouths all around us as the cars careened straight down. I jolted forward against the security bar —and into Kess's grip. She held me, pumping lightly, as a gasp of excitement slipped from her own lips. A laugh sputtered from mine, mingling with a moan of pleasure I couldn't totally contain. If my nerves had been sparking before, now they were outright crackling.

As the train sped upright again and swayed into an undulating sideways loop, Kess shifted away, removing the pressure. A sigh escaped me. I was half relieved that I didn't have to regret my lack of a change of pants and half desperate to feel her hand on me again. I snuck a peek at her as the train slowed momentarily before the final huge hill, and this time she was looking at me. Her eyebrows arched when our gazes locked. Her fingers traveled back up my inner thigh. I just smiled and tipped my head against the seat. If every roller coaster had come with *this* sensation, I'd have been a much bigger fan.

When the cars coasted to a halt, I scrambled out after Kess, my pulse thrumming. I caught her arm and she grinned at whatever she must have seen in my eyes. I didn't have to speak or even gesture. As one being, we surveyed the grounds and dashed for a shed to the right of the coaster's entry station.

Behind the small building, a cluster of trees provided enough shelter for me to kiss Kess without an audience. She wound her arms behind my neck as I nudged her against the wall. Her hips canted against mine, making me hard all over again. Her tongue slid into my mouth, her fingers tangling in my hair. I traced my hands up the smooth skin of her back beneath her tank top and then down to her slim thighs. While I'd appreciated the view the shorts gave me of her long, lean legs before, now I wished for her usual dresses, the skirts I could have edged up and eased under.

"Mateo," she murmured, the longing in her voice as she spoke my name igniting me the way it always did. I dipped my hand between her legs, cupping her through her clothes the way she'd held me. She sighed and pressed against my palm. Desire sang through my veins with every hitch of her breath and mine, but no matter how much I burned to, I didn't quite have the bravado to strip her down and plunge into her here with so many park-goers just a few feet away.

That sense of caution was reinforced a moment later when footsteps rasped over the dirt by the side of the shed. I jerked back and tugged Kess's shirt straight just as an adventuring kid came around the corner. He peered at us suspiciously. Kess covered her mouth as if restraining a giggle.

The kid tramped off, but the intrusion had dampened my lust. I kissed Kess on the temple. "I think we'd better finish this at home," I said.

An odd, almost dazed expression came over her face. "Home," she repeated.

"Well, I mean, my apartment," I said, rubbing the back of my neck awkwardly. Kess had spent every night there with me since our reconciliation on the beach, but while I was at work I knew at least some of the time she returned to her own plane of existence. Even as much as she'd changed, in some ways she must still be more comfortable there. "I know you have your actual home... wherever exactly that is... but whenever you're on this side, you can consider my place yours too."

She blinked at me, her eyes suddenly serious. "Mateo," she said, and hesitated. "Are you sure?"

I frowned. "Why—" Then it hit me: the reason she'd reacted this way, the reason she looked afraid I might take back what I'd said once I realized.

Glowers could only come onto private property if invited. Every night Kess had spent with me, I'd let her in with permission expressed either verbally or physically. But what I'd just offered was a blanket invitation. Permanent access to my apartment at her whim, no further permission required, as if it belonged to her as much as it did me. I didn't know whether I could ever revoke that invitation if I confirmed it now.

Gazing into her uncertain eyes, my mouth set. I'd been sure when I'd said the words, even if I hadn't thought through the implications. I did trust her. Maybe my superiors at the Tether Society would have panicked at the idea, but my home was completely separate from my work. It was only mine, to share with whomever I wished.

And I wanted to share it with her.

"Yes," I said firmly. "You can come any time you want. It's always open to you."

For a moment, she didn't speak, only stared at me, until I started to wonder if I'd said something wrong after all. Then she clutched my head and pulled my lips back to hers. She kissed me hard. I wrapped my arms around her, holding her to me. Holding the two of us together, with love.

Caught in the Burn

DEMONS OF FAME #4

One

"THIS PLACE IS HAPPENING," I SAID TO MRS. TSUNG AS WE stood by the main doors to The Platform, the loft-style base of the hottest new video game company in the country. From what I'd been told, Macro Play's business offices were hidden behind the clouded glass wall at the back of the expansive room. The rest of the space was open to the public. Macro's employees encouraged indie designers to visit and make use of The Platform's large communal area and often joined the up-and-comers for brainstorming and beta testing sessions. Right now, at least twenty men and women, most no more than a few years older than me, were clustered around the espresso station, lounging on linen couches with laptops open, or hunched over the black glass coffee tables sharing sketches and notes. Everyone kept their voices low, but added together the loft was humming with conversation. Around them, framed art from Macro Play's games hung on the exposed brick walls.

"That's why Macro has become concerned," Mrs. Tsung said, her wide-set brown eyes scanning the room. "Aydin

Demirci prefers to work mixed in with the crowd, but the nature of the space means there's little regulation of who comes and goes. He says he needs the energy of the community; they want to protect their star designer. So they hired us to keep an eye on things. The initial contract is only for the next month, and only when he's here or at gaming-related public events— you won't need to monitor him at home. There's a lot of attention on them and him right now with their new title on the verge of release. If we see no cause for concern, they'll ease off and we can focus on other clients."

I wound a strand of my strawberry-blonde hair around my thumb. That didn't sound like too much pressure, but you never knew with this job. "Do you think all the publicity will bring out the Glowers?"

"We haven't seen them insinuating themselves into the newer creative industries very often," Mrs. Tsung said. Her eyebrows arched. "Like us, they're somewhat stuck in their traditional ways. But they have been even more unpredictable of late. It's difficult to predict anything these days. In a few months, we may be *facilitating* a Glower partnership for Demirci."

Her tone was disbelieving. I rubbed my pale arms, though the room was warm even with the air conditioning at full blast. When I'd first started training into the Tether Society eight months ago, all anyone had talked about was the dangers the Glowers posed. The demons attracted creative types with the inspiration they could supernaturally spark in their targets— which I guessed was how the first one I'd seen had gained the street painter's trust. They used their targets' desire for fame or genius to manipulate them into a deal that left the target marked with an unbreakable connection. And then they fed off all the positive emotions their inspiration stirred up in their marks, leaving the marks increasingly hollowed out and depressed, increasingly hooked on getting that next brief spark... until despair took over completely. I'd seen what happened then.

I knew now that the street painter hadn't been drunk or high —or, at least, that hadn't been his biggest problem. The way he'd talked, the sob I'd heard, stuck in my memory. Whether his fatal climb had been an attempt to feel something beyond the emptiness the Glower had left him with or a decision to end the cycle the only way he could find, I had no idea. But my witnessing the demon taking its final meal had left me with the ability to spot its kind by their unnatural glow, a talent that had brought the Society to my door. At least I could hope to stop anyone else from reaching that point.

But it seemed *how* we dealt with the Glowers might be changing. The new strategies the Society had been trying out were increasingly effective, and the Glowers had turned to desperate measures to survive. At least a few were willing to make peace with us if it meant avoiding starvation. Mateo—one of the other younger Tethers—and Sterling—one of the supervisors—had been campaigning for a trial compromise, which they claimed would stop the escalating conflict between our groups and mean reducing or maybe even eliminating markings. If we could regulate the inspiration the Glowers offered, stop them from taking too much joy in return, the clients would benefit from those sparks of inspiration without any harm done, and the Glowers would survive as well.

At least, that was the theory. I'd heard the same skepticism Mrs. Tsung had expressed from a lot of my colleagues in the last two months. After fighting so long, it was obviously hard for them to see the Glowers as anything other than an enemy. It didn't help that Sterling was so sick he'd spent much of the last month in the hospital and Mateo had only a few years of experience under his belt.

"You should find the transition to taking lead a relatively smooth one," Mrs. Tsung said, drawing me out of my thoughts. "I don't imagine Demirci will give you too many challenges. But, of course, you can turn to your observer if you need support."

I glanced toward the door. "Where is my observer?" This was my second placement, and my first where I was supposed to take the primary role in protecting the client. I definitely didn't feel ready yet to try to handle everything alone.

"Shawn should be here within the next half hour," Mrs. Tsung said. "Unfortunately there was something of a critical situation with his previous client this morning, and it seemed wisest to let him step in. He contacted me not long ago to say that had been resolved and he was on his way. In the meantime, why don't you meet your client?"

She headed deeper into the loft, and I followed. We stopped at a narrow bar-height table where a couple guys and a young woman were working intently on their laptops. One of the guys, a tall man with shaggy black hair and an aquiline nose, looked over at us and sighed. He picked up the large mug on the table next to him and took a gulp.

"Mr. Demirci," Mrs. Tsung said. "I'm Edith Tsung from the Tether Society. I assume you were informed that we'd be coming today. This is Sofie Martel, who'll be working most closely with you for the next month."

"Hi," I said, with a tip of my hand.

Demirci nodded brusquely. "I don't think I need the 'protection,'" he said. "These are my people—they come here to learn and share, not to stir up trouble. But if Macro feels hiring you is what they've got to do..." He shrugged. "Make yourself comfortable wherever."

He turned back to his computer. Well, at least he hadn't been overtly antagonistic. And if he was right about the atmosphere here, then I wouldn't need to interfere much at all.

Mrs. Tsung lingered, obviously not wanting to leave me on my own any more than I wanted to be left. I drew in a breath. I needed to find a way to settle in, to show I could handle myself and treat this like the job it was.

My skin prickled as I crossed the room to the coffee bar, but only a few people even glanced my way. Obviously this was a crowd used to new faces. No one around me gave off even the slightest glow, so we were off to a good start there. I was already starting to relax when I reached the sideboard.

I ignored the more complicated looking machines in favor of the standard pot of coffee, mixed cream and plenty of sugar into my mug, and ambled back to Demirci's table. A cluster of armchairs circled a side table behind him. I sank into one of those, and Mrs. Tsung took another.

From the angle I was sitting at, I could see Demirci's screen. For the first few minutes, I couldn't make out exactly what he was doing, other than tweaking lines on a graph paper-like background to form a complex shape that looked like little more than a vague blob. Then he started adding textures. Finely bumped brown skin here, worn gray stone there. As he shaded it in, a creature emerged against the background: an enormous upright toad with a castle tower teetering on its hunched shoulders. It looked like an illustration out of the children's books I'd hoarded from the library as a little kid. A smile curled my lips.

When I'd finished my coffee, I stood up so I could get a clearer view. Demirci had skills—anyone could see that. I'd never thought about drawing on a computer before, not seriously. Never thought pixels could produce anything that felt as vibrant as paint on paper. Maybe I'd been wrong. As I watched him bring the toad fully to live, images bubbled in the back of my head. My fingers itched with a familiar desire to let them out.

Demirci stopped and leaned back in his chair to stretch his arms. He studied his creation as he drained the last of his current cup of coffee. Before I could catch myself, I'd stepped closer, a question popping out of my mouth.

"How did you get the skin looking like that—rough, but still alive? I always have—had—trouble with animals. The ones without fur, anyway."

Demirci blinked his heavy-lidded eyes, and my throat clenched up. I must have sounded like a total amateur. But then he smiled and nodded to his picture. "A lot of it's the color scheme," he said. "You want to make sure there's always at least a little warmth, even with cold-blooded things. That, and using dips and wrinkles to show the skin is moving over flesh rather than a mechanical structure."

I saw what he meant as he gestured at the screen, my mind leaping to how those approaches might translate onto canvas.

Not that I was going to apply them to canvas. That part of my life was over. I closed my hand against the itch, my eagerness snuffing out. "Thanks," I said, and pulled myself back. I was here to keep Demirci safe from demons, not to learn painting techniques.

"I hope that's the last time I see you interrupting a client," a husky voice said behind me.

I suppressed a startled flinch and turned.

A well-built guy with a sheen of dark hair had joined Mrs. Tsung while I'd been focused on Demirci's work. It was hard to read his age from his smooth brown skin, but I guessed he was in his late twenties or early thirties. His penetrating ebony eyes fixed on me as he rubbed his angular jaw. My pulse hiccupped. He was cute. No, not just cute—*hot*.

Then my brain caught up and reminded me what he'd said. My uncertainty made me stammer.

"I—I'm sorry?"

"Shawn," Mrs. Tsung said, mildly chiding. "Advise rather than condemn, please. Sofie, this is Shawn Joyner, who'll be your observing Tether for this placement. Shawn, meet Sofie Martel. She's been with us less than a year, but she's picked up—"

"I read her file," Shawn said, smoothly enough that it hardly sounded as if he'd cut her off. He nodded to me, those intense eyes slipping down over my body and back to my face without any indication of whether he approved of what he saw. Not that I needed his approval of my *body*. God, Sofie, get it together. I resisted the urge to cross my arms over my chest.

"This is the first piece of *advice* I'm going to give you," Shawn went on. "Stay out of the client's way. We only intervene and make ourselves noticed if the client turns to us or if it's necessary to protect them. Otherwise we're just part of the background. Understood?"

I nodded back, my lips pressing tight. Heat crept into my cheeks. I knew that rule from training. But saying that after he'd just caught me forgetting the rule wasn't going to win me any points, clearly.

I was going to have this guy breathing down my neck for the next month? Holy hell. I'd like to trade the eye candy for someone a little less intimidating, please.

"I know you're new," Shawn added, his voice low. At least he wasn't making a scene, though I suspected that was a matter of keeping face for the Society rather than for my benefit. "That doesn't mean I'm going to go easy on you. This is a serious job handling serious business—the business of keeping our clients *alive*. WIth that kind of responsibility, we can't afford to slack off, even for a minute."

Under that stare, I felt very young and very small, even though he couldn't have had more than ten years and half a foot on me. Because he was right. My thoughts slipped back to the street painter's crumpled body, to the moments before when I could have spoken up and made a difference... and hadn't. I swallowed thickly. Maybe intimidating was what I needed if I was going learn how to do this job properly.

"I know," I said. "I understand completely. It won't happen again."

Two

"Hey, Sofie, have you got a few minutes?"

I paused by the Tether Society's front door and waited as Mateo loped over to me from the office he was now sharing with Sterling, though these days Sterling was rarely there anyway. It was late—I'd come here for an advanced first aid tutorial after finishing my third full shift with Demirci—and I didn't really feel like talking, but Mateo was on track to becoming my boss. And even if the vibe between us sometimes felt a little awkward because of our one failed date a few months back, I knew he was a good guy. The fact that _he_ was here this late working out the details of his Tether-Glower cooperation plan was proof of that.

Mateo stopped a few feet away, careful as always of my personal space. He gave me a lopsided smile. "Sorry," he said, with his faint Spanish accent. "I'm sure you're wanting to get home."

"It's fine," I said. After seeing the state of my former abode, Mrs. Tsung had arranged for me to receive enough of an advance on my Society paychecks for me to move into a small but cozy one bedroom with a proper kitchen and no cockroaches shortly after I'd started training, but I still didn't exactly look forward to spending time there. It was a place to sleep and make meals, and that was about it. "Why don't we grab a coffee and you can tell me what's up?"

"Sounds good."

There was a tiny indie cafe on the right side of the building's first floor, so we didn't have to leave the air conditioning and venture into the August heat, still so stifling even this late in the evening. There'd been a forest fire nearby in the morning, with an evacuation warning for a couple suburbs. The taste of burnt cypress smoke had filled my mouth on my walk over here from The Platform.

I ordered a latte, decaf, and Mateo got a double shot espresso, so I guessed he was planning on staying at the office a while longer after this conversation. He didn't look tired, though. Even before he took his first sip of his coffee, there was an exuberance to his movements, like restrained anticipation. He was excited about his proposal, even if no one else in the Society fully believed in it. I liked that about him too.

The one date hadn't failed because I'd lacked interest. It'd failed because Mateo had gotten himself entangled with a Glower in a rather personal way. I still wasn't sure how I felt about *that*, but as long as it was working for him, it wasn't my business.

We sat down at one of the four little tables, and Mateo curled his thin fingers around his mug. "So you started your second placement," he said. "Is it going smoothly?"

I wondered if he was asking as a friendly colleague or a concerned almost-supervisor. "There hasn't been much to it so far," I said. "No Glower sightings. The client isn't keen on having us there, but he's not actively resisting either." My thoughts drifted to Shawn. To the heady warmth that still flicked through my body whenever he fixed me with one of his particularly penetrating stares. To the flush of embarrassment that so often followed, because he only gave me that stare if he was about to point out something he felt I'd screwed up. "My observer's a bit of a hard-ass, though."

The corner of Mateo's mouth twitched up in amusement. "You've got Shawn, right? He can be a little... slow to warm up." He paused, and his smile faded. "He's never told me this directly, so I don't know for sure that it's true, but I've heard that his first solo assignment when he was starting out, years ago— his client ended up getting marked."

"Oh," I said. My hands tightened around my own mug. Knowing a Glower had managed to get its hook into your client on your watch, that it was your *fault* the person was going to die... I couldn't imagine how awful that must feel. "I can see how that could turn someone into a hard-ass." I felt the need to add, in case I'd sounded over-sensitive, "He hasn't been *mean* or anything. He just doesn't say much to me unless it's to point out something I should do differently. Which is what he's there for, after all."

"The job gets easier with practice," Mateo said. "You'll find a grove." He leaned back in his chair, studying the tabletop. I was about to break the growing silence when he sucked in a breath and raised his gaze to me again.

"The main reason I wanted to talk to you is to ask you for a favor," he said. "It's a really big one, and I know that, and I won't hold it against you if you say no. But I hope you'll at least think it over, because it's also really important."

The back of my neck prickled with anticipation. "What are you talking about, Mateo?"

"You know what I've been working on," he said. "You know

most of the senior Tethers... well, most of the Tethers of all levels of experience... aren't totally on board. I think part of the problem is it's hard for them to accept that a Glower could actually interact with a client without hurting them. So I think the key to making sure they give this proposal a fair shot is showing them what's possible. I have a Glower I trust for that side of the process."

"Kess," I said. The name tripped off my tongue. I'd met the slim, sharp-faced beauty a couple times now, but it still felt odd to think of her as a *person* rather than a monster.

Mateo inclined his head. "I need a creative to work with her, to accept her inspiration—and to give some of that energy back to her to complete the cycle. I need it to be someone who's going in with a full understanding of what's being asked of them, who can make an educated decision about how far they're willing to take it."

"So it has to be someone within the Society..." My voice trailed off with a catch in my throat. Oh. "You're asking me. You want me to let her into my head."

"It's not like that," Mateo said softly. "She's done the transfer of energy with me a few times now—a feeling comes over you, slowly, and then it's slowly taken away again, and you feel the same as you did before you started. She doesn't see what you're thinking; she won't affect that part of your mind. And it won't hurt—it never has to. That's what we need to show everyone."

"So why don't you use yourself as a demonstration?" I said.

He made a frustrated sound. "I'm not an artist. My creative inclinations are pretty limited. I can't do anything that will really show how the partnership would benefit our clients. And I'm not sure people will trust me to report the aftereffects accurately. It's my project. I'm biased."

"I'm not an artist either!" I protested. My stomach had

started to churn. I turned the mug in my hands, not sure I was going to be able to force the rest of the latte down.

"You were," Mateo said. "You have the talent. I know you said you've put that part of your life on hold, but that could be even more reason to try this. Maybe working with Kess will help you figure out why you stopped and find a way you'd want to move forward. And if it doesn't, well, you could stop again as soon as the Society's satisfied with the demonstration."

"It's not that easy," I said, and Mateo's eyebrows drew together. I shut my mouth.

I couldn't explain it to him. Couldn't explain how even thinking about throwing myself into the act of painting again made my gut knot. Most days I could hardly explain it to myself. What was easy was leaving it in the past. The past couldn't touch me, couldn't hurt me. But if I let a Glower start messing with my emotions, prying inside me, jostling all the memories loose... anything could happen.

The only reason I was okay right now was no one had any control over my life or my feelings other than me.

But even as I instinctively resisted, I couldn't ignore the tendril of hope unfurling in my chest. What if Mateo was right? What if Kess could simply help me find and believe in the inspiration I'd used to be so close to inside myself, set me on a path through the wreckage of the past toward something better? Maybe making art could feel good again.

It used to be the most magical thing in my life.

"I don't want you to answer right away," Mateo said. "Take at least twenty-four hours to think on it. Just... please do really think about it?"

"How would it work?" I heard myself asking, even as my muscles tensed further. "If I decided to try it, what would happen next? How much would you need me to do?"

"Well, I guess first I'd have you sit down with Kess and talk with her about what would happen, any boundaries you want to set. Make sure you're totally comfortable going forward after that. Then we'd give it a short trial run, privately, so you can see how the transfer feels. If you were willing to continue after that, we'd arrange for a meeting with the senior Tethers where you'd go through the process with them watching. They might want you to complete several sessions with Kess and make notes, maybe get a medical examination, to confirm that there are no ill effects, but you wouldn't have to do that unless you were okay with it. You'd always be able to decide to stop. And I don't want you to start unless you're sure you're okay with it. All right?"

He shifted forward as he said the last words, the genuine concern on his face reminding me why I'd agreed to go on that date with him, why I was listening to him now. He cared so much—about people, about this job, about doing the right thing. It was impossible to spend more than a few minutes in his company and not see that.

"All right," I said. "I'll think about it. And when I figure out what my answer is, I'll let you know."

I drank a little more of my latte, but it was cooling and my stomach was still unsettled. Mateo gulped down the rest of his espresso. "If there's anything else you want to ask me, don't hesitate," he said.

I shook my head. "I can't think of anything right now. If something comes up, I'll call you."

Normally I walked to my apartment, as I'd used to from my old job to my old room, even though the hike from the Society office took nearly an hour. The Society reimbursed us for taxi rides to and from work, but that generosity didn't sit well with me. Why should they pay money that would be better spent elsewhere when I was capable of making my way under my own steam? Anyway, getting into a small vehicle with a stranger at the wheel tended to make my skin creep. But today I was exhausted and my head was whirling, so I flagged down a cab and spent the drive home turned toward the window, resting my forehead against the cool glass.

I *was* going to think about Mateo's request. I just needed a little more time for my emotions to settle before I could do that clearly. Sleep should help with that.

I was too wired to fall straight into bed when I got up to my apartment, though. I pulled the curtains tight across the main room's square windows and curled up on the plush-cushioned couch I'd picked out at a consignment store, partly for the faint scent of wild clover that clung to it like a childhood dream. Nibbling on a piece of peanut brittle I'd grabbed to supplement my hastily eaten dinner, I opened my laptop.

I'd thought to myself that the past couldn't touch me, couldn't hurt me. Maybe I needed to show that to myself before I decided what I showed anyone else. I was making a new life here completely separate from the people and places I'd left behind. It shouldn't affect me at all to look at them from a distance.

I hesitated, and then gritted my teeth and opened the web browser.

I'd deleted my old Facebook account, but too many people didn't keep up to date on the privacy filters. There were Mom and Dad at a dinner party at a friend's house, everyone holding up martini glasses to toast the photographer. There was Kerri-Ann, her arms slung over the shoulders of two of her basketball championship teammates. A small smile tickled my lips—she must be over the moon about that win.

There was a selfie of Hannah in full make-up before a business do, her dark eyeliner making those pale green eyes I'd always envied even larger than usual. There were Renata and Brandon, making cheesy scrunched-up kissy faces, on the verge of bursting into laughter. There was the whole gang at the lake, Hannah and Renata and Brandon, Kim and George and Jasmin, Sven and—

My gaze halted on a slightly blurred face toward the back of the group. My stomach dropped. My hands moved without consulting the rest of me, slamming the laptop shut. I sat there staring at its sleek silver top, trembling.

Can't touch me. Can't touch me. Can't touch me, I repeated to myself. My heartbeat slowed, but a lingering nausea remained.

I couldn't be completely sure of that. And hadn't I learned a thousand times over that someone didn't need to touch you to wound you bone deep?

Three

✳

Because it never rains but it pours, the next day I faced my first Glower in The Platform.

Shawn and I had fallen into certain patterns over the course of the week. I gave Demirci a wide berth, wanting him to feel free to move around within the loft and wanting to show Shawn I had no intention of interrupting any more of the designer's work. So I usually claimed one of the armchairs close to the front door. I could still see Demirci anywhere he went in the room, and I could also monitor every newcomer who arrived as they walked by me.

In turn, Shawn was giving *me* a wide berth, I guessed to encourage my independence. He normally found a seat on the opposite side of the room near the coffee bar and spent most of the shift nursing a series of cappuccinos. So far, he'd only talked to me a few times a day other than hellos and goodbyes—to suggest I find a way to blend more with the crowd, to chide me for appearing to get too distracted by the design magazine I'd picked up to achieve the first purpose, that sort of thing. Maybe after hearing Mateo's story I could understand why Shawn was so anal, but the guy was still a pain in the ass.

Yet an annoyingly attractive ass it was. I didn't look at him often, but when he stood and gave his shoulders a stretch or helped one of the shorter loft-goers grab something from the shelf over the coffee bar, my eyes were immediately drawn to his muscular body, which had all sorts of lines I would have enjoyed painting. I tried to keep my appreciation to the artistic side, but I couldn't help also speculating that those lines would feel amazing to touch.

Other than those occasional enjoyable visuals, the job was pretty uneventful. I'd decided to start bringing my laptop as both a tool for blending in and a way to stop myself from completely zoning out from boredom. I was on it that morning, making notes on the patrons I was beginning to recognize as regulars and forcefully ignoring the niggling question Mateo had posed me with that had disturbed my sleep all night, when a demon walked in.

To anyone else, she would have looked completely human: a tall, elegant black woman with a cascade of delicate box braids. To me, her skin lit up with an eerie glow that even the bright overhead lights couldn't obscure. As she paused to survey the room, my hands clenched around the sides of my laptop. My gaze slid to Shawn automatically. He was watching me with his usual penetrating intentness, his dark eyes offering no hint of direction.

I wasn't supposed to need directions. I was supposed to show I could handle a Glower's intrusion on my own.

One factor working in my favor: I was pretty sure this Glower hadn't come with a particular target in mind. From her casual perusal of the room, it looked as though she was simply trolling, considering her options. Not that I was keen on her getting her hook into any of the artists making use of this space, but at least that would make her a little easier to dislodge. A Glower who'd already committed to marking one particular person tended to be more stubborn, from what I'd seen in my admittedly limited experience.

My first step was obvious. As the Glower eased farther into the loft, I pulled out my phone and dialed a number I'd programmed in on the first day. The Macro Play execs had assured the Society that the security company they'd contracted would respond to any threats we reported. At least one security guy should be on the premises right now.

The phone on the other end rang and immediately cut off to a voice mail service, as if the line were already in use. I hesitated, my own phone still at my ear, studying the Glower more closely as she prowled through the room.

The demons had been coordinating their operations more and more in the last few months, according to the other Tethers I'd talked to. I'd seen it a couple times during my first placement. If this one had already noticed a Society presence here, I wouldn't be surprised if she had a buddy or two keeping security busy while she scoped out the place. Of course, if she knew there were Tethers on the premises, it'd have been easier for her to scope out some place that wasn't protected. Apparently that used to be more the norm too—simply having Tethers around provided plenty of protection in itself. These days, in defiance of the Society's new efforts to crack down on their activities, some of the Glowers were taking a perverse pleasure in challenging us directly.

Well, without security on the way, it was up to me to see her out. I stuffed my phone into my pocket and set my laptop on a side table, debating the best approach. The Glower hadn't talked to anyone yet. Maybe this *was* only a scouting mission, in which case I'd be better off not tipping my hand, letting her know I was someone to watch out for, if she didn't already know that much. On the other hand, if I gave her a chance to start talking to someone, intervening would become more complicated. My heart thumping, I got up.

It wasn't likely that she'd try to hurt me. Glowers didn't usually go in for physical violence—from what Mateo said, intense physical sensations seemed to ground them more in our chaotic human world, making it harder for them control their reactions. But who knew what any individual demon might resort to now? Still, the far bigger risk was me looking incompetent in front of my observer.

I squared my shoulders and walked toward the Glower, just as she stopped by a couple women discussing their work in hushed voices. Whatever they said in response to her quick question, it turned her head toward Demirci's usual table. My skin chilled. *Oh no you don't.*

I adjusted my course to intercept her, but she glided to the high table too quickly for me to catch her. She drew up beside Demirci with a light touch of his arm to catch his attention. A touch that transferred a tiny spark of her energy into him. My pulse thudded harder as I hurried over. She was already trying to manipulate him, to inspire whatever emotional response she thought would make him most open to her influence.

Demirci looked up, and the Glower said something in a silky voice too soft for me to make out. A little smile that I didn't like at all crossed his face. He answered quickly, and the Glower started to gush about one of his games as I came around the table to confront her.

"I'm sorry," I said, pulling my five-foot-four frame as tall as I could manage and fixing the Glower with my best authoritarian stare—which probably wasn't a great stare, but it was a work in progress. "I need to go over a few things with you before you spend any more time in The Platform."

"Oh," the Glower said with a careful arch of her eyebrows. "Has there been a change in policy?"

"What's this about, Sofie?" Demirci put in, frowning.

"I'll explain later," I told him. To the Glower, I said, "It'll only take a minute, as long as there aren't any issues."

As I spoke, I rested my hand on her forearm, making use of a trick one of the other young Tethers, Fiona, had taught me when she'd helped me pick through the Society's selection of Glower repelling tools. I'd chosen a ring much like the one she wore, with a speck of malachite embedded in the underside. The stone was too small to affect a Glower through proximity, but touch it directly to their Earthly form and they'd get a zap of discomfort. Enough discomfort to let them know I meant business—in theory, anyway.

The Glower's arm twitched at the contact. Her mouth pressed flat. But her voice stayed just as silky as she said to Demirci, "I hope I'll be right back. I can't wait to hear your thoughts on component association."

I led her to the least busy part of the room, near the wall. "We both know why you're here, and that I'm not going to let you get away with it," I said, trying out my stare again. "Why don't you go find some other hunting ground where you won't have someone like me getting in your way? Or better yet, get in on the deal Kess is arranging so you can receive the energy you need without any trouble at all?"

"Aw, where would be the fun in that?" the Glower purred. "Everyone knows a Tether sighting means there's a particularly tasty meal to be had, and I'm going to keep him all for myself."

I suppressed a shudder. "No one here is going to be any

demon's meal," I said. "Are you going to leave or do I have to force the issue?"

She blinked at me innocently. "What exactly are you going to do?"

"Let me see." I reached into my purse and fumbled momentarily before my fingers closed around the vial of oregano oil I'd stashed there. I popped the lid and dribbled a bit onto my finger without bringing it into view, exactly the way Mrs. Tsung had shown me. Then I flicked it onto the Glower's dress before she had a chance to so much as flinch.

She did flinch afterward, her lips curling in disgust as the smell rose up. Her hands flew to tug the fabric away from her false skin underneath. She looked as if she wanted to rip the dress right off herself, but her awareness of the audience around us stopped her even as her chest heaved and her jaw clenched in pain.

"Now are you ready to leave?" I asked. The demon made a face at me that was almost a snarl, her cool broken by the concentrated herb, and whirled toward the doorway. She'd barely made it into the hall when I saw her form blink out of this plane of existence.

Relief washed over me. I leaned back against the wall, catching my breath. As the tension faded, a smile came to my lips.

I'd done it. I'd gotten rid of a Glower completely on my own.

Shawn was ambling to join me. I straightened up, bracing for an account of how I should have done one thing or another slightly more effectively. But before he reached me, Demirci stalked between us, halting in front of me.

"What did you say to her?" my client demanded, his eyes stormy.

"I, uh—" I'd expected to have more time to think up an explanation if he asked. I'd expected him to stay at his work, not rush over to defend her. She'd barely spoken to him—why was he so upset?

I groped for one of the Society's standard lines. "We've seen her around. She's a con artist, makes her living exploiting creative types. I wanted to make sure she didn't try her scams on anyone here."

"She didn't seem like a scammer to me," Demirci said. "I know what a desire to learn looks like, and that was all I saw in her."

That spark of inspiration she'd passed into him, I thought. She'd encouraged him to see her as an eager novice in need of his expertise.

"She's very good at her act," I started, and he cut me off with a jab of his hand.

"Or maybe you're too quick to judge. People come to their passions in all sorts of ways, not always by the most ideal route. If she wants to join this community now, I say we give her a chance. I should be a better judge than someone like you— someone who doesn't have a clue what really giving yourself over to creating something means."

His last sentence sliced through me, jarring loose a memory of a voice aimed to cut even deeper. *You're so rigid. Never letting anyone else have a say. That's why you'll never make it as an artist, you know. For that you'd have to really give yourself over, and everyone knows that's the last thing you'd ever let yourself do.*

Cold flooded me from head to toe. Suddenly my pulse was racing again, twice as fast and frantic as before. I opened my mouth, and a sob rose up my throat.

No. I held on to enough self-control to force the sob down.

To keep my arms rigid at my sides. For long enough to say, "I'm sorry you feel that way. You'll have to excuse me for a moment."

I spun and hurried toward the foyer as fast as I dared to go. The second I pushed inside the single stall bathroom, tears leaked down my cheeks. I shoved the door closed and turned the lock. Then I sank down on the floor, gulping air as I hugged my knees. A shiver rippled through me.

Jace lied, I reminded myself, my teeth gritting. *He told you all kinds of lies so you wouldn't leave. But you did. You did, and now you're free of him.*

Except he hadn't lied about *every*thing. Some things he'd said to me had been true, even if he'd only said them to hurt me.

Knuckles rapped on the bathroom door. Shawn's husky voice carried through. "Everything all right, Sofie?"

I hugged my knees harder. I didn't want to hear what he thought of this freak-out.

"Just give me a minute," I said, as steadily as I could manage. I swiped at my face. My heartbeat was starting to settle again, but my legs still felt shaky as I stood up to examine my reflection in the mirror.

My skin looked even paler than usual, but the whites of my hazel eyes had reddened. I dabbed cold water from the sink around their edges to bring down the puffiness. That was one useful thing Jace had forced me to learn: how to hide what was really going on inside me.

"Sofie," Shawn said, softer than before. "Come out and let's talk. That's what I'm here for."

To be a sympathetic confidante? He could have fooled me. But he didn't sound frustrated or annoyed, only concerned. Maybe that was what gave me the courage to unlock the door and step out.

Shawn eased back to let me by. His gaze lingered on my

face, and I suspected that despite my efforts he could guess that I'd been crying.

"I'm sorry," I said quickly. "I don't normally get overwhelmed like that. It shouldn't happen again. There was just — Something the client said, the way he said it, hit me in a bad place, that's all."

I turned to head back into the loft, but Shawn stopped me with a hand on my shoulder. A hand that was unexpectedly gentle. I was suddenly aware, with a heat that prickled over my skin, of how close we were standing to one another, the firm muscles I'd admired just inches from my fingers.

"Hey," he said. "It's okay to take a breather. I'm not going to judge you for an incident like this, all right? We all have crap in our past, considering how we got into this line of work, and the work itself can be triggering. It happens to everyone now and then. Is there something about this particular assignment that's a bad fit for you?"

The steadiness of his voice soothed the last of my shakiness. "No," I said honestly. "I think I should be fine. It was just the specific choice of words... I don't think it's likely to come up again."

"Good," Shawn said, and dropped his hand. My body protested at the sudden loss of contact for an instant before his next words warmed me in a totally different way. "You handled that entire situation well, especially moving the Glower off. I was impressed."

My cheeks flushed. I'd want him training those dark eyes so intently on me all the time if they always looked the way they did now: kind and appreciative. Yes, that look made me want to do all sorts of things for the man in front of me.

I swatted at that thought. He was a senior Tether, and my

observer. Not the sort of person I should be entertaining ideas like that about.

"Thanks," I said. "It matters a lot to me to hear you say that. I can tell you don't give compliments indiscriminately."

The side of his mouth quirked up. I wondered if he'd guessed how much I'd chaffed at all the opposite-of-compliments he'd given me during the week. "They wouldn't mean much if I did," he said.

I couldn't help smiling back. "No," I agreed. "They wouldn't."

We stood suspended in the moment, smiling our little smiles, our eyes locked. The little murmur in my head that hadn't completely shut up started to speculate about what might make him touch me again.

As if he'd heard it, Shawn jerked his head to the side, breaking our connection. "Well," he said, his typical gruffness creeping back into his voice, "if you're sorted out now, you'd better get back on the job."

He strode back into The Platform ahead of me, leaving me wondering if I'd imagined that momentary bonding. Not that it made a difference to what I needed to do either way.

Inside the loft, Demirci had gone back to his computer, but he lifted his gaze when I came in. He was still frowning. I was going to have to talk with him more, make some kind of peace. Especially since that specific Glower might come back. My gut twisted. I'd have to steer that conversation carefully away from any discussion of my artistic commitment or lack thereof.

Caution would hold me over for now. But no matter what Shawn had said, I couldn't help clients properly if one stray comment could break me down. I was supposed to be over all that.

Maybe the problem was that I didn't totally believe in myself yet, I thought as I headed to the high table. I didn't have the confidence to stand up to the memories. Because I hadn't really challenged them. If I could prove Jace had been wrong, prove I could do more than he'd said, then those words wouldn't matter at all. I just had to take that leap.

Four

"You're nervous," Kess said.

I glanced up at her. Her head was cocked, her sleek black hair slanting against her narrow shoulder as she considered me. The glow that seeped from her body was fainter than that of most of the Glowers I'd met, but it was still visible enough to make it impossible to forget she wasn't human.

Identifying people's moods—so they could figure out how to use those emotions to their advantage—was one of the demons' primary skills, so I shouldn't be surprised she'd noticed. Hell, anyone who knew what I was planning to do here should have been able to guess that I'd be a little nervous.

We were poised in the living room of Mateo's apartment across from the tall, narrow windows. A coarse sheet was spread on the hardwood floor under the easel and stool he'd borrowed from I didn't know where on my specifications. The table to the right of the easel held a selection of oil paints, brushes, and a palette. The canvas on the easel was primed with that faint but distinctive gesso smell. I had the urge to suck even more of it into my lungs. God, it had been ages.

The stool held my weight easily, as if it'd been made for me. Kess had come over to stand beside me as I'd appraised the set-up. Mateo was hovering in the doorway, prepared to jump in as an intermediary if he thought it necessary, I guessed.

"Yeah," I said to Kess's comment. "I think that's pretty understandable, don't you?"

She nodded, her thin lips curling into an awkward smile, and abruptly I saw the humanity in her that Mateo must all the time. She wasn't presenting the untouchable, unflappable Glower persona I was used to in her kind. There was something real about her even if her physical presence in this world wasn't totally natural.

"That's why we should talk beforehand," she said in her smooth, slightly clipped voice. "I should tell you what my limitations are: I can make you feel more enthusiastic and confident about creating art, but I cannot guarantee that the art you choose to make will appeal to anyone other than yourself, although in my experience art that has come from enthusiasm is more likely to accomplish that than art that hasn't. I cannot make you interested in a creative practice that didn't appeal to you before. Otherwise I could transform Mateo into a prodigy."

She shot him an affectionate grin that he returned. Seeing the love so blatant on her face dampened the last of my worries.

"Okay," I said. "And then afterward, you take that energy away?"

"Yes," Kess said. "What I will do to start this experiment, if it is all right with you, is offer you a small push of inspiration. I won't stay connected to you for any longer than five seconds. I will give you whatever time you need to finish a single piece of art to your satisfaction. When you are finished or inclined to move on, I will… feed. I will only take the energy I gave and the additional energy generated by your creative efforts following that. You will be left feeling much as you do now."

"You haven't seen any lasting effects in someone being… fed from like that?" I asked.

Kess and Mateo exchanged another glance, this one more serious. "There's always the risk of an addictive effect," Mateo said. "Marked or not, if you enjoy the feeling of the inspiration, you may find yourself craving to experience it again. But that shouldn't be as much of a problem without the lows that would come after a full feeding, and if we allow some time between the periods of inspiration… But we're not completely sure. That's why we're starting small."

"If you want to stop the experiment at any point, you only need to say so," Kess added. "It's very important to us that all participants are fully willing. Do you have any requests you'd like to make of me?"

They'd already covered pretty much everything I'd have been concerned about. I bit my lip. It had been a long time since I'd sat in front of a canvas. Underneath my anticipation, I couldn't ignore the prickle of dread that had nothing to do with Kess and her demonic talents.

"If I… if I seem upset or, I don't know, distressed in any way about what I end up painting," I said, gesturing to the easel, "can you stop it early? Take away the energy so I won't feel compelled to keep going?"

To my relief, neither Kess nor Mateo pressed for further details. "Of course," Kess said. "Creation should be a joyful process. If I stir up pain accidentally, I'll spare you from it."

I drew in a breath long and slow, and let it out. My fingers curled against my palms.

"All right," I said. "Let's try it."

Kess barely moved, only rested her hand lightly on my arm just below my shoulder. Where Shawn had touched me a couple days ago, I remembered, with more warmth than I liked. He hadn't *shown* me any more warmth the rest of that day or the next.

But yesterday, one of the designers who'd dropped by The Platform had sketched the most amazing landscape. It'd reminded me of— Oh, I'd love to capture that.

Without thinking, I reached for the palette. I squeezed a dollop of a few different colors onto the palette's surface to start, movement following movement as if I'd still been doing this every day. Apparently the practice never left you. Then I dipped a brush into the indigo and streaked a thick line sloping across the middle of the canvas.

Yes. There, that was where it began.

Excitement tingled through my chest as I layered in reds and oranges, a hint of yellow here, a dab of purple there. The image I could see behind my eyes swallowed up every other thought. I leaned forward, the paint fumes filling my nose, to speckle puffs of clouds across my sky, to texture the bark of the gnarled tree and the rope dangling from its lowest branch. Grass sprouted yellow-green beneath the smaller brush along the base of the gap-toothed picket fence; sunflowers leaned over its jagged posts. The hues of sunset tinted everything with an edge of violet. As I leaned back to stare at the landscape, I could almost taste the lake breeze and the tickle of sweet clover under the oil paint tang. It was perfect.

It was home.

That recognition smacked into me just as the exhilaration of the moment faded. I registered Kess's hand on my shoulder, my fingers tacky around the brush I was still gripping, the hush in Mateo's living room, where the sunlight was now fading. But I couldn't tear my eyes away from the image I'd brought to life.

It was the field by the lake. The field I'd played in almost every day when I was a kid. The field I'd crossed to lounge by the lake with my friends as a young teen. In starker, bolder colors than I'd normally have used, but somehow that gave it a depth I wouldn't have imagined until I saw it now.

My stomach knotted. Why had I wanted to capture *that*?

"Wow," Mateo said, coming over. "That's lovely. The vivid colors combined with what would normally appear to be a placid setting... The UCLA art department would have taken you in a second, you know that, Sofie?"

My face heated even though the rest of me stayed cold. "I did have some help."

"In bringing it out," Kess said softly. "The ability was already in you. Do you feel all right? I didn't take too much?"

I wondered if she would have asked anyway or if I'd betrayed some of my distress. "No, no," I said. "I'm fine. It was fine."

That wasn't entirely true. She'd said I'd be left feeling the way I had before I'd started painting, and instead fear was crawling through me. But that wasn't because of anything she'd done. That was because of what *I'd* done, the memories my mind had chosen to throw onto the canvas.

I didn't like her and Mateo seeing those memories. I didn't want anyone seeing them. That place wasn't home anymore, and the only way I could stay separate from everything that had happened there was if I kept it buried.

If we did this again, though, I might not have a choice. Who knew what the next session would provoke?

"Do you think—" Mateo started, and I hopped off the stool.

"I should go," I said. "I need time to—to process. I'll give you a call later."

And then I fled.

Bass thumped throughout The Platform as video game images glowed on three massive projector screens and bodies jostled in the sporadic light between them.

So this was how Macro Play launched a new game. I hung back near the wall, watching the crowd, trying to keep an eye on my client. For the first bit, Demirci had been standing on the temporary stage erected under the primary screen with the other key staff as they'd given a brief speech, but now I had to track him by glimpses of his crimson T-shirt amid the mass of bodies. The projected shapes at the edges of my vision weren't helping matters. The color scheme Demirci and the others had chosen for this game—rich blues and reds and purples—kept tugging my mind back to the painting I'd abandoned in Mateo's apartment.

"Heads up, Sofie," Shawn's voice said by my ear. I hadn't heard him approaching. I glanced around in time to see Demirci vanishing through the doorway into the hall with a few of the other guys. Damn—I almost hadn't noticed him leaving.

Without a word to Shawn, who was no doubt having all sorts of gloomy thoughts about my job performance, I hurried to follow. We hadn't seen any sign of last week's Glower or any others tonight, but Demirci was more vulnerable outside the building, where we had no private security force I could call on for back-up.

I was grateful to discover that Demirci and his companions didn't intend to venture any farther than the pizza joint a couple storefronts down from The Platform. After they'd placed their order and settled into a booth near the back, I asked for a soda and claimed one of the tables near the door. As much as I usually enjoyed pizza, I didn't have the stomach for greasy cheese tonight.

Shawn slid into the seat across from me. He peered toward Demirci's group and then turned back with his usual impassive expression. I could never tell whether he was pissed off at me or unconcerned.

What I'd really like, if I let myself admit it, was for him to give me that little smile he'd offered up after my freak-out in the washroom. For him to fix those eyes warmly on me and tell me how impressed he was.

Not very likely after I'd almost lost our client.

"Sofie," Shawn said, and I snapped back to the present. He was looking at me, but his eyes were stern, not warm. "You need to stay focused. You've been zoning out all night."

I ducked my head. "I know," I said. "I'm sorry. I'm trying, I really am."

He paused. Then he admitted, with the same gruffness, "I haven't seen you like this before. Is something going on that's gotten you distracted? If there is, I should know."

I circled my finger around the rim of my soda can. I hadn't talked to Mateo again yet, though he'd texted me a couple times since Saturday. Was I supposed to be keeping the arrangement with Kess a secret? It couldn't be a secret, though, if the whole point was to use me as a demonstration for the rest of the Society. Maybe it *was* the sort of thing Shawn should know about while he was observing me. I'd like him to at least know I was distracted by something for the Society.

I dropped my voice so I didn't have to worry about anyone in the pizza place overhearing me. "Mateo asked me... You know his proposal for cooperating with the Glowers? He wants to show everyone how it would work, so they can see that the Glowers don't *have* to hurt the clients. I used to do art—painting—before I moved to L.A., and he thought I'd make a good example—"

"*What?*" Shawn said, so sharply I lost the train of my words. I blinked at him, tensing as I took in his grimace, the angry set of his eyebrows. My pulse stuttered. Maybe I should have kept my mouth shut.

"It's okay," I said, struggling to keep my tongue from tripping. "I mean, it's not as if Mateo was pressuring me or anything. He and Kess were *really* clear that I don't have to do anything I'm not sure about. And when we tried it, it wasn't bad at all. It was actually kind of good."

"You've already let her feed from you?" Shawn said before I could go on, his face even darker than before. My back stiffened. I had the urge to pull myself into a ball, as if I could shield myself from the weight of his disapproval.

"Never mind," I said, hugging myself instead. "I shouldn't have mentioned it."

Shawn's expression softened. "Sofie," he said, "I'm not upset at you. I just— I can't believe—" He made a frustrated noise that was almost a growl. "It's bad enough that Sterling and Mateo want to expose the clients to the things we're supposed to be protecting them from, without getting trainee Tethers caught up in the whole mess too."

"You don't think we should try Mateo's plan?" I said.

"Hell, no. These are demons we're talking about. Beings that have been murdering us for who knows how many centuries. And now we're going to just trust them to play nice? I know Mateo hasn't been with the Society that long, but I'd have expected Sterling to be less naive, even given his condition." He leaned forward, pinning me with his gaze. "You're not going to do it again, are you? It's bothering you; that's why you're distracted. You have to tell Mateo you changed your mind. You have every right to."

His vehemence had the opposite effect to what I suspected he wanted. I opened my mouth, and something twisted in my chest. He was wrong. It wasn't Kess or what she'd done that was bothering me. It was what was inside *me*. That was my mess to deal with. I shouldn't let it ruin what Mateo was trying to accomplish. I didn't know enough to say whether he was being naive or not, but surely it wasn't misleading anyone to simply let them see what Kess could do with me?

"I don't know," I said.

"Sofie," Shawn started, and at the same moment Demirci's group got up. They were bringing their pizza back to The Platform, it looked like. I sprang to my feet, eager for the excuse to end the conversation. Shawn fell silent, but I felt his gaze on me the whole way back to the loft.

Five

Late that night, I found myself on Facebook again. Nothing much new had gone up since my last peek. After flipping through the profiles of former friends and family, I almost shut the laptop. Instead, my hand hesitated. My old email address was still active—I hadn't bothered to delete it, since there was no risk of *it* accidentally revealing when I was online or where I was located. I just hadn't signed in to the account in ages.

Maybe seeing how quickly everyone else had let go would help me to do the same. No doubt they'd stopped reaching out ages ago. Barely anyone had been talking to me during the last year before I'd left anyway. I'd shut them out, all of them except Jace, to avoid the concerned looks, the digging questions, looking for proof I was losing it. To avoid the remarks Jace would end up dragging out of me later, to hold up as *his* proof that this person or that one couldn't be trusted.

Jace. My "protector." Running himself ragged trying to keep

his girlfriend together while she fell to pieces. That was what they'd all seen, wasn't it? Otherwise they wouldn't still be inviting him to hang out down at the lake.

Without giving myself a chance to rethink the decision, I tapped out the username and password. The inbox loaded in a blink, showing a massive line of unread messages. Spam, spam, more spam— Oh. My hand froze over the touchpad.

Hannah had written to me just last week. I swallowed hard and forced myself to open the message.

Hey darlin'! I just wanted to remind you how much we all miss you. Whatever's going on with you, if you read this, get in touch, okay? I'll always have your back.

My hand clenched. *But you didn't*, I thought. *I needed you so goddamn much and you didn't even see it. You thought the problem was* me.

It was easy for a person to spout platitudes when she didn't really believe I'd answer. Had she written that to reassure me or to make herself feel better?

I skimmed a little farther down. My fingers halted again with a lurch of my stomach.

Jace had written me. *Love you*, the subject line read. My vision blurred as nausea swelled inside me. Fifteen days ago, he'd written that. I'd been out of his life nearly a year, and fifteen days ago he'd still been making claims on me.

The mouse cursor jittered. Because I was shaking. I started to recoil, then snapped my arm out to close the browser window and push the laptop away. As it slid to the edge of the coffee table, I lowered my face into my hands.

I was okay. I had a job. I had a decent place to live and enough food to eat. I had... maybe not friends, but at least supportive acquaintances and colleagues. That was all I could hope to ask for. Even if Hannah had meant what she'd said, replying to that email would mean putting myself back into Jace's orbit. I'd promised myself I was never letting him near me again. And this was the only way I could manage that.

So why did I feel as though I were teetering on the edge of catastrophe?

"You don't need to *do* anything today," Mateo said when we paused outside the Society office's largest conference room. "Sterling and I will only be setting the stage for the next few months, getting feedback on the official plan of action. But I thought you should be here for that, since you're going to be an important part of that plan. Other than you and me, it's only senior Tethers—people with at least ten years' experience in the field."

"Kess isn't coming?" I said.

"Kess can't come," Mateo said, a hint of bitterness coloring his tone. "The directors insisted on having this meeting here, and there are too many protections on the building for her to even stand out front. That's one of the topics we need to discuss —finding a neutral meeting location."

It would be pretty difficult to come to a compromise with the Glowers if we weren't even wiling to talk to them directly, I thought as we squeezed into the room.

Some twenty Tethers were already inside, sitting around the long conference table or, because there weren't enough chairs, standing along the walls. I spotted Mrs. Tsung, who gave me a quick nod that suggested she knew why I was there, and Shawn, who either hadn't noticed my arrival or was studiously ignoring me. I hung back as Mateo strode through the waiting figures to the head of the table, where Sterling was waiting. If I was here only to listen, I should be just fine fading into the background.

I'd only met Sterling a few times since starting training. I'd understood why he hadn't been more involved when news of his cancer diagnosis had spread through the Society a couple months ago. Today, he was sitting in a wheelchair with a stack of papers in front of him on the table, his posture rigid straight but his dark skin dulled with a sickly cast. Chemo had left his narrow skull completely bald. His body looked so emaciated and his sunken eyes so weary I was surprised he wasn't confined to bed-rest.

Maybe his doctors had ordered that, and he'd simply decided not to comply. From what I'd heard, Sterling turned stubbornness into an art form. That must be why he and Mateo got along so well, though I'd hate to see what would have happened if they'd been on opposite sides of a debate.

I leaned against the wall, watching the two of them from my spot near the door as they called the meeting to order. The murmuring that had filled the room a moment ago fell away, but I didn't like the frowns I saw on so many faces. Mateo had an uphill battle ahead of him.

But it was a battle that deserved to be fought. I'd grappled with my fears over the last few days, with Shawn's words piercing deep, but I hadn't been able to shake two certainties: Kess, whatever she might have done in the past, meant to help not harm now, which meant other Glowers might be capable of the same, and every qualm I had about continuing was based on my personal issues, not anything she or Mateo had done. I didn't want to see this proposal fail simply because I'd refused to contribute. So I'd called Mateo yesterday and told him as much.

Mateo and Sterling laid out their recommended timeline, Sterling taking the lead and Mateo picking up the thread frequently when the older man tired. When they brought up the need for a location to meet with the Glowers, a middle-aged Tether I whose name I didn't know spoke up from a seat at the table in front of me.

"How will we even be able to confirm that we're speaking to the same individuals each time? With their shape-shifting abilities, any demon could show up and say whatever they want, misdirect us, take advantage of the situation."

"Kess will always be supervising on the Glower side of things," Mateo said. "She's capable of identifying every individual, and she'll restrict her invitations to the negotiations to those she's sure are committed to making peace. Once we get to know the other Glowers who are on board for this initial stage, we'll be able to start identifying more who we trust enough to help with management so it isn't all on her."

"Trust a Glower," someone muttered with a scoffing sound. Mateo's eyes narrowed, but he said nothing.

A broad-shouldered woman with a cloud of bronze-brown hair stood up from her chair abruptly. "Forget identifying them," she said in a gravelly voice. "How can we know they won't turn this into a trap, if they get that many of us together in an unprotected location?"

A muttering of agreement followed her question.

"As I said, Kess will be choosing who she invites carefully," Mateo said. "None of the other Glowers will even know when the meeting is happening, let alone where it is. She understands the need for caution just as well as we do, Rafaela."

Someone else cleared their throat as if to add to the

protests, but Sterling spoke up first. "I know some of you have many doubts," he said with a rasp. "You've made them very clear over the last two months. But this is the best chance we've had in the entirety of the Society's existence to expand the number of people we're protecting. When we focus on keeping individual clients unmarked, we're only saving those few. The Glowers we put off simply find less prominent creatives to target. But every Glower we can bring into this... program, who'll feed without harming or marking, means one fewer Glower leaching life away from *anyone*. The potential benefits are immense. I know you see that, or we wouldn't be—"

He broke off with a bout of coughing.

"Aren't the Glowers only considering working with us because we've made it so difficult for them to feed at all already?" Rafaela said. She hit the tabletop with her closed fist. "If we're already so close to stamping them out, why help them now?"

"Desperate creatures take desperate measures," Mateo said. "We've already seen how much bolder some of the Glowers are acting, how they're challenging us more directly, working together to trip us up. We should be concerned about what strategies they might turn to next, if they see no alternative. If we can give them an easier option than fighting, it'll be safer for us and our clients too. The Glowers who refuse to compromise, *they'll* be stamped out—while we have others of their kind on our side to help us accomplish that. And why shouldn't we take advantage of what the Glowers can offer our clients? Why shouldn't we not just protect them, but offer them a new way to boost their creativity?"

"I doubt they'd see it as a good offer if they knew it meant letting demons meddle with their minds," the man by me said.

"How can we be sure of controlling their feeding? How can we know they *won't* hurt the clients?"

"We're going to develop the program slowly, starting with the Glowers we're completely sure of," Sterling said. "We'll be monitoring every transaction, with herbs and malachite ready to shock them out of the feed if we can see they're overindulging."

"I still don't like it," someone else said.

"I know," Mateo replied. "That's why, as part of the planning process, we're going to have one of our Tethers who has an artistic talent work with Kess for you to observe. You'll be able to see how the process works first hand: how much it can help an artist, how little negative effect there is. We can arrange the first demonstration for you before we even meet with any of the other Glowers, if that will help ease everyone's fears. I want you all to feel comfortable with at least trying out this proposal, even if you still have questions or aren't ready to fully support it. Any concerns you have, we'll address them."

A murmur passed through the group. A couple gazes flicked toward me. Instinctively, I pressed back against the wall.

"As a space we can book that will be neutral ground for both parties, I'd suggest—" Sterling began, but Rafaela cut him off. She still hadn't sat back down.

"Now we're using our own people as test subjects? I have concerns about *that*."

"The volunteer received full disclosure and decided to participate of her own free will," Mateo said. "We wouldn't *force* anyone."

"No, but you're awfully passionate about this... cause," an older man put in. "Maybe you didn't intend to pressure anyone, but the effect is still the same."

My skin tightened. This felt far too familiar. People deciding how I must feel, what I must want, amongst themselves, without bothering to really listen to me. *She's so on edge these days. We wouldn't want to upset her. You're right, Jace; you know what's best for her.* My hands balled.

As Mateo hesitated, I pushed myself off the wall. My heart was thumping in my ears, but I had to say something. I'd spent too long staying quiet already.

"I wasn't pressured into agreeing," I said, loud and clear. From the corner of my eye, I thought I saw Shawn's head jerk toward me. My pulse pounded a little harder, wondering what he'd make of this, but I didn't let that stop me. I understood why he'd been upset, I appreciated that he'd worried that much about me, but it was my decision, not his. "Mateo never made me feel I couldn't say no. He and Kess were completely upfront about the possible risks. But I think giving this compromise a shot is important, for all the reasons Sterling and Mateo have said. And I think if you let yourselves talk with Kess a little, you'd see that Glowers can be a lot less monstrous than you expect. So don't dismiss Mateo's proposal on my account. I'm all for it."

My throat closed up after those last words. Everyone was staring at me now. So much for fading into the background. Even Mateo was staring. But then his mouth tipped up with a little smile, and across the room I saw Mrs. Tsung smiling too. The racing of my pulse ebbed.

"Perhaps we should have that demonstration before we move forward," Sterling remarked.

"Yes," Mateo said. "And you all *should* talk with Kess, as Sofie said. She'll be able to answer so many of your questions. You'll be able to see for yourselves that she isn't using supernatural influence to change anyone's minds. She wants this to be an honest working relationship too."

"We already had a general meeting booked for next week,"

Sterling said. "If I can arrange an appropriate space, why don't we use that time?" His gaze settled on me. "Are you available on the 28th, since you'll be the... star of the show?"

It was already happening. I was going to let Kess crack me open in front of all these people, and they'd see whatever spilled out of me. For an instant, I couldn't breathe.

"Yes," I managed to force out. "I can be there."

"SEE YOU TOMORROW, I GUESS," DEMIRCI SAID AS THE Platform's manager locked the place up. He gave Shawn and me an ironic salute and trotted down the stairs without waiting for an answer.

"He really doesn't like us hanging around all the time," I said to Shawn as we took the same route more slowly.

"The clients almost never do," he said. "You'll get used to the attitude."

"Yeah." I wondered if that attitude might change if Mateo's plan worked. If we became not just bodyguards but facilitators for a wellspring of inspiration. After the way Shawn had responded the last time I'd mentioned that plan, though, I figured it was better not to express my wonderings out loud. He hadn't mentioned my defense of the proposal at the meeting, and I was happy to keep the subject under wraps.

A car whizzed by as we stepped out onto the street, its horn blaring and a passenger waving a huge foam hand from an open window.

"What's that about?" I said.

Shawn tipped back his head in thought. The vulnerable curve of his throat, so at odds with the power the rest of his body exuded, made a funny fluttery feeling happen in my stomach. I tried not to notice.

"I'm going to guess baseball fans," he said. "Today is... August 25th. Yeah. The Dodgers are playing the Giants. That always gets people riled up. If you're into that sort of thing."

From his tone, I guessed he wasn't. But his comment jarred me for a different reason. August 25th.

"Oh," I said with a startled laugh. "It's my birthday." I'd literally forgotten. I hadn't found there was much need to pay attention to the exact date on any given day as long as I knew where I was supposed to go after I woke up, and it wasn't as if I'd had anyone to remind me or make plans with.

Shawn gave me a quizzical look. "You must be eager to get going then. What number is this?"

"I, ah—" I shouldn't have let the remark slip out at all, I realized. This wasn't the birthdate I'd given the Society, the birthdate on my fake ID. That one wasn't until September. But I didn't think Shawn would have committed that to memory during his glance over my file before he'd even met me. At least I'd remembered in time to make sure I gave the right age. I was twenty-one today, but the fake ID also said I'd already passed that milestone.

"Twenty-two," I said. "Nothing too exciting about that."

"I think the twenties are all worth celebrating," Shawn said. "But that's coming from a guy who unwillingly left them five months ago, so maybe I'm biased. Here, I'll flag you a cab so you can get wherever you're going."

"No, that's okay," I said quickly. "I don't actually have anything planned. I can walk home from here."

He fixed me with that unreadable gaze again, as if he were looking right inside my head. It took all my self-control not to squirm. Now he was going to think I was a loser on top of whatever other judgments he'd already made.

"You're not doing anything?" he said. "That seems like a shame."

"Well, I... I haven't been living here that long," I said. "There's no one I'm close with who lives nearby. It's not a big deal. I'm sure by next year I'll be ready for a big party or something."

He was still looking at me. Something in his eyes had shifted, in a way that sent a tingling warmth over my skin.

"If you did have people you wanted to celebrate with," he said, "what would you have wanted to do?"

"I don't know," I said automatically, and then realized that wasn't true. Every birthday since I'd been old enough to fake my way in, until Jace had put a stop to those excursions, I'd always wanted to do the same thing. And I had a lot more selection of venues here than there'd been in the one city easy driving distance from my hometown. "I haven't been clubbing since I moved here. I probably would have gone dancing."

"You still could."

I shook my head. "I wouldn't know where. And I never liked going alone."

The dance floor could be beautiful with its mishmash of lights and colors, bold clothes and brash voices, but it was also a bit of a jungle. The thought of being dragged into it without anyone to reach out to if I felt overwhelmed made my lungs clench up.

"So I'll take you," Shawn said, as casually as he'd offered to flag me a cab. "My evening's free. I know a good place. It's been a while since I went, but I don't think it'll have changed too much."

I considered him, that funny fluttery feeling coming back. "You're offering to take me clubbing? Is this an excuse to keep an extra eye on me for your evaluation?"

"If it's an excuse for anything, it's to get to watch a pretty girl dance," he said, with a sudden grin like the sun dawning. I'd forgotten how striking his smile could be, he showed it so little. My pulse stuttered, and suddenly I found it difficult to speak.

He'd made the comment lightly, like this whole conversation. He'd kept the same professional distance from me standing here since we'd come out of the building. If he was flirting, he meant it more teasingly than seriously.

The problem was, if I was honest with myself, I wanted him to be serious.

Well, that murmur I'd never been able to completely silence said, *maybe this is your chance to* make *him serious.* He'd called me pretty. He must like what he saw at least a little.

"Okay," I said before I could second-guess the impulse. "But I've got to stop by my apartment first. I can't go dancing in this." I motioned to my plain T-shirt and jeans, chosen for comfort and blending in with The Platform's crowd. Half the fun of dancing was making myself up into a sort of work of art.

Having agreed out loud didn't stop me from second-guessing my decision after all. My skin itched as I sat in the back of the cab with Shawn just a couple feet away. His grin had vanished into his usual cool expression. Maybe *he* was already having second thoughts? He wasn't technically my boss in the grand scheme of things, and the Society seemed to be pretty easy-going when it came to socializing between colleagues, but he was overseeing my performance in this placement. Did that make hanging out together in a totally nonprofessional way weird?

I was pretty sure it did. But I didn't care quite enough to call off our little adventure myself.

"I'll be fast," I promised when the cab pulled up at my building, and dashed for the elevator. In my apartment, I dug through the closet, dismayed to rediscover how focused I'd been on practicalities during my hasty pack for the move. But there was the flirty sea-green halter dress I'd bought in a brief burst of exhilaration after I'd gotten my first real Society paycheck. That would do.

I pulled the dress on, relieved to find the soft fabric hadn't formed any wrinkles, dabbed ruby-red stain on my lips and mascara on my eyelashes, and stepped into the only sandals I owned that had any heel at all. Well, semi-practical shoes made for easier dancing. As I rode the elevator back downstairs, I pulled the waves of my hair into a loose twist and clipped it into place behind my head. If I left it down, it'd be in my face the second I hit the floor.

Shawn made no comment when I ducked back into the cab. If anything, he looked outright grim. "Ready?" he said, and I nodded, my stomach sinking. Maybe this was a bad idea.

He leaned forward to give the driver directions. His work clothes would fit in fine for dancing, I thought—thin button-up shirt with a sharp collar and fitted slacks. I caught myself watching the shape of his muscular shoulders as he shifted back in the seat and quickly yanked my gaze away.

"If you changed your mind…" I forced myself to say. "We really don't have to do this."

"We're going," he said evenly. "You've got your nice dress on now. It's your birthday. Someone ought to take you out."

So I was a pity case. I restrained myself from gnawing on my lower lip, focusing on the view out the window. But when the cab stopped in front of a three-story warehouse converted into a nightclub, the flash of the lights and the beat of the bass that trickled onto the sidewalk made my heart leap as much with anticipation as trepidation. I clung to the former as I followed Shawn inside.

It was early enough in the night that the place wasn't packed yet, but a decent-sized crowd swayed across the pitch-black dance floor just inside. Shawn headed straight for the marble-topped bar and spoke to the bartender. I trailed behind him.

"You want anything, birthday girl?" he asked me.

"No, thanks. Not right now, anyway." I didn't want to risk getting tipsy in a totally unfamiliar place, especially when he'd be watching if I made a fool of myself.

"Go ahead," he said, nodding to the dance floor. "I'll 'keep an eye' on things, make sure no one hassles you."

Ah. Even if he wasn't pitying me, he was going to treat me like a client. Stay out of my way unless I needed help. Had I really expected more than that? It was good enough. I still knew I wasn't alone.

I gave him a thumbs-up and turned to the dance floor. The DJ blended one song into another, and I let the rhythm carry me into the crowd. The dress had been a good choice, I decided as I shimmied between the undulating bodies. The smooth fabric licked over my limbs and swirled with my movements like a partner.

A guy in a silver silk shirt sidled up to me. I danced with him for a few minutes, letting him spin me at a flourish in the music, but something about the grasp of his fingers against my palm sent a chill down my back. When he released me, I drifted away. A cluster of women around my age caught me up, and we all bobbed and laughed through a couple songs before they started to split off with approaching guys.

An older man with gray speckled in his tawny hair beckoned me over. Why not? We matched each other's steps until he reached for my waist and that panic washed over me again. I shook my head and slipped away.

The pulse of the music no longer felt quite so invigorating. My own pulse was thumping faster. There were too many strangers surrounding me, a sea of unfamiliar faces with none I could latch onto for comfort.

Almost none. My gaze darted over to the bar. Shawn was there, lounging on one of the stainless steel stools, watching me as he'd promised. He tipped his head to me the second my eyes met his, and the warmth of just that acknowledgment carried away my earlier chill.

I knew what I wanted. Why shouldn't I go for it? The worst that could happen was he'd say no. He couldn't accuse me of lack of professionalism when he was the one who'd suggested this entire outing.

I wove through the other dancers to the bar. Shawn started to frown as I reached him. "Everything all right?" he said. "You looked like you had the situation under control."

"I did," I said. "Now I want you to dance with me."

He really hadn't been expecting that. His eyes widened for a second before he schooled his expression. "Me? I— Sofie, that wasn't the idea."

"Well, you weren't very clear on what exactly the idea was," I said. "I figure taking me dancing should include some actual dancing. You've obviously danced before or you wouldn't know this place. I won't judge if you're out of practice. Please?"

I wouldn't have thought that last word would change his

mind, but the second the plea fell from my lips, his eyes softened. He rubbed his face.

"All right," he said. "One song. If that's what you really want."

This time, I took the lead, pushing onto the dance floor with him following behind. Shawn stayed close—not touching, but near enough that I felt his presence all through my body. I turned to face him as the music swelled. His dark gaze locked onto my face with its usual intensity, threatening to melt me. I swallowed hard and made myself start moving.

We swayed with the music, at first tentatively, but after a minute I could see Shawn relaxing. A mischievous glint lit in his eyes. He stepped up his pace, sidling closer and swiveling away, shooting me a challenging look as if daring me to keep up. I gave myself over more fully to the beat, slinking up to him with a dip of my shoulders and then pulling back just as he had. A grin broke over his face that lit a flame low in my belly. He drew up to me with a swagger that told me he hadn't suffered that much from his lack of recent practice. My breath came faster as I matched him move for move, barely managing to keep up. I whirled in an attempt to take over the lead, and my body brushed against his. The fire inside me sparked even hotter.

Shawn caught my hand, letting me spool out and then whirl back toward him. With a careful hand on my waist, he turned me so my back met his front. His hips grazed mine with a swivel as we moved together, lower and higher again. His palm burned against my side. My pulse was racing. Was he feeling even a bit of what I was, or was this just meaningless play to him?

That was the question I'd wanted to answer from the start, wasn't it? It was up to me to find out. I reached back as we dipped again, tracing my hand down the firm muscles of his forearm. Just before my fingers slid over his, Shawn spun me to face him again, putting a foot of space between us. Too much. I smiled up at him as I raised my arms, making my dress flirt around me. His gaze held mine again. He wasn't grinning anymore, but that intensity shone even hotter. *Yes.* I dared a touch, teasing my fingers across his chest, those planes I'd admired so often. I could feel the curves and ridges of his torso through his shirt even with that light contact.

He caught me, his palms on my ribs just below my breasts now, and I lost my breath altogether. "What do you think?" I said, leaning close so he could hear me. "This is more fun than sitting at the bar, isn't it?"

He took long enough to answer that I started to worry I'd misjudged. This was a bad idea. I *was* making a fool of myself, and I couldn't even blame it on a drink. But then he pulled me right up to him, easing me down and up with him through a loop in the rhythm, and I couldn't bring myself to care.

"We didn't come here so *I* could have fun," he murmured, the words spilling hot down my neck. "Are *you* having a good time?"

God, yes. I needed this. I deserved it. To feel desire that wasn't tangled up in shame or fear, even if it wasn't returned. To hope it might be returned.

"It could get even better," I said in a purr of a voice I hadn't known I had in me. Unbidden, my fingers trailed up over his chest and shoulders to twine with the short, wiry curls of his hair. Shawn's expression stuttered.

"Sofie," he said, almost pained. I started to let go, thinking that was a protest, but before I had time to drop my hands, he'd pressed his lips to mine.

Seven

Everything fled my mind but the sensation of Shawn's kiss. It set off sparks along all my nerves. I clasped his head, pulling my body against his, reveling in the feel of his muscular frame. The club's lights danced through my closed eyelids. Shawn tipped his head a little farther, coaxing open my mouth. I couldn't suppress a tiny whimper as his tongue teased over mine. A pleasant tremor swept through me.

We were barely moving amid the crush of dancers, but the music still carried through us. My hips brushed his, and his fingers tensed around my torso. His thumbs arced up, tracing the undersides of my breasts. *Yes. Yes, please.* It had been so very long since anyone had touched me like that. Anyone I'd really wanted to, at least.

One of the other dancers jostled against us, and Shawn jerked back. He stared down at me, his face inches from mine, his hands tight around me. His eyes were wide, but they looked as troubled as they did hungry. I hesitated, torn between the longing to drag his mouth back to mine and the fear that he'd recoil if I tried to.

He reached up and caught one of my hands where they had lingered on his shoulders. Without a word, he tugged me to follow him.

His palm was hot against mine as we wove through the crowd. I hoped mine wasn't sweating. My whole body felt shivery and blazing all at once.

We passed the bar without slowing and squeezed past the expanding stream of newcomers in the hall. Shawn kept walking several paces beyond the front doors, and I matched his stride as well as I could. Then he stopped and turned toward me. The harsh light of the streetlamps in the night cast his face in sharp contrast. As he dropped my hand, his gaze tripped down me with the hunger I'd seen inside the club. He closed his eyes. His chest rose and fell. Then he looked at me firmly, his mouth flattening.

"I'm sorry," he said. "I shouldn't have let things go that far."

The glimpse of his attraction, the knowledge that I hadn't imagined it, steadied me enough that I could say, "You don't need to apologize. I'm not complaining about what happened."

"Maybe not now," Shawn said. "But I'm your observer for another three weeks. I'll be writing up your evaluation. I don't want you to have to wonder, if I praise or criticize you, whether my comments were influenced by factors outside of your work. I don't want *myself* to have to wonder. And I'm not going to put you in a position where you'd have to worry about saying no, in case it might affect my professional judgment."

That last possibility hadn't even occurred to me. Maybe it should have. But Shawn had given off such a strict, responsible vibe from the first moment I met him that even hearing him say that, I found it impossible to imagine him lying about my job performance simply because I'd decided to stop kissing him. I had on doubt he cared more about making sure the Society's clients were properly protected than getting in my—or anyone else's—pants.

"Okay," I said. "You don't seem like the vindictive type to me, but I get why you might by concerned about that." I paused. I found I couldn't quite stop myself from lifting my hand to rest my fingers against his side. To steal a little more of his warmth. I looked at them, pale against his midnight-blue shirt, grazing the taut muscles beneath. He didn't stir. Suddenly it seemed very hard to meet his eyes. "So does that mean... when this assignment is done, and you're not evaluating me anymore... maybe then we could see where this goes? I mean—" A chill shot through me. "You don't have a girlfriend or anything, do you?"

"No," he said roughly. "No, I never would have— I don't mess around on people."

I glanced up at him then, but he'd dropped his gaze to the sidewalk. He swallowed audibly. Then he placed his hand over mine, moving my fingers from his side but staying wrapped around them, his thumb circling my palm.

"Do you think you'd want that?" he said. "To see where this could go?"

With me? those questions implied without speaking his uncertainty outright.

Did he really find it so odd that I would want him? My own anxieties eased back. He wasn't sure I'd think him good enough for *me*? The thought made a laugh bubble up inside me.

"Well, I guess I've got a few weeks to get to know you better and make sure," I said, letting a teasing note enter my voice.

"But initial impressions say yes. As long as you promise not to start ordering me around outside of the job."

A hint of his earlier grin crossed his lips. "I think I can manage that. And I don't think there's any conflict of interest in simply getting to know each other better."

I felt myself beaming. "All right," I said. "Then it's a deal."

My first demonstration with Kess for the Society was set up in a conference room in the basement of one of the city's public libraries. Mateo had brought the easel, the stool, and all my supplies. I paced around them uneasily as the senior Tethers filtered into the room. The lighting wasn't great, just those yellowish florescent panels overhead, but it was late evening anyway, so I wouldn't have had natural light anywhere. Besides, I didn't need to create a masterpiece. The point was just to show that Kess wasn't hurting me.

It was weird to think that all those people already eyeing me would see the transfer happen. They'd see the glint of inspiration dart from Kess into me in a way I wouldn't even register myself. Because it happened *inside* me.

They'd observe whatever picture welled up in response as it spilled out across the canvas. They'd identify the forms before I'd gotten to a place where I was noticing more than depth and color. I had no idea what was going to come out of me today.

I halted in front of the easel, my skin tight. What would I paint right now without Kess's nudge of inspiration? *Nothing*, I thought. There was nothing I wanted to mar that perfect blank space with. What was the point? Nothing I created was going to be all that special.

No. Those were Jace's words. Jace's voice still twined with my own thoughts. I shook my head as if I could jostle his influence loose and cast it away. It'd been almost a year. How much longer would it take for me to shed his influence completely?

When the rows of chairs were full, Mateo and Kess ambled over to me. "Where's Sterling?" I asked.

"He's had a bad couple of days," Mateo said with a regretful grimace. "When he isn't even fighting for his right to leave the hospital, you know it's serious."

"I hope... I hope he isn't suffering too much." I didn't know what else to say. The only people I'd known who'd died had gone suddenly—a childhood friend in a car accident, my grandfather to a heart attack. How did you talk about someone everyone knew was dying while they were still hanging on?

"The doctors have a wide range of medications to keep him comfortable," Mateo said. "At least when he's doing this poorly, he lets them help rather than fretting about keeping his head clear." He peered at our audience. "Are you ready?"

I dragged in a breath. "Yeah. Sure." Might as well get this over with.

I sat down on the stool and Kess stepped up beside me. She studied my face as Mateo offered a few introductory remarks to the assembled Tethers, the same basic pitch he'd given me when asking for me to participate.

"What is it you're worried about?" Kess asked me.

Glowers and their damned emotional sensitivities. I groped for an explanation I thought she'd accept that didn't reveal more than I wanted to. "I've never painted in front of a bunch of people like this before. I mean, there was art class, but then everyone was focused on their own work, not mine. This is a little... intimidating."

She nodded. "That's understandable. If you would like, if it would make this easier for you, I could adjust what I offer you to take those concerns into account. Along with the boost to your confidence and openness, add a little pride in sharing what you can do?"

The idea was tempting and unnerving at the same time. "It'd go away after you feed, though, wouldn't it? I'd feel less bothered *while* I was painting, but after, the discomfort of knowing they watched me would come back."

"Most likely," she said. "I'm sorry. I don't think I can avoid that. The feeding... It isn't precise."

"That's all right," I said. "I think it'll be better for me to deal with those feelings in the moment. But thank you for suggesting it. Really."

She gave me that thin smile of hers that somehow managed to convey more warmth than almost any other I'd seen. I guessed it wasn't often she got honest gratitude from someone who knew what she was.

Kess's kindness relaxed me for a moment. Then Mateo motioned to me and said, "We owe many thanks to Sofie Martel, a relative newcomer to the Society, who has agreed to make herself the subject of these demonstrations. Sofie, can you explain briefly why you agreed and what your history with creative practice is?"

I'd known I was going to have to speak this time, but my throat closed up for a second all the same. I swiveled to face the audience fully, my heart thumping. I didn't let myself look at Shawn—didn't want to see him frowning his disapproval— though I was intensely aware of his presence in the back corner all the same.

"I've been interested in the visual arts since I was a kid," I said, letting the words come out as I'd rehearsed them. "Mostly painting. I did a lot of creative work when I was in my teens, but I let that practice slide over the last few years. I can tell you that the energy Kess offers, it helped me tap back into my creative side without self-criticisms or doubt getting in the way. And there wasn't anything painful about her... feeding, afterward. I haven't felt any ill effects since our first trial run ten days ago. I wouldn't be here if I had. I don't— I haven't been part of the Society long enough to feel any particular allegiance to anyone or their cause. All that matters to me is figuring out what really is best for the work we do. So I hope you'll believe what I tell you and what you see from me today. I don't have any reason to lie. If this process could hurt someone, I'd want to know that, and I'd want you all to know too. I promise I wouldn't hide it."

My tongue stumbled a little toward the end. I couldn't tell whether the skepticism I saw in so many of the gazes trained on me was directed at me specifically or the proposal in general. Well, there wasn't anything more I could do to persuade them by talking. I turned to the easel.

Kess shifted forward and explained in her clear, fluid voice how she would use her powers to encourage my creativity. Then she rejoined me. She lay her fingers on my forearm as she had before. My body tensed, unbidden. Kess's brow knit.

"You need to be ready to accept it," she murmured to me. "If you're resisting the idea of painting at all, it will take more effort on my part than I think is wise."

"Sorry," I said. I inhaled, pushing away the anxious thoughts that rose up in my mind. It was just a painting. Even if what I produced meant something to me, no one here knew me well enough to read anything into the image that I didn't explain. I was safe because they were strangers.

My arm moved without me thinking about it. I picked up

the broadest paintbrush. Twirling it between my fingers, I considered the paints. A pang reverberated through my chest as a vision of sparkling eyes flitted through my mind. I reached for the yellow, the red.

The figure came to life with each stroke of the brush and each layer of color, homesick excitement swelling inside me alongside the image. Cupid's bow lips. Delicately arched nose. Those wisps of fly-away hair only the most delicate brush could capture, that would never stay in their ponytail no matter how carefully slicked down. And those eyes. Crystal blue, never failing to catch the light even when they glistened with unshed tears. Not that they teared up very often. No, this face ought to have a smile, because that was the expression that most naturally came to it.

The pinks and greens of her bedroom—did it even still look like that? I hadn't been in there in years—filled out the background. A little more shading on her cheeks and through her hair. Then I was setting down the brush, staring at the bright-eyed girl gazing back at me.

I hadn't seen Kerri-Ann face to face in over a year. My little sister. Not so little, though. Eighteen now, and presumably heading off to college any day now. I wondered if she would smile at me like that if she really were here, or if she'd turn away like she probably thought I'd turned my back on her.

"Sofie?" Kess whispered beside me. I'd choked up without realizing it. She must have sensed the shift in my emotions—maybe thought it was her fault.

"I'm okay," I said, exhaling sharply. And I needed to be. The other Tethers had gotten up from their seats. A few at a time, they walked over to examine me from head to toe. Checking for lingering flickers of Glower energy? Making sure I hadn't developed any gaping wounds? Their thoroughness struck me as absurd, but I stayed put on the stool and managed to put on a smile of my own. My sister's image hovered at the edge of my vision. But as long as I didn't look straight at it, I could pretend it didn't affect me.

Eight

"No," Demirci muttered to himself, scowling at his laptop's screen. "Why can't you just—" He shook his head in frustration.

Everyone in The Platform had opted to give him a wide berth today. He was sitting at the high table near the back of the loft alone. It'd been obvious from the moment he'd arrived that he'd woken up on the wrong side of the bed. I couldn't even mentally mock him for his artistic temperament, because I'd had my share of dramatics when a piece of work wasn't turning out quite the way I needed it to.

Shawn ambled over to join me when I went to grab a coffee from the bar. He mixed cream into his own mug, leaving a foot of distance between us, but ever since that night at the club there'd been a companionableness to his silence. I wasn't worried anymore than his lack of comment meant he was judging me. Of course, I gave him the same space as always—I didn't want him to think I was shirking my responsibilities here. The job came before any sense of anticipation I got when his body was so close to mine.

"I wonder if what Kess does could get him through whatever block he's struggling with," I said in a low voice. Shawn's jaw twitched, and I immediately regretted bringing up the Glower. Too late now.

He peered at Demirci, his eyes narrowing. "There's something to be said for working through problems by your own effort, don't you think?" he said. "Why take the risk just to make it a little easier?"

"You still don't think I should be letting her work with me," I said.

He paused and sipped his coffee. "No," he said. "But I don't think this is the right time or place to get into an argument about it. And... from what I've seen you've thought the decision through. You made it because you believe in what you're doing. It took some guts to say so in front of a bunch of people you know aren't on the same page. Even if, with everything I've seen, I don't agree either, I do respect all of that, Sofie."

The way he said my name, a shade softer than the rest of his words, sent a tingle over my skin. "Well, good," I said, doing my best not to smile like a giddy schoolgirl. It took some effort.

Normally I would have headed back to my usual post, but Shawn stayed where he was instead of returning to his chair, and it was hard to just walk away. He drank a little more of his coffee. Then, his gaze still fixed on Demirci, he said, "In the interests of getting to know each other better and that sort of thing, is it all right if I ask about the girl you painted? Is she someone you know? It looked like—from what I've seen, watching other artists—you were working from memory."

The choked-up feeling that had hit me yesterday filled my

throat again. I managed to speak around it. "Yeah," I said. "She's... She's my sister. Three years younger."

"Any other siblings?" Shawn asked. His even tone smoothed out my emotions. He wasn't expecting this conversation to lead to a big confession. He just wanted to know the basics—about me. I did let myself smile then, just a bit.

"My little brother. He's only ten. Surprise baby. Not that my parents minded. My mom just didn't think it could happen again at her age. How about you? Any brothers or sisters?"

Hell, he could have *kids*, it occurred to me. He'd indicated that he was thirty, and just because he didn't have a girlfriend at the moment didn't mean he'd never gotten that serious with someone. He could have been married in the past for all I knew.

I didn't think so, though, once I considered it. The few divorcees I'd known back home had all seemed a lot more jaded about relationships than Shawn had acted with me.

"One sister," he said. "My twin—fraternal, obviously. She and... my niece, they're the only family I'm close with."

Well, that answered the kids question too. "How old is your niece?" I said.

He smiled then, but his jaw tightened at the same time, turning his expression bittersweet. Damn if it didn't still look lovely on his handsome face. "Nine," he said. "She had a tough start of it, but she's a fighter. Strongest person I know."

His serious tone and the distant look that had come over him stopped me from asking about her any further. "So your parents aren't really around?" I said, hoping that wasn't too sensitive a subject.

He shrugged, the tension I'd seen a moment ago fading. "My father was never around much to begin with. Same old story of the white guy who thinks the girl from the hood is fine enough to hook up with, but add a couple kids to the mix..."

I winced. "I'm sorry."

"Don't be. Nothing to do with you, and it taught me what kind of guy I *didn't* want to be. And I don't hold it against the other pale folks." He tapped my elbow playfully. "The guy who pulled the same move on my sister was darker than me. Anyway, my mother never really liked this city. By the time Sherice and I were ready to leave home, she hated it. So she moved as soon as we were out of the house. I guess your parents are back wherever you came from?"

"Yeah," I said, my voice catching. I felt I owed the implicit question some sort of answer. "Arizona. Little town no one's heard of who wasn't born there."

"So what brought you to L.A.?"

God, how to answer *that*? No one I knew had ever talked about coming here. It was far enough away that I didn't think anyone would just happen to stop by. It was big enough that I could become an anonymous figure in the crowds. Most people thought of Los Angeles as a place to go when you wanted to get noticed, to make yourself into a star, but it was also an awfully good place to disappear. But telling Shawn any of that would provoke questions I wanted to answer even less.

There were a few true things I could say. "The focus on the arts here," I said. "All the theaters and galleries and movies being made—I like being around that. And—"

I halted as my gaze snapped to the tall man with a sprinkling of silvery hair who'd just strolled into the loft, taking in the lay of the land through black-rimmed glasses. He would have stood out anyway given that he looked at least twenty years older than the next oldest person in the room, but what had grabbed my attention was the unearthly shimmer emanating from his skin and his Hawaiian shirt.

Beside me, Shawn stiffened. I reached for my phone. It

might be another lost cause, but I should at least give security a try before intervening directly.

Before I could pull the phone out, Shawn touched my arm. The firm press of his fingers against my bare skin made my pulse shiver. It took a second for me to register the menace in his eyes. He was glaring at the Glower, his teeth gritted.

"I'm going to handle this one," he said.

"But—" I started. He'd already moved, striding over to confront the Glower. Why was he taking over? He was supposed to step in only if I needed assistance, and he hadn't even given me a chance to address the situation.

A sly grin crept across the Glower's face as Shawn approached, and the demon gave a little nod. It could have been just bravado, but the sense tickled over me that he'd met Shawn before. That could explain it, if this was a Glower Shawn had past dealings with and had recognized. Maybe he was a particularly dangerous demon, and Shawn had felt he should head him off before he made any headway at all, no time to coach me through it.

My suspicion solidified as I watched. Shawn didn't go for the usual tricks, no malachite charms or herbs. He said something I couldn't hear from across the room with a sharp motion of his hand, and the Glower replied with a languid shrug. Then Shawn pointed to the doorway. I straightened up as they marched out.

Where were they going? Did Shawn have a plan to banish the Glower that involved getting him out of view? I waited, my gaze sliding between Demirci still fuming at his laptop and the open doorway. Minutes ticked by. Shawn didn't return.

Uneasiness coiled in my chest. My hand dropped back to my pocket over my phone. If there was a major problem, if I thought we'd gotten into a situation the two of us couldn't handle alone, I could call Mrs. Tsung for additional backup. But what would I tell her? I had no idea what was going on or where Shawn was now. Calling in other Tethers might mess up whatever strategy he was using. It'd only been ten minutes.

As I debated with myself, a ringtone pealed out from a different phone, the one next to Demirci. My client sighed and scooped it up. At the sight of the call display, his scowl turned even darker. He brought the phone to his ear with a jerk of his hand.

Whatever the person on the other end said, it only seemed to tick off Demirci even more. He made several abrupt nods as he spoke, biting off his words with a vigor I could see even if I couldn't hear his words. After a minute, he wrenched the phone from his face and shoved it into his back pocket. Then he pushed his laptop shut, lurched off his seat, and stalked toward the front door.

Damn. Where was *he* going? I hung back, hoping he'd change course at the last second, but he barreled on out the door. My gut twisted as I hurried after him. I had no choice but to follow, with or without Shawn. Protecting Demirci was my first priority, and I couldn't do that without keeping the guy in sight.

He must have heard my sneakers tapping down the stairs to the ground floor behind him. I came around the landing halfway down to find him standing there, waiting.

"What are you doing?" he snapped.

That attitude, and the stress that had been building in me since seeing his bad mood when he'd walked in, loosened my tongue. "My *job*," I said. "My contract says I need to be with you when you're on company time. Which includes right now."

"This has nothing to do with Macro Play," Demirci said, with such a desperate note in his voice that I forgot my own frustration.

I studied him. "What *is* it about?"

"It's none of your business either," he said, retreating into his previous hostility. "I just need an hour. Do you really think I'm going to get into that much trouble in an hour?"

"That's not up to me to decide," I said. "Look, I'm not going to get involved. You don't even have to acknowledge my presence. I just need to be able to see that you're safe. All right?"

He grimaced, but he was already edging toward the next set of stairs. Wherever he was going, he felt he had to get there fast. "Fine," he said. "Just keep your distance. I expect to be able to conduct a private conversation."

"Not a problem," I said, and he hurried on.

I gave him a ten-foot head start as he strode down the street, since distance seemed to be such a priority for him. As I went, I scanned the road and the sidewalk opposite for any sign of Shawn. He hadn't been in the hall outside The Platform or in the stairwell. What was he going to think when he came back to the loft and *I* was gone?

He'll see that Demirci is gone too, I told myself. *It'll be obvious what must have happened.*

That reassurance wasn't enough to calm my nerves. It occurred to me that I had Shawn's phone number too, to get in touch if I was going to be late for a shift. I hadn't ever expected to need to use it while on the job, because I'd always expected to be *with* him. I wasn't sure it was a good idea to call him when I had no idea what he was doing that I might interrupt, but I could at least send a text message.

Still keeping an eye on Demirci, I tugged out my phone and typed a quick message. *Client left building. I'm following. Everything OK with you?*

I kept the phone in my hand for another minute, hoping for the hum of a response, but it stayed quiet against my palm.

Shawn must still be occupied. What if this Glower had decided to try to hurt him? He might not have been prepared for that. I swallowed thickly.

Before I could decide what to do next, Demirci veered off the sidewalk into a bar. One of the staff was setting out the placard announcing the lunch specials—the place must have just opened for the day. I ducked in after my client. The ozone-y smell of an air conditioner on the fritz hit my nose.

Demirci was settling onto a stool at the bar, so I grabbed a small table near the door where I could watch him without being obvious. This had better be enough privacy for him.

A waitress came by, and I ordered an iced tea. Demirci appeared to put off the bartender's inquiries about drinks. The guy raised an eyebrow and let him be. I guessed there were few enough customers at the moment that he wasn't concerned about losing the bar space.

Demirci drummed the bar counter, scowled some more, and ran an anxious hand through his shaggy black hair. My iced tea arrived. I sipped it slowly, puzzling over my client's behavior.

My phone vibrated. I snatched it out of my purse, and my breath rushed out of me in relief at the message that popped up on the screen. *Thanks for the heads up. Need help? If not, I'll meet you back at Platform. All's well.*

Did I need help? Not so far. And Demirci would probably get even more edgy with another person watching him. I texted Shawn the name and location of the bar in case he felt the need to check up on me, but told him I thought I could handle the situation. *No Glowers involved.* Hopefully I wouldn't need to do anything other than watch.

As I was setting down my phone, a lanky guy with a headful of messy, straw-pale hair sauntered past my table. Demirci caught sight of him, and his shoulders squared. The newcomer hopped onto the stool next to him.

He was just an ordinary guy, as far as I could see—no supernatural glow. But he had some significance to my client, clearly. They spoke in hushed voices for a minute, and then the straw-haired guy threw his head back with a wild laugh. Demirci cringed, glancing around the bar as if he was afraid of the attention the sound might draw.

"Cut it out," he hissed, loud enough that I heard the protest.

"Aw, man," the other guy said, still guffawing. "You're really something."

Whatever words they exchanged next, they dropped their voices again. The guy slid his fingers over the counter as if drawing something, and Demirci shook his head with an angry flash in his eyes. The iced tea soured in my mouth.

I didn't know what was going on, but it looked important. Screw privacy. I couldn't protect my client if I didn't know what trouble he might have gotten himself into.

Heart thudding, I abandoned my drink and ambled over to the bar, still leaving several feet between me and Demirci. I asked the bartender for a Coke, and studied the napkin dispenser as he poured it, my ears perked. I could pick up most of the conversation from here.

"You can't keep doing this," Demirci was saying. "At some point someone's going to notice. I've given you everything I can already."

The guy shook his head. "Not everything. You still owe me, Aydin. You know you do. And I'm going to keep asking until you've paid me back in full. Or I can go have a chat with your boss, maybe?"

Demirci let out a harsh sigh. His hand balled on the

countertop. "Are you actually going to do something with the opportunity, or are you going to piss it away like always?"

The guy's dark mutter in response was too muddied for me to make out, but it caused Demirci to look away. I didn't hear his answer either, but it appeared he'd given in to the guy's request. Demirci handed him something that he stuffed into a pocket. The guy took his leave with a loose bob of his head. As he passed me on his way out, he scratched the light stubble on his cheek, and I noticed his fingernails: cut or maybe bitten to the quick, ragged at the edges.

My client had slumped on his stool. The bartender came back, and this time Demirci ordered something. A beer, it turned out when the foaming glass was plunked on the counter in front of him. Demirci eyed it for a long moment, and then took a swig.

I guessed the vital business of this excursion was complete. I was about to take my soda back to my table to wait for Demirci to leave when another figure approached him. This time it was a woman: a tall brunette with an hourglass figure poured into a bright red blouse and pencil skirt. She glimmered brighter than the bar's dim lights could account for. My fingers tensed around my glass.

"You look like you could use some company," the Glower said to Demirci in a smoky voice. I couldn't tell whether she was a random demon trolling for prey or whether she knew who he was, but it didn't matter. Either way I had to get him out of here. And fast. If this went bad, there wouldn't be time for Shawn to get here to back me up.

I hopped off my stool and hustled over as Demirci raised his head. Before he could answer the demon, I'd nudged his shoulder.

"Time's up," I said. "You need to get back to work."

Demirci's gaze shifted from the woman to me, his expression strained. "I don't think you get to decide that," he muttered.

"Definitely not," the Glower agreed with a smirk. The tremor of energy flowing off her rippled over my skin in a vaguely familiar way. She might be the same demon who'd approached him in The Platform the other day, just in a different guise. "We all need a break now and then."

"Not right now," I said. I hesitated, and decided it was worth playing the best card I had. "Especially not if there are already things about you that your boss would be upset to hear."

Demirci jerked around to stare at me straight on. His mouth worked. He obviously hadn't realized I'd overheard any of his conversation. "You..." he said in a low voice, but he didn't seem to know how to follow that.

I set my hands on my hips. "It sounds to me as if you're in enough trouble as it is. Let's not add to it, all right?"

"Well, now," the Glower started, but Demirci was already getting up. He grasped my elbow, his fingers digging in uncomfortably tight. I managed to keep my legs steady as he walked us to the door.

"What do you know?" he rasped, bending close. The smell of the beer carried on his breath.

Not as much as I needed to, I thought, but all I said was, "Enough."

Nine

The library conference room felt even more claustrophobic today, though there were fewer people in it. Mateo had asked me to come along so that I could speak up on Kess's behalf, and therefore on behalf of any Glower who wanted to feed without marking, but otherwise the gathering had been limited to only select senior staff. About a dozen of them circulated around the table, no one seeming to feel comfortable enough to sit down. Shawn was among them, somewhat to my surprise—most of the others who'd been invited were middle-aged or older. He'd given me a brief nod as he'd come in, but that was it.

Mateo stood near me by the table where a couple of catered platters had been set out: cookies and veggies with dip. His arms dangled loosely at his sides, but I saw his fingers working the seam of his slacks pocket. He was on his own again, Sterling too unwell to attend. And I was sure he could feel the thread of hostility in the air as well as I could.

We were waiting on Kess and the delegation of Glowers she

was supposed to escort here. In the interests of security, she hadn't told any of them where this meeting would be taking place, so she had to bring them directly. She'd promised to vet those she allowed to join us carefully, but I could tell most of the Tethers here still saw every Glower as an enemy.

"I can't believe we're allowing this," the woman who'd spoken up in protest at the earlier meeting—Rafaela, Mateo had called her—muttered under her breath to the man standing next to her. "If Maxim had been around to see this..."

"We're here now," her neighbor replied. "We might as well hear them out. But I'm not holding my breath that I'll believe anything they have to say."

"Do you really think this can work?" I asked Mateo. "I mean, you've been working with the Society a lot longer than I have. Is there *anything* the Glowers can do that'll convince people to trust them?"

"Kess convinced me," Mateo said, but his voice was tense. "She managed to even though the last thing I wanted to do was believe in a Glower. It's possible."

If he could just figure out *how*, he didn't say.

A barely audible *pop* carried through the air, as if the atmospheric pressure had shifted. Then Kess stepped through the doorway into the room, leading four other Glowers who were in the guises of middle-aged men and women. To match the Tethers they'd come to speak with, I suspected. It seemed a little unfair to me that they were so outnumbered, but Kess must have agreed to that imbalance for the Society's comfort. Or else there were only four other Glowers she'd managed to find who were committed to exploring this compromise. Maybe the demons were as hesitant as our side was.

From the edge of my vision, I saw Shawn sidle closer, stopping by the far end of the refreshment table. I kept my attention focused on the Glowers. The unnatural gleam to their bodies made my muscles tighten up, even though I was fairly at ease with Kess on her own now.

It didn't matter how well I knew her. I was going to have trouble trusting every other Glower I met, just like the rest of my colleagues.

Mateo stepped forward to welcome the Glowers. "Thank you for coming," he said, the bob of his head acknowledging the entire delegation. "I hope this can be a productive meeting for all of us."

"We trust that Kess has been conscientious in her evaluation of you," one of the Glowers said in a tremulous voice. "We will listen to your proposal. If you are not truly ready to bargain with us, then we will leave."

Kess said something softly to her companion in their own language, and he frowned.

"So this is it?" Rafaela said. "Out of all the Glowers, only five are considering taking us up on this very generous offer?"

Mateo gave her a sharp look. "There are others who are interested," he said. "Out of respect for the concerns the *Tethers* have expressed, we're taking this slowly."

"And our people want to be sure that your motivations are honest before they appear before you," Kess put in. "But I have talked to many who would rather feed more carefully in exchange for freedom from additional interference."

"As if the Society ever would leave off interfering," another of the Glowers muttered.

I hadn't realized they might be quite *that* skeptical of us. It was hard to imagine their perspective—how could they blame us for trying to stop them from killing our fellow human beings? I wondered how the situation looked from their point of view. Did they feel their hunting was a right, some sort of process of natural selection that we were unfairly restricting? Just thinking that made my stomach knot. I couldn't see any way to sympathize with that complaint.

But they were here. They were standing with Kess. That meant these ones were willing to meet us halfway, at least.

"All right," Mateo said with a clap of his hands. "We're here to talk, so let's sit down and talk—openly, in good faith."

The first Glower who'd spoken shifted on his feet. "I prefer to stand." The others nodded. At their refusal, the few Tethers who'd moved toward the chairs around the table halted.

"Fine," Mateo said. "We can stand. This is how we'll structure the meeting. Glowers, I know Kess has explained the basics of our proposal to you. I'll go over the plan in more detail. My fellow Tethers will stay silent during this part, because they're already familiar with those details." He shot the group at large a warning glance. Rafaela grimaced but kept her mouth shut. "I'll answer any questions you have about the proposal. Then you may state any remaining concerns you have. I'll address those, with feedback from the other Tethers in an organized fashion. Once we're clear on what each side is able to offer, we'll adjourn the meeting so that both groups can talk amongst ourselves. I hope that we'll come away from this more confident and willing to move beyond simply talking by the next time we convene. Any questions before I start?"

"No," the second Glower said. "That sounds reasonable."

"Good." Mateo stepped back to lean against the edge of the table, still facing the Glowers. "The program we're proposing should benefit both us and you. We would regulate who you feed from and how you feed to ensure no one is harmed, and you would get access to the artists we'd normally be protecting —some of the greatest creative talents in the city. You'd be able to feed without conflict, and the artists would benefit from your inspiration without the lows that follow unrestricted feedings. Here's how we see the program actually structured: The Society would draw up a list of clients who are interested in your services. We'd present you to them as creative coaches. Glowers who wish to participate and have been vetted by Kess and whomever she chooses to help her as the program expands would be able to choose people from that list to exchange with. Over time, we'll develop a system of identification so we can be sure of which of you we're dealing with at any moment. Those who join the program would make a formal vow that you will not mark any clients, that you will offer them productive inspiration, and that when you feed you will leave them at the same emotional level as before the process began. When you meet with the client, their Tether will always be present to monitor the transfer."

"Once we've made a vow, we must stick to it," one of the Glowers spoke up.

"Kess has told us that," Mateo said. "But we still need to confirm that the Glower who shows up is a Glower who's made the vow, and it will make the Society more comfortable if we can see for ourselves that no one is trying to find a loophole. You can inspire and feed while watched. Maybe if this goes well, once it's gone on long enough without issue, we'd be able to let you work more independently."

A few sounds of consternation passed through the assembled Tethers as they shifted uneasily. Mateo raised his hand. "That's something we won't be seriously discussing for some time, if at all, so let's not get sidetracked. Now, one other factor is—"

My ears popped the way they had just before the Glowers walked in, with a faint sting that pierced through my senses and left me blinking. When my eyes refocused, the group of Glowers was gone.

I stared at the spot where they'd been standing as if maybe I just wasn't looking hard enough. Mateo had jerked upright. He swiveled, taking in the room. The Tethers' previous mutters rose.

"Looks like the demons weren't so committed to compromising after all," Shawn said darkly.

"Where's the 'good faith' in that performance," Rafaela demanded. "They didn't even listen to all of your opening explanation!"

Mateo was shaking his head. "It doesn't make sense. *Kess* wouldn't have—" He cut himself off abruptly and strode to the doorway. His mouth twisted as he toed something there with his loafer.

"Who did this?" he said, his voice shaking. "Who's responsible for this?"

He snatched up the object from the floor, and I saw it was a string—the same white as the tiles, knotted and no doubt rubbed with herbs the way Mrs. Tsung had shown me. My heart sank.

The Glowers hadn't left intentionally. Someone had arranged to banish them. I crouched down and spotted more of the string running along the room's baseboard. It must go all the way around, against the wall where no one would have noticed it. The perpetrator would have to have left it open at the doorway, though, so the Glowers didn't sense it as they'd come in. Somehow he—or she—had prepared it so they could pull it closed and complete the banishing circle after the demons were in the room.

The tone of the murmurs changed as everyone glanced around at one another. I looked too, taking in expressions of uncertainty and confusion. Rafaela looked a little pleased, but she was searching the faces of those around her as if wondering who to thank.

It could have been anyone.

Mateo tossed the string on the floor. When he spoke again, his tone was uncharacteristically harsh.

"Whoever set this up, you should be ashamed," he said. "We *need* the Glowers to trust us if this compromise is going to succeed. That stupid trick might have set us back so far they'll never agree to meet us again."

Only a couple enthusiasts were waiting at The Platform's doors right at the ten a.m. opening time. Feeling awkwardly out of place and blearily unfocused, I hung back by the entrance as they shuffled over to grab coffee and claim their favorite seats. Demirci's usual work period was eleven to eight, but after tossing and turning all night, I'd been itching to get out of my apartment. Just wandering the streets hadn't settled me down. I was too aware of the fact that every person I passed had no clue about the life and death conflict being waged behind the scenes of every arts community in the world. At least here I could feel a little more connected to my current purpose.

I plopped down into my usual armchair, but I didn't take my laptop out of my bag. Instead, I stretched out my legs and tried to relax as today's soundtrack, a medley of wind instruments, drifted from the speakers near the ceiling.

"Hey," a low voice said. My heart leapt as Shawn sank into the chair next to mine. I straightened up, suddenly overly aware of the loose fit of my T-shirt, the no-fuss approach I'd taken to my hair. I didn't normally get dressed up for work, but last week I'd been giving my style choices a little more thought. Today I hadn't found the energy—and now, with his eyes on me, I regretted it.

"I got your text," Shawn went on. "I was feeling pretty restless myself. Thought I might as well stop by and see if you wanted to chat about it before our shift starts. I assume last night's meeting is at least part of what's on your mind?"

"Yeah." I looked at my knees and rubbed a nub in the thin denim with my thumb. "I just... I know people in the Society are nervous about trusting the Glowers. *I'm* nervous about trusting any of them other than Kess. But to go behind Mateo's back and purposely screw up the meeting like that—it's awful. How could anyone we work with justify that even to themselves?"

"I don't know," Shawn said. "They must have thought it was the right thing to do, for everyone, but obviously it wasn't an acceptable way of making a protest."

"There isn't even anything to really protest against yet," I said. "We don't know what the Glowers might have asked for. Maybe they'd be fine with everything Mateo suggested. If everything happens the way he wants, I don't see how anyone would be in danger. Why can't we just *try* it?"

Shawn was silent for a moment. "I don't want to get into an argument with you," he said. "You know I have issues with the whole idea of a compromise. We've been in conflict with the demons for hundreds of years—they've always been looking for ways to screw us over—even if one or two can change, I don't think it's worth the risk that the others might find some way to turn this program around on us. These are creatures that can suck the life out of someone and laugh while they're doing it. They don't feel guilt. They don't feel compassion. We'd be better off focusing on strategies to get rid of them completely. But... I don't want one person to force our hand. Whatever we're going to do, we should decide as a group, no sneaking around."

"Well, we can agree on that last part," I said, glancing at

him. He was gazing toward the opposite wall now, with a distant expression that made me think he was remembering something beyond this room. He looked sad, too. A twinge of concern rippled through me.

"It was really bad, wasn't it?" I said. "When you first saw— Whatever happened that let you see the Glowers." Had that one laughed? Or the one that had marked his first client? No wonder he found it so hard to trust them.

Shawn blinked at me. His mouth twitched but didn't quite frown. "You don't have to tell me," I added quickly. "I know I probably shouldn't have even asked."

"It's all right," he said. "That first one was bad, sure, but I think the first experiences are for everyone. There's no way you can be prepared. Yours was bad, wasn't it?"

The image of the street painter swaying on the peak of the sculpture flashed through my mind. I cringed inside. "It was."

"I've dealt with a lot of Glowers since then," Shawn said. "I haven't met one that didn't seem to enjoy causing us pain. That one Mateo's taken up with, maybe she's something special. But most of them are the worst kind of predators, and if we give them an inch, they'll take everything they can. And it's the innocent people, the people they'll mark, who'll suffer because of that mistake."

He had mistakes of his own that he regretted, I could tell from the way he spoke. I thought again of what Mateo had told me about Shawn's first client, but it seemed even less wise to bring *that* up. If he wanted to talk about his past, I should let him do it on his own timetable.

"Sterling seemed to think it was possible," I said. He had more experience in the field than Mateo and Shawn combined.

Shawn shrugged. "Sterling isn't at his best right now. With all the treatments he's undergoing, who knows how his thinking has been affected. I have huge respect for the man, but on this subject..." He rubbed his jaw. "Enough about that. Are *you* okay?"

"I think so. Enough that it shouldn't get in the way of me doing my job."

He tipped his head toward me, with enough warmth in his intent eyes that my skin tingled. "I'm not asking just because of the job."

"No?" I said, brave enough to tease. There were still only two other people in the loft, and technically I wasn't on the clock yet. So I gave in to my urge to extend my hand past the arm of my chair to brush the backs of my fingers against his sinewy arm. Shawn caught my hand and gave it a quick squeeze.

"Two more weeks," he said with a crooked smile. "Are you still making up your mind about what you're going to do then?"

I couldn't help smiling back. "I'm pretty sure I already know, actually."

The look he gave me then was outright scorching, but his voice stayed cool. "I'm glad to hear that. I know I gave you a hard time at first, Sofie, but that's what all the trainees need. Everything I've seen from you since has made me think that you'll handle this job just fine... and that I'd really like to see more of you. If that's what you want."

"I think I've already been pretty clear on that point," I said.

He exhaled with a broken chuckle. "Well, I can't tell you how quickly I'm hoping those two weeks go by, then." He tapped my knee, a casual gesture of acknowledgment that lingered just long enough to send sparks up my thigh. Then he stood up. "Do you want anything to drink?" he asked.

For a second, I found myself unable to do anything other than gaze up at him. At this good man. Everything I'd seen from *him* told me he was a man who held his beliefs strongly, who cared most about protecting those who couldn't protect themselves. Who was protecting me even when his own desire pulled him in the opposite direction. Maybe I didn't think I needed that protection, but it was still a nice—no, a *wonderful* —feeling to have my security placed first, for real and not just for show. Not like Jace.

A burst of panic flared in my chest. Jace had known me so much better than Shawn did now. What if the girl Shawn wanted to do all that for wasn't truly who I was? Could I really hope that someone as... as good as him would care that much about someone like me?

My fingers curled around the chair's arms as I squashed down that doubt. Those were Jace's ideas, not mine. I couldn't let them be mine. I deserved so much better.

I managed to keep smiling as I said, "If you could grab me some of that hazelnut blend, with cream, that would be great."

Shawn was just turning toward the coffee bar when his ringtone sounded. He paused as he pulled out his phone. His brow furrowed.

"Hey," he said, answering the call. "Joyner here. Yeah. Oh. *Oh.*" His voice dropped. "Hell. Okay, definitely. I'm really sorry to hear that. Pass on my condolences."

I watched him as he hung up, my throat abruptly tight. Condolences for what?

Shawn grimaced at the floor and then raised his head to meet my gaze. "Sterling passed away this morning," he said. "The Society is making arrangements for a funeral this weekend."

Ten

THE ONLY FUNERAL I'D BEEN TO BEFORE STERLING'S WAS MY grandfather's, and that had been a quiet, mostly-family affair. It seemed the entire Society had turned up for Sterling's, though I supposed at least a few must have been unable to leave their clients. Some fifty people had gathered around the gravesite where the priest was now offering a few final words. It was only mid-morning, but the August heat was already scorching. The smoky smell of some new forest fire on the city fringes flavored the air.

I shifted from foot to foot on the yellowed grass, my arms folded awkwardly over the bodice of the navy sheath dress I'd originally bought for job interviews. The polyester fabric was thin but held the heat. I didn't know the people on either side of me. I'd barely known Sterling. But coming to give my respects had seemed like the right thing to do.

The three other Tethers close to my age—Mateo, Fiona, and Avery—had ended up on the other side of the grave. Avery stood with her boyfriend, Colin, who I was more familiar with from a recent music video that showcased his flashy grin and guitar work than any in-person interaction. His demeanor was subdued now, his arm around Avery's waist.

Mateo had brought Kess. Her shine was even dimmer than usual as she stood in her modest dress suit, but I noticed several of the other Tethers aiming glares her way.

Shawn had shown up at the funeral home just before the initial service had started, looking agitated, but now he stood solemnly next to a portly woman I suspected was Sterling's sister given the resemblance in their features. I hoped it was only Sterling's death that had upset him and not some new problem as well.

When the priest finished his final prayer, those who'd felt closest to Sterling shuffled forward to pay last respects. I gravitated toward Mateo and the other younger Tethers. I'd just reached them when Rafaela brushed past the group with a sneer directed at Kess.

"*She* doesn't belong here," she said under her breath. Mateo watched her go, his shoulders tensed. Kess touched his arm.

"It's understandable for people to feel more hostile in the face of a loss," she said.

"This isn't the place for expressing it," he replied. "Glowers didn't kill Sterling—cancer did."

"I heard you ran into some problems at the first joint meeting too," Avery said, tucking a strand of her bright brown hair behind her ear.

"Yeah," Mateo said. "I would have liked to think our colleagues are above outright sabotage, but apparently not. I'm not sure whether or not I should be glad Sterling wasn't in any state to hear about what happened before he passed. It might have been nice to get his advice." He gave a hoarse sort of laugh and rubbed his temple. Kess squeezed his arm.

"Were *your*... colleagues upset?" I asked her.

"I've been talking with the others," she said. "They were unsettled, but they're able to see why some members of the Society might lash out. It may take a few more days before they're calm enough to consider another meeting, though. I suppose we'll have to be more restrictive in who we allow to attend."

"We can't restrict people much more than we already are or they'll feel we're going behind their backs," Mateo said. "In the end, everyone in the Society needs to be on board or the plan isn't going to work." He sighed. "But we shouldn't be getting into this subject here. This is supposed to be Sterling's day."

"Hey," Fiona said with her usual sly grin. "He was pretty invested in your plan. I don't think he'd mind."

Mateo nodded, but he still looked uncomfortable. I wondered how much he'd been relying on Sterling's support. Sterling had been a supervisor and had worked with the Society for decades, from what I'd gathered. He'd only just begun grooming Mateo to take a management position. How much would the other senior Tethers listen to Mateo without Sterling's backing?

Shawn's comment from the other day came back to me. They'd already had their doubts about Sterling's judgment because of his illness. It was only going to be harder to convince them to agree with him now that he wasn't here to speak for himself.

"How's Will doing?" Colin asked Fiona.

Her olive skin lit up at the mention of her boyfriend even as her mouth twisted. The sluggish breeze lifted briefly, flicking her fine black hair across her cheeks.

"He's good," she said. "It looks like he'll be moved to the L.A. office permanently next month, so we'll be able to see each other a lot more. He offered to come down for the funeral, but, you know, then everyone would have to be watching what they say around him..."

"Because he doesn't know about us?" Kess said. "He doesn't *see?*"

"No," Fiona said. "I met him through a client. God, I hate lying to him. But it's not like I can just say, 'By the way, I defend people from demons for a living.'"

"Why not?" Kess said. "He knows you. Wouldn't he believe you?"

"It's more complicated than that," Fiona said.

"Most people, at least in this country, think any kind of magic or supernatural beings are just made-up ideas," Avery put in. "They can't wrap their heads around it no matter who's telling them. The only reason *we* can accept it is because we can't help seeing it."

"And I'm not arranging for Will to witness a Glower killing so we can change that!" Fiona added with a wry shake of her head.

Kess was silent for a moment. "That isn't the only way," she said. "If you wanted... We lack the control to maintain our cover during the final feeding, but we can allow our powers to be visible to any human's eyes at other times as well, if we choose to. I could let him see. If you think it would help."

She peered at Fiona tentatively, as if worried the other woman would take offense. Fiona stared at Kess for a second, her lips parting. Then she seemed to collect herself.

"Oh," she said. "I didn't know that. I— Let me think about it. Thank you for offering."

Kess inclined her head.

A movement near the crest of the hill that overlooked Sterling's gravesite caught my eye. A figure—a young man, I thought at a glance—was striding between the saplings there. A shimmer flared off the edge of his body, and my lungs clenched. A Glower? Why would any other than Kess be here?

As I shifted position to try to get a better look, the sun blazed into my eyes. I blinked away the glare, and the figure was gone. Light beamed around the branches of the trees where he'd been walking. The tension in my chest eased, but didn't quite disappear.

I must have mistaken the effect of the rising sun for something supernatural, I decided. There *wasn't* any reason for another Glower to be wandering around in a graveyard. It hardly seemed like an ideal hunting ground in which to find artists to mark.

"It was good of your mother to offer to host the wake," Mateo was saying to Avery.

"Well, Sterling was the one who brought both of us into the Society," Avery said. "He always looked out for us, even if he got a little overbearing about it sometimes. She wanted to help out somehow." She turned to me. "I guess this has been a pretty chaotic introduction to the Society for you, Sofie. Changing our entire approach to handling Glowers, getting together for funerals... I hope it hasn't been overwhelming."

"Well, I don't know anything different," I said with a smile, touched by her concern. I hadn't spent much time with Avery, but she had a warm, sure presence that I liked. "Mostly I'm glad to be a part of *something*—something that matters. I didn't have much going on in my life one way or another before this."

"Sofie has a strong spirit," Kess said quietly. "She knows how to keep herself steady in a storm."

I met her burgundy-brown eyes, startled, and she gazed back at me calmly. For the first time, I wondered what *she* had seen in me when she'd inspired me to paint. It had been Mateo and the other Tethers I'd fretted about before, but Kess was the one who'd actually connected with me.

But then, she also knew all about keeping secrets. I found her comment didn't bother me. In fact, it hardened a sort of resolve that was forming inside me.

Yes. I was strong. I'd survived an awful lot to make it here. Maybe I hadn't made it unscathed, but I'd gotten out when I needed to. Jace's storm hadn't dragged me down.

"Has Shawn eased up on you at all?" Mateo said.

I stiffened—I'd forgotten about complaining to Mateo—and my cheeks warmed in a way I hoped didn't show. I ducked my head just in case. "He seems happy with how I've been handling things," I said. "We're getting along all right."

I thought I saw Fiona's eyebrow twitch as if in amusement, but before I could come up with a change in subject, a new scent tickled my nose. Smoky, but not the dense tang of wood smoke that had been carrying from the forest fire. That was still lingering in the air, but another smell, lighter and crisper, was lacing through it. I looked around, and my gaze stopped on the crest of the hill again. A figure—the same guy as before, or someone else? I couldn't tell, seeing him mostly in silhouette— was peering down at us. Sunlight gleamed from behind the form, but this time I saw for sure an unearthly glimmer that revealed just a hint of the short-cropped hair and blunt-nosed face turned toward us. My pulse stuttered.

Something was wrong. Alarm bells were going off in my head, and even if I didn't know exactly what they meant, my instincts had served me well in the past.

"There are Glowers around," I said, but even as I nodded toward the hill, the figure slipped away.

Kess followed my gaze, frowning. "Strange," she said. "I wouldn't have expected any presence here. Let me take a look."

She hurried away with steps so fleet she looked as if she were gliding over the grass.

"Why would Glowers be hanging out in a graveyard?" I said to the others.

"It's not something they're known to do," Fiona said. Avery's brow had knit. Colin set his hand on her shoulder.

"There are more Tethers here than you usually see in a week," he said. "If the demons are up to something, they don't stand a chance of getting away with it."

That depends on what they're up to, I thought. The breeze rose again, bringing that lighter burnt smell more strongly to my nose, and the sweat on my back chilled. It didn't seem we could predict anything about the Glowers' behavior these days.

I kind of wished I *had* been brought into the Society during a time when their approach and the responses we could expect had been much simpler.

With a faint crackle, Kess appeared in our midst. Her face was drawn, her eyes wide. "Call the fire department," she said. "And everyone needs to leave."

"What's going on?" Mateo said as he pulled out his phone.

"Someone's started a fire," Kess said. "The grass was dry enough... The blaze is moving this way."

She'd barely finished speaking when one of the mourners on the other side of the gravesite gave a cry. A flickering ripple of flame wavered over the crest of the hill with a wash of that crisp smoke. My pulse skipped. I started backing away as the Tethers around me swiveled to see and then to retreat, jostling against each other and me in their confusion. Fiona grabbed my arm and the bunch of us headed toward the road.

My mouth had gone dry. All I could taste was the smoke. I glanced back at the fire. It was streaming down the hill now, closing in on Sterling's grave. My eyes slid to Kess.

"The Glowers did that," I said. "The one I saw—they did it on purpose." To disrupt and ruin the funeral service?

"Whoever it was had left when I arrived," Kess said. "We can't know..." Under my gaze, she faltered. "If my kind were involved, they weren't the kind that matter," she added firmly. "Some are against any of us associating with the Society. They are the ones we mean to shut out, not any you'd ever work with."

"No one will blame you for this," Avery said, but Mateo looked grim as we hurried on. The smoke was chasing us faster now. Urgent voices carried around us as the other Tethers hustled to their cars.

Of course someone would blame the Glower in our midst for this crime if they realized the demons were behind it. They'd been blaming Kess simply for showing up. Rafaela, or someone like her, would probably claim she arranged the whole thing.

If they realized. It struck me then, with a trickle of cold straight down to my gut, that I might be the only one who'd seen the figure on the hill. The only one who could offer proof of what must have happened.

Eleven

WE REACHED THE ROAD WHERE MOST OF THE MOURNERS
had parked their cars. The other Tethers were piling into their
respective vehicles. Kess gave Mateo a quick kiss and blinked out
of our plane of existence. Colin motioned for Mateo and Fiona
to join him and Avery in his maroon Mercedes. I thought the
gesture might have included me too, but before I could follow, a
firm hand caught my arm.

"Sofie," Shawn said. "Did you take a taxi here?"

"Yeah," I said, "but—" The smoke gusted over us, filling my
throat before I finished my sentence. I couldn't restrain a
shudder. Shawn gazed down at me, his jaw tight. Something
wild had come into his eyes. I was staring at him now, but I
found I didn't want to look away.

"Come on," he said. "I'll give you a drive home. We've got
to get out of here."

I hurried after him to a dented blue minivan toward the
back of the parking area. The heels of my shoes wobbled as the
matted grass clung to them. I dropped into the front passenger

seat after Shawn opened the door for me, but my throat still felt raw, my limbs shaky. The wail of a siren sounded in the distance.

The Glowers hated us so much that they'd gone out of their way to desecrate our commemoration of a dead colleague. Maybe there *wasn't* any way we could ever compromise with them. Maybe Shawn was right to refuse to let down his guard.

That knowledge sat heavy in my gut as Shawn pulled around the cars still parked and turned us toward the gate. I expected him to comment on the fire, to speculate about how it might have been started, maybe even to ask if I'd seen anything, but he stayed silent. All the same, I couldn't relax.

He pulled out onto the main road just a few seconds before the first fire truck careened into view. We'd been driving a few blocks, his knuckles pale where he clutched the steering wheel, before he said, "I guess it'd be easier if I asked you to remind me of your address."

"You didn't memorize it last time?" I heard myself say. "I'm disappointed."

The joke fell flat, at least in part because of the quaver in my voice. We stopped at a red light, and Shawn let go of the steering wheel long enough to squeeze my hand.

"Are you okay?" he said.

"Just a little shaken up," I said. "It's not every day you get run out of a funeral by a flash fire, right?"

"No, it's not."

I gave him the address of my apartment building, and we drove on in silence. He'd already been heading in the right direction, so I guessed he'd at least noted the neighborhood when we'd paused there on our way to the club the other night.

The smoky smell dissipated as the air conditioning licked over us. I sank lower in the worn leather seat and closed my eyes. When I did, the image of the glimmering figure at the top of the hill stared back at me. I tried to blink it away.

Why were there so many beings in the world who did so many horrible things?

I trained my gaze instead on the pine air freshener dangling from the mirror. The minivan rumbled along with periodic thrums of its engine.

"This isn't exactly the car I'd have pictured you driving," I said to break the silence.

Shawn's lips crooked up into a half smile. "My mother left it behind when she took off," he said. "It may not be the most stylish ride, but you can't argue with free. And it's useful when Lisa—my niece—and her friends need carting around."

His niece. Talking about her had dredged up that sadness in him when he'd spoken about her before, so I didn't ask more about that. "Makes sense," I said, and then couldn't think of anything else to add. Then all of a sudden Shawn was pulling into the drive outside my building.

I glanced over at him as he set the car into park. I could imagine myself stepping out, walking to the elevator, down the hall, and into my apartment alone—feeling the emptiness of the space around me echoing with all the people I'd left behind. The thought made my stomach knot.

The wake wasn't for another couple hours. I wasn't sure I'd even want to be there, surrounded by people making accusations about the fire. People who might be looking for answers I wasn't sure I wanted to be the one to offer.

I didn't want to think about home, or Glowers, or any of the rest of the mess in my life.

"Will you come up?" I said to Shawn. "There are visitor spots in the parking garage."

Shawn gave me a long look. I could feel him considering my

suggestion in the warmth his gaze traced on my skin. He smoothed his hand over his knee. "I'm not sure that's a wise idea," he said.

"I just... I'd really like some company right now," I said. "But if you don't want to stay—"

"You should know it has nothing to do with what I *want*," Shawn said dryly. "I'm trying to make sure I do the right thing here."

"Shouldn't what's right be at least partly up to me? Anyway, I'm not scheming to drag you into bed the second we get up there."

"No?" he said, with an arch of his eyebrows so devilish I wanted to reconsider scheming.

I made myself shake my head. "We can make a pledge. All clothes will stay on. Safe enough?"

He let out an amused sound as if he still wasn't convinced, but he took the car out of park. "A little saf*er*, at least. Where are those visitor spots?"

I knew asking him up had been right as soon as we stepped into the elevator. Because then I *couldn't* think about the Glowers or anything else—I couldn't think about anything except Shawn standing there just a couple feet from me. Wanting to touch him, knowing I wasn't supposed to. It was a perfect, torturous distraction.

I didn't even consider the state of my apartment until I was unlocking the door. But then, I usually kept my belongings pretty tidy. You learned to avoid taking up much space when a beloved item you happened to leave sitting out might end up bagged in the trash without warning.

Shawn took in the main room with a slow turn of his head. "You moved in here after you were recruited, right?" he said.

I evaluated the place through an outsider's eyes. I'd bought a few things just for my own enjoyment—the brightly patterned quilt draped over the back of the couch, the glazed ceramic bowl I tossed my spare change into—but most of the furnishings were practical, the cheapest stuff I could find that looked like it would hold together. I didn't have any pictures to hang on the walls, photos to stick to the refrigerator's door. Somehow I hadn't felt quite ready to seek out little pieces of meaning to bring home. The space had been comfortable enough without those, but I guessed it might also look unfinished. I remembered Mateo's apartment with its bold paintings hanging on every wall, and longing pinched my gut. I had money now. Maybe I should start making the apartment completely *me*.

"A few months ago," I said, even though it was closer to nine now. "Do you want anything to drink? I've got lemonade and Sprite... and water, of course."

"Lemonade sounds perfect for a day this hot," Shawn said. He hovered by the counter as I opened the fridge. I shooed him away.

"Go sit down," I said. "After this morning, I think we both should be taking it easy."

When I returned to the main room with two sweating glasses of lemonade, Shawn was sitting at one end of the couch, with lots of room left for me. I sat down at the other end, knowing he wanted that distance, resisting the urge to see how much I could close it.

Shawn accepted the glass I handed him and took a long swig. "Homemade?" he asked.

I laughed. "No, I'm a little lacking in the culinary skills department."

"Ah, well, maybe I'll have to teach you a thing or two sometime."

"Are you a kitchen whiz, then?"

He shrugged with a little smile. "I like food, and I've lived on my own since I was nineteen. It was either pick up a few skills or spend way too much money on takeout."

Nineteen. When he'd joined the Society? He couldn't have been much older than that when he'd seen his first Glower, or he wouldn't have the ten years' experience to place him among the senior Tethers.

"All right, the verdict's in," I said teasingly. "Clearly you are the perfect man."

He laughed this time, a rough chuckle. "Oh, I'm far from perfect. You don't know me that well yet."

"I think I know enough." I dared to reach out my leg and nudge his calf with my toes. Shawn shot me a look so smoldering I nearly fanned myself. I gulped my lemonade instead. "So what do you like to cook?"

"Sometimes I go for stereotypical guy foods: burgers, wings, steak. But I appreciate a good curry too, even if I can't replicate restaurant quality. And pad thai. I make a mean pad thai, if I do say so myself."

"Okay, then you definitely need to teach me some things," I said.

"Thai fan?" he said.

"Anything spicy. There was hardly anywhere to get it near... near where I grew up." That was one thing I'd loved about L.A. from the start. But remembering home, with the single Chinese restaurant with its white-people level spicing, brought back that hollow feeling inside that I was trying to escape.

"Pretty small town, I take it?" Shawn said. Interest had lit in his eyes. I decided I could manage to talk about it as long as I focused on him.

"Really small. But there were a few other little towns nearby, so we used the resources available in all of them. One had a library. One had the schools. One had the best shopping. You got to know which direction to head in depending on what you were looking for."

"That's hard for me to imagine after growing up here. You don't find the big city overwhelming?"

I bit my lip as I considered my answer. Shawn's gaze dropped to my mouth, and a flush tingled over my skin. "I did a little, at first," I said honestly, forcing myself to stay on topic. "But I'd been to Phoenix a bunch of times, so it wasn't as if I'd never seen any cities at all. And I do like all the energy here."

"I bet you do," Shawn said, his eyes on mine again, with a grin that was almost a smirk.

He hadn't complained the first time I'd nudged him, so I did it again, letting my toes linger against his slacks this time. "What's that supposed to mean?"

"Only that you seem like the kind of woman who likes to be in the middle of things."

"I guess that's reasonably accurate." It was too hard just sitting here while he smiled at me, looked at me, like that. My self-control was slackening, and I hardly cared. I set my glass on the coffee table. Then I extended my arm along the back of the couch so I could touch his shoulder.

Shawn closed his eyes as I ran my fingers over the sharp curves of the muscles there. "Sofie," he said, softly but with a warning note.

"I want to paint you some time," I said, ignoring his tone. I hadn't realized how true that statement was until it came out of my mouth. "You have... a very nice form."

I was pretty sure *I* was smirking now. Shawn chuckled again. "Is that what the ladies are calling it these days?"

"That's what I'm calling it."

He caught my hand as it started to trail farther down his arm, his gaze turning serious.

"So what about you?" I said, scrambling to divert him from telling me I'd pushed too far. "You must have gone to some huge high school here before you ended up with the Society, right? Isn't it weird taking classes with so many other people you don't even know all their names?"

His eyebrows twitched, but he accepted my change in subject. He kept my hand in his almost like an afterthought, his thumb tracing the lines of the bones in a way that made it difficult for me to focus on his answer.

"It doesn't feel that isolating while you're there," he said. "You get to know more people than you might think. And you have your group of friends that you mostly hang out with—they're your community."

"Do you still see any of those people?" I asked, thinking back to the conversation with Fiona in the graveyard. "Or is it too awkward when you can't talk about what you really do?"

"I hang out with a few of the guys sometimes. Watch sports, catch a movie. We just don't get into anything too personal."

"You don't like letting people in," I guessed, shifting forward so I could tap his chest. His grasp on my hand slid to my wrist. I could smell him now, a warm tart scent like mulled apple cider over a more primal musk. My heart skipped a beat.

"The more tangled up you get with people, the more complicated life becomes," Shawn said. He halted my arm before I could trace my fingers down his sternum. Our skin slid together, pale and dark, the coarse hair on his forearm sending pleasant shivers through me.

"This is getting dangerous," he said.

"I know," I said. "I don't care. I can handle it."

"Sofie," he started, that serious expression coming back.

"You don't get it," I said before he could go on. "You don't know how long it's been since I've felt this *good* with a guy. I promise you, you're not going to hurt me in any way close to what I've already been through. If you really want to keep waiting, I'll respect that. But what *I* want is to have as much of that good feeling as I can get away with, as much as you're willing to share with me right now. So please, don't stop for my sake."

Shawn stared at me. His chest rose and fell with his breath, less than an inch from my fingertips. His grip tightened around my arm.

"Screw it," he said, and tugged me in for a kiss.

He kissed with the same heat as in the club, sure and powerful. The taste of the lemonade lingered in both our mouths, deliciously sweet and sour. Kneeling on the couch next to him, I kissed him back until I was dizzy. His hands laced into my hair and then slipped down over my shoulders. I explored the planes of his chest that he'd guarded from me a minute ago. As he turned more toward me, my thumbs found the nubs of his nipples through the smooth fabric of his shirt. He sucked in a breath as I circled them. His tongue tangled around mine, drawing me in even deeper.

His hands roamed down to the back of my dress. As they ran over the zipper there, I pulled back just far enough to murmur, "Clothes stay on, remember? That was the deal."

"Right," he said. "Right." The haze of lust in his eyes cleared into a wicked sharpness. "I can work with that. Let's see how good you can feel, Sofie."

He cupped my breasts through my dress, holding my gaze. The thin polyester hardly diminished the heat of his skin, the pressure of his palms. His thumbs arced up against the thicker covering of my bra. Not so thick that it prevented them from finding my already hardening nipples. A gasp caught in my throat. Shawn smiled as he flicked his thumbs over those two little points. Then he pushed himself forward to catch my mouth again.

I leaned back on the couch, my whimper of pleasure muffled by the kiss. My hips canted up of their own accord as Shawn teased my nipples even tighter. He followed me, his knee sliding between my legs. The texture of his slacks against my bare inner thigh radiated over my skin. The skirt of my dress had ridden up, but that wasn't the same as taking it off. That seemed completely unavoidable in the midst of the pleasure spiking through me.

Shawn trailed his lips over my cheek and down my neck, still caressing my breasts. I pressed against him, wanting even more. My hips bowed up again, and a moan broke from my mouth as the core of me brushed against his leg. God, I wanted him so much.

"Ah," Shawn muttered against my throat. One of his hands left my breast to travel over my side, along my thigh, and into the space between my legs. I moaned again as he stroked me through my panties, and he let out a groan in return.

"The things I'd like to do to you," he said.

"I can't wait," I said, breathless as he tongued my collarbone. His hands stilled. He lifted himself up a few inches so we could look each other in the eyes. My body ached at the loss of contact.

"If you ever change your mind, or you feel we're going too far, I want you to tell me," he said. "Stopping this—I swear I wouldn't let it affect your job, your place in the Society—"

I set my hand against his chest, feeling his heart thumping against my palm.

"I know," I said. "I'm not afraid of you. Now come back here."

He gave a halting laugh and bent over me again. As he kissed me, hard and hot, he reached down to adjust our position so my legs splayed around his hips. Then he ran his hand down my back to my butt, urging me up toward him. The core of me lifted to meet the hard bulge in his slacks. He eased himself up and down against me until I pulled my lips from his to cry out. The friction sent tremors up to my head and down to my toes. I raised my knees to give him better access, arching into him with each thrust of his thighs.

"I want you inside me, so badly," I murmured, and gasped as he rocked against me even harder.

Shawn made a choked sound. "Not yet," he said. "That'd be breaking the rules."

I didn't care anymore about the rule I'd set down, but the spiraling high of pleasure was carrying me too far away for me to say that. I gave myself over to the sensations, riding them as my hips started to tremble and my breath caught. My orgasm crashed over me like a wave, shaking a sigh from my lips. I kept moving with Shawn, stretching the moment as far as I could. Then, with a grunt, he pressed his mouth to my shoulder. We sagged into the couch cushions, swaying to a stop together.

Shawn burrowed his face into my hair for a few seconds before he rolled to the side, cradling me against him. "Holy hell, Sofie. I haven't been with a woman who could make me come in my pants since I was fifteen."

Without thinking, I slid my hand down. Dampness was spreading across the crotch of his slacks, even wetter than my panties must be. My face flared.

"I'm sorry. I've got tissues, or—"

He wrapped his arm around me before I could get up,

pulling me against him. "Don't apologize for that. I'll clean up when I'm ready to let go of you. It's just a pair of pants. More than worth it. You're spectacular, Sofie."

At the unbridled satisfaction in his voice, my body relaxed. I nestled against him, listening to the rush of his breath over my hair, and for a moment or two I truly did feel spectacular.

Twelve

EVEN THOUGH EVERYONE IN THE CONFERENCE ROOM WAS
keeping their voice low, the tension in the air was thick enough
that I could taste it.

"With Sterling gone, we need to table any discussion about
this proposal."

"It can't work when we're never going to be able to trust the
Glowers."

"Don't you think *she* must be getting something out of this
that she's not saying?"

The *she* in question, Kess, stood close to Mateo at the front
of the room. She'd come alone, the only Glower who'd been
invited, and then only at Mateo's insistence. The senior Tethers
had refused to meet with a larger Glower delegation again.

"We're still willing to move forward," Kess said now. "My
people understand that the interruption of our last meeting
wasn't an intentional move by the entire Society, only a rogue
protester."

"And what about the fire in the cemetery?" Rafaela said, her voice rising. "Are we really going to pretend we don't know the Glowers must have been responsible for that? Do we want to deal with creatures who can't even respect our grief for the dead?"

"We don't *know* it had anything to do with the Glowers, or even with us," the man next to her pointed out. "It could have been a random prank."

But it hadn't been. I knew that. My teeth gritted. Was it better to say something or to stay out of the argument?

My eyes caught Kess's. She was watching me, not pleading or accusing but simply observing. As if she knew the dilemma I was working through.

Mateo had been there for our conversation. He wasn't mentioning what I'd seen. But then, I supposed he could justify staying silent on the basis that he hadn't witnessed anything incriminating himself. Now, he sidestepped the issue completely, lifting his voice above the others to get the whole group's attention.

"Nothing has actually changed," he said. "You all know Sterling would have wanted us to proceed with this program. Shouldn't we respect *his* opinions by giving it a real chance?"

There was a momentary silence. Then Shawn spoke up. My skin warmed at his voice even as I dreaded hearing what he'd say on this subject.

"Why not at least put proceedings on hold and wait until we've had time to adjust to Sterling being gone?" he suggested. "The Society isn't going anywhere; the Glowers aren't going anywhere. It seems to me that rushing ahead is going to cause more problems than being cautious. If the Glowers react badly to a little delay, well, then we'll know they weren't that committed in the first place."

I let out my breath. His words hadn't been half as critical as I'd feared they'd be. And he had a point.

Why was I hiding something so important from my colleagues? They should have all the facts so they could make a reasoned decision.

I'd almost convinced myself to open my mouth when Rafaela let out a huff.

"How can anyone believe they're really committed even now? Look at what they're doing *every day*! Come on, people— don't let this one fool you with her pretense at being human. She's just as much a shark as the rest of them. A predator. A *monster*. We can't afford to give them even a sliver of a chance. I've been saying it all along, and it's time the rest of you woke up."

Kess didn't quite manage to restrain her wince as a few voices muttered in agreement. Mateo grabbed her hand. My stomach turned.

No. Rafaela was wrong. I'd touched souls with Kess, and I hadn't felt a single predatory impulse in her.

But my discomfort prickled even deeper than that concern. The sort of expansive, exaggerated talk Rafaela was using, poking at people's fears, making the situation seem all or nothing—I'd heard it before. Jace had liked to talk that way. It was how he convinced people he was an expert on one thing or another. Sometimes that he was the expert on me, or on something I wanted to do that he didn't think I should. And people listened, then and now.

I swallowed down the admission I'd been about to make. What good was speaking up going to do if it would only upset people even more? Sure, what I'd seen was a "fact," but it was a fact that wasn't even relevant to the debate. Kess had been right when she'd said the Glowers who'd set the fire had nothing to do with the proposal. They were trying to stop it, just like Rafaela and whoever had set up that banishing circle the other day—if it wasn't her. If anything, the Glowers who'd interrupted Sterling's funeral were on the *same* side as her.

That last thought hit me with a lurch in my gut. I looked around the room again, hearing the voices now near shouting, seeing the angry flush coloring so many faces. My hands balled at my sides. I did need to speak up. I just had to make sure I was saying something that mattered.

"Stop it!" I said before I could think twice.

The Tethers quieted. Kess peered at me curiously. Shawn was staring at me too, his brow furrowed with what might have been worry or discomfort. I couldn't let myself wonder which. I'd watched one life career out of existence because I'd been too scared to speak. I wasn't going to risk this plan and all the dozens, hundreds, thousands of people *it* might save.

"You're being ridiculous," I barreled on. "Maybe I haven't been in the Society for very long, but I have to say it. I *haven't* been part of this organization very long, but I'm still willing to take a chance, to see if the Glowers can work with us instead of against us. Why aren't the rest of you? If your first priority really is your clients and not avoiding anything that makes you nervous, then you should be trying every possibility that comes your way to put them in a better situation. Do you *really* think we're so incompetent that we wouldn't notice if our trial runs end up doing more harm than good, so we could stop the program then? All this arguing, all this resistance to even giving it a shot... I expected people here to be above that."

Rafaela's mouth had fallen open. For a moment, no one spoke. I couldn't tell whether the expressions aimed at me were ashamed or annoyed or what. But I'd meant every word I'd said.

I was glad I'd said it. The certainty of that burned like a tiny flame in my chest.

Rafaela drew in a breath as if to say something, but Mateo beat her to it. "All I'm asking for is another meeting," he said. "They come, we talk with them, we work through all our concerns. We can pull out at *any* stage if we see a real reason to. Please. This mattered so much to Sterling. Give it a fair try."

One by one, heads around the room began to nod. My hands unclenched. Maybe the whole proposal would still come falling down, but at least we were going to see it through as far as we could.

The convention center was buzzing even late in the day. Amid the throng of video game enthusiasts, the humidity kept rising, the vast building's air conditioning struggling to keep up. I swiped at the back of my neck as I followed Demirci, who'd just finished speaking on his last panel, along the carpeted path to the glass-walled foyer.

Demirci accepted greetings and compliments as he went, but his gaze kept scanning the crowd beyond his obvious fans. At one point he stopped, frowning and staring, before pushing himself onward again. I didn't like how jumpy he seemed. I hadn't noticed any Glowers around this afternoon, and Shawn hadn't mentioned any sightings either, but our client clearly had other troubles.

I caught up with him at the security boundary only official guests could cross. "Everything all right?" I said.

"What do you mean?" Demirci asked, the look he shot me so sharp it was almost a glare.

I eased back a step. Antagonizing the client would only

make my job more difficult. "You look as if you're expecting to see someone in particular. Maybe... that guy you talked to in the bar the other day?"

Demirci's expression shuttered. "Maybe you should mind what's actually your business. Who I talk to? Isn't." He turned away, shaking his head and muttering something about stalkers that I suspected was referring to Shawn and me.

Shawn had come up beside me. I rubbed my mouth. "Well, that didn't go so well," I said. "Something's up with him, though."

"From what you said you saw, it doesn't have anything to do with Glowers," Shawn said. "At least not so far. So it isn't our domain. We'll keep on keeping an eye on him. If there's something we can help with, it almost always comes out eventually."

He didn't sound worried, but he hadn't seen how Demirci had looked when he was talking to the straw-haired guy. Anything that threw off our client's mood made him easier prey for Glowers. And now he was done his work here. We didn't have license to protect him beyond the convention center doors.

But I was going to stick with him at least that far. Demirci had grabbed the shoulder bag he'd stashed in the special guest area. He stalked past us to the main entrance without a word. I hurried along after him. I was so focused on him, wondering what was up and who that mystery guy was, that I didn't register there was something different about the crowd around the security point until voices started hollering.

"Aydin Demirci, can you give a few comments for Game Watch?"

"Mr. Demirci, The Interactive Report would love to hear your thoughts on the new developments in the indie scene!"

Demirci slowed and raised a hand that appeared partly

acknowledging and partly waving off. "I'm on three more panels tomorrow," he said. "You can hear me speak and ask me questions then. A guy needs a break after a whole day here talking."

"Mr. Demirci!" the chorus started up again as I reached his side. This time it was with the click and flash of cameras. The flickering light caught my eyes. Caught *me*.

My pulse stuttered. They were taking photos of him for their magazines and blogs—photos I could end up in. Photos *anyone* could see.

My first reaction was complete instinct: I flinched, my arm shooting up to cover my face, my feet stumbling backward. A hand touched my shoulder. I was already jerking away when Shawn's voice washed over me.

"Sofie," he said. "What's the matter?"

"I just—" My mouth was too dry. Demirci had stopped to say something to one of the journalists a few feet down the line. The flashes were still going off, brilliant bursts of light. Each one made my chest clench tighter. I grasped Shawn's arm. "I don't want to be in any photos," I managed to say.

"Come on then," he said gently. "Let's follow the client. I'll stay on this side of you."

We walked together, Shawn's muscular frame hiding me from view. Demirci moved on, and we trailed a careful distance behind. What were the chances the news sources would use a photo I'd been in? *Very low*, I thought in an attempt to reassure myself. No one cared about some random girl who happened to be walking near the star video game designer. They'd pick an image with just him. It'd be okay.

My heart thudded on, unconvinced.

On the sidewalk outside, Demirci gave us a wary nod before flagging a cab. Then he was gone—off to his condo, I hoped, and not anywhere a Glower might find him in his current emotional state. I dragged in the hot, heavy air and swallowed thickly.

Shawn rested his hand on my back. Even as I longed to lean into him for comfort, I didn't want to look at him. I'd totally freaked out, for the second time this month. And this time in public. That couldn't have looked good. Our relationship, whatever it was, wouldn't be what screwed up my place in the Society. My inability to function properly on the job was screwing that up all on its own.

"Let's walk," Shawn said.

I let him guide me away from the convention center. Beyond its floodlights, the streets were dim, only a faint glow of fading sunlight penetrating the murky clouds overhead. Thunder rumbled distantly. At least if it rained, the downpour might wash away some of the stickiness in the air. I was sick of sweating buckets.

There weren't many people out on the street once we'd left the convention center several blocks behind. I kept my gaze on the sidewalk, barely noting the buildings we passed. Waiting.

"Are you going to tell me what that was about?" Shawn said finally.

"Do I have to?" I muttered.

I sensed his wry smile. "Technically I can't *order* you to, but... it would help me a lot if I understood where you were coming from. Why you reacted that way. And I'm not just asking as your observing Tether. You were scared. If there's something you feel you need to be scared of, I'd like to know, in case I can do something about it. Because I care."

He cared. About me. A lump rose in my throat. I hadn't really thought it through, jumping into this thing with him. If the relationship was going to turn into something real, something more than a make-out here and there, then I was going to have to be real with him. As much as *that* scared me.

I'd trusted this man with my body. I'd trusted him with my career. I should trust him with the truth about my past too. He deserved it.

I raised my head, and recognition struck me. We'd wandered in the direction of my former workplace. The art gallery with its giant airplane parts pigeon-shaped sculpture was a few blocks ahead of us. My entire time with the Society, come full circle. My journey to becoming a Tether had started here. Maybe telling Shawn the truth would mean that journey came to an end. But I was carrying so many secrets now. One needed to come out.

I inhaled deeply, past the tightness in my throat.

"I'm not who I told the Society I was," I said. "My name's not even Sofie."

Thirteen

We kept walking, side by side. Shawn stayed silent, as if giving me space for my confession. I twisted my hands together in front of me.

"I got into a... bad situation, back home," I said. "This guy I was with— At first it was really good. One of those whirlwind teenage romances. Maybe there were warning signs, but I didn't see them. But then he started picking away at all different parts of my life, making me question everything. Whether my family and friends were really looking out for me, if they even *liked* me. Whether there was any point in trying to make it as an artist. Whether I had anything important to say about anything. Whether anyone else could ever be remotely interested in me as a girlfriend."

I paused to take a breath. Shawn reached out and took my hand. The pressure of his palm against mine reminded me how wrong Jace had been.

"I was only sixteen when we first got together. I'd dated a couple guys before but nothing at all serious. I didn't know...

what was normal. And the bad parts just sort of crept up on me. Before I realized it, I was acting kind of weird around everyone I knew, and they started acting as if there were something off about me—and he was always there to step in and reassure people that I was just dealing with some 'tough emotional stuff' or whatever, making it sound like he was my stoic protector and I wasn't right in the head. By then I was eighteen and he was twenty, he'd gotten his own place, and he'd convinced me to move in with him even though my parents weren't keen on it. He'd do things like spend all day talking about how this person or that person thought all these awful things about me, until I didn't want to do anything but stay buried in bed, and then he'd go out to whatever get-togethers were happening and tell everyone that I'd decided I didn't care about hanging out with people anymore. I know it sounds stupid when I just say it. It's not like he ever hit me or pushed me around. He never hurt me physically. But for such a long time, I felt so alone. I felt like I *was* going crazy."

"You're not crazy," Shawn said. There was an edge in his voice. His hand tightened around mine. "And a person doesn't have to hit you to be hurting you."

"I know," I said. "The situation got to the point where I knew I'd ruined my relationships with everyone I used to be able to turn to, but I was so miserable with him that I couldn't stand to stay. But I was afraid of what he'd do if I tried to leave the regular way. Afraid he'd find a way to convince me I should stay. Afraid he might start getting physical then. Afraid if I asked anyone for help, they'd go to him for guidance and believe his version of what was going on over mine..." My voice caught. Thunder rumbled again as I gathered my words. "The only way I was sure he'd leave me alone was if no one knew where I was. So I ordered a fake ID with a new name over the internet. I grabbed all the stuff I thought I needed, and one day when he was at work, I got on a bus and came here. So I could find out who I was, without him there."

"And have you found out?" Shawn said.

"I guess," I said. "Mostly. But I was with him for three and a half years, and that kind of damage, it stays with you. It sticks in your head. I have to spend a lot of time arguing against the things he would have said when I'm trying to think for myself. And I'm still scared of what he'd do if he found out where I am. I think it'd piss him off more than anything that I managed to get away from him so completely."

"That's why you didn't want to be in the photos," Shawn said. "In case he came across them and recognized you, figured out where you are."

"Yeah," I said. We came up on the edge of the art gallery's courtyard with its bizarre statue. The spot where I'd seen my first Glower. I halted there, toeing the cement tiles. "I didn't try to disguise myself—change my hair, my makeup, any of that. I thought I was far enough away, anonymous enough, that there was no way I had to worry about being caught. Maybe I should have done something after I started this line of work."

"I can't blame you for not thinking of it," Shawn said. "It's not as if it's a problem that comes up often. Normally the press focuses on the client and we're keeping enough distance to be out of the picture. You probably only ran into that situation with Demirci because the convention was so informal."

"So you think I can still be a Tether, even with... everything?" I said.

He touched my cheek with his free hand, tipping my face as I looked into his eyes. "Of course," he said. "I think you have all the makings of a *great* Tether. I think that even more than I did before. You know what it's like to be in the grip of a predator.

You know how important it is to save people from experiencing that. You've shown you're strong enough to fight for yourself. I know you'll do the same for the clients."

"Yeah," I said softly, entranced by his gaze. Those intent brown eyes held mine. He was right, I thought. Speaking up against Rafaela at the meeting, puzzling out what was bothering Demirci, it all made me feel even stronger. More like myself, or who I was meant to be. "Are you going to tell the Society that I lied to them—I mean, about my name and all?"

Shawn hesitated. "I don't see any reason to right now," he said. "Do you think they should know?"

"No," I said. "The fewer people who have my real name, the fewer places it could turn up, the safer I feel."

"I understand that." His thumb stroked up down the side of my face, sending shivers of anticipation in its wake. "Can I ask you what your real name is? Just for me to know. I won't tell anyone."

I found I wanted him to know. One last step to being completely real. "It's Sarah," I said. "Sarah Johnson. I always thought it was such a plain name—I wanted one that sounded more exotic, like a European debutante or something." A short laugh jerked from my throat. "That seems silly now. But it felt good when I picked it."

"Nothing wrong with feeling good," Shawn said, the roughness in his voice sending another shiver through me. "I think 'Sofie' suits you. And you know what else? I like that it's a name that other guy has no hold over. I don't want you to ever have to think of him when you're with me, when I talk to you. If I do anything that rubs you the wrong way—"

"You haven't," I said quickly. "I don't think you would."

"So that's why you didn't have any friends to celebrate your birthday with," he said. "You've lost everyone you would have counted on before. That's got to be tough."

I shrugged. "It is. But not as tough as staying there living the way I was. And I'm finding new people to count on. Like you."

He gazed down at me as I smiled up at him. His hand stilled against my cheek. In that instant, I was sure he was going to kiss me. I wanted him too, so badly my lips ached.

Then the thunder boomed directly over our heads, and the sky opened up, letting loose a torrent of rain.

In a second, I was drenched. The rain washed away the day's heat and sweat, streaming through my hair and into my clothes. Shawn swore, but with a hint of laughter underneath. Grinning, I grabbed his hand and pulled him toward the art gallery's long, arched portico that sheltered the area in front of the doors.

Ducking out of the downpour into that space was like stepping into a dim room. The museum doors were dark—it was a couple hours past closing. The rain gushing past the portico on the other three sides drowned out all but a glint of the streetlamps.

Shawn swiped a hand over his wet hair, sending droplets of moisture flying. His shirt was plastered to his chest, showing off every detail of that impressive musculature. I wasn't content just to look. Giddy with the weight of so many secrets spilled out of me, I shook my own hair back from my face, brought my hands to his shoulders, and bobbed up on my feet to kiss him.

He kissed me back hard, his lips slick with the rain. His body warmed mine where it pressed against me, fending off the chill of the damp. I wound my arms behind his neck. His came around my waist. We kissed and kissed as a deeper heat kindled in my chest and between my legs. His thumbs ran back and forth over my ribs, sending an eager tremble through me.

"Damn it, Sofie," he muttered as his mouth broke from

mine. He walked me backward a few steps to the side of the building. I let myself lean against the glass-paned door, gazing up at him in the near dark. His throat worked. He brushed his mouth over my cheek, my jaw, the curve of my throat. His hands slid over my body, down my sides and back up to my breasts. I arched into his touch, the contact feeling too distant with my bra in the way.

Shawn seemed to have the same idea. He withdrew his hands to my murmur of protest, only to slip them up under my damp shirt. I sighed as his hot fingers trailed over my skin.

"Clothes stay on," I reminded him, though my commitment to that rule had never been shakier.

Shawn chuckled. "I'm not taking anything *off.* Just... adjusting."

He eased me away from the door so he could reach behind me. His hands found the clasp of my bra and unhooked it. Then his thighs pinned me to the glass again as his fingers shifted the bra to explore the naked territory beneath.

A sharp gasp escaped my throat as he rolled my nipples with his thumbs. My hips canted against his. Shawn caught my mouth again, drinking in my sighs and whimpers as he teased one peak pebble-hard and then the other. He edged the bra up so it lay against my collarbone and lowered his head.

Sparks of pleasure shot through me as he suckled me through the thin fabric of my shirt. My head tipped back against the glass. The rough texture of the wet fabric and the delicate movements of his tongue combined in a sensation so heady I couldn't hold back a moan. I clutched Shawn's head as he released one nipple to attend to the other. His hand took over where his lips had been, caressing the tip even harder.

When he raised his head to kiss me on the mouth again, I took the opportunity to reach under his shirt in turn. His muscles tensed as my fingers roamed over them, his skin hot, his heart thumping as fast as mine. He shifted against me, and the thick bulge of his hard-on fit into the space between my open thighs. I sucked in a breath as he rubbed against that needy part of me. I wanted him *in* me, but against me to the point of release would do for now if that kept his conscience clean.

"Sofie," Shawn muttered again. His hand traced down the curve of my torso to rest on the button of my jeans. "Not taking anything off," he repeated. "Just adjusting."

"Adjust away," I said, breathless.

He leaned his head close to mine as he popped open the button and eased down the zipper. My skin burned in anticipation.

"A week from now," he murmured in that low, husky voice that had made me melt from the very first time I'd heard it, "I'll be stripping the pants right off you. The panties too." He dipped his fingers down over those panties to my core. I gasped, bucking to meet him. He rubbed me there, smiling at the whimpers I tried to muffle against his neck. Then he retreated just far enough to slip his hand under the soft fabric, cupping me skin to skin.

"I'm going to slide right inside you," he went on, as his forefinger did just that. I moaned again, riding his hand. "Fill you up. Take you all the way over the edge. As many times as you want me too." He added a second finger, plunging all the way to the pressure point inside that sent a wash of pure bliss through me. My arms tightened around him, my legs wobbling. "I'm going to make you come like no one else ever has. I want to give you everything, Sofie. I want you to feel as spectacular as I know you are."

He sped up his rhythm, and I was helpless to do anything but cling to him, swaying as he took me closer and closer to that edge. My scalp tingled and my breath shuddered. Pleasure swept through me again and again, cresting higher each time. Then it crashed over me with fireworks behind my eyes. My limbs went slack, my body contracting around Shawn's fingers. He carried me through with several more gentling strokes, and then bent to kiss me.

"Is that a promise?" I asked through my haze of bliss. "Everything you just said?"

He grinned. "You can count it as one if you like."

I did like. I liked it so much that for one brief shivering moment, it scared me.

Fourteen

"So that's the entire plan, as we see it now," Mateo said. "Does it sound reasonable to you? If you need time to discuss amongst yourselves, that's fine, of course."

The group of senior Tethers and Kess's delegation of Glowers had gathered again, this time in a corporate rental space in a building just a few blocks from the Society's office. Mateo had come in first to check the floor, walls, chairs, and scattered tables for any sign of tampering. He'd only given Kess the go-ahead to bring the others when he was sure the room was safe.

"It is mostly as we expected," said the Glower standing next to Kess, who'd taken the form of a burly, bearded man. "But we would appreciate some clarifications. For example, how often would any of us be allowed to feed from the same client? With smaller feedings, we will need them more frequently to properly sustain ourselves."

"I've managed with one a month," Kess said to him quietly.

"Not all of us find toeing the edge of starvation an acceptable situation," he retorted.

Even from the back of the room, I'd sensed since they first appeared that some tension had lingered after the last meeting's unexpected banishing. Apparently it extended even to their own. I bit my lip.

"The frequency will depend in part on the clients' wishes," Mateo said, drawing their attention back to him. "They're agreeing to this exchange for their own benefit, remember. If they're getting good work done because of the pairing, I don't see any reason they might not want your 'services' as often as once or twice a week."

His gaze sought me out through the other assembled Tethers. I stepped a little closer. "From what I've experienced during the trial transfers I've done with Kess, I don't see any reason that wouldn't be true," I put in, raising my voice so everyone could hear. "The process hasn't had any lingering effects that I could see making someone hesitate."

"That might change in an on-going arrangement," one of the Tethers near me remarked.

"Well, then we could adapt how we're handling the arrangements based on the data we're seeing, couldn't we?" I said. "Or I can work with Kess twice a week for a few months and see if any issues develop before we move forward. If that's what it takes, I'm okay with that."

Shawn had been leaning against one of the tables near the broad window. Now he straightened up. "You don't have to go that far, Sofie," he said.

It was the first time he'd acknowledged me as someone he knew in front of the other Society members, I realized. I looked back at him, reading the concern in his eyes, not entirely comfortable with it. I liked that he made *me* feel safe, that he wanted to protect me, but I knew far too well that I didn't want to be over-protected.

"I know," I said. "I wouldn't offer if I didn't feel sure."

He bowed his head in acknowledgment, and the tightness that had clenched my chest released. He wasn't Jace. He wasn't anything like Jace at all.

"I think once a week should be fully satisfactory," the Glower who'd spoken up allowed.

"There's also the matter of availability," said one of the other Glowers, who looked like a girl not out of her teens. "There are many of us. How many clients will we be given access to?"

"Again," Mateo said, "that will depend on their interest and agreement. But if you make the experience productive and pleasant for them, they're more likely to want to continue. We would do our best to make sure every Glower who wishes to work with us is in a position to do so. That's an area where you might be able to offer additional support, if you wanted. If you help us keep those of your kind who still wish to mark and kill away from our existing clients, we'll be freed up to bring more clients on board. Everyone wins."

Except the murdering demons, I thought. And good riddance to them.

A third Glower murmured something to Kess in their language. "One minute," she said to the rest of us. The group of Glowers turned away, drawing together near a corner of the room. The conversation I could overhear was all unfamiliar words, but the tone was urgent.

"Are you sure it would be a wise idea handing over some of our protective duties to *them*?" one of the Tethers said to Mateo.

"It isn't something we've discussed," Rafaela added, with a sharp look at Mateo.

"No," Mateo agreed. "But it's something Sterling and I had talked about. We didn't think it should be included in the initial proposal, so we hadn't brought it up. But it *is* a possibility, if all is going well and we feel we can trust the Glowers who've allied with us. I wanted to let them know the option might be there. If anything, it'll give them more incentive to work with us rather than against us."

"I think we're better off if they don't see any other choice," she muttered.

"No," I said, unable to stay quiet. I faltered when Rafaela turned her glare on me, but managed to find the words I'd wanted to say. "When a person agrees to something because they think they have no options, they're always looking for a way out. They'll jump at a chance to get away even if it isn't a good one, just because they feel trapped. It's so much better having the choice and making it properly."

I hoped it wasn't obvious I was speaking from personal experience. I felt Shawn's gaze on me, but I didn't let myself look at him.

Rafaela sighed. "We'll see," she said.

On the other side of the room, the teenager-looking Glower had split off from the others, her expression unhappy. She paced to the wall and back a couple times before wandering restlessly along the edge of the room. She paused just as I noticed small sheaf of folded paper sitting on one of the side tables. Her brow knit, and she reached to pick it up.

"What's that?" I said to Mateo, nodding toward the Glower. "I don't remember there being papers sitting out before."

Mateo followed my gaze and stiffened. "There weren't," he said. "Did someone put something down there?" He glanced around the Tethers and was met with only puzzled expressions. When he got no response, he spun on his heel. He'd barely taken two steps when the Glower gave a cry. She rushed to the others, waving the papers and shooting a dark look toward us.

Mateo reached the Glowers just as Kess took the papers. She

frowned as she perused them. When she offered them to Mateo, the Glower who'd found them tried to snatch them back.

"Don't give that to him," she snarled. "He'll make up some explanation like he did for the banishing. It's obvious what their real motivations are. We shouldn't listen to another word."

Kess ignored her and handed the papers over. Mateo scanned them, his mouth twisting. When he looked up at the rest of the Tethers again as we clustered closer around him to find out what was happening, frustration radiated off of him.

"Who did this?" he snapped. "Why can't you let us work things out properly? Who here is so selfish that you can't care about anything other than how *you* want to see this turn out?"

"What is it?" I asked.

"A report outlining our supposed 'plan' for controlling the Glowers and forcing them into servitude," Mateo said with a scoff. He held it out for a moment. I skimmed the first several lines, my stomach sinking. It looked almost legit. It looked like exactly the sort of thing the Glowers would suspect us of.

Mateo turned back to the Glowers. "This isn't true," he said, waving the fake report. "We've never talked about, and would never talk about, anything like this. Someone made it up and left it for you to find so they could break up our negotiations all over again."

"Why should we believe you?" the bearded Glower asked.

"If for no other reason, because hopefully you can at least believe that if we *were* planning something like this, we'd never be so stupid as to leave a report about it lying around in a room we've never used before today, where we knew you'd be coming to talk to us?" Mateo said. "Or because it's an *idiotic* imaginary plan if you stop to think about the details for two seconds? None of this would actually work in practice."

Kess touched his arm. "Mateo," she said gently.

"I'm sorry," he said. "I just— This is a childish prank. This should be below everyone in this room. I feel sick knowing I'm working with anyone who'd rather play games like this than talk through whatever their problem is, the way civilized people are supposed to."

"Lies," the teenager Glower said with a flounce. "How can we listen to anything they say after all this?"

"Let me see it," the bearded Glower muttered. Mateo gave him the fake report without hesitation. The Glower read it over as the others stirred uneasily beside him. The teenager one shook her head and disappeared with a faint *pop*.

I considered the Tethers around me as I had before, but as before, I couldn't read guilt on anyone's face.

It wasn't right. I didn't care how scared any of them were—it wasn't *right* to try to take away our choices, to force our hand.

"He's telling the truth," the bearded Glower said.

"Are you sure?" one of his companions asked.

"At a glance, it looks concerning," he said. "But if you give it more consideration, it's clear the plan is illogical. As soon as they attempted to implement anything in this way, we would recognize the problem and simply refuse. There is no danger here. And it's also true that it's unlikely they would be so careless as to leave this out where we could find it—for any reason other than one of them wanting to trick us. I say we continue the discussion. Do not let their prejudices win. We can show we are better than they think."

"You stay, and we'll keep talking," Mateo said, relief washing over his face.

The bearded Glower inclined his head. "I will."

"I don't like this," another said darkly, and disappeared as the teenager Glower had. So we were left with only three—and one of those was Kess.

It's better than none, I told myself, but inside I felt just as sick as Mateo had sounded.

———

I was pouring myself a cup of coffee in The Platform when Shawn ambled past me. He paused just long enough to touch me, tapping his fingers on my shoulder. *One, two, three.* I smiled to myself as he walked on.

Three days left until our contract with Macro Play was done. If the company decided to continue using the Society's services, a more experienced Tether would take over from me. Whatever they had me doing next, I wouldn't be working under Shawn anymore.

Which meant it would be completely fine for me to be under him in more literal ways.

My good humor didn't change when I glanced over at Demirci. He'd been in a better mood than usual today, joking with some of the regulars before he'd settled into his usual spot at the high table near the back. Now he was humming to himself as he polished up his latest design. Maybe he'd sorted out his troubles all on his own. I'd be perfectly happy to let go of that responsibility.

That thought had only just passed through my head when an expectant cough carried from the loft's front door. A familiar figure was standing there, leaning against the frame: the guy Demirci had met at the bar last week. His straw-like hair was limper and messier than before, and his eyes were red-rimmed. The twitch of his hands as he waited to be acknowledged sent an uneasy tremor through me. I hadn't had much experience with illicit substances back home, but it hadn't taken a lot of time in L.A. for me to learn the identifying characteristics of a druggie. Was *that* what this whole problem was about—drugs?

Demirci had noticed the arrival of his "friend" too. He stiffened on his seat, his jaw clenching. Then he shut his laptop and leapt down. A few heads turned as he stalked across the room to the doorway. I sidled closer.

"What are you doing here?" Demirci demanded of the other guy in a low voice.

"Seems like I've got to make a big show to catch your attention these days," the guy replied, too loud. He waved vaguely. "Gotta collect on what you owe me!"

More people were staring now. Demirci's back had gone rigid. "I told you we'd talk when I get off work, remember?"

"Not good *enough*!" the guy proclaimed.

"Fine. Fine. I have to finish one thing first. Go... wait in the pizza place on the corner. I'll meet you there in half an hour."

"You'd better," the guy said, waggling a finger. "There are so many things I'd like to talk to the people behind that big glass wall about."

"You do that, and I won't owe you anything," Demirci spat out, quiet but sharp. Sharp enough that the guy seemed to focus for a second in the midst of his spaced-out haze.

"All right," he said. "Half an hour. I'll see you over pizza!"

He sauntered to the stairwell. Demirci exhaled, his shoulders slumping. As I came up beside him, I realized he was trembling.

No more, I decided. This trouble had gone on long enough.

"Hey," I said, and he flinched.

"Don't start," he said. "Not—"

"It looks to me as if it's already more than started," I cut in, "whatever *it* is. What I'm concerned about is finishing it. I've got to do my job here, Mr. Demirci, and that means I need to know if someone's got a hold over you. I don't want to make a public exhibition of it. I'm not asking you to tell anyone other than me. But if you're still not going to talk to me, I'll have to go ask your 'friend' there, and it seems he's in the sort of mood where he'll be happy to vent."

Demirci's jaw worked. He sighed. All at once, hopelessness washed out his expression.

"All right," he said. "Let's go to my office. We can talk there."

Fifteen

I HADN'T REALIZED THAT DEMIRCI HAD A PROPER OFFICE, given that he seemed to spend all his work time out in the loft. But back beyond the fogged glass wall where management had their larger private rooms, there was a little space about the size of a walk-in closet with a door bearing Demirci's name. The desk inside was cluttered with sketches. The air smelled like stale marker ink.

Demirci opened up a folding chair for me and pushed his wheeled desk chair to the wall so we both had room to sit. It was a tight fit, but the large skylight overhead stopped the space from feeling suffocating. I was glad Shawn had opted to hang back, though he'd given me an approving nod as I'd headed in here.

"So what's the story?" I said when Demirci didn't speak. He was busy examining his hands. "What happened between you and that guy?"

"Josef," he said in an empty voice. "His name's Josef. We

went to school together. We were friends—both of us loved games and art. But before we graduated, we'd already started growing apart. I was serious about the industry. I wanted to put in the hours, the effort, to make a go at a career. He wanted to sit around and smoke pot, or maybe crack if he could get his hands on some, and do a doodle here and there if he happened to be in the mood."

"Okay. And then?"

Demirci ran his hand over his face, grimacing. His tone became even more strained. "He was a slacker, but he had some pretty cool ideas. We used to play around with each other's concepts... The big boss in my first game with Macro, the one that got everyone excited about the game... I built it off a design he drew."

My stomach sank. "And you didn't credit him. You didn't get his permission?"

He shook his head. "I didn't think he'd even *notice*. He was so out of it most of the time by then. And at that point I wanted so badly to just get my foot in the door, and it seemed fair—I mean, we'd bounced off each other so much, maybe something I'd said had inspired the idea in the first place. But it wasn't okay. I knew that as soon as they brought me on to really make it. I just... It seemed like it was too late then. Saying something would have meant throwing away my big chance."

"But he did notice," I supplied without any trouble. "And he's been threatening to tell the rest of the company about it. What's he been asking from you to keep him quiet?"

"Mostly money," Demirci said. "Recently he's been pushing for an in to a job. As if it wouldn't screw me over just as badly to put in a good word for someone who'd show up acting like *that*." He gestured toward the loft. "But all of the work I've done since then has been mine. Three more games that I don't need to credit anyone else for."

My thoughts tripped back to the day the first Glower had shown up at The Platform. The way Demirci had reacted when I'd sent her off. "Is that why you're so touchy about supporting new designers?" I asked. "Trying to make up for taking advantage of one?"

"I'd like to think I would anyway. But it's one way of paying back, paying forward."

A way that made him vulnerable to demonic manipulation. A weakness like that, guilt burrowed down that deep, was the perfect sore spot for a Glower to exploit.

Which meant I had to find a way to dig it out and set things right, no matter how I felt about his conceptual theft.

"I just don't know when he's going to stop," Demirci went on. "I don't know when he'll feel I've paid everything I owe. And he's getting more demanding, not less."

I drew in a breath, trying to speak as dispassionately as possible. "Look," I said. "Taking his work and passing it off as your own, that wasn't okay. But you obviously know that. Have you kept records of everything you've given Josef?"

Demirci nodded. "Not at first, but when it became obvious he was going to keep coming back, I started making notes."

"How much have you given him so far?"

"Just cash? About eighteen grand. And then there've been purchases he's asked me to make: new computer, new TV, that kind of thing."

"And how much would an unknown designer normally get paid to have a concept used as one part of a game by a company that hadn't had any hits yet?"

Demirci blinked at me, looking startled and then grim. "Not that much."

"Then you've more than paid for your mistake, don't you think?"

"I suppose," he said. "But how do I get Josef to see it that way?"

I frowned. That I didn't know. I had training in conflict resolution, sure, but for the purposes of keeping good relations between Tether and client. I didn't have a clue how the games industry or internal company politics worked.

"There has to be a way for you to sort things out," I said. "Now that I have the big picture, I'll come up with something." In the two and a half days I had left here? Damn. I pressed on, not letting doubt take over. "You go meet with Josef, do what you need to do to keep him happy for right now, and it'll be the last time you ever have to deal with him."

I hoped. But if I couldn't figure this out, what was I even here for?

"Sure," Demirci said, sounding weary. I couldn't tell whether he believed I could pull off a fix or he just didn't want to argue about it.

We got up and stepped back into the loft. Demirci grabbed the sunglasses he'd left on the table next to his laptop. I caught Shawn's eye and tipped my head toward the front door. We'd give Demirci space for his conversation, but we needed to be around in case a Glower happened to prowl by.

Demirci was just heading for the door when one of the admin staff poked his head out of the office area. "Hey," he said, peering at me. "You two from the Tether Society—I just got kind of an odd call."

A cool prickle ran over my skin. "What do you mean?" I said. Demirci paused to wait as I approached the admin guy. Shawn came over to join us.

"Well, the guy says he saw the photos from last week's

convention online, and he wanted to know who the woman with Aydin was," the admin guy said, scratching his head. "I wasn't sure how much we're supposed to be saying about your involvement with the company..."

The prickling deepened into a flood of cold. My heart started thudding. "You didn't tell him my name, did you?" I said, too loud, too fast, but I couldn't hold back the words. "Or who I work for?"

"No, nothing," the admin guy said. His eyes had widened. "I mean, he's still on the line, waiting for me to get back, but I told him I had to ask Aydin."

"Did the caller give *his* name?" Shawn asked, and the guy shook his head.

I swallowed hard, tensing my muscles to stop them from shaking. It had to be Jace. Who else would have recognized me and gone this far to track me down without offering any explanation?

Shawn rested his hand on the small of my back. A simple gesture, but it grounded me. The panic in my chest loosened slightly. I found the wherewithal to say, "Tell him no one here knows that woman. That it was just someone passing by. I shouldn't have been in the photos anyway."

"Go it," the admin guy said without hesitation. The tension inside me relaxed even more as he ducked back into his office as if I'd made a completely normal request. I guessed in his eyes I had.

But that chill was still shivering through my nerves. My past had gotten so close. If the admin staff hadn't been as cautious as they were... If Jace had decided to show up here without calling first... My hands clenched at my sides.

"Give us a minute," Shawn said to Demirci, who nodded. He sat down in one of the armchairs while Shawn guided me into the front hall. There, I turned toward him, wanting to lean against his solid frame and knowing that wasn't appropriate yet, not in public, not on work time. I settled for grasping his forearm.

"You're okay," Shawn said, his low voice washing over me. "He doesn't know anything. He can't get to you."

"He knows I'm in L.A.," I said. "Or at least that I was on that day."

"He can't even be completely sure it's *you*," Shawn said. "I saw the pictures that went up online. You were moving when the photographer took them—you're a little blurry. He saw enough to wonder, because he's obviously got an obsessive screw loose, but no one could look at those and definitively ID you. Do you really think he'd come all the way out here on the basis of a couple of photos with a woman who looks like she might be you?"

I considered. "No," I said. "Or... I don't know." I pressed my palm to my temple. "I have no idea how he's thinking now. But the call got handled. I can keep working."

"I know you can," Shawn said. "But if anything else comes up—if you see any reason to worry—you let me or someone else at the Society know, all right? We'll look after you. He's never going to hurt you again, Sofie. I swear it."

His voice, his touch, and his certainty steadied me. I nodded, and he moved to get Demirci. But even before I lost that contact, skin to skin, I knew it wasn't enough. Jace still had a hold on me that not even Shawn could break. And I'd spent too long letting other people "look after" me. That was how I'd gotten here in the first place.

It was up to me now. I had to find my own way to cut Jace out of my life for good.

Even though I assumed she could pop into our plane of existence in the middle of my living room if she wanted to after I'd invited her in, Kess arrived with a knock on my apartment door from the hall. I saw she had a good reason to use conventional methods of transportation when I opened the door. She was carrying the art equipment I'd used at Mateo's and in the demonstration for the other Tethers. Maybe she couldn't bring all that through the Glower's realm. Or maybe she simply believed in politeness. Either way, I appreciated the effort.

"Thanks for coming," I said, letting her in.

"I was happy to," Kess aid. I wasn't sure what she and Mateo had been up to when I'd texted him asking if he could pass a message on to her, but he'd indicated she was with him. Not anything too... intimate, I hoped, given how quickly she'd made it here and how unruffled she appeared. But then Kess almost always appeared unruffled. She glanced around my apartment with a mild expression and glided toward the couch.

"This would probably be the best place to set the easel, for the light, I think," she said. "If we just move the coffee table... Would you agree?"

"Yes," I said, startled, and then remembered that she was probably more of an expert at this than me. Who knew how many artists she'd played muse and succubus to before her current reformation?

I hurried over to help her unfold the easel and stool and arrange the rest of the tools, setting one of the canvases Kess had bought on the frame as Kess rested the few spares against the wall.

"Is there a specific reason you felt we should have another

session now?" Kess asked when she straightened up, sweeping her sleek hair out of her face.

There was. I didn't feel quite up to explaining it, though. It had been hard enough talking about my past with Shawn.

"I just feel as if I need to let some things out," I said. "Painting was always the best way I had of doing that before."

"That sounds reasonable," Kess said. "Let me know when you're ready to begin."

I settled onto the stool and eyed the blank canvas. I wasn't sure what *was* going to come out. The fear and hurt inside me had twisted into an enormous knot. I had to untangle it if I was going to find an answer. I had to draw Jace and his lies out of me for good.

"Okay," I said.

Kess gave me the same light touch as before, on the back of my arm. As always, I didn't feel anything change. There was just the slightest shift when a glimmer of an idea came into my head, and my hand was reaching for the palette before I was entirely sure where I was going with it.

I kept my focus on that painful knot as I brought a brush to the canvas. It was so dark inside. So dark and wound so tight. My hand slashed paint across the white: dark blues and purples and then a brutal maroon. That narrow-eyed look he would shoot me that could freeze me from across the room. His fingers pressing me forward at the back of my neck. The way his voice could snap from a soft sneer to a crackling yell in a split second. My chest tightened as the wave of memories crashed over me, but I pushed all that emotion through me. From my heart along my arm and into the brush.

Black. Sickly brown. Then more blue, washed out shades fading into gray. The averting of my friends' eyes when I passed them on the street. The murmurs between people that hushed when I came near enough to hear. That sarcastic comment Kerri-Ann had bitten out at me the last time I'd seen her. I jabbed and swirled and scraped the paint, faster, faster. Sour saliva filled my mouth.

But then, suddenly, the clouds in my head began to clear. The darkness broke with a streak of yellow, brilliant gold, glinting white. A brighter blue. The murk still clung to the edges of the image, but there was a path through it.

There was hope inside me too.

I was breathing hard when I came back to myself, paint fumes thick in my nose and my hand aching from gripping the brush. I was leaning over the canvas, not even on my stool anymore. But it wasn't the canvas I'd started with. As my mind caught up to the present moment, I noted two other paintings set against the coffee table. One all dark emotional violence, that made me think of Jace. The other a lonely fog. And in front of me, the light I'd started to find on my way through it.

Because I had found a way through. With the Society, with Shawn, with the friendships I was forming. Maybe I'd had to leave a lot behind, but I'd escaped. He hadn't owned me.

And he never would.

"You were so wrapped up in the process, I didn't want to stop you," Kess said. "I waited until it seemed you were starting to come down on your own."

"Thanks," I said. "I think I needed all of this." To remind myself of not just what I'd been through, but where I was now.

So here I was, I thought, considering the paintings. Like my other work with Kess, they were so much bolder, more vivid than the delicate lines I'd preferred before. There was all my fear and hurt and even anger, outside of me, where it could stay without messing up my life. Because I was bolder and more vivid now too.

But getting out wasn't enough, was it? Jace was still out there in the world, living and breathing. I might have a new path, but I had the feeling I was going to need everything I had in me to defend it.

Sixteen

I walked toward the Society's office Friday morning
with a weight in my gut. It was my last day with Demirci. I still
wasn't sure what advice to give him. Maybe solving his problem
was beyond my abilities. It wasn't even the sort of conflict that
was technically my responsibility as a Tether. But I couldn't
shake the feeling that if it wasn't resolved, some Glower would
manage to mark him before the end of the year. I'd already seen
those two prowling around him.

I hadn't slept well last night. My mind had been too busy
trying to hash out potential strategies. I'd figured I might as well
stop by the office and talk to Mrs. Tsung before my shift started
to see if she could give me any guidance. As my direct
supervisor, that was *her* job, after all.

Rush hour had passed, but the traffic was still pretty dense.
Watching the cars maneuver around each other, honking and
sputtering exhaust, I was glad I'd opted to walk.

As I reached the block with the office building, an oddly
amplified voice reached my ears over the growl of the traffic. My

gaze shot to a cluster of figures standing right across the street from the Society's building. Half a dozen, lined up at the edge of the sidewalk, with the two in the middle holding loudspeakers. And all of them were gleaming with an unnatural light.

My legs locked. Why had a bunch of Glowers staked out our building? That was obviously as close as they could get to it, with all the protections it had in place. What did they hope to accomplish from over there?

"Tether Society!" hollered one of the Glowers with a loudspeaker. "All your work is useless. Anyone who says they will compromise with you is lying. We are the truth, and we say you can't change us. We will take all the lives we can devour."

A passing pedestrian stared at them and then shook his head, probably dismissing them as crazies. My shoulders had tensed. So they were more of the same troublemakers trying to ruin Mateo's proposal in any way they could. I wanted to think my colleagues would be wise enough to realize what these ones said had nothing to do with Kess or her allies, but considering that the Glower's words echoed what a lot of them had already been saying themselves... Hearing the demons taunting us certainly wasn't going to *help* the situation.

My discomfort hardened in my chest. It took me a moment to recognize the emotion as anger. Mateo was already having enough trouble getting the rest of the Society to give his proposal a fair shot. Why did this have to be so *hard*?

Then a second thought popped into my head. The Glowers there, the Glowers who were against the compromise—they must be truly terrified that the proposal would work. If they actually thought any association between their kind and ours would fall apart, that it couldn't threaten those among them who wanted to continue marking and killing people, they wouldn't be wasting their energy on spectacles like this.

We could win this. Even they thought so. But we only could if we didn't let them get in the way.

With that rush of confidence, my feet started moving again. Probably not too many of my colleagues had seen the Glowers' demonstration yet. Most of the Tethers worked on location with clients, not in the office, after all. As the day went on, more would be coming and going—hearing those shouts, seeing whatever else the demons had planned for their audience—unless someone cared enough to step up.

So I didn't stop at the office building. I walked a block farther to a gardening shop I'd noticed before and bought a spray bottle. The clerk gave me a strange look when I asked if she could fill it halfway with water, but she went to the staff restroom and did so. Outside, I opened it up and poured in the entire contents of the vials of oregano and rosemary oil from my purse. I twisted the nozzle to its most powerful spray setting. Then I crossed the street, shaking the bottle hard as I went.

Oil and water might not mix completely, but they'd mingle enough for the water to carry that oil along just fine. I'd seen the process in action with Mom's ever-present homemade salad dressing spritzers. And a carrier for the oil was all I needed.

I strode up to the congregation of Glowers without hesitating, shutting out every doubt that tried to pry its way past my sense of conviction. The first demon noticed me when I was ten feet away. I kept walking as he nudged the one next to him. They'd all turned to face me, some looking puzzled, others with eyes narrowed in hostility, by the time I was within range.

"You'd better back off, Tether," snarled the woman Glower with one of the loudspeakers. She must have recognized me from somewhere, I thought distantly. Every other bit of my focus went to aiming the spray bottle.

I caught three of them with the first blast. Pumping quickly,

I splattered water mixed with the herbal essences Glowers found most toxic into their midst five, six times before it even started to take effect. The demons scattered, clawing at their skin, their clothes, a few of them shrieking in distress. The few I'd missed scrambled away, but I walked on, waving my arm as I worked the spray bottle. One darted into the shadows to vanish, and then another, and another, as the discomfort overwhelmed them. I leveled one last blasted into the faces of the two with the loudspeakers who'd bumped against each other as they dodged. They cringed as they wisped away from our plane, one right after the other.

Alone on the sidewalk, I dropped my arm. My breath was raw in my throat. It took me a moment to notice I was smiling. Grinning, really—broad and open. All the tension I'd been carrying inside me had dispelled into the air just as the Glowers had.

I hadn't felt this free in months. Maybe in years.

Understanding struck me with such force that a laugh jolted out of me. That was it. That was the answer. You looked your problem in the face and shoved it out the door.

"Are you sure about this?" Demirci asked as we stood outside the office room where he was supposed to meet with the heads of Macro Play in just a few minutes. He'd agreed to call the meeting when I'd first given him my suggestion, but now the jitters seemed to be getting to him. He rubbed his arms, shifting his weight from foot to foot.

"You've made these people a lot of money in the last few years," I reminded him. "You just tell them you borrowed that one concept, you feel bad about it, and you want to add Josef's name to the credits and have the company direct a small share of your royalties from that title to him. You don't have to mention how he's been hounding you or what you've already done for him. You're making up for a past mistake. People respect that. And it's not as if it costs *them* anything, really."

"You can't know for sure they'll see it that way. Artistic integrity is an important issue in this industry."

"Well, maybe you should have thought of that before you adapted Josef's design," I said dryly. When Demirci scowled at me, I added, "You're nervous about telling them. I get it. But you were nervous before you decided to do that too. Josef has been making you nervous for *years*, because you never know when he might decide to tell someone. Someday he probably will tell. The only way you can stop him from controlling your life is to take that power away from him. Stand up for yourself instead of letting him bully you into submission. You're nervous right now, but after you've confronted the problem, I promise you'll feel *so* much better."

He sighed. "You can be very convincing, you know. That all makes sense. I still hate having to talk about it."

"I doubt they're going to enjoy it much either," I said, tipping my head toward the office door. "So after today, you probably won't ever have to talk about it again—*they're* not going to bring it up. You won't even have to think about it, or Josef. The payments can be automated, right?"

"Yeah." Demirci rubbed the back of his neck. "That will be nice, not ever having to talk to him again."

A moment later, the door opened. Macro Play's owner and senior programmer motioned Demirci inside, with a raise of his eyebrows at me. I held up my hands. "Just keeping him company while he waited. I'll be out front if you need me."

Despite having said that, I lingered for a few minutes in the hall. Long enough to watch through the narrow window beside the door as Demirci sat down at the small conference table with his three superiors. To see him look at his hands, clasp them together, and start talking. To recognize from the surprise and then sympathy on the others' faces that he'd told them what we'd discussed, and that they weren't going to tar and feather him for his crime. I exhaled, a tingle of satisfaction passed through me.

I'd done all right by my client. He was going to be okay now even without a Tether, I had a feeling.

I headed back into the loft area. Shawn had gotten into a conversation with one of the artists who'd been sketching near the windows. When he saw me emerge, he exchanged a few more words and then ambled over.

"He went through with it?" he asked.

"As far as I could tell. It looked as if they were taking it well, too. Which they should. I mean, it was a crappy thing for him to do, but twenty-year-olds do stupid things sometimes. I should know."

"Nothing you've done or did was stupid, Sofie," Shawn said.

I waved him off. "I could have made better choices lots of times. But anyway, Demirci's done tons of other work that's all his own. Even that one design, he only used his friend's concept as a starting point. He's proven himself, and he wouldn't feel so torn up about that one thing if he wasn't a decent person. I think they'll see that. And from a more practical standpoint, it's not as if they can afford to fire their star designer with their next game in the middle of development."

Shawn chuckled. "I assume you didn't mention that last line of reasoning to Mr. Demirci as part of your pep talk."

"No," I said with a grin. "I'm definitely not *that* stupid."

"So, last day," Shawn said, glancing up at the clock on the

wall. He eased his hand over just slightly to trail the back of his fingers from my elbow down to my wrist. The contact sent a slow burn of heat over my skin.

"Last day," I agreed, resisting the urge to return the touch. There would be lots of time later. "Four more hours until we're off the clock."

Shawn smiled. "I have the feeling it's going to be a very good night."

Seventeen

THOSE LAST FOUR HOURS PASSED LIKE MOLASSES, SLOW AND creeping. Demirci came out of his meeting looking worn but relaxed. He gave me a thumbs-up from across the room, and I relaxed completely too. For about five seconds, until the tickling anticipation of what I'd be doing when the clock hit eight started building again.

Demirci gathered up his things at the end of the day, and stopped to shake my hand.

"Thank you," he said. "I thought you being here was kind of pointless at first, but I'm really glad they had you come on board. Let me know if there's ever anything I can do to help you out, all right?"

"Of course," I said. "Good luck with the new game. I'll be watching for its release. And stay away from anyone who tries to promise something that sounds too good to be true, okay? You've spent enough time tangled up in a bad situation with someone."

"Don't worry," he said with a smile. "From here on out, I'm going to be *very* careful who I make any commitments to."

Then he was gone, and Shawn and I were left by the doorway.

"Shall we?" Shawn said, with so much promise in those two words that a pleasant shiver rippled through me. I nodded, and we headed down the stairs. Shawn took my hand, teasing his fingertips back and forth over my palm.

I didn't want to wait. I'd been doing so much of that already. When we got to the bottom of the stairs, I reached up to pull him into a kiss. His tongue slid over mine as he coaxed my mouth open, his powerful arms coming around me, and in that moment I would almost have agreed to fulfilling the promise of the night right there, possible spectators be damned. Shawn was breathing hard when he drew back.

"Soon," he said, and I smiled despite the burn inside me. No, the wait, the anticipation, it was only going to make this first time more delicious.

Outside, Shawn hailed a cab. "No minivan today?" I said.

"That thing's a beast to drive downtown," he said. "I avoid it when the Society's footing the transport pill. This will be a bit of a trip," he added after he'd given the driver his address. "My place is up north near the wilderness."

"Sounds exciting," I said with an arch of my eyebrows.

He grinned. "I helped my sister get a place up there too, so my niece could go to a good school, get away from the smog, all that. I wanted to be nearby. Lisa is clamoring to take up horseback riding now." Abruptly, the light faded from his eyes.

"Are you okay?" I asked.

"Yeah," he said, shaking himself. A sliver of his grin came back. "Just thinking how much there is I want to give her a chance to do."

"She's lucky to have an uncle who cares so much."

"Yeah," was all he answered. He turned his gaze to the window, still pensive. It bothered me seeing that something seemed to be bothering him, but if he didn't want to explain further, I wasn't going to push. I took his hand and held it on the back seat between us, and he started tickling his fingers over my palm again.

I knew he'd put whatever he'd been thinking about behind him when he slipped that touch up to the sensitive skin on the inside of my wrist. A flutter of warmth raced up my arm. He still wasn't looking at me, but his lips had curled slyly. He ran his fingers up to my elbow and down again, and just that was enough to kindle a flame at my core. I hoped this drive wasn't going to be *too* long.

The streets beyond the cab's windows widened, businesses and apartment buildings giving way to houses and lawns and parkland. The driver pulled to a stop outside a stretch of stucco townhomes. The yellow light of the streetlamps highlighted neatly trimmed hedges bordering walled patios.

I'd started to taste a hint of something ashy in the air, but it was only when we climbed out onto the sidewalk in the growing dark that I fully registered the smoky smell. Sharp and cedary, lingering after the passing of the breeze. Shawn glanced to the north.

"Must be another brush fire," he said. "We're close to the forest up here. The fire department will be on it." He gave my hand a tug, a glint in his eye. "Come on. There's another kind of fire I'm planning to start."

I laughed as he led me to one of the wooden doors. "I don't know about that line."

"Needs a little refining?" he said. We stepped into his shadowy front hall. He shut the door behind him and flicked on the light. Then there was just us, in a space no one else could reach. My pulse kicked up a notch.

"I think we should completely forget about talking," I said. There were no more rules. I knew what I wanted. I grasped the hem of his collared shirt and pulled it upward. Shawn's gaze turned smoldering as he worked it the rest of the way off. Then he was standing before me, bare from the waist up. My eyes drank in the planes of his stomach, those tightly defined abs, the gorgeous curves of his pectorals, his biceps. My hands followed, splaying against his skin, rising with the hitch of his breath. I traced the lines of him as if painting them into my memory.

"Sofie," Shawn said in a strained voice. I leaned in so close the warmth of his body radiated over my face, and breathed in the tart, musky smell of him. Then I let my lips brush his chest. He inhaled raggedly, running his fingers into my hair.

I dipped my head to follow the contours of his muscles to one taut nipple and slicked my tongue over it. At another rasp of his breath, I smiled and made my slow, careful, nibbling way over to the other. Shawn's hands slid around to the back of my head and drew my mouth up to his.

We kissed as if we'd been starving for it, demanding lips and hot tongue. Shawn jerked himself away just long enough to yank my shirt over my head. As he dove in to continue the kiss, his touch roamed up to my spine to the clasp of my bra. With another yank, that item of clothing was dropping to the floor. I wrapped my arms around him, humming happily at the feel of his naked skin against mine.

With a growl, Shawn lifted me off the floor, leaning me against the wall as he guided my legs around his waist. He devoured my mouth before trailing his lips over my jaw to my neck. Then, as he offered a scrape of his teeth that made me gasp, he turned us toward the stairs. With steady strides, he carried me up and into the second-floor bedroom.

I caught only a glimpse of his wicked grin before he'd tossed me onto the feather duvet covering the bed. The breath jolted out of me with a giggle. He bent over me, kissing his way down to my breasts. My giggle turned into a sigh as he nuzzled around my nipple before sucking it into his mouth. He worked it over with tongue and teeth until I was whimpering.

"So much easier doing this without clothing in the way," he murmured against my skin, and another giggle wriggled out of me.

He reached down to my jeans as he shifted his attentions to my other breast. One-handed, he undid the button and eased down the zipper. I raised my hips to help him pull the jeans off and kicked them over the end of the bed. He glided his fingers across my legs from one side to the other, outer thigh to inner, making me squirm. Finally, he rested them against the hungry place between my legs. He stroked me gently until I pressed against his hand, needing more. Pleasure spiked through me at the firm weight of his touch.

Shawn lifted his head to kiss me on the lips again, more tenderly but with no less passion, as he caressed me through my panties. My hands traveled over his shoulders, his back, wanting to pay him back in kind, but he'd positioned himself so I couldn't reach the most sensitive part of *him*.

"I'm all for equality," he said as he pulled back. "But this is one area where I believe in ladies first."

He slid my panties off and lowered his head between my legs. I swallowed a squeak of surprise and bliss as he kissed me there. My hips arched to meet him, out of my control. I couldn't focus on anything except the waves of pleasure he was provoking. He massaged my thighs as he lapped his tongue over me, slicking it down to my opening. Then he placed his whole mouth on me, licking and nibbling as the waves built and built. I moaned, my head spinning. My fingers curled into the duvet. I careened up and away with the crash of my orgasm, panting and boneless.

Shawn kissed his way back up my torso. I managed to find the wherewithal to grasp the top of his slacks. He grinned against my cheek as I tugged them open and down his thighs. He sat up to peel them off completely and stripped off his boxers in turn. The sight of him, fully erect and stunningly hard, send a fresh tremor up from my core, even though the aftershock of my orgasm had barely faded.

I pulled him down over me, one hand on his shoulder, the other slipping down to grasp his length. He groaned as I gripped him. The silky-firm feel of him against my palm made me shiver in delight. I pumped him a few times, flicking my thumb over the head of his hard-on to spread the moisture beading there, but I was greedy. I wanted what I'd been craving since that first kiss in the club: all of him, inside me, now.

Shawn must have been thinking the same thing. He stretched out to grab a condom packet off the top of the dresser —he'd left it there this morning, I thought, knowing we were going to be here, knowing we'd be doing this, an idea that sent another wash of heat through me—and ripped it open. I guided it over his length, stroking him even harder with the heel of my hand.

I opened my thighs and tipped my hips upward to give him access. Shawn didn't hesitate. He plunged into me, all the way to the hilt. I gasped, and he paused, gazing down at me.

"I'm good," I reassured him. "I'm wonderful."

His lips canted up. "You're spectacular," he informed me.

I was wet and ready for him, every nerve quivering as he

eased even deeper inside. He held my hips against his as he slid in and out at an escalating tempo. The friction of him filling me set my whole body ablaze. I whimpered as I bucked to meet him, driving toward that final highest peak that seemed just out of reach. Higher, higher, his hand squeezing my backside, my nails digging into his, pleasure coursing through me like a flash fire. Then it burst behind my eyes, shuddering up from my core to melt my muscles and slacken my jaw. A sigh slipped out.

Shawn thrust into me even faster as I clenched around him. With another groan, he sank over me. He kissed the crook of my neck, still holding me to him as he gave over to his own release. Then he rolled over, gathering me beside him. I rested my head against his chest, listening to the heady beat of his pulse.

"Worth the wait," he said, "if I do say so myself."

"More than worth it," I murmured, snuggling closer. My eyelids drifted shut. Now there was nothing I wanted more than to fall asleep curled up next to him—and to wake up tomorrow to do this all over again.

I woke up buried in Shawn's duvet with his spicy scent all around me. The space next to me was warm, but his presence gone. As I pushed back the duvet, a thicker, smoky smell filled my nose, acrid enough to make me grimace.

Shawn appeared in the doorway. I would have taken more time to appreciate the sight of him in fitted jeans and nothing else if his expression hadn't been so serious.

"What's going on?" I said, sitting up.

"That forest fire from last night spread too fast for the fire department to contain," he said. "It's moving in this direction, and they're not sure they'll be able to put it out before it reaches the residential neighborhoods. I was just listening to the radio—they're recommending people evacuate until the situation is more stable. It'll be a couple hours at least before we'd be in any real danger, and it's not likely the fire would make it this far down, but I'd rather not take the chance and leave it to the last minute."

Damn. So much for tender morning-after sex. I started grabbing my clothes off the floor. "I guess you could come back to my place. If you want, I mean."

He managed a small smile. "I appreciate the invite, but I need to check in on my sister and Lisa. Sometimes Sherice doesn't take these warnings seriously, and if she puts it off until the evacuation is an actual order, it's going to be chaos on the roads."

I nodded and stepped into my panties. As I pulled on my jeans, Shawn handed me my T-shirt and bra, and touched my arm. "I do plan on seeing you again, Sofie," he said. "I hope I've made it clear that I'd want more than just a one-time hook-up."

"You have," I said with a smile back. "It's all right. I like a guy who looks out for his family."

"Well, good," he said. "Because I like you too. Meet me at the front door? I've got to grab a few things I'll want to keep safe, just in case the fire does get down here."

"Of course. Is there anything I can help you with?"

"Nah, it'll only take a moment. This isn't the first evacuation warning I've followed—I keep everything in good order. You just make sure you have all of your things."

He vanished downstairs as I rehooked my bra. I tugged on my shirt and then glanced around. My sneakers had ended up on their sides by the door, but I only spotted one of my socks lying on the carpet. Where had the other one gotten to?

I peeked into the mesh laundry hamper in case Shawn had accidentally scooped it up with his clothes and then got down on my hands and knees to scan under the bed. There. Somehow it had ended up a couple feet back in that shadowed space.

As I reached for the sock, my arm hit a crumpled piece of printer paper that had taken up similar residence. It rolled out into the thin sunlight streaming through the window. I wouldn't have given it any attention, except that my gaze happened to fall on it while I was slipping on my socks. My eyes caught on a couple words visible by one of the folds. *Glower* and *initiative*.

I hesitated. Then curiosity got the better of me. I picked up the paper and smoothed it out on my knee.

In the first few seconds, looking at it, I felt only mild confusion. I recognized the text: it was the fake report on how to enslave Glowers, the one that had been left on the table at that last meeting. Why had Mateo let Shawn bring it home with him? Why had Shawn made notes on it, a thin scrawl of blue pen?

Then I read more closely, and dread crept up through my chest. This wasn't the same report after all. I'd read the first several lines of that one. This one started differently, and the bullet points were in a different order, with different wording. Wording that the pen scrawls were revising.

I blinked at the paper, but I couldn't shake away my dawning understanding. This wasn't the same report because it wasn't the final version. It was an earlier draft. Which meant...

I could only think of one thing it *could* mean: Shawn was the person who'd written the fake report in the first place.

THE FLOOR CREAKED, AND MY HEAD JERKED UP. SHAWN came to a stop on the threshold, his stance going rigid when he saw what I was holding, the expression on my face.

"Sofie," he said, and then didn't seem to know how to continue.

"*You* did this?" I said, getting to my feet. I waved the paper at him. "*You* put it in the meeting room to try to screw up the negotiations? Were you the one who banished the Glowers the first time we tried to talk with them too?"

I didn't need him to answer. His wince told me enough. I crushed the paper and threw it at his chest. It bounced off the shirt he'd put on since I'd last seen him. That was fine. I didn't want to think about how attractive I'd found him just a few minutes ago, about the fond thoughts I'd been having for him over the last few weeks. While he lied to my face.

He'd always been against the compromise, of course. He'd never made any secret of that. But—

"I talked to you about the sabotage. You said you thought it was wrong!" Sounding so reasonable, so thoughtful, when all along...

"I still think it was wrong," Shawn said, his voice strained. "I didn't do it because I *wanted* to, Sofie."

"What other reason is there?" I demanded.

He rubbed his jaw, looking at the floor. "It's complicated."

"I'll bet it's complicated. You betrayed people who are supposed to be your friends, your colleagues. You almost ruined the first chance the Society has had at maybe completely ending this conflict with the Glowers. You pretended you were innocent with me. I'm going to need a little more explanation than, 'It's complicated.'"

"Well, then, how about, 'It's a long story, and I don't think this is the time to get into it'?"

"I think," I said, "that either you're going to find a way to explain it to me now, or I'm going straight to the Society office and telling them what you did. Because unless you can give me a good reason *not* to do that, they deserve to know."

Shawn let out his breath in a rush. "All right. All right. Can you just— I'll call Sherice and make sure she's getting her and Lisa's things together. Then we'll talk."

"Okay."

I followed him into the hall and down the stairs, my feet meeting the floor tentatively as if my body expected it to prove unsteady. While Shawn went into the kitchen with his phone, I perched on the thickly padded arm of his couch. It was pretty comfortable, which annoyed me. I didn't want to feel comfortable in this situation at all.

Shawn strode back into the living room a few minutes later. He set a duffel bag by the front door. Then he turned to me. From the twist of his lips, I could see how much he didn't want to have to talk about this. But I didn't let the pang of sympathy divert me.

"Go ahead," I said.

"You have to understand, Sofie," he said. "I didn't want anything to do with this. I don't believe collaborating with the Glowers is a good idea, but I also don't believe in using underhanded tactics to push that belief on people."

"But you did use them."

"I did," he said, "because I didn't have any choice. You've seen that some of the Glowers aren't too happy about the talks with the Society either. One of them approached me, a little after Kess first started talking up the idea among her kind. He wanted someone inside the Society who could help disrupt the meetings. And he knew exactly how to get a hold over me."

A chill prickled down my spine. "And that was...?"

"Lisa," Shawn said, in a tone so pained it wrenched at my heart. "He marked her. She's only a kid—she didn't have any idea what she was agreeing to! But he managed to weasel his way in. And there's no way I can break that connection. If I hadn't done what he'd asked, he would have fed on her. Drained her. Murdered her. Because of me. I couldn't let that happen."

For a moment, I couldn't speak. Horror clogged my throat. A nine-year-old girl, marked. I'd never heard of a Glower targeting anyone younger than mid-teens. But this wasn't about their normal practices. It was about controlling Shawn.

"You couldn't have told the Society what was going on?" I said.

"What could they have done?" Shawn said sharply. "No one there has any idea how to break a marking! The protections don't work once the Glower already has a direct in. I would have been killing her."

I knew he was telling the truth. His frustration and

desperation radiated off him. But as sick as I felt, one piece of his story didn't sit quite right with me.

"You said the Glower knew how to get to you," I said. "How? Why did he pick *you*? There are tons of more senior Tethers who would have had more influence."

The anger in Shawn's face crumpled. He fell silent for a long moment. Then he said, "He picked me because he was able to get to me before."

"Before?" I said, and a memory crept into my head. Mateo, telling me that Shawn's first client had been marked. Had died.

"I was just starting out," Shawn said, his voice dropping. "I didn't totally understand how vicious the Glowers could get, that they were all the same... The first client I was assigned to solo, this Glower had been eyeing her for a while. He approached me and offered to make a deal. I would look the other way for half an hour here and there, give him a sporting chance. And he'd give me anything I asked for that he could provide. Lisa was only six months old. She'd been born premature, spent weeks in ICU. She'd already had two operations and needed at least one more. Even with the Society paycheck, I couldn't help my sister enough to cover all the medical fees. The money he gave me made sure Lisa survived."

Until the Glower had come back to collect a second time. I swallowed tightly. "And in exchange, you gave him your client's life," I said. His guilt over that decision was written all over him. I'd heard it in his reprimands about handling my own clients. But I couldn't help being even more horrified than before.

"I didn't know everything I do now, and I was stupid, and frantic," Shawn said. "I thought... I thought the client was smart enough, strong enough, not to listen to him. I'd been working with her almost a year when the Glower approached me; she was starting to use some of the independent protections, some of the time. And I didn't agree to let him mark her, only spend time with her. I really believed he wouldn't get anywhere. But I was wrong. If I could do it over, I would never have made that deal. I hate that I ever did. That's how it started, though. That's how he knew how to manipulate me."

We sat there for a minute without speaking. I couldn't find the words to express even a fraction of the turmoil inside me. Only one clear thought broke through. "You should have tried talking to the Society. You should have asked for help. I know how much you care about your niece, but Mateo's proposal could mean hundreds of people who would have died now won't."

"*Could*," Shawn said. "And I think it's a pretty slim chance. This is the sort of creature we're dealing with, Sofie. The sort of creature who'll mark and kill a *child* just to get his way. They can't be saved. They're monsters."

"You should have at least *tried*," I repeated.

His jaw clenched. "Are you really in a position to tell me that?" he said. "Who did you turn to, when you were faced with an awful choice? You didn't trust anyone in your life to help you deal with your problems, did you? So how can you blame me? I needed to deal with this on my own. I did it the best way I could. If you can't accept that, then..."

The truth in his words jabbed at my gut. "The only one who was affected by what *I* did was me," I said. "You had a responsibility to the Society. To your clients. To the client you failed last time."

"I had a responsibility to my family."

"I don't see why that has to be two opposing things," I said. I stood up, nausea rolling over me. I didn't think I could handle any more of this conversation. "I'm going to go. I'll call a cab. You look after your sister and Lisa."

"Are you going to report this to the Society?" Shawn asked with a nervous twitch of his eyes. He still cared what they thought of him, I realized, even if he hadn't trusted them to help.

"I don't know," I said. "It's a lot to process. If I decide to, I'll let you know first. I think that's only fair. But I also think *you* should be the one to tell them."

I hesitated, half expecting him to make some further gesture, say something more, that would make my decision clearer. When he gave me nothing, I squared my shoulders and walked out the front door.

The impact of my discovery didn't fully hit me until I'd walked through the doorway of my apartment. I stopped in the hall, looking at the couch where Shawn and I had sat just a couple weeks ago, where he'd made me feel so wanted and so powerful, and something cracked open inside me. Tears spilled down my cheeks. I crouched down on the floor, my hand covering my mouth, as if I could hold in the pain expanding through my chest.

I stayed there for a long while, until the tears slowed and I felt less as if my ribs were going to wrench apart. Then I sat right down, wiping my cheeks with my sleeve. An itch rose up inside me, to work out the pain the way I'd used to. To throw it onto a canvas where it could be mine and apart from me at the same time.

The rest of me balked. That wasn't who I was anymore. I'd left the creative side of me behind. That was what the murmur in the back of my head wanted me to believe.

But it wasn't true. I'd made art with Kess. If she'd been able to coax it out of me, I should be capable of finding a way to do that on my own. The ability was still in me, somewhere.

I got to my wobbly feet and went to the closet where I'd stashed the art supplies Kess had left after her visit. There was one canvas left—a small one, but maybe that was better as a starting point. Less intimidating.

I didn't bother with the easel, just lay the canvas on the floor and squeezed paint onto the palette. My hand hesitated as I picked up the brush. The blank white surface stared back at me.

What is even the point? Jace's voice echoed through my mind. *Do you really think making pretty pictures is going to get you anywhere?*

There doesn't have to be a point, I thought back. *And the pictures I want to make aren't* pretty *now.*

I jabbed down at the canvas. A streak of raw red, bleeding into bruised purple. Harsh oranges and yawning blues. The canvas turned into a flowing river, carrying blood and reflecting dim sunlight, washing away everything I'd thought I'd known.

When I finished, I was panting. My back was stiff from hunching over the canvas. But I felt cracked open in a completely different way. As if I'd shoved open a door I'd thought was locked and walked into a place I'd spent years searching for.

This was where I belonged. This was who I was. I'd always found myself in the act of painting. And then I'd let Jace pollute that place, take it away from me.

As I leaned back against the wall, my thoughts crept back to Shawn. To the anguish on his face as he'd explained what he'd done. To his accusation: *Who did you turn to? You didn't trust anyone.*

He was right. I didn't agree with what he'd done, it made me sick to think he'd hidden it from me, but when I let myself think beyond that, I understood why he'd acted the way he had. I'd acted out of self-preservation. He'd acted to protect the most important part of his family. I'd hidden an awful lot from him, from everyone I'd met here in L.A., trying to cover up where I'd come from. It was different, but it also wasn't.

I'd held Shawn accountable for not outing his issues to the entire Society when until this moment, I'd still been letting my fears control me to the point that I hadn't lifted a paintbrush on my own, even though I hadn't been near Jace in months.

I glanced at my computer, remembering the emails I'd seen. The people I'd left behind hadn't completely forgotten about me. Who was I kidding? My parents wouldn't ever have stopped thinking about me. I was their daughter. Maybe Jace had skewed the story so they weren't sure who I was anymore, just as I hadn't been sure of myself either, but every minute since I'd left, I'd let him keep doing that. He could only separate me from the people I cared about while I allowed him to control the story of who I was and why I'd withdrawn from them.

When I'd been younger, my family and my friends had been my comfort, true protectors when I'd needed them, just as I'd looked out for them in turn. Maybe I didn't have to see them as lost. Maybe I should give them more of a chance to show who *they* really were, without Jace in between us.

A flicker of hope trembled inside me. I grabbed my phone and sat down on the couch. My heart started thumping.

I still had to be careful. Jace was still *there*. I'd been using a prepaid phone so I didn't have to worry about registering under any name. I didn't have to tell anyone where I was or what name I was using until I was sure it was safe to. But I was so tired of hiding. It was time to open all the other doors I'd closed and find out what was really on the other side. Time to stop hanging back in the shadows, afraid of what would happen if I raised my voice.

I drew in a long breath. Then I dialed my parents' home number. My stomach knotted as the phone on the other end rang, and rang again. A flash of panic shot through me. My thumb twitched toward the End Call button. As I restrained myself, there was a click, and my mother's warm, dry voice traveled into my ear.

"Hello?"

A lump rose in my throat. "Mom?" I said. It came out more of a croak.

"Sarah!? Oh my goodness, honey, are you all right? We've been so worried. Where are you? Do you need help?"

The flood of questions—all concern, no judgment—made me tear up again. It took me a second to gather myself.

"I'm okay," I said. "I'm sorry it's been so long. I—I was scared. I don't want to tell you where I am yet. Because... Because of Jace."

I braced myself as soon as I admitted that. My parents had seemed to approve of him, had listened to him, enough that it hadn't taken them long to come around to accepting us living together so young. He'd had so much time to spin the story his way even more. She was going to be confused, or chide me for paranoia, or—

"Oh, honey," Mom said. "What did he do to you?"

I really did start crying then. She understood what I meant. She was ready to believe me. And sobbing there on the couch hundreds of miles from the voice on the phone, I felt less alone than I had in years.

Nineteen

I'd thought calling home had been hard, but it turned out that walking into a building I'd entered dozens of times in the last nine months was even harder. I halted outside the front doors below the Society's office, my gut knotting.

You don't have to do this, I told myself. *They don't need to know.*

They didn't. But if I expected Shawn to trust the Society to help him, I ought to trust them to help me too. They understood predators. I hadn't lied to them about anything that made a difference to my work. They shouldn't be *that* upset.

But I was also a new, unproven trainee who at least half the senior staff were probably already suspicious of because of my association with Mateo and Kess.

I bit my lip. Then I pushed myself forward. Past the door, up the stairs, tuning out the erratic thump of my pulse.

Mrs. Tsung was expecting me. We were supposed to talk about my experiences during my placement with Demirci and about my next assignment. All I had to do was walk straight to her office—

I hesitated again just inside the main room with its row of cubicles and sitting area, but this time for a very different reason. Mateo had officially taken over Sterling's office, though he'd left much of Sterling's decor in place, which I could see because like Sterling he was keeping the door open. He was standing behind the broad oak desk with Kess beside him. And facing them from the other side of the desk, his back to me, was Shawn.

As I caught myself staring, Kess glanced over and saw me. Shawn followed her gaze, turning. We looked at each other for a long moment, his dark eyes inscrutable, my heart pounding even harder than before. I hadn't seen or talked to him in two days. Not since I'd left his house Saturday morning.

He raised his hand and gestured for me to come over. I went, my throat tight. What was going on?

"I should give Sofie credit," Shawn said as I joined them in the room. "She figured out what was going on and convinced me that coming clean about the situation was the best option. She was right. I should have figured that out for myself.

He looked at me again, his expression so solemn my heart wrenched. So he'd told them.

"And you've come to me first?" Mateo said.

Shawn nodded. "I thought this was the right place to start, so you can do whatever you need to do to make up for my mistakes. It's your work I'll have hurt the most. And I'm honestly sorry for that. I'll tell the rest of the senior Tethers too, of course, and face whatever consequences the directors decide are necessary. I just... We need to find a way to protect Lisa from the fallout."

Kess's eyes flashed, her usually subdued glow flaring. "Your niece—you said she's nine years old?"

"Since January," Shawn said. He eyed her cautiously.

"It's unacceptable," she said. "I would say that anyway, but even those of my kind who still feel marking is reasonable practice would not normally consider feeling off one so young. A child." Her voice crackled with anger.

"I didn't realize it mattered to you," Shawn said.

"We have standards," Kess said. "A few of us have always recognized the unfairness of preying on humans not fully matured, unable to make decisions on the same level. And there is also..." She paused and grimaced. "I don't like to speak of it this way, but it's how most of the others still think. Before a certain age, before the body and spirit finish developing, the energy contained within is not... fully satisfying. It is a waste, to the detriment of all of us, to cut off a life before it has even come close to its full potential."

Before the person could provide a bigger meal, one that could keep them from starving longer, she meant. I winced inwardly at the thought, but Shawn's expression didn't shift.

"Obviously this one didn't care about that," he said.

"And that will be his undoing," Kess replied. "We won't let this injustice stand. He will face his own consequences. I may have to speak to the others from the old perspective, but I can get it done. The one who marked her, who came to you, did he wear the same form each time?"

"Yeah," Shawn said. "Older guy, like sixty-ish? Gray hair, tall, thick-framed glasses."

The description jolted a memory from my head. The Glower who'd come by The Platform a couple weeks ago—the one Shawn had headed off, that I thought he'd recognized. So he had. The demon hadn't been there for Demirci or the other creatives. He'd come *for* Shawn. To show how easily he could disrupt Shawn's life?

Kess's mouth had twisted. "Ah. Yes. I'm not surprised. Stay here. I'll need your confirmation."

She vanished into the air with that *pop* of released pressure. Shawn blinked at the spot where she'd been standing.

"What exactly is she going to do?" he asked Mateo.

"I'm... not entirely sure," Mateo admitted. "I suppose we'll find out before too long."

Shawn turned to me. He held himself a little stiffly, as if he was afraid of how I'd react if he moved even an inch closer to me. My skin still tingled with the awareness of his body near mine.

"I sent in my report on your placement yesterday," he said. "There's nothing in it you'd need to worry about."

"Oh," I said. I hadn't even been thinking about that. I guessed I'd still trusted him in some ways, more than I'd realized. "Thank you. I'm glad you decided to get the Society's help."

"Like I said, you were right that I should."

I dropped my gaze and swallowed thickly. Part of me wanted to take his hand, to offer some sort of affectionate reassurance, but a larger part of me was still too off balance from Saturday's revelations. Nonetheless, it seemed only fair to give him as much as he'd given me.

"I should go talk to Mrs. Tsung," I said. "There are some things I've been through that I decided the Society should know too."

When I looked up at Shawn again, he tipped his head in acknowledgment. "I'm sure she'll do whatever she can to make circumstances easier for you."

"When you're done talking with her, can you ask her to

meet us in the front room?" Mateo said. "I think we should get all the senior Tethers who are available together to let them know the latest... developments, so we can decide how to proceed from here."

"Of course," I said.

I felt a little lighter as I crossed the room to Mrs. Tsung's office door, until I raised my hand to knock and trepidation gripped me again. Ignoring it, I rapped the wooden surface. My supervisor opened the door a moment later.

"Good to see you, Sofie," she said. "We have lots to discuss."

"We do," I agreed. "And before we get started, there's something about me I need to explain."

<hr>

About an hour later, I walked out of Mrs. Tsung's office feeling shaky but relieved. My supervisor had listened thoughtfully as I'd shared the story of my past with Jace and my concerns for the future. "I understand," she'd said afterward. "It shouldn't be any problem to place you with clients who aren't likely to be targets for spontaneous photography. We can put a note in your file about that. I don't even need to say why; the others will accept it. You won't have to air your personal history with the entire Society."

She'd offered additional security arrangements for my apartment, too, and suggested that with the Society's contacts they might be able to trace Jace's financial activity so we could be alerted if he showed signs of heading to L.A.—buying a bus or plane ticket, booking a hotel.

"Yes," I'd said. "Please. It would be amazing to know I'd at least have some warning."

The thought of seeing him again if I had the Society and people back home supporting me didn't seem quite as scary.

In the front room, Mateo had already gathered half a dozen of the senior Tethers, including Rafaela. She frowned as Mrs. Tsung and I came over to join them.

"Are we going to hear what this impromptu meeting is about now?" she demanded.

"It's very simple," Shawn said before Mateo needed to speak. "I'm the one who interfered with our meetings with the Glowers. It's my fault that relations with the ones who say they're willing to try a compromise are strained. I was being... blackmailed, by a Glower who didn't want the proposal put into action, but that's not a good excuse. I'm coming to you now. It's late, but at least now we can do something about it."

"I'm not in a position to say how we should deal with the violation to Society privacy and security," Mateo put in. "As far as the proposal goes, I think the most important thing is having Shawn meet with Kess's colleagues to tell them personally that he was responsible and why, and to offer an apology. I think that could do a lot to mend relations and make sure we can keep moving forward."

"Are we sure that's what we want to do?" Rafaela said. "Maybe this is just—"

Before she could finish her thought, the air in the room outright thrummed. Kess reappeared near the doorway, along with an oddly-grouped cluster of fellow Glowers. Six of them stood in a tight circle around a central figure, a stout young man who appeared to be straining against their hold. Their supernatural light formed a thick circle linking them, one that didn't so much as shiver as he squirmed against it.

"I believe this is the one who committed a crime against you and your niece, though he has chosen a different form in an attempt to confuse matters," Kess said, her gaze on Shawn. "Can you confirm?"

Shawn's eyes hardened. He stepped away from us to approach the Glowers, studying the one they held. The faint hum of energy their presence gave off tickled over my tongue. A little of it felt familiar, probably because Kess would have called on her usual associates. Shawn must have been feeling out the prisoner's vibe. He scowled.

"That's him," he said. "That's the one who marked my niece."

The Glower in the middle bared his teeth with a furious hiss. If he meant to say anything after that, the others didn't give him the chance. The cluster around him vanished, taking him with them back to their plane. Only Kess stayed behind. She gave us a thin smile.

"They will see to it that he receives the proper punishment for his transgression," she said. "And the mark on your niece will be severed."

"You can do that?" I said, startled out of my silence.

"When we all agree circumstances call for it, yes," Kess said. "It requires a capital punishment."

Rafaela was gaping. "You're going to kill him? Just for marking someone?"

Kess narrowed her eyes at the woman. "For marking a child. For marking not to feed but to play games to manipulate the rest of us. I know how you feel about my kind, but even those without much conscience when it comes to yours can see when a line has been crossed. This harms all of us. And it isn't the first time he's shown what damage he may do. He has had his chances to reform."

The firmness of her voice chilled me, even knowing what that Glower had done to Shawn's niece. I guessed this was justice among demons. It wasn't our place to police how they handled their internal conflicts any more than it was theirs to police the Society's. At least, I hoped they saw it that way.

Shawn must have been thinking along similar lines. "How will they feel about my part in this?" he asked.

"They understand your participation was coerced," Kess said. "You are more victim than accomplice."

He bowed his head. "Thank you," he said. "I'll admit, I wouldn't have expected you to even care. I'm sorry for misjudging you."

A murmur passed through the group, agreement or acknowledgment. I noticed Rafaela's expression had softened. Maybe even she was seeing the Glowers a little differently now.

"So we move forward?" Mateo said, and every other person in the room nodded along with me.

Twenty

As the final applause started to fade and the curtain dropped, the actress rushed to the wings of the theater's stage, where several of us Society members and associates were waiting. She clasped the hand of the pixie-ish Glower who'd passed her a spark of inspiration two and a half hours earlier when the play was beginning. Kess, Mateo, and Mrs. Tsung, there to monitor the proceedings from their respective points of expertise, stayed close. Mateo was recording everything on his phone, so he'd be able to show the rest of the Society this first official run of the joint Tether-Glower program later. But he'd invited me along to witness it firsthand as a thank you for my volunteering as Kess's test subject.

"It's a moment for history," he'd said. "We might not have gotten here without your help. If anyone should be there to watch our first success, it's you."

I kept a respectful distance now, my back by the thick curtain, but even from there I could see the glitter of exhilaration in the actress's eyes, hear the awe threaded through her voice.

"That was great," she said, letting go of the Glower's hand so her own could gesture wildly. "I've never felt so connected to the role, so sure of what she wants and how she'd express it... It was *wonderful.* I don't know what the secret to your meditation trick is, but sign me up for another round, please!"

The Glower ducked her head almost shyly. "I'm pleased it worked so well for you," she said, in the slightly formal tone her kind usually took when speaking to humans. She patted the actress's elbow, and I saw the feeding happen: just a flicker, a quick stream of shivery light traveling from the actress's chest down her arm and into the Glower.

The actress's bubbling enthusiasm quieted, but she looked only relaxed, not let down. My own stance relaxed, the tension washing out of my body. The Glower had kept her word, had taken no more than she'd agreed to. From what we understood from Kess, the demons shouldn't be *capable* of breaking their word when given as a vow, but it was difficult to completely trust that idea just on hearsay.

"We can definitely set up another session," Mateo said. "I don't want to stop you from celebrating that great performance with the rest of the cast, though. You can set something up with us later. Right now, enjoy the moment!"

"I will," the actress said. Her beaming smile might be more restrained now, but it was no less warm. "Thank you," she said to the Glower. Then she hurried into the depths of the theater to find her colleagues.

Mateo put away his phone and dipped his head to the Glower. "That was exactly how we hoped the scenario would go. If every session runs this smoothly, we can keep up this arrangement as long as you'd like."

"It was satisfying for me as well," the Glower said. She turned to Kess to consult in their own language, and Mateo turned to me.

"What do you think?" he said, breaking into a grin.

"I think you already know that went perfectly," I said, unable to help smiling back. "It really worked. You should be proud."

"I'm not ready to call it an all-around success yet," he said. "I'm sure there are still hitches to come. But it was an awfully good start. And you should be proud too. You really stepped up for me—and Kess—even though this whole situation is pretty new to you. I'm not going to forget that."

"Good," I said with a playful knuckling of his arm. "Well, I'd better get going."

"We were going to go out and grab dinner for our own celebration," Mateo said. "You should come."

I shook my head. "Thanks, but I've got other plans."

I didn't mention that technically I hadn't nailed down those plans yet. I'd only made them as I was watching the actress on stage, living her character. Wrapped up in the career she loved.

We only had so much time to do that—to go after the things we cared about. The people we cared about. And I couldn't deny that I'd been carrying an ache of loss inside me all month, one that my friendships and my tentative outreach to people back home hadn't eased.

I headed down the stairs and through the hall that ended at the lobby, pulling out my own phone. Holding my breath, I sent the message I'd decided on. Then I ambled over to the wide glass doors to wait.

It only took a minute before my phone buzzed. *I'll be there in ten*, the answer said. I read it more than once, not sure how much the jittery feeling growing inside me was nerves or happiness.

Exactly ten minutes had passed when a dented blue minivan pulled up at the curb. Shawn leaned toward the open window from the driver's seat.

"Hey," he said, looking cautious but hopeful too.

Suddenly I wasn't sure what to say. "You were in the area?"

"I'm supposed to pick up Lisa from gymnastics class. The place is just east of here."

"Oh," I said, my cheeks warming. "I didn't mean to hold you up."

"No, no," he said with a wave of his hand. "This was just a little detour, and I was going to be early anyway. And I thought... It might be good for you to meet her. Before we talk."

My throat tightened. "Yeah," I said.

I got in, sinking into the worn leather seat. Shawn's warm, spicy scent filled the space underneath the tang of the pine air freshener. It warmed my body as I sat there next to him.

He drove on down the street and around a corner, stopping a few minutes later at an athletic center. We'd only just stepped out into the parking lot when a girl with a head full of twists and an open smile came hustling over to meet him. As she grabbed him in a hug, I noticed the faint scar that ran across her chest just above the neckline of her tank top. Leftover from those infant surgeries Shawn had mentioned?

What I didn't see in her chest, to my immense relief, was any hint of a Glower's mark. She was just a normal, untouched nine-year-old girl. Kess had said the demon who'd marked her had been dealt with, but it was better seeing the confirmation directly.

As she let her uncle go, Lisa's brown eyes settled on me,

curious. "Lisa," Shawn said, his hand on her shoulder, "this is my friend Sofie. She works at the Society with me. You know how you were feeling kind of under the weather last month? She's the one who helped me figure out what the problem might be."

"Hi," I said, hoping I didn't sound too awkward. "I hope you're feeling better now."

"I am," Lisa said. "Thank you." Her gaze shifted from me to Shawn and back again. I suspected she was speculating about what exact variety of "friend" I might be—a suspicion confirmed when she cocked her head and asked, "So are you two going on a *date* after this?"

Shawn tugged one of the twists of her hair. "Is that an appropriate question to ask someone you just met?"

"I just want to know," she said with a roll of her eyes. "I'm getting older. You don't have to pretend about this stuff with me."

"I think I get to treat you like a kid for at least a little longer," he said. "Come on. Your mom's waiting."

"You should take the front," I said, reaching for the back door. From the smile Lisa gave me at that, I had the feeling I'd won a boatload of points with her right there.

As Shawn turned the minivan north, he asked Lisa about her class and she eagerly described the floor routine she was working on. She sounded so normal, so apart from the work Shawn and I did, that it was hard to imagine a month ago a Glower had been hovering around her. The thought of that, of what it must have been like for Shawn to see the mark glowing over her heart, to hear how it was already affecting her, to be aware of the awful fate that had met every other person he'd known who'd been marked, left a pain in my gut.

I hadn't felt angry with him in a while. Seeing the life he'd been protecting, I couldn't even say I didn't understand why he'd panicked.

"So you do all that Society stuff too?" Lisa said, twisting in her seat to look at me. "Protecting famous people, keeping them from getting into trouble? Have you worked with any really big stars?"

"Um," I said, "not really. Not yet. I only just started."

"And we're not allowed to talk about what goes on with our clients anyway," Shawn reminded her. "You know that."

She let out a dramatic sigh, but I saw the corner of her mouth turn up as she looked at him. I was pretty sure she was just as devoted to him as he was to her.

We dropped Lisa off at a bungalow with a wide front yard. Shawn waved to his sister when she came to the door to meet her daughter, while I climbed into the now-vacant front seat. Then he aimed the van toward his townhome.

"She's a good kid," I said.

"She's the best," he replied.

I wanted to reach out and grasp his arm or his knee, to make some kind of contact, but I hesitated. There was still so much left unsaid between us, and trying to have a serious conversation while he was driving didn't seem like a great plan.

"I guess we'll go back to my place?" he said.

"Sure," I said. "It's closer."

We were there in barely a moment. Shawn parked the minivan in the garage built into the house and let us inside through an inner door. We came to a halt in the living room.

"So..." he said.

"I'm sorry I've been keeping my distance for so long," I said quickly. "I just... I didn't know what to say. And I've been working through some things with my family and other people back home. I've had a lot going on."

He nodded. "So you got back in touch with them?"

"Yeah," I said. "It's going slowly. I've only talked to my parents and my sister and one of my friends. My ex is still involved socially with a lot of people there. I don't want to trust anyone with information until I'm sure they won't let it get passed on to him. But it's good knowing... that I was wrong. I shouldn't have given up on them. They hadn't given up on me."

"Better finding that out late than never," Shawn suggested with a soft smile.

"Yeah." I looked up at him. "I didn't want it to become 'never' with you either."

"I've got to tell you, it made my day seeing your name pop up on my phone," he said. "I've been hoping... But I didn't want to push you. I know what happened must make you question trusting *me*."

"It did," I said. "But maybe I put you on a bit of a pedestal before I'd really gotten to know you, and that's my fault too. So I figure, the second time around, we could take everything a little more slowly."

He raised a questioning eyebrow. "Second time around?"

"Yeah," I said. "I'd still like to see where this goes. If, I mean —if you want to too."

"Hell, yes," he said. He stepped toward me then, and I moved to meet him. He touched my cheek, his face bent close to mine. The scent of him washed over me, sending a tingle right to my core. I'd forgotten how much of an effect just being near him had on me.

"What about this side of things?" he said, his voice dropping even lower than usual. "Are we back to rules, or can we pick up where we left off?"

I drew in a breath shaky with anticipation. "I don't see any reason to go backwards in that particular area."

"Good," he said, and kissed me.

It was deep but gentle, his lips sliding against mine and teasing them apart, our breaths mingling for several seconds before his tongue ventured over mine. I wrapped my arms around his neck, pressing my body to him, and he humming in approval. His hands traveled down my sides to my hips, shifting the skirt of the dress I'd worn for the theater. Then they slid back up and stopped against my ribs just beside my breasts.

Our kisses grew hungrier, needier, as his thumbs traced arcs over the thin cotton. I let my hands fall so I could start unbuttoning his shirt. I got distracted halfway down by the heat of his chest. My fingers ran over the planes of the muscles there, tweaking his nipples in a way that brought a rough sound from his throat.

Longing rushed through me. After all that waiting, we'd only had that one full moment before this. I'd missed his touch.

As I finished unbuttoning his shirt, Shawn tugged at the sleeves of my dress. The stretchy fabric gave, letting him ease the neckline down, down, until I pulled my arms free. He pressed a kiss to the top of each breast, just above the cups of my bra. My pulse shivered.

"Come here," he said, shedding his shirt. He pulled me with him onto the couch and settled me on his lap with my dress pooled around my thighs. I could feel how hard he already was, the length of him firm through his slacks where it pressed between my legs. I arched into him with a whimper of longing. His chuckle came out breathless.

He made short work of my bra, but he caressed my breasts with the same gentleness as our first kisses. Soft strokes over my skin, closer and closer to the peaks, until he flicked his thumbs over the nipples. I gasped and pressed my mouth over his. We devoured each other as he rubbed my nipples tighter, until I could hardly bear the torture. I ground against him with a growl and reached for the zipper of his slacks.

Shawn let me tug his pants down and off. Then he drew me to him again, sliding his hands up my thighs under my dress. He massaged my hips as he angled me against his boxers, his hard-on straining between us. I kissed his neck, adding teeth when the friction overwhelmed me. Shawn groaned.

"Off," he said, grasping my dress. I helped him yank it the rest of the way down. He paused to stroke me through my panties. I flexed against his hand with a moan, the pressure carrying me higher. Then he tugged the panties off too and stripped off his boxers. When I sank back onto his lap, his naked length pressed against my core. My bare breasts brushed his chest. I sighed, every inch of my skin on fire for him.

Shawn produced a condom and slicked it over himself. I didn't wait for him to guide me, but steadied myself over him and took him in, the whole hard length of him. He groaned again, gripping my thighs. We started to move together, up and down, in and out. His gaze locked with mine. We were naked from head to toe, face to face, locked in the most intimate embrace, and there was nowhere I wanted to be more. I'd had sex before, with Jace, with the boyfriend before him, but this was the first time it had ever felt like making love.

Shawn shifted his angle to fill me even more completely, and pleasure spiked up inside me. I tipped back my head, letting the sensation carry me away. Our pace sped up, a perfectly matched rhythm, each pump of his hips sending a fresh pulse of bliss through me. On and on, until with a shudder my muscles clenched and my eyes rolled back. I came around him, lost on that peak.

Shawn thrust harder, faster, gazing up at me. He cupped my face with one hand to bring my eyes back to his. The pleasure started to build again, even more intense than before. I whimpered as he hit that pressure point within, pushing me higher, farther. But I didn't break from his gaze this time. I stared straight into his eyes as they grew hazy with his own pleasure. Watched his lips part as it took him over. With a grunt, he filled me one last time, and I came apart again, sagging over him.

We stayed twined together like that as our panting slowed. I leaned into him, my sweat-slick skin against his, wanting to sink inside his warmth. Shawn ran a hand up and down my back with a tenderness that brought a lump to my throat.

He wasn't a perfect man, but I wasn't a perfect woman either. He'd seen my flaws as I'd seen his. No one in this world was perfect—not Kess or Mateo, not any of the other Tethers, not my loved ones back home. But what we created together was no less beautiful for it.